THE SKELETON TREE

THE SKELETON TREE

Diane Janes

SEVERN
HOUSE

First world edition published in Great Britain and the USA in 2021
by Severn House, an imprint of Canongate Books Ltd,
14 High Street, Edinburgh EH1 1TE.

Trade paperback edition first published in Great Britain and the USA in 2022
by Severn House, an imprint of Canongate Books Ltd.

severnhouse.com

British Library Cataloguing-in-Publication Data
A CIP catalogue record for this title is available from the British Library.

ISBN-13: 978-0-7278-5019-5 (cased)
ISBN-13: 978-1-78029-779-8 (trade paper)
ISBN-13: 978-1-4483-0517-9 (e-book)

All Severn House titles are printed on acid-free paper.

MIX
Paper from
responsible sources
FSC® C013056

Typeset by Palimpsest Book Production Ltd.,
Falkirk, Stirlingshire, Scotland.
Printed and bound in Great Britain by
TJ Books Limited, Padstow, Cornwall.

In Memory of
Capulet Janes Esq.

the village for odds and ends. Wendy liked the walk, turning left out of Jasmine Close into Cyclamen Drive, then right into Magnolia Road, often pausing to exchange a word or a wave with someone who was busily shaving their lawn with the compulsory hover mower, or rehanging their net curtains, fresh from the sweaty labour of the ironing board; faces recognized from PTA meetings, or the night classes in cake decorating or Spanish for Beginners.

The point where Magnolia Road formed a T-junction with Green Lane marked the end of the estate, and from there it was a left turn on to Green Lane, which ran in an almost straight line until it met the High Street. Unlike the estate, Green Lane had existed for centuries, its direction determined long before the existence of motorized traffic, when the quickest way to anywhere was also the slowest way and did not involve a bypass. Midway between Magnolia Road and the High Street, a gentle kink in Green Lane indicated the existence of some long-forgotten obstacle, a giant tree perhaps or a patch of boggy ground, long since felled, or drained, or otherwise eliminated. For many years it must have been lined by hedgerows, flanked to either side by open fields, but by the time the Thorntons moved into the village, Green Lane was lined with houses and bungalows. Unlike the neat little estate on the edge of the village, there was no uniformity to the dwellings in Green Lane, which had sprung up piecemeal as Bishop Barnard expanded southwards and represented a whole variety of twentieth-century fashions. Wendy liked to look at the different houses. There was one row of six rather dull semis, where a builder had evidently managed to acquire a substantial stretch of land, but most had been individually designed: mock-Tudor monstrosities which looked down on their neighbours in every sense, here a wrought-iron balcony serving a central upstairs French window, there a mini-mansion with art-deco curves and stained glass top lights.

It would have been easy to overlook number thirty-seven alto-gether, because it stood much further back from the road than all its fellows and was mostly hidden by the overgrown hawthorn hedge which separated the front garden from the pavement. Apart from the brief interval it took anyone to pass the front gate, you couldn't see the house from the road at all. Even the gate itself was different to every other garden gate in Green Lane, having the appearance of a farm gate, sturdy, rectangular and always closed. A rectangle of wood had been fixed to the gate at some point in the past, with the name of the house burned into it. It had been there so long that the wood had weathered until the whole piece was almost as dark as the name itself, but it was still just possible to make it out: *The Ashes*. At some stage the house number had been added to one of the gateposts. A three and a seven, barely noticeable; the sort of small wooden numbers that could be obtained cheaply from a hardware shop. The numbers had once been black, but had long since acquired a greenish tint like the gatepost itself, and the screws or nails which secured the numbers had gone rusty. Everything was in need of a good clean-up and a lick of paint.

Wendy knew next to nothing about architecture, but even she could tell that the house was old, probably the oldest building on Green Lane. It was built of brown brick – smaller bricks than its modern neighbours, bricks which belonged to an earlier age – and it had a grey slate roof. She guessed that it must once have stood alone, probably the only dwelling on what would then have been a quiet country lane. In fact, it seemed to her that the house had remained a little bit aloof, as if it had never quite come to terms with having neighbours.

From the very first time she saw it, the house had intrigued her. Its front aspect looked like a house in a child's drawing, with a central front door, flanked by two downstairs windows, taller than they were wide, with a pair of matching windows on the first floor. She had probably walked past it a hundred times, holding Katie by the hand, pushing Jamie in his pram, then holding his hand, and eventually walking on her own once he had started school. But whenever she passed, she invariably glanced over the gate and down the drive, which ran along one side of the plot and presumably continued along the side of the house, though the view was obstructed by a pair of head-high wooden gates which stretched from the side of the house to the perimeter fence. Above the gates, she could see that the side wall of the house continued for some distance, suggesting that the building went back quite a long way. The front garden clearly needed more attention than it ever received, and as the years went by the whole place achieved an increasingly neglected air.

The occupant or occupants were a complete mystery. She had never seen any signs of life, though whenever she glanced down the drive after dark she could see the glow of an electric light behind the closed curtains of one downstairs window – always the one to the right of the front door. It was the sole indication that anyone lived there at all.

Much later she would remember how she had drawn the children's attention to The Ashes on a couple of occasions when they were all walking down to the village together. On the first of these she had declared that she would love to see inside the house.

'It looks pretty decrepit,' Tara had commented. 'Helen at school says some old relic lives there, all by herself.'

On the second occasion, Wendy had asked Katie if she wouldn't like to live in a house like that.

'Oh no,' Katie said. 'There might be ghosts.'

'Nonsense,' Wendy said. 'It looks to me like the sort of house where you might have an adventure.'

Katie wasn't having it. 'It just looks spooky to me.'

By the summer of 1979, the area behind the hawthorn hedge bore little resemblance to a garden. The grass, which had not been cut at all that year, had grown knee-high and run to seed, while the stone sundial which had once been clearly visible in the centre of the lawn was so overgrown with brambles that it might not have been there at all. A coterie of nettles had risen beside the wooden gateposts, impudently poking their heads out and leaning across the pavement, while bindweed snaked its way all over the cracked concrete of the drive. The onset of autumn and winter only increased the sense of dereliction. Plants and weeds turned brown, drooped, rotted, then frosted. The house maintained its expressionless air.

The arrival of the 'For Sale' board that bitter January day stopped Wendy dead in her tracks. The wind was stinging her face, so she had her head down and was level with the gate of number thirty-seven before she saw the board, but its presence had the most extraordinary effect on her. It was almost as if someone had delivered a blow to her chest, leaving her gasping for breath. All her impotent longing to see over the house surfaced in a rush.

Viewing by appointment only, the board said. Well, why shouldn't she make an appointment? It wasn't really right, said a voice in her head. She would only be wasting someone's time. It was true that they were planning to look for another house – a bigger house – but not one like this. This was a detached, double-fronted property, sitting on a large plot of land. She knew perfectly well they weren't in that league.

The board belonged to a local firm of estate agents who had an office in the High Street. She searched their window display in vain for the house, but it was not on show. As she stood there, she could hear Bruce's voice in her head. Her husband shared most people's healthy scepticism when it came to estate agents. '"Quaint" means old and poky, "spacious" means draughty and impossible to heat, "deceptively spacious", on the other hand, means it looks small and it is, while "would suit first-time buyer" translates as no one who isn't blind with love, or green as grass, is going to touch this with a barge pole.'

Since the house was not among those advertised in the window, she decided to go inside and enquire. There couldn't be any harm in it. Half the people who go to view houses are just timewasters, satisfying their idle curiosity, she told herself.

The receptionist greeted her with a smile straight out of a toothpaste advert.

'Good morning,' Wendy said. 'I want to enquire about viewing a house called The Ashes.'

The young woman smiled. 'Of course,' she said. She rose from her desk and crossed to the rear of the office, opening one of the filing cabinets and clicking through the dividers until she reached the section she wanted, then produced a single printed sheet, which she handed to Wendy.

A mature detached property set in a large garden in need of extensive renovation but offering a rare opportunity to provide a house of character.

'We're asking for offers in the region of twenty thousand pounds,' the young woman said, as if twenty thousand pounds was well within anyone's budget. 'But prospective buyers need to bear in mind that the property will require at least another ten thousand spent on it, depending upon what is required.'

Some sort of reaction was evidently expected, so Wendy nodded and said, 'Yes, of course,' in a knowing sort of way, as if she had a sock full of fifty pound notes at home, which would make such a proposition even remotely possible. 'What are the major things that require attention?' It was surprisingly easy to keep up the pretence, she thought, once you'd embarked on this fantasy persona of a woman who could afford to acquire a mature detached house of character in need of extensive renovation. 'Is it possible to make an appointment to see round the house?'

The woman smiled again. 'The property has generated consider-able interest, so we have decided to open it up for two general viewings this week, firstly on Thursday afternoon between one until four and then on Saturday morning from ten until twelve.'

'So anyone can just turn up between those times?'

'That's right.'

For a woman who was only going to have a nose around a house she didn't have a cat in hell's chance of buying, Wendy felt ridiculously excited.

She waited until they were all sitting down to tea that evening before she announced, 'You'll never guess! That old house on Green Lane – you know, the one I've always liked – is up for sale. They're holding some open viewings and there's one on Saturday morning. Why don't we all go and have a look?'

'Whatever for?' asked Bruce. 'We couldn't possibly afford to buy it.'

'Just out of interest,' Wendy said. 'I've always wanted to see inside.'

'What for?' Bruce asked again. 'Jamie, don't reach across like that. Ask your sister to pass the sauce, if you want it.'

'Didn't some scary old woman used to live there?' queried Tara.

'What happened to the scary old woman?' Katie wanted to know.

This stymied Wendy completely. She had taken it for granted that the elderly occupant had died. That was the usual reason for a long-neglected house suddenly appearing on the market, but she was reluctant to introduce that idea – she seemed to recall that Katie had already raised the possibility of ghosts and she badly wanted them all to like the house, even if there was no realistic prospect of it ever actually becoming theirs.

'We don't know anything about who lived there before,' she said. 'And anyway, that doesn't matter. The great thing is that it's a good chance to see inside the house. Once it's sold there may never be another opportunity.'

'I still don't see the point,' said Bruce. 'It sounds like a complete waste of time to me.'

Wendy turned to Tara, hoping for some support but receiving none. 'Yawnsville,' her eldest said, theatrically patting her hand against her mouth.

'Well, all right.' Wendy laughed off their indifference. 'I'll go up there myself, on Thursday afternoon.'

Wendy spent Thursday morning busying herself with what Bruce jokingly referred to as her housewifely chores. At lunchtime she sat at the dining table for a solo lunch of crispbread and cottage cheese, and after that she went upstairs to exchange her jeans for a smart skirt, selecting a bag that matched her shoes. Somehow it felt important to dress the part of someone who could actually afford to buy The Ashes.

She was relieved to find Jasmine Close and Magnolia Road deserted. Friendly neighbours might ask where she was going, all dressed up on a weekday afternoon, and now that she was actually on her way it suddenly felt silly to have smartened herself up merely in order to go nosing around someone else's house. Her own family clearly thought so. When she had mentioned the viewing to Bruce that morning as he left for work, he'd just laughed and warned her to look out for dodgy floorboards. 'Otherwise, you might find yourself having an unexpected look around the cellar.' Afterwards she'd wondered whether it was a roundabout way of letting her know that she was putting on weight, hence the cottage cheese lunch.

As soon as she turned into Green Lane, she could see what the woman in the estate agents' office had meant by 'considerable interest': there were far more parked cars than was usual for the time of day, and before Wendy had reached the gate herself, three lots of viewers had entered ahead of her. She arrived simultaneously with a couple who'd approached from the opposite direction. The woman was slim and pretty, huddled in a coat with a fake fur collar. Her companion was an older man in a heavy, dark overcoat. He held the gate open for both women, but once they were on the drive Wendy paused politely, allowing them to go ahead of her; she wanted to savour the moment.

Now that she was finally standing on the drive, she could see things she had never noticed before. There was a holly bush planted next to the path which ran between the drive and the front door. No need to buy holly at the greengrocers each Christmas, she thought, and there were some laurels – badly in need of attention – at the further side of the garden. More Christmas evergreens.

The front door was wide open, allowing all-comers to walk straight into the narrow, panelled hall, which was dark after the brightness of the winter afternoon. The man who'd entered ahead of her flicked a light switch up and down a couple of times, but the electricity had evidently been disconnected. Wendy was forced to pause and allow her eyes to adjust, while she tasted the stale air and listened to the sounds of other people's footsteps and voices as they echoed against the uncarpeted floors and bounced off the high ceilings. Along with these tastes and sounds came the unmistakable smells of damp and neglect, but finally, most strongly of all, came the strange and overwhelming sensation that the house wanted her.

'It wants to be loved.'

Oh, for goodness' sake, had she spoken out loud? Fortunately, everyone else had already moved on from the hall and her own entrance seemed to mark a lull in arrivals.

Three or four steps took her to the point where the panelling ended and the hall broadened out to double its initial width, with doors opening to the right and left, a staircase ascending immediately ahead of her, and to the right of the staircase a passage continued towards the rear of the house. As she hesitated, deciding where to begin, she noticed that the open door to her right had a paler patch of wallpaper alongside it, suggesting the ghost of a low, narrow doorway, suitable for a slender child. It was the outline of a clock. Wendy pictured it standing there, marking the minutes, hours, days, years. She smiled, satisfied by her powers of observation. It was like finding a clue.

She chose the doorway on her left, noticing as she entered the room and walked across the bare floorboards that her feet seemed to be making less noise than anyone else's, as if hers was not such a great intrusion. The room was empty. The wallpaper had faded to an indistinct pattern of yellows and browns and someone had pulled off a strip, revealing that the back of the paper was grey with mould. The plaster behind it had crumbled to expose the brickwork. Aged wiring hung from a central point in the ceiling, where a light fitting should have been, and the fireplace was filled with crumpled newspapers and lumps of dirt. In spite of this, she could see that the room had once been beautiful. It felt light and spacious, and around the perimeter of the ceiling there was a plaster border of intertwined leaves and flowers. Her reverie was interrupted by a trio of viewers who entered the room, talking loudly.

'It's difficult to say,' said one of the women.

They walked past Wendy as if she was not there. It's as if I'm part of it, she thought. As if I belong here and they don't.

She left the newcomers without acknowledgement and crossed the hall to look inside the other front room. This was a slightly larger room than the first and in a marginally better state. It was still possible to discern a pattern of roses on the wallpaper. Wendy remembered that this was the room from which she had sometimes seen a light shining: the room which had still been in use, when the rest of the house had perhaps been all but abandoned. There was nothing left to provide clues of its former occupant now, except that a fire was laid in the grate. A little layer of coal, a few pieces of kindling, neatly placed, only waiting for a match. Someone had laid the fire, expecting to light it, but fate had intervened. It was like the previous owner leaving a small gift for the new occupants. Welcome to your new home . . .

It was very easy to mentally kindle that fire, furnish the room with comfy chairs and a fireside rug, see the younger kids lying around in their pyjamas, staying up to watch Saturday night telly, their older sister, Tara, affecting teenage sophistication but enjoying *The Generation Game* as much as anyone, and herself with Bruce's arm draped around her shoulders as they sat, side by side, on the sofa. Just visualising it all took the winter chill from the room.

Returning to the hall, she noticed that the passage leading to the back of the house had a slate floor. It was illuminated by a window at its furthest end, but the daylight was being obstructed by a plump woman who was standing in front of the window, addressing an unseen third party. 'You're surely not going down there, are you, Jack?'

Jack was evidently standing out of sight, where the passage made a right angle turn to run along the back of the house. 'I certainly am.'

'There'll be nothing to see down there.' Even as she protested, the woman sounded resigned. Wendy didn't catch the unseen Jack's reply.

'Honest to God.' The woman turned her attention to Wendy. 'Men. They're nowt but little kids, the lot of them.' She adopted an expression of shared conspiracy. 'Fancy going down the cellar!'

Wendy smiled, uncertain how to respond.

'It's in a right state, isn't it?' the woman added, making a movement with her head to encompass the property as a whole. 'It'll take a mint of money to put it right.'

Wendy nodded.

'He loves anything like this, our Jack does. Old houses, traction engines, the lot.'

'It's a beautiful old house.'

The woman gave Wendy an odd look. 'All right if you like that sort of thing, I suppose. Did you want to come by, pet, or are you going in there?'

'In there' was a door at the end of the passage on the right-hand side. It led to what had once been a big, old-fashioned kitchen. Wendy entered to find the room already occupied. A small boy was looking out of the window into a cobbled back yard. Following his gaze, Wendy saw the back garden was screened from the kitchen by a range of single-storey outbuildings, whose roofs had mostly fallen in.

'There'd be room to stable Femo,' the little boy said in a high, piping voice.

'I hardly think that Daddy will buy it on the strength of that, darling.' The boy's mother was sizing up the ancient cooking range which occupied part of the wall opposite the window.

She doesn't like it, Wendy thought. Why did no one else seem to get it? Couldn't anyone else sense its yearning? All The Ashes needed was someone to love it properly.

Two more women entered the room, obviously curiousity viewers like herself.

'Eee, will you look at that!' exclaimed the younger of the pair, pointing at the range.

Two men arrived immediately after them and began poking about in a big built-in cupboard. 'It's a wonder it's never burned down with the state of this wiring,' one of them said.

'You'd have thought she'd have had that seen to, if it were dangerous,' the older woman said. Wendy wasn't sure if the two pairs were together, but the situation made for conversations between strangers.

'Dangerous?' This from the same man as before. 'It's bloody lethal!'

'You know these old ones,' the younger woman put in. 'They don't realize. They think things last forever.'

'Still,' her companion said. 'I'm surprised at Mrs Duncan. It's not as if she were short of a penny or two. I mean, just look at the place. It's not what I was expecting.'

'Did you know her then?' asked the man, who had not yet spoken.

'Well . . . by sight, you know. Not really to speak to. I've lived in Green Lane since 1938 and she's been here all that time.'

The other woman glanced at her watch, as if sensing the possibility of a delay. 'We'd better get going,' she said. 'We haven't seen upstairs yet and I need to be back home for our Gary.'

'Our mam used to say she was never right after . . .'

Wendy did not hear the rest, for the women were gone, their places taken by the couple who had arrived at the gate when she did. She tried to ignore the other viewers and concentrate on taking in the room, committing it to memory, because she would probably never see it again. There were windows on three elevations in the kitchen. One faced across the courtyard towards the outbuildings, which even the estate agents' handout had described, in a rare rush of candour, as 'semi-derelict'; another looked out to the side, where a stout fence and a shield of trees and shrubs separated the plot from its immediate neighbour; and finally there was a narrow window which looked up the drive towards the road. Wendy had not realized that the rear of the house was slightly wider than the front. Until today that window had always been hidden by the tall double gates which stood partway along the drive, but now they had been opened and this enabled anyone standing in the kitchen to keep an eye out for someone entering the property from the road. Wendy imagined herself looking out for Bruce . . . putting the kettle on, or pouring him a drink, as she saw his car pull into the drive.

When she left the kitchen, she found her progress along the rear passage was still blocked by the same woman who had spoken to her before. The man called Jack was just returning from his exploration of the cellar, torch in hand.

'Thank goodness for that. I thought you was gone for good,' his wife chided, holding the door open for him as he emerged.

Jack exchanged a smile with Wendy as he stepped up from the wooden stairs and closed the cellar door behind him.

'Where to next?' His wife consulted the agents' particulars which she held in her hand. 'Utility room and storeroom?'

'This must be the store.' Jack stepped through an opening next to the cellar door and flashed his torch around the darkened space. Wendy peered in from the doorway, grateful to have fallen in with Jack and his torch at just the right moment. The space was lined from floor to ceiling with dusty wooden shelves, though this still left sufficient space for several people to cram inside, should they choose to.

'I wonder why they've boarded up this window?' Jack mused, shining the torch directly ahead of him.

'Come on out of there,' said his wife. 'Poking about in that dusty hole.'

Jack ignored her, advancing further into the storeroom while Wendy retreated into the passage. This ended in what the estate agents described as a utility room, though it had clearly seen recent use as a kitchen. There was a big ceramic sink under the window, large enough to bath a small child, its lower plumbing on show and lagged in old sacking. To one side of that was an ancient gas cooker, and at right angles to the cooker was a freestanding two-tier kitchen cupboard of the variety favoured by her own mother in the 1950s. One of the bottom doors was missing and the patterned Perspex of the upper cupboards was cracked and dirty. Wendy experienced a sudden sense of desolation, picturing a lonely old lady who had not been short of a penny or two, cooking her solitary meal in her big, empty house. The outside door opened at that moment, admitting the little boy with the high-pitched voice and his mother. The woman wrinkled her nose. 'Pretty squalid, isn't it?' she remarked as she passed through.

'It must have been lovely, once.'

The woman made a dismissive noise as she headed back to the main part of the house. Wendy followed, electing to leave the yard and back garden until the end. She walked along the passage, made the right-angle turn at the kitchen and so returned to the widest part of the hall, where she encountered Jack and his wife again. He was backing out of a closed door – smaller than the norm – which stood between the first room she'd explored and the foot of the stairs.

'Big walk-in cupboard,' he informed her. 'It backs on to the storeroom. If you took down the back wall of this cupboard, it would lead you straight into it. Open it up, get rid of all them shelves, and it would make a nice little study for somebody, that would.'

Wendy nodded, noticing as she did that his wife was starting to look impatient. She sidestepped the wife and began to climb the stairs. The bannister was smooth and solid, the dust already polished from it by the passage of numerous hands. A tall, arched window faced her on the half landing, where she was confronted with another choice: to mount the trio of stairs to her left, which led into a short corridor, or to follow the main staircase as it turned back on itself in order to gain the upper landing. She decided on the latter. The upper landing was almost square and offered five doors to choose from, one of which was slightly smaller and evidently led to the attic. All four bedrooms were large – certainly bigger than any of their bedrooms in Jasmine Close. As she explored each in turn, Wendy inwardly named them: Katie's, Tara's and Jamie's. 'Our room' was the biggest of all. It had a cast-iron fireplace and its window overlooked the front garden, which by a trick of the light took on a much better appearance when viewed from above. The grass appeared shorter, the shrubs tamer, the weeds less profuse. While she was contemplating this illusion, she was joined by a trio she had not seen before, two women and a man, who was saying, 'Derek would know the cost better.'

'Well, I don't think it's suitable at all,' said the shorter of the women. 'I was expecting six bedrooms.'

'There's really only four,' the other woman agreed. 'You can't count those two little rooms at the end of the passage, where the slaveys slept.'

'Couldn't you run a partition through this room?' asked the man, indicating the largest bedroom.

'What about the window? That would complicate things,' said the taller lady, apparently oblivious to Wendy's meek, 'Excuse me,' as she tried to squeeze past them and on to the landing.

'It would probably make two decent singles, I grant you,' the man mused, while Wendy felt tempted to shove him down the stairs. To even consider the idea of destroying the symmetry of that lovely room!

She managed to escape them and attempted to explore the attic, but this proved impossible: a flight of steep, narrow stairs ascended into complete darkness. With the electricity disconnected and no torch, it was an impossible task. She did not mind all that much. She had always been slightly spooked by the thought of attics. The moment anyone in a film went up to the attic, you just knew

something bad was going to happen. Not here, of course. Not in
a lovely, friendly house like this. Instead she descended to the half
landing, where she found the bathroom. The plain white bath,
basin and toilet were grimly old fashioned and set against chest-
high, once-white wooden panelling. In one corner the greying
paper was coming away from the ceiling. It was easily big enough
to install a shower cubicle as well as a bathtub, she thought.
Beyond the bathroom, the passage ended in a door and, when she
reached it, Wendy could see at once what the women in the
bedroom had been talking about. These had indeed once been
the servants' rooms, one leading directly into another. Though
both rooms were about twelve feet wide, the roof sloped up from
floor level on each side, making the effective space much smaller.
An icy draught was penetrating a gap where one of the skylights
in the sloping roof no longer fitted snugly. She realized that she
must be in the small wing which extended out above one side of
the outbuildings that formed the rear courtyard.

After the few seconds it took to glance around the servants'
quarters, Wendy made her way back to the stairs. The people who
had discussed the possibility of vandalizing 'our bedroom' were
gone. As she paused on the half landing, the sunshine flooding in
through the arched window seemed to grow brighter. For a moment
she allowed herself to imagine Katie and Jamie, racing up and
down the stairs, playing hide-and-seek, bobbing in and out of the
numerous doorways. It couldn't happen, of course. Even though
it had always been her special house, it was only a dream. It could
never actually *be* her house. She descended the stairs slowly,
enjoying the solid feel of the balustrade, taking in the plasterwork
around the light fittings, noticing the paler patches where pictures
had once hung. After standing aside to make room for yet more
new arrivals, she made her way out of the front door, along the
garden path and down the drive towards the rear of the house,
which brought her to the yard she had seen from the kitchen
window. It was enclosed on two sides by the house and on the
third by the semi-ruinous brick-built sheds. The fourth side of
the square, where the drive ended, was protected from the neigh-
bouring garden by a sturdy six-foot wooden fence, which appeared
to be in better and more solid repair than almost anything else she
had seen so far.

The outbuildings didn't occupy her for long. The one nearest the drive still had most of its roof intact and contained a small amount of kindling in an old log basket and a part-used sack of coal. The second and third in the row had lost pretty much all of their roofs. The section of the building which stood beneath the servants' bedrooms had a pair of arched double doors, wedged open but leaning dangerously. Peering beyond them, Wendy could make out a couple of wooden stalls. The little boy had been right about the existence of stabling.

The entrance to the back garden ought to have been as wide as the drive, but the contents of what had once been a border producing vegetables or flowers had rioted unchecked until, even in winter, only a narrow track of flattened grass was left between the minia-ture jungle and the wall of the outbuildings. Wendy worked her way along for a few yards, taking care to avoid the treacherous, slippery patches of mud, where multiple feet had already trodden that day. It reminded her of a fairy tale, where the traveller strug-gles through the wilderness until he or she can enter the hidden garden, which always turns out to be a magical, secret place, but when she reached the point where the garden should have opened out to the full width of the plot, she was disappointed to find that she could go no further. The garden at the front had merely been neglected. The area behind the outbuildings had obviously been allowed to run wild for years. It wasn't even possible to see how far the garden extended – though it was clearly a large area. A confusion of trees and bushes, dead brown stalks, and mouldering, indistinguishable hummocks all struggled to catch a glimpse of the sky from beneath cloaks of ivy and convolvulus. A blackbird startled her, screeching as it flew from one branch to another. She had no alternative but to admit defeat and edge back the way she had come, only to find that the courtyard was becoming quite crowded.

'I'm sure Marcus could never bring himself to live in such an ugly house,' a woman in a duffel coat and boots laced to the knee was telling her companion.

'Dreadful old place,' declared a man in a check jacket. 'The best thing they could do is demolish the whole thing. You'd get half-a-dozen starter-homes in this plot, if you planned them running sideways from the road.'

'Decrepit is the word I would use, dear.' A woman in pale green patent shoes had just emerged from the back door and was picking her way across the cobbles, her face a study in disgust.

It isn't fair, Wendy thought. I'm the one who really loves it, but I can't have it.

At teatime that day, the rest of the family took very little interest in Wendy's account of her visit to The Ashes. Bruce uh-huhhed a couple of times, before Tara jumped in to change the subject. In spite of their lack of encouragement, Wendy couldn't get the house out of her mind, and when she and Bruce climbed into bed that night, she said wistfully, 'You should have seen the size of the biggest bedroom. We could have easily fitted a king-size bed in there.'

'I know we need to look for somewhere with a bit more space,' Bruce said, 'but are you really that unhappy here?' He sounded puzzled, even a little anxious.

'No, no, of course not. It's just a lovely house, that's all. I've always felt like it was my special house. My dream house, I suppose.'

'Well, OK . . . But you know we couldn't ever afford to buy it?'

'Of course I know that.'

'Then . . . don't you think it's a bit weird to keep going on about it?'

'I'm not going on about it. I was just interested to see inside, that's all.'

There was a pause before he spoke again. 'And you're not . . . unhappy?'

'I'm perfectly happy. I couldn't be happier.'

'You're not bored? Being at home all day?'

'I don't have time to be bored. I've always got loads to do.'

'Good. That's OK then.' He kissed her and she kissed him back. It was a familiar preamble to love-making, but that night Bruce turned over and went to sleep, leaving her wakefully pondering her weight gain, her approaching fortieth birthday, and the rather odd way Bruce had asked about her state of happiness.

Why would he think she was unhappy? She had known happiness and unhappiness. She knew the difference now, even if she had once been mistaken. She had been much younger then. It had been easy to believe that happiness lay just where she expected to find it. Robert had been her childhood sweetheart. She couldn't even recall a time when she hadn't known him. People liked Robert. Older people approved of him. Her parents used to say things like, 'Robert is terribly clever,' as if being clever was something she ought to have been a little bit afraid of – and perhaps it was. Robert had taken her to the school dance and then to the pictures, after which it had been generally understood that they were going out together. There had been one long, glorious school summer holiday, with more visits to the pictures, and days out to Whitby and Scarborough, both easily accessible on the train from Middlesbrough and all financed by Robert's Saturday job at the local greengrocers, and they had engaged in endless sessions of snogging on the sofa in her parents' front room. By the time Robert left for university they were already engaged . . . but it was going to be a long engagement. 'We are going to wait,' they would tell people virtuously, as if by waiting they would be getting something better at the end of it.

Robert's three years at university had faded in her memory: a jumble of homecomings and departures, interleaved by waiting. Waiting on the platform for Robert's train to pull in. Waiting for her building society savings to reach the magical figure of one hundred pounds, so that she could write and tell him. Waiting for Robert's letters to slip through the letterbox and onto her parents' bristly doormat. Waiting, always waiting. Robert changed over the course of those three years. His hair grew longer, his temper a little shorter, but it never occurred to her that their future together would be anything but rosy. They were engaged. They loved each other. That was happiness.

After he graduated, Robert was offered a job in Coventry. She hadn't expected that. Wendy had been working in the typing pool at Bradshaws for three years by then and they were able to use her savings to put down a deposit on a tiny terraced house. Robert moved in immediately and the long-awaited wedding took place at the parish church four months later, just shy of her twenty-first birthday.

The move to Coventry had been a disaster from the start. She missed her friends and family and failed to settle into her new job, where colleagues teased her for her accent and called her 'Geordie' (which was more than slightly annoying to a girl who came from Teesside). Her new social life was equally fraught. Robert had a natural flair for making friends, but they were mostly single graduates, who no more than tolerated his funny little wife from up north. When they laughed at her for thinking Siegfried Sassoon was a painter, Robert joined in. In public Robert was Mr

Bonhomie, but it was a different story at home, and like a confused child who does not know why she is being punished, Wendy began to cry at every angry look or cross word, which in turn drove Robert to distraction. 'Don't turn on the tears,' he would storm, which invariably made her sob even harder.

Her mother had always said that every baby is a miracle, so Wendy believed that Tara's arrival would make things better, but a tiny, perpetually grizzling baby was not the miracle they needed. Rows escalated, becoming louder and more frequent, often conducted to a soundtrack of Tara's screaming, until one night in August 1963, when Tara was ten months old and they were engaged in a series of arguments stretching back intermittently over days, Robert had picked up a glass ashtray and flung it at the chimney breast, where it shattered into a trillion fragments, one of which bounced back, cutting his cheek. Previously their violence had been verbal. The broken glass and the sight of blood on Robert's cheek represented a frightening escalation. As Wendy cowered in a chair, her husband picked up his car keys and left without another word.

As the sound of his car faded into the distance, an oppressive silence had settled over the house. Wendy stayed in the chair for some time, staring at the broken glass. Eventually she roused herself sufficiently to clear it up, taking the infinite care of a mother whose baby is liable to crawl across the scene of destruction the moment she is set down the next morning. About two hours after Robert's abrupt departure, the silence in the house was broken by the telephone ringing. She hesitated to answer it. Suppose it was her mother, or Robert's mother, to both of whom the union had always been represented as completely blissful? But the caller was persistent. Someone who was not prepared to give up. Someone who knew she was at home.

'Hello?' She tried to sound calm. And when there was a moment's silence from the other end, 'Who is it?'

'It's Dennis – you know . . . Robert's friend, Dennis. Is that you, Wendy?' (A silly question, she thought – who else would be picking up their phone?)

'Yes,' she said, trying even harder to keep her voice level. 'Do you want Robert? He's out at the moment.'

'Robert's here with me. He doesn't want to speak to you himself. He's asked me to tell you . . . are you still there, Wendy?'

'Yes,' she gasped through the tears which came immediately, partly due to the humiliation that Robert must have confided their problems – at least to some degree – in Dennis. How could he do that? How could he break the traditional, unspoken code of presenting a united front to the world? She felt exposed, betrayed.

'He wants me to tell you that he doesn't want to live with you anymore.' Dennis spoke like a schoolboy actor, delivering carefully rehearsed lines, breaking the news as kindly as he could. 'He says the situation has become insupportable. He says that if you need any money, there is some in the Toby jug.'

What felt like a very long silence followed, while she stood holding the phone to her ear, choking back sobs as the tears rolled down her cheeks, dripped on to the hand that was holding the phone and eventually fell onto the front of her dress, creating a series of damp splotches on the fabric.

'Are you all right, Wendy?'

She could tell from his voice that Dennis felt sorry for her and didn't enjoy having to give her Robert's message. He would do it though, because he liked Robert, and it occurred to her that as well as being sorry for her, he was probably even more sympathetic to Robert.

'Yes, thank you. I'm perfectly all right.' It wasn't even a well-told lie, but it must have been enough to satisfy Dennis, because he said goodnight and replaced the receiver.

In spite of the telephone call, she had initially assumed that Robert would come back. After a couple of days she had swallowed her pride and called Dennis, but though he admitted that Robert was staying with him, he also conveyed to her that Robert declined to come to the phone. Later the same day she returned from a shopping trip and found that Robert had sneaked into the house during her absence and removed all his personal belongings. She tried ringing him at work, but he was never available to take her calls, and after three weeks, though still shell-shocked and disbelieving, Wendy finally accepted the situation. She packed a suitcase, put Tara into her pushchair and took a taxi to the station, where she used the last of the money from the Toby jug for the train ticket, which brought her back north to the safety of her parents' house in Middlesbrough.

Robert had evidently been monitoring her movements, because the first of the envelopes arrived a few days later. They appeared at a rate of one per month, each containing a cheque, always made out in neat black ink, in Robert's distinctive handwriting. There was never an accompanying note, not even a card at Christmas. At first these wordless arrivals wounded her, but she eventually grew hardened to them, extracting the monthly cheques without bothering to run hopeful fingers around the inside of the envelope in case she had missed something.

In the meantime, Robert's solicitor began to communicate with hers. Her mother never quite got over the shock. There had never been a divorce in the family. Respectable women of her mother's generation didn't get divorced. They didn't 'give up' after a mere three years of marriage, preferring the comparative dignity of sitting in winged armchairs on opposite sides of the fireplace to their husbands, fading slowly, like the wedding photographs on the mantelpiece.

Wendy's mother stayed in touch with Robert's. Sometimes Wendy gave her mother photographs of Tara to give to Robert's mother. She guessed that some of these photographs were destined for Robert himself, but she never enquired or commented on it. She would have sent him photographs of his daughter if he had asked for them. But he did not ask, not directly at least, for any photographs or news of Tara. Sometimes she wondered how much you needed to hate someone in order to cut them off so completely, but as the months passed she realized that the route to survival lay in trying to achieve an equal detachment. She slotted back as far as possible into her former life, even getting her old job back in the typing pool at Bradshaws, returning home each evening to a dinner cooked by her mother, who made no complaints about minding Tara through the day. Eventually the abnormality of Robert's behaviour became less strange to her than the fact that she had once shared her life with him. She never saw him and never spoke to him. As her divorce progressed, he became like one of those characters in a television play, who is apparently central to the plot yet never appears.

Her first encounter with Bruce took place on a chilly December afternoon in 1967. Rain was slating down from a leaden sky and the gutters were awash. It was the sort of day when umbrellas are up and heads are down, but Wendy had forgotten her umbrella and was relying on a little plastic rain hood, from which strands of her hair were escaping in wet tendrils. A passing car had splattered the front of her tights with dirty brown slush and, to complete her humiliation, when she was in the middle of the zebra crossing her carrier bag decided to capitulate to the downpour and give way completely, leaving her clutching string handles attached to shreds of brown paper. Bruce – then a complete stranger – had followed her on to the crossing and, seeing what had happened, took pity and stopped to help her retrieve the spilled shopping, piling the various items into her arms so that everything was saved except for an exploded paper bag of sprouts, which had to be left to their fate.

When they reached the opposite side of the road, Bruce insisted on her taking shelter in a bank doorway while he ran into a nearby shop and bought a string bag. He introduced himself while she repacked her shopping, then waited with her under the dripping awning of a nearby butcher's shop until her bus came, the two of them watching the grisly demise of the scattered Brussels sprouts, as they were crushed beneath the passing traffic. For years afterwards it would bring a private smile to her lips, remembering how he had made her laugh, drawing her attention to one particularly intrepid sprout which had rolled to and fro across the road, just managing to avoid the wheels of passing cars and lorries, until it was eventually flattened by a furniture van and they let out a simultaneous 'ooh' of disappointment, which drew surprised glances from others waiting at the bus shelter. Telephone numbers had been exchanged and a rendezvous for a drink agreed before her bus arrived.

Her mother had not initially warmed to the idea of Bruce. The expression 'on the rebound' was employed. Fortunately, Bruce was the sort of chap her father described as 'steady', and even her mother was won over when it became apparent that Tara had taken to Bruce from the off.

They had not been dating very long before Bruce poured out the story of his own doomed love. He had been engaged to a girl called Frances in his native Ashby-de-la-Zouch, and they too had played the waiting game, saving up for a house deposit while Frances finished her teacher training. During Frances's final year at college, Bruce was despatched on a temporary posting to Teesside. The courtship had continued via letters, phone calls and only occasional meetings. Then Bruce had received a promotion which made the Teesside posting permanent, and while he continued to write of setting a wedding date and doing some house-hunting, Frances's letters began to cool, until the day one arrived informing him that she wanted to break off the engagement altogether. She had talked it over with her mother, Frances wrote, and decided that she would be making a mistake in marrying him. She said that while she was very fond of Bruce (an awful get out, 'very fond'), she had realized that she did not love him enough to uproot herself, leaving her family and all her friends, for a place where she knew no one but him. 'My heart was broken, of course,' Bruce said. 'But that was before I met you.'

It certainly appeared that Frances's instincts had been proved right. Bruce's meeting with Wendy had taken place a matter of weeks after her Dear John letter, while Frances herself had wasted very little time in marrying one of her old friends from college, after what Bruce's mother described as a whirlwind romance. There had been nothing of the whirlwind about Bruce. He and Wendy became acquainted slowly and carefully, like a pair of children building a castle out of Lego bricks. They married in 1969: a quiet register office affair, though Tara cajoled Bruce into letting her have a bridesmaid dress and a posy. People warned them that Tara might be difficult, but Bruce was the father she had never known and Katie the baby sister she claimed to have always longed for. All the pieces fitted together beautifully – and that was happiness, Wendy thought.

There had been occasional moments of self-doubt, particularly as her fortieth birthday loomed large on the horizon. Sometimes she wondered if she ought to be doing more with her life. Other women were embarking on Open University courses or netting second incomes after training to be nurses or teachers, whereas she and Bruce just kept on going in the same old way, ferrying the children about, Bruce playing squash once or twice a week, Wendy going to night classes (her cake decorating surpassed all, but she never really mastered conversational Spanish). She wasn't sure that the Open University offered very much for failed Spanish conversationalists.

*The act itself was all too easy, too fast. It was the conceal-
ment, the clearing up afterwards that took the time. Blood
everywhere, staining everything, turning from scarlet to rusty
brown. And all the time, expecting someone to come. Fearing
discovery.*

*You can't get bloodstains out, not once they've dried. Don't
believe all that stuff about soaking things in cold water, or
using Vanish soap. That's why I had to build a bonfire in the
back garden. It was the only way I could think of to get rid
of the clothes. There were no rules against having bonfires
back then, and it was November. A good time for bonfires.*

TWO

February 1980

Though she had no real hope of buying The Ashes, each
time Wendy drew level with the gate she was almost afraid
to look. Roughly a fortnight after the public viewings, the
sign she had been anticipating finally appeared, tacked across
the original sale board on the gate: *Sold – Subject to Contract.*
That was it. Her numbers had not come up on the pools in time.

The telephone call came on a weekday evening while they were
having tea (or what posher folks would have called dinner). Wendy
was sitting in the seat nearest to the door, so she got up to answer
the phone. In an era of nuisance calls from purveyors of fitted
kitchens and double glazing, her 'Hello' was cool and cautious.

'Is that Wendy Thornton?'

She didn't recognize the voice, and then misunderstood the
initial introduction, so it took a moment or two of confused interaction before she eventually realized that the caller was a distant
cousin, Larry, who was barely more than a memory from half-
forgotten weddings and funerals.

'Oh, Larry . . . what a nice surprise. How are you?' She was conscious that her enthusiasm sounded artificial (though the surprise was genuine enough: she couldn't recollect Larry ever calling her before). Through the open door of the dining room, she caught a glimpse of Bruce, frowning. They had only just sat down to eat and he objected to this interruption in their normal routine. She turned away before he had a chance to mouth anything about ringing back. Small patches of warmth had already formed on her cheeks, born of the embarrassment of her initial hostility. She could hardly compound the felony by telling Larry that it wasn't a convenient time.

Her husband and children had fallen silent, forking in their food while listening in on her half of the conversation. First there was a lengthy pause while she gave her full attention to what Larry was saying. Then, 'Yes . . . yes . . . oh, yes, very sad.' Another pause. 'But of course, she was a good age, wasn't she? I did think about coming down for the funeral, but it's such a long way for me and I would have had to arrange for someone to collect Jamie from school . . .'

Out of the corner of her eye, Wendy saw seventeen-year-old Tara exchange bemused looks with her father across the table. Even as she uttered the words, Wendy knew that they probably came across as a thin excuse to Larry, who was a childless bachelor and, in any case, very probably recognized it for the lie that it was. She would not for a moment have contemplated travelling all the way down to London for the funeral of an ancient relative whom she had not seen in years. Her most recent visit to her mother's one surviving aunt had been at least five years ago and had only been undertaken because it coincided with some other family excursion south.

Back in the dining room, eight-year-old Katie, the first to decide that the telephone call was of no particular interest, asked her father whether he intended to watch a programme that night on BBC2.

'Ninety-one? Well, there, I knew she was getting on . . .' Wendy knew she was prattling, but it was hard to know what to say, with Larry being a virtual stranger and her having no idea what had put it into his head to contact her at all. The reveal came a sentence later.

'A beneficiary under the will? Me? Goodness, I never expected that!' A moment of genuine sincerity there, she thought, though if anything, the conversation became even more strained as she felt obliged to reiterate the difficulties she would have experienced in travelling down for the funeral.

Larry had clearly tired of excuses regarding the funeral, because he cut across this with a piece of information that all but stunned her into silence. After that Wendy stopped attempting to make polite conversation and just listened. Then she said, 'Thank you.'

When she finally returned to the dining room – a space so restricted that when all five of them were seated at the table, the backs of the chairs almost touched the wall on one side and the sideboard on another – she found the children all talking at once.

'But it's a programme about horses,' Katie was protesting.

'You know we always watch *The Rockford Files* on Tuesdays,' said Tara, in the voice she used when attempting to crush any dissent from her younger siblings.

'Why can't I stay up to watch *Dallas*? All my friends at school watch it.' Jamie was getting tired and becoming querulous.

'Be quiet a minute, all of you,' said Bruce. 'Your mother looks as if she's seen a ghost.'

'Ooh, have you, Mam?' Katie had a tendency to take things rather literally.

'It's just an expression, pet.' Wendy resumed her seat and glanced down at her plate, where the gravy was congealing around her slice of home-made chicken and mushroom pie. She hesitated, taking in each of the faces around the table before she said, 'Though, actually, I have had a bit of a surprise.'

'A nice surprise?' asked Tara.

'Oh, yes. Definitely a nice surprise. You remember I told you that my aunt Adi had died?' She addressed the family in general, but Bruce in particular, continuing, without waiting for his acknowledgement, 'Well, it turns out that she's left me some money. One of my cousins – well, strictly speaking, I think he's one of Mam's cousins – Larry – is the executor of her will, and that's what he rang to tell me. She left the money to Mam, but under the terms of her will, since Mam is already dead, the money will come to me instead.'

'How much?' asked Bruce, not bothering to beat about the bush.

'Thirty-seven thousand pounds.' She said it slowly, savouring the taste of it. Their house wasn't worth thirty-seven thousand pounds.

'Bloody hell!' Bruce was not much given to swearing, and certainly not in front of the children.

'Flipping heck!' exclaimed Tara. 'No one ever told me we had rich relations. Are there any more out there? Who on earth was this Aunt Adi, anyway?'

'She was your nanna Burton's cousin. Adeline Crawley, her name was. I hardly knew her, to tell you the truth. Her part of the family went down south years ago, before I was born. Mam always said they'd done well for themselves. The thing is, there were a lot of sisters in that branch of the family and, apart from Larry's mother, none of them got married, so I suppose as the others died off, the money gradually got passed along to Aunt Adi. According to Larry, she left everything to be split equally among her cousins, but she's lived so long, it's mostly her cousins' children that'll be benefitting and there's none too many of those.'

'Lucky for you she thought blood was thicker than water,' said Bruce. 'She could easily have left it all to the cats' home.'

'Lucky for all of us.'

'I suppose this means I can have that dress from Topshop after all,' said Tara, with a hint of mischievous sarcasm. The dress in question had been pronounced of dubious quality and too expensive during a mother and daughter shopping expedition to Middlesbrough the previous Saturday.

Never slow to scent an advantage, Jamie chipped in with a request for a new bike.

'Hold on, hold on,' Bruce protested. 'Your mother hasn't even got the money yet and you're already spending it. I'm sure there will be a chance to each choose something nice in due course, but we won't be spending it all at once, you know.'

'I've already decided what to do with most of it,' Wendy said. 'It's like a sort of sign, isn't it? The money coming just now . . . It means we can buy that house.'

The morning after the phone call from Larry, Wendy timed her walk down Green Lane and into the High Street to coincide with the nine a.m. opening of the estate agents' office. She just had to pray that the legalities accompanying the sale had not progressed too far. Whatever the prospective purchasers had offered for The Ashes, she would simply offer more.

The same young woman with the toothy smile was manning the front desk. 'Good morning. Can I help you?'

'Yes, please. I've come about the house in Green Lane. The Ashes.' Wendy took in the look of mild surprise but ploughed on regardless. 'I want to make an appointment to view the house with my husband, and after he has seen it, we will be making an offer.'

The teeth flashed back into smile mode. 'Well . . . goodness me, doesn't word get round quickly? We only heard that the sale had fallen through yesterday. We haven't even had time to readvertise or take down the sold plate.'

Wendy sat down heavily in a convenient chair. The sale had fallen through. It was an omen. Not only did she want the house, but the house wanted her. She felt as if she had successfully pulled off a conspiracy with someone she had never met. On the way home, when she looked over the gate, she wondered if she ought to pinch herself.

Her joyful mood was only slightly dented by the general air of surprise which greeted her announcement over tea that she had made an appointment for the whole family to view The Ashes.

'Good grief, Wendy, I didn't think you were serious,' Bruce said. 'You've got to think about the running costs of a house like that. It would be far more than we're used to. Even with an efficient system, the heating alone would be prohibitive, and I hate to think what the council rates would be. To say nothing of maintenance. Even after you've done the place up, old houses are invariably money pits.'

'But we'll have no mortgage to pay,' she reminded him. 'And once this house is sold, we can invest the money we get from it.'

Bruce nodded, but without much enthusiasm. 'I suppose there's no harm in taking a look.'

Jamie, who had been ploughing through his mashed potatoes, now looked up and asked, 'We're not going to move house, are we? I don't want to move unless we can live next door to Andrew Webster.'

'Don't worry, Jamie, you will still see Andrew at school every day.'

'But I don't want to move, except next to him.'

'Don't be silly,' said Tara. 'You don't live next door to him now, do you?'

'Andrew Webster is my bestest friend and I only want to move if I can live in the house next door to his house.'

His voice had developed a whining note. Wendy decided that he was overtired. 'I haven't told you about the special presents yet, have I?' she said brightly.

The younger children eagerly confirmed that she had not. In fact, she had not even thought of the scheme until that moment, but she improvised frantically. 'We'll each have a hundred pounds to buy something we've always really wanted.'

'Except for your mother,' muttered Bruce, 'who will have twenty thousand pounds to buy herself something she's always wanted.'

Wendy ignored him. 'What will you choose, Tara?'

'A stacking system. The one I really like is a bit more than that, but I can put the rest to it out of my building society account.'

'Can I have a proper motorbike?' enquired Jamie. 'A real one, with an engine?'

'Too much,' said Bruce. 'A hundred pounds will buy you an ordinary bike, but you only had a new one at Christmas. Think of something else.'

'A digital watch then, like Andrew Webster's.'

Bruce and Wendy exchanged glances. The digital watch question had come up before. They both knew that such a fragile article wouldn't last two minutes strapped to Jamie's wrist.

'How about you, Katie?'

'Is it enough to go to Disneyland?'

'Not nearly enough, I'm afraid.'

'Though if we are careful with the money,' Bruce paused to give his wife a meaningful look, 'we could use it to go to all sorts of interesting places.'

'I suppose there's no hope of a pocket money raise?' asked Tara.

The appointment to view the house had been arranged for Saturday morning, so that the whole family could see it together. Wendy attempted to rush everyone into readiness with a haste that was completely alien to their normal weekend routine.

'For goodness' sake,' Bruce complained. 'The house isn't going anywhere. It will still be there if we're five minutes late.'

'Oh, I don't know,' said Tara. 'It's always looked about ready to fall down to me. I bet it stinks too, if it's been shut up for a long time.'

'I'm not going to live in a house that smells nasty.' Katie wrinkled her nose.

'You mustn't be put off by any funny smells,' Wendy said. 'It's a bit damp and dirty now, but once it's been done up, it will be wonderful.'

The young man from the estate agents was waiting for them at the gate. Wendy had pictured the younger children's excitement as they all but ran up the drive, so she was disappointed by the way they hung back, following at a distance and waiting with resigned expressions while the young man stood on the front doorstep fumbling with a bunch of keys.

Jamie peered through one of the front windows, putting his face up close to the dirty glass. 'The wallpaper's coming off the walls,' he said. 'It looks horrible.'

Katie edged closer to Bruce and slotted her hand into his.

'Here we are.' The young man sounded relieved as the door swung open. 'I understand you've been round once before, so I expect you know your way. I'll just wait out here for you. Call me if you have any questions. Take as long as you like.'

In the hall Bruce paused to admire the panelling. 'That's a nice feature. You'd need some pictures to break it up a bit. Some old-fashioned hunting scenes would look just right.'

'Not fox hunting!' exclaimed Tara.

'Only pictures, Tara. No one's advocating that the Zetland pursues a fox through the back garden.'

'It does smell a bit, doesn't it?' said Katie.

'A bit is putting it mildly,' said Tara.

'It only needs the doors and windows to be left open for a while,' Wendy said. 'Fresh air makes a huge difference.'

'I think it needs a bit more than that,' said Bruce.

Wendy watched their faces anxiously as the little group moved from room to room.

'You could turn this into a splendiferous kitchen,' said Tara, when they reached the big room with the old-fashioned range at the back of the house. 'It would be massive, like a house on the telly . . . But could you put all this right?' She nudged a lump of fallen plaster with one foot.

'It would take a hell of a lot to put it right,' said Bruce. 'Time and money. And you wouldn't be able to live here until it was all done, either.'

'But we wouldn't need to,' Wendy said. 'That's the beauty of having a house already and not needing to sell one in order to buy the other.'

'Is there enough money to do it?' asked Katie.

'I honestly have no idea, my pet.' Bruce sounded slightly exasperated. 'You'd have to ask a builder – that is, if you were going to buy it.'

Wendy had taken the precaution of bringing a torch.

'Mind how you go,' Bruce cautioned, as she led the way into the cellar. 'These stairs may be rotten.'

In fact, the stairs were remarkably sound. Even so, Katie hung back and declined to join the others as they followed Wendy down.

'Wow,' said Tara, when they all reached solid ground and Wendy played her torch around the room. 'Look at that for a wine rack.'

The structure in question, made in dark wood and covered in cobwebs, occupied the whole of one wall from floor to ceiling. Their wine rack at home was a self-assembled rectangle with room for a dozen bottles.

'Hullo.' Wendy's torch beam had reached the wall to the left of the stairs. 'There's a gap here. It must lead into a second room.'

'I expect the cellar runs the full width of the house,' said Bruce.

The other half of the cellar was divided into three parts. One had a broad stone shelf built into it, one had rusty hooks dangling from the ceiling, and the third was empty.

'Cold slab,' Bruce said, indicating the stone shelf. 'As good as a fridge for keeping your dairy produce cool. I expect the hooks would have been to hang meat.'

'Uhh,' Tara shuddered. 'It's dead creepy. Think of coming in here and seeing half a dead pig or something.'

'They didn't have Asda to pre-pack everything then, you know.'

'Daddy, Mam, where are you?' Katie's voice sounded faintly from the cellar door.

'It's all right, pet. We're coming back now.'

When they reached the first floor, Jamie was impressed by the size of the bedrooms, and Wendy encouraged him to see beyond the peeling paper and bare boards, to a time when a railway track might command space in one of them. On their arrival in what had once been the servants' quarters, Wendy found another unexpected convert in the shape of her eldest daughter. Character won out over space as far as Tara was concerned. 'I could have these two rooms as a sort of bedsit. My bed in there . . .' She indicated the furthest room. 'And my other stuff could be out here with beanbags for my friends to sit on. It wouldn't matter how loud we had the stacking system, because we'd be miles away from the rest of the house. You'd need to put some radiators in here, though.'

'You haven't got a stacking system,' Katie said.

'No, but I will have. It's going to be my special present, remember?'

As they were on the point of returning to the ground floor, Wendy remembered that they hadn't been up into the attic.

'Is there any point?' asked Bruce. 'There won't be anything to see up there.'

'Well, we want to see all over . . .' Wendy said.

'And there might be lots of things to see,' suggested Tara. 'Whoever cleared out the house might have forgotten about the attic. There might be all sorts of stuff up there.'

All five of them trooped back up to the main landing, then followed Wendy as she led the way through the attic door and up a short, steep flight of stairs. Whereas the cellar had been larger than she had anticipated, the attic was much smaller, a single space constrained by the slope of the roof. The house clearers had been more efficient than Tara had anticipated, however, leaving only spiders and dust. There was nothing to see.

'Do you suppose this was used for servants as well?'

'I doubt it. There aren't any windows and there wouldn't have been any electricity when it was first built. It was probably just used as storage.'

When they went outside, there was collective disappointment at the discovery that it was impossible to penetrate any distance into the back garden.

'Dear God,' said Bruce. 'You'd have to start with a flamethrower.'

'Look on it as an exciting project,' Wendy said.

'I have exciting projects at work, thanks. When I come home I want to relax and enjoy life. You can't even see what you're taking on. Look how far it must go back. Even after it's been sorted out, it would be a full-time job keeping it up.'

'We could turf most of it,' Wendy said. 'I can easily keep the grass cut.' She turned to see that Katie had drifted back into the courtyard, where she was looking up at the arched window which lit the stairs.

'Do you like the house, Katie?'

Katie turned to face her mother, apparently caught between the desire to please and telling a fib. 'We-ell,' she began. 'It's not a very nice house . . .'

'It's not very nice now,' Wendy plunged in. 'But once it's been cleaned up and decorated nicely . . .' She turned to Bruce, hoping for support.

'It's no use even thinking about it until you've had proper advice from a builder.'

'But do you like it?'

'Wendy, it's no good anyone liking or not liking anything unless you can afford to make it habitable. Assuming you *can* make it habitable.'

'But if we really could?'

'If. If. It's all ifs. If you really want to, then I suggest you get in touch with a builder – a reputable one who knows his way around old buildings. You need proper advice to find out what needs doing and how much it would all cost.'

'The estate agents can probably recommend someone.'

'I daresay. In the meantime, don't go getting your hopes up.'

'A builder,' Wendy said brightly. 'Job for first thing on Monday.' She folded her arm through Bruce's. 'Would you like to walk round again?'

'No. That young chap is waiting to lock up, and anyway, it's no use getting the kids all excited if in the end it turns out not to be doable. Jamie, stop clambering about in that shed – you'll break your neck in there.'

Wendy smiled. That was it, of course. Dear, steady, sensible Bruce, treading cautiously, not wanting to get the children's hopes up. It wasn't that he didn't like the house, just that he was taking things step by step, avoiding the risk of a possible disappointment.

Disposing of a body isn't easy. Burial is the traditional way, and there's a lot to be said for sticking with tradition. Do things the traditional way and you can't go far wrong. Except that you can – easily – go wrong.

THREE

March–May 1980

The estate agents recommended Mr Joseph Broughton of Broughton and Sons, Master Builders, a recommendation which was fully endorsed by Ted, a squash player of Bruce's acquaintance, who was something to do with building controls on the local council. 'Sound as a pound,' Ted said. 'You won't go wrong with Joe Broughton. A bit on the expensive side, but he'll see you right.'

Bruce declined to take an afternoon off work to meet Mr Broughton. 'I don't need to be there,' he said. 'We'll want everything in writing, anyway, before we decide to go ahead.'

Wendy therefore met the builder alone. He was a short, stocky man of few words, who explored in an unhurried manner and seemed reluctant to be drawn into any kind of conversation. He managed a lit pipe between his lips, while his hands were busy pulling away bits of crumbing plaster, poking into the backs of cupboards, and periodically working a stub of pencil against the pages of a dog-eared notebook. He began his inspection by standing in the front garden, where he shaded his eyes, peered up at the chimney stack, then shook his head before making a note, and he finished it in the little courtyard at the back of the house, where he finally removed the pipe from his mouth and used it to gesture up at the landing window. 'D'you know what that is?' he asked.

Deciding that 'a window' was not the correct answer, Wendy shook her head.

'That's a Venetian window, that is. You don't see so many of them about now.'

'No.' Wendy thought she had probably never seen another like it.

'About two years ago I had a client who got us to brick right across the arch; blocked it up completely, to accommodate some double glazing.' The recollection seemed to so incense Mr Broughton that he knocked out his pipe against the outhouse wall and replaced it in the top pocket of his jacket, as if unable to enjoy his tobacco in the contemplation of such vandalism.

'I want to keep this one just as it is.'

Mr Broughton nodded. 'In a right bad way, this lot.' He gestured to take in all the outbuildings.

'I would like them repaired and reroofed. Apart from installing things like central heating and a modern kitchen and bathroom, I want to restore all the actual buildings so that everything is as close as possible to how it was originally. The only exception to that is the place I showed you where I would like the hall cupboard and the pantry knocked into one, to make a small study.'

The builder grunted and wrote down something else, but her commitment to retaining the building – as far as possible – in the spirit of the original seemed to thaw him, and he unexpectedly volunteered the information that the bricks had probably emanated from a local brickworks, affectionately patting the wall alongside the kitchen door as he did so. 'Course,' he said, stepping back inside and hauling a strip of mouldering wallpaper away from the wall, 'them old chaps had never heard of damp courses. They seen the water travel down the walls, but they didn't appreciate that it could travel up them and all. They knew craftsmanship, though.'

'But can you sort out the problem with the damp?'

'Oh aye,' he said, as they made their way back through the house. 'There's nothing here as can't be fixed. It'll take time though, and it won't be cheap. I'll make you out a full estimate this evening and get it in tomorrow's post . . . No, Mrs Thornton, I'll not be giving any rough guesses. That's not the way I do business. Let me lay it all out proper so's you and your husband can think about it. By but it's a grand old place, I'll say that.' He extended his hand and smiled for the first time, nodding as he headed towards the front door and repeating by way of a farewell, 'A right grand old place.'

*   *   *

Though the estimate was well within the scope of Wendy's inheritance, Bruce remained unenthusiastic. 'Broughton is sure to go over budget,' he said. 'Builders always do.'

'It doesn't really matter. Even if it costs almost twice as much, we can still easily afford it.'

'But surely you don't want to fritter away every penny? You have to consider whether you will end up spending more than the house is worth, just in order to make it habitable. It's not as if we need a house that big.'

'But surely we can have some things that we want, whether we need them or not. Isn't that the definition of having enough money? Even if Mr Broughton goes over budget, there will be plenty of change left out of thirty-seven thousand. To say nothing of the equity from this house.'

'Well, we won't be frittering that away on any mad schemes like this, I can tell you. This house is a shared asset.'

'Oh, Bruce, we won't be frittering anything away. We're using the inheritance money to get ourselves a lovely home. I don't understand why you are being so negative about it. And the money I've inherited is a shared asset too. All my worldly goods with thee I share.'

'For richer, for poorer.' Bruce laughed. 'Anyway, those weren't the promises you made to me. We were married in the register office, remember? But as you're so determined, you'd better go ahead.'

Wendy jumped out of her chair and hugged him.

'Hold on . . .' He held her at arm's length, laughing. 'I haven't finished. The condition is that you will have to take responsibility and deal with the builders. Your dream house, your project.'

'I know you're just teasing. You know I don't know anything about DIY.'

'I am not teasing. And this is a bit more than DIY, my girl. You are going to have to be the person the builders answer to because I've got a huge amount on at work. If you want to go ahead then you will have to take responsibility and manage things.'

Wendy took a deep breath. 'Mr Broughton knows what he's doing. He won't need much managing, but I will be keeping an eye on things, because while he is working on the house I'm going to start sorting out the garden.'

'The garden is a pretty big project in its own right.'

'There's no need to sound so doubtful. I've picked up quite a few gardening tips from the television, and if I run into trouble there's a whole section on gardening in the library. If the worst comes to the worst, I can get a gardening firm in to do some of the heavy stuff.'

So it began. Though he oversaw the work, Mr Broughton was seldom actively involved. He subcontracted the electrical work to a trusted local firm, but pretty much everything else was done by three of his employees. Kenny treated Wendy with exaggerated deference each time she arrived on the premises, which she did on an almost daily basis, her jeans tucked into her wellingtons and old anorak over her gardening jumper, addressing her as 'Missis', which seemed to be his equivalent of 'Your Ladyship'. Kenny's sidekick was the much younger, perpetually cheerful John, who bore a faint resemblance to Robert Redford, a resemblance which he had played on by growing a Sundance Kid-style moustache. John wore a sleeveless T-shirt in all weathers and whistled as he worked. His accent betrayed him as a Brummie, and his habit of ending the day with the words 'tara-a-bit' took her back to her Coventry days. The third member of the team was Peter, a hulking giant of a man, who wore a permanently sorrowful expression, which probably derived from his principal interests in life: Hartlepool Football Club and the mournful songs he sang about penitents being in a jailhouse and elderly hobos dying on freight trains.

One afternoon Wendy met John carrying a length of pipe across the courtyard while Peter's voice was issuing from somewhere within the house. It was a song Wendy had heard him sing so often that she knew the words herself.

'What are those songs that Peter sings?'

'It's that country and western stuff.'

'Like Dolly Parton?'

'Oh no,' John said. 'Peter doesn't think much of them. He's got a thing about some old bloke who used to drive an engine.'

'A railway engine?'

'I think that's right. Peter . . .' John raised his voice above some hammering that had begun upstairs. 'Peter! Come and tell Mrs Thornton about your engine driver.'

The song came to an abrupt halt, just as someone was a kissin' with Nellie Bligh, and Peter's huge frame appeared, filling the doorway.

'He were a brakeman. The Singing Brakeman, they used to call him.' Peter's speaking voice was grave and steady. He would have made a marvellous undertaker, Wendy thought.

'Yes, but what was his name?'

'Jimmie Rodgers – the Singing Brakeman.'

Wendy did not like to enquire what a brakeman actually did, so she said, 'Are all the songs you sing his songs?'

'Mostly. I know all of them.' His features attempted to reconfigure themselves into a smile, but the unaccustomed effort was too much for them.

'And he worked on the railways,' John prompted.

'Aye. He worked on the railways in Mississippi. That's in the Deep South.' Peter imbued the words with the kind of awe some people might have used a century before, when referencing the Mysterious East. 'He were a genius. He died of TB.' Peter nodded to himself, as if these two factors were inextricably linked.

'Thank you for explaining,' Wendy said, for some kind of comment was clearly required.

As Peter disappeared into the house again, John winked at her as if sharing a joke, before he went on his way, pipe balanced effortlessly across his shoulder.

Wendy put her tools away in one of the reroofed sheds and headed for the front gate, where she paused to glance back at the house. The external appearance of The Ashes was vastly improved, now that the slate roof had been replaced with modern terracotta tiles and the old brown brickwork cleaned and repointed. After an initial period when the place had looked more like a warzone than a dwelling, the house was coming alive again just as she had always known that it would. The garden was progressing too. Soon she would be able to start buying plants from the newly opened garden centre at the other side of the village. From inside the house, she could hear Peter singing something about being a thousand miles away from home, just waiting for a train.

It was only when she opened the gate and stepped on to the pavement that she noticed a vaguely familiar figure a couple of yards down the road. It was a woman she had seen a few times, walking along Green Lane. Someone encountered often enough for them to be on nodding and smiling terms, although they had never exchanged a word. Today the woman was not smiling, but she did appear to be hesitating, on the point of speaking.

Though something about the woman's demeanour made her feel
slightly uneasy, Wendy smiled and said 'Hello,' as she emerged
from the gate.

'Hello.' Encouraged by the friendly overture, the woman stepped
closer, simultaneously glancing towards the house, as if she was
trying to make sure that the front hedge concealed her from anyone
who might be looking out of a window.

'Is there something the matter?' Wendy asked.

'I'm Mrs Parsons. I live just opposite. Well, not exactly opposite . . . across the road, a few doors down. Look . . . I don't
know . . . well, I don't want you to think I'm poking my nose
in or anything, but those men who're working on your house – it
is your house now, isn't it? Well, do you know who that big, tall
one is?'

'Do you mean Peter?'

'The big one,' Mrs Parsons repeated. 'Peter Grayling, his name
is.' She paused again, but then continued when she realized that
Wendy was none the wiser. 'He's the one what was arrested over
that girl what disappeared. Leanne Finnegan, her name was. You
must remember it. Happened up Hartlepool way, two years back.
Police never charged him, but everyone knew it was him as did
away with her.'

'Oh . . .' Wendy could see that her soon-to-be-neighbour was
expecting a reaction, but she had no idea what to say. At least
half-a-dozen possibilities ran through her mind all at once. 'But
. . . people can't be sure,' she said, hesitantly. 'I mean, if it was
certain . . . if there was actual evidence, the police would have
charged him, wouldn't they?'

Mrs Parsons pursed her lips and shook her head. It was almost,
Wendy thought, as if the woman considered that she herself was
complicit in some felony for allowing Peter to work on the house
and therefore facilitating access to the neighbourhood for this
dangerous individual.

'Well, I just thought I ought to warn you. You've a teenage girl
yourself.'

'Thank you,' Wendy said. 'That's . . . very thoughtful of you.'

There was a pause, which became increasingly awkward with
every passing second.

'Well, I expect we'll be bumping into each other again,' Wendy
said. 'Seeing as we're going to be near neighbours.'

'Aye. Maybe.' Mrs Parsons turned away, heading down the road, presumably towards her home.

Wendy thought about the encounter all the way home. What had Mrs Parsons meant, saying 'maybe' in that way? That she would not be going out of her way to mix with someone who had clearly not been willing to immediately act on her warning? Or that she doubted it because Wendy might end up disappearing as comprehensively as the girl from Hartlepool? She didn't keep things from Bruce as a general rule, but he had been inclined to worry over the new house since the very beginning, and the idea that someone working there had been suspected of abducting and doing away with a young woman wasn't exactly going to reassure a man with a wife and two daughters. Surely there was no need to give him anything additional to worry about – another reason to question the purchase of The Ashes in the first place? After all – and she had intimated as much to Mrs Parsons – the police (and 'everybody') couldn't really know that Peter was the guilty party. If there had been any evidence against him worth talking about, he wouldn't still be at liberty to replace her rotten floorboards while singing his Jimmie Rodgers songs and spending his Saturday afternoons at the Victoria Ground?

She considered speaking to Mr Broughton about it, perhaps even asking him to move Peter to another job, but that seemed very unfair. Suppose there wasn't another job? It must be bad enough having the finger of suspicion pointed at you by everyone, without losing your job on top of everything else. Well . . . no, not pointed at you by everyone. She herself had not associated him with the disappearance of Leanne Finnegan. Nor, obviously, had Bruce, who would surely have said something about it if he had.

She only vaguely remembered the case. The disappearance had been all over the local papers, and at one stage a man had been detained to help police with their enquiries, but now she came to think about it, the girl had never been found and the man had not been named. There had been a brief flurry in the local media and then a couple of days later came the news that he had been released without charge. There would always be a grapevine, though. Neighbours, work colleagues, friends of friends who could put a name to the man involved. Word would spread along that spiderweb of contacts, a whisper in the pub, a nod in the supermarket.

Mrs Parsons had evidently heard the story and knew what Peter Grayling looked like well enough to recognize him as he arrived to work at The Ashes, though she clearly wasn't a friend.

It came to Wendy, as she turned into Jasmine Close, that if you wanted to settle an old score against someone who was not a friend, suggesting something that might result in his immediate loss of employment was a nifty way to go about it. After all, she had no way of confirming whether or not what Mrs Parsons had told her about Peter had so much as a grain of truth in it. That decided her. It was far better not to bother Bruce with the story at all, particularly when everything was coming on so well, what with Mr Broughton saying they were still on budget and all the major works on target to be finished in little more than two or three weeks. After that they would need time to allow for things to dry out before they could paper and paint. No point rushing to move in until everything was perfect.

They would be in by summer. At Christmas she would be snipping holly from their own bush and putting up their tree in The Ashes. A proper evergreen from now on, not that artificial one they had in the loft. She visualized the tree's arrival, Bruce unloading it from the roof rack, being helped (or hindered) in the process by overexcited children. Fairy lights reflecting in the front downstairs window. Maybe they could rig up some lights in the garden too. It was a bit posh, having lights strung in your front garden, but the kids would love it. Bruce would know how to do it safely (and tastefully).

When she reached home, she changed out of her gardening clothes, taking a moment to consider the state of her hands and nails. Gardening was hard on the hands, in spite of wearing gloves, but the results were rewarding. Spring had crept through the garden as she worked. She had cleared a good deal of it herself, working relentlessly day after day until the area at the front of the house was transformed: rediscovered flowerbeds formed three sides of a square around the stone sundial, each of them newly planted with rose bushes where nettles had previously held sway. The last of a succession of skips had gone from the drive, which was no longer home to pallets of bricks, roof tiles and other sundry materials which had arrived amid the sound of reversing wagons, then gradually been swallowed up by the house, inside which, though the litter of building work was still scattered about, rooms were beginning to emerge as all but finished. Some were already wearing the various wallpapers she had picked out. The newly installed bathroom suite was surrounded by shiny tiles. It was all coming together and it was all going to be perfect.

Two days later Wendy was putting her gardening tools away when a deep voice behind her said, 'Before you go, I thought you'd like to see this.'

For a big man, Peter moved remarkably quietly. She had jumped violently on hearing his voice and couldn't disguise her alarm on discovering that he had followed her into the outbuilding and was only a couple of feet away.

'Sorry, Mrs Thornton. I didn't mean to startle you. I thought you'd'a heard us coming like.'

'No . . . I didn't hear you, you made me jump.' Wendy found herself wondering where Kenny and John were.

'It's just that I found this. I thought you might like to see it.'

She looked down and saw that he was holding out a framed photograph. 'Let's go outside, into the light,' she suggested, and was relieved when Peter readily complied. Though for heaven's sake, she told herself, what on earth did she imagine he was going to do with two other men within earshot on the premises? She should not have listened to that crazy Parsons woman from across the road.

When they were both standing in the yard, he handed her the object of supposed interest. It was the size of a postcard, a photograph of a young man, mounted in a cheap wooden frame. Peter had evidently rubbed some of the dust from the glass in order to see what the frame contained, and she used a forefinger to complete the job. It was a black and white photograph: a youth of indeterminate age, leaning on a garden wall, the shot showing him from the waist upwards. He was wearing an open-neck shirt, with sleeves rolled up to the elbow, and he had fair, curly hair. Though he was smiling, his eyes were screwed up against the sun. Little could be seen in the background, except the lupins and gladioli growing in the garden behind him. For a moment Wendy wondered if the photograph could have been taken at The Ashes, but she decided it had not, for there was no matching garden wall anywhere. It was impossible to date the picture. Men's fashions changed so little. That shirt and haircut could have belonged to almost any point in pretty much any time before the 1960s.

'Where did you find it?' she asked.

'I was working up in the attic and I noticed there was a loose floorboard. It sprung up a bit when I stood on the end of it. I was going to nail it back down, thinking it was a trip hazard, like. Only then I saw that there wasn't no nails in the other end neither. It was just a little section of board, see, what could be lifted out completely. The picture was hidden in the gap between the boards and the bedroom ceiling.'

'I wonder who put it there.' Wendy held the photograph out for him to take it back, but he shook his head.

'It's yours by rights,' he said. 'Found in your house.'

'I suppose it is. Thank you.'

'S'aright. I suppose someone had their reasons. For hiding it, I mean.' Peter turned back and entered the house, leaving her holding his treasure trove. As he disappeared up the hall, she heard him start to hum. She recognized the tune as 'In the Jailhouse Now' – it was one of his favourites. A sudden shiver ran through her – a phenomenon her mother had always referred to as a goose walking over your grave. It was a funny expression, which made no sense at all, now she stopped to think about it.

She followed him into the house and put the photograph down on the windowsill while she went to wash her hands at the sink. When she was drying her hands, John appeared in the doorway. In spite of the plaster dust in his hair, he could almost have doubled for the Sundance Kid, she thought.

'All done for the day?' he asked cheerfully. 'Knocking-off time, is it?'

'I have to get back in time for Jamie and get started on tea.'

'Wednesday,' John said. 'Steak and kidney pie at my digs.'

'You know what you're getting in advance?'

'It doesn't change, week by week. Roast on Sundays, bacon, egg and chips on Mondays, chops on Tuesdays, steak and kidney on Wednesdays. Friday is best – fish and chip night.'

Wendy advanced towards the door, conscious that time was passing. 'That must get a bit boring,' she said.

'Don't get me wrong, she's all right, Mrs MacIntyre, but she doesn't have much imagination. I get myself a Chinese sometimes, to ring the changes.'

'Goodness.' Wendy glanced at her watch. 'I need to be off.'

'See you.' He stood aside to let her pass.

It only occurred to her as she was walking up the road that she had forgotten to pick up the photograph. She didn't mention Peter's discovery that evening, as she thought everyone would be more interested when she actually had the object to show them, but when she went into the kitchen at The Ashes next morning, the photograph had gone. She considered asking if anyone had moved it, but if they all denied it, that could become awkward. It might be interpreted as an accusation. What if Peter had decided to take it as a keepsake of the job? She had initially tried to give it back to him, so he might have assumed that she had left it lying about because she didn't really want it. It would very likely get him into trouble if she started asking after property which he had removed from the premises. And she wasn't exactly certain of her ground . . . had she really left the photograph on the windowsill? She had occasionally put things down in the past, only to find them weeks later somewhere that they shouldn't have been . . . And anyway, what did it matter? It was only an old photograph of someone she didn't know.

I had already bought the tree, its roots wrapped in sacking, in readiness to conceal the freshly dug grave. A tree would deter any future gardeners from disturbing the spot I had chosen. I don't know how long it takes to happen, but eventually the flesh and internal organs of the body rot away, leaving only the bones. Sometimes I imagined the tree roots, creeping down, winding their way around the rib cage, twisting in and out of the eye sockets, working their way through the skull. The blossom is profuse every spring, as if drawing life from what lies beneath it.

FOUR

July 1980

The builders had started the process of clearing the back garden early on, hacking a way through to what would eventually be the centre of the lawn and burning a load of old floorboards on a bonfire which had lasted three days. As moving day approached, the entire family laboured alongside Wendy to complete the clearance, in order for the newly delivered turf – 'like lots of giant swiss rolls', said Katie – to be laid. Wendy was delighted that her initially reluctant brood had become more enthusiastic, now that actually inhabiting the house was an imminent possibility.

On the first Monday of the school summer holidays, The Ashes was filled with industrious noise. Kenny was installing the last of the long-awaited kitchen units (there had been a problem over the delivery of part of the original order), while Peter could be heard proclaiming that it was peach-picking time in Georgia as he installed insulation in the roof space of Tara's wing. With the turf down and the surrounding beds prepared, Wendy had engaged in an orgy of planting, while Jamie and Katie were released from acting as garden labourers and spent the latter part of the afternoon riding their bikes up and down the drive, just as Wendy had envisaged them doing during her first viewing of the house. Tara had spent the day with friends, but she called to check on progress as she made her way home down Green Lane. Tara's arrival was a reminder that tea would soon be required in Jasmine Close and, calling to the children that it was almost time to go, Wendy put her tools away in the designated shed. She smiled to herself as she walked through the house. It was all turning out just as she had imagined. In a few days' time they would actually be living here. Not just Peter, but the house itself seemed to be singing. Sunshine flickered around the rooms. The smell of decay had been superseded by fresh paint. She breathed in deeply.

As she crossed the hall she heard Tara's voice coming from somewhere out of sight upstairs. She didn't catch what her daughter said but, pausing at the foot of the stairs, she heard John's reply: 'Whereabouts in Coventry were you born?'

'I don't know. We moved back up here when I was still a baby. I don't remember anything about living in Coventry at all.'

'Is that where your dad's from – Coventry? I knew he wasn't from round here, but I couldn't place the accent.'

'Oh, that's not my real dad. My mam and dad got divorced. Bruce is my stepfather.'

Wendy placed a hand on the bannister. She was about to call Tara's name, but something prevented her.

'There's a lot of it about,' John said. 'My sister, the one who lives in Erdington, she's divorced. Mind you, she says she won't get married again. He was a right one, her old man.'

'When Mam married Bruce, I was bridesmaid,' said Tara. She laughed. It was a funny, half-hearted kind of laugh.

Wendy was unexpectedly stung with surprise and embarrassment. It was perfectly true, but something in the way Tara had spoken made her second wedding sound vaguely sordid.

John laughed too. 'A bit funny, being bridesmaid at your own mother's wedding.'

They both laughed again.

From the foot of the stairs, Wendy called, 'Tara, is that you?'

'Hello, Mam.' Tara's head came into view above the bannisters on the top landing.

'I'm just going to wash my hands in the kitchen,' Wendy said. 'Then I'll be ready to go.'

'Water's off again, I'm afraid, missis.' Kenny had come into the hall behind her.

Wendy felt her cheeks flush. She wondered if he had seen her eavesdropping. More sharply than she needed to, she said, 'Come on, Tara. We may as well go home.'

Partly to get away from Kenny, she walked briskly towards the rear passage, where she found the cellar door standing open. The light was switched on, but when she called 'Hello' there was no response. She wondered whether someone had been down there for something and forgotten to turn out the light. Descending half-a-dozen steps brought the main section of the cellar into view. It was interesting, she thought, how much clutter had already accumulated down here, even though they hadn't moved in. Mostly it was packing material from items which had already been delivered, but there was also an unidentified pile of sacks – or were they dust sheets? She would have to remind Kenny to remove any builders' stuff before they finally departed.

Peter emerged from the doorway linking the main cellar to the smaller ones. She managed to stifle an exclamation of surprise. Surely she'd heard him singing upstairs only a few minutes ago? It was very unnerving, the way the man could loom up out of nowhere.

'Aw reet, Mrs Thornton? Did you want summat?'

'No. I saw the light was on and I wondered if anyone was down here, that was all.'

'Oh aye. It's only me.'

'You won't forget to take this stuff away before you finish, will you?' She waved an arm to encompass the various bits and pieces which were scattered about.

'Oh aye. It'll all be moved, like. You'll be wanting to get at the wine rack, likely.'

Wendy laughed. 'I don't suppose we'll ever use it. We don't drink that much, so I expect we'll just keep whatever we need in the kitchen.'

'It's a fine auld piece of woodwork.'

'Yes, yes . . . it's nice to keep things as they were originally.'

'I'm not sure this is where it was originally.' Peter considered the fixture with the seriousness he applied to all topics. 'I reckon it's been moved from one wall to another at some time. You see here . . .' He stepped across and indicated a tall, solid strip of wood about six inches wide, which ran horizontally from floor to ceiling at one side of the rack. 'That's been put in to make it fit, and over here . . .' He pointed to the brickwork of the wall which was at right angles to the rack. 'That's the marks of where it used to be.'

Wendy moved a couple of paces closer and peered obediently at the places he was indicating. Sure enough, there were ghostly imprints, reflecting the distinctive shape of shelves which curved in regular semi-circles, intended to accommodate the individual bottles.

'Goodness, yes, I think you're right. I wonder why it was moved?'

'They must ha put the false back in at the same time,' Peter said. 'Thing like that would normally be flush against the wall. It must ha been like that originally t' ha left those marks.'

'Why would they do that? Put a false back on it?'

Peter considered. 'I cannae guess,' he said eventually.

'Well, I'd never have noticed,' Wendy said. 'Anyway, I'd better be getting back.' She turned awkwardly and mounted the stairs.

She did not refer to the conversation she had overheard between John and her daughter as she and Tara walked back to Jasmine Close, or later when she was alone with Bruce, but it replayed itself uneasily in her mind, troubling her although she would have been hard pressed to explain why.

Wendy had been able to do a great deal in advance of the actual removal men, ensuring that the kitchen was fully functioning, with stocked cupboards and everything in its place before any of the larger items of furniture from Jasmine Close had been unloaded. In the dining room, a new table and chairs, complete with matching sideboard, had already been delivered, so instead of the fish and chip supper eaten among a chaos of boxes which had characterized previous moving days, the family sat down to a properly cooked meal of roast chicken at a table laid with a snowy cloth. To mark the meal as an occasion, Wendy's silver-plated candelabra formed a centrepiece and two bud vases of freesias (arranged by Katie) stood to either side of it. The best wine glasses (a wedding present from Bruce's well-heeled aunt) were filled (three with wine, two with raspberry-flavoured pop) and raised to toast future happiness in their new home.

'I can't believe we're actually living here,' Tara said. 'I mean, to start with it all seemed utterly preposterous. In fact, when they first started work, everywhere was such a mess that it didn't look as if anyone would ever be able to live here again.'

'Well, we are here. And I know we're going to be happy.' Wendy glowed in the fulfilment of an ambition achieved.

'Do you know what would be really useful?' Bruce said, as they began to clear the table at the end of the meal. 'A little trolley on wheels. I know we'll mostly eat in the kitchen, but when we do use the dining room, it wastes a lot of time, carrying everything along the passage to and from the kitchen. It's not like Jasmine Close, where we could just pass everything through the serving hatch.'

'That's a good idea—' Wendy was never sure afterwards how it happened, but perhaps in half turning to respond to Bruce on her way to the kitchen, she lost her concentration and missed her footing. Maybe she was a little bit unsteady after the wine, but at any rate she felt herself stumble, collided with the doorpost, and in a hopeless attempt to save the tray of wine glasses, ended up sprawling across the hall floor.

Voices came from all directions.

'What's that noise? What's happened?'

'Look out, Jamie, don't tread in that broken glass!'

'Mam, are you all right?'

For a moment, Wendy was not at all sure. She had come down hard. Tentative movements reassured her that all limbs appeared to be functioning.

Bruce took command. 'Stand back, you two. Tara, find the dustpan and brush. Wendy, be careful! Don't try to stand up without me helping. There now, you've put your hand down on some glass and cut yourself. Just stay still a minute. Let's make a safe space for you to get up.'

'Oh, Bruce! I'm so sorry. Every one of your aunt May's glasses is broken.' She could hear her voice shaking, in spite of her attempts to be brave in front of the children.

'Never mind the glasses, they're not important. Here now, give me your hands, I'm going to help you get up without leaning or kneeling in all this mess. Katie, go and fetch the first aid kit – oh, damn it, where will it be?'

'Kitchen cupboard, bottom right,' Wendy supplied.

'Damn,' said Bruce again. 'No one else knows where anything is in this place.'

Bruce and Tara chivvied Wendy and the younger children away, while they set about clearing up the broken glass. Wendy's wounds turned out to be superficial. There was only one actual cut, but it was on the ball of her thumb and bled profusely until it was finally stemmed with kitchen roll and then covered with a plaster, eagerly provided by Katie, the appointed first aider for the occasion.

In spite of Bruce's assiduous care, when Wendy came downstairs next morning, the first thing she noticed was a speck of glass glittering against the skirting board at the foot of the stairs. As she bent down to carefully retrieve it, she saw that there was a dull red stain on the stone-flagged floor nearby. How very peculiar, she thought, to have made a bloodstain on the floor the very first night we moved in – and acquired some bruises.

No one else was up. She noticed that the morning paper had already been pushed halfway through the letterbox. It gave her a sense of satisfaction to see it. The arrival of the newspaper, such a small thing, so easily arranged, nevertheless gave a sense of permanence. As if this had always been home and always would be. She pulled the paper towards her slowly, easing it out, not wanting the letterbox to snap too loudly, then carried it through to the kitchen, where she tossed it on to the table, put the smidgeon of glass into the bin and filled the kettle in readiness to make a cup of tea. It was very quiet, the silence only disturbed by the slap of her mules on the floor and the whisper of the kettle as the heat increased. She spread the paper flat on the table while she waited for the water to boil.

New lead in Leanne Finnegan case, the paper claimed. She picked it up again, in order to focus better on the text. 'Cleveland Police have confirmed that following information from a new witness, who believes they may have seen the missing teenager on the day she disappeared, a man is helping them with their enquiries. A police spokesman last night refused to confirm whether this was the same man who had previously been held in connection with the case but later released without charge. Police have declined to comment on speculation that the Leanne Finnegan case is being linked with the disappearance last month of Leah Cattermole in Darlington.'

Wendy read swiftly all the way to the bottom of the piece,

but it merely reiterated the few known facts about the disappearance of the two teenagers. The similarities were striking: both
girls were in their late teens, similar in appearance, and even
their names began with the same three letters, though that was
perhaps just a weird coincidence. She had hardly been aware of
the second case. They were all so busy at the moment, what with
the move and everything. Besides which, Darlington, though it
was only about fifteen miles away, never felt very local. It was
somewhere they drove to once a year to have lunch in an Indian
restaurant, followed by the matinee of the pantomime at the Civic
Theatre. She wondered if the man being questioned was Peter.
They might have been in daily contact with a killer, without
being aware of it. As the kettle began to whistle, she pulled
herself together, recalling that apart from some unsubstantiated
gossip from a woman she'd only spoken to once in her life, there
was no reason to believe that Peter had ever been involved in
Leanne Finnegan's disappearance at all. But if he had been . . .
it meant that he might have abducted another girl while actually
working here, in their home. Well, no, there was no reason to
think anything of the kind. In fact, it was downright hysterical
to even contemplate such a thing.

She was suddenly in need of fresh air. Having made her tea,
she unlocked the door, walking round the side of the house and
up the drive. It would be OK going into the front garden in her
dressing gown. There was hardly anyone out and about to be
passing the gate to see her. She stood on the front lawn, ignoring
the way the dew was soaking into her slippers, admiring the transformation. The sun made the bricks glow a warm, welcoming
orange. The front door opened and Bruce appeared. He had pulled
on a pair of jeans and a T-shirt.

'I saw you out of the bedroom window. What on earth are you
doing out here?' He advanced across to the grass to join her.

'I was just looking at the house – our house.'

'Why? Is there something wrong?'

'No, no. Just the opposite. Look at it, Bruce. The house is
smiling.'

He laughed and draped an arm around her shoulders. 'If you
say so.'

'I'd better come in and do some breakfast.'

'There's no rush. The kids are all still in bed.'

Wendy smiled up at him. 'Just you and me and our happy house.'

Bruce laughed again. 'Come on in, you barmpot,' he said. 'Your slippers are getting soaked.'

In summer, I used to see faces in the shadows made by sunlight on the leaves. In autumn, the dried-up leaves clung on too long, whispering their secrets as the wind tried to prize them away. In the winter, the bared branches showed through, ending in twigs that were thin and knobbly, like miniature finger bones. Eventually I stopped looking at the tree. I stopped going into that part of the garden altogether.

FIVE

August 1980

During the first few weeks in the new house, Tara made the most of her bedsit, inviting friends from sixth form college to lounge about on the beanbags in her room, or to sunbathe in the garden. Jamie and his friend Andrew Webster seemed to alternate between constructing enormous Lego space-ships on his bedroom floor and racing their bikes up and down the drive, while Katie and her friends gravitated onto the back lawn, which had sprouted a swing-ball set and some croquet hoops. Often Katie sat out in the garden alone, drawing the trees and flowers or reading a book. She had always been the quietest of the three children.

From the local news, Wendy learned that the man who had been detained in connection with the disappearance of Leanne Finnegan had been released without charge. The case slipped out of the news cycle and she did not think about it overmuch. There was no reason to believe that Peter had any connection with the girl's disappearance, and even if he had, he was just a man whose life had briefly run alongside theirs. Now that the work on the house was finished, it was unlikely they would ever see him again. Besides which, Wendy was thoroughly enjoying herself: baking and flower arranging and keeping up the constant battle against the weeds which were keen to make a comeback in her freshly planted flowerbeds. The house absorbed her in the same way as a new baby. It had a personality and needs. Even after all these months, there was something slightly unreal about its acquisition. The money arriving when it had, the other buyers dropping out. The magic of it all made her heart leap when she turned in at the gate, knowing that she could call it home.

They had only been living there for about a fortnight when she decided to broach a question with Bruce. 'I've realized that something is missing. It will probably be a bit expensive, but we must have a grandfather clock to stand in the hall, next to the sitting room door. I know it's the right place for it, because I saw a lighter patch on the wallpaper in that exact spot when I first came to see the house.'

'Just because there was a clock before, it doesn't mean there has to be one there again.' Bruce sounded irritable. He was often irritable lately. She put it down to his having such a lot on at work. 'Honestly, Wendy, you sometimes talk as if this house doesn't belong to us at all.'

'Of course it belongs to us. I don't know what you mean.'

'The way you talk about there being a right place for things, as if it's all been pre-ordained. There is no right place or wrong place for anything, only places where we decide to put things.'

'But I just know that *is* the right place for it. Where there's always been a clock before.'

'Oh, so it's down to women's intuition then?' He sounded sarcastic.

Wendy decided to let the matter drop for now. A grandfather clock was an expensive item. She really ought to have gauged his mood before bringing it up in the first place.

'I see they've confirmed the identity of that girl.' Bruce nodded towards the television, where the early evening news was on in the background and had reached the local section. 'It *is* that kid from Darlington who went missing in June – Leah, I think her name was.'

'Her poor family . . . what they must be going through.' Wendy directed her full attention towards the detective, who was appealing for anyone who had seen a necklace the girl had been wearing on the day of her disappearance. He held up a similar one, which the camera zoomed in on.

'It's not all that distinctive,' Wendy said. 'Lots of girls have got those necklaces at the moment. They make them up themselves from little kits of coloured wooden beads, with their names picked out, like alphabet blocks. Or you can get them ready-made in the gift shops at Whitby and places like that.'

'But there won't be many necklaces with Leah on them,' Bruce pointed out. 'It's not a common name, is it, Leah? Not like Tracey, or Michelle, or Julie?'

'I s'pose not.' Her response was half-hearted. The bulletin had already moved on to a story about a robbery at a butcher's shop in Middlesbrough. She stood up and crossed the room to stand beside the window.

'Don't you love the way the smell of roses comes in from the garden in the evenings?'

'I can't say I've ever noticed it.'

Wendy thought of telling him to come over and stand next to her, but she decided not to. He was already a bit umpty over the grandfather clock. He never seemed to understand how important it was to get the details right.

The only part of the house that definitely didn't feel right was the study. Mr Broughton's men had knocked through the cupboard in the hall to combine it with what had originally been the pantry off the kitchen passage, and with the shelves removed and the window unblocked there was plenty of space for a desk and some bookcases, but in spite of having this purpose-built area at his disposal, when Bruce brought work home he still spread his papers on the dining table and worked in there. And it wasn't just Bruce. Tara steadfastly refused to consider doing her homework anywhere but in her own rooms. Wendy was forced to admit to herself that the study was not as pleasant as the rest of the house. She had chosen wallpaper printed with tendrils of green ivy, but she realized now that it wasn't right for such a small space. It made her feel crowded. She invariably hurried over the hoovering and dusting, in order to be in and out of the room in the minimum amount of time.

The school holidays were almost over when Bruce's parents came to stay. His father admired the house to an extraordinary degree and insisted on taking lots of snapshots, including one of Bruce, Wendy and the children posed outside the open front door. 'We'll show them to your auntie Greta,' he said. 'She'll be thrilled to see how you're going up in the world.'

'We're not going up in the world,' said Bruce. 'I've already told you that we only bought it because Wendy came into some money.'

Bruce's mother, though politely complimentary, managed to inject a less positive note, saying that she hoped the burden of taking on such a big old place didn't turn out to be too stressful, later taking Wendy to one side and asking whether she thought Bruce was quite well.

'Of course he is. They've got a lot on at work, that's all.'

Bruce's mother always fussed over him, Wendy thought irritably.

'I don't think your mother liked the house,' Wendy said.

Bruce's parents had been waved away that afternoon, and they were relaxing on the sofa in the sitting room. The younger children had been put to bed, though Tara remained in the sitting room, half-watching a television documentary about a North African nomadic tribe.

'She said she liked it.'

'I know she wasn't being genuine.'

'Each to their own.' Bruce stretched his legs out in front of him, flexing his feet. 'You can't expect everyone to like your house.'

'Did she say why she didn't like it?' asked Tara.

'Not as such. It was just carping, I suppose. "You must have to walk miles every day in this kitchen" . . . "I'm surprised you find time to manage this enormous garden" . . .'

Tara laughed. 'You've got Gran's voice off to a tee.'

'I'm sure she was only making conversation,' Bruce said.

'I saw this wonderful white dress today, on my way home from college,' Tara said.

'By itself?' asked Bruce. 'Or was it out with its owner?'

'It was in a shop. It was only eleven ninety-nine.' Tara gazed wistfully at a couple of turbaned men who were herding goats.

'You've had your pocket money for the month,' said Bruce.

'Couldn't I take it out of my building society account?'

'No, that's for special items only.'

'This is a special item,' Tara wheedled, focussing her attention on Bruce. 'It's an absolutely gorgeous dress and I've been invited to that eighteenth at the Cons Club next month . . .'

'How much was it again?' asked Bruce.

'Eleven ninety-nine. That's a really good price for a dress, these days. It's not like when Mam was young and you could get them for one and ninepence or something.'

'I'm forty, not four hundred!' Wendy exclaimed in mock outrage.

'All right then.' Bruce pretended to capitulate reluctantly.

'Thank you, Dad.' Tara grinned. She knew that her mother would not have given in, if necessary marching her upstairs to examine the contents of an amply-filled wardrobe and pointing out all the perfectly suitable dresses she already owned.

'Now that your mission for the evening is successfully accomplished, I suppose you'll be off upstairs to listen to The Flying Reptiles,' Bruce said.

'You know they're called The Flying Lizards,' Tara said, rising to go, as he had anticipated. 'And they are so last summer. Actually, I'm going to play Blondie.'

'Oh well, they're all right,' Bruce said.

'All the dads like Blondie.' She tipped him a cheeky wink as she skipped out of the door.

'You know,' Wendy said, after Tara had gone, 'I've been wondering who lived here before we did.'

'Some old lady, wasn't it?'

'Mrs Duncan,' Wendy said. 'I meant before that. She can't have lived here since the house was built. It's well over a hundred years old.'

'If you really want to know, you could have a look at the deeds of the house. There must be earlier documents than the ones we signed. Do you mind if I turn over? That play is starting on the other side.'

'The deeds are with the bank.'

Bruce's attention was on changing the television channel. 'Ring them up and ask them if you must. But they're sure to charge you for any information.'

'OK, I will.'

The last few days of the school holidays were marked by a spell of glorious weather. On the final Monday, Tara went to spend the day with friends on the beach at Redcar, Jamie had been invited to play at Andrew Webster's house, and Bruce was at work, which left Wendy and Katie to enjoy a lazy day in the back garden. Wendy had set up a pair of sun loungers with a picnic table between them where they had eaten cheese and tomato sandwiches at lunch time, before settling down to read their respective books. Katie had her well-loved copy of *Alice's Adventures in Wonderland*, while Wendy was tackling a novel which had not lived up to the interesting blurb on the back cover. She had just allowed the novel to slide down into her lap and was relishing the luxury of doing absolutely nothing, when she heard a voice coming from the direction of the house.

'Hello-o-o . . . hello-o-o . . .' It was a woman's voice, rather posh, calling out as though trying to make herself heard down an uncertain telephone line.

The novel fell onto the grass as Wendy scrambled to her feet. 'Who on earth can this be?' she asked of no one in particular, as she headed towards a point where she could see down the drive. As soon as she reached it she saw that there was a woman standing level with the back of the house. A stranger who was considerably older than herself, short and rather plump, wearing a summer dress which exposed pale, freckled arms. She was carrying a large handbag, from which dangled a set of car keys on a fob shaped like a monkey. She spotted Wendy immediately.

'I'm so sorry. I knocked at the front door but there was no answer, so I came down the side of the house. I do hope you don't mind.' It was definitely a well-spoken voice. Someone who'd once been to a private school, Wendy thought.

'I was sitting in the garden,' Wendy explained. 'You can't hear the front door from there, I'm afraid. We'll have to rig up a much louder bell for when we're outside.'

The visitor paused, then said, as if slightly embarrassed, 'You will probably think this is the most dreadful cheek, but . . . well . . . I knocked at the door to ask if I might see around the house. You see, my aunt, Elaine Duncan, used to live here when I was a girl. I used to spend quite a lot of my summer holidays here.' She hesitated again, then hurried on. 'I knew that Aunt Elaine had died and the house had been sold, and when I drove past today and saw how it had been done up, I couldn't resist coming up the drive, even if I was given my marching orders when someone answered the front door.'

'Of course you can see around the house. I'd love to show you what we've done.' Wendy all but grabbed her visitor by the hand, for here, surely, was an opportunity to discover something of the house's past. 'Why don't you come into the back garden first and we can have a cool drink? It's such a hot day, isn't it?' She led the way as she spoke, noting how her visitor's eyes ran curiously around the courtyard. 'We had to reroof all the outbuildings. The roofs had mostly fallen in when we bought it. I'm Wendy, by the way. Wendy Thornton.'

'Joan.' The woman extended a surprisingly dainty hand. 'Joan Webb. This is most awfully generous of you. You're sure you don't mind?'

'Not a bit. Actually, I'm thrilled to meet someone who knows a bit about the house's history. This is my daughter, Katie. Katie, this is Mrs Webb.' (She had taken in the wedding band and a large, old-fashioned engagement ring.) 'Pop into the kitchen and fetch a clean glass, would you?' She gestured to one of the sun loungers and Joan Webb willingly sank into it. Wendy noticed that her feet were swelling in the heat, making her cream sandals bulge.

'Is she your only one?' Mrs Webb asked, as Katie obediently skipped off towards the house.

'No. I have a seventeen-year-old daughter called Tara and a six-year-old boy called Jamie.'

'How lovely. It's nice to think there are children in the house again.'

'Mrs Webb—'

'Please call me Joan.'

Wendy smiled. 'Joan, if you're not in too much of a hurry, will you tell me all about the house as you remember it – in return for seeing round?'

'Gladly, if you've got time to listen.'

Katie returned with the glass and Wendy poured out lemon squash all round.

'How much do you know already?' Joan asked.

'Hardly anything, except that the previous owner was a very old lady who had lived here for a long time before she died.'

Joan thought for a moment, as if deciding where to begin. 'I never actually lived at The Ashes, of course, but I did spend a lot of time here.'

'Was it always called The Ashes?'

Joan smiled. 'Yes, but I've no idea why. I don't ever recall there being any ash trees here.'

'I've always supposed that there must have been some, once upon a time.'

'Well, not in my day anyway. Of course, the house had been here a long time before Aunt Elaine and Uncle Herb came.'

'Our builder said he thought maybe 1840.'

'Well, there you are. My aunt and uncle bought it when they got married, which was practically straight after the war, so 1919 or 1920. There was a story in the family that there was a bit of a row over them buying it. Uncle Herb's parents thought they were over-stretching themselves. It is a big house . . . but of course they had help in those days, a cook and a maid, I think . . . everyone did back then. It was all too much for Auntie in the end, I expect. It's far too big for one old lady living on her own. It's a family house.'

'And did your aunt Elaine have children?' Wendy prompted.

'Four: two boys and two girls. It was wonderful for me when I came to stay, because I was an only child, so I loved having some playmates. I was only a few months younger than Dora so I fitted in nicely.'

'Was Dora the eldest?' Wendy was as eager to keep Joan talking as a child who senses the approach of bedtime.

'No, Dora was the youngest. Ronnie was the eldest, then Hugh. The boys were only about twelve months apart. Then came the two girls, Bunty and Dora. Four children in seven years.'

'Hugh . . .' Wendy repeated the name as if trying it out. 'I wonder, could that have been the person who signed the conveyance?'

'Hugh's dead. He died about three years ago. I think his son, Charles, would probably have been the one who dealt with the estate. I expect Aunt Elaine left everything to be divided between her three grandchildren, but none of them would have wanted the house. Charles never did like The Ashes. I don't imagine either of Bunty's girls would have been overly keen either – and of course none of them live up this way.'

'Oh dear, why didn't Charles like it?'

'Well, of course, he only ever knew it as a gloomy old place where his grandmother lived. He'd tried to persuade Auntie to sell up and move somewhere smaller. I believe they had quite a row about it. Charles thought the old lady was a bit of a liability, pottering about here all alone. Days would go by without her seeing or speaking to anyone. Uncle Herb had been dead for a long time by then, and most of her friends too I suppose, and

Charles lived too far away to keep an eye on her, and his wife wouldn't come at all, on account of the state of the house. I was abroad until just after she died, but I last saw her about ten years ago and things were going downhill then. It was sad to see everything getting in such a state.'

'Poor lady. She must have been very lonely.'

Joan appeared to think about this. Eventually she said, 'I think she'd gone a bit funny at the end. At least, that's the impression one got from the rest of the family. Charles said she always insisted that she didn't mind being on her own, or even seem particularly pleased when anyone did go to see her. I called in on Fiona a couple of weeks ago. That's Bunty's eldest. She said she'd been to see her grandmother a few weeks before she died and Elaine had talked a lot of nonsense.' Joan hesitated, glancing across the garden to where Katie, still within earshot but apparently uninterested in the conversation, had gone to play with the swing-ball.

'If you've finished your juice, let's go and look at the house,' suggested Wendy. 'What sort of nonsense?' she asked, once Joan had levered herself out of the lounger and they had put the outhouses between themselves and Katie.

'Apparently she talked as if she thought Uncle Herb was still alive. Fiona said it was most disconcerting, almost as if he might walk back into the room at any moment. Then she kept on saying, "I was wrong about Ronnie. I was wrong about everything." I suppose she must have been dwelling on the past. You see, Ronnie had been taken prisoner by the Japs and we never heard a word until the war was over, but all through the war Aunt Elaine was convinced that he had survived. No one knew then, the terrible things the Japs had done to our boys. We found out afterwards that Ronnie had died in a POW camp in 1944. He was only twenty-three.' The two women stood for a moment in the cool silence of the kitchen passage.

Joan sighed. 'One heard such terrible stories. Men being starved, beaten, tortured to death. Apparently they picked on the tall men worst of all, because the guards didn't like looking up to anyone – and I can't imagine Ronnie bowing to some Jap officer. It wasn't in him.'

In the passage, Joan exclaimed over the grandfather clock. 'Is it Elaine's?'

'No, or at least not as far as I know. I bought it from a dealer last week.' (It had been a good price, impossible to resist. Bruce had been forced to admit that it was a bargain.)

'Well, it's just like hers, and in exactly the right place. Well done you.'

As they moved from room to room, Joan was full of approval. 'How lovely you have made everything. If you don't mind my saying so, you haven't spoiled it at all.'

At the end of the tour Wendy offered her visitor a cup of tea and they sat at the kitchen table to drink it. Joan needed very little encouragement to reminisce. Visions of long past summers swam before Wendy's eyes, the characters coming to life as Joan's memories floated by. There was Elaine Duncan in a shady hat, tending her garden while the children played nearby. Dora stuffing the bedclothes in her mouth to stem a fit of irrepressible giggles when she and Joan traded jokes long after they should have been asleep. Ronnie, the daring elder brother, always running faster and climbing higher; the captain when they played at pirates and the general when they arranged battles with the toy soldiers. The one who never cried when he scraped his knee or got caught when they went scrumping for apples. Hugh was the natural second-in-command, a quieter boy. Bunty was the pretty one who hated spring cabbage and woodlice with almost equal passion.

After pausing to take a breath and glancing down at the last few sips in her teacup, which had long since gone cold, Joan asked, 'Have you ever noticed anything odd about this house?'

'It's got a lot of . . . unusual features . . . but I don't think that's what you mean, is it?'

Joan laughed. 'It's silly, of course, but as children we always believed the house was haunted. It was all Ronnie's fault. He and Hugh used to come creeping into our room after bedtime and tell us ghost stories. Ronnie had a tremendous imagination and it was all the usual stuff, clanking chains and haunted rooms where people died of shock after trying to sleep there for a night, you know the type of thing. But then one night he told us that there was a ghost here at The Ashes. It wasn't like his usual stories. It was sort of . . . matter of fact.'

'What was the story?'

'I can't properly remember. Bear in mind I was only about eight years old at the time. I do remember that the ghost was supposed to have been a girl who only haunted certain parts of the house.

The thing is that a couple of nights later, Dora needed to go to the bathroom in the middle of the night, and when she was out on the half landing she had absolute hysterics and woke the whole house, claiming that she'd seen the ghost. Well, of course, Aunt Elaine quizzed her the next morning and when she got it out of Dora that Ronnie had told us this story, she was absolutely furious. She took Ronnie into the dining room (it was always the dining room for a severe telling off, I don't know why) and we could hear her shouting, even from upstairs. When he came out, Ronnie was actually crying. I don't think we'd ever seen him cry before. Aunt Elaine said we were none of us to ever talk about it again – and after that there were no more ghost stories.'

'Goodness me, your auntie sounds pretty fierce.'

'She wasn't usually, though she did occasionally show flashes of temper. I remember Dora telling me that she'd once seen her get into a terrible, scary rage, but I never saw that side of her. In fact, I really can't imagine it. Aunt Elaine was such a lady.'

'And do you think Dora really had seen something, that night on the landing?'

'I have no idea. We weren't exactly afraid of Aunt Elaine, but children respected their elders then. Or at least, children who'd been brought up like us. So we never spoke of it again. Or none of them did in front of me. I suppose it's possible they discussed what had happened among themselves later on, but certainly not in my hearing.'

'But you think there could have been something in it?' Wendy asked.

'I don't know. Elaine was probably just furious with Ronnie for frightening us younger ones, but when I thought about it much later, what struck me as odd was how it was different from his normal stories. No people dying of fright or being walled up in a nunnery and all that kind of rubbish. I rather wondered if he'd overheard the grown-ups telling the story, or maybe the servants.'

'But you've never asked any of the others?'

Joan smiled sadly. 'I wish I could, but Ronnie was lost in the war, Bunty died in 'sixty-seven and Hugh about three years ago. They're all beyond my reach now, I'm afraid.'

'What about Dora?'

'What about Dora?' Joan repeated the question thoughtfully.

Her attention seemed to have been caught by a blackbird which had perched on the guttering of the outhouse and was therefore just visible through the kitchen window. 'Dora disappeared in 1943. She went out on her bicycle and never came back. No one ever saw her or the bicycle again. People mostly believed she was murdered, but I suppose we will never know. I hope I haven't upset you. I never intended for all this to come out. Ghosts and murders. It isn't the kind of thing one ought to be telling people when they've just moved into a house.'

Wendy ignored the goosebumps on her arms. It came to her that there had been nothing more reported about the Leanne Finnegan case . . . or Leah Cattermole, subsequent to the discovery of her body. No news of any further arrest. Whoever had abducted those girls, he was still out there. Suppose it had been Peter? Peter who knew his way around The Ashes and knew exactly who lived there. Maybe she should have gone to Mr Broughton after all. But if she had got Peter dismissed from the job, wouldn't that have given him a reason to dislike her and want revenge? If someone bad came into your life, it wasn't always possible to be easily rid of them. She pulled herself firmly back to matters in hand. 'Please, it's fine. I asked you to tell me all about your family and you have. I'm not at all upset about it. Not by something that happened so long ago . . . but it must have been terrible for all of you?'

'As it happens, I wasn't living up here at the time, because my father's work had taken us down to Surrey, but I felt it very deeply, because Dora and I had been so close.'

'Didn't they find any clues about what had happened to her?'

'Nothing much. So far as I remember it, the last known sighting was of Dora going along the track which led to Holm Farm, but even that wasn't very reliable. The lady who saw her was a bit short-sighted and all she could say was that she'd seen a girl on a bicycle, wearing a blue frock. And Dora was wearing a blue frock that day.'

'Where's Holm Farm?'

'It's gone now. There's a new housing estate where it used to be. Magnolia Road starts at the place where the farm track used to run off Green Lane. It was all open land across there when I was a child. We often used to walk or bike along the track. The Coxes kept Holm Farm, and before the war you could buy your milk from them.'

'Do you suppose Dora might have been going to the farm?'

'It's possible. The day it happened Bunty was staying with a school friend in Yorkshire and Aunt Elaine was out visiting for part of the afternoon. Uncle Herb was up in Scotland, doing some kind of war work, and the boys were both in the forces, so Dora hadn't told anyone where she was going – that much I do remember. She might have been heading beyond the farm, down towards the river perhaps. The funny thing is that on almost any other day, one of the Coxes would certainly have seen her, but that particular day they were all out in the motor. That hardly ever happened, what with petrol rationing and everything, but Old Mrs Cox had a hospital appointment and her son and daughter-in-law had gone into town with her. There was a big search, I believe. The police were probably a bit stretched, but I think they got local volunteers and some soldiers to help. They never found anything.'

'How awful. Did Elaine believe . . . you know, like she did with Ronnie?'

'Not that I heard. The strange thing was that though she clung to the idea of Ronnie coming back, after a while she never spoke of Dora at all. Bunty said it was because Ronnie had always been her favourite, but that's probably unfair. I think she suffered more over Dora, but she suffered in silence. We were able to hold a memorial service for Ronnie. There was no body, but at least we knew what had happened to him. You couldn't have a service for Dora because no one could ever be quite sure . . .'

'None of them lived to be very old,' Wendy mused. 'Poor Elaine! Imagine outliving all your children.'

'I know. Poor old Ronnie was twenty-three and Bunty was forty when she went down to cancer. Hugh was only in his fifties – of course he always was a reckless driver.' Joan pulled herself up abruptly, as though indulging in a thought which she ought not to have entertained. 'Killed outright, a great tragedy. And Dora was fifteen when she . . . went. Well, I think I've kept you long enough. I must say you have been awfully generous and hospitable.'

'It's been great. You must come again.'

'Well, that's very kind of you. If you would like to see some photographs of the family and the house as it was in the old days, I have several albums.'

'I would love that.'

There was an enthusiastic exchange of telephone numbers. Joan lived less than ten miles away, which made keeping in touch perfectly feasible. As the two women walked up the drive together, Wendy explained that she had approached the bank just a few days previously, in the hope of finding out more about who had owned the house from its earliest days.

'How fascinating,' said Joan. 'You must promise to share whatever you find out with me.'

Wendy stood in the gateway to wave her visitor goodbye. The gate was always propped open these days, to facilitate the passage of their car. As she turned to go back to the house she was horrified to see Jamie approaching, hand in hand with Mrs Webster, mother of his best friend. Jamie's face was smudged, as if he might have been crying.

'Jamie, what's happened?'

'It's quite all right,' Andrew Webster's mother assured her. 'It's just that you did promise to collect Jamie at four o'clock, and when it got to nearly five he became a bit anxious so I brought him along. You see, Jamie, I told you it would be all right. Nothing bad has happened to Mummy, she's just been delayed, that's all.'

Wendy gathered up her son, red-faced, apologetic and more than a little ashamed of herself, while the expression on Mrs Webster's face conveyed better than words that some mothers would never forget to collect their own children.

'Come on, Jamie.' Having wiped his face with a tissue from her pocket, Wendy took his hand and, thanking Mrs Webster one final time, led him up the drive and into the kitchen.

'I thought you weren't coming,' Jamie sniffed.

'Don't be silly, darling. I had a visitor and lost track of the time, that's all. Look at the clock! You sit down there and I'll get you some orange juice, and then I must sort something out for tea.'

Bruce arrived home soon afterwards and found Wendy kneeling in front of the freezer. 'Hi,' he said, as he dumped his briefcase on the kitchen table and turned to the fridge for a drink. Looking up, she noticed that his shirt was sticking to his back, where it had been compressed against him by the seat of the car.

'Are you getting some ice out?' he asked.

'Actually, I'm looking to see what I can give everyone for dinner. There's been a menu change because I forgot to defrost the chicken joints. Here's the ice.' She passed the tray across to him as she spoke. 'You'll never guess who came to the door today.'

'You're right. I won't.'

'A lady called Joan Webb. She was old Mrs Duncan's niece. She used to spend a lot of time here as a child and she asked if she could look around the house.'

'Bloody cheek! I hope you sent her packing.'

'Of course I didn't. She stayed most of the afternoon. She's been telling me all about how things were when her aunt lived here. It was absolutely fascinating.'

At that moment Katie appeared at the kitchen door. 'I'm too hot,' she said.

'It must be the hottest day so far,' Bruce said. And then in an altogether different tone, 'Good God! Come here, Katie.' He turned her round. 'Look at her shoulders!' he ordered Wendy. 'You've surely not let her run around outside all day wearing just a swimsuit?'

'Oh dear.' Wendy inspected her daughter anxiously. 'You are rather burned, pet. Does it hurt?'

Bruce thumped the glass he had been filling on the worktop. 'She should have put on a T-shirt hours ago. Why on earth didn't you make sure she did? You know how easily she burns.'

'I'm sorry, Katie,' Wendy said. 'Don't get upset, darling, come up to the bathroom and I'll put some aftersun cream on for you.'

By the time mother and daughter returned to the kitchen, Bruce had talked with Jamie and heard all about his abandonment at the Websters' house. This did nothing to improve his mood. 'As soon as Tara gets in I'll fetch a takeaway,' he said. 'Since you couldn't manage to remember that we'd all need a meal tonight as usual.'

'Please calm down, Bruce. It's not the end of the world. It only happened because I got a bit distracted by what Joan was telling me.'

'Naturally, complete strangers take priority over the needs of your own children.' He stalked out of the kitchen and along the hall.

It's the heat, she told herself. This run of hot weather was hell for people who had to sit in an office all day. At the same time, she knew that she had failed badly on the domestic front. Amends ought to be made. She followed him to the sitting room where he had taken up a position behind the newspaper.

'Why don't I take the car down to Asda and pick up some things so I can put together a nice salad? That would be better for everyone than a takeaway on a warm evening like this.'

'I'd rather wait for Tara, then fetch something. It will be quicker. Particularly if you get waylaid en-route.'

'I won't get waylaid. How on earth could I get waylaid?'

'Distracted then.'

'I won't. Oh, please don't be annoyed with me, Bruce. I've said I'm sorry.'

'And I've said I would rather have a takeaway.'

Unfortunately, Wendy had also forgotten that Tara had told her she wouldn't be back in time for tea. It was well after seven o'clock before she returned, announcing that she'd had a wonderful day at the beach.

'At last,' Bruce said, when Tara finally drifted in. 'Now we can all eat.'

Wendy refrained from pointing out that her salad plan could have been brought to fruition a good deal earlier, with a portion plated up and put in the fridge for Tara.

'Sorry,' Tara said. 'Have you guys waited? I didn't expect you to wait for me. Mam, I told you I'd be late.'

'It isn't your fault,' said Bruce. 'Your mother has completely lost her marbles since some nosy old bat arrived, wanting to see over the house, of all things. We can't expect her to remember little matters like what time any of her family are expected home.'

Wendy's attempts to lighten the mood as she unpacked and plated the containers of sweet and sour chicken, beef chow mein and fried rice mostly fell on deaf ears. Katie and Jamie were subdued and Tara picked up on the atmosphere and contributed little to her mother's tentative attempts at conversation. Wendy decided that it was not a good time to talk about Joan Webb's visit.

They had eaten so late that she sent Jamie up to get into his pyjamas while she cleared everything away. She had just finished when the telephone rang, and since Bruce made no move to answer it and the children had all gone upstairs, Wendy went into the hall and lifted the receiver. The voice was male and vaguely familiar, though she couldn't place the owner.

'Could I speak to Tara, please?'

'Hold on.' She put her hand over the mouthpiece and bawled, 'Tara . . . telephone . . .'

Tara came flying down the stairs and Wendy wordlessly handed the phone over. It was a well-practised manoeuvre as the majority of incoming calls were for Tara.

'Hello,' she heard her daughter say as she went into the sitting room, closing the door behind her. Bruce was in his usual chair, flicking through the *Radio Times*. The window was open admitting birdsong and the scent of flowers from the front garden.

'Who was on the phone?' he asked, with no particular interest.

'Someone for Tara. I'm not sure who it is.' As she spoke, a memory clicked in her head, of an accent which had once been part of her everyday life – yet that made no sense at all. She picked up a stray glass which had been left on the coffee table and headed back into the hall, closing the sitting room door behind her.

'Yes,' Tara was saying. 'And when they threw her in . . . oh, I know, it was brill.'

A silence followed. Evidently the caller was speaking. Wendy went into the kitchen where she put the glass into the dishwasher. As she moved away from the machine back in the direction of the kitchen door, she heard Tara's voice, coming from out of sight round the corner in the hall. She was speaking more softly now and in a very different tone.

'It was special for me too . . . Of course I will . . . You know I do . . .'

'Ma-a-am,' Jamie's voice came from the upper landing. 'I can't find my Flintstones book.'

'Hold on, I'm coming up,' Wendy called. 'Have you cleaned your teeth yet?'

Tara was still glued to the phone ten minutes later, by which time Wendy had settled Jamie in bed, having first inspected his teeth and retrieved his favourite bedtime reading matter from under the bed.

'Is Tara still on the phone?' Bruce asked, as Wendy re-entered the sitting room. 'I wish she'd think of the bill.'

'Don't worry, this one's on his parents.'

'Oh, it's a him, is it?'

'Yes.' She hesitated. Ought she to provide a more concrete identification? But then she herself was not absolutely certain.

At that moment the door opened and Tara entered the room. 'That,' she said, evidently making what she perceived as an important announcement, 'is the new love of my life.'

'Is it anyone we know?' Bruce smiled. It was his first genuine smile of the evening, but Wendy suddenly knew that she ought to have forewarned him.

'Yes, you've both met him loads of times. It's John.'

Bruce was clearly none the wiser. 'John who?'

'John McIlroy. He worked on our house.'

'One of those brickies?' Bruce looked as if he couldn't believe his ears.

'Yes, John.' Tara sounded impatient. Her announcement had clearly not generated the effect that she was hoping for.

'You are joking, of course.'

Wendy wanted to shout, *Oh no Bruce . . . Don't go at this head on . . . That will be a terrible mistake . . .* But she had no opportunity to say anything at all.

'Of course I'm not joking.' Tara was full of seventeen-year-old haughtiness and outrage.

'Are you trying to tell me that you have been seeing this John? Behind our backs?' Bruce seldom ever got angry with Tara, but this was an exception.

Tara raised her voice to match his. 'I'm not *trying* to tell you anything. I *am* going out with John. I spent most of today with him, as a matter of fact.'

'You told us you were going to spend the day with friends.' The accusation in Bruce's voice was inescapable.

'I did spend the day with friends. John happens to be one of my friends. I don't see anything wrong with that.'

'Don't you? *Don't you?*' Bruce had gone red under his sunburn. 'Well, I'll tell you what's wrong with it, shall I? To begin with, he's years older than you. Secondly, he's the type who's out for only one thing. A pig-ignorant yobbo, who goes around picking up naïve young girls while he lays cement and fixes up other people's toilets.'

'You snob!' Tara yelled. 'There's nothing wrong with laying bricks or cement, or doing an honest day's work. For your information, John is really intelligent and sensitive. He's a good person. You'd have found that out if you'd taken the trouble to get to know him.'

'I don't "get to know" people I've paid to do jobs at my house,' Bruce sneered.

'I'm sure he is a very nice person.' Wendy managed to put in a word. 'It's just that you've sprung this on us, Tara. We're used

to your boyfriends being from college, or lads you've met at the
ice rink. People of your own age. Your dad and I just want what's
best for you. We don't want you to get into bad company. It isn't
that we object to John in particular.'

'As a matter of fact, I do object to John in particular,' Bruce
interrupted. 'And I forbid you to see him again.'

'I'm old enough to please myself who I see,' flashed Tara.

'You'll do as you're told!' shouted Bruce.

'Don't try to come the heavy-handed father with me,' stormed
Tara. 'You're not even my real father.'

'Tara!' Wendy was horrified. How had things helter-skeltered
into this? Bruce had always been Tara's father – she'd known no
other.

'Well, he's not.' Tara turned her ire on her mother. 'It's no use
you trying to pretend. I'm a big girl now, you know.'

'Tara,' Wendy pleaded. 'There's never been any pretence. You've
always known that Bruce isn't your biological father, but he's the
person who's brought you up—'

'I don't have to do what he says. I'm eighteen soon and after
that I don't have to do what you say either.' She turned back to
Bruce. 'I don't have to listen to your pathetic, snobbish lecturing.
I shall go on seeing John and anyone else I want to see.' She left
the room, not slamming the door as Wendy had half expected her
to, but closing it emphatically, like a victor removing themselves
from the field of battle.

Bruce's face was a strange mixture of emotions.

'You know she doesn't mean it,' Wendy said.

'Doesn't she? It's true, after all. I'm not her father.'

'You have been – are – a wonderful father,' Wendy began, but
Bruce stood up and walked out of the room, not bothering to shut
the door behind him.

Wendy jumped to her feet and pursued him to the bottom of
the stairs, but he didn't look back. For a moment, she hoped that
he might be following Tara up to her room, intending to talk things
out and make up, but when he reached the half landing he turned
the other way. He must be going to their own bedroom. She
considered following him, but then she remembered that he was
already angry with her too. If she had not put him in such a bad
mood to start with, Wendy reflected, he might not have lost his
temper so quickly with Tara.

She stood debating for a moment, before returning to the sitting room, where she noticed that it was very still, as if the room was holding its breath, nervous after the drama just witnessed. Bruce and Tara had always been so close. She couldn't remember them ever quarrelling like that before. Bruce had always lavished so much love on Tara, almost as if he was trying to compensate for the absent father she had never known. No wonder he was wounded by this abrupt rejection. If only he had not been in such an irritable mood . . . Bruce wasn't a snob. Normally he would have laughed off the Brummie brickie as no more than a teenage fad. Tara fell madly in love with a different boy on an almost weekly basis – announcements about the latest 'love of her life' were a regular source of mutual amusement. Tara wasn't about to do anything silly. She had her mind set on a place at university. It would be all right. Bruce would have a lie down, reflect that it was all a storm in a teacup and come back downstairs soon. He was always so sensible . . .

She continued to wait for him in the gathering dusk. The only sounds in the room came from the birds in the garden and occasional cars passing along Green Lane. The other four occupants of the house might not have existed. The sense of drama and unease had dissipated, replaced by more familiar sensations, as the comfort and safety of home wrapped itself around her. The steady tick of the grandfather clock soothed her. When it was almost completely dark she closed all the downstairs windows and locked up for the night. She found Bruce in bed, fast asleep. On reflection, she couldn't help feeling that it was rather pathetic of him to have come up to bed like this: it was reminiscent of a child in a sulk.

She slipped along to Tara's room, but the door was closed and Tara failed to respond to a quiet repetition of her name from the landing. Perhaps she too had already gone to bed. Only when she returned to the upper landing and noticed that Katie's door was ajar did Wendy remember that she and her younger daughter had not wished each other goodnight. She opened the door another foot and saw that Katie had fallen asleep lying on top of the bed. *Alice's Adventures* lay on the duvet cover beside her. Wendy slipped across the room and closed the curtains. There was still a little bit of light in the sky and the nearest street lamp in Green Lane created a paler patch at the top of the drive. She contemplated trying to get Katie under the duvet, but it seemed a pity to disturb her, and anyway it was such a warm night. Deciding it would be best to leave her be, Wendy crept into her own room, undressed among the soft, familiar shadows and climbed into bed, where she eventually succumbed to a restless, uneasy sleep.

A child's screams woke her. She was immediately aware of Bruce, swearing under his breath as he sat up and fumbled for the bedside lamp. As it illuminated the room, they both leaped out of bed and raced for the landing. Bruce was several strides ahead of her and reached Katie's room – the source of the noise – before Wendy. He flung open the bedroom door and she saw him taking Katie in his arms in the same moment as she heard a sleepy voice behind her.

'Mam? Mam, what's happening?'

Wendy diverted from her original intention in order to intercept Jamie. 'It's nothing, pet. Katie's having a nightmare, that's all. Come on now. You come back to bed.'

By the time she had reassured Jamie and settled him back into bed, then gone to check on Tara, who had apparently heard nothing and was fast asleep, Bruce was emerging from Katie's room.

'Is she all right now?' Wendy asked.

'She's gone straight back to sleep.'

Wendy followed him into their bedroom. It was so airless, she could hardly breathe. 'She hadn't . . . she didn't say she'd seen anything, did she?'

'Seen anything?' Bruce turned to face her. 'What do you mean, seen anything?'

'I just wondered . . . when I heard her scream like that, it reminded me of Dora.'

'Dora? Who's Dora? What are you talking about, Wendy?'

'Dora was one of Mrs Duncan's children. Joan thinks she may have seen a ghost here one night—'

Bruce didn't allow her to get any further. 'What the bloody hell are you talking about? Have you been filling Katie's head with all this rubbish?'

'Of course I haven't. And for heaven's sake keep your voice down. You'll wake the children again. I wouldn't tell them about a thing like that. It's just that Katie waking up and screaming reminded me of Joan's story, that's all.'

'Your daughter is overheated through too much sun and all you can think about is some stupid ghost story?'

'No, it isn't. You're being very unfair. It was only that, as children, Joan and her cousins all thought the house had a ghost and—'

'Look, Wendy, I don't care what that stupid old woman told you. I don't want to hear about it. Let me tell you, if you start harping on about this kind of nonsense again, the house goes straight on the market, do you hear me?'

'I'm surprised half of Green Lane can't hear you. There's no need to talk to me as if I was a child.'

'Then stop acting like one. Oh, for goodness' sake, don't start crying.'

'You know I can't stand it when you shout at me.'

'I'm not shouting. Here.' He threw a box of tissues across the bed.

She caught it and drew out a tissue, which she used to dab her eyes and blow her nose.

'I'm going to open our window wider,' she said. 'It's still awfully stuffy.'

He grunted an assent as he climbed into bed, waiting until she had finished with the window and climbed in beside him before switching off the bedside light.

Bruce's breathing soon assumed a steady rhythm, but it took Wendy a long time to get back to sleep. Even when she laid on top of the bedclothes, she felt stifled, as if the heat covered her like a dense, dark blanket, and when she awoke the next day it was with a sense of unease. The all-important happiness of the household had been disturbed, she thought, and the problems which had led to this state of affairs remained unresolved.

Bruce – never much of a conversationalist in the mornings – made no reference to Katie's nightmares or the fracas of the previous evening with Tara. Katie appeared to have forgotten all about her bad dream and Wendy decided not to mention it. Tara rose long after Bruce had left for work, rebuffed all of Wendy's overtures and absented herself for the day, saying that she was going to her friend Helen's house. Later, she phoned to say that Helen had invited her to stay for tea. As it was Bruce's night for playing squash, only Wendy and the two younger children were eating home-made quiche with salad and new potatoes at the kitchen table when Jamie enquired, out of the blue, 'Why were you shouting out last night, Katie?'

'I had a bad dream.' Katie concentrated on securing another

piece of cucumber on her fork. 'Daddy said it was just a bad dream.'

'What was it about?'

'Now, Jamie,' Wendy intervened. 'It doesn't matter what it was about.'

'It's the dream about the nasty man,' Katie said. 'I've had it before. But when I wake up, the man isn't there.'

'Which is what always happens with dreams,' Wendy said. 'Because dreams aren't real.'

'I've only dreamed it since we moved to this house.' For the first time, Katie looked up from her plate and met her mother's eye. 'I never used to dream it in my old bedroom, in our old house.'

'Well, I expect that's just a coincidence, pet.'

'It's probably because people make too many noises in this house,' Jamie asserted. 'I wish people would stop going up into the attic after my bedtime. Their feet make too much noise, walking about up there. Maybe you should put carpet in the attic. That way I wouldn't keep hearing people when they walk about.'

Wendy hesitated. A part of her was curious, especially after Joan's tale about Dora and her ghost. Then she remembered Bruce's views on the subject. It would be a mistake to take too much interest in these supposed footsteps in the attic, particularly when Jamie appeared unconcerned about any aspect of them apart from their potential for noise. 'Yes,' she said. 'Some carpet would be a good idea. When we get round to it.'

When the younger children had gone to bed, Wendy lounged on the sofa, still failing to engage with the paperback which had looked so promising when she'd bought it in WHSmith. The usual comfortable, familiar stillness had fallen over the house. Muffled birdsong, occasional traffic; Elaine Duncan must have heard this same soundtrack on innumerable nights down the years, she thought. In her mind Wendy replayed all the stories Joan Webb had told her. There had been no opportunity to tell anyone about any of it yet. Bruce had indicated that he didn't want to know. Tara would certainly be interested, but she must be warned not to breathe a word in front of Katie, who was such a sensitive child and probably close to the age when poor little Dora Duncan had imagined that she'd seen a ghost.

What on earth could have happened to Dora Duncan? Fifteen,

Joan had said. Fifteen was older then, almost an adult. Before the war there had been lots of people who left school and started work at fourteen. Perhaps Dora had run away? Poor Elaine Duncan, losing her children, one after another. So much sadness . . . but even so, she had refused to leave The Ashes – the house she had loved, the house she had wanted enough to fall out with her in-laws.

Bruce and Tara arrived home almost simultaneously, Tara entering through the front door just as Bruce's car nosed between the gateposts. Wendy offered coffee, which was accepted by both of them. They appeared to have arrived at some kind of unspoken agreement to remain civil, neither of them making any reference to the argument of the night before. At least they weren't yelling at one another, Wendy thought, but she longed for them to drop the polite facades and return to their usual teasing, Bruce feigning ignorance over Tara's music, while Tara stood behind his chair, rumpling his blond hair and pretending to find bald spots.

When she carried the tray bearing three mugs into the sitting room, Wendy found Tara explaining that her friend Helen's father had been tracing his family tree.

'He found the whole lot of them, still living in the same house in 1861,' she was saying. 'He's a member of the local history society.'

'He would be,' said Bruce. 'He's into everything.'

It was no secret within the family that Bruce had no time for John Newbould, father of Tara's friend Helen, ever since the two men had once served together on a committee which had been formed in response to proposals to resite a rubbish tip.

As she deposited the tray on the table and handed round the mugs, Wendy suddenly grasped the potential significance of what Tara had been saying.

'Do you mean that you can look up addresses of old houses and see who was living in them?'

'I think it's only in certain years.' Tara thought for a moment. 'Census years, I think he said.'

'There's a census taken every ten years,' said Bruce. 'But I think it's meant to be confidential. I don't think it's made available to the general public.'

'I think Helen's dad said you can see the ones that are over a hundred years old. I could ask him if you like, next time I'm round at their house.'

'That would be brilliant,' Wendy said. 'We could look up The Ashes and see who lived here.'

'I thought you were getting that information from the bank,' said Bruce.

'I've written to ask, but the deeds will only tell us who owned the house. According to what Tara's just said, the census would tell us the names of everyone who lived here.'

'What on earth do you want to know that for?'

'Because it would be so interesting,' Tara chimed in in support of her mother. 'Think of all the people who must have lived here before us . . .'

'No thanks,' said Bruce. 'The here and now is exciting enough for me. Anyway, Wendy, I thought you said that woman who came here yesterday told you everything about the house since the year dot.'

'What woman?' asked Tara.

'Joan. You were out when she came. She turned up on the doorstep yesterday. It was a lovely surprise.'

'Infernal cheek, more like,' Bruce said. He picked up his coffee mug and headed off somewhere, but Tara listened eagerly while Wendy summarized what she had gleaned from Joan's visit.

'I wonder what happened to Dora Duncan,' mused Tara. 'I suppose she might still be alive somewhere.'

'It's possible, but not very likely. It wouldn't have been hard for her to get a job, I don't think, but as it was the wartime she would have needed ration cards, things like that.'

'Could she have been killed by a bomb?'

'I think people might have noticed if a bomb had dropped on the farm track that day.'

'Mmm. But suppose she wasn't on the farm track? Suppose she'd gone a bit further afield and been killed? Maybe they wouldn't have been able to identify her.'

'It's an ingenious theory. There were a lot of bombing raids around here in the war,' Wendy said thoughtfully. 'Your Granny Burton used to talk about it. Teesside was the real target: the docks and all the heavy industry and ICI at Billingham, but some of the towns and villages were definitely hit. Thing is, though, I think that mostly went on at night, not on a summer day in broad daylight.'

'But maybe it wasn't anywhere near here. You can get a long

way on a bike, especially if you have a whole day. I wonder if they knew where she was planning to go?'

'Apparently no one did. Though I don't think Joan knows that many details herself. She was only young, and don't forget it was over thirty-five years ago.'

'I bet there would be some stuff about it in old newspapers,' said Tara. 'They keep microfilm of newspapers going way back at the main library. Mrs Hillyer brought some printouts of stuff into school when we were doing our history project in third form. We could easily go and have a look.'

'Turning detective?' Wendy laughed.

'Why not? I mean, poor old Dora's almost one of the family, right?'

People don't just vanish into thin air. Everyone knows that. But a thousand searchers won't find them if they're not looking in the right place.

SIX

September 1980

The letter from the bank arrived one Saturday morning while Bruce and Wendy were eating breakfast at the kitchen table. Tara had only just joined them, yawning and still in her dressing gown. Jamie and Katie had already finished eating and gone off to play. The letter opened with a preamble about consulting the title deeds and ended by billing for the time taken, but Wendy was only interested in the meat of the sandwich and skimmed over the rest. The little history began with the transfer of a parcel of land comprising five acres from Mr Joseph Heaviside Esquire to Mr James Coates in 1848, and ended with a conveyance to Mr Bruce Geoffrey Thornton and Mrs Wendy Ann Thornton in 1980.

'James Coates must have built the house once he'd bought the land,' Wendy said. 'Because when it was transferred to his son, George Frederick Coates, in 1876, it's described as *the house known as The Ashes and all that piece and parcel of land adjoining Green Lane . . .*'

'What a funny way to describe it,' said Tara. 'Imagine all that soil spilling out of the string and paper . . .'

'George Coates must have been dead by 1919 because it's described as the estate of the late George Frederick Coates when it was acquired by the Duncans. Less land, too. Most of it must have been sold in the Coates's time, because the plot the Duncans got was the same dimensions as it is now.'

'So the Duncans lived here the longest,' said Tara.

'That depends what you mean,' said Bruce. 'The house was owned by the Coates family for over seventy years. Of course, they might not have lived here at all. They may have rented it out.'

'There you are, Mam, you've got seventy years to beat.' Tara helped herself to the last piece of toast from the toast rack, examined it and, deciding it was still edible, reached for some butter.

'I don't think there's much chance of that.' Bruce laughed. 'Your mother would need to live to be over a hundred.'

'Oh, I don't know . . . if you're counting continuous occupation by one family and we left the house to Jamie, he could easily live to be in his eighties,' Wendy said, cheerful and unthinking.

'*Thorntons* living here eighty years from now.' There was an odd inflection in Tara's voice as she laid the emphasis on Thornton. On Wendy's remarriage, Tara's surname had never been changed to match.

'He'll need to have a jolly good job then,' said Bruce. 'Have you any idea how much the electricity bill is?' He tossed the offending item (which he had just opened) across the table. It slid to a halt against a used knife, acquiring a smear of marmalade at one corner.

'I'll have to ring Joan and tell her about this,' Wendy said.

'What on earth has it got to do with her?' asked Bruce.

'She said she'd be interested. I promised to let her know whatever information we got back from the bank.'

'She's probably not interested at all. Just wanted to come gozzing around to see what we've done to the place.'

When she telephoned Joan later that morning, however, Wendy took a small, private degree of satisfaction from the fact that Bruce was completely wrong. Joan's response was highly enthusiastic and she reissued her invitation for Wendy to visit her for the purpose of viewing some old family photographs.

Wendy chose lunchtime to announce that Joan had invited her over. 'I'm going a week on Tuesday evening. You won't need the car, will you?'

'What?' Bruce's attention was divided between his sandwich and the weekend paper, which he had folded to a suitable size so that it fitted between the edge of the table and his plate. 'The car? No, I don't need it on Tuesdays. Though goodness knows what you want to be going off to see that woman for.'

'You know I said I was going to make the invitations for my

eighteenth?' Tara said. 'Well, I'm starting to think we'll need to buy them after all.'

'I knew you'd never get round to doing them,' Wendy said. 'You'll have to go into town and choose something.'

'That means they'll be really ordinary. Couldn't we get something printed up specially?'

'You should have done them in the holidays,' Katie said. 'I told you I would help you with the colouring in.'

Tara pulled a face at her sister before saying, 'Please, Mam, I bet we could get something much nicer if we had them made up specially.'

'I daresay we could . . . at a price. But when we costed everything out at the start, you said you were going to make them yourself. We haven't budgeted for a lot of bespoke invitations. What do you think, Bruce?'

'It's nothing to do with me. I see the paper's full of this Lady Diana Spencer again.'

Wendy turned back to Tara. 'I suggest you have a look at what's available, while you're in town this afternoon. You might see something really nice.'

Bruce had finished with one section of paper and was making heavy weather of refolding it in readiness to read something else. He was about to flatten the pages into their next configuration on the table when he made a wordless exclamation.

'What's the matter, Daddy?' asked Katie.

'It's nothing,' Bruce said. He folded the paper in half, enclosing whatever it was he had just seen, put it down beside him and leaned his elbow on it, which prevented anyone else from picking it up to investigate. 'So, what's everyone planning for this afternoon? I don't suppose anyone wants to come with me to watch Billingham Synthonia in the cup?'

'Yawnfest,' said Tara. 'Anyway, I'm going into town.'

'I'm going to stick my stamps in,' said Katie.

'Have you tidied all that other stuff off your bedroom floor, like I asked you to? You've to do that before you go getting anything else out,' Wendy cautioned.

'I'd like to come,' Jamie assured his father solemnly. 'But I have to ride my bike.'

Seeing that Wendy had finished her lunch, Bruce caught her eye and left the kitchen, the newspaper stuffed artlessly under his arm. She followed him to the sitting room, where he closed the door behind them and thrust the paper at her, opening it out as he did, so that she could read what he had seen.

'Peter Grayling,' he hissed. 'Isn't that the big bloke who worked for Broughton?'

Wendy was reading as she spoke. 'Goodness,' she said. 'Peter's been arrested. Mrs Parsons was right after all.'

'What do you mean?'

'When they were doing the house up, Mrs Parsons – she lives on the opposite side of Green Lane – told me that the police had questioned him about this Leanne Finnegan's disappearance when it first happened. She's sure that he killed her.'

Bruce was incredulous. 'And you didn't see fit to mention this?'

'It was just gossip.'

'Pretty accurate gossip, by the sound of it. You mean to tell me that you knew this man was *a suspected murderer* and you never so much as breathed a word? You just let Tara and Katie wander freely around here? You didn't even have much to say when Tara started going out with one of these men. I mean, what is wrong with you?'

Tara chose that moment to bob her head around the door. 'Having a not-in-front-of-the-children moment, are we? What's the big news? I saw you being all secretive with the paper.' Though she and Bruce had never officially made up their spat, their relationship had to all intents and purposes slipped back into its former groove.

Bruce took the paper from Wendy and thrust it at Tara. 'It's that bit, there. See the headline? Man held in connection with Hartlepool murder. You see what type of person Mr Broughton employs?'

'That's very unfair.' Tara was obviously shocked by the news, but Bruce's words brought colour to her cheeks. 'It's not fair to judge other people by something someone else has done. Has it occurred to you how horrible this must be for John? Having worked with someone who's done a thing like that?'

'Are you still seeing John?' Wendy asked.

'From time to time.' Tara sounded cagey.

'Well, you know what I think. But you're eighteen in a few weeks and I'm not your father anyway . . .'

'Oh, Bruce, don't say that,' Wendy protested.

'I'm not your father,' he continued, 'so you don't need to take any notice of me, but if you end up dead in a ditch somewhere, it won't be anything to do with me either.' He stomped out without affording a right of reply.

'I wish you'd never spoken to your dad the way you did,' Wendy said. 'It's never been properly sorted out and now there's always this . . . this edginess between the pair of you. Things were all right before you went and upset him like that.'

'For you, maybe.' Tara spat the words out before taking her leave in equally dramatic fashion.

Wendy noticed that Tara had taken the paper with her. She would probably show it to her girlfriends later and they would all enjoy the frisson of excitement that came from a brush with a newsworthy story. And really, she reflected, there was nothing for Bruce to get upset about. Peter Grayling was in custody. Any danger he might have represented was nullified now. She thrust away the thought of his voice echoing through the house, singing those odd, mournful songs, the times he might have watched herself, or Tara, or Katie from a window. On second thoughts, she supposed that Bruce was right. She should have told him what Mrs Parsons had said. Lies and deliberate omissions always came back to bite you, if you got found out.

She wondered how often Tara was still seeing John. He hadn't been mentioned since the original argument, but that didn't really mean anything. Tara came and went pretty much as she pleased. When she said she was going into town with Joanne or round to Helen Newbould's house, they had no way of knowing if it was true, and until now Wendy had carefully avoided mentioning John or asking Tara directly if they were dating, because there was no point in needlessly provoking a row. Besides which, forbidden fruit was always the sweetest. Rule number one with teenage daughters: parental disapproval inevitably renders any undesirable boyfriend ten times more attractive.

Wendy returned to the kitchen and cleared away the lunch things. Bruce called from the hall to say that he was heading for the match and Tara called a goodbye in turn as she was going into town. The younger children had gone off to play, leaving Wendy to deal with their leftover crusts and contemplate whether or not to run the mop over the kitchen floor. Bruce had been right about the amount of maintenance involved in taking on The Ashes, she thought. The floor area must be at least treble that of the house in Jasmine Close, if not more.

There had been no opportunity to smooth things over with Bruce before he went off to watch his football match. Wendy had decided to apologize. She had been wrong to say nothing, she recognized that now. She would make it right with him when he came in, she thought, as she stacked the dishwasher and turned it on.

There was an old Tyrone Power movie on BBC2 and, after checking on the children (Katie had seated herself at the dining table, where she was gravely sorting out her stamp collection, while Jamie was riding his bike up and down the drive, emitting sounds in imitation of a Harley Davidson at full throttle), she settled down in the sitting room to watch. The performances were stagey and the plot creaked, but it was pleasantly reminiscent of wet Sunday afternoons spent with Mam and Dad, everyone cosy in front of the glowing coal fire, and she stuck with it until the credits rolled. As she stood up, she noticed Tara and her friend, Joanne, coming up the drive. She met them as they entered the kitchen. 'You're back sooner than I expected.'

'It's these shoes,' Tara said, pointing down at the offending items. 'They're rubbing me. I couldn't stand it any longer. Jo's mother's just got a microwave oven. We should get one, they're amazing.'

Wendy ignored the abrupt change of subject, introducing one of her own. 'Did you see any suitable invitations?'

'Oh, no. Sorry, I completely forgot to look. We went into Topshop though and I got this amazing T-shirt.' Tara fumbled with her bag and dragged out a skimpy-looking vest which she held up for inspection.

Wendy declined to be amazed. 'Oh, Tara! The one thing you should have been focussed on and you forgot all about it. The clock is ticking, you know. The party is only six weeks away. If you don't give people proper notice, they won't be able to make it.'

'Relax. People can always make a good party. I'm starving. Do you fancy some toast, Jo? We've got strawberry jam, marmite or peanut butter. Oh . . . and also a scrape of lemon curd in the bottom of the jar.' Tara held up the jar in question, assessing the quantity that remained.

'I'll make a pot of tea,' Wendy said. 'And it's about time the children had a drink. Slip out and ask Jamie if he wants tea or juice, will you?'

'Where is he?' asked Tara.

'He's riding his bike. Didn't you pass him as you came in?'

'We passed his bike. It was lying on the drive. Jamie wasn't there. He's probably in the back garden.' Tara headed outside and across the courtyard. Wendy heard her calling her brother's name as she disappeared round the corner of the outbuildings. She was back a moment later. 'Not there,' she said, as she crossed the hall. 'He must have gone up to play in his bedroom.' A second later her voice sounded loudly from the foot of the stairs: 'Jamie . . . JAMIEEEE.'

A heaviness was growing in Wendy's chest. It seemed to press against her lungs, making her conscious of each breath.

'Oh, bugger!' exclaimed Tara as she re-entered the kitchen. 'Now I've gone and burned the toast. Ouch, that's hot.' She extracted the blackened slices from the grill and dumped them in the pedal bin. 'We ought to get a proper toaster. We must be the only family in the world not to own one. And one of those toasted sandwich-makers. Helen's Mum . . .'

Wendy wasn't listening. She hurried outside, but Jamie was not in the back garden. His bike had been abandoned, just as his sister had said, lying on its side in the middle of the drive. She automatically picked it up and placed it on the grass, so that Bruce's return in the car would not be impeded, glancing up at Jamie's window as she did so. There was nothing to be seen apart from the stickers he had put there on first moving in. She entered the house by the front door. The obstruction in her chest was getting bigger. From the kitchen came a burst of laughter. At that moment Katie drifted out of the dining room.

'Is it teatime?' she asked.

'No, not yet. I'm making a drink in the kitchen. Do you know where Jamie is?'

'No. Are there any biscuits?'

'Yes . . . no.' Wendy almost pushed Katie out of the way, ignoring her puzzled expression. She took the stairs two at a time, gained the top landing and entered the rooms, each in turn, then ran down to the lower landing, checking the bathroom, then Tara's little suite. No Jamie. The attic? Surely not. All the same, she returned to the upper landing and checked, but one glance from the top of the attic stairs was sufficient. She descended to the ground floor in a helter-skelter of panic, her breath coming in ragged gasps. Katie had joined the other girls in the kitchen. 'Oh my God.' Tara laughed. 'I've burned the flipping toast again. What's wrong with me today?'

'You're not concentrating on what you're doing,' Katie said reprovingly.

'Tara,' Wendy gasped. 'Jamie's gone. He's disappeared.'

'He's probably just hiding somewhere. Pass me the bread, Jo, third time lucky . . .'

'He's not hiding! He's gone!'

'Don't fret, Mother. We'll soon find him. Come on, Jo.' Tara abandoned the loaf on the kitchen worktop. 'Katie,' she instructed, 'you double check the garden, make sure he isn't hiding in the bushes or something.'

'He's not out there,' Wendy said, her voice rising. 'I've already looked.' She knew he wasn't in the garden. None of their shrubs had achieved the maturity necessary to conceal a six-year-old boy. She stood helplessly in the centre of the kitchen while Tara and Joanne took the same fruitless trip from room to room which she had taken moments earlier. Katie had evidently taken her mission seriously, leaving no stone unturned, but she arrived back simultaneously with the older girls, reporting a negative.

'He's lost,' Wendy said. Tears started up in her eyes. 'We have to ring the police.' She sank on to one of the benches beside the kitchen table.

Tara took charge. 'Of course he isn't lost,' she said briskly. 'Now think,' she addressed her mother. 'Think. When did you last see him?'

'It was hours ago.' Wendy looked down at her hands and saw that they were shaking. 'He was out on the drive, riding his bike. It was just after your dad went to the football.'

'That *was* hours ago. You must have seen him since then?'

Wendy stared stupidly at her trembling hands and shook her head.

Tara turned to Katie. 'What about you?'

'I don't remember,' said Katie, in her most absentminded voice.

For a moment Wendy thought Tara was going to shake her little sister. 'Yes, you do. Come on, you must remember. Think, think. Where have you been this afternoon? What were you doing?'

'Sticking in my stamps.'

'Where?'

'In the dining room.'

'All the time? The whole afternoon?'

'Yes.' Katie's voice contained a suspicious note of hesitation.

'Tell me the truth, Katie. Did you go outside? Did Jamie come in to talk to you?'

'Ye-es.' Katie spoke reluctantly.

'Which? When? What time?'

'I don't know.'

'Oh, come on, Katie. You must know.'

'I don't know. It was ages ago. I didn't look at the clock when he came into the room.'

'All right. What did he say? Where did he go?'

'He didn't say where he was going.'

'Well what *did* he say then? Come on, Katie, this is important. He must have said something.'

'He said he was going to hide.'

'Hide where?' Tara and Joanne chorused.

Katie shook her head.

'Was he running away from home?' asked Joanne.

'Why did he say he was going to hide?' demanded Tara.

Katie fidgeted her hands and looked down at her feet. 'He kept bothering me to play with him. I didn't want to, because I was sticking my stamps in, so in the end I said, "All right then, hide-and-seek. You go and hide first."'

'This is wasting time,' Wendy said. 'We should call the police. He's been taken. I know he's been taken.'

'Do calm down, Mam,' said Tara. She turned back to Katie. 'But you didn't go and look for him?'

Katie shook her head again.

'Why not? Look, don't you start crying as well. You're not in trouble, we just need to find out what's happened. Why didn't you go to look for him?'

'I didn't really want to play. I was sticking my stamps in and he was bothering me, so I said—'

'Yes, yes, we know what you said.' Tara was becoming increasingly impatient. 'So what you're saying is that Jamie went off to hide on purpose. You don't know exactly when and you've no idea where. Did you see which way he went?'

'No . . . but he said he was going to hide in a really good place where no one would ever find him.'

Wendy emitted a low wail of distress.

'Don't worry, Mam, we'll soon find him. Has anyone checked in the outhouses or the garage? I expect he thinks he's being clever, keeping hidden for so long.'

Wendy waited for them in the kitchen. She felt paralysed, unable to do anything. It was every mother's fear. This identical sense of hopelessness must have gripped Elaine Duncan when Dora had failed to come home all those years ago. Perhaps she had even been in this very room when the realization hit. As if in the midst of some terrible nightmare, Wendy watched the two older girls moving swiftly about the yard, with Katie trailing in their wake. As they returned, she overheard Joanne saying, 'already looked under all the beds,' and Tara saying, 'we'd better look again, just to be sure.'

'It's not in Jamie's nature to stay hidden,' Wendy said. 'He's never still for five minutes.'

'Could he have gone to a friend's house?' asked Joanne. 'Someone who lives nearby?'

'Jamie never goes anywhere on his own.'

'Maybe we should try at Andrew Webster's house, just in case,' Tara said.

Joanne was dispatched to enquire, with Katie to show her the way.

'We have to call the police,' Wendy repeated. 'We mustn't waste any more time.'

Tara capitulated. 'Shall I do it?'

Her mother nodded, head in hands. It was like one of those dreams where you urgently need to move but cannot. A nightmare, in fact, where you become an onlooker, trapped in the path of whatever horror is approaching. She heard Tara asking for the police, providing names, addresses: 'Yes . . . yes . . . six years old . . . missing for several hours . . . no, nothing like that. No . . . never been missing before . . . Not allowed out on his own, no . . .' Then Tara reappeared in the kitchen doorway. 'They're sending someone,' she said.

Bruce's arrival almost coincided with the police. Tara had only just admitted two uniformed officers when his car turned into the drive. Noting the presence of the police car in Green Lane, he leapt out and sprinted the few yards required to join everyone in the increasingly crowded kitchen, where one of the two police officers, after a glance encompassing the teenage girl who'd let them in, another teenager who was in the process of making a pot of tea, and a much younger girl who appeared to be white-faced and frightened, was just suggesting that it might be better if they spoke with Wendy somewhere more private.

Jamie chose this moment to emerge from the cellar. He stared at the assembled company and was clearly startled by his mother's abrupt rush in his direction and the way she started to sob all over him.

'I went to hide in my den,' he said, in response to questions fired from all sides.

'But you must have heard us calling you?'

'No. I was hiding from Katie. I got under my covers and I waited for ages and then I fell asleep.' He looked from one face to another. 'In my den,' he repeated, as if this clarified things.

'What den?'

'I built it myself. It's a secret den. In the cellar. I knew Katie wouldn't look for me down there, because she's frightened of the cellar, but I'm all right, because I can leave the light switched off and have my torch.'

'And apparently no one else thought to look down there either.' Bruce's disparaging glance was mainly directed at his wife.

'But how could you possibly have gone to sleep in the cellar?' Wendy asked. 'It's so cold down there.'

'I've got blankets.' Jamie glanced up at the policemen. 'I took them from the airing cupboard when no one was looking. That's not really stealing, is it? Not when they're things from my own house?'

'It's true, look at this.' Tara had gone to the cellar door, switched on the light and descended a couple of stairs.

Some of the others followed her. Jamie's secret den was admirably elaborate. He had utilized an old clothes horse and some abandoned boxes and packing cases, over which he had draped a couple of redundant curtains from Jasmine Close, which had found their way into the 'to keep' pile by mistake during the move. This had created a tent-like structure which Jamie had furnished with a bed made from a variety of pillows, cushions and blankets purloined from the family stock. There was also a child-size plastic chair and play table, which Katie had outgrown and donated to her brother some time before. Part of a child's plastic tea set was on the table, alongside a part-eaten packet of Maryland cookies.

Bruce managed to contain his fury until the police had departed.

'Have you gone completely mad? What on earth possessed you to get Tara ringing the police before you'd even searched the house properly?'

'We did search. All of us.'

'Not thoroughly. The child was found inside the house, for God's sake! The police probably think you're deranged, calling them out and saying your child is missing when he's hidden in the house all along. They'll think you're an attention-seeker. If we ever call them out in a genuine emergency, they probably won't attend.'

'Don't be ridiculous. Once Jamie had explained everything, they understood perfectly how it had happened.'

'Oh, they did, did they? Because I can't understand how it happened.'

'Please, Bruce, do stop shouting. No one thought of the cellar, that's all. Not just me, we none of us did.'

'Never mind the others. They're just children. You are supposed to be the adult. You're supposed to be the one in charge and you didn't even know Jamie had a den down there.'

'Well, did you?'

'*I* am at work all day.'

'I don't think you understand what I've just been through. I was terrified, Bruce. I imagined all sorts.' For a moment she considered raising the spectre of Dora – that previous disappearance involving a child and a bicycle – but she knew it wouldn't help. It would probably make things worse.

'And you don't seem to understand that you are entirely responsible for this whole charade. Did you see poor Katie's face? It can't do a child's confidence much good to see her mother go to pieces like that.'

'I didn't mean to. I was so scared that something had happened to Jamie.'

'Do you know what scares me, Wendy? The increasing sense that my wife is losing her mind. You need to get a grip.'

Digging is not a good thing. Digging about in the past.
Digging up a corner of the garden. I'm not in favour of any
of it.

SEVEN

October 1980

J oan had been looking out for Wendy and met her at the front door of her bungalow. 'Come in, come in,' she said, waving her visitor into a small sitting room, into which had been crammed a pair of overlarge armchairs, an enormous, old-fashioned sideboard and what seemed like innumerable side tables, two of which were positioned adjacent to the armchairs, each already endowed with a glass of sherry, positioned on matching silver coasters. 'How are you keeping? Family all well, I hope?'

Space was at such a premium that Wendy had to sidestep into the chair which Joan indicated she should take, and when Joan seated herself in the other armchair, their knees all but met across the intervening gap.

'Chin, chin.' Joan raised her glass and took a sip of sherry before saying, 'Now you mentioned on the phone that you wondered why George Frederick Coates didn't leave the house to anyone in his family, and that set me thinking. I have a feeling that he did have a son who was killed in the First World War. I'm not absolutely sure where I got that idea from, but I suppose Aunt Elaine may have said something about it at one time or another. I don't believe she and Uncle Herb actually knew these Coates people themselves, but of course there are always people living round and about who do remember things.'

Wendy was abruptly reminded of the nosey parker who lived across the road and had been so eager to tell her things about one of her builders. Joan was right. There were always people who knew – or thought they knew – things. Aloud, she said, 'That would be a strange coincidence – a casualty of the First World War and then one from the Second, both growing up in the same house.'

'Not really,' Joan said sadly. 'When I was a child there didn't seem to be many families who hadn't lost someone in the first war, and plenty lost a son or a sweetheart in the next war too. A terrible lot of men from these parts were killed. You only have to look at the war memorials in the villages.'

'Of course!' Wendy exclaimed. 'The Bishop Barnard war memorial is in the churchyard. I can easily go down there and check if there's anyone called Coates on it.'

'Wendy.' Joan raised her glass in salutation. 'You have a first-class detective mind.'

'My daughter Tara has given me some ideas too. Her friend's father is a bit of a family history fan and he's found out a lot by looking at old census records and that sort of thing.'

'Oh, how interesting! And you are going to do that for The Ashes, are you . . .? Well, when you get round to doing all this, would you mind awfully if I tagged along?'

'Not at all. It would be more fun with two of us. Though it might be a few weeks yet. We've got my daughter's eighteenth birthday coming up and one or two other things going on.'

'My time's my own, dear. Whatever suits you. Unless of course you have already arranged to take your daughter. I wouldn't want to intrude.'

'Tara tends to blow hot and cold. She enjoys hearing about the history of the house, but I'm not sure she would actually want to go and do any research. In any case she's at college through the week and it's her A-level year, so that keeps her pretty busy.'

'In that case I am happy to offer myself as Doctor Watson to your Sherlock Holmes. Now . . . to the photographs.' She reached to one side of the chair as she spoke and lifted an old, black, leather-bound album from the top of a disparate pile. 'These belonged to my mother. They were all in storage while we were living abroad, but I must say they have survived remarkably well. I've got them in chronological order, to make things easier.'

The earliest images in the album were of Joan's grandparents, a pair of formal Victorians, sometimes pictured with infants and toddlers who were hopelessly overdressed in layers of petticoats, their heads invariably covered by hats, caps or frilly bonnets. Their identities had been neatly inscribed on the page by Joan's mother, Dorothy, in ink which had faded to a bluish mauve. There were not many pictures of Dorothy and her sister Elaine until they were aged about ten or eleven, at which time the frequency of the photographs increased, proclaiming as clearly as a written memo the point at which the family had acquired a camera. A vanished world of Edwardian picnics unfolded before Wendy's eyes, where families clad in their best, from the tips of their polished boots to the beribboned hats on their heads, sat laughing on a series of rugs spread anywhere from Whitby Sands to the ruins of Rieuvaulx Abbey. *Dodo's birthday*, an older and wiser Dodo had written underneath one particular shot.

The second album opened up a new era. The album itself must have been expensive. It was covered in a soft, dove grey fabric and each page of mounted photographs was faced with one of tissue paper. The opening page was entirely taken up by a portrait labelled *Elaine aged 21*.

'She was very pretty,' Wendy ventured.

'Everyone said so.'

The pages of the album steadily marked the passage of the years. First Elaine, then Dorothy, on the arms of their new husbands. By the end of the volume their hat brims were narrower and their skirt hems had risen to reveal shapely ankles.

It was not until the third album that they were positively able to identify The Ashes. By this time they were sharing the books across their knees, eagerly pointing things out to one another. The Ashes first appeared as a backdrop to what was evidently a christening party, presumably Ronnie's, as there was no sign of any other young children. The group had gathered alongside the sundial in the front garden for the shot, but big hats must have been in vogue that year, for the women's faces were all in shadow, while the baby itself was no more than a bundle in its mother's arms, trailing ghostly white lace.

'I wonder what colours those dresses were,' Wendy said. 'It's such a pity that everything is in black and white.' It was strange, she thought, the way nothing had really changed. The sundial was still there, the rose bushes a perfect match for the ones she had recently planted herself, and in the background the front door stood open invitingly. The whole party might have dressed up twenties' style and slipped into the garden to take the picture that very afternoon. On another occasion a family group had posed outside the front door, like a pre-enactment of the shot Bruce's father had set up just weeks before.

Though the albums had belonged to Dorothy, she had evidently been in close touch with her sister because many of the photographs were of Elaine and her family, particularly Ronnie, who as Dorothy's godson presumably merited special attention. As a result, his progress was lovingly recorded: a small boy holding a wooden sword aloft, a taller boy in a school uniform, a youth in a Roman toga worn for a fancy dress party, in the uniform of a Boy Scout, and eventually a young man who looked rather dashing posed astride a motorcycle above a caption which read *Ronnie, July 1939.*

The last few pages were devoted to Dorothy's pre-war holiday in the Lake District, which included shots of Joan waving from a pleasure steamer. Between the last page and the back cover someone had slipped a loose enlargement. It was face down, but there was a sprawling diagonal message across the back, the writing far more flamboyant than Dorothy's. *For Aunt Dodo. See you soon. With love from Ronnie.*

Joan turned it over and Ronnie smiled up at them, his eyes forever focussed on something just above the photographer's left shoulder. Unbearably young, handsome and confident.

The war years marked a downturn in the number of photographs. 'You couldn't get the film,' Joan explained.

The post-war era contained fewer appearances by Elaine and her family, but enough for Wendy to mark some changes. Ronnie and Dora were absent, while Bunty, Elaine's remaining daughter, had grown tall and slim, sported a heavily lipsticked mouth and a fiancé called Bill Webster. Elaine's surviving son, Hugh, though bearing some physical resemblance to the lost Ronnie, seemed like a pale imitation of his brother as he posed self-consciously with a cricket bat. There was a difference in Elaine Duncan too. She was still slim and elegantly dressed, but her face appeared to have lost the art of smiling. It was strange, Wendy thought, the way it seemed as if she was and yet was not the same woman.

Joan said quietly, 'When you're young, you are more resilient. Terrible things happen, but you can get over them. Life went on and I used to assume that Aunt Elaine must have got over what happened to Ronnie and come to terms with the fact that Dora would never come back, but since I've been widowed, I've come to realize how wrong I was. There's never a day goes by when I don't think of my George, but of course you can't tell people that. And although everyone is very kind, they don't really want you to go on about it. "Get over it" . . . that's the expression, isn't it? You can get over illnesses, but I'm afraid there's no cure for death.'

'You just have to live with it . . . Sorry, that was an awfully stupid thing to say.'

They turned back to the albums, which had moved into a third generation of christenings. There were Bunty and Bill Webster, wearing fashions Wendy recognized from her own childhood. Joan's wedding to George Webb was lavishly recorded, before she sailed away for years of exile in South Africa and Canada, but glimpses of The Ashes became increasingly rare as Dorothy's encounters with her sister and the extended family either happened less frequently or went unrecorded.

'Mother died in 1964,' Joan said. 'So that's the end of her albums. I was abroad mostly, but I've managed to find two more photographs of Elaine. Apart from the family groups at various weddings, where she's just a speck in the background, that is. I don't know who took this one.' She handed across a shot of a couple sitting in deckchairs at some unidentified resort. 'I suppose someone sent it out to us. People often used to include a few snaps with their letters. There's Aunt Elaine and Uncle Herb. That's Hugh's wife, standing up behind them, so it was probably Hugh behind the camera. And this is the very last one.'

Wendy took the proffered snapshot. This time it was of Elaine alone, sitting in the courtyard at the back of The Ashes. She was occupying a sturdy-looking, square-backed canvas garden chair which had flat wooden arms on which she had rested an elbow. She looked very old, her face wrinkled, almost skeletal, framed by grey hair in a tight perm. The fingers which had strayed up to touch a string of beads around her neck were bony. She was wearing a navy and white polka dot frock and the broad blue shoes of the geriatric over thick, pale stockings. There was a white cardigan draped around her shoulders in spite of the sunlight. On her wrist was a delicate ladies' watch, the image so precise that the time – a quarter to three – could be made out. Elaine, though unsmiling, had inclined her head slightly to one side in what appeared to be a single concession to a photograph she didn't want to have taken.

'Thank you,' Wendy said. 'It's made them more real for me now. I do hope we can find out more about the Coates family too.'

'Well, why don't we make a start tonight? Let's go and have a look at that war memorial. There's a street light almost right above it, if I recall. And I've a torch in my car. Oh, hold on, though . . . I forgot . . . my car is in for its service.'

'That doesn't matter,' Wendy said. 'I'll drive. There's a torch in our car.'

'Oh, but then you will have to double back to bring me home.'

'That doesn't matter.' Wendy felt lightheaded, like a child setting off on an adventure. 'Bruce is on babysitting duty and he's not expecting me back at any particular time.'

'Tally ho then!'

Joan's enthusiasm was infectious. They laughed all the way to the northern edge of Bishop Barnard, where the parish church stood behind a lychgate across the road from what remained of the village green. Wendy parked her car in the layby reserved for 'official church business only' and they entered on foot via the gate. The war memorial was only a few feet inside the churchyard, an impressive stone cross set on a raised square plinth, which was, as Joan had correctly recalled, well within the orbit of the tall, modern street lamps. On one side an inscription stated that it was dedicated to the memory of the men of Bishop Barnard who had given their lives in the Great War of 1914–18. Below this, a further inscription exhorted everyone to remember also those who had died in the 1939–45 war, whose names were recorded within the church. The remaining three sides were filled with the names of the young men who would never return. Between Private James Campbell and Sergeant Charles Copeland was Albert George Coates. Joan jotted the name down in a notebook she had produced from her handbag.

'He won't be buried in here.' Wendy glanced around.

'No, but other members of the Coates family might be.'

'Let's have a look.'

Assisted to some extent by the street lamps on the Green, together with the lights set at intervals on the path which ran between the lychgate and the church, they began to traverse the rows of graves, navigating their way among headstones and monuments by the light of Wendy's torch.

Wendy giggled. 'If my kids could see me now . . . I feel like something out of the Secret Seven.'

'Lucky it's nowhere near Halloween,' Joan said. 'Or we'd probably be accused of witchcraft and arrested on suspicion of performing forbidden rituals within sacred grounds.'

'We won't be able to go much further in. It's going to be too dark to see where we're going, even with the torch, if we get much beyond the street lights. Mind you, if they're here, they won't be buried in the modern part of the churchyard . . . Oh! Hold on, Joan, look at this.'

As an example of Victorian ostentation, the monument could scarcely have been bettered. An almost life-size marble angel stood poised for flight on a knee-high marble block. This formed a centrepiece for an ankle-height marble kerbstone, mostly hidden in the grass, which Wendy had almost tripped over. By the light of the torch they could see that the angel and her support were covered in a greenish-grey layer of grime, and she had been crowned by multiple bird droppings, but the inscription on the angel's plinth was still easily readable.

In Loving Memory of
Maria Coates
1828–1873
Well done thou good and faithful servant
Also of
James Coates
1819–1876
Thy will be done
Also their children who lie near this spot
Amy died 1857
James Henry died 1859
Philippa died 1860
Catherine died 1865
Sophia died 1867
Francis Michael died 1871

'Six children, all dying before their parents,' Wendy said.

'The Victorian infant mortality rate was truly awful.' Joan was writing busily, apparently unhampered by the lack of light.

They almost missed the inscription on one of the kerbstones: *Sacred to the memory of Charlotte Coates born 14 April 1854 died 7 September 1915. Daughter of James and Maria Coates.*

They agreed that it was too dark to search for any more long-dead members of the Coates family in the further reaches of the churchyard.

'I'm sure Aunt Elaine and Uncle Herb are buried not far from here,' said Joan, casting about to get her bearings. 'I think it's just along this path, beyond the big tree.'

The path made it easy to reach the place she had indicated. The Duncans' monument was a plain rectangular headstone with a vase incorporated at its base. The vase was empty, its metal rose rusting. 'I suppose I really ought to bring some flowers, one of these days,' Joan said, in a tone that did not suggest to Wendy that she ever really meant to do so.

They returned to the car and Wendy drove back to Joan's bungalow. The trees and hedges had long since melted into dark shadows against a backdrop of grey-black sky. Wendy declined Joan's invitation to go in, saying that she had better get back. On the homeward run the car was quiet without the clamour of the radio or Joan's conversation, but Wendy hardly noticed. Her head was full of golden sunsets and brave young soldiers marching into them, and she was still experiencing a faint sense of exhilaration from engaging in something a little bit adventurous and out of the ordinary. She knew the back lanes well and negotiated the twists and turns rather faster than usual. It was not as if there was any traffic about at that time of night. At the notorious right-angle bend halfway between Bishop Barnard and Cleveley, where she would normally have changed down to second, she found herself on the wrong side of the road and was forced to swerve and brake, narrowly avoiding an oncoming vehicle.

In the split second of the near collision, she observed that the car she had almost hit carried the livery of Cleveland Constabulary. The stab of panic she had experienced at the sight of the approaching car was replaced by the sickening knowledge that unlike most other drivers, the person behind the wheel of this vehicle was unlikely to merely curse the stupidity of women drivers

and continue on his way. She had come to a halt at an angle to
the road, with one wheel on the grass verge, and a glance in her
mirror confirmed that the other car had also stopped, though in a
much more orderly fashion, a few yards down the lane. As one of
its uniformed occupants got out, she briefly entertained the idea
of driving off. It would take them a moment or two to turn the
car in the lane. No, that was a stupid idea. Even if they hadn't
already clocked her registration number, they would easily catch
up with her. Far better to be contrite. Tell them she was sorry. It
was not as if she had actually hit them or anything. There was no
harm done.

The approaching officer did not look much older than Tara.
Wendy wound down her window and smiled up at him, launching
off immediately. 'I'm really very, very sorry, Officer, but I'm afraid
I misjudged the bend . . . so tricky in the dark . . . didn't realize
it was coming up . . . have to take it more carefully in future . . .'

'May I see your driving licence please, madam?' He was
deadpan.

Her handbag was on the passenger seat. She fumbled inside the
bag until her fingers closed on the slim plastic wallet.

'Is this your own car, madam?'

'Yes. Well, I suppose technically, no. It's registered in my
husband's name, but we share it.'

'Would you mind getting out of the car please, madam?' He
opened the door and held it for her, like a flunkey at the front of
a posh hotel, she thought. There was something slightly surreal
about it. She thought about declining, but she wasn't sure of her
rights, and anyway, she wanted to follow up on the good impression she must surely have made by her apology, so she climbed
out and stood on the tarmac, separated from him by the car door,
which formed a chest-high barrier between them. He considered
her driving licence and she found herself thinking that he must
have jolly good eyesight to be able to make it out with only the
car headlights to help him.

'Have you been drinking, Mrs Thornton?'

'No . . . I mean . . . well, yes, not drinking exactly. I've had a
sherry.' Actually, it might have been more than one. Joan had
topped up the glasses while they were looking at the albums – once
. . . maybe even a couple of times? She had not been paying that
much attention.

She was shocked at the mention of the word 'breathalyze'.

'But this is ridiculous. I only took the bend a little bit too quickly. I haven't been in an accident.'

'It's an offence to drive a motor vehicle when under the influence of alcohol, Mrs Thornton.'

There was something vaguely obscene about the way he assembled the little kit at the roadside, she thought. It induced the same nauseous panic as seeing a doctor putting on a pair of plastic gloves in readiness to conduct an internal examination. A couple of cars went by in quick succession, slowing in order to pass them safely, the occupants taking the opportunity to have a good look and see what was going on. She prayed that it wasn't anyone she knew.

There was something equally surreal about being handed the kit and asked to blow into the plastic tube. The crystals turned green.

'That's a positive result.'

'What happens now?' she asked. Was she shaking because it was getting colder, or was it the thought of being arrested?

'You will have to accompany me to the station, Mrs Thornton, to give us another breath sample and, if it's positive, you'll be charged.'

'But I want to go home.' Wendy knew it sounded childish. It was shameful, standing at the side of the road, trying not to cry. 'My husband will be getting worried.'

'You'll be able to call him from the station. One of my colleagues will drive your car there and your husband will be able to pick you and the car up from there. He's licensed to drive, is he? Your husband?'

She nodded dumbly. What would Bruce say about her being arrested? Drunk driving was detestable. Something she had always associated with sozzled, middle-aged men who drove recklessly and killed other people's children. She was barely able to concentrate on the policeman's questions. Had she had a drink in the last twenty minutes? Did she smoke? It all had a bearing on the test, seemingly. I'm not a drunk driver, she thought. How can this have happened? I've never so much as had a speeding ticket before. She half wished that the policeman would stop being so polite and correct. If he had bawled her out, she might at least have had the satisfaction of shouting back and maybe kicking his shins.

At the police station they asked her to blow into a bigger, static machine. The station was quiet, with Wendy the only source of interest for the greying desk sergeant, who seemed surprisingly cheerful for someone confined to such a barren environment. The only decorations were a very old poster showing different breeds of dog, and an African violet dying in a pot on the windowsill. By the time the machine had spat out its official verdict, she had begun to cry in earnest. The desk sergeant gave her a tissue to wipe her nose, while they filled out various forms.

With the formalities completed, she was allowed to sit in the waiting area, head cast down, not making eye contact with the flotsam and jetsam of people who had begun to trickle in as the hour grew later. An auburn-haired officer came to confirm that her husband was coming to collect her, but Bruce didn't actually appear until almost eleven o'clock.

One look at his face was enough to see that he was furious, but just the same, she assumed a hopeful smile as she stood up. Bruce neither looked at her nor spoke to her, deftly sidestepping as she moved forward to greet him, as if to avoid contamination with a person who had been defiled by arrest. Wendy began to wish she really was so sodden with drink as to be immune to Bruce or her surroundings. He was coldly polite to the desk sergeant who handed over the car keys, then stiffly thanked the constable who showed him where the car was parked. To Wendy he said nothing until they were clear of the car park and he had driven beyond the street lights and switched the headlamps to full beam. Only then, when even the sharpest-eared policeman could not possibly have heard him, did the outburst begin.

'What the bloody hell were you playing at?'

'Nothing. I didn't really do anything at all. I just took a bend too fast . . .' The words tumbled out.

'You've been done for drunk driving, you silly bitch! That's not nothing.' He swerved sharply to avoid a parked car.

'Now who's driving dangerously?'

'Don't tell me about driving. What the hell do you know about driving? You never take the car anywhere except to do the shopping.'

'Only because you never let me.'

'Drunk driving! Bloody hell! Drunk driving! How many have you had? It's fucking humiliating, Wendy. What will people say when it gets round? It's bad enough when a man gets nicked, but a woman . . . People will wonder what on earth you were doing. You know what they'll think? That you were out with some fancy man.'

'That's ridiculous. And I wasn't. Please don't use that language. You never say that word.'

'That's what people will think. You'll have to appear in court. You realize that, don't you? You'll lose your licence. That's going to be an embarrassment – and an inconvenience. I shall have to start taking you shopping and running the kids around. Then there's things like the dinner dances, particularly at Christmas. We've always relied on you driving us back. I can't sit drinking bloody Britvics all night.'

Why not? she wanted to say. I always had to.

'It's going to cost us a fortune in taxis. It's all so ridiculous, Wendy. Whatever possessed you?'

She shrank back into the seat, saying nothing. He was right. How could she, who normally drank so little, who never got tipsy, let alone staggeringly drunk, explain to people that she couldn't drive anymore because she had lost her licence? She would be condemned as some kind of secret alcoholic, a drunkard, a failure. A failed drunk in fact, as she hadn't managed to escape detection.

'I got a taxi to the police station.' Bruce was steaming on. 'I could have asked Alec Wilson or Jack Mitchell, but what the hell was I supposed to say to them? I've got to go and collect Wendy from the cop shop. An accident? Oh no, Alec, she's been run in for drunk driving.' He pounded remorselessly on and on until the car finally came to a halt in the courtyard and she was able to escape the car and rush headlong into the kitchen, where Tara was sitting at the table, a magazine spread in front of her. She looked up anxiously as they entered the room.

'Are you all right, Mam?' Tara asked uncertainly. 'Do you need some coffee?'

'No, thank you. I'm going to take a shower.' Dear God, did Tara imagine that she needed to be sobered up, like a teenager returning from a party?

She headed straight upstairs, unable to face Tara and desperate to escape Bruce. In the bathroom she bolted the door, shed her clothes, then ran the shower for a long time, not stepping out of it until steam all but obscured the bathroom and she had freed herself from the sense of the police station. Wrapping herself in a thick, pink towel, she consigned every stitch of the clothing she had worn that evening to the linen basket, then crept across the half landing and up the remaining stairs to their bedroom, switching out lights as she went. Bruce had left the bedroom door an inch ajar and the soft glow of a bedside light came through the gap. When she entered, she saw that Bruce was lying with his back to the door. She guessed that he would still be angry. In the car he had railed against Joan for abetting such disgraceful behaviour, but mostly against Wendy herself. He was right, of course, but now she needed his understanding. It had been a foolish mistake, two glasses of sherry instead of one (or maybe three instead of two – what did it matter now?).

She let the towel drop to the floor and lifted the bedcovers high enough to admit herself, sliding the front of her naked body down his backside, then letting her hand caress his arm and glide over the slope of his belly.

'Bruce?'

He shifted slightly, jolting the hand away. 'Please put the light out. It's late.'

The coldness in his tone froze her fingers.

'You do still love me, don't you, Bruce?'

'Not particularly, at this moment, no.'

She withdrew her hand sharply and pivoted to switch off the light. It was intended to be a sharp, decisive move: a demonstration that she could be angry and spiteful too, but her fingers fumbled the switch and she had to turn over fully and clumsily to engage with it, which rather spoiled the effect.

They lay back to back, keeping their bodies uncomfortably taut to avoid anything that might be construed as an invitation to intimacy. After what seemed like an eternity, Wendy heard his breathing deepen and, with all pretence gone, she turned to snuggle her body against his in the darkness.

By an unfortunate coincidence of timing, Bruce's parents were due to stay that weekend. Wendy invariably found these visits a trial, not least because Bruce's mother, while never offering direct criticism, always managed to imply a fault of some kind in the housekeeping arrangements. Wendy was on tenterhooks the whole weekend lest some mention be made of the episode which had resulted in her visit to the police station, but neither Bruce nor Tara made any reference to it and the younger children had been kept in ignorance. Even so, it was more of a relief than usual to wave them off the premises and, as if to expunge the house of their presence, as soon as she had closed the front door behind them, Wendy ran upstairs and stripped the spare room bed. She had just returned from the utility room after filling the washing machine when Tara came in and flopped down at the kitchen table.

'Where's my father?' she asked.

'You know perfectly well that he's taking Granny and Gramps to get the train.'

'Not him. I mean my real father.'

Annoyed by the derogatory tone employed for 'him', Wendy said crossly, 'He is your real father. The best and most real father you'll ever have.'

'Oh, don't give me all that crap.'

'Tara!' Wendy was shocked. Tara never spoke to her like that.

'I don't want to hear all that stuff about him being better than this or that. I want to know about my *real* father. I've got a right to know. I don't even have a photograph. I never see him.'

'Perhaps he doesn't want to see you. Have you ever thought about that?'

'All this make-believe,' Tara continued. 'Let's pretend Bruce is Tara's real dad. If we all pretend hard enough, maybe we'll start to believe it.'

'That is most unfair. We've never pretended to you. We've always told you the truth. If anything, Bruce has always spoiled you, over and above the others.'

'You never told me anything about my father. Not anything I wanted to know.'

Wendy's emotions left little room for a considered response. 'All right,' she shouted. 'You want to know about your real father, as you call him. The man who walked out on us when you were a few months old. The man who has never asked to see you in seventeen years. The man who has never sent you a birthday card. That's how much he cares about you, Tara. That's how interested he is. He doesn't even know if you're alive or dead!' She stopped abruptly. The words had emerged much more brutally than she had intended, and through tear-spangled lashes she saw that she had just scored a tremendous own goal.

'Well, that's your side of the story,' said Tara. 'Perhaps one day soon I'll get to hear his.' The chair scraped violently against the stone floor as she stood up.

'Tara . . .' Wendy held out her arms. 'Tara, I didn't mean . . .' But her daughter was already pounding up the stairs. When Wendy followed and called her name, she didn't respond. Wendy slowly retraced her path back to the kitchen. She must remedy this. It had to be put right. She would go and reason with Tara and apologize for losing her temper. She turned back towards the hall, just in time to hear the front door opening and closing. Tara had only run upstairs to fetch her coat and bag. Dashing over to the window, Wendy could see her marching down the drive. She could run after her, of course, but suppose Tara refused to stop? She would look like an idiot, trailing her almost grown-up daughter out of the gate and along the pavement. Strictly speaking, Tara was not supposed to leave the house without saying where she was going, but on balance it seemed best to let it go. Tara seldom adopted the persona of a moody teenager. She would calm down and come home and then they could talk it out.

When Bruce returned from the station, he didn't enquire as to Tara's whereabouts and Wendy thought it best not to mention anything about her sudden departure or the conversation which had preceded it. There had been an uneasy truce between herself and Bruce since the night of the breathalyzer and Wendy decided not to jeopardize it by instigating the debrief that usually took place following the departure of his parents, which generally entailed her venting all the irritation she had bottled up throughout the visit, while Bruce assured her that his mother hadn't intended to be uncomplimentary, critical or downright provocative.

Tara returned to the house just in time for tea, said little throughout the meal and disappeared to her bedroom the moment she had finished. Wendy cleared away in the kitchen, pondering the wording of her apology. She decided it would be best to postpone it until later in the evening. The more time Tara had to calm down and reflect on the real nature of her relationship with Bruce, and how truly lucky she had been to have him as a stepfather, the easier it would be. They had been later than usual with their meal, and once everything was tidy in the kitchen it was time to chase the younger children into bed. It was after nine when Wendy eventually joined Bruce in the sitting room, where he had settled himself in front of the television. Perhaps, she thought, it was time to apologize again to him too, over what she thought of as the 'police station affair'. (The words 'drunk driving' were too shameful. How had they ever become applicable to her? She had been such a fool.)

'Bruce,' she began hesitantly.

'What?'

At that moment the door opened and Tara made an entrance. There was something in her body language that stopped Wendy in the act of drawing breath to speak. Bruce had evidently sensed it too, because his attention immediately switched from Wendy to Tara, watching her as she crossed the room and sat down in the chair nearest the fire.

Well aware that she had their full attention, Tara announced with no little satisfaction, 'I made a phone call today, from my friend Helen's house.' She paused, but received no response. 'I spoke to my father. My real father . . . Robert.'

There was a short silence. Invisible electricity seemed to flicker about the room.

'Well, that's very nice for you,' said Bruce. It was the voice he used for waiters or petrol pump attendants who tried to strike up a conversation with him. He stood up and left the room.

To Wendy, his exit seemed both dignified and tragic. As the door closed behind him she turned on Tara. 'Why did you do that? How did you do it? Who gave you the number?'

'No one gave me the number. I heard Grandma Burton saying years ago that he'd moved somewhere just south of Birmingham. I knew from my birth certificate that his initials are R.G. All I had to do was pop into Stockton Library. I went last week. They've got phone books for the whole country there. It didn't take Sherlock Holmes.'

'But to announce it just like this. Can't you see how much you've hurt your father . . . Bruce. It's like a betrayal, Tara, don't you see that? Good God, it's so, so ungrateful.' And earlier that day, Wendy thought, when Tara was asking about Robert, she already had his phone number.

'I didn't realize it was gratitude he wanted,' Tara snapped back. 'For taking on poor little orphan Annie.'

'You've hurt him,' Wendy persisted.

'What about Robert, my real father? Don't tell me he hasn't been hurt. Don't try to tell me he doesn't care about me, because I've spoken to him. Did you know that he has photographs of me? That he's always wanted to see me? Do you know what his first words to me were? "Tara," he said. "Is it really you? This is wonderful." That's the word he used. "Wonderful". He wants me to go and stay with them. Next weekend. He says he can't wait to meet me.'

Wendy cut short the flow. 'That's out of the question. You're not going. He has no right—'

'He has every right. And so do I. He's my father and you can't stop me. I'm eighteen in a couple of weeks.'

Wendy was unused to dealing with outright rebellion. She stood up abruptly and went in search of reinforcements. She found Bruce sitting in the kitchen, the crossword spread out in front of him. He was using a pencil which she recognized as one of Katie's. It was topped with a miniature horse's head, fashioned in pastel-coloured plastic, from which a straggle of nylon mane was dangling. The scene looked ridiculous, not least because Bruce never did the crossword.

'Bruce, will you please come and help me talk to Tara? She's got some ridiculous idea into her head about going to spend the weekend with . . .' She hesitated, not wanting to say 'her father'. 'With Robert.'

Bruce didn't look up. 'Has he invited her?' His enquiry implied a complete lack of interest.

'Apparently.'

'Then she may as well go. She'd better find out where he lives and check the times of the trains.'

'Don't be so ridiculous, she can't possibly go.'

'I don't see how you can stop her.'

Wendy stood for a moment, struggling to gain control of her feelings. Being confronted by the same truth from two separate parties was not helping.

Eventually she said, 'I don't want her to go.'

Bruce raised his head and regarded her with an expression she could not read. 'Don't be childish, Wendy. If she wants to go, I don't see any problem with it.'

'Me be childish! Who was it went sulking out of the door the minute Robert's name was mentioned?'

'I was not sulking. I don't happen to think that this has anything to do with me. It's between you, Tara and her father.'

'You're her father.'

'No, Wendy, Robert is her father.'

'This is ridiculous. We're going round in circles.'

'Shut up then,' he snapped.

'Bruce, you don't seem to understand what is happening.'

'Wendy, will you kindly stop screaming at me? Tara wants to spend a weekend with her father. It's perfectly reasonable that she should. He's not a child molester, is he? The more you carry on and make a thing of it, the more determined she is going to become. It's hardly surprising that she's curious and wants to see him. And she's very nearly eighteen years old, which is quite old enough to make a journey by herself.'

'That's not the point.'

'Then what is the point? You say you don't want her to go. Why not? You say you don't want her to meet her own father – again, why not? Surely that's a decision for Tara? I think you've created this fantasy in which he's the big, bad wolf, which in reality he's not. He's just some ordinary bloke who'd like to see his daughter.'

'So you're on his side.'

'Oh, for God's sake! I'm not on anybody's side.'

In the days that followed, however, it felt very much to Wendy as if Bruce was on Tara's side. It was Bruce who paid Tara's train fare, Bruce who offered to run her to the station, and Bruce who gave her extra pocket money for the trip. In the meantime, Wendy reluctantly adopted his advice, affecting to pretend that she did not mind about the trip, ignoring Tara's air of smugness in arranging it all, while pondering on the way in which, over a period of years, Tara must have hoarded the information that had helped her to find Robert.

It was arranged that Tara would travel down on Friday evening, catching the 18.33 from Darlington. When Jamie announced that he wanted to go to the station and see the trains, Katie hadn't wanted to be left behind, so in the end the whole family had piled into the car to see Tara off, just as they had done in the past when she was heading off on school trips to France and the Lake District.

It had proved unexpectedly difficult to explain Tara's destination to Jamie. 'If Robert is Tara's other daddy, he must be my other daddy too. Why can't I go and see him?'

Katie had been more interested in the news that Tara's other daddy had children, and on learning from Tara that these children were of a similar age to themselves, Jamie wanted to know when they would be coming to stay on a reciprocal visit.

A holiday atmosphere prevailed as Bruce drove towards Darlington. The children began to play a game with the registration numbers of the cars they passed, though Wendy noticed that no one invited her to join in. They arrived on the platform with ten minutes to spare and, having already received his weekend pocket money, Jamie insisted on being taken to the shop to buy some sweets. Tara followed Jamie and Bruce, saying something about getting a magazine to read on the journey, while Katie wandered along the platform to look at a notice board about the old Stockton to Darlington Railway. Wendy was left alone with Tara's suitcase. Judging from its weight, she assumed that her daughter had packed her entire wardrobe.

Katie returned first. 'This was the first railway station in the whole world,' she said.

'Was it really?' Wendy's attention was focussed further up the platform. Catching trains made her nervous. Trains did not wait for people who had dispersed to buy confectionery or visit the loo.

'When is the train coming?' Katie asked.

'In about four minutes. I wish they'd all hurry up.'

'Shall I go and fetch them?'

'No, it's all right. Here they come now.' She managed to stop herself making hurry-up gestures with her hands. She knew it irritated Bruce. Instead she glanced up at the clock again.

'Who's that man?' Katie said. 'The one who's waving at us.'

Wendy swivelled round at the same moment as Tara arrived beside her.

'Oh, look, it's John,' Tara said. 'Hello . . .' she called down the platform to him.

John raised his arm again in greeting, picked up an enormous black barrel bag, which he swung effortlessly over his shoulder, and strolled across to join them. Wendy spared a hasty glance at Bruce.

'Tara, Mr Thornton, Mrs Thornton.' He nodded politely at them, his blond hair flopping forward slightly as he spoke. Wendy noticed that he still had his moustache. She wondered if Tara had ever reported back Bruce's comments about him being just a bricklayer.

Tara had not mentioned him for weeks and Wendy had therefore assumed that she was no longer seeing him. Now his presence on the platform conjured up a variety of alternative possibilities.

'Going on holiday?' he asked Bruce.

'We're here to see Tara on to the train.'

'I'm going to see my father in Solihull.' Tara beamed.

'No? Straight up? You'll be going all the way to New Street then?'

The train was approaching the platform. The lad's surprise seemed genuine, but Wendy was not convinced. Were the bricklayer and her daughter playing out an elaborate charade?

'Are you going to Birmingham too?' Tara asked.

'Yup. Going down to Brum to stay with Mum and Dad.'

Neither of them looked displeased by the discovery that they would be travelling on the same train.

'Well, this is great,' John said. 'Now I'll have someone to talk to. The journey doesn't half drag otherwise.'

The train doors were being flung open. 'Plenty of seats,' he said. 'Here, I'll carry it.' He picked up Tara's case, making light work of both their bags as he waited politely while she pecked each of the family on the cheek and Jamie demanded that she bring him back a present. As John led the way on to the train, Wendy watched him warily. There was something almost threatening about his masculinity. He seemed different from the John she had seen on an almost daily basis when he was working on the house. She had not properly noticed then how dangerously attractive he was. Tara followed him on to the train and turned to slam the door closed behind them. They momentarily disappeared from view, emerging a moment later in the windows of the carriage. John was looking back at Tara as she followed him down the aisle, laughing at something she said. They got a table to themselves, Tara seating herself beside the window and waving happily as the train began to move, while John finished stowing the luggage. The coaches moved steadily along the platform until Tara was carried beyond their view, just as John took the seat opposite her.

'Can we stay and see some more trains?' Jamie was asking.

'No, we can't. Come on, don't you want your supper? It's Chinese takeaway, remember.' Bruce seemed relentlessly cheerful. Wendy kept glancing sideways at him in the car, but it didn't appear to be an act.

They left the children sitting in the car outside when they went in to pick up the takeaway. 'You're very quiet,' Bruce said, after he had placed their order and they had moved across to the waiting area, which was furnished with plastic-covered bench seats and a coffee table with an ancient *Woman's Own* and a somewhat distressed copy of the *Daily Mirror.*

'That's because I'm worried sick.'

'Why? Now what's the matter?'

Wendy was incredulous. 'Well, do you really think it was an accident? Them meeting on the station platform like that?'

'What, you mean Tara and that John?'

'Of course. Who on earth else would I mean?'

Bruce shrugged. 'I don't know. The bloke was going down to see his parents. He probably goes down every other week, gets his washing done and eats them out of house and home. You know what young lads are like.'

'You know what young lads are like,' she echoed, incredulous. 'Well, you certainly thought you knew what they were like when you first kicked off about her seeing him. We should have stopped her going.'

'Wendy, we've been through all this before. She's entitled to go and meet Robert if she wants to.'

'This isn't about Robert, it's about John.'

'For heaven's sake, I can't keep up with this. She'll sit with him on the train for a couple of hours, then they'll both get off at New Street and go their separate ways.'

'But will they?' She lowered her voice, conscious that a fat, middle-aged man who had placed his order just before them was becoming increasingly interested in their conversation.

'What exactly are you trying to say?' Bruce asked.

Wendy hesitated, ever more aware of the eavesdropper. He didn't know them, but that didn't matter. 'Oh Bruce, don't be so obtuse. You know very well what I'm getting at. Suppose Tara isn't going to stay with Robert at all?'

'Well, if she isn't, there's damn all we can do about it. You can't run after the train, and if you think I'm driving all the way down there, you can think again.'

'So you're taking the line that as she's not really your daughter, it's not your responsibility, is that it?'

'Not at all. But you need to recognize that kids grow up fast these days. Tara's seventeen. Some people would say it's none of our business who she chooses to spend her weekends with. She's not a child any longer and everyone kicks over the traces sooner or later.'

'Bibbings.' The woman who served behind the counter called out the name, and as the fat man stood up she began to reel off the contents of two bulging carrier bags, starting with prawn crackers and spare ribs.

'You're condoning it!' Wendy was astounded.

'I'm not condoning anything. I'm suggesting that Tara has reached a point in her life where some things are none of our business. I don't suppose you liked your mother prying into your teenage sex life.'

'I didn't have a sex life, not until I was married.' Thank goodness the fat man had left and the woman had disappeared into the rear of the premises again.

'Well, not everyone is as . . . restrained as you were.'

'What do you mean by that?'

'Face facts. A lot of people sleep together before they're married. You may not have done . . .'

'I didn't.'

'But a lot of people did.'

'Did you?'

'Yes.'

'I didn't know that.'

'You never asked me.'

'I just thought . . . How old were you? The first time?'

'Nineteen.'

'Thornton?' The query was unnecessary, since they were the only customers waiting. 'One sweet and sour chicken, one beef curry, one prawn chow mein, one chicken in oyster sauce, two egg fried rice, one boiled rice, two banana fritters.'

'I hope you're not going to have some sort of mid-life crisis about my ex-girlfriends,' Bruce said as he held the shop door open for her. 'It was a long time ago and they were all before I met you.'

'Well, of course not,' she said, mentally noting his use of the plural. 'It doesn't matter a bit.' It did matter, she thought. It mattered that she had never known. Everything she thought she knew, everything she had always taken for granted, had somehow begun to unravel.

Tara telephoned much later that evening. Bruce happened to be passing through the hall at the time, so it was he who picked up the call. 'Hello . . . Tara? . . . Good, fine. Did you want to speak to Mam? . . . No? OK . . . Yes, yes, have a nice time . . . See you on Sunday.' He turned to Wendy, who had appeared in the kitchen doorway. 'It was Tara to say she's arrived safely. The train was on time and Robert was there to meet her at the station.'

'Did she say anything about John?'

'No.' Bruce sounded irritable. 'What would there be to say?'

Bruce and the children collected Tara from the station on Sunday evening while Wendy stayed at home to cook, steeling herself to be politely interested in hearing about the trip.

There was no need for her to ask any questions, because Tara scarcely drew breath over dinner, so eager was she to share the fun she had had with 'Bob' – as her father had suggested she call him – his wife and other offspring. The whole family had gone on a shopping expedition into the city centre, during which they had lunched in an Italian restaurant and 'Bob' had bought a necklace for Tara and encouraged her to pick out a dress and some perfume at his expense.

Wendy attempted to catch Bruce's eye over the table, as Tara detailed these blatant attempts to buy her affection, but Bruce was concentrating on his roast lamb and appeared entirely unperturbed.

While Wendy cleared the plates in readiness to serve the apple crumble, Tara dashed off to fetch a Polaroid photograph from her bag and Wendy forced herself to appear pleased by the smiling image of her eldest daughter standing with Bob's hand resting proprietorially on her shoulder, with his two boys, Alexander and Richard, grinning in front of them, the perfect little family group.

'Bob always kept his distance because he didn't want to complicate things for me.' Tara smiled across the table at them, making it sound, Wendy thought, as if this was some kind of incredibly generous act of sacrifice on Robert's part. 'But of course things will be different, now that we're back in touch. They want me to go and stay again soon.'

Looking at the middle-aged man in the photograph, Wendy found it difficult to believe that she had ever been married to him. She noticed that he had put on some weight since their Coventry days and developed crow's feet at the corners of his eyes. She realized that Bruce was watching her as she studied the photograph. She quickly passed it back to Tara.

'They've suggested I might like to go away with them on holiday,' Tara was saying. 'They've got a timeshare in Portugal. It's no wonder they're all so brown. Look, here's another one with me and the boys and Mel.'

'Mel?'

'It's short for Melissa.'

Wendy regarded the slim, undeniably attractive Melissa and wondered how it was that the man she had once been married to had transformed from Robert into Bob. It made her feel foolish, the way she had always referred to him as Robert. It was as if they had never been on sufficiently intimate terms for her to know what his real name was. She handed the photograph across the table to Bruce. 'And how was the journey down, with John?'

'It was great to catch up with him. He's been accepted at the Polytechnic, in Birmingham. He's going to live back at his parents' place while he does his degree.' Though she was responding to her mother, Tara directed her words at Bruce, her tone unmistakably challenging, but if she had been hoping for any acknowledgement that he had misjudged John, she was disappointed. Bruce merely asked Katie to pass him the custard.

Next morning, Wendy decided to give the bedrooms a thorough clean. She was still wondering whether John had featured more in Tara's weekend than her daughter had admitted, but she found nothing left lying about in Tara's rooms to indicate that. Wendy was not normally given to snooping on her children, and by the conclusion of her unsuccessful operation she felt rather ashamed of herself, particularly as she did not even know what she had been expecting to find. Her mood was not improved by the discovery that not only was Katie's room as untidy as usual, but her previous efforts at tidying when last instructed to do so had consisted of pushing everything out of sight under her bed, where it now lay like the detritus left behind by the retreat of a tidal wave.

On Katie's return from school Wendy marched her upstairs and demanded that she lift the valance to reveal the mess.

'I want all this stuff picked up and put away properly,' Wendy said. 'You're to stay in here until it's done, do you understand?

And when you've finished, I will be coming up here to check that you've done it properly.'

Katie mumbled that she did understand and Wendy departed, closing the door behind her. In truth, she was less annoyed by the mess than by the way Katie had lied to her, assuring her that everything had been tidied satisfactorily, when it so clearly had not.

She half expected Katie to reappear after half an hour and claim the job was done, but the clock ticked towards five and there was no sign of her. At a quarter past, beginning to feel suspicious, she crept up the stairs, intending to check that tidying, as opposed to any other activity, was still in progress. When she reached Katie's door, she heard crying within. For a moment she hesitated, hand an inch from the door handle. It was horrid to think of Katie, sitting inside, sobbing amid the mess, but then she remembered that the situation was entirely of her daughter's own making, and that there had been lying involved too. Katie was learning a valuable lesson. She slipped quietly back down to the kitchen.

It was perhaps a quarter of an hour later when she heard Katie start screaming and pounding on the door with her fists – or possibly kicking it. Katie never threw tantrums – or not since she was a toddler anyway. Well . . . let her scream and shout. The room had to be tidied and throwing a wobbler was not going to make any difference. Tara had phoned to say she was calling at a friend's on her way back from college, and Jamie was playing outside, so there was no one around to hear her.

Two minutes later, Bruce's car pulled into the drive, rather earlier than his usual time.

'Good grief!' he exclaimed, as he walked in at the back door. 'What on earth is happening up there?' Without waiting for an answer, he raced up the hall and Wendy heard him taking the stairs two at a time.

She thought about following him or calling after him, but on second thoughts, she would let Katie explain for herself. When Bruce discovered that she was merely playing up, he would be just as annoyed by their daughter's behaviour as she was herself. From the kitchen, Wendy heard the screaming and pounding stop abruptly. After a few minutes she heard Bruce's approach and turned to face him as he entered the kitchen. His expression was oddly serious.

'I've sent Katie to wash her face before she comes down.'

'And got her to stop that caterwauling too,' Wendy said approvingly.

'Caterwauling? The child was terrified. What on earth were you thinking of, letting her get herself worked up into such a state?'

'She worked herself up. It was nothing to do with me.'

'She says you locked her in her bedroom.'

'Don't be silly, Bruce. I found a whole stack of stuff shoved under the bed from when she said she'd tidied up before, and I told her to stay in there until she had sorted it all out. How could I possibly have locked her in? There aren't any keys. You can't lock any of the bedroom doors. She was just having a tantrum, that's all.'

Bruce hesitated. She could see that the point about the lack of keys had hit home.

'Katie doesn't have tantrums,' he said.

'Well, she had one today.'

'She was frightened. She thought she was locked in.'

'Oh, really? And did you have to break the door down to release her?'

'No, of course not.'

'There you are then.'

'The door must have jammed. She was obviously terrified. You should have gone up to her to see what was the matter.'

'I know what the matter was. She had been caught out fibbing and not doing what she was told and she didn't like having to sort it out. And what's more, you ought to be backing me up on this, not criticizing me. Whatever happened to showing a united front and not allowing the children to divide and rule?'

The conversation might have continued but for the arrival of Jamie, asking what was for tea, and then Katie herself appeared, red-eyed and crestfallen. In response to Wendy's question about her bedroom, she said, without meeting her mother's eye, that she had finished putting everything away and Wendy said briskly, 'That's good then.'

The episode was not quite over, however, for not long after they had settled into bed and Bruce had switched out the light, the quiet was disturbed by yet more screams from Katie's room.

'No, Mammy, no! Oh, don't please, Mam, don't!'

Both parents raced across the landing, as they had done once before, and Bruce was again the first to arrive, hushing Katie and holding her to him as he sat beside her on the bed. Wendy hovered in the doorway, anxious lest the noise had woken Jamie, but there was no sound of him getting out of bed.

'Was it a bad dream, poppet?' Bruce was asking.

'It was a horrible dream. I was up in the attic and there was a horrid old woman and she said, "What have you got there?" and I said, "Nothing." And then I tried to run away and at first I couldn't get out and she was going to hurt me,' Katie's words tumbled out. 'Then I was running down the stairs and out into the yard and the old woman had turned into Mam, but she was frightening and she was going to hurt me too . . .'

'Now then, now then . . .' Bruce was coaxing, soothing. 'You know that Mummy would never hurt you.'

'I know that, but in my dream . . .'

'Why not let Mummy go and get you a nice glass of water and you just calm down and stop thinking about this nasty dream? Where's Huey? Here, look . . .' Bruce reached down and located the bear in question. 'You take Huey . . .'

Wendy heard no more, having taken her cue to fetch a glass of water, but by the time she returned, Bruce was emerging from Katie's room, waving her away as he carefully closed the door behind him.

'What *did* you do to that child this afternoon?' he asked when they were safely back inside their own room.

'What on earth do you mean? You're surely not blaming me for this?'

'Whatever you did, she's absolutely traumatized.'

'For heaven's sake, Bruce!'

'You heard her . . . "Don't Mammy, don't!"'

'This is ridiculous. She was dreaming. All kinds of weird things happen in dreams that bear no resemblance to real life. Katie got herself into a strop this afternoon because she'd been told off for not tidying up her bedroom. She was made to spend her afternoon doing something she'd been told to do days ago and she didn't like it, so she lost her temper and got herself worked up and overheated and this is the result.'

'Well, I think you need to be more careful. Katie's oversensitive.'

'Overindulged, more like,' Wendy muttered as she dragged the duvet back into place, but either Bruce did not hear her or he chose not to reply.

As she settled back into bed, she considered asking Bruce if he did not feel that Katie's latest little exhibition might have been fortuitously timed for their own bedtime, but she decided that suggesting Katie had been faking would only inflame the situation. And what had Katie been up to, pretending that she'd been locked inside her bedroom? It would be difficult to manage the children if Bruce was about to start undermining her. First the business with Tara, and now Katie . . . She comforted herself with the thought that if Katie continued with such blatant fictions as suggesting that it was possible to confine her in a room without a working lock, Bruce would soon see through her games.

The sound above the ceiling was so faint that at first she wasn't sure whether she had heard anything at all. She lifted her head clear of the pillow and concentrated. She was aware of Bruce's breathing and the muted passage of a distant car. Nothing else. She was just deciding that she had been mistaken when it came again. A faint series of creaks, commensurate with footsteps crossing the attic floor.

'Bruce?' she whispered. She didn't want to wake him over nothing, but if he was awake already . . .

No reply.

'Bruce . . .' She tried a little louder.

Still no reply.

Was there someone up there? Impossible, surely? If Tara had come up the stairs from her wing, she would have had to pass their bedroom door and they would surely have heard her. Katie was hardly likely to venture up there when she'd just had a bad dream. Bruce was sleeping beside her. Jamie then? She remembered Jamie and the wretched secret den in the cellar. Perhaps he had made some similar arrangements in the attic. He'd once drawn attention to hearing some footsteps in the attic himself. Could that have been some kind of elaborate ruse to cover his own after-bedtime activities up there? Surely not! He was barely out of infant school.

She ought to go and check. If it was Jamie, then he ought to be sent back to bed.

Trying not to wake Bruce, she slid out of bed into the velvety darkness without recourse to the bedside light. It was easy to navigate her way out of the bedroom, because the night light which was always left burning on the landing glowed under the door. The landing was deserted. The silence within the house had begun to feel oppressive. She put an exploratory hand on the handle of the attic door, as cautiously as if she expected it to burn her, turned it slowly and allowed the door to swing open. The night light only reached as far as the first two treads leading upwards; the rest of the staircase was in darkness. She felt around on the wall until her fingers encountered the switch. She flicked it on, but no sound came from above.

'Jamie,' she called softly. He might be playing a game of some kind, pretending not to be up there, just as he had done in the cellar. He would know perfectly well that he was not supposed to be up there at this time of night, so he probably wouldn't answer. The only way to check would be to ascend the stairs and see for herself, but even with the benefit of the electric light, she baulked at the thought of going up to the attic at this hour.

'Jamie . . .' It occurred to her that from where she was standing, if he was awake, he could just as easily hear her from his bedroom as he could from the attic. Then she remembered that she could check on his whereabouts by simply looking into his bedroom. Feeling rather stupid at the way this obvious solution had escaped her, she crept across the landing and pushed Jamie's door until his pillow, complete with tousled, fair head, came into view.

As she turned away from his room, it was all she could do to stifle a scream. Bruce had appeared silently outside their bedroom door.

'Is everything all right?'

'Yes, fine. You startled me. I was just checking on Jamie.'

'Why are you creeping about at this time of night? What were you doing in the attic?'

'Nothing. I haven't been in the attic.'

'Then why is the door open and the light on?' He reached in and snapped the switch off, turning to close the door.

'I thought I heard someone up there. I thought it might have been Jamie.'

'Jamie? At this time of night?'

'Well . . . there were footsteps . . .'

'Footsteps my eye. It's these boards creaking. I often hear it.

For goodness' sake, come back to bed. Some of us have to be up for work in the morning.'

He was right, of course, Wendy thought. Old houses were full of funny noises. The wood expanding and contracting as the temperature changed, as if the house yawned and stretched at night, like a living thing, settling to sleep. It was a comforting thought.

The tree has haunted my dreams. One recurring sequence finds me approaching the tree in winter. The leaves are gone, but the branches are not empty. The finger bone twigs are painted gaudy colours and a strange assortment of small articles hang from them, like decorations placed among the branches in readiness for Christmas. I recognize some of the items. The belongings of the dead mock me.

EIGHT

November 1980

When Wendy arrived outside Joan's bungalow to collect her for their trip to the county record office, she experienced an uncomfortable sense of déjà vu. She had spoken to Joan several times on the telephone but had not mentioned the outcome of the last occasion on which she had given Joan a lift. She was still waiting to receive a date for the case to be heard, but Bruce seemed to think it certain that she would receive a ban, at which point she knew that people would become aware of the episode, because she would have to explain why she wasn't driving. Embarrassment flooded through her every time she thought of it.

Joan had evidently been looking out for her, because she emerged from the front door without Wendy needing to get out of the car.

'Well, this is nice,' Joan said, settling herself into the passenger seat and arranging her large handbag between her feet before clipping her seat belt in place. 'It's jolly good of you to give me a lift.'

'It makes sense not to take two cars. It wasn't a problem – I dropped Bruce at the office and I'll pick him up again tonight. That way I get to use the car all day.' (Actually, Bruce had tried to turn it into a problem, grumbling even though the arrangement made no real difference to him at all.)

'I've been looking forward to this,' Joan said. 'It's very intriguing, isn't it, all this delving into the past? You know, I think after I've cut my teeth on this little project, learned the ropes as it were, I might have a go at my family history. There's always been a rumour that we're related to the Howards – the Norfolk Howards, that is – way back on my grandmother's side.'

Wendy, who had no idea who the Norfolk Howards were, decided to gloss over the point. 'I'm sorry it's taken so long to get this trip organized,' she said. 'It's just been one thing after another at home. Of course, Tara's eighteenth took up a lot of time.'

'Your daughter's party – of course. How did that go?'

'It was super. The food was a big success and everyone danced.' Wendy smiled at the recollection of herself and Bruce joining the youngsters on the floor for 'Oops Upside Your Head', and later dancing close together when the DJ played Streisand's 'Woman in Love'. It had been such a happy evening, to which thankfully it did not seem to have occurred to Tara to invite either her newly discovered father and stepfamily, or the wretched John, about whom nothing further had been said since the apparently coincidental meeting at Darlington station. It only served to show that they were a happy, united family, Wendy decided. Everyone went through tricky patches, but underneath they were rock solid.

Like Joan, she had been looking forward to seeing the county archives, but on arrival her initial emotion was disappointment. She had anticipated the faded elegance of the central library in Middlesbrough, with its antique radiators, glass-fronted cabinets and inviting alcoves, but Durham's archives were housed in the modern basement of County Hall, and instead of paper documents, she and Joan were faced with microfilm machines, which were fiddly to work and lacked the romance of the anticipated ancient volumes.

They shuffled two chairs in front of a single machine and, after several false starts, managed to load the film containing the 1851 census for Bishop Barnard. This revealed that The Ashes had been occupied by James Coates, aged thirty-two years, who described himself as being of independent means. He lived with his wife, Maria, and they had one daughter, Elizabeth, who was just a year old. The Coates family were outnumbered by their resident servants: a cook, a manservant and various maids, the youngest of whom, Mary Mason, was just thirteen years old.

'Where the slaveys slept' – the words returned to Wendy's head unbidden. 'Poor Mary Mason,' she said aloud. 'I hope they didn't work her too hard.'

By the 1861 census, the Coates family had increased considerably. James, Maria and Elizabeth had been joined by young Ann Maria, George Frederick and six-year-old Matilda, and all the domestic personnel had been replaced by newcomers.

'We could probably find baptisms for these Coates children in the parish registers,' said Joan. 'They have them here.'

'Let's finish the census first. We've only got 1871 left,' Wendy said.

'I suppose 1881 will be available in a couple of years,' Joan said. 'What a nuisance this hundred years' business is.'

By 1871 James and Maria's family had increased still further. Elizabeth – a young woman of twenty-one – was still at home and now had another four siblings, Eleanor and Joanna, who were 'scholars', Madeline Victoria, who was three, and baby Francis Michael, who was just two months old. In contrast, the number of servants living in the house had reduced to just three: Hannah Colbeck, aged twenty-five, Alice Croft, aged eighteen, and Edward Graves, aged twenty-nine, none of whom had been at The Ashes ten years earlier.

The searchers turned their attention to the parish registers next. These were also on microfilm and the two women were soon cursing the Victorian incumbent of Bishop Barnard, whose handwriting was extremely difficult to decipher. In spite of this, they quickly realized that the census had under-represented James and Maria's progeny. It was a rare year in which the couple had not presented an infant for baptism, but the burial register provided an answer for the absence of Charlotte, Amy, James Henry, Philippa, Catherine, Sophia, and even poor little Francis Michael had not survived many weeks beyond his 1871 census appearance. In 1873 Maria Coates herself was laid to rest in the churchyard.

'What an existence,' said Joan. 'Married at twenty, pregnant for the next twenty-three years, dead at forty-five. Thank heavens for birth control! Let's go and find some lunch.'

In the afternoon they followed up the various Coates children in the parish registers. All the daughters had been married in Bishop Barnard. George, heir to the house, had married elsewhere, but his four children had been baptised in the parish church. Three had pre-deceased him, and the only surviving son, Albert George, was identifiable from the name they had seen on the war memorial. With George Coates's burial in 1919, entries in the name of Coates ceased to appear in the parish registers.

'It's quite sad, really,' Wendy mused. 'I imagine when James Coates built his house he thought his family would be there for generation after generation, but in spite of having all those children, the family barely lasted seventy years.'

'We've still got well over an hour before they close,' Joan said. 'What do you say we have a look at the local newspapers for the time when Dora disappeared?'

Wendy had been privately hankering after exactly the same thing but had hesitated to say so for fear of upsetting Joan.

'*The North Eastern Gazette* was worth three halfpence of anybody's money,' Wendy said a few minutes later, when they had fetched the relevant film and fitted it on their reader. 'Look at this "Join the Silent Column". And the cinema listings! You could have gone and seen a different film every night of the week. I love these advertisements too. "Ladies lock-knit directoire knickers, exceptionally well cut, all colours two shillings, usual price two shillings and eleven pence.'

'Sounds like a bargain.'

Wendy wound the reel on again.

'Look.' Joan's voice rose slightly above the archive-appropriate whisper. 'Here's the first mention of it. "Dora Duncan, aged fifteen, the daughter of Mr and Mrs Herbert Duncan of The Ashes, Bishop Barnard, failed to return home yesterday evening after going for a cycle ride. Local police are appealing for anyone who may have seen Dora to come forward. She has blonde hair, blue eyes and was wearing a blue cotton dress. She was last seen riding a black bicycle".'

The following day, the paper carried a much bigger piece explaining that Dora had left home alone in the afternoon and was believed to have been cycling along the track leading to Holm Farm at around three p.m. Concern was mounting, the report added, since there was no known reason why Dora would have absented herself from home. Police and volunteers were searching fields and woodland nearby. The photograph of Dora which accompanied the article had not reproduced well, and it was impossible for them to be sure from the grainy microfilm whether Dora had even been smiling for the camera. Only the shape of her hair and the white semi-circles of her collar stood out with any clarity.

Concern was mounting! Wendy could only imagine the state she would have been in if it had been Tara or Katie who was missing.

Though the paper continued to devote some space to Dora each day, with subsequent editions naming Dora's siblings and explaining that she had been doing well at school and had numerous friends, there were no fresh developments until a full week had gone by.

'Fresh lead in schoolgirl's disappearance,' Joan read. 'Child witness, nine-year-old Peggy Disberry, has told police that she believes she saw Dora Duncan on the afternoon she went missing. Peggy Disberry was unavailable for comment yesterday, blah, blah . . . police are pursuing this new lead . . . blah blah . . . But what is the new lead? What did this Peggy Disberry see?'

'Wind the film on to the next day,' Wendy said. 'There might be something there.'

They combed the following day's edition, and the next day and the day after that, but the coverage of Dora's disappearance had faltered to a halt due to lack of new information.

'I wonder what the child saw?'

'It may have been nothing. Particularly as it took her a whole week to come forward.'

'She may have been attention-seeking.'

'Well, we've found out an awful lot about the Coates family,' said Joan, as they walked towards the car park.

'But nothing new about Dora. I was just thinking what a lot of babies have been born at The Ashes. Did your aunt Elaine have her children there too?'

'I don't know. Probably. Women mostly did have their children at home in those days, though I suppose she could have afforded a nursing home if she'd wanted one. I'm still thinking about that Peggy girl in the newspaper. What was her name again?'

'Disley?' Wendy flipped open the shorthand notepad she was carrying and thumbed through a couple of pages. 'No, sorry, Disberry. Unusual name.'

'That's what I was thinking. We might be able to find her, if she still lives around here. She was nine in 1943, so she'd only be forty-six now.'

'She's probably got married. Her name will be different.'

'Even so, we might be able to track her down with an unusual name like that. Of course, you're quite right, some children are terrible fibbers.'

It was only after she had dropped Joan off that Wendy remembered the photograph Peter had discovered in the cellar. She'd intended to mention it on both occasions she had seen Joan following her initial visit. Not that she could remember much about it, or even whether the young man in it could be said to resemble any of the family members in Joan's album. It was just that she thought Joan might have had some suggestion as to what it had been doing, hidden under the attic floorboards – perhaps it was connected with some sort of game the children had all played together? The trouble was that she and Joan always got talking and the mystery photo slipped her mind.

Wendy was eager to share her discoveries over dinner, but the rest of the family were no more than politely interested. Katie wanted to talk about her forthcoming school play, in which she had been cast as a fox. It wasn't a speaking part, which was fortunate as she would need to wear a mask. Tara was in a hurry to get away from the table and phone a friend – allegedly about a shared college project. Bruce merely said, 'It was very clever of you to find out so much. It's great that you've satisfied your curiosity, because now you'll be able to get the whole thing out of your system.'

Wendy had stuck to the information regarding the Coates family, deciding that it was better not to mention anything about Dora (since this was a chapter of the house's history that Bruce considered an inappropriate topic for the ears of the younger children). She said nothing at all about the fact that she and Joan had spent part of the journey home speculating about the possibility of tracking down Peggy Disberry.

I find it better not to dwell on anniversaries. Christmases and birthdays, special occasions which some people will never again be able to share with the lost ones. But there are some anniversaries that you aren't allowed to forget. The blood, the dirt, the digging – the desperate, desperate digging.

NINE

December 1980–January 1981

The drink driving case came before the magistrates a couple of weeks before Christmas. The bench was unmoved by Wendy's explanation of a single mistake in an otherwise unblemished decade of driving, or the notion that the loss of her licence would cause difficulties for her during the occasional periods when her husband's work took him away from home. Having listened, stern-faced, they handed down a ban of twelve months, while Wendy stood in the dock, trying not to cry. She supposed that she ought to be cross with Joan – as Bruce was – for unthinkingly encouraging her to drink and drive, but it wasn't as if Joan had done it on purpose. I have to take responsibility, Wendy thought. It was my own stupid mistake.

It was a nuisance, no doubt about it. Bruce had to take her supermarket shopping now, and missed his Saturday afternoon football match to accompany her on a foray into Middlesbrough for Christmas presents. He didn't openly complain, but she knew what he was thinking.

The Christmas shopping went much more smoothly than Wendy had anticipated and by eleven thirty they were laden with bags and had already ticked off most of the items on her list.

'Let's go and have a coffee,' she suggested. 'I know a nice little place just round the corner, well away from the plastic cup and hamburger fraternity.'

'Good idea.'

They were passing a shop which advertised 'picture framing, quality paintings and personal service' when Wendy stopped abruptly. With bags in both hands, she was unable to point. 'Look,' she said, nodding towards a painting propped on the easel which formed the centrepiece of the window display.

The picture was of a young woman in a full-length dress, who was smiling down at her sleeping child. The woman's face had a wistful quality to it, Wendy thought. And the child looked utterly peaceful, cocooned from the world by the transparent draperies of its crib.

'Oh Bruce! Isn't it lovely?'

He nodded. 'Very pretty.'

'I wonder if it's an original. I'd love to know who painted it.'

'I should think it's a print. I can't see a price on it.'

'It's quite big. And it's a posh shop, so it's sure to be expensive.'

'I'll go and ask.'

To her surprise he dumped his bags on the pavement and entered the shop, disappearing immediately among the various items on display inside. He returned two or three minutes later.

'Is it very expensive?'

Bruce laughed. 'Horribly. But at least I've found out what you wanted to know. It's a print of a painting done by a French woman. Morisot, the chap said her name was, from a French school apparently.'

'A woman,' Wendy said thoughtfully, taking a last long look at the picture, as Bruce adjusted the shopping he was carrying before they set off again in search of caffeine.

Though Bruce was forever watching the pennies, the balance of Wendy's legacy and the equity from the house in Jasmine Close meant that they were comfortable enough for regular treats, and it crossed Wendy's mind that he might have arranged to buy the painting as a Christmas present for her, but there was no tell-tale flat, rectangular present under the tree on Christmas morning and instead she simulated appropriate excitement over her favourite perfume from Bruce and thanked his parents profusely for their misguided gift of a sandwich toaster (of rather more benefit to the children than to herself, Wendy could not help thinking). Only when all the other gifts had been opened and the sitting room floor was covered in torn paper and bits of sticky tape, did Bruce take her by the hand and lead her across the hall and into the dining room, where he had secretly hung the Morisot reproduction on the chimney breast late the night before.

Wendy was speechless. She could only turn and bury her face in his chest, as Bruce's parents and the children crowded into the room behind them. It was the clearest possible sign, she thought, that she had been forgiven.

The celebrations were such a success that if Bruce's mother considered anything sub-standard, she did not think to mention it. Christmas lunch was perfect, there was no squabbling over Monopoly or Charades, and no one cavilled about joining in with the Boxing Day walk, regardless of what was showing on television. When Tara insisted on telephoning 'Bob' and his family on Christmas morning, no one made a big thing of it. It was only after Bruce had set off to drive Tara and his parents to the station – the senior Thorntons homeward bound, Tara on another trip south to see in the New Year with Robert and his family – that Wendy had a real opportunity to stand before the fireplace in the dining room and have a long, uninterrupted look at her picture. She had read somewhere that the positioning of a painting is all important. It had to be hung in the right light, and surely that must be the explanation here. The painting was evidently in the wrong place. How else to explain the way the woman's expression was so sad, the way she looked so tired as she rested her face against her hand while she watched over the sleeping infant? It was only when Wendy gave her full attention to the child, lying unnaturally pale behind the drapes, that she suddenly understood. The baby was dead.

Silly, she told herself. It's just the light.

She decided to put off stripping the bed in the guest room until tomorrow. Nor would she get the hoover out and deal with the day's shedding of needles from the tree. (A real tree was all very well, but it did dry out fearfully quickly in a room with the benefit of both central heating and a log fire.) It was still the holidays – the more so with the departure of Bruce's parents – and she was entitled to a break. She would go and make herself a well-deserved cup of tea. She paused to glance in at the sitting room where Jamie sat cross-legged on the rug, watching some old adventure film – *Jason and the Argonauts* perhaps? *The 7th Voyage of Sinbad*? It was such a lovely scene, she thought. The room decorated with their own evergreens, the tree dripping with baubles and twinkling fairy lights. The Ashes lent itself to moments like this. There had been a scattering of snow on Boxing Day – nothing to get excited about, not enough for a snowman or a snowball fight, but enough to outline windowsills, to make the view from the gate like something from the front of a Christmas card. She had always known the house would look wonderful at Christmastime.

The kitchen bore evidence of the season too, dotted about with the detritus of that period between Christmas and New Year. A discarded novelty from a cracker lying on a windowsill, the big platter which they only ever used for the turkey standing out on the surface, waiting to be put away on a shelf that only Bruce could comfortably reach, and a part-eaten box of cheese biscuits, for which there was no space available in the cupboard, standing alongside it. When she opened the fridge, she was confronted by various clingfilmed leftovers which no one was ever likely to eat. Who wanted cold stuffing?

As she shut the fridge door, milk in hand, she glanced around the room and smiled. It had come to life, she thought, this once sad, neglected building. Their very first Christmas here. Full of warmth and happiness, just as she had imagined. 'Thank you, house,' she said.

'Mam!' The urgency of Jamie's yell sent her racing back to the sitting room, still holding the container of milk.

'Oh my God! Jamie, get back.'

For a few seconds she stood transfixed in the doorway, staring at the surreal site. Where a few minutes before there had been one fire cheerfully burning in the grate, the original now had a fellow, a much smaller blaze, centred on the hearth rug.

'Quickly, to me.' She beckoned her son urgently as he skipped across the room to join her. 'Run upstairs,' she ordered. 'And tell Katie to come down. Then you are both to go straight outside. Both of you, do you understand?'

'What are you going to do?'

'I'm going to put out the fire.' I have to, she thought. If I don't do it right away, it'll get across to the Christmas tree and that will go up like a torch and set the whole house ablaze. Having sent Jamie on his way, she raced back to the kitchen, grabbed the biggest vase from the cupboard and filled it with cold water. As she ran back up the hall, she heard the children's voices on the landing.

'Hurry up!' she shouted. 'Get out of the house!'

In truth, the fire on the rug was a small one. A single vase of water quenched the most serious flames, though it created a billow of smoke, through which she could still see glowing embers. She passed the children in the hall as she was dashing back to the kitchen. 'Get outside,' she repeated, not pausing for discussion or explanation.

A second vase full of water appeared to extinguish everything, but she made sure of the job, retracing her steps another three times. By now the sitting room was full of smoke – or more likely steam – and an unpleasant smell of charred carpet filled her nostrils. The place where the fire had been was marked by an irregular blackened patch on the rug, with the soaked, charred remnants of a couple of Christmas cards lying on top. The rug was a goner, but apart from a mark on the carpet underneath, once the smoke had cleared, there was no other damage. The house, the children and everything else had been saved, but her heart was still hammering in her chest. It could so easily have been different. Imagine if Jamie had not been in the room to give an immediate alarm.

'It's not worth trying to claim on the insurance,' Bruce said, as he inspected the scene. 'We'd be better off just replacing the rug. That will hide the mark on the carpet and be cheaper than having to pay the excess on the policy. What I can't understand is why the fireguard wasn't in front of the fire.'

'I suppose the last person to put a fresh log on forgot to replace the guard. But I still don't see,' Wendy continued, 'how the fire got started in the first place.'

'I should have thought that was obvious. A draught must have blown a couple of cards down off the mantel shelf and they caught light. There should never have been cards standing on there in the first place. It's an obvious fire hazard.'

'So obvious,' Wendy said, 'that you never thought to mention it until after the event.'

'It's no use arguing with you about how you want things arranged,' Bruce retorted.

'Oh, naturally it's my fault!' Wendy turned to Jamie, who was hovering in the hall behind them. 'Jamie, you must have done something, just before the fire started. Were you jumping about? You won't be in trouble – we just need to understand how it began.'

'I wasn't jumping about. I wasn't even moving. I was lying on the rug, watching TV and then I heard a crackle and when I looked round, the rug was on fire, right behind my feet. I jumped up then, because I was scared my feet were going to get burned.'

'That really can't be true,' Wendy said. 'Those cards have been standing there for two or three weeks without falling down. Why would this mysterious draught happen all of a sudden this afternoon? And why would the cards bounce into the fire and then out again on to the floor? Just when the fireguard happened to be out of the way. Jamie, please tell me the truth. Did you move the fireguard after I'd left the room?'

'No, I didn't. I'm telling the truth. Perhaps it was the bad lady.'

'What bad lady?'

'The bad lady who chased Katie. In the dream. Or maybe the nasty man . . .'

'That's enough of that nonsense,' said Bruce. 'Why don't you run upstairs and play for a bit while I talk to Mummy.' He closed the door of the sitting room, closeting himself and Wendy inside. In a lower voice, he said, 'Did you see the fireguard in place before you left the room?'

'I don't honestly know. It's usually there when the kids are around. When I picture the room, I see it there, but that's because I'm expecting to see it, if you know what I mean. But Jamie must have been responsible. Maybe he was chucking something around and it knocked the cards into the fire. Perhaps he tried to rescue them by dragging them out on to the rug, only now he's afraid to own up. I expect it was all just an accident.'

'Well, I hope so. Otherwise we've got a budding arsonist on our hands.'

'Jamie's not an arsonist, Bruce. Don't overdramatize.'

'And what's all this about bad people?'

'What do you mean?'

'The bad lady who chases Katie, and the nasty man.'

'Katie must have told him about those dreams she had.'

'You're sure no one else has been talking about ghost stories? Putting ideas into his head?'

'If you mean me, then of course I haven't. Give me some credit. As if I would tell Jamie a thing like that!'

'Do you think Katie's still having those dreams?'

'How on earth should I know? She hasn't said anything to me

about them and I don't see the point in stirring it all up again by asking her. It was probably just those couple of times. Don't forget that she woke Jamie. He probably asked her about it.'

'I suppose so.' Bruce looked doubtful. 'Anyway, I suggest we go out tomorrow and see if we can replace that rug. We don't want to sit looking at a black mark on the carpet. There might be something in the sales.'

'What about Jamie? Shouldn't we try to get to the bottom of how the fire started?'

'Better to leave it. If he did it by accident, he isn't going to admit it. If he did it on purpose . . . well, we might have a problem on our hands . . . and I suppose it could have been a freakish accident – a door closing somewhere, creating a sudden draught.'

Wendy was about to point out that no one had closed a door at just that moment, but she decided that Bruce was right. It would be best left alone.

Once the Christmas festivities were over, they didn't use the dining room again until Bruce's birthday in January. Wendy had cooked his favourite gammon steaks and they opened a bottle of Gran Ponte Spumante, which even Katie and Jamie were allowed to taste, using two of the little coloured liqueur glasses that Bruce had won years ago on a tombola. After they had finished eating, Bruce helped her to carry things through to the kitchen (the wheeled trolley had yet to be purchased) while the children dispersed to use the telephone, watch television and play with a racetrack respectively. When he'd placed his stack of plates safely on the draining board, Bruce turned and put his hands on Wendy's shoulders. 'Leave all this,' he said. 'I've got a secret to share with you.'

She smiled up at him, responding to his mischievous tone. 'Ooh . . . good secret or bad secret?'

'Very good secret.'

'Come on then, tell me.'

His smile became a grin. 'I've been promoted.'

'How lovely! Congratulations!'

'Effective from April. District Director for Leicestershire.'

'Leicestershire? Won't that involve an awful lot of travelling?'

'Not once we've moved down there.'

'But I don't want to move to Leicestershire.' The words were out before she could stop them.

Bruce's smile faded. He adopted the patient tone which she recognized as the one he used for the children, when they didn't understand the finer points of their maths homework.

'Darling, you haven't had time to think about it yet. It's my fault for springing it on you like this. Once you get used to the idea you'll love it. It's a real step up the ladder. Quite a lot more money.'

'But you don't have to say "yes"? I mean, they can't make you go, can they? You said it was a secret. It's not official yet, is it?'

'I had the official offer today. Naturally I wasn't going to turn it down.'

'You mean you've accepted the job? You've been negotiating for a job in Leicester behind my back and you've accepted it without even consulting me?'

'I didn't want you to get all stirred up for nothing. It's a brilliant opportunity. We'll be able to afford a lovely house down there, somewhere handy for my parents in Ashby.'

'Any advantages of living somewhere handy for your mother completely escape me.'

'As well as more money, I get a company car. That means we could easily afford a second car, so you could have a little runaround of your own.'

'Great. I suppose you've forgotten that I've lost my licence.'

'Driving bans don't last forever. You'll be back behind the wheel before the end of the year. We have to look to the future.'

'And what about the children? They'll have to change schools, leave all their friends behind.'

'Good heavens, they'll soon make new friends. Now is as good a time for a move as any, before Katie starts senior school. And Tara will be going to university in September, so it won't make much difference to her. She'll come home to Leicester in the holidays instead of Durham.'

'But she's in the middle of doing her A-levels.'

'She'll be sitting them well before we actually move down there. The move won't be instantaneous. There's this place to sell, and you know how long it takes for house sales to go through these days. We're sure to become involved in some interminable chain.'

'So it's all decided then?' Wendy asked angrily. 'We're definitely going. The master has spoken.'

'Look, Wendy, I know this has taken you by surprise and maybe

I should have mentioned before that I was going for it, but you have to understand that if I turn this down, it puts my career into a siding, possibly permanently. I can't afford to pass up an opportunity like this at my age.'

'But you're only forty-one.'

'Exactly. I'm still young enough to move up again, if I take my chances. If I don't, I'm going to get stuck at the same level, bypassed by younger men. I know you don't really understand things like this . . .'

'But I thought you were happy doing what you do now. It's not as if we actually need more money. Not really.'

'People always need more money. You moaned last month when I said we couldn't afford a microwave oven without dipping into savings.'

'No, I didn't.'

'Well, on the new salary, you can have as many microwave ovens as you need.'

'But only if I go to Leicester.'

'Come on, Wendy. You always knew we might have to move. We'd never have met at all if I hadn't been transferred up here. You must try to see this from my point of view.'

'Have you tried to see it from my point of view? All my roots are up here. We've just made The Ashes into a lovely home and now you're asking me to leave it. I don't even like it down south.'

Bruce was struggling to contain his growing annoyance. 'Firstly, Leicester is not in the south, it's in the Midlands. As for your so-called roots, your parents are dead and you've got one cousin who lives in London and one who lives in Peterborough, both of which are actually closer to Leicester than they are to here, and the others are all so distant that they're no more than names on a Christmas card list. And the prospects for the children will be much, much better. It's a far more prosperous part of the country, with far more jobs available.'

'What about The Ashes? What about all the work we've put in?'

'Look on it as an investment. It will fetch much more than you paid for it. Wait until you start house-hunting down there. We could have one of those big splooshy new builds, four or five bedrooms, an en-suite for us, somewhere fuel economical. You have to admit that this house isn't exactly practical.'

'In what way?'

'The sheer size of the place. The layout. Huge gardens, back and front. These houses were designed for people who could afford to keep servants. You know it's too much for you to keep up with. I went into the study for some Sellotape the other day and you could write your name in the dust. It's not that I'm being critical . . .'

'Well, I do let the study go a bit, because no one seems to go in there very much.'

'My point entirely. It isn't used. Absolutely surplus to requirements.'

'But Bruce, I love this house.'

'Who's to say that you won't find another house you like even better?'

'I won't.'

'You might at least try,' he snapped.

'I'm sorry. I know I ought to be pleased for you and everything, but you don't understand how I feel. I thought we were happy here. I thought we were here to stay.'

He had let his hands drop from her shoulders, but now he raised his right hand and gave her left shoulder a squeeze. 'I shouldn't have sprung it on you like this. We'll find another house which you'll like even better than this one, and you'll soon make lots of new friends. There will be all the usual things, I expect. PTA and coffee mornings and such like. It's not as if it's a completely new area to both of us. We can look up some of my old friends. Most of them are married now. Then there will be the other wives from work. We'll be doing a bit of entertaining. That will help you get to know people.'

'What sort of entertaining?'

'Oh, the odd buffet supper, things on sticks. Just the usual. The type of stuff that Ray and Jan lay on when we go there.'

'But Jan's a brilliant cook!'

'You don't need to be brilliant to put cheese and pineapple on sticks.'

'Jan has never given us cheese and pineapple on sticks. What was that thing she gave us last time? Something Maringo?'

'It was chicken, wasn't it? Sweetheart, the sauce probably came out of a packet. You should be flattered. It was partly because of you that I got the job at all.'

'Why? What do you mean?'

'Well, John Crimmond approves of you tremendously. Ideal company wife, capable of putting on a bit of a spread, chatting to the other wives, being supportive and keeping the home fires burning. Now Keith Tulley's wife Marianne, you see, she's a career girl, might cut up rough about moving in case it affected her job.'

'But everyone just assumes that I will move without any fuss.' Her tone was bitter.

'Well, you haven't got a job, so obviously we're mobile. Good Lord, Wendy, lots of families have to move about the country – the world, even – at regular intervals. It's not as though it's going to cost us anything. The firm will cover all our relocation expenses.'

'It's going to cost me my home.'

'Is that all you can think about? This precious bloody house? You can be very selfish at times.'

'And I suppose you're not being selfish at all? Uprooting the whole family just because it suits your work.'

'Can I remind you that it's my work that keeps this whole show on the road?'

She paused then, thinking guiltily of her status as a non-working wife, the expensive gift at Christmas, a day spent at the county archives while the dust in the study built up, and the bumper crop of carrots from her father-in-law's allotment sat waiting to be made into something for the freezer. 'I expect you're right,' she conceded. 'It will all be for the best in the end.'

'Of course it will.' He leaned forward and kissed her forehead.

She accepted the kiss then turned to face the sink, not wanting him to see the deceit in her eyes.

We live in a scary world. People go missing every day. Some of them turn up, some of them are never seen again. But they can't pin it on you without a body. That's always been my assumption. My hope.

TEN

February–April 1981

Wendy was surprised at how well the children took the news of the impending move. It was probably because of the way Bruce had sold the whole scheme to them – in the guise of a great big adventure, she thought. He wasted no time in putting The Ashes on the market, and booked a week's holiday from work to coincide with the children's half term, with the intention of devoting the time to house-hunting. To Wendy's considerable annoyance, Tara decided at the last minute that instead of accompanying the rest of the family to Leicestershire, she preferred to go and stay with Robert in Solihull.

'But I want you to be part of choosing the new house.'

'What's the point? I'm going to uni soon and in future I'll be spending half my holidays with Bob and Mel. Anyway, I didn't help choose this house. You just said we were buying it and that was that.'

Nor did Wendy relish the prospect of a week with her in-laws in Ashby-de-la-Zouch. Her fears were well founded. By Wednesday night she and Bruce were exchanging sharp, if muted words, in the privacy of their bedroom.

'Can you please ask your mother to stop feeding the kids a constant diet of sweets and chocolate?'

'It's only for a week. It's not doing them any harm.'

'She's only doing it to undermine me.'

'Don't be so silly.'

'Yes, she is. True to her usual fashion, your mother is indulging the children to a ridiculous degree, with the result that Jamie in particular is playing us all off one against another and generally behaving atrociously.'

'Jamie has picked up on the atmosphere you have helped to create and is taking advantage of it.'

'What do you mean "the atmosphere I've helped to create"?'

'Well, you aren't exactly being cooperative, are you?'

'I am being extremely cooperative. I have spent the last fortnight keeping The Ashes spotless and showing people all over it like some kind of tour guide, followed by the last three days being driven from one new development to another, looking around house after house.'

'You might at least pretend to be enthusiastic.'

'I am doing my best, Bruce, truly I am. But after the first half-dozen developments, one Laurels or Westmoreland starts to look very much like another. The children have lost interest completely, and today they just ended up racing around, squabbling about who's having which bedroom.' She faced him in a direct appeal. 'The houses are all starting to look the same. This afternoon we found we were looking at a design we'd seen yesterday on another estate. Honestly, I've got to the stage where I'm not even sure we aren't looking at the *same* houses we walked round the day before.'

'And none of them are right,' he said, with more than a hint of sarcasm in his voice. 'In one the kitchen's too small, in the next one the kitchen space is adequate but the bedrooms don't suit, and so it goes on.'

'I'm trying to be constructive. You said we didn't have to make our minds up right away.'

'But you don't seem to want to make your mind up at all. Several of these firms will accept our old house in part exchange. If we went for one of those deals, we could be on the move in a matter of weeks. You know I have to be in post by the end of March, and Tara's last exam is the first week in June. I don't want to be staying at Mum and Dad's through the week and shuttling up and down the motorway at weekends on a permanent basis.'

'But a new house, Bruce . . . It's a big decision. It isn't easy. And anyway, it isn't just my decision. You must have a preference.'

'I don't recall you being too worried about my views when you bought The Ashes. I've told you, that double-fronted place at

Whitwick would suit me. Or the Wolverton – that's a great design, I don't see how we could go wrong with that. To be honest, I'd be fine with just about anything we've seen, so long as you're happy with it. There are pros and cons with all these new places. There's no such thing as the perfect house and you know it. And please don't try to tell me that where we live now is perfect, because you and I both know that is very far from being the case.'

'You see, that's the thing . . . I'm wondering if we shouldn't look for something older.'

'Now, you know we discussed this before. I don't want to get involved in some chain which collapses when someone further down the line pulls out and everyone else has to start all over again. Besides which, a new house needs nothing doing to it. No more wrecks and projects. These old places are money pits. We want somewhere we can move straight into.'

Wendy reached for the pile of brochures on the bedside table and began to consider them in what she hoped Bruce would take as a positive fashion. 'Which ones are we going to look at tomorrow?' she asked.

At the conclusion of the week nothing had been decided and the journey north was mostly accomplished in silence. A little pile of post was lying on the hall floor and the light was blinking on the telephone answering machine. Wendy pressed the button to rewind the tape, then pressed play. When she realized that it was Joan, she was rather glad that everyone else had already dispersed further into the house. Bruce was unaware that they were still on the trail of information about the house's former occupants, and Wendy strongly suspected that he wouldn't approve.

'I've made a breakthrough on Peggy Disberry,' Joan said, after a brief preamble. 'Do ring me back as soon as you can.'

Wendy waited until the following day when she had the house to herself before she returned Joan's call. They had touched on the possibility of locating Peggy Disberry several times, without ever reaching any particular conclusion on the subject.

'How on earth did you find her?' Wendy asked.

'Simplest thing, my dear. I just got it into my head to look in the phone book. There are only two Disberrys and the first one happened to be her brother. He was a bit cagey at first and I had to tell a couple of little fibs, I'm afraid. I told him we were

researching a history of Bishop Barnard – well, yes, I know . . .
I said it was for a little book we were putting together. Anyway,
to cut a long story short, he gave me her address and telephone
number and I rang her up. It's so lucky you've rung back just now,
because I've arranged for us to go and see her this afternoon. I
was on absolute tenterhooks in case I didn't get you in time. You
can come this afternoon, can't you? I can pick you up if you don't
have the use of the car today.'

'Bruce has taken the car to work . . . And I have to be home
for Jamie at three.' As she spoke, Wendy felt the weight of her
omission in failing to explain to Joan that even if she had half-a-
dozen cars sitting on the drive, she would not have been able to
use one of them.

'That's not a problem. Peggy Disberry lives in Stockton, so it
won't take us long to get there and back. Say I pick you up at
one? I can easily get you home for three. Must dash now, my dear,
I've got a hair appointment.'

Joan arrived on time and kept the engine running while Wendy
trotted down the drive to the gate. They screeched away at high
speed, with Wendy still fastening her seat belt.

'Is it far?'

'No,' said Joan. 'It's that rather rough estate on the edge of
Stockton. It won't take us long to get there at this time of day.'

An unnecessary observation, Wendy thought, since the speed
at which Joan was driving meant it wouldn't take long to get
anywhere at all.

'Any luck with the house?' Joan asked.

'You mean selling? Nothing definite. One couple seemed keen,
but they haven't sold their own house yet.'

'House purchase is such a nightmare these days,' Joan said,
jamming her brakes on as the lights ahead turned red. 'And it's
not like the old days, when people shook hands on a price and
kept to their word. Today everyone thinks they can start horse-
trading about the price at the last minute. One has to deal with
such a different type of person these days.'

'Bruce is quite keen to do one of those part-exchange deals on
a new house, so we don't get involved in a chain.'

'Don't you rather lose out on the price of your own house with
those sorts of things?'

'Bruce thinks it's worth losing a couple of thousand, just to move quickly and avoid hassle. He says that if you don't sell quickly, you often end up having to reduce the price in any case.'

'And what about you, my dear? What do you think?'

'I can't decide. And the trouble is . . .' It was somehow easy to confide in Joan. 'I don't really want to leave The Ashes. We haven't even lived there a year.'

'George and I did an awful lot of moving about,' Joan said thoughtfully. 'Wouldn't have missed it for the world, of course, but I sometimes used to think how nice it would be to settle down – and I always thought of this area as home.'

'That's how I feel.' Wendy's words came out in a rush. 'The Ashes is home. The home I've always wanted. It's the place I wanted to end up in, not a stop on the route. But once it's sold, there won't be any going back to it.'

'I suppose you couldn't rent it out while you live somewhere else? Have it to come back to, once you were able.'

'We can't afford to buy another house and keep The Ashes on, unless we take out a mortgage, and Bruce won't hear of that now we've been able to pay the old one off. Besides which, I think Bruce sees the move south as potentially permanent. He's from Leicestershire originally.'

'Ahh . . . So Bruce's direction of travel isn't necessarily the same as yours when it comes to an eventual finishing line,' Joan said thoughtfully. In a completely different tone, she asked, 'How much have I told you about this book we're working on?'

'Book?'

'Our history of Bishop Barnard. That's officially what we're going to talk to Peggy Jones about. Her married name is Jones, did I mention that?'

'You haven't told me anything about the book.'

'Well, I told this Peggy Jones that we're including a chapter on unsolved mysteries in Bishop Barnard.'

'Are there any – apart from Dora?'

'Of course not! Well, none that I know about anyway, but if necessary I'm going to waffle a bit about some missing medieval church plate. I didn't get the impression that we're dealing with an academic, or the sort of person who's going to know about that kind of thing. Oh yes,' Joan added, 'I also told her that we wouldn't be able to pay her anything for talking to us. You know what people are like . . . they read about the *Daily Mail* paying thousands for someone's night of passion with a great train robber and imagine that some half-remembered anecdote is going to make their fortune.'

'Am I supposed to be your secretary?'

'Of course not. You're my co-writer. I brought along my notepad and pencil from the record office to make us look a bit more convincing. I thought about bringing a cassette tape recorder, but that might be a bit inhibiting. People don't always like being recorded.'

The residents of the estate where their quarry lived were divided into those who cultivated their front gardens and those who left a square of beaten earth to be fouled by the local canines. The house inhabited by Peggy Jones had a square of lawn, fronted by a privet hedge which appeared to have expired in one or two places. It was easy to pick out because the number seventeen had been painted in large, childish numerals alongside the front door. There was a smirking garden gnome on the doorstep and the net curtains at the front windows were an alarming shade of primrose yellow.

Wendy followed Joan as she walked briskly up the path. The bell, when pressed, emitted an agonized rendition of the opening bars of Greensleeves.

Joan just had time to mutter, 'Eat your heart out, Vaughan Williams,' before the door was opened and the frame filled by a large, plump woman whose body had been squeezed into a skirt and sleeveless jumper which appeared to be at least two sizes too small. Her freckled arms were a completely different flesh tone to her made-up face, which included lashes and brows which had been blackened until they matched the unnaturally black hair piled into a sort of plaited loaf on top of her head. However, Peggy Jones afforded them such a genuinely warm welcome that Wendy experienced more than a pang of guilt at Joan's deceitful method of gaining entry to her home.

'Call me Peggy,' their hostess instructed, as she ushered them into the living room. 'Everyone does, ever since I were a bairn.'

She insisted on making them tea, in spite of Joan's protestations that she need not, so while Peggy was busy in the kitchen and Joan was readying her notebook, Wendy occupied herself in looking around the room. There were lots of photographs of small children, all displayed in cardboard frames, some of them faded through long exposure to the light, and all having a slightly jaundiced appearance thanks to the effect of the net curtains. There was a very large television set and a number of china and glass ornaments, but not a single book, or even a newspaper. She could not help concluding that Joan had been correct in her assumption that Peggy would not detect them in their fraud.

'Do either of yous take sugar?' Peggy appeared in the doorway to enquire.

Neither of them did.

A moment later she appeared again, this time carrying a plastic tray on which three cups rattled in their saucers. The tea was incredibly strong and unmistakably laced with sterilized milk.

'Now then.' After handing round the teacups, Peggy slid herself into a black vinyl armchair, which received her with a sound somewhere between a squeak and a sigh. 'Tell us all about this book you're writing.'

To Wendy's astonishment, Joan launched into a potted history of Bishop Barnard – how much was made up and how much genuine, she had no idea – quite quickly reaching a point which implied that they had stumbled on the story of Dora Duncan pretty much by accident. 'Although,' Joan said, favouring Peggy with a winning smile, 'I would love to know more about it because I'm distantly related to Dora Duncan.'

'But you never knew she was murdered, like?' Peggy seemed surprised.

Ha! Wendy thought. You've slipped up there. But Joan never faltered. 'Well, I knew she'd disappeared, but I never knew the details. And I didn't know it had happened in Bishop Barnard, the very place we're writing about. When I first saw it in the old newspapers I gave quite a jump, didn't I, Wendy?'

Wendy smiled and nodded, uncomfortable in endorsing these lies. Peggy Jones seemed such a nice, ordinary woman. Had the subterfuge really been necessary? Mightn't she have agreed to talk with them even if they had explained their actual connection to the case?

Joan had clearly missed her vocation. '"My goodness," I said. "That's Dora. She was my mother's cousin's girl, or something like that." I wasn't sure of the relationship. One never is in big families like ours.'

'So how did you find out about me? Old newspapers, you said?'

'That's right. The report said you came forward to say that you saw Dora on the day she disappeared.'

'Eee . . . how funny, that you should come asking us after all these years. Mind, I cannot tell you owt what I didn't tell the police at the time.'

'Of course not,' Joan agreed. 'But we'd like to hear first hand from you what you remember.'

Peggy seemed to be in no hurry to impart what little she knew, firstly pressing them to have more tea (which they both declined) and then apologizing about the lack of biscuits, which, she explained, had all been eaten by visiting grandchildren the day before. Wendy noted that Peggy appeared much older than her forty-six years and had evidently embraced motherhood at an early stage in her life. Once they had surmounted the topic of refreshments, Peggy wanted to know how one went about looking things up in old newspapers. The idea that her brief moment of fame was preserved for posterity on microfilm seemed to appeal to her. At last she began to relate her story, scanning the faces of her visitors for a reaction, slowing almost involuntarily when she noticed Joan jotting down a word or two.

'Well, I'd been bad, you see. I was often poorly as a bairn, on account of me chest, so the day it happened, I wasn't out playing. Usually we'd have all been playing out. There was three of us. Me, I were the eldest, then our Joey, then Roger. Our Peter wasn't born until after the war. There was big families in all the houses round by us, so the streets was just full of bairns the whole day long, only that day while they was all outside, I was up in the bedroom, on me own.

'It were a lovely sunny day, so I were kneeling up, looking out of the window. We used to live in one of those houses off Chester Place, in Bishop Barnard. They're still there, but there's that new estate at the back of them now. I wouldn't mind a house on there meself. Very nice they look, but they're nearly all private, and even if we could get one, our lad would never agree to move from here. Too far from his club and his darts team . . .

'Anyway, when we lived in our old place there was nothing at the back of us. You could look right across the fields. You couldn't see nothing from downstairs, because of the hedge, and it were all blocked off at the back to keep the chickens in and all. You weren't supposed to keep chickens, the landlord said, but they turned a blind eye when the war was on. Upstairs, though, you could see right across to the farm. We used to watch them getting the harvest in. They often used to bag rabbits and stuff, when they cut the last of it.'

'That would be Holm Farm? So you could see the farm track?' Joan prompted.

'Aye. Part of it, not all. We couldn't see the start of it, like, where it came off Green Lane, nor the end of it up by the farm, because there was trees and stuff in the way, but you could see a good long stretch of it, and I saw that Dora, all right. They said old Mrs Gregory was wrong, because of her eyes, and they said I was probably wrong too, being so young and probably just romancing, but it was her all right and some chap was following her.'

'Did you know Dora?' Wendy asked.

'Not properly. Not to speak to. They were a right stuck-up lot. Lived in a big house on Green Lane. I recognized her, though. It was the hair. Blonde and curly. The opposite of mine. Course, I have to help mine now or I'd be mostly grey. By, I'd look a right mess if I didn't dye it.' Peggy chuckled to herself.

'Did you recognize the man who was following her?' Joan asked.

'I can't say that I did. It's a pity I never got a better look at him, because it must have been him what done it.'

'So you think she was murdered?'

'Well, it stands to reason, doesn't it? If a girl goes out and never comes back.'

'They never found a body,' said Joan.

'Not looking in the right place, was they? I reckon that fella had got it all sorted out by the time the police started looking. Short-handed, they would have been, I suppose, what with the war and all.'

'Do you think Dora knew she was being followed?' Wendy asked. 'I mean, was the man close behind her? Did she look back or anything?'

Peggy paused, as if attempting to replay the faded memory in her mind. A black cat emerged from behind the chair and began rubbing its head against her legs. 'I know she never spoke to him or owt like that. I remember the police asking me and me saying no. He wasn't all that close behind her, not really. In fact, he was a good long way back, so she might not have known he was there. Old Mrs Gregory, she said she was cleaning her top window when she saw them, though no one really believed her – she was blind as a bat, poor old thing. Anyway, she reckoned this chap weren't following Dora at all. Said she thought he turned off towards the bridge what goes over the beck while that Dora carried on along the track. There was a couple of paths led off the track before it reached Green Lane.'

'But you don't think he turned off?'

'Well, I don't know. I never saw him turn off. Not that I saw him doing anything else either. They was both just walking. Her pushing her bike and him just walking along, ordinary like.'

'And they just carried on walking until they both went out of sight?'

'I suppose so, yes. But you see I only saw them when they was partway along. Then I went back to playing. I mean . . . I suppose he could have turned off without me seeing.'

'And you never saw anyone coming back . . . later on?'

'How do you mean, coming back?'

'Well, if Dora and the man were heading along the track towards the farm . . .'

'Oh, no. They wasn't walking towards the farm when I saw them. They was both walking back in the opposite direction.'

'Back towards Bishop Barnard?' Wendy couldn't conceal her surprise. That wasn't how she had pictured it in her mind at all.

'That's right,' said Peggy. 'I suppose she must have walked the other way first, but you see, I wasn't looking out of the window the whole time. Some of the time I was playing in my bed. I would'a had my doll and some books to look at and that.'

'So really,' Joan said, 'it was lucky you just happened to be looking out at that particular time and saw them.'

Peggy laughed, startling the cat, who shied away and disappeared behind the chair again. 'I don't see that it was very lucky. It didn't do her much good, did it? Nor the police. Questioned me left, right and centre, they did, but it didn't make no difference. I couldn't tell them what I didn't know.'

Joan nodded. 'If you don't mind me asking, why did it take you so long to tell the police what you'd seen?'

'That weren't my fault.' Peggy's swift, defensive response suggested someone accustomed to having the world's wrongs unfairly heaped on her shoulders. 'That was our mam. She never told bairns anything, our mam, so when I saw the police searching all along the track and in the fields and that, she pretended not to know what it was all in aid of. Said somebody must have lost summat on the farm.

'It wasn't until a day or two later, when I was better and playing out again, and some of the kiddies in our street said they still hadn't found that Dora Duncan, and the mams was all telling everyone not to go over to the farm, that I realized it must have been her what they were looking for. I knew it were no use asking our mam anything, so I went and asked me grandad. He was a grand old chap, me grandad. He used to tell me all sorts. Well, when I told him I'd seen that Dora on the day she went missing, first off he told me to keep quiet. He didn't hold with the police, didn't Grandad. Never had no time for them. Only then our mam got to hear about it and it was straight into her best hat and coat and down the police station with me.

'There was a lot of chew over it after, what with policemen coming to the house, traipsing all over, wanting to look out of our back bedroom window. Our mam wasn't happy about that. In the end I think she wished she'd listened to Grandad. It never did any good anyway. They never found that Dora, did they?'

'Even so, you did the right thing, going forward,' Joan said. 'It could have been very important.'

Peggy shook her head, half smiling at the recollection. 'It didn't half start some trouble between Mam and Grandad. Grandad lived with us, you see, and he liked to think he was the man of the house, with our dad being away in the army. Grandad was that mad at having the police in the house, he threatened to tittle off to me auntie Margaret's. He was swearing under his breath when the police came looking round.'

'Perhaps he'd had some trouble with them,' Wendy suggested hesitantly.

'Oh aye. He didn't like them. Our Uncle Billie got put away during a pit strike before the war. He was a miner, Uncle Billie, and there'd been some trouble over the men stealing coal. Me grandad told me all sorts. I was his favourite, see? Being the only girl and a bit sickly, like. Wouldn't think so, to look at me now.' Peggy's bosom heaved up and down with laughter. 'He used to tell me all sorts of stuff from when he was a boy. Lived in Bishop Barnard all his life, he had. You wouldn't have needed to see anyone else for your book if you'd have had me grandad.'

'I daresay his memory would have gone back to the last century,' Joan said.

'Oh aye. He died just before VE Day, and he were a fair age then. He used to tell me all about the hunt. They used to meet up at the Green, where the old Grange was. All the nobs from the big places round and about used to come riding up the lane, Grandad said, expecting you to get out of their way and touch your cap when they passed you. Grandad wouldn't do it, mind. "Sod 'em," he used to say. "Stuck up buggers. They ain't no better than us, they've just got more bloody money, that's all."' Peggy laughed again.

Joan had closed her notebook and replaced it in her handbag. She caught Wendy's eye, but Peggy was still in full flow.

'Mind you,' Peggy continued, 'he could be a right old scrounger, Grandad. I remember he thought that Dora's family should have given me something. A reward for coming forward. They didn't, though. Not that I expected anything, but Grandad said they should have done. Them not being short of a bob or two and our mam at home with three bairns and the breadwinner away fighting for his country and all. Mind, he said he didn't envy them their luck, losing a daughter like that. Unlucky house, Grandad said it was. And it was funny, when you think about it. Two murders in the one house.'

'Two murders?' Joan looked up from her bag, interest abruptly rekindled.

Wendy stared at Peggy but said nothing.

'Two murders?' Joan repeated. 'Are you sure? At The Ashes, where the Duncan family used to live?'

'The Ashes . . . Aye, that was the name of the place.' Peggy nodded to herself.

The cat had slipped out from behind the chair and began clawing the upholstery.

'Stop it, you naughty girl!' Peggy batted the cat away. 'I thought you'd know about that already,' she said. 'Seeing as how you're looking into the history of the village and all.'

'No,' Joan said. 'You're the first person who's mentioned it.'

'Well, me grandad told me, so it must have been fairly common knowledge.' Peggy regarded them doubtfully, like a child who is starting to question stories about Santa Claus.

'We haven't long begun our research.' Joan was fishing in her bag for the notebook as she spoke. 'Do tell us what your grand-father told you about this other murder.'

'It was years before that Dora Duncan. Grandad didn't tell me too much. It was our mam, you see. She didn't like him telling us anything like that. Grandad reckoned everybody knew that house was unlucky. The people what owned it before the Duncans lost their son – or was it their grandson? – in the first war. Grandad used to say that the old chap what owned the house died of a broken heart after that. Just shows that money doesn't bring happi-ness, I suppose. Not but what a bit extra wouldn't go amiss now and then.' Peggy chuckled again.

'But the other murder . . .' Joan prompted.

'It must have happened a long time ago. Grandad was only a little lad, I reckon.'

'But who was murdered? Did they catch anyone?' Joan persisted.

'It was something to do with a young girl. I think she had a tiff with her fancy fella and did him in, in a fit of temper. All the bairns round about used to say the place was haunted. Not that any of us was ever inside there. Them Duncans kept to their own sort. They went to boarding schools and didn't mix with the likes of us, not even in the school holidays. I suppose it was the ghost of the fella what was murdered. There's probably two ghosts in there now, keeping each other company.' Peggy's bosom heaved in time with another chuckle. 'Me grandad had heard some tale about that Dora getting in wrong with her mother for hanging about with a lad from the village. "Her folks wouldn't have liked that," he said to me. "Thought they were too good for the likes of us." But it were just gossip. I don't suppose there was anything in it.' Peggy laughed again.

Wendy joined in nervously. She wondered what Peggy would say if she discovered that the present owner of The Ashes was sitting barely a yard from her.

Joan attempted a few more questions, but it soon became clear that while Peggy would have been more than happy to devote the whole afternoon to sharing recollections of her childhood and her grandfather, she could add nothing more about past events at The Ashes.

'Well,' Joan said, when they were back in the car and Peggy had waved them on their way. 'What did you make of all that?'

'It's incredible. We've got to get to the bottom of it. You don't suppose she was making it up . . . or had got the wrong house?'

'I don't think she was making it up. Of course, her grandfather might have been romancing. You know how some men do love to tease children with tall stories. And I suppose he might have mistaken the house, although she said he'd lived in the village all his life and actually remembered it happening.'

'She said he was getting on a bit. Old people sometimes get very confused.'

'One thing's for sure. Ronnie's story must have come from the local children – though goodness knows how he got hold of it. As she said, they didn't really mix with the village children. But it can't be a coincidence because it fits so neatly with what Peggy told us . . . except that in Ronnie's story it was a young girl who was doing the haunting and in Peggy's version it's supposed to be the murdered boyfriend. I say, Wendy, it's jolly lucky you're not the nervous type.'

'There's nothing to hurt me at The Ashes. I don't believe I've ever known such a welcoming house.' It was true that the house had seen more than its share of tragedy, but every run of bad luck had to end sometime.

'Well, there we are.' Joan nodded approvingly. 'Nothing hysterical or imaginative about you. Or indeed Aunt Elaine. I shouldn't mention it to any prospective new owners, though. Not everyone's as sensible or down to earth as you are.'

'These ghost stories can't still be current,' Wendy said. 'My kids have all been to school in Bishop Barnard and they've never mentioned them.' She pushed aside the recollection of Jamie's talk of footsteps in the attic. A few creaking boards – that was all it was.

'I suppose a lot of local people have moved away since the war and the stories have died out,' Joan said. 'People are far more mobile these days. It's not like the pre-war generation, where all the agricultural labourers had lived in the same parishes since Domesday. It's also a very long time ago. Let's face it, my dear, you were barely born when Dora disappeared. And the first murder – if there was one – happened even longer ago than that.'

'How do we find out about it? Another trip to the archives in Durham, I suppose?'

'If there was a murder, it would be sure to have made the newspapers,' Joan speculated.

'The problem would be where to start looking,' Wendy mused. 'We knew exactly when Dora went missing. This time it's much vaguer. It was at some point during her grandfather's childhood, according to Peggy, but we don't really know when that was.'

'Didn't she say her grandfather died around VE Day? That's 1945, so if he was ninety, that would mean he was born around 1855, but if he was only in his sixties, it could be as late as 1885. Goodness, I see what you mean. Oh dear! Sorry to swerve like that.'

Wendy stifled a gasp as the car narrowly avoided a collision with a cyclist while Joan's mind had been preoccupied with questions other than the road ahead. When she could breathe again, Wendy said, 'The microfilm would send you bonk-eyed. It might take days to cover all those years. There must be a shortcut?'

'Do you think there's a real book? A history of the village, I mean? There might be something in the local interest section of the library.'

'I've never noticed anything like that. Oh, I know!' Sudden inspiration made Wendy's voice rise. 'I could ask Tara to ask her friend's father about it. The one who put me on to the census. I believe he knows quite a lot about local history. You know,' she added, 'I was a bit surprised when Peggy said that Dora was going back in the direction of Green Lane when she saw her. To think that she was almost home and never made it.'

'It's strange what she had to say about the man, too,' said Joan. 'Perhaps the other witness – the old lady with the bad eyesight – was right. He might have turned off and had nothing to do with it. But that doesn't make sense, does it? It's always the sinister stranger on the lonely path. And he wasn't identified, was he? An innocent person would have come forward.'

'I'm not so sure. A lot of people mightn't want to get involved. And if all he saw was a girl pushing a bike along a track, he might think, what's the point? I can't tell them anything they don't already know.'

On balance, Wendy decided it best not to mention the visit to Peggy's in front of Bruce. He had such a lot on his plate at the moment. On the other hand, she would have to explain at least some of the details to Tara if they were going to enlist the help of John Newbould via her friend Helen. Best mull it over, she thought, and not do anything right away.

*   *   *

'Do you think the papers will go a day between now and the wedding without printing something about this blessed engagement?' Bruce turned a page of the Saturday morning paper, spreading the sheets wide, then folding the whole newspaper into a smaller shape which could be accommodated more easily on a corner of the breakfast table, while he indulged in a weekend treat of bacon and eggs.

'I suppose it's because it's Prince Charles and she'll be the queen one day. And it makes a change from the unemployment figures.'

'A chap at work said he'd only been put up to marrying her to distract people from what a mess the country's in.'

'I like Lady Diana.' Katie looked up from a bowl of cornflakes. 'She's very pretty.'

'A dumb blonde,' said her father. 'You'd have thought Charles would have gone for someone with a few more brains. I mean, what does she know of life? A young girl of nineteen? She's barely a year older than Tara, for goodness' sake.'

'Who's barely a year older than me?' Tara, still in her dressing gown, entered the kitchen in time to hear the tail end of the sentence.

'Lady Diana,' Wendy explained. 'I'm doing bacon and eggs, Tara, do you want some?'

'Uggh, no thanks. So what about me and Lady Diana then?'

'I was just saying to your mother that she's far too young and inexperienced to be getting married – particularly to a man who's so much older.'

'I don't see why.'

Oh dear, Wendy thought. First thing on a Saturday morning when Tara was barely out of bed was not the best moment to take issue with her on anything.

'Well, you would see exactly what I mean if you were a bit older yourself.'

No, no, Bruce, Wendy wanted to say, but it was already too late.

'It's older people who have got the world into such a mess,' Tara said, not even looking at Bruce as she reached into the fridge for the juice. 'If she's in love with Prince Charles – though why anyone would be, I can't imagine – then of course she should marry him. Younger people know a lot more than older people think they do.'

'Tara, please don't take that tone with your father.'

'He's not my father. I do wish you'd try to get your head around that.' Tara had moved from the fridge to the counter, where she poured some juice into a glass.

'Irrespective of blood lines,' said Bruce, 'you shouldn't be speaking to anyone in that tone of voice. Not me or your mother. And while you're living under my roof, you'll show some respect.'

'Or else what?' For the first time since she had entered the kitchen, Tara looked Bruce straight in the eye. 'Go on . . .' she goaded. 'What are you going to do about it?'

'Tara, please . . . we were all just sitting here, having a nice family breakfast . . .'

'And it's all been spoiled by the cuckoo in the nest.' Tara shrugged. 'Well, don't worry, I'm not stopping you. Carry on with your nice family breakfast.' She invested the final words with contempt.

'For heaven's sake!' Bruce exclaimed, but Tara had already gone, leaving the juice carton out on the counter. Wendy automatically turned away from the stove to put it back in the fridge.

Katie rose from the table and sidled out after her sister.

'Katie!' Wendy called. 'What about your bacon?'

'I don't want any, thank you,' came a voice from the hall.

'But you said . . . oh for goodness' sake, now I've cooked far too much. Bruce, Jamie, can you each eat another rasher?'

A few minutes later, Wendy said, 'You shouldn't take any notice of her. She's on edge over her exams.'

'Her exams are weeks away.'

'You know,' Wendy said, when Jamie had finished his extra bacon and she was left alone at the table with Bruce, she still finishing a bacon sandwich, he lingering over a second coffee while he read the paper, 'this all started when you objected to her seeing that builder boy.'

'Of course. My fault as usual,' Bruce grunted, not bothering to look up from whatever he was reading.

'I didn't mean it like that. I just think he's at the root of all this trouble. I think she's carried on seeing him behind our backs. There's someone she rings, someone she's always a bit secretive about. If I come through the hall sometimes, when she's on the phone, her voice changes and she shuts up sharpish, as if it's a conversation she doesn't want me to hear.'

'She's eighteen. There's probably a lot of conversations she doesn't want you to hear.' He lifted the paper, shook it back into shape and turned another page. 'As for her continuing to see that John, or whatever his name is, why would she bother to keep it a secret? She was pretty defiant about it when I first challenged her.'

'She's put Birmingham down as her first choice.'

'It's a good university – and it's near to her father too.'

'It's also where he's all set to go to the Polytechnic.'

'Birmingham's quite a big place, Wendy. It's not like them both being in Bishop Barnard, you know. Oh . . .' He paused, his attention clearly caught by something he had spotted in the paper. 'Talk of the devil . . . or devils, I suppose, in this case. That other labourer of Broughton's, Peter Grayling . . .'

'Yes?'

'Well, the trial finished yesterday and he's been found not guilty.'

'I didn't even know the trial had started. I suppose that's good then.'

'What's good about it?'

'It means he didn't do it and now he'll be set free.'

'Good God, Wendy, you can be so naïve. All I can say is what a good thing it is we'll all be moving away from here very soon.'

'What on earth are you talking about?'

'Don't you get it? This chap knows the layout of the house and exactly who lives here.'

'But he's been found not guilty.'

'There's no smoke without fire, not in cases like this. The difficulty they've had all along in bringing it home to him is that they've never found the body, but the police wouldn't have made an arrest if they hadn't known it was him. You'll need to be very careful with security when I'm not here. No forgetting and leaving the back door unlocked all night.'

'That was only one occasion.'

'Well, you'll have to be very careful,' Bruce repeated.

She had hoped to have a day free from all mention of Bruce's impending departure, but they were right back on it again, she thought. It cast a cloud over everything, coloured every conversation. One more week as a family, before Bruce took up his new post, which would mean staying with his parents during the week. At least he would be home at weekends.

*   *   *

When they assembled to kiss Bruce goodbye on the front doorstep a week later (all except Tara, who was out with friends), Wendy experienced an awful sense of foreboding. Suppose he was killed on the motorway and never made it? It was quiet on Sunday afternoons, but even so . . .

'Don't forget to ring me when you get to your parents' house,' she said.

He did ring, but it was Tara who happened to answer the telephone. From the sitting room, Wendy caught a perfunctory exchange before Tara rang off and popped her head around the door.

'That was Dad.' (It was funny, Wendy thought, the way Tara attempted to make a point of addressing him as Bruce, but as often as not forgot herself and still called him by that old familiar label.) 'He just called to say he got to Granny's OK.'

'Is that all?'

'What were you expecting him to do? Declaim from Shakespeare or recite the Magna Carta? He's only been gone a few hours. He said something about going out for a walk, to stretch his legs after the drive.' Tara withdrew, shaking her head theatrically, as if in wonderment at the stupidity of parents.

Alone in the sitting room, Wendy considered the TV schedule and found nothing of interest. Katie joined her and they played best of three games of draughts (later extended to best of five) before it was her bedtime. At nine thirty she took Tara a cup of coffee in her lair, but Tara had settled down with her books and her headphones and was clearly not disposed for a chat. Back downstairs and mindful of Bruce's warnings, Wendy checked that all the doors and windows were locked. She returned to the sitting room, wondering if the children felt the same sense of absence as she did. Did they feel any less safe now that Bruce was gone? And what would she do, supposing some maniac were to break into the house while she was there alone with just the children? She opened the sitting room curtains a crack and looked out on to the drive, the furthest end of which enjoyed sufficient illumination from the street lamps to confirm that it was empty. The rest of the front garden was in deep shadow. There was no moon and the high hedge and trees obscured the light which spread freely down the drive. Half-a-dozen crazed axemen could have been lurking unseen.

'Stop it,' she said to herself. 'This is The Ashes. It's your home. There's nothing to be afraid of here.'

Monday began like any other, with the usual struggles to get everyone up and out on time: Katie being slow and sleepy and losing her socks; Jamie fretting over a missing toy car instead of focussing on eating his breakfast; Tara impossibly grumpy and best avoided. Jamie was the last to leave, collected at the door by Andrew Webster and his mother. Wendy and Andrew's mother had arrived at an arrangement some weeks previously, whereby they took it in turns to walk the boys to school and collect them at the end of the day, and it happened to be Mrs Webster's turn.

Left to her own devices, Wendy cleaned the kitchen floor to within an inch of its life and was about to turn her attention to the stone flags in the hall when she glimpsed the sad-eyed Morisot through the open dining room door. She had never liked it but hadn't wanted to upset Bruce by removing it from the position he had chosen. It didn't look right there – in fact, it was downright depressing – and since he wasn't around to see that it had gone . . . She marched decidedly into the room, reached up, took a good hold on either side of the frame and carefully lifted the picture down. She carried it across to the window and, not without difficulty, held it up at different angles, but it failed to transform itself into the image that had so captivated her when she had first set eyes on it in the shop window. She could not imagine how it would fit in with the sort of modern property that Bruce now appeared to be set on acquiring. Her picture, her grandfather clock . . . the new dining suite? Probably all sorts of lovely things would be thrown onto the bonfire for which his career had laid the foundations. She supposed she shouldn't mind. They were only things. Family was what mattered . . . but oh, it felt so wrong, so very, very wrong to be leaving this house.

She stood, hesitating, before the window, picture in her hands, not seeing the daffodils bending on their stems in the breeze which was raking across the garden. She decided to put the picture in the study. Bruce would notice it was gone when he came home at the weekend, but she could make up an excuse, or even replace it temporarily. She carried it into the study, where it would be out of the way. No one ever used the room for anything. It was, as Bruce had said, just wasted space, its doors mostly kept closed.

It provided a natural shortcut from the rear passage to the front hall, but Wendy had never noticed anyone using it as such, and she herself invariably walked the long way round, passing the entrance to the cellar and turning the corner by the kitchen door. Ever since Bruce's explosion over Joan and her half-remembered ghost story, it had never seemed politic to query why everyone else avoided the study, but as time passed, she had been forced to admit to herself that the room had a slightly unpleasant atmosphere. Perhaps because it was not quite large enough or light enough to make a good study. Perhaps because the dark green and white wallpaper made it feel a bit claustrophobic.

She managed to manoeuvre the door open while continuing to grip the picture in both hands, entered the room and bent to prop her burden against the end of the bookshelf. As she did so, the previously indefinable sensation of something unpleasant in the room finally crystallized. It was a feeling she had experienced once before, many years previously, when she had been at a dance with some girlfriends while Robert was away at university. One of her friend's brothers had persuaded her to dance with him, and afterwards, when she slipped out to the ladies, he'd been waiting for her in the passage. He'd said something to arrest her progress, then made a grab, pressing his body aggressively against hers, his beery breath contaminating her mouth as he'd managed to land one kiss before she pulled away. The feel of his hands on her back, hot and clammy through the thin cotton of her summer frock, had nauseated her. She shuddered at the recollection. It must have been more than twenty years ago, but it came back to her now, as clearly as if it had happened only moments before. She drew back from the room, shutting the door. Her heart was racing. Ridiculous, of course. The blood must have rushed to her head when she bent to put the picture down – and the picture itself must have been heavier than she'd thought, to make her feel all giddy like that. She abandoned her plans with the mop and bucket in favour of a cup of coffee in the kitchen. All was well in there – everything was safe and normal. A listener's dedication was being read out on Radio Two. She put on the kettle and made herself a coffee. She would have a chocolate digestive with it, if the kids had left her any. She smiled as she noticed the way the fridge hummed to itself when Johnny Cash began to sing about 'A Thing Called Love'. No wonder she was a bit on edge, she thought, with all this change in the air. Bruce must have been quite nervous, starting his new post. Not that he ever showed anything like that.

There was plenty to keep Wendy busy through the day. The ironing pile alone was enormous. Three shirts per day, courtesy of Bruce's job, the younger children's school uniforms and, judging by the amount of items belonging to Tara, her eldest must be changing her clothes at least three times a day! When the children came home from school she gave them fishfingers and chips for tea by way of a treat (their meals usually involved proper vegetables, which canned baked beans were not). They weren't showing any particular signs of missing their daddy, she thought. And tonight she would allow herself no licence to indulge in silly fantasies about hatchet-wielding maniacs lurking in the garden. Just to show herself that she wasn't scared, Wendy made a point of using the study as a shortcut when she went to check that the back door was locked.

She had thought that Bruce would ring and tell her how his day had gone, but he didn't. Perhaps he was waiting for her to call and ask. After all, he knew she wasn't really reconciled to the move. She decided it would be a nice gesture to take the initiative. It wasn't quite ten; he wouldn't have gone to bed yet.

Bruce's mother answered. 'Wendy? Is everything all right?'

'Yes, perfectly, thank you. Can I speak to Bruce, please?'

'He's not in, I'm afraid.'

'Oh.' She tried to smother her disappointment. She could hardly have been expected to know that he wasn't there, but she felt, foolishly, as if she had been caught out in not knowing.

'He went out at about eight for a drink with some of his colleagues.'

Wendy noted the use of 'colleagues'. It was the sort of word Bruce's mother liked. It gave her son status to be consorting with 'colleagues', rather than just the chaps he worked with.

'Was it anything important? Something Digby and I could help you with?'

Digby. Wendy thought for perhaps the millionth time what a good thing it was that Bruce's parents hadn't been tempted to name their son after his father. 'No. Everything's fine. I just thought I'd have a quick chat, that's all.'

'Are you and the children all right?'

'Yes, of course.'

'Good, good. Well, I'll tell Bruce you rang, shall I?'

'Thank you, yes. Are you and Digby OK?'

'Mustn't grumble. Give our love to the children, won't you? Tell them how much we're looking forward to seeing them.'

But not to seeing me, Wendy thought, as she exchanged farewells and rang off. She had never quite forgiven Bruce's mother after overhearing her telling Digby, 'Of course they don't realize that Wendy isn't really common. It's just that everyone talks like that up there.'

Bruce telephoned her on Tuesday evening. He was in a call box and their conversation was preceded and then punctuated by the sound of him shovelling more coins into the box at the prompting of the pips.

'Why are you ringing from a payphone? Aren't you at your mother's?' Wendy asked.

'I'm at a pub. I bumped into some old friends last night and they invited me to come out for a drink.'

'Well, I'm so glad you're enjoying yourself.'

'There's no need for sarcasm, darling. Is there any reason why I shouldn't be allowed to go out and enjoy myself? It's only a sociable drink with some people I haven't seen in quite a few years. Is there something wrong up there? Has something upset you?'

'Oh, not at all. I suppose I should count myself lucky that you've bothered to ring. You didn't find time last night.'

'For goodness' sake! I've barely been down here two days, what on earth do you think I had to say? And I have to think of Mum and Dad's phone bill. Long-distance calls are expensive, you know.'

'I'm sure you could offer to pay them for the cost of the calls.'

'You know they've refused to accept anything for having me here, which means I can't start freeloading by spending half the night on their phone.'

'Well, that's typical of your mother. She refuses to take any money but will make an issue of the phone bill. Don't you see what a clever way that is of limiting your calls home?'

'Don't be so silly. The way you talk about my mother, anyone would think she was an ogre. Anyway, I didn't think I was expected to ring you every night.'

'Naturally, I don't expect you to think of us when you are so busy enjoying yourself.'

'Oh really, Wen—' Bruce's voice was drowned again by the incessant mechanical demand for further payment. He had either run out of patience or run out of change because this time the pips ended in the distinctive burr of a dead line.

On Wednesday evening he called from his parents' house, and after a perfunctory exchange he had Wendy call the children to the phone, one at a time, to talk to him. On Thursday they merely confirmed the arrangements for his weekend visit home. By then she was regretting their spat. It couldn't be easy for him, settling into a new job while moving back in with his parents, where there would be a thousand and one pinpricks and irritations for an adult accustomed to having their own place and ordering their life in the way they wanted it.

She planned his Friday evening homecoming carefully. Supper for two at the kitchen table, with candles lit and a bottle of wine, to be finished in front of a log fire in the sitting room. She would put fresh sheets on the bed. Everything would be made just right for his weary arrival home after the long drive, and on Saturday they would do something nice together, the whole family. A walk perhaps, or a visit to the cinema.

She had already made most of her preparations for supper when he called her late on Friday afternoon to say that the car had developed a fault and the garage could not get the part they needed until the following morning. On Saturday he phoned again, hours after she had thought him already on the road, to say that the garage had been let down over the delivery of the part and, as a result of this further delay, he was only just setting off. An accident blocking two lanes of the motorway created yet another hold-up, so that by the time he arrived, tired and disgruntled, Tara had already gone out for the evening and the salmon which Wendy had prepared for them was on the edge of dried up. Katie and Jamie picked up on the atmosphere and fractiously competed for their parents' attention throughout the cheerless meal that followed.

When dinner was over, Wendy shooed Bruce from the kitchen and dealt with the various dirty pans herself while the children got ready for bed. When she finally went to join him in the sitting room, she found the fire smoking and her husband fast asleep in one of the armchairs, his head lolling at an uncomfortable angle. Though she flapped a magazine about and chinked a glass, hoping for some sign that he was looking forward to the sort of passionate night an absence was supposed to engender, Bruce slept on, eventually waking with a half-hearted apology, admitting that he was all in and heading upstairs where he wasted no time in shedding his clothes and resuming his slumbers.

Wendy could not help but reflect that she might just as easily have spent the evening alone and taken a good deal less trouble about it. She eventually drifted into an uneasy sleep in which she dreamed of being at a 50/50 dance with Bruce, who unaccountably turned into a different man, who went too fast when they played a foxtrot and refused to let her go when she tried to pull away, instead thrusting his face towards her as he attempted an unwanted kiss, his hands everywhere, groping her until she woke up with a little sob. It was dark and she lay still and quiet for a long time, fearful of a resumption of the dream if she went back to sleep, eventually dropping off again as the first hints of daylight crept around the edges of the curtains.

She was eventually drawn out of bed by the sounds of movement on the landing. Leaving Jamie unsupervised in the kitchen was a recipe for disaster, so Wendy dragged her dressing gown around her and descended to organize her son's breakfast. Bruce appeared soon afterwards in search of coffee and the papers.

'I was just wondering what you wanted to do today.' She greeted him brightly and felt crushed when he gave a pseudo-groan.

'Do we have to do anything? Don't forget I need to be on the road again this afternoon.'

'No, of course we don't *have* to do anything. I just thought you might like to do something . . . well . . . nice. All of us together, because we've been apart all week.'

'Well, at the moment my idea of something nice would be a cup of coffee and a quiet hour with the Sunday papers.'

'Yes, of course. Sorry.' Actually, she thought, I'm not sorry. Why am I apologizing? It isn't my fault that the car went wrong or there was a sodding traffic jam.

In a repeat performance of the weekend before, Wendy and the two younger children stood outside the house to wave Bruce off. It was less than twenty-four hours since his arrival. He hugged each of the children in turn and then pecked Wendy's cheek.

'It was hardly worth it, was it?' she said lightly.

'No, it wasn't.' Bruce turned away and climbed into the car.

Feeling as if she had been slapped, Wendy laughed, trying to show the children that it was just a little joke between Mummy and Daddy. Bruce reversed the car down the drive and the children trotted after him, readying themselves for a final wave from the front gate. Wendy followed a pace or two behind them. Once out in the road, Bruce put the car into forward gear and waved his hand as he moved off, but she knew that the wave was for the children. Back in the kitchen, she contemplated the wrecked weekend while she burned the muffins intended for the children's tea and snapped at Katie because her bedroom was untidy again. Had any of it been her fault? Of course not. Was it her fault that he worked so far away? Or that the initial interest in The Ashes seemed to have dried up? A lull in the market, the agent said. None of it was her fault. It was very unfair.

Even so, she felt moved to apologize to Bruce, and was ready to issue some platitudes for the sake of making up this quarrel, which they hadn't exactly had, so when he had not telephoned by eight thirty on Monday evening, she dialled his parents' number.

The phone was answered by Bruce's mother, who greeted her without enthusiasm and said she would call Bruce to the phone. Her mother-in-law did not ask after her or the children. Wendy wondered how much Bruce had said about his unsatisfactory trip north, or how much his mother might have picked up, merely from his manner and general mood.

'Hello?'

Now that he was on the phone, all the useful, well-intentioned phrases she had rehearsed seemed to have stowed themselves in some locked box in the back of her mind. In their place came the sort of polite, mechanical conversation which one can only have with people to whom one is entirely indifferent or with whom one is very cross. Bruce offered her no help, enquiring after the children, the weather and what they had all eaten for tea. Neither of them raised the spectre of the weekend and, after three or four minutes, he reminded her with sickening politeness that they ought not to stay on the line too long because of the phone bill.

'No, of course. Goodbye then, Bruce. Love you.'

'Goodbye.'

'Bye-ee.' As she said it, she heard the click of the call being ended. She must not be upset, she thought. The telephone in his mother's house was strategically placed so that anyone's conversation could be heard pretty well all over the house. Naturally Bruce wouldn't want to have any kind of private discussion or intimate conversation when he knew that his mother was probably hanging on every word.

They spoke every evening that second week. Bruce made it his habit to ring just after six, which not only took advantage of the cheaper call rate, but also enabled him to speak to the children before anyone needed to think about going to bed. On Thursday he explained that he had decided not to attempt the drive home next day, as there were overseas clients expected and he might need to work late.

'After last week I've realized that it just doesn't work – driving up on Saturday and having to be back on Sunday – so I'm not going to attempt it. I'll be owed some time, so I can probably get off at lunchtime next Friday and that way we can make a full weekend of it.'

'Of course,' Wendy said, burying her disappointment. 'You're right. It's silly to drive all that way, just for a few hours.'

It's going to be different, she promised herself, next time Bruce comes home.

And it was. The candlelit dinner, the love-making, followed by a day dodging the rain in Middlesbrough, the whole family dashing from shop to shop, laughing too much, like one of those glossy, too-good-to-be-true families in a TV advert, Bruce spoiling the children, spoiling her. It was as if a page had turned, transporting them into a completely new story. The entire weekend was an orgy of friendliness and cooperation, during which Bruce made no reference at all to the sale of The Ashes, and the pile of brochures and pamphlets promoting new-builds in Leicestershire lay gathering dust on the desk in the study where Wendy had tidied them away during the week.

This new spirit of affability and compromise barely survived Bruce's next call home. The new wave which rocked the paper boat was generated by the approach of the Easter holidays. Bruce's parents had invited the whole family to come down, representing it as another opportunity to do some house-hunting, but as soon as she got wind of the plan, Tara protested that she wanted to stay at home and revise for her A-levels.

'I think I should stay too,' Wendy informed Bruce the next time they spoke. 'In fact, maybe we should all stay here. You could come home for the Easter weekend.'

'Don't be ridiculous. Tara crying off for revision is one thing, but it hardly creates an excuse for the whole family.'

'I'm not happy about her being here on her own.'

'If Tara says she doesn't mind, then I don't see your problem. She's perfectly capable of feeding herself for a few days, and I don't suppose she'll burn the house down or organize any wild parties while you're away,' said Bruce. 'She has her faults, but she's always been conscientious about schoolwork.'

'It's all very well her saying she doesn't mind. If you ask me, she's suspiciously keen on the idea. And it isn't wild parties that worry me. I'm sure she's still seeing that John boy.'

'I don't know why you're being so prudish. If she and that lad want to sleep together they'll have found a way by now. She'll be at university in another few months anyway.'

'Well, I'm not leaving her here on her own.'

'In that case I'll have to come and fetch Katie and Jamie and leave you up there. The kids have been looking forward to coming down, and Mum and Dad are looking forward to seeing them. Mum can't wait for us to move down here and have her grand-children on the doorstep. We'll never be short of babysitters, even when Tara's gone to university.'

'But the holidays are an opportunity for us all to be together. You know we never feel comfortable sleeping in that room next door to your parents. The walls are paper thin in that house. If you were at home, we could let ourselves go a bit. It isn't as if we get enough . . . time together now. That first weekend you came home was a complete washout.'

'And whose fault is that? Mine, I suppose,' Bruce said bitterly. 'Can I help it if I'm tired? I didn't realize I was expected to perform to order. Fulfilment of stud duties as well as everything else. It puts a strain on a relationship you know, living apart.'

'It wasn't my idea to move to Leicester.'

'It still isn't your idea to move to Leicester, is it? You're quite happy staying up there.'

'Oh, Bruce! That's not fair!'

'Well, I don't see you jumping at the chance to look for a new place. How are we going to continue with the house-hunting at Easter if I'm down here and you're up there?'

'This isn't about that. It's about not leaving Tara on her own.'

'Whatever you say.'

'We still haven't found a buyer for The Ashes. There haven't been any viewings at all these last ten days.'

'Hardly surprising. Interest rates are high and there's a limited market for places like The Ashes. Maybe you should have thought about things like that before you railroaded us into buying it in the first place.'

'Your mother won't mind me not coming.' Wendy changed tack abruptly. 'She's never pretended to like me.'

'That's all in your imagination.'

'No, it isn't. Your mother has never got over the fact that I'd been married before we met. Nor my accent. Every time the kids call me Mam, she makes a point of referring to me as "Mummy". Your mother plays spiteful little games like that all the time.'

'Don't be silly.'

'Oh, come on, Bruce. You know the tricks as well as I do. She's forever talking about people you know and I don't as a way to exclude me from the conversation. She even goes on about your ex-fiancée, Frances. "Such a nice girl," your mother always says. For a while, I began to wonder if that was her name, you know, a hyphenated name, Frances Such-A-Nice-Girl.'

'Why are you dragging Frances into this? What on earth has put her into your head all of a sudden?' he asked sharply.

'Oh, I don't know . . . I'm so tired of all this bickering.'

'Well, let's stop it then. We'll discuss this when I come up at the weekend.'

The conversation regarding plans for the Easter weekend did not resume until Saturday afternoon, when Wendy was annoyed to discover that Bruce had yet to appraise his parents of the fact that she did not intend to accompany him and the younger children to Leicestershire.

'I thought you might have changed your mind.'

'That's very unfair,' Wendy said. 'Because now your mother will be able to say that I cried off at short notice.'

'I really don't see—'

Bruce never finished the sentence, his protest cut short by the sound of the doorbell. Wendy went to answer and found Helen's father, John Newbould, standing smiling on the doorstep. Inwardly deploring his timing, she showed her visitor into the sitting room. A couple of weeks had passed since she'd asked Tara to make enquiries with him as to whether anyone in the local history society happened to have come across anything of interest regarding The Ashes. She knew that it was disingenuous to pose her enquiry in that way, but she guessed that any violent episodes in the past would be grist to their mill, and although involving John Newbould opened up the possibility that Tara would get to hear about the murder, Wendy figured that her eldest would be more interested than upset, and this way, if Bruce got to hear about it, it would be via a channel that didn't involve Joan or Peggy Disberry. Bruce still knew nothing about the visit to Peggy Disberry, not least because Wendy knew that he would disapprove of Joan's deceitful method of gaining Peggy's confidence, and it therefore naturally followed that he knew nothing of the story of the supposed Victorian murder either.

She assumed that John Newbould hadn't said anything to his own daughter about the murder, because Tara certainly hadn't mentioned it a couple of days ago, when she'd told Wendy in passing that Helen's father intended to call round and talk to her about the house. Wendy had hoped the visit would take place on a weekday evening when Bruce was safely down in Ashby, not just because this avoided him getting wind of the murder story, but also because Bruce did not particularly like John Newbould and would be irritated by Wendy's having extended an invitation to him.

'It's John,' Wendy announced brightly, as she ushered him into the sitting room. 'Goodness, how long is it since you two talked rubbish together? John's helping to organize the big party for the Royal Wedding.' It was just possible, she thought, that she might divert John onto this topic long enough for Bruce to be fooled into thinking that it was the main purpose of his visit.

Bruce did not even smile at her attempted joke about their one-time membership of the rubbish tip committee. 'Oh yes?' he said. 'Weren't you on the committee for the Silver Jubilee party as well? Are some people still not speaking after the big fall out over the Under Eights Fancy Dress?'

John Newbould laughed. 'Well, after 1977 I did say "never again". I think we all did, but the village likes a bit of a show on these national occasions, and if it's going to happen, someone's got to bring it all together.'

'I'm sure everyone appreciates what you do,' Wendy said quickly. 'Have you brought your catering lists?'

'I have as it happens. I noticed I hadn't got you down for anything yet and I know you can always be counted on to volunteer.'

'How about sausage rolls?' Wendy suggested. Anyone could make a success of them, now that you could get those bags of frozen ones.

John consulted a rather battered sheet of paper. 'No . . . I've got sausage rolls covered. Moira Cox is doing some, and so are Thelma Scott and Pat Gilby. I still need 100 toffee apples . . .' As Wendy blanched, he continued, 'Oh, no . . . Barbara and Josie have promised the toffee apples . . .'

He pulled out a pencil and made a swift annotation, while Bruce took the opportunity to give Wendy a look.

'What about things on sticks?' John asked.

'I think even I can spear cheese and pineapple.'

'Say two hundred cheese and pineapple and I'll get someone else to do the sausages on sticks.'

Wendy's mouth dropped open, but John was making another mark on his list and failed to see her expression.

'Now then,' John said, refolding his sheet of paper as he spoke. 'To what I really came about.'

Bruce shot Wendy a questioning look which she pretended not to see.

'I asked around at the local history society and, sure enough, someone came up with this.' John produced a thin booklet from his jacket pocket with a flourish. 'Fascinating stuff. Apparently the chap who produced it was a retired schoolteacher. Real old character from what I can gather. Seems to have spent his entire retirement at the record office. What he didn't know about the history of Bishop Barnard wasn't worth knowing. Self-published several of these little booklets about the local area. And to a jolly high standard for an amateur. He did a lot of good work on census indexing for the Family History Society as well.'

Wendy noticed that Bruce was managing to look irritated, mystified and bored, all at the same time.

'And The Ashes is mentioned in this book?' Wendy prompted.

'Yes, indeed! The whole business was obviously a cause célèbre at the time. I'm amazed I'd never heard about it before: something that happened just over a hundred years ago, in our own village. Here it is . . .' He handed the booklet across to Wendy. 'The place is marked.'

The pale blue paper cover, no thicker than the inner pages, had the words 'Local Law Breakers by J H W Warmsworth' printed on the front. A bookmark commemorating a visit to Ripon Cathedral had been inserted at page nine, where the heading was 'Alice Croft 1853–1872'.

Wendy scanned the words swiftly, giving less than half an ear to John's attempts to engage Bruce's interest regarding the wisdom or otherwise of hiring a bouncy castle for the Royal Wedding bash.

Alice Croft stood trial for the murder of Edward Graves in 1872. Murderess and victim were both servants in the employ of Mr James Coates Esq. of The Ashes, Bishop Barnard. Little is known about either party, though they were said at the trial to have been of sober habits. The law prevented Alice from entering the witness box at her own trial, but in the statement she made to the police, she claimed that she had acted in self-defence, alleging that Graves had frequently made advances to her, which she had always repelled. According to Alice, on the night of the tragedy, which happened to be St Valentine's, Alice had begun to suffer from stomach pains and had descended to the kitchen to avail herself of some powders which the cook kept there. She claimed that having obtained a powder and a glass, she went along the passage to the scullery, to get some water and here she came upon Graves, who had let himself in through the scullery door. Graves, having made a lewd suggestion, forced the girl into the pantry, which was adjacent to the scullery and, as they struggled, Alice's hand fastened on something in the darkness – she would later claim that she had not realized it was a knife – and in defending herself she had pushed the unseen object at Graves once or twice. He groaned and fell, and it was only when Alice had pushed past him and retrieved her candle from the scullery that she realized he was stabbed.

The cook, Hannah Colbeck, gave evidence that she had heard and seen nothing until Alice shook her awake, when she saw by the light of the candle that Alice had blood all across the front of her nightgown. On following the girl downstairs, the cook found Edward Graves lying on the pantry floor, his shirt soaked in blood and the skillet knife, gory to the hilt, on the flags beside him.

There were several problems with the tale told by Alice Croft.

Mr Coates testified that nothing improper had ever been tolerated beneath his roof and that any suggestion of behaviour such as that described by Croft would have resulted in dismissal. The cook echoed her master regarding the strict proprieties observed within the household and was unable to support Alice's story of having gone downstairs only moments before the attack took place. It seems that the layout of the servants' quarters meant that Croft would have needed to pass through Colbeck's room to get downstairs, but Colbeck had not heard her do so. Colbeck explained that she was a particularly heavy sleeper, but this did not really do much to support Croft's story. The Crown also elicited from Colbeck that Edward Graves was known to have a sweetheart who lived on a nearby farm and questioned the likelihood of Edward Graves having let himself into the house at an hour approaching midnight, just at the very moment when Alice Croft happened to be fetching a glass of water from the scullery. More potentially damning evidence came from the cook, Colbeck, who, when asked about the knife, agreed that it was not normally kept in the pantry. Household knives, she said, were kept in the kitchen, and it was most unlikely that one would be left lying about. Worse still, the last person known to have handled the skillet knife happened to be Alice herself, who had received all the knives back from the travelling knife grinder on the previous afternoon and been charged by Colbeck with putting them away in their rightful places.

The Crown's case was that Alice had been in the habit of slipping down to meet Graves when the rest of the household was asleep, taking advantage of the cook's propensity to deep sleep, and they suggested that the girl had become jealous when she learned of his other sweetheart and had decided to take her revenge for his faithlessness by arranging a final tryst, planting the newly sharpened knife in a spot where she knew how to find it, luring him into the darkened pantry and then stabbing him to death, but pretending it was an accident. The significance of the date was also stressed.

Reports of the trial offer more questions than answers. Did Alice Croft accidentally kill her fellow servant while defending her honour, as she claimed? Or had she premeditated cold-blooded murder, planting the knife in advance and stabbing Graves twice in the heart? The jury concluded that the Crown's explanation was the correct one. They found her guilty but made

a recommendation for mercy. Alice received none. She was
hanged at Durham jail on a May morning in 1872.

The pantry . . . which was now the study . . . Wendy gave an
involuntary shiver as she looked up and realized that both men
were watching her. She wondered how long ago they had stopped
talking.

'Well,' said John. 'What do you think of that?'

'I suppose it's not too much to ask what's so exciting about
that booklet?' Bruce enquired.

'History, old man. Jolly violent history at that. This booklet
proves that a murder was committed within a few feet of where
you're sitting.' John's ghoulish enthusiasm was unmistakable.

'Here,' Wendy said. 'Would you like to read it for yourself?'

Bruce's expression was stony. He ignored the proffered pages.
'No, thank you,' he said coldly.

'You've never seen over the house, have you, John?' she said
quickly. It suddenly seemed imperative to get him out of the sitting
room before Bruce said or did something really rude. 'Come on,
I'll give you a tour, show you where it all happened.'

Bruce banged his coffee mug down so hard on its coaster that
Wendy was sure she heard it crack. She ushered her visitor into
the hall, grinning like a maniac, in a vain attempt to make up for
her husband's manner. Fortunately, John Newbould's curiosity
subsumed any concerns he might have had about the degree of
his welcome.

'I suppose the layout of the house has changed a bit in a hundred
years,' he said, as he followed Wendy towards the back of
the house.

'No, no. Hardly at all. This is the kitchen.' She flung open the
door. 'There was no water supply in this part of the house until
we had the pipes run through.'

'But this was the original kitchen?'

'Yes. You can see the shape of the original fireplace and where
the range used to be.'

'So if Alice had fetched a powder from here . . .'

'She would have had to go to the scullery for water, which was
just along here, where our utility room is now.'

'And those outbuildings . . .' John glanced out of the window
as they crossed the back passage. 'They look original as well.

There was nothing unusual about a manservant sleeping outside at that time – and of course people didn't always bother to lock their doors.'

'Servants slept in the outbuildings?'

'Oh, yes. The men frequently bedded down in barns and outbuildings and thought nothing of it at all. People were grateful not to have to share a bed. The average agricultural labourer was lucky to have a two-room cottage for himself and his entire family: one up, one down. They had big families back then, so miladdo was probably extremely grateful to have a shed to himself. Would have seen it as a step up in the world.'

'This is the scullery. Let me show you outside.'

They went into the yard, speculating about which building might have been occupied by Edward Graves. 'Probably not that one,' John said, when Wendy explained about the wooden stalls which had still been fixtures before the space beneath Tara's rooms had been turned into a garage. 'More likely one of these, facing the kitchen.'

'I've got it!' Wendy exclaimed abruptly. 'I bet the jury weren't brought here. If they had been, they'd have seen it too.'

John Newbould looked at her expectantly, so Wendy continued, 'It says in Mr Warmsworth's book that they couldn't see how Edward Graves would have just happened to be inside or even known the right moment to enter the house and accost Alice, unless Alice had pre-arranged it, but standing here, you can see exactly how it's possible. You see that end skylight there? Well, that's the room where Alice Croft would have slept. From here in the yard, and also through the window of this end shed, you can see that skylight. You would be able to see the light of a lamp or a candle in that window, and you'd see the light moving as the person carrying it moved through into the next room – see that skylight there? Well, that was the cook's room, and you still have to walk through there to access the rest of the house from the little room at the end. After that, the light would show in the window of the upstairs passage, and then in that tall, arched window as she walked down the stairs. Edward Graves would have known that was Alice's light, because it started in her room, and he would be able to see exactly where she was without even moving from his window. He would have seen the light moving into the kitchen and then along the back passage, where he would have been able to slip inside and intercept her in the scullery. Poor thing. You know, I'm sure she was telling the truth. Come back inside and I'll show you what used to be the pantry.'

When they got inside the study, Wendy explained the alterations which had been made, showing her visitor where part of the wall had been taken out to link what had originally been the old pantry and the big walk-in cupboard off the main hall. 'When we first bought the house there were floor to ceiling shelves all the way round, which made it much smaller and more cramped.'

'So there was only one way in or out.' John nodded. 'Just the place to corner and rape the kitchen maid, in fact. The knife might have been left in the pantry accidentally, or Graves might have brought it in himself, in order to threaten her.'

'Do you suppose *he* intended to murder *her*? Otherwise, if he'd raped her, wouldn't she have given him away later?'

'Probably not. There wasn't much sympathy expended on servants back then, and the family might have chosen to disbelieve her. It's much more likely that any suggestion of immoral goings on would have meant her being dismissed as well as him. Didn't you notice the way that Mr Coates was more interested in denying that anything improper could possibly have been going on between his servants than he was in establishing who had murdered whom? And the cook's evidence isn't to be relied on either, because if she'd admitted that she'd known anything was up between Edward and Alice, she would probably have got her marching orders for not telling on them sooner.'

'But if she'd told her master what was going on, both her fellow servants might have been dismissed, even though one of them hadn't done anything wrong?'

'Exactly. And without good references it would have been pretty much impossible to get another job.'

'That's awful.'

'No one ever said that life in the 1870s was fair.'

'It's a funny thing, but this is the only room in the house that I've never much liked. When we first saw it, the window was boarded up, but even with the window as it is now, the room is still rather dark.'

'Has anyone . . .' he hesitated. 'Has anyone actually *seen* anything?'

'No. There used to be stories that the house was haunted, but

that was a long time ago and the actual details are a bit vague.'
She didn't want to discuss her own experiences in the room. They
were the sort of things not easily explained to a mere acquaintance,
and she could imagine how her story might translate on retelling:
'Wendy Thornton says that she's been groped by a ghost, you
know . . . Oh, isn't she the one who drinks? Lost her licence,
didn't she?'

Wendy led the way out of the room. It had occurred to her that
if she took John through the courtyard at the back, it would avoid
any need for him to say goodbye to Bruce.

'It's quite a remarkable survival, you know,' John said, as he
followed her out of the back door. 'A great many houses of this
age have been altered beyond recognition. You've managed to
retain a lot of the original features. Our chairman has been talking
about the possibility of getting up a little tour, taking in some of
the local buildings of interest and finishing with a few jars in a
local hostelry. A lot of our members would love to see over The
Ashes, I'm sure. You could show them around, tell the story and
offer them your theory about the murder. Everyone loves a ghost
story, after all.'

As they reached the corner of the house, they all but collided
with Bruce, coming in the opposite direction. He had clearly heard
the last part of the conversation and his face was pale with anger.
His expression stopped Wendy dead, so John automatically stopped
too.

'No one will be seeing over this house unless they're a
prospective buyer,' Bruce growled. 'This is a family home, not
a bloody peep show.'

'We couldn't make any definite arrangements,' Wendy blundered
in, trying to smooth things over. 'Not with us liable to move at
any time.'

'If you're interested in the house you'd better make an appointment through the estate agents,' Bruce said. 'Other than that, you
and your ghoulish weirdo friends can keep away.' He stalked past
them and entered the garage, all but brushing John Newbould
aside.

Wendy felt like weeping with embarrassment. The momentary
silence that followed seemed like an eternity.

'I'm sorry, Wendy, that I seem to have said the wrong thing.'
John's voice betrayed both self-righteous annoyance and a degree

of nervousness. 'I regret that my little suggestion appears to have upset Bruce, but I don't think he needed to be quite so offensive. No . . . please don't apologize.'

Wendy had said nothing at all. She was still floundering, trying to form her mouth into appropriate shapes from which suitable platitudes could issue.

'I do think, though, that you might have forewarned me about Bruce's views on this matter.' His voice had developed an aggrieved whine. 'When all is said and done, you *asked* me to find out about the house for you. I gave up my own precious research time to look into it, and in return I have received a string of insults and what might well be construed as threatening behaviour. I can only say that I consider our friendship is at an end.'

'I'm so sorry.' Wendy found her voice as she accompanied him down the drive. 'I really didn't expect . . . you see, Bruce . . . well . . . I never thought . . .'

At the gate John paused to bluster about how it was fortunate that Wendy had been standing between Bruce and himself, as he wouldn't normally have taken that kind of thing from anyone. Wendy stood stupefied with embarrassment, not only at her husband's behaviour, but now at John Newbould's too. She wasn't much troubled by the withdrawal of the friendship, since the Newboulds had never been much more than acquaintances, but the thought that a version of the scene would soon be circulating the PTA, the squash club and every other village organization in which John Newbould had a finger – which was pretty much all of them – was deeply humiliating.

'I trust,' he said, 'that I can still rely on you for the cheese and pineapple?'

'Oh, yes . . . yes, of course.'

She found Bruce in the kitchen.

'Why on earth were you so rude to him?'

'He needed it. He's the sort of prat that people ought to be rude to at regular intervals. And I don't want him coming round here, spouting that sort of rubbish.'

'It's not rubbish,' she said. 'It all happened.'

'Have you forgotten that we have children living in this house? Is that the type of thing you think you should be talking about? Murders? Ghosts? Is it any wonder the kids are having nightmares?'

'That was weeks ago. Months ago . . . If you don't want them to hear about it, then I suggest you keep your voice down. You're shouting fit to wake the dead.'

'The sooner Katie and Jamie are away from this house the better. I thought you'd gone far enough with this nonsense before, but guided tours? Christ, you're getting worse.'

'It wasn't my idea. I hadn't agreed to it.'

'No, but you would have done. Admit it, you would have let him go ahead if I hadn't been here.'

'I don't know. I expect I would have said "no" if I'd only had the opportunity, before you started laying down the law and acting the heavy-handed husband.'

'Of course you wouldn't have said "no". You'd have jumped at the chance of showing the house off to a bunch of strangers, because you always do. Because it's your house. Wendy's blasted dream house. It would never occur to you to consider anyone else, not when it comes to this house. It wouldn't matter if the kids were going to be scared to death, because nothing can get in the way of Wendy and her ego trip about her great big house.'

'That's absolutely not true, Bruce. Why are you saying these horrible things?'

He turned away, as if he was considering some invisible item on the kitchen table.

'Bruce? You know these things you're saying aren't true.'

'Of course they are. Ever since we came here . . . in fact, before we came here. Ever since you got hold of that money and became obsessed with this place, you've thought of nothing but this precious bloody house.'

'I don't know why you keep saying it's my house. It belongs to all of us. It's our home. We've always shared everything.'

'It's never been mine. Your aunt left you the money. Your house, your choice, not mine.'

'Oh, I see it all now!' Angry tears glittered in her eyes. 'It's all right for you to be the big man, earning the money and buying everything, but when I contribute something, you can't cope with it. It upsets your image of yourself as the provider and you don't like it.'

'Spare me the Women's Lib crap, Wendy. It doesn't suit you.'

'It's true, though, isn't it?' Her anger was getting the better of her good sense. 'You need me to be dependent on you. You thought my coming into money threatened our traditional roles. Is that why you never want to have sex with me anymore?'

'Don't be so pathetic. You know, you've always had this remarkable facility for obscuring the true nature of any argument with the most ridiculous fantasies.' He had stopped shouting now, delivering this latest pronouncement in a lofty tone which enraged her.

'You're the pathetic one,' she shouted back. 'You've let this stupid resentment about money take you over. It's even made you impotent.'

He made a swift move towards her, and for a split second Wendy thought he was going to strike her, but then he turned and walked out of the room. She heard his footsteps going along the passage and the sound of the sitting room door closing behind him, while she remained rooted to the spot. Bruce had never been violent towards her before, but she knew how close he had just come. She realized she was shaking. It had never occurred to her to feel afraid of her husband, and the discovery that he could be frightening was like a previously unnoticed crack in the mirror, or smudge on a painting.

It was my own fault, she thought. I pushed him too far. I trespassed way beyond the boundaries that people who love one another are allowed to go. It was all my fault.

She took a few deep breaths then followed him into the sitting room. She found him sitting in one of the chairs, leafing through a book of wildlife photographs which Katie had brought home from the library in connection with a school project.

'Bruce,' she began. 'Bruce, I'm really, really sorry.' She knelt before him on the carpet, hoping that he would put down the book and take her into his arms.

'Forget it.' He wasn't even looking at her.

'Please, Bruce. I was wrong to say that. Living apart has put a strain on our relationship, but we can work this out.'

'Just skip it, will you?'

'If there are things you would like me to do . . . I know we've never been very adventurous, but if you wanted . . . I could buy some of those silky French knickers, stockings, suspenders . . .'

'Don't be ridiculous.'

'Bruce, we can't just skip it, we have to talk.'

He said nothing. Having reached the end of the book, he began to flick through the pages in reverse, from the back to the beginning.

'It's childish to pretend that you can't hear me.'

'I am not pretending that I can't hear you. I am not responding to you. I don't want to talk about the house, money, bed, you, me, or anything else.'

Her tears came again, in greater quantity and accompanied by a series of choking sobs.

'Oh, for heaven's sake, Wendy, don't turn the tears on.'

She began to sob in earnest at that. 'You've never said that to me before. It's hateful of you to say that. You're only saying it because you know that's something Robert used to say to me all the time.'

'Poor sod,' Bruce said, rising from his chair and crossing to the door. 'He must have had a lot to put up with.'

A few minutes later she heard the car heading down the drive. Bruce never went anywhere without saying where he was going; it was the abrupt departure of a sulking teenager, she thought. It had been wrong of her to goad him, but he too had said cruel things.

She had to gloss over his absence from the tea table for the children's benefit, not wanting to alarm them with the unexpected information that Daddy had gone out and she did not know where he was. He had probably gone to the pub, she reasoned. (It was Saturday evening in Bishop Barnard. There weren't all that many options.) Perhaps he would have a few pints, get up some Dutch courage and be ready to ravish her when he got home. The idea of making things up in bed was an appealing one, and she decided to help things along by having a scented bath, putting on a night dress which she knew Bruce had always liked, then awaiting his return in their double bed.

It was long after eleven when she heard the car returning. She had left the hall light on for him and she pictured him, letting himself in, coming upstairs . . . sure enough she heard him reach the half landing and enter the bathroom. There was a pause followed by the indistinct sound of the toilet flushing, water moving through the pipes, and at length she heard the bathroom door opening and his footsteps on the short flight of steps which brought him to the upper landing. She waited for the bedroom door to open, a welcoming smile fixed on her face, but the door did not open. The main landing light clicked out, leaving just the glow of the night-light showing under the bedroom door, and as the seconds became minutes she realized that he had gone to sleep in the spare bedroom. For a moment she thought that perhaps he was too upset and ashamed to come to her. She was on the point of going across the landing to join him. She would slide into bed beside him, they would kiss . . . but then she considered the possibility that the retreat to the guest room was intended not to punish himself, but instead to punish her. She contemplated the hideousness of attempting to entice him into love-making, only to be coldly rejected. She had assumed it was his fault. He might say that it was hers – that she failed to stimulate desire in him, because she had grown too old and unattractive. She stayed where she was, trying not to cry.

When he drove south the following day, nothing had been resolved.

In the beginning, you think everyone will guess what you have done. You imagine that the guilty knowledge will shine out from your face, but it doesn't happen like that. Lives are full of secrets, invisible burdens weighing each one of us down, some heavier than others.

ELEVEN

May 1981

When Bruce and the children had driven away for the Easter weekend the previous month, Wendy told herself it would be a wonderful opportunity for some peace and quiet, but Katie and Jamie had scarcely been gone a few hours before she began to miss them. She had equally anticipated spending some quality time with Tara, but when not dutifully engaged in her revision – even insisting that Wendy plate up her meals so that she could eat them up in her den – Tara would slip out to spend a couple of hours with her friends. One way or another, it was a huge relief when Bruce's car finally pulled back on to the drive and the house was filled with childish noise and untidiness again.

After the Easter break, life fell into a regular pattern. Bruce came home at the weekends, and though he did not resort to the spare bedroom again, nor did he make any physical overtures in her direction. Fearful of outright rejection, Wendy accepted the invisible wall between them, and they lay chastely in their shared bed like siblings forced to share in an overcrowded house. All couples go through difficult patches, she reasoned. It would be different when they were not living under this strain of constant departures, engaging in stilted telephone conversations with the spectre of his mother listening in the background. At weekends they never seemed to be alone together. Bruce insisted on letting the children stay up much later than usual, because he said he didn't get enough time with them anymore, and Wendy felt she could not argue with this, though she feared for the reinstatement of proper bedtime routines when the move to Leicestershire was finally made.

That particular horizon seemed no nearer. Certainly they were no closer to selling The Ashes. Viewings had effectively dried up. The agent said it was all the uncertainty over interest rates. However, when Wendy attempted to raise the possibility of a part-exchange deal on a new-build, Bruce seemed far less keen on the idea than he had been before. 'You lose quite a bit doing it that way,' he said. 'And anyway, I thought you didn't like any of the new-builds. We should leave things for the time being and see if a buyer for The Ashes comes along.'

His reaction made her wonder if he was being contrary on purpose. Hadn't he been positively urging that they take this route only a matter of weeks before? She said nothing. She didn't want to quarrel with him, because rocking the boat with Bruce would only upset things even further.

In the middle of May the agent rang to say that there were some people who wanted to see over the house – a Mr and Mrs Taylor. They were moving up from the London area and had already sold their property. Wendy said she was happy to show them around herself and an appointment was arranged for the same afternoon. She spent the next couple of hours getting the house to look its best, plumping cushions, tidying Katie's bedroom, wiping down every surface in the kitchen in case of imaginary smears.

She watched the couple arrive from the window in the kitchen which looked up the drive. They paused partway along, looking up at the front façade while he said something to her and she nodded approvingly. That was good, Wendy thought. A positive first impression. The Ashes was living up to the photograph on the particulars. Just one couple who really liked the house – that was all they needed. And she wanted them to like it, of course she did. There was no future in carrying on the way they were.

She conducted them round the ground floor, not saying too much. 'Never try to oversell the house to anyone,' the agent had warned her. 'Buyers are very wary of people who keep pointing things out. It makes them feel you might be trying to distract them from things you don't want them to see. Just smile, answer any questions they have and let the house sell itself.'

'The agent told us you haven't lived here very long?' Mrs Taylor sought confirmation as they crossed the hall from sitting room to dining room.

'That's right. We've owned the house for over a year, but we only moved in last July, when all the work was finished. We intended to stay long term, but my husband's job has taken him unexpectedly south, so we have to sell.'

Mrs Taylor laughed. 'That's a bit like us. We'd no sooner finished doing up our place and Dennis's job meant a move to the barren north. Not that our house was anything like this. You can get so much more for your money up here, can't you?'

The Taylors nodded approvingly over the dining room and Mrs Taylor exclaimed in pleasure when they reached the kitchen.

They're the ones, Wendy thought. At last, we've found our buyers. As she conducted them through the study, the utility room and out into the little courtyard, she imagined phoning Bruce that night to tell him they'd got a buyer. He would be so pleased.

'You know,' Mrs Taylor said, when they were standing in Jamie's bedroom. 'We wouldn't need all these bedrooms. You could knock two of these upstairs rooms into one and have that full-sized snooker table you've always wanted.'

A cloud moved across the sun, altering the level of light in the room as effectively as a dimmer switch. For a second Wendy fancied she heard a footfall, almost directly above their heads, but any sound was drowned by Mrs Taylor exclaiming, 'Goodness! Doesn't the sunlight make a difference?'

'It's quite dull in here now,' her husband said. 'It's these old-fashioned windows, I suppose. You'd get more light in if you changed them . . . though you'd soon start to rack up the costs.'

Wendy tried to keep smiling. Why on earth would anyone want to vandalize her house? Though of course it would not be her house, if the Taylors bought it.

'You'd need to change them all, so they matched,' Mrs Taylor said. 'And anyway, we agreed, no more major projects. I don't want to live in any more building sites, thank you very much.'

'Well, it was you who suggested knocking a wall down.' He laughed, while Wendy's hopes plummeted.

'I wasn't really serious. Come on, let's see the rest of it.' Mrs Taylor's voice had transformed into that of a person who feels they must go through the motions. Someone resigned to the convention that it would be impolite to say outright to a homeowner that you have seen enough of their property to know that it is not what you are looking for.

Wendy ushered them across the landing and into the master bedroom, sparing a swift glance up at the white, impassive ceiling as she did. Why now? It was only the second time she'd heard those sounds, and this was not a good moment for any mysterious creaking to manifest itself.

Feeling that it was her turn to ring Bruce, Wendy tried the number at around eight that evening, but Digby answered and told her that Bruce was out. 'I'm not sure whether he's working late,' he said vaguely. 'I'll get him to ring you when he comes in, shall I?'

It was well after ten when Bruce rang back. 'I popped out for a drink with some people after work,' he said. 'Are you all right? How are the kids?'

'Everyone's fine. Some people came to look at the house today.'

'Oh yes?' Bruce sounded cautious. 'What did they say?'

'Nothing very much. I don't think they'll go for it. She suggested knocking through two of the bedrooms, of all things.'

'I was thinking of fetching the children down here again for the spring bank holiday weekend,' Bruce said. 'Obviously you'll want to stay up there with Tara.'

'Well . . .'

'Better if you do. Spring bank holiday is the sort of time when you might get a few more people wanting to see over the house.'

'The estate agent has a set of keys,' Wendy began, but Bruce wasn't listening. He'd started telling her something about a chap at work who had offered to put him up for membership of a local squash club.

Wendy wished that she had never made such an issue of not leaving Tara alone. For all she had seen of her eldest over Easter, Tara might as well have been there on her own, and there had been no sign of any boyfriend on the scene at all. Now it seemed to be taken for granted that Bruce and the children would spend another weekend at his parents' house without her. It was like being separated or something. Rather than tackle the question on the phone, she decided to talk it over when Bruce came home for the weekend, but that intention was thwarted when he unexpectedly announced that he wouldn't be able to make it due to a works meeting being scheduled on the Saturday.

'I don't believe it,' she said, when he told her. 'You've never had a meeting on a Saturday before.'

'What do you mean, you don't believe it? Are you saying that you think I've made it up?'

'No, of course not. I didn't say "I don't believe it", as in you're not telling the truth. I was just . . .'

'Incredulous?'

'Yes, incredulous. That's the word.'

'Well, things are different down here. It's not like it was on Teesside. I've got a lot more responsibility now.'

'Yes, yes. Of course, I can see that.'

Wendy was a little hurt to witness the children's enthusiasm as they clambered into Bruce's car in readiness for another jaunt to Leicestershire without her. Of course, they did not view time spent with his parents in quite the same way as she did. To compensate for their absence, Wendy persuaded Tara to join her at the kitchen table for supper. 'I've made a prawn curry,' she said. 'One of your favourites.'

'I've decided to go and stay with Bob and Mel once my exams are finished,' Tara announced, after downing her first mouthful. 'It'll give me a good chance to find my way around Birmingham – assuming I get the grades to go there. And then I'm going to go out to the villa with them in the summer holidays. I bet I come back with a lovely tan like Mel's. And I'll also be able to catch up with John.'

'John?' Wendy knew perfectly well who Tara was referring to, but it was the first thing she latched on to in a stream of unwelcome information.

'You know very well who I mean. He's living down there at his mum and dad's, waiting to start at the Poly.'

'Oh. That John. I didn't think you'd been seeing him.'

'I haven't been seeing him. Didn't you hear me? He's been living in Birmingham, so how can I have been seeing him? I've been keeping in touch with him, though, and he can't wait to see me again, if you know what I mean . . .'

'I don't think it's a good idea, Tara. He's so much older than you . . .'

'Four years. Four years is nothing.'

'It's quite a lot at your age.'

'Oh, Mother! Do stop being so fucking ridiculous!'

'Tara!'

'Well, just jack it in, will you? I'm an adult. I'm not some silly little fifteen-year-old virgin. I know what I'm doing.'

Wendy felt herself go rigid with anger. Her cheeks burned. She stared at her daughter while Tara continued to eat her prawn curry, chewing steadily, regarding Wendy with thinly disguised contempt.

'Tara . . .' Wendy began at last. 'I don't know what to say.'

'Then I suggest you don't say anything.' Tara remained cool as the proverbial cucumber. 'If I was you, I'd focus on your own problems in that department and leave me alone.'

'What the hell do you mean by that?'

'These rooms aren't soundproofed, you know. If you scream at someone when you're in here, anyone who happens to be coming down the stairs can hear every word.'

Wendy looked down at her plate. The food she had eaten seemed to be churning in her stomach, trying to force its way back up her throat. She stood up slowly and walked across to the pedal bin, which she opened with her foot, slowly scraping the mostly uneaten curry downwards, so that it fell into the liner on top of a muddle of onion skins and tea bags. She would not cry. She kept her back to Tara while she put her scraped plate into the dishwasher, then got a glass from the cupboard and filled it with water at the kitchen sink. She must not cry. She heard the scrape on the floor as Tara got up from the table and left the room. Wendy turned to see that her daughter must have continued to eat in silence, for her plate was empty.

During the next forty-eight hours, Wendy replayed their conversation again and again. This was what things had come to. Her family life was breaking apart. But it could be fixed. She had to believe that it could all be fixed, starting with Bruce.

When the children scrambled out of the car on Monday afternoon, she was waiting for them on the front step. Jamie returned her hug with his usual exuberance and hurled himself into the house and up the stairs. Katie, on the other hand, seemed uncharacteristically reluctant.

'What's the matter, sweetheart?' Wendy asked.

'Nothing.' Katie obliged with a kiss, but sidled into the house without meeting Wendy's eye.

'What's wrong with Katie?' she asked as Bruce approached,

carrying the children's bags, which he had paused to retrieve from the boot.

'Nothing that I know of.' He bent forward and pecked her on the cheek, in a gesture as perfunctory as Katie's had been.

'She's not been in trouble, has she?'

'Katie? No. I expect she's just having one of her funny moods. You know Katie.'

'I do . . . and she doesn't have funny moods for nothing.'

'Oh, come on . . . Katie's capable of throwing a wobbler over all sorts of things. We saw a dead badger run over in the road earlier. It might have been that. If I was you, I'd ignore her and wait until she snaps out of it. Quizzing her will only make it worse.'

'There haven't been any more people coming to look at the house,' Wendy said, as she stood aside to let Bruce pass and then followed him down the hall. 'I think we should give up on trying to sell independently. Let's just cut our losses and do a part-exchange on a new house, like you suggested in the first place. We can afford to do it and at least it would mean we were all properly together again, the way we should be.'

He didn't answer immediately. 'You're probably right,' he said eventually. 'Tell you what, let's just give it until the kids break up for the summer holidays. That's barely six or seven weeks away. Shall I take these bags straight upstairs, or do you want them down here? Jamie's is mostly stuff for the washing machine.'

Sometimes when I look back on those things that happened so many years ago, it's hard to be sure how much of it was real. The house is real all right. The house is always there. Still standing. Solid. Permanent. Much harder to destroy a house than to destroy a life. I thought of burning the bloody place down once . . . but of course I couldn't.

TWELVE

June 1981

Though Wendy had wasted no time in conveying the information about the murder of Edward Graves to Joan on the telephone, she had not actually seen her since their afternoon with Peggy Disberry so, feeling rather guilty about unreciprocated hospitality, she invited Joan to supper. She fed the younger children early (with her exams finished, Tara had already decamped to her father's house in Solihull) and laid the table in the dining room for herself and her guest with a vase of flowers. They had three courses, including a lemon mousse dessert that she was rather proud of, decorated with tiny rosettes of piped whipped cream. Joan appeared to thoroughly enjoy herself, regaling Wendy with the adventures she had shared with George, whose work as an engineer had taken them to almost every continent.

'I always went along,' Joan said. 'It might have been different, I suppose, if we'd had children, but as it was only the two of us, we could be flexible. We scarcely had what you could call a permanent home in almost thirty years. The place we stayed longest was Oakville in Ontario. We had a lovely house there. And the Canadians are such lovely people. George used to say that I could make a home anywhere, given twenty-four hours, but then he never really cared very much where he was, so long as we had a bottle of gin and his gramophone. He loved Beethoven. The Emperor, the Pastoral Symphony . . . I think he'd have been happy sitting on a packing case, so long as we got the gin flowing and the gramophone records on.' She laughed indulgently, as if contemplating the foibles of a mischievous toddler.

'The house in Oakville was one of the few where I had time to plant things in the garden and see them come up. Our garden in Surat was a marvel, but sadly we were only there for four months . . .'

They took their coffee into the sitting room, where Wendy continued to listen as Joan moved seamlessly about the globe. She felt as if Joan's life had been lived on a fast train, while her own had consisted mostly of standing on the platform, waving a hankie as the train ran through. Only when the hour approached eleven did Joan return to the subject that had first brought them together.

'The inhabitants of The Ashes have always been stay-at-homes,' she said. 'Here for the duration, as it were. Except for you. Barely a year . . . but we must go wherever life takes us. Has anyone made you an offer for the house yet?'

'Not so far, no.'

'Didn't you once tell me that you and your husband could be eligible for a part-exchange scheme?'

'We could.' Wendy hesitated. 'We'd lose out a bit financially doing it that way, but it's a possibility. Bruce was very keen on the idea at one time, but he seems to have lost interest in it. He said we should keep trying for a buyer ourselves until the schools break up, and when I mentioned it again on the phone last night, he said something about holding out until the end of the school holidays. For some reason he's completely gone off the idea.'

Joan's face took on a serious expression. 'If I were you, my dear, I'd talk him back into it. I've been thinking a lot about what Peggy Disberry said, and in your place I would get myself down there to be back with my husband as soon as possible. Well, I must be going.' She pushed herself up using the arms of the chair. 'Look at the time! Dear me, I have gone on and on . . . and I have to be up for a dentist's appointment at ten in the morning. It's just a check-up, fortunately.'

Wendy stood up too, smiling and saying what a nice night it had been and how they must do it again. As they exchanged farewells, Joan leaned forward, unexpectedly placing her hands on Wendy's shoulders and brushing her lips across Wendy's cheek, something she had never done before. Wendy stood on the front

step and watched Joan reverse her car down the drive, saw the arc
of her headlights as she straightened up in the road, and then the
tail lights, no more than a red glow through the hawthorn hedge
as Joan's car headed away up Green Lane. She wondered what
Joan had meant about Peggy Disberry.

Three days later the telephone rang mid-morning, interrupting
Wendy in the act of hoovering the sitting room.

'Mrs Thornton?' It was no one she recognized.

'Yes? Hullo?'

'My name is Fiona Huntley-Wilkes. We haven't met, but I
believe you knew my aunt, Joan Webb.'

Wendy instantly grasped the implication of the past tense. 'Yes,
I do. I did. Has something happened to Joan?'

'I'm so sorry to have to tell you, but she was killed in a car
accident on Tuesday morning. She was on her way to the dentist
and there was a lorry coming down the hill in the village. It was
her right of way, but his brakes failed and the lorry just came
straight out of the side road and shunted her car into the wall. If
it's any comfort, they believe she died instantly.'

Fiona Huntley-Wilkes sounded almost dispassionate. It occurred
to Wendy that hers must be one name on a very long list of people
who had to be told. Joan's niece must have said these same things
so many times now that it had become hard to invest them with
meaning. 'The accident was on the local news, but no names were
mentioned, so you mightn't have connected it with Auntie. I don't
know how well you knew her,' the voice continued. 'But my sister
and I are her next of kin and we're going through her address
book, telling everyone. Her funeral is on Monday at the cremator-
ium. That's what she wanted. She'd left instructions. Oh . . . and
it's family flowers only, please.'

Wendy fetched a pencil and took down the details like an
automaton. The time of the funeral, the address to send donations
in lieu of flowers. She didn't tell her caller that Joan had been to
supper the night before she died. It was hard enough trying
to stifle the tears as it was.

It was only when she replaced the handset that she realized she
must have been talking with one of Elaine Duncan's granddaugh-
ters. Someone who, with Joan's address book open before her,
must have realized that she was speaking to the person who now

lived in her grandmother's old home. Funny that she had made no reference to it. Well, perhaps there was no reason why she should. She was probably too busy for small talk. She would have a lot of people to call.

Poor Joan. Tears welled in her eyes as she returned to the hoover. When she switched it back on, she realized that it wasn't sucking properly and, on checking, she found that the bag was full. A tear overlapped her lower lid and dripped on to the vacuum cleaner as she removed the bag and headed for the kitchen. The pack of refills was normally kept on the top shelf of a kitchen cupboard, but when she opened the door and reached up, she found that they had somehow got pushed towards the back of the shelf, so that her questing fingers only made contact with the polythene packaging. When she attempted to get a grip on it, she only succeeded in sliding it further away.

'Dammit,' she hissed. No one but Bruce was tall enough to reach things at the back of the top shelf without standing on something.

She was about to carry a chair across when she had another idea and instead grabbed a fish slice from the jar of utensils alongside the hob. Angling it until contact was made with the back wall of the cupboard, she brought it down and pulled forward. She scarcely had time to appreciate that there was more resistance than might be expected from a lightweight pack of hoover bags, when both the bags and a second object came hurtling towards her head, forcing her to take swift, evasive action. The unexpected item smashed against the floor, shattering glass across a wide area and splitting two bits of wood apart at a corner joint.

For a second Wendy was puzzled, but then she recognized the wooden frame amid a sparkle of broken glass as the picture Peter had given her all those months before, when he had found it in the attic. What on earth was it doing in the kitchen cupboard? She supposed that one of the workmen had seen it lying about and tucked it on to the top shelf of the cupboard to get it out of the way while they did some job or other, and then it had been unknowingly pushed to the back by the insertion of the pack of hoover bags. And now there was another mess to clear up . . .

She took up what was left of the frame and carefully picked away the remnants of glass. The photograph of the smiling young man was easily extractable now, and she slid the image free and automatically turned it over, wondering if a tentative identification might be available. The writing on the back was faint, the silvery grey remainder of a pencil dedication: *To Dora from Johnny with all my love.*

Wendy gave a little gasp. Oh, Joan . . . Oh my goodness. This surely must have been the local boy about whom Peggy Disberry had spoken. A photograph hidden under a loose board in the attic, where Dora's disapproving parents would not find it. Where no one had found it, not for over forty years. Hadn't one of the children said, on that very first day when they all came to view the house together, that attics were always full of secrets, or something of the kind?

As she fetched the dustpan and brush to clean up the glass, she wondered whether she had been directed to break the photo frame, today of all days, just after hearing the news of Joan's death. Bruce would have dismissed it as a coincidence, but so many aspects of her relationship with the house and its past seemed pre-ordained. Look at the way she had come into the money in the first place; it was as if she had been meant to have the house . . . as if her fate had been tied to it. She double-bagged the glass before putting it into the bin, moving about the kitchen like an automaton. Could there be other clues up in the attic? Things Peter hadn't found? After all, he had only discovered the photograph by accident. It wasn't as if he had been searching up there. It wasn't as if anyone had ever searched up there.

Though the electricity supply to the attic had been restored, the provision of lighting did not amount to more than a couple of bulbs, suspended from wires which hung from the ceiling: good enough not to fall over anything, but no good for a proper search. Wendy armed herself with the big torch, checking the batteries before she mounted the stairs to the upper landing.

At the attic door she hesitated, just as she had done that night when she'd thought she'd heard someone moving about up there. Bruce was probably right about that. Old houses always creaked, their woodwork subject to changes in temperature and humidity. She opened the door, switched on the light and slowly mounted the stairs.

Up in the attic, her footsteps echoed around the large, relatively empty space. So far, they had made little use of its storage potential. The cardboard boxes containing the Christmas decorations were up there, and some boxes of old toys which should rightly have been donated to the Scouts jumble sale but had somehow been overlooked. There were a couple of slowly deflating lilos leaning crazily against the boxes of toys, probably the result of some sleepover in Tara's den, but that was about all. There was nothing to be afraid of. Wendy moved around the perimeter first, shining her torch across one patch of brickwork after another, looking for any possible cranny which a young girl might have utilized to conceal love letters or a diary, but nothing presented itself. When she reached the furthest corner from the stairs, she thought she heard voices, whispering. She turned back so that she was facing into the room.

'Who is it?' she asked. 'What do you want?'

She stood for a few moments, feeling foolish in the silence. It was probably just the wind on the roof slates or something. And yet there had been so many rumours of ghosts.

'I want to help,' she said aloud.

Laughter? Surely, that had been the sound of laughter, faint but definite? A moment later, she caught the faint whoops and shouts of some boys, passing in the road outside, probably on their way home from school for lunch. That must have accounted for the other noises too. They were just sounds coming in from outside. Kids being loud. Maybe. For an unheated space it was surprisingly warm. Airless, too.

When her search of the walls produced nothing, she turned her attention to the floorboards. So far as she could remember, Peter had implied that he'd discovered the hidey hole by accident, having trodden on a loose board. She tried to remember exactly what he had described, as she crossed and recrossed the attic floor, hoping to identify the place. No boards sprang up when she stepped on them, or even seemed particularly rickety. Think, think, what had he told her about the place where the picture had been? Then it occurred to her that it must have been a short section of wood. A young girl couldn't have lifted the kind of long planks which made up most of the attic floor. She began to search again, this time looking for shorter sections of wood, of which there were very few. Only half-a-dozen and none of them loose . . . But of course, Peter would have nailed the board back into place . . . and here was a length of board no more than a foot long if that, held in place by nails which were much shinier than those holding the adjacent boards in place. As she headed down the attic stairs in search of Bruce's tool basket, that strange laughter came again, sounding uncannily as if it was coming from within the attic itself, though she knew that it must really be seeping in from outside.

Peter had done his work well and Wendy found it impossible to extract the nails, which had been hammered home flush with the wood. Next she attempted to work the prongs of a claw hammer into a tiny gap at the end of the short board, but there wasn't enough room and eventually she had to use a narrow metal file, which dug painfully into her hands as she attempted to prise the end of the board up. When the nails eventually loosened their grip, the board jerked upwards so suddenly that Wendy was all but thrown backwards. Once she had recovered her balance, she held up the end of the board with one hand while holding the torch in the other, angling it so that it shone into the little cavity where Peter had almost certainly located the photograph of Johnny. She was astonished to see that he had missed something. It appeared to be a string of beads. She reached in and picked it up in order to get a proper look, expecting something dulled with time, another keepsake given to Dora by her forbidden boyfriend.

'No . . .' She whispered it. It was hardly a word, more of a groan.

The beads had lost none of their modern brightness. She stood the torch on the floor and used a finger of her spare hand to twist them until they lined up the right way round and spelled out their owner's name: Leah.

'Oh God, oh God,' she whispered.

Leah Cattermole had gone missing while Peter had been working on their house. He had hidden the necklace in their attic. He had already been acquitted of murdering Leanne Finnegan through lack of evidence. Now she was holding the evidence that would convict him of murdering Leah.

A board creaked ominously behind her. She jumped and turned, almost expecting to find Peter himself behind her, but the attic was just as empty as before.

She ought to go straight to the police. But what about the children? What about the house itself? The police would be sure to want to take the place apart, searching for more clues showing Peter's involvement. Perhaps they would dig up the garden, searching for the girl's body. That would be horrible – and totally unnecessary as Peter couldn't possible have buried anything in the garden without her noticing the freshly disturbed ground when she had been working there herself. Bruce would be furious. And he would blame her . . . Oh yes, he would perceive it as all her fault for failing to convey Mrs Parsons' original warning.

Why on earth had Peter hidden the necklace in their attic at all? She had read somewhere that rapists and killers sometimes retained trophies, but what would be the point of hiding such a thing in a house which belonged to someone else? She fingered the beads, twisting them so that the letters of the girl's name appeared and disappeared. If Mrs Parsons was right, Peter had been a suspect in the first murder and might have realized that he would be a person of interest in the second case too. Perhaps he had initially planned to keep his trophy then, realizing the police might get a search warrant but unable to bring himself to discard the necklace completely, he had decided to hide it in a place where he knew it was unlikely to be discovered by anyone. Except that she had discovered it. Thanks to the photograph. Almost thanks to Dora. Was one victim pointing the way to justice for another?

A police investigation would very likely create problems in trying to get a house sale through. Once the police became involved, the press might get hold of it too. Prospective buyers might be put off by the notoriety or the second-hand association with a murder. She twisted the beads until all the letters were hidden against her palm. Peter had already got off on one charge. She didn't know any details, but he must have very clever lawyers. How would anyone be able to prove that it had been Peter who had placed the necklace in the attic? In handling it, she had probably smudged any fingerprints. He would say that someone else must have put it there. Good grief, he might even say that Bruce could have put it there! And what about Katie and Jamie, who were already a bit funny about the attic? How could it be kept away from them that a bad man had put a dead girl's necklace just above the ceilings beneath which they slept?

She recalled Joan's final advice to her: to rejoin her husband as soon as possible. More than ever, she wondered if rediscovering that photograph today had been a sign. If it hadn't been for her smashing the photo frame, she wouldn't have found the necklace. Someone, something, maybe even The Ashes itself, had wanted to warn her about its presence, but even so she now wished that she had not found it. Ignorance is bliss. The answer was to put it back, pretend she had never seen it, say nothing to Bruce or indeed anyone else. She replaced it carefully and slotted the board back into place, stifling her conscience with the thought that her silence on the subject did not have to be permanent. A point might come, at some stage in the future, when she was able to drop a hint in the right place. Maybe even provide an anonymous tip-off. Not a nice thing to do to the new owners, of course . . . But perhaps there were other clues anyway? Maybe justice would catch up with Peter Grayling without her ever having to become involved.

Joan Webb's funeral took place the following Monday and was well attended. Wendy recognized no one, though she guessed that the slim, handsome women in the front pew must be Bunty's daughters. Not technically Joan's nieces, though they had evidently been accustomed to calling her 'auntie'. She found herself a seat at the back, glad for Joan's sake that so many people had turned out. At the end of the service the women she had earmarked as Fiona Huntley-Wilkes and her sister took up positions at either side of the outer doors, along with a tall, dark-haired man, who must be their cousin Charles, in order to greet the emerging mourners.

'So good of you to come.'

Wendy recognized the voice of Fiona Huntley-Wilkes. 'Thank you for taking the trouble to let me know,' Wendy said. 'I'm Wendy Thornton. I live in Elaine Duncan's old house. I think she was your grandmother.'

'Really? What an interesting coincidence that you should know Auntie Joan.' The tone was polite, rather than interested.

'It isn't really a coincidence. You see your aunt . . . Joan . . . approached me. She was interested in the house because she used to stay there as a child.'

'Yes . . . yes, I suppose she would have been.'

Wendy realized that the woman was waiting for her to move on and stop blocking the way for the handful of people who were still attempting to exit the building. 'Thank you for letting me know,' she repeated, as she moved down the steps, allowing Fiona Huntley-Wilkes to greet an elderly couple, both leaning on sticks.

'So good of you to come,' Wendy heard her say.

The small funeral reception at Joan's bungalow was limited to close family. As Wendy rode the bus home she reflected that Fiona and her sister probably had not known Joan all that well. She hadn't even been their auntie – a cousin of some degree, if truth be told. A middle-aged relative who'd spent a lot of time abroad and was therefore something of an unknown quantity. Someone who must not be accidentally omitted from wedding guest lists (even if she lived too far away to attend), a name on a reciprocal Christmas card each year. Someone who'd moved about a lot, making a mess of a page in their address books.

Fiona and her sister would care nothing for Joan's precious albums of photographs. The information that she, Wendy, lived in the same house where her grandmother had lived and their own mother had grown up, had elicited not the slightest flicker of interest. Had Joan bequeathed her photographs to anyone? Wasn't there a danger that they might end up trashed in a skip? That would be awful. The precious archive – and in particular photographs of The Ashes itself – lost forever. And surely, if Joan had known what was going to happen, she would have offered to pass on some of those images herself?

When she got off the bus in the village, Wendy all but ran along Green Lane. She had no idea where Fiona Huntley-Wilkes or her sister lived, and it was no use writing to them care of Joan's bungalow, because by the time the letter got there, a house clearance firm might have been in and done their worst. Her only concrete hope of getting to Joan's relatives was here and now. As soon as she entered the house, not even bothering to take off her coat, she turned up Joan's details in the book which sat beside the telephone.

Suppose the line to the bungalow had already been cut off?

But it had not. It was answered immediately. Someone must have been standing right beside the telephone.

The woman who had answered sounded slightly startled. No doubt she had not been expecting the phone to ring.

'Hullo,' Wendy said. 'I'm sorry to disturb you. Is that Fiona Huntley-Wilkes?'

'No. Hold on, I'll get her for you. Who's calling, please?'

'My name is Mrs Thornton. I'm a friend of Joan's. I was at the funeral today.' She heard the faintest of clicks as the receiver was put down. The woman must have laid it on the little polished side table where Joan's telephone was kept. There was a faint murmur of voices, then another sound as the receiver was lifted.

'Hello? Fiona speaking.'

'Hello. This is Wendy Thornton. You were kind enough to let me know that Joan had died. We met today at the funeral.'

'Yes. I remember. How can I help you?'

'I live in The Ashes, you see. The house where your grandmother used to live.' Wendy paused, uncertain how to proceed, hoping for a little encouragement.

'Yes, so I recall.' Very cool. Precise diction. Almost certainly someone who'd been privately educated.

'I don't know whether you know this . . . but Joan has quite a number of photographs – old photographs – which show the house. And I was wondering . . .' Wendy began to stumble, the impudence and impropriety of her call belatedly flooding her consciousness. 'Well, I was thinking . . . that perhaps you wouldn't want all of them. I wondered if I might be able to have one . . . just a snap . . .'

'I'm aware that Aunt Joan had a lot of family photographs.' Was it Wendy's imagination, or was particular emphasis placed on the word 'family'? 'My cousin Charles has offered to deal with all that kind of thing. I will pass your request on to him. We already have your name and address, in Aunt Joan's address book.'

'Thank you . . . thank you so much. So sorry to intrude.' Wendy stumbled through a farewell, red hot embarrassment prickling her entire body. She imagined the conversation as Fiona Huntley-Wilkes explained the interruption in proceedings to the rest of Joan's family.

'The nerve of it!'

'If there are any pictures of Grandma Elaine, then naturally we will want to have them ourselves.'

'What a peculiar woman. Must be off her head.'

Grandma Elaine. Wendy continued to stand alongside the telephone table in the hall. Grandma Elaine, so very much loved by her family, but who had – according to Joan – occasionally shown terrible bursts of temper. The photograph of Johnny, the local boy, which Dora had chosen to hide in the attic and never retrieved. Dora going out alone for a bike ride, not telling anyone where she was going. Her own words returned to her: to think that she was almost home and never made it.

An unlucky house, Peggy's grandfather had said, because it had been associated with two murders. Her own mother had always adhered to the superstition that deaths came in threes, and so, it seemed, did murders, because Peter's made three. She shuddered as she remembered him looming up behind her in the outhouse, waiting to show her the photograph he had found, not accidentally as he had suggested, but more likely because he had been hunting around for a place to hide something himself. There had been another occasion when he had startled her. In the cellar. Where he had drawn her attention to the wine rack . . .

Her hands were shaking as she collected the torch again, and she was afraid her legs would give way as she descended the cellar stairs. The light in the cellar was better than that in the attic, so she did not need the torch in order to check the state of the nails which held the panel installed to make the wine rack appear to fit the wall, but they were all reassuringly rusty. Nothing had been interfered with recently, but the more she looked at it, the odder it seemed to be. Why go to the trouble of moving a purpose-built fixture in the first place, and why install a false back to it? She tried to picture the layout of the floor above. If the wine rack had been repositioned to create a secret cavity, it couldn't be more than two or three feet deep at most. A closer investigation, this time employing the torch to illuminate the recesses of the racking, suggested that the false back was little more than hardboard – something easily confirmed when she fetched the tool basket and attacked it with a screwdriver, punching her implement of choice repeatedly into the back of one of the wooden compartments. Then it occurred to her that making an obvious hole at head height might be spotted if a particularly nosey prospective purchaser chose to peer too closely into the empty rack. It would be more sensible to commence her investigation in one of the floor-level compartments, where the rest of the structure would hide the damage from anyone who wasn't crawling about on the cellar floor.

She dragged a flattened cardboard box over and used it to kneel on. (Jamie's den had long since been dismantled and its soft furnishings relocated upstairs.) Using a long chisel and belting it with a hammer while taking great care not to hit any of the surrounding framework, Wendy gradually managed to create a hole at the back of one section. The noise of the hammer, greatly magnified by the enclosed nature of the cellar, made her head ring. She longed to stop, but the need for knowledge forced her to continue. When the hole was the size of a tennis ball, she exchanged the tools for her torch and shone a light into the dark void: a space created by someone with something to hide.

Peering at a tiny section of a largely hidden object reminded her of a regular feature in the old quiz show 'Ask the Family', when the screen would be filled with a close-up of some mystery object and the contestants vied to guess its identity as the camera gradually panned out. Wendy had never been good at guessing the mystery objects, but then – unlike now – she'd had no advance warning as to what the object might be. On this occasion she knew at once that she was looking at the spokes of a bicycle wheel, rusted with age, but unmistakable. A bicycle which had been hidden even longer than the necklace.

A millstone of knowledge pressed down upon her as she carried the torch and the tool basket back up the cellar stairs. The bicycle, the necklace, the photograph of Johnny . . . burdens she must carry alone, for none of these things could be shared. The house had revealed its secrets to her, and now she fervently wished that it had not.

I have learned not to expect good things. After all that has happened, I still don't know how much is pure bad luck, how much is natural evil and what is pre-ordained.

THIRTEEN

29 July 1981

Wendy could not help feeling that in common with a good proportion of British citizens, Katie had become somewhat obsessed with the royal wedding. 'Suppose it rains . . .' she said anxiously the night before.

'It won't,' Wendy said. 'The forecast is for sunshine. Now you just get off to sleep and stop your worrying. It's not you who's getting married, you know.'

It struck Wendy, as she opened the fridge the next morning and took a last look at the stacked Tupperware boxes and washed-out margarine tubs, the contents of which represented hours of threading cubes of cheese and pineapple onto cocktail sticks the night before, that today would be one of those defining moments in people's lives. In decades to come, people would recall how they spent the day of the royal wedding. It would be to one generation what the Kennedy assassination or the outbreak of the Second World War had been for others. And it was going to be a happy day for everyone, a day of celebration. A day to forget the bicycle, standing in the darkness, mere feet away from where Jamie had constructed his den, the necklace positioned in a cavity which lay directly above Katie's head as she slept.

After they had washed, dressed and eaten breakfast, Wendy and the two younger children settled down in front of the television in the sitting room to watch events unfold. Katie seemed full of nervous excitement about the wedding itself, though Jamie was much more interested in the party to be held on the village green later in the day. Bruce was down in Ashby and Tara was in Portugal with her father and his family, but she had informed Wendy that they would be watching the wedding on a television specially set up by the pool. Wendy had considered ringing Bruce to wish him Happy Royal Wedding Day but decided against it. He probably had enough to contend with. His mother was an ardent royalist and had apparently been talking of little else for weeks.

She joined in as Katie oohed and ahhed over the various dresses of the female guests and the bridesmaids, but after all the anticipation, Lady Diana's dress was rather a disappointment.

'It looks all creased,' Katie mourned.

'You're right, pet. It looks as if it could do with a good iron across it.'

Katie lived the ceremony, visibly wincing when the bride stumbled over her future husband's names, but Jamie grew bored and eventually got up from the sofa and drifted across to the window.

'Mam,' he said, beckoning. 'Come over here and listen.'

Wendy joined him, mystified. 'I can't hear anything,' she said.

Jamie nodded. 'The whole world must be watching the wedding,' he said.

She realized then what he meant. Not a single car had travelled along Green Lane since proceedings in St Paul's had begun. No voices, no vehicles, nothing but birdsong disturbed the stillness of the glorious summer day.

They ate cold chicken and salad for lunch, the children being allowed fizzy drinks while Wendy had a large glass of white wine. The whole world was celebrating, so why not? She noticed that Katie seemed even more het up than before. Jamie was excited too. They were both wound up about the party, she supposed.

After lunch she took the various plastic boxes from the fridge and packed them into her largest shopping bags. There were too many to fit into just two bags and she had to press the children into service as porters. It was times like this when you really missed having a car, she thought. And thank goodness the children hadn't been dragooned into donning fancy dress, which would surely have created an added complication. They walked up Green Lane and along the High Street to the village green. The route had been festooned with flags and bunting, pretty much every shop and dwelling on the High Street joining in. Cardboard crowns covered in kitchen foil jostled with garish pictures of the newlyweds, some cut out of newspapers, some hand-drawn. There had been nothing like it since the Silver Jubilee in '77. If anything, John Newbould and his team had exceeded their previous efforts, for on the village green they encountered displays from a ferocious-looking troop of Viking re-enactors, a bouncy castle, and a carousel whose inbuilt barrel organ competed loudly with the kazoos, drums and glockenspiels of the local junior jazz band as they marched about and twirled their batons in unison.

'They must be hot in those uniforms.' Andrew Webster's mother had appeared alongside Wendy, holding a cloud of pink candy floss on a stick, which she used to gesture towards the youngsters in the jazz band, who were now effecting a complicated-looking manoeuvre which entailed two groups crossing one another on opposing diagonal routes.

'It is hot,' Wendy said. 'I'm afraid I'm getting a headache, what with the noise and the heat.' And possibly also the unaccustomed wine at lunchtime, she thought.

Mrs Webster turned to study her face. 'You do look a bit flushed,' she said, raising her free hand and placing it uninvited against Wendy's forehead. 'You're not going to pass out on us, are you?'

'Oh, no . . . I shouldn't think so. The trouble is I don't want to take the children home when they're having such a good time.'

'Oh, don't you worry about that. I'll look out for them. Me and our Barry will be here until the fireworks tonight. Why don't you go home and put your feet up for a bit? You'll probably feel better in a while.'

Wendy made no more than a token protest. Mrs Webster was right. Her head was getting worse and she felt the need to lie down. After swiftly explaining the arrangements to Katie and Jamie, she set off to walk back to The Ashes. Just the prospect of lying down in her cool bedroom made her feel a little better as she left the cacophony on the green behind her. Most people who were attending had long since made their way to the village green, but there was a middle-aged couple approaching along the deserted High Street, and when they got nearer, Wendy saw that it was Mrs Parsons, accompanied by a man who was probably Mr Parsons. Wendy had not seen the woman to speak to since the occasion, over a year before, when she had stopped her in the street to inform her that Peter Grayling was a suspect in the Leanne Finnegan case. Wendy would rather have avoided speaking with her now, but they were approaching each other on the same side of the road and it was impossible to cross over without being pointedly rude, so she smiled and would have passed by with a 'hello' had Mrs Parsons not stopped and effectively blocked the pavement.

'I suppose you saw the news yesterday?' the woman said.

Wendy admitted that she had not.

'Well, they've found that girl's body. Leanne Finnegan.' There was an almost triumphant glint in Mrs Parsons' eye. 'Poor lass. The family have identified her by her jewellery. Of course, they can't get him now, that Peter Grayling. You can't try a person twice, seemingly.'

'Double jeopardy,' the man put in gravely. He had a surprisingly deep voice.

'But . . . are they sure he killed her? Peter Grayling, I mean?' Wendy tried not to allow the knowledge of the necklace in the attic to impinge on her expression.

'Everyone in Hartlepool knows as he did it.' Mrs Parsons spoke impatiently, as if she could not countenance the stupidity of someone in Bishop Barnard failing to comprehend a fact universally accepted in Hartlepool.

'Well, that's terrible,' Wendy said, uncertain what exactly she meant by that and just wishing that Mrs Parsons and the man would move aside and let her pass.

'So we've a dangerous killer in our midst,' Mrs Parsons continued grimly, her tone implying that Wendy might be in some way responsible for this sorry state of affairs – which, Wendy guiltily reflected, was truer than Mrs Parsons could possibly have known.

At this the man who was probably Mr Parsons demurred, rumbling something to the effect that he'd heard Peter Grayling had been forced to leave the area because things were getting too hot for him in Hartlepool.

Wendy managed to stop herself from responding that she didn't think it would ever be too hot for anyone in Hartlepool, because it had been pretty chilly on every occasion that she'd ever been there. Instead, she made some anodyne response about being sure they had nothing to worry about before sidestepping politely and continuing on her way. She would have to try to forget about the necklace. She ought never to have gone snooping about in the attic. It hadn't been her own idea, something had made her do it. No . . . no . . . that was silly. She was only thinking like that because her head hurt.

It was a relief to turn into Green Lane, where the jamboree became so muted as to be barely noticeable. When she reached the gate she heard the sound of a hover mower starting up somewhere in the distance. Apart from herself and the lone gardener, it seemed that the entire village was down on the green, enjoying the party.

She let herself into the house, took some aspirin and went upstairs to lie on the bed. The duvet was pleasantly cool to her touch, the sun already far enough round to leave the room mostly in shadow. It was gloriously peaceful.

When she woke, the small patch of sunlight on the wall had moved much further across the room, and by turning her head to bring the digital alarm clock into range, she confirmed that it was half past four. Her headache seemed to have gone and there was still plenty of time to go and join the children at the party. She would have a cup of tea first. She indulged in a slow, luxuriant stretch, sat up and swung her feet towards the carpet, where her sandals were lying cock-eyed where she had kicked them off.

The first sound she heard was so faint that she thought for a moment it might have been her own movements. Even so she stayed still, listening, to see if it came again. There were lots of possibilities. The floorboards sometimes creaked of their own volition and the pipes emitted odd sounds from time to time. Butterflies and once even a small bird had been known to fly in through an open window and become trapped. She hoped it wasn't a bird. They made such a mess and were terribly hard to catch.

It wasn't a bird. Footsteps. Where? For some reason her mind flew immediately to the attic. She looked up automatically, as if she expected to be able to see through the bedroom ceiling. But the sounds were not coming from above her head. A distinctive creak helped her to locate their position: it was someone descending the stairs. Someone who had started from the landing, a couple of feet from her bedroom door. Not the children. They were still on the green – and anyway they never walked at that pace or with that heavy tread. A burglar then. A burglar taking advantage of the royal wedding bash on the green. Someone who had assumed that the house was empty. Someone – a man – who thought the occupants were all elsewhere, stuffing down jelly and sausages on

sticks. The telephone was down in the hall. Why on earth had they
never had an extension run upstairs?

The image of Peter Grayling entered her mind. Peter Grayling
knew the layout. Could he possibly have got a key cut for himself,
all those months ago, while working on the house? Had he returned
to collect his trophy from the attic?

She waited, holding herself painfully rigid, but the sounds did
not immediately come again. Perhaps she'd allowed enough time
for him to get clear? Then a new thought struck her. Peter had
nailed down the board which secured the hiding place, but she
had wrenched the nails out of the wood, interfering with it in such
a way that it would open too easily. He would know that someone
had discovered the necklace, and that person's life would be worth
very little to a man who had already killed twice.

Minutes passed. She gradually relaxed her muscles and let out
her breath. The idea of Peter Grayling entering the house, creeping
up and down the stairs, making it his business to silence her for
what she knew, seemed increasingly melodramatic. In the silent
bedroom, she began to question whether she had really heard
anything at all. Had she been properly awake? Might she have
imagined it?

The soft, steady tread ascended the stairs again. For a moment
she froze, half expecting the bedroom door to swing open, revealing
Peter's huge frame blocking the doorway, but the unseen feet
bypassed her room. Wendy strained her ears, listening for their
direction. Katie's room. The softest of clicks registered the closure
of Katie's bedroom door. This wasn't a burglar. To begin with,
how could a burglar have accessed the house without breaking in?
She'd carefully locked up before they all left for the party and
then let herself back in using the Yale key. She had definitely shut
the front door behind her. Breaking in necessitated some noise,
surely? Had she really been that deeply asleep? And there was
nothing to interest a burglar – or for that matter, Peter Grayling
– in Katie's room. No money, no jewellery, no electrical gadgets,
not even a transistor radio – just a little girl's clothes and toys.

As she sat on the bed, toes flexing against the bedroom carpet,
Joan's words about Peggy Disberry returned to her. There was
Joan herself, so attached to the house and recently cremated. Maybe
. . . maybe it wasn't a real, here and now, kind of visitor?
Maybe if she got up from the bed, crossed the landing and opened

Katie's door to have a look, she would find that there was no one there at all.

Wendy stood up and silently moved towards her own bedroom door, which stood slightly ajar, the way she had left it. Or was it? Hadn't she been able to see more of the landing before she went to sleep? Hadn't the door been standing further open? Suppose a burglar had come up the stairs, checked on her while she slept and adjusted the door to prevent an easy view from the bed as he made his way up and down the stairs? No, that was ridiculous too. No thief would have risked her waking up, just for the sake of garnering a few second-hand toys. She swung her bedroom door open to reveal the deserted upper landing. There was no sound from Katie's room, but then the door was solid and well fitted. She crept across two yards of carpet and placed her hand on the door handle. Still no sound.

In a single movement, she twisted the knob and flung the door open, half hoping, half expecting the room to be empty.

It wasn't.

His name came out in a cry of surprise: 'Bruce!'

He paused momentarily in the act of reaching down a last handful of books from Katie's top shelf.

'What are you doing?' It was a stupid question, she knew that. A fraction of a second had been enough for her to see what he was doing. There was a cardboard box on the bed, into which he was stowing the books from Katie's shelves. There was a second cardboard carton on the floor, which appeared to be full of jigsaws, with Katie's old teddy bear, Huey, sitting on top. Katie never slept anywhere without Huey.

'I'm packing up Katie's things.' He placed the last handful of books into the box on the bed and set about closing it, overlapping the four flaps one over another.

'I can see that. Why are you doing it?' She was still gripping the doorknob. She felt sick and lightheaded. This is how it must be, she thought, when women walk in on their husbands doing something indecent – shagging the babysitter, perhaps.

Bruce took a deep breath. 'I'm taking all the children's things, Wendy. They won't be living here anymore.' He had closed the box on the bed and now set about doing the same for the one on the floor. He had to lie Huey flat to do so. Then he lifted one box on to the other and advanced towards the door.

She automatically stood back to let him pass, staring stupidly. As he reached the head of the stairs she regained the powers of speech and movement, pursuing him as a gibberish of questions tumbled out. Where was he taking the children's things? What on earth was he talking about? What was he thinking?

He half turned his head as he reached the lower landing. 'I'll talk to you when I've finished loading the car.'

It was the calmness, the sheer ordinariness of his tone that frightened her most. He had gone mad. Bruce had gone completely mad. She raced back into Katie's room, all but falling over a cushion which had somehow become dislodged from the little wicker chair which stood beside the toy cupboard. The bookshelves, the top of the wardrobe and the dressing table were all bare. She began to career wildly from cupboards to drawers, flinging them open to reveal bare interiors. Katie's possessions had been stripped from the room. Emitting high-pitched whimpers of distress, she hurtled into Jamie's room, trembling at the same scene of desolation. Even his Superman duvet cover was gone. Tidy to the last, Bruce had left the duvet folded neatly across the bottom of the bed. Sobs forced themselves up her throat. Back on the landing, her knees buckled and she had to grab the balustrade for support, before making it down to the hall, where she met Bruce heading for the open front door, carrying Jamie's personal mug which he had just collected from the kitchen. Evidently nothing was to be forgotten.

'Explain,' she demanded.

'Why don't you sit down?' He gestured towards the sitting room and she obeyed, sinking into her usual chair, keeping her eyes fixed on him, much as one would a dangerous escaped lunatic with whom one has been unexpectedly placed in close proximity.

He remained standing. 'Our marriage is over. I'm sure you realized that some time ago.' She attempted to speak, but he continued in the same dispassionate tone. 'I know you are very good at pretending, but you know perfectly well . . . I live in Leicestershire now and the children are coming down there to live with me.'

'They're at the party,' she said. 'I won't let you—'

'They're not at the party. Frances has already collected them. They'll be well down the A19 by now.'

'What? What are you talking about? Frances who?'

'You know very well who Frances is. Frances is the woman I should have married. It's fate really. I bumped into her by sheer chance on my very first night home and she told me that she'd separated from her husband. I think we both realized straight away that we'd made a terrible mistake, marrying other people. We will be moving into her house at first, until things get sorted out and we can find somewhere more suitable.'

Wendy was close to laughing hysterically. 'But you don't love Frances. You were never in love with her. You told me that yourself.'

'I was wrong. Frances and I were meant to be together. It was you and I that was a mistake.'

She leapt from the chair and flung herself at him. A mistake? Twelve years of a life shared, dismissed as a mistake? She managed to land one good blow and tear his shirt before he grabbed both her wrists.

'Stop it,' he said. When she writhed and attempted to lash out again, he tightened his grip. 'Pack it in. You know I could hurt you far worse than you could hurt me. Don't make me lose my temper.' He pushed her back towards the chair and flopped her into it, relinquishing his hold but standing over her.

'The children . . .' she stammered.

'The children will be living with me. They met Frances during their last visit and they both like her. Frances loves children. She's never been able to have any of her own—'

'So she thinks she can steal mine! Well, she shan't have them. They're my children. I'll fight you through the courts for them. She won't get away with kidnapping them.'

'No one has been kidnapped. That's exactly the sort of dramatic accusation which will convince any judge in the land that you are unbalanced. Katie and Jamie are my children and they will be far better off with me in every sense. Frances has already given in her notice so that she can be a stay-at-home mum and take care of them. Believe me, Wendy, you will make life far easier for everyone if you simply accept the situation and don't start all the fuss of a custody case. For goodness' sake, surely even you can see that the children are better off in a stable, two-parent household?'

'She isn't their parent.'

'Your parent is the person who brings you up, gives you love and cares for you. Doesn't that sound familiar? Isn't that what you always said about Tara?'

'That was different. Robert deserted us. This woman is stealing my children. And I helped her to do it.' Her voice rose. 'If I'd just moved down there with you right away, I'd have been there that first night when you met her. I'd have been there all along. When you wouldn't sleep with me, it wasn't because you were tired, was it? It was because you had her . . . and you didn't want to be unfaithful to her. I even stayed back here at Easter and Whitsun, leaving you clear to set up meetings between her and my kids. You made them keep it secret, didn't you? You made my children keep your dirty little secret. It's this house! It's been like a spell, but I see it all now. This bloody house is cursed. Everyone who comes here loses their children. It's all happening, just like it did before.'

Bruce's slap brought the tirade to an abrupt end. She reeled back in the chair, lifting an exploratory hand to her cheek. They stared at one another. When he finally spoke, it was the genuine concern in his voice that wounded her most of all.

'Quite frankly, Wendy, I think you should seek some professional help. This house has become an obsession for you. It's one of the reasons I would give if this ever comes to court and I need examples to illustrate why you are unfit to take proper care of the children.'

Love is exceedingly dangerous. Love makes people reckless. It makes them cruel. In my experience, love does not always turn out well.

I am alone now. It's safer. The only safe way. Then again, don't ever become a hater . . . that's my advice. That never turns out well.

FOURTEEN

November 1981

Wendy declined to initiate divorce proceedings. She didn't want to make it easy for Bruce to disentangle their finances or be free to marry Frances, and besides, she was giving him time in which to change his mind. This Frances thing was an infatuation, some kind of crazy mid-life crisis he was going through. She told him so when he brought the children up to stay with her in the October half term. The children were not themselves. They seemed almost tongue-tied in her presence, and it tore her heart to see the way they ran out to greet their father at the end of the visit, and in particular the way in which Katie entwined her arms with those of the hated Frances as soon as she got out of the car. Wendy ignored Frances, pretending that she was not there.

The children had been supposed to visit her again on the second weekend in November, but Bruce telephoned to inform her that they did not want to come up and he wasn't going to force them. Wendy railed against him in vain, while he declined to put either of them on the line.

'I'm not going to let you upset them again. When you get your licence back you can come and see them down here. Take them out for the day, that kind of thing, but they won't be coming to stay again. Not unless they say they want to.'

She had seen nothing of Tara since her departure for university.

It was hopeless trying to get hold of her via the payphone in the halls of residence, so Wendy had to make do with the occasional phone calls initiated by Tara herself. From what Wendy could gather she was seeing a lot of Robert and his family and remained in touch with John, the one-time bricklayer.

'It would be lovely if you could make it up here for a weekend,' Wendy found herself saying with monotonous regularity, to which Tara invariably responded by saying that she'd see what she could do.

'I'll come up and surprise you one of these days,' she said, and Wendy thought sadly that it would be a surprise because, on bad days, she sometimes wondered if she would ever see Tara again.

She had been to see a solicitor in the village for advice regarding access to the children, but he told her it was complicated. There was nothing to say that she had a right to have the children living with her. If she took her case to court, the court would consider what was in the best interests of the children, and she had to appreciate that they had perhaps settled into new schools by now and made new friends. They might well say that they preferred to live with their father and his new partner.

'Well, of course they would,' Wendy said angrily. 'They've been brainwashed.'

On her way home, as the wind stung her face and made her eyes water, Wendy concluded that it was Frances (who had turned out not to be a 'nice girl' at all) who was at the root of the problem. Bruce could not have stolen the children without her complicity. He would not be able to manage them now if it wasn't for Frances having given up her job to take care of them. Even some old fool of a judge would see that Bruce could not juggle his job and the care of his children alone. The question was how to remove Frances from the equation. Once she was out of the picture, the children would have to come home and she could win Bruce back . . . Everything could return to the way it used to be. To a time when everyone was happy.

A letter from Jamie helped to crystallize her plan. Wendy sensed the editing hand of some southern schoolteacher in play.

Dear Mummy,
    We are writing letters in class so I am writing to you.
Daddy and Franny are well. So is Katie. Franny says I can

have a rabbit if I promise to look after it myself. Daddy is
going to Belgium all next week and he will bring back special
chocolate. I hurt my knee when I was in the playground
yesterday because I fell over but I am fine now.

Love from Jamie xxxxxxxxxx

She waited until midway through Bruce's week in Belgium
before she telephoned, reasoning that this would minimize the chance
of Frances speaking with him again before his return. She timed her
call for after the children's bedtime, thereby ensuring that it was
Frances herself who answered the phone and removing the likelihood
of there being any inconvenient witnesses to the conversation.

'Hello . . . Is that Frances?'

'It is. Who's speaking, please?' Frances sounded guarded, as if
she knew perfectly well who was speaking and was already
suspicious.

'It's Wendy. Listen to me, Frances. Don't put the phone
down. I need to talk to you.'

'If it's about the children or the separation, you need to speak
to Bruce.'

'No, no. It's about Bruce. I need to speak to you.'

'To me? What about Bruce?'

Wendy caught the note of alarm. That was good. She had got
her interested. 'There's something I have to tell you about him.
Something I can't say on the phone. It's something you need to
know.'

'What are you talking about? Wendy . . . have you been
drinking?'

'I don't drink. Very rarely anyway.'

'Yes, you do. You know you do. You were caught drunk driving.'

'That all happened *because* I hardly ever drink. I wasn't used
to it. Someone else gave me a drink and I hadn't realized what
was in it. Believe me, I would never drink and drive on purpose.
I was always the one on the Britvics so that I could chauffeur
Bruce home after work dos. I bet he's got you doing that for him
now.'

A short silence at the other end told Wendy that she had hit the
mark.

'What is it that you want?' Frances asked. 'Why have you rung?'

'I know Bruce is away. Jamie wrote a letter to tell me. That's

why I'm ringing you now, so that Bruce doesn't find out. I want
you to get a babysitter for the children and come up here to see
me. Come on Friday night. Don't tell Bruce anything about it and
don't mention anything to the children. Then I can explain.'

'Don't be ridiculous. Surely you can tell me whatever this
mysterious thing is on the phone?'

'Come on Friday night. I can't tell you on the phone. And don't
tell Bruce I rang, or let anyone else know. He mustn't find out.'

'You're mad,' Frances said.

But Wendy noted that she didn't sound very sure of herself.

In the forty-eight hours that followed, Wendy laid her plans
carefully. She fluctuated violently between deciding that Frances
would ignore the invitation, dismissing the whole thing as nonsense,
and feeling strangely confident that she would not be able to resist
turning up.

When the street lamps came on in the late afternoon of Friday,
Wendy noticed that the one that usually illuminated the top end
of the drive was flickering. It created a somewhat sinister effect,
she thought, like something in a B-movie. She switched on the
sitting room light and drew the curtains. That way, to anyone
passing the house or approaching from the road, it would appear
that she was in there as usual, reading or watching the TV. She
took care to leave the hall and passage lights, as well as the lights
in the kitchen, switched off. She did not want anyone who came
up the drive to be aware of her silhouette as she stood watching
them from the kitchen window. She had eased the window open
an inch. It allowed a lot of cold air into the room, but it was
important that she be able to call up the drive at the right moment.
She huddled a coat around her as she waited, stuffing her hands
into the pockets to keep them warm, not daring to leave her post
and place them against a radiator. When the moment came,
she would need to be on the spot so that she could act quickly.
Timing would be everything. Otherwise she would lose the element
of surprise.

At just before eight o'clock the flickering street light gave up
altogether, immediately plunging the end of the drive into shadow.
Wendy gasped. That wasn't in the script at all . . . but as she stared
towards the gate, she realized that the section of the drive nearest
the road was not in complete darkness. Once you let your eyes
get used to it, there was still enough illumination from the next

closest street lights to make out the open gateway. She would still be able to see anyone as soon as they came onto her property.

But of course Frances would not come. Wendy's earlier certainty had been extinguished as surely as the street light. It seemed childish now, this plan of hers, to lure her husband's mistress more than 150 miles north. She might as well give up her vigil, close the window and get warm by the sitting room fire.

She decided to give it until nine. Surely Frances wouldn't time her arrival any later than that? Not that she was likely to come at all. It had been a stupid idea, stupid, stupid.

Then she saw her. It was all she could do not to cry out as the figure, unmistakably female, hesitated for a fraction of a second before heading smartly up the drive. She was carrying a bag of some sort. That was as much as Wendy could make out before the figure was lost completely in deeper shadows.

'Come down to the back door,' she called out, before racing out of the kitchen and into the courtyard. She knew she had no more than seconds to be ready. Any hesitation would be fatal. She reached the corner of the courtyard as the figure turned round the side of the house. Drove the knife in hard, with a strength she had scarcely known she possessed, and as the woman collapsed forward against her she was already withdrawing the knife and striking again, driving in a second blow before her victim had time to speak. Before that single, desperate gasp of 'Mam.'

'Tara. Oh my God! Tara! What are you doing here? Oh my darling, my sweetheart . . .' The words tumbled out as Wendy sank to her knees, dragged to the ground as she attempted to support the weight of her dying daughter.

Tara did not answer.

NOVEMBER 2011

S he died in my arms. I didn't know what to do. I would never get my children back if anyone found out that I had killed one of them. So I carried part of my original plan through. I washed the knife and replaced it in the kitchen drawer. I made a bonfire of the clothing. I began to dig the grave in the corner of the back garden, close to the wall of the outbuildings, but I barely got down a foot before I hit something hard. Scraping away the earth, I easily identified what I had found. I didn't explore any further. From the day I saw the spokes of that bicycle, I had understood why it was that Elaine Duncan couldn't leave. Dora had last been seen heading homewards . . . In one way or another, the house always claimed its victim. Two victims sometimes – the one who was buried and the one who stayed to guard the place. The one whose continuing ownership precluded any accidental discoveries.

I laid one daughter of the house above another then planted the tree, leaving the sacking loosely wrapped around the roots as the man in the garden centre had suggested. It has grown tall now. Much taller than me.

The university alerted me to Tara's disappearance. She had said something to a friend about going home for the weekend, but no one was sure which home she meant. When Robert called me to ask about her, I cut him off short. 'You wouldn't speak to me for nearly twenty years,' I said. 'Why should I speak to you now?'

She was listed as a missing person, but there was some doubt about whether or not she had actually come to any harm. As one policeman said, in a voice no doubt designed to reassure, 'Just because a person has chosen not to communicate, it does not necessarily mean they are missing in the accepted sense, it's just that not everyone knows where they are.' One girlfriend thought Tara had not been altogether happy on her course. Another said she'd been having boyfriend trouble. Someone else thought there had been a plan to run off with some unidentified boyfriend. Yet another fellow student said that things between Tara and John *had become more intense. None of them had known her above a matter of weeks. She'd had no time to develop any special confidantes at university, but had seemingly already drifted apart from her old friends in the north. The police had that John boy in for questioning but it got them nowhere. He didn't know where she'd gone.*

I know where she is. She is here, with me, every day and every night. I have tried putting a padlock on the bedroom door – not my bedroom, but the one that belonged to her and to that other victim, Alice. But padlocks cannot hold that kind. She watches me. Always.

Frances never answered my summons. It was never mentioned by anyone again. Presumably it was dismissed as another of my eccentricities. I gave Bruce his divorce and he married Frances. Katie sent me a photograph, which I burned on the sitting room fire. I was allowed to keep The Ashes and much of what remained of my legacy. Bruce took the proceeds of the house in Jasmine Close and everything else I had ever held dear. Now they are grown up, the children come to visit me from time to time, Jamie less frequently than his sister. Katie does her best to make conversation, but there is always something strained about it. Tara watches me from the corner of the room.

Justice caught up with Peter Grayling. It was no thanks to me. I couldn't afford to attract any police interest in The Ashes. The little necklace of wooden beads lies where he hid it, beneath the attic floorboards, waiting for some future explorer to discover it, pluck it from its hiding place and wonder over the fading letters, spelling out the name of a girl long dead. No, it was a different form of justice for Peter. I saw the story in the local paper. He lost control of his car on a bend and hit a tree. No other vehicle was involved. Divine justice. I like to think he saw a figure in the road as he took the corner, and tried to swerve out of the way with disastrous consequences. There were no witnesses, according to the press. But in my mind there may have been one – the girl in the road, who watched him die before quietly fading away.

My contacts within the village have dwindled. I had not realized how much of my life was lived through my husband and children. As time went on my chats in the supermarket grew shorter and less frequent, as I carried my sad little wire basket down the aisles where I would once have pushed a full trolley. Then I noticed that people had started to avoid me. Well, what could they say? They must have wondered about what kind of terrible woman I am, to have been abandoned by two husbands and become estranged from all my children.

Money has become an increasingly pressing problem. Economies have had to be made. Just a fire for the sitting room now, no question of running the central heating. It doesn't matter much. I don't go into all those empty bedrooms, nor eat alone at the dining room table. I never enter the study at all. One afternoon when I was weeding in the garden, the sensation of watching eyes from the study window became too much. I got a sheet of hard-board, a hammer and some tacks and I boarded it up. That window isn't visible from Green Lane, so there won't be tittle tattle in the village.

The gardening grew more difficult, particularly after I passed my seventieth birthday and became less and less inclined to kneel down and engage in the never-ending battle with the weeds. When the time came that I couldn't afford to have the electric mower repaired, I let the back garden go completely. The nettles have long since taken over. It doesn't matter anyway. No children have played on the rusty climbing frame since 1981.

The front garden is still reasonably neat. I manage the grass with shears, doing it a bit at a time. Roses still bloom in the beds and I have repelled the convolvulus from the sundial for another year. I am resigned to the peeling paint on the doors and window-sills. I expect passers-by have noticed that the house is beginning to look run down. Newcomers from Magnolia Road and Cyclamen Drive glance curiously over the closed gate, wondering about the house's name, curious as to who the unseen occupant might be.

I had the agents remove the sale board in November 1981. I have resigned myself to the fact that The Ashes will be my home until I die . . . and maybe even after that.

ACKNOWLEDGEMENTS

I would like to record my thanks to the family and friends who have offered so much support during the period when I have been working on this book: Sam and John, Ash, Richard, Clare, Arthur and Daniel, Les and Sarah, and of course Erica and Pete. Thanks are also due to all at Severn House for their patience, in particular to Kate Lyall Grant, Sara Porter and Natasha Bell, and finally to Jane Conway-Gordon, who remains the best agent anyone could hope for.

Faces of Feminism

Faces of Feminism

A Study of Feminism
as a Social Movement

OLIVE BANKS

Martin Robertson · Oxford

First published in 1981 by Martin Robertson & Company Ltd., 108 Cowley Road, Oxford OX4 1JF.

British Library Cataloguing in Publication Data

Banks, Olive
    Faces of feminism.
    1. Feminism — History
    I. Title
    301.4'2   HQ1154

    ISBN 0-85520-261-0
    ISBN 0-85520-260-2 Pbk

Typeset in 11/12 pt AlphaComp English
by Pioneer Associates, Flimwell
Printed and bound in Great Britain
by The Camelot Press, Southampton

Contents

1

Introduction

Feminism as a subject of study is no longer, as it once was, a neglected area of study, a change for which the new feminist movement itself is in large part responsible. Nevertheless, in spite of the large volume of writing in what has come to be called women's studies, feminism as a social movement has been of less interest than the documentation of and explanation for women's continuing inequality. Consequently most studies may be said to deal more directly with women's place in society than with the efforts of an organized women's movement to change it. Certainly the position is no longer what it was even ten years ago, as the list of sources in the bibliography should itself make abundantly clear. Nevertheless, while studies of aspects of the feminist movement are now, in some respects, becoming plentiful, most of them deal with relatively restricted areas of both time and place. Very few have attempted to set feminism in a historical context that takes us from the earliest beginnings of an organized movement through all the stages in its development. Even those studies that attempt such a perspective frequently end with suffrage as if that ended the feminist movement, and O'Neill's (1969a) account of the American feminist movement, which includes a survey of the 1920s and 1930s, does not cover the rise of the new feminism. The new movement, it is true, has its own chroniclers but these do not, save perhaps for a brief introduction, concern themselves much with nineteenth-century feminism. The present study, then, is at the time of writing (and to the best of my knowledge) the only one that attempts to see the old and new feminism as one single historical process and to assess systematically how one movement developed into the other.

1

The inclusion of a greater time-span than usual is not, however, the only way in which this book tries to be different. It also attempts to be comparative. On the whole, it has been customary to study the manifestations of feminism in a single country and this is largely true even when only a single aspect of feminism is under discussion. There are of course exceptions, but those that attempt a systematic comparison of two or more countries are very few. One of the earliest is O'Neill's (1969b) attempt to compare Britain and the United States, but this is a sketch rather than a systematic study, and in any case does not take us beyond 1920. Another relatively early work is Paulson's (1973) study of women's suffrage and prohibition. While dealing with only a limited aspect of feminism, it is very widely comparative including not only Britain and the United States, but France, Australia and Scandinavia. The most recent attempt at comparison is Evans' *The Feminists* (1977), which includes material on Europe, America and Australasia, but this too is limited in time, and covers only the years between 1840 and 1920.

There is, of course, a very good reason why comparative studies of feminism are so rare, since such a study carries with it the risk of superficiality if not of downright error. The earlier neglect of the subject has meant that our knowledge of it has been so limited that studies in depth on many different aspects of its history were an essential prerequisite for any attempt to draw a broader picture. Only in recent years has it been possible to make the kind of comparative study attempted by Evans or, in a somewhat different form, in the present study. Moreover in the course of making this attempt, it was frequently all too obvious to me that the gaps in our knowledge are still formidable, and that it is indeed all too possible that the attempt is still premature. The justification, however, lies in the belief not so much that we now know the answers, but that only by trying to take the longer and broader view is it possible for the researcher, whether historian or sociologist, even to ask the right questions. It is in this faith that the enterprise was undertaken.

The decision to include the whole history of feminism from its earliest beginnings as a movement to the present day gave the study an exceptionally long time-span. In consequence, and unlike both Paulson and Evans, only one other country was chosen for comparative purposes, and that one the easiest in terms of the availability of published material, the United States of America. While certainly losing some of the advantages of wider comparability, I believed that this was justified by the greater depth it allowed. In particular I hoped that such a comparison would throw fresh light on feminism in both Britain and the United States, since both their similarities, which are indeed striking, and their differences reveal aspects of feminism that are concealed by attending only to its manifestation in a single country.

By the choice of the comparative method, and by the decision to cover so great a time-span, the character of the study as an analysis of mainly *secondary* sources was, however, determined in advance. In consequence I am more than usually dependent on those whose work in the field has made available data without which the present study could hardly have begun, and I hope that this dependence has been duly acknowledged in the citations of sources. Inevitably, however, there have been gaps, some of them serious, and it is for this reason that the study must be regarded as tentative, and as suggesting questions, rather than providing answers. The pace of work in this field is moreover rapid and, in some areas certainly, work already in progress may change our perspective, so that the interpretation given to certain events in this study may soon need to be challenged. This, however, is the fate of all interpretations in time, and this should not, in itself, be regarded as a serious shortcoming. Moreover, where lack of data makes the interpretation appear particularly speculative, the reader's attention has been drawn to this in the text.

Having attempted to justify the methodology, it is now necessary to define the scope of the study further, by an examination of the concept of feminism itself. This is not self-explanatory, and on its definition will rest our understanding of exactly who the feminists were and what they were trying to achieve. For the purpose of this study the concept has been used in the broadest possible way. Any groups that have tried to *change* the position of women, or the ideas about women, have been granted the title of feminist, and the great variety of ways in which they have tried to do this has been allowed for by exploring the different varieties, or, as the title of the book phrases it, the different faces of feminism. This has seemed more fruitful than adopting a narrow definition, which would have left many groups and many ideas significant for feminism outside the scope of the study, even though it meant including certain activities that some might like to consider as not really feminism at all. Anti-feminism is less easy to define because feminist goals have often been opposed by those who, using my definition, are feminists themselves. In this study, therefore, I have been less concerned with anti-feminism as an ideology than with the opponents of feminist goals at particular points in time. An analysis of the reasons for the opposition often indicates a complex system of motivation in which anti-feminism, in the sense of a traditional view of woman's place, is only one part.

In writing about feminism, and particularly the feminist movement, the chief aim has always been to gain an understanding of the reasons for the emergence of feminism as a social movement in a certain limited number of countries and at a certain specific time. Those who have tried to explain the rise of feminism have noted that it is associated, invariably, with liberal Protestantism (Evans, 1977, pp. 17–18). This is not to suggest that Protestants were necessarily feminists by any means but there are certainly aspects of Protestantism, absent from Catholicism, that seem to provide a suitable environment for the growth of feminist ideas. These include ideas of religious individualism, alongside ideas on the nature of marriage and the family, and on sexuality itself, all of which were later to be significant for nineteenth-century feminists. Within Protestantism, moreover, some radical sects allowed women a considerable degree of religious freedom and even, to some extent, of religious authority; such sects, and particularly the Quakers, were later to be a source not simply of feminist ideas but of feminist leaders. Certain extremist sects also advocated doctrines of 'free love', which were again to play an important role in feminist history.

The political ideas of the Enlightenment as developed not simply by the Enlightenment philosophers but more practically in the events of the French and particularly perhaps the American revolutions also represent an important if not indeed a vital aspect of feminist ideals and aspirations. It is impossible to understand feminism at all without seeing it as one aspect of the Enlightenment doctrine of natural rights, and much of nineteenth-century feminism in particular was part of the general adoption of political democracy.

Structural changes in society have also been noted as important reasons for the rise of feminism. Of these perhaps the most significant are those that forced middle-class women in particular to attempt to redefine their role in society (Evans, 1977, p. 30). The separation of home from work, as the process is usually described, affected, it is true, both middle-class and working-class women, but it affected them differently, and it was amongst the middle classes that dissatisfaction turned into the kind of channel that

produced the feminist movement. The precise manner in which
that occurred was complex, but it involved on the one hand a
greater gap between men's and women's lives as man's sphere, for a
variety of reasons, expanded (O'Neill, 1969b, p. 17) and on the
other an attack by the feminists on the doctrine that confined them
within a constraining and indeed even a contracting woman's
world.

The preponderance of the middle-class woman throughout the
whole history of feminism has perhaps given rise to the most
comment and has indeed led many to argue that the feminists for
that reason are unrepresentative of the needs of women as a whole.
Certainly working-class women have their own sources of
discontent, and by and large these have appeared to be less a result
of their sex than of their class. Nevertheless, although it would be a
mistake to see middle-class and working-class women as always
having common interests, it is equally true that working-class
women do not always have a common cause with working-class
men. It will be one of the purposes of this study, therefore, to
examine the interplay of sex and class in the history of feminism
and to explore, in particular, the relationship between feminism,
socialism, and the labour and trade union movement.

The preponderance of middle-class women in the feminist
movement should not in itself, of course, occasion any particular
surprise. They alone had the education and the political skills
necessary for rebellion and, indeed, the leisure time that made it
possible for rebellious ideas to be translated into political action.
Moreover, for them, much more than for working-class women, it
was clear that their discontent was linked to their position as
women, rather than to their class. It should not be imagined,
however, that middle-class feminists were concerned only with
their own position. Much of their work was for others, and the
place of philanthropy in feminism is an issue that will be explored
in some detail in subsequent chapters. Nevertheless, it is probably
true to say that their view of the needs of working-class women was
coloured by their own class position, an aspect of feminism that
again has given it a distinctive character.

Variations in demographic patterns have also been seen as
important causes of feminism, and certainly the surplus of women
in nineteenth-century Britain was one of the reasons both for
pressure for the improved education of girls and for expanding
employment opportunities for women. On the other hand,
according to some accounts, it was the *shortage* of women that

produced the advances in women's suffrage in the American West. The proportion of women in the population may therefore be an aspect of their position in society that has its part to play in the rise of feminism, but the effect that this has will vary with the circumstances (Evans, 1977, p. 28).

Much the same point can be made if we examine some of the reasons given for the rise of the modern feminist movement. It is explained, for example, as a response to such aspects of the social structure as the fall in the birth rate and the increase of women, particularly married women, in the work force. There is a sense in which this explanation is a plausible one, but again it would appear to be too simplistic. Feminist ideas can be a response to the exclusion of women from production as well as to their entry into it in large numbers. Moreover, neither the entry of women into employment in two world wars, nor their rapid exclusion from it afterwards, led to a rise in feminism but was instead accompanied by its decline. The relationship between feminism and the birth rate is also a highly complex one, and women's attitude to the size of their family may be a consequence of feminist ideas, as well as a cause of them.

More promising perhaps are Juliet Mitchell's suggestions that modern feminism was a consequence of the contradictions between the ideology on women's role and their actual position in society. She cites as examples the contradiction between the domestic ideology and women's productive role, the contradiction between their role in the family and in the work force, and the contradiction between the ideology of sexual freedom and women's actual sexual exploitation (Mitchell, 1971, p. 174).

It is possible therefore that the idea that there is a single cause or set of causes for feminism is itself mistaken. The explanation for feminism is thus perhaps less urgent than a greater understanding of the nature of feminism itself, and it is with this that this book is chiefly concerned. In pursuing this issue, I shall attempt to discover not only who the feminists were, and who supported them, but why their fortunes changed over time to such an extent that by the end of the 1920s feminism appeared to have died, and why by the late 1960s their resurgence was complete. In presenting this analysis, particular attention will be paid to what may be called alliances.

I shall argue that both the fortunes of feminism and its character were deeply influenced by its need to join forces with other groups for their mutual aid. Sometimes this occurred between feminists themselves working for rather different goals, but frequently it was between feminists and groups working for ends outside of, although congruent with, feminism itself. The most obvious of these is the anti-slavery movement, but there are many others, ranging from temperance and the purity crusade to various branches of left-wing politics. In addition to the alliances, there were also cleavages both between different groups of feminists, and between feminists and other groups whose interests ranged them against feminist goals. An obvious example here is the opposition by brewing interests to women's suffrage, an opposition that certainly owed its virulence not to the idea of women's suffrage in itself, but to the alliance between suffrage and temperance. Periods of decline in feminist support were often brought about by cleavages of this kind, sometimes amongst feminists themselves, as in the years after the vote was won. The suffrage campaign itself, on the other hand, was characterized by a strong sense of unity amongst feminists of all persuasions as they came to see the vote as the answer to their own particular problems.

Within feminism, three intellectual traditions have been distinguished, each taking its origin in the eighteenth century but continuing to operate as differentiating principles even to this day. The first of these traditions to be examined is that of evangelical Christianity. Both Britain and the United States were, in the late eighteenth and early nineteenth centuries, swept by revivals that gave a fresh meaning and significance to religion in their zeal for conversion. Primarily missionary in intent, the movement was eventually led into a concern with social issues, of which perhaps the most significant was the campaign against slavery. More important for our purpose is the extent to which women were drawn in, at first as subordinates, later as active partners. Under its influence women began to emerge from domesticity and take on a public role, as they became increasingly involved in issues of moral and later social reform. Accompanied by ideas of the moral superiority of women, it finds its most modern expression in the 'pro-woman' sections of radical feminism.

The second tradition is that of the Enlightenment philosophers. Among the principles they bequeathed to feminism is the appeal to human reason rather than tradition and its most influential feminist propagators have been Mary Wollstonecraft and John Stuart Mill. Within this tradition, differences between men and women are seen as shaped by the environment rather than as natural, and its whole tendency has been to emphasize the potential similarities between the sexes, rather than the differences. Women, like slaves and other oppressed groups, are seen as excluded from their natural rights and the emphasis is on an end to male privilege. It is from the Enlightenment thinkers, too, that the feminists draw their emphasis on self-realization, freedom and autonomy. The heir to the Enlightenment tradition is equal rights feminism, the rise and fall of which is sometimes treated as the rise and fall of feminism itself.

Socialist feminism has its roots, not in Marxism, but in the much earlier tradition of communitarian socialism, and derives chiefly from the Saint-Simonian movement in France. The Saint-Simonians were significant for feminism because of their attacks on the traditional family and their advocacy of a system of communal living that would take the burden of child-rearing away from the individual and place it on the community. Alongside these changes in family life went changes in the sexual relationships between men and women, often described, not always very accurately, as 'free love'. Doctrines such as these, it is true, never represented more than the views of a tiny minority of feminists. Nevertheless they have been a persistent undercurrent in both feminist and socialist thought. They reappear in a somewhat different form in Marxism, with its advocacy of state-provided child care, and are strongly in evidence within much radical feminism at the present day.

It is not suggested that there are three different feminist movements, although feminist groupings are often characterized by an adherence to one or other of these three traditions. On the other hand, I shall argue that they represent different and indeed sometimes contradictory approaches to feminism; this makes it difficult to conceive of it as a single movement, let alone a single ideology. Deriving from separate origins, representing different goals and holding very disparate images of women and their proper place in society, those three traditions comprise the several faces of feminism with which this study is concerned. There are often alliances of a temporary nature between the different traditions and sometimes feminists draw on more than one tradition without being aware of their contradictory nature. At other times, however, the different traditions may give rise to violent opposition between feminists.

In Part I, which now follows, these three traditions will be described in more detail, and their influence on the early years of feminism will be explored. Later Parts take the story further, examining in chronological sequence all the stages of feminism including, finally, an attempt to assess the present-day scene. It will be argued that the three intellectual traditions do not lose their identity but, even if no longer clearly recognized for what they are, continue to differentiate between feminists and their goals. The consequences for feminism of this differentiation will be explored in the Conclusion.

PART I

The Early Years, 1840—1870

2

The Evangelical Contribution
to Feminism

The evangelical movement that re-awakened religious enthusiasm in both the United States and Britain was based upon the individual's personal experience of conversion. It spread widely into both the Church of England and the nonconformist denominations on both sides of the Atlantic. The Evangelicals with the Church of England like Wilberforce and Hannah More had much in common with Congregationalists, Presbyterians, Baptists and Methodists (Heasman, 1962, pp. 16—17; Carwardine, 1978). From the individual's personal experience of salvation came the desire to convert others, and it was this proselytizing zeal that led to the revivalism that was perhaps its most characteristic feature. There was also a seriousness of purpose that lent the movement its strong moral emphasis, so that the drive to save souls was accompanied by a crusade to stamp out sin, an endeavour made more immediate by the millenarianism that pervaded evangelical thinking. Moreover it was this blend of religious enthusiasm, moral indignation and millenarianism that turned so many Evangelicals towards the cause of both social and moral reform, of which perhaps the crusades against vice, drunkenness and slavery were to be the most important.

At first sight the religious revivals that were such an important feature of both British and American society in the late eighteenth and early nineteenth centuries seem unpromising ground for the emergence of feminism, since Protestantism, except in certain of its radical forms, did not challenge the accepted view of women as subordinate to their husbands (Hamilton, 1978, pp. 57—75). Moreover the Protestant emphasis on the family and domestic virtues was, as we shall see, to become an essential ingredient in Victorian anti-feminism and the doctrine that woman's place was in the home. Yet in spite of this the evangelical movement in the United States, and to a lesser extent in Britain, was to be a significant factor in the development of feminist consciousness. To understand how this came about it is necessary to look at the way in which successive revivals impinged with particular immediacy on the lives of women.

Already in the opening years of the nineteenth century women were prominent in the revivalist campaign. There is evidence from the United States, for example, that female converts in the New England Great Awakening between 1798 and 1826 outnumbered males by 3 to 2 (Cott, 1977, p. 133). Moreover the years after 1800 saw a phenomenal increase in the number of female missionary societies. The chief aim of these groups, as of evangelicalism generally, was the task of religious conversion, and the distribution of Bibles and tracts was an important part of their work. But if conversion was the chief aim, charitable enterprise was often associated with it, and many of these organizations became involved in the relief of destitution and in fund-raising for the provision of asylums and refuges (Berg, 1978, pp. 163—73). Nor was this activity confined to the United States. By 1830 there was considerable development of such ladies' societies in England (Brown, 1961, p. 249). According to Prochaska (1974) the period 1795—1830 saw the emergence of no fewer than seventeen ladies' societies, several of them with numerous provincial branches. Women were involved in the work of lying-in charities and in the provision of asylums for the deaf, blind, destitute and insane. By 1857 the *Lancet* was able to report that 'there was not a town in the kingdom which did not have its lying-in society, female school, visiting association, nursing institute and many other charitable organizations exclusively managed by the "gentle sex"' (Donnison, 1977, p. 65). Although much of the work done by women was of a routine nature, and carried out under the direction of men, Prochaska has pointed out that women sometimes had a direct responsibility for the regular operation of the organization, so that they gained experience of such activities as drawing up regulations, the election of officers, taking minutes, overseeing accounts and corresponding with other ladies' societies.

It should not be supposed that evangelical fervour was the only reason for this enormous proliferation of female societies. Another cause was the increase in leisure time for women of the middle classes with the separation of home and work and the decline in household production. Women, and especially perhaps unmarried women, turned to religious and charitable exercises as a way of filling up empty time with purposeful activities. At the same time the emancipation of middle-class women from many of their previous household duties provided religious and charitable organizers with an army of part-time helpers eager to run bazaars, collect signatures for petitions and distribute tracts and charity to the poor.

It was, however, in the United States that the emotions awakened by the evangelical revival were to lead most obviously and directly to feminism. The proliferation of female associations in the 1820s led women into a variety of activities that involved them directly in the lives of the poor, but it was perhaps in their work for prostitutes that they showed most daring and initiative. Inspired by the revivalistic preaching of Charles Finney and the missionary work of John R. McDowell, the New York Female Moral Reform Society was founded in 1834 to convert New York prostitutes to evangelical Protestantism. The work required courage because McDowell's report on brothels had shocked New Yorkers and he was accused of sensationalism. The women were highly committed however, and a journal was founded, the *Advocate of Moral Reform*, which became one of the nation's most widely read evangelical journals. From the start the society adopted the policy of staffing the journal as far as possible only with women. In 1836 two women editors were appointed, and in 1841 their male financial agent was replaced by a woman book-keeper. By 1843 women even set the type. Efforts on the part of men to take over the journal in 1837 were indignantly repulsed, although at this time men still chaired public meetings of the society and read out the women's report (Rosenberg, 1971, pp. 98—124).

The emerging feminism shown by the staffing policy of the journal was also evidenced by its tone and concepts. There were countless articles refuting the charge that moral reform was destructive of female sensibility, and woman's right to an individual conscience was repeatedly appealed to. Moreover in their attack on the double standard of sexual morality they were outspoken in their claim that the men involved should also be treated as guilty. There were threats, for example, to keep vigil at brothels and to publish lists of clients (Berg, 1978, pp. 182—7). By 1840 there were 555 organizations linked to the original society. By this time too the scope of its activities had widened and it was more determinedly feminist in its activities than ever. During the 1840s the journal carried articles challenging the idea that a woman's only happiness came through marriage, attacked low wages for women as a cause of prostitution, and, in 1846, attacked the male monopoly of professions and skilled work and advocated the vote for women as a means to compel lawmakers to listen to their arguments. In New York in 1845 a delegation of women proposed to make seduction a state prison offence, and this was followed by relentless pressure for three years until a bill was introduced and became law in New York. By the 1850s the journal was an expressly feminist publication arguing for women's need to be independent, attacking their low wages and demanding expanded employment opportunities (Berg, 1978, pp. 212—51).

In England there is little evidence that the early evangelical involvement in moral reform led to the rise of a specifically feminine consciousness. Not until Josephine Butler's campaign against the Contagious Diseases Acts in the 1870s was concern for the prostitute linked specifically to feminist arguments about the relationship between men and women in society. There were certainly early examples of female initiative, and in 1804 a Ladies' Committee for Promoting the Education and Employment of the Female Poor was founded by the Clapham Evangelicals who saw a connection between prostitution and the want of work for women (Donnison, 1977, p. 51). Prochaska too describes a Forlorn Female Institution in which in 1813 women interviewed prostitutes (Prochaska, 1974, p. 432). On the whole, however, refuges for fallen women seem to have been largely punitary and there was little if any concern with the kind of issues that interested the American Female Moral Reform Society. Indeed there seems to have been a reluctance on the part of women in England to get involved in this work at all. In 1843 a plan, largely unsuccessful, was launched to set up female branches, although with male secretaries, to include women in rescue work, since at this time virtually all rescue workers were men (Bristow, 1977, pp. 62—3). In 1858 a Female Mission on the Fallen was established with paid women missionaries (Walton, 1975, p. 41). One of its initial objects was to go out into the streets at night to distribute tracts and other literature, and by 1871 nine districts in London had a woman outdoors worker for this task. From 1860 onwards many small rescue homes were opened and it was during this decade that

Josephine Butler and Ellice Hopkins started their work (Heasman, 1962, pp. 153—60).

Clearly, therefore, women were beginning to take an active interest in work with prostitutes even before Josephine Butler's campaign brought out its feminist implications. It was still, however, conceived of in mainly religious terms, its aim the reclamation of the individual. When once the concern for the welfare of the prostitute became an attack on the double standard of morality, the campaign was to take on more of the characteristics of the American Female Moral Reform Society. There seems little doubt, however, that this was a later development in England, coming in the 1860s and 1870s rather than the 1830s and 1840s, by which time a more general feminist movement was already well under way.

The field of temperance is another area, evangelical in inspiration, that was to be of great significance for feminism, although again there is evidence that it was a more important source of feminist consciousness in the United States. A large number of studies have drawn attention to the relationship between the temperance movement and feminism (Paulson, 1973; Harrison, 1971) although the closest ties between the two movements were forged after 1870 and, in consequence, are beyond the scope of this chapter. Even in the early years, however, there is evidence of what may be termed a natural affinity, which springs in large part from the links between temperance and moral reform. Both drunkenness and sexual immorality were defined as moral weaknesses, which could be overcome by self-discipline. They were therefore both aspects of the evangelical striving after perfectability (Gusfield, 1972). At the same time a direct link was made between alcohol and sexual excess. Frequently moral reformers also worked actively in the temperance cause. Drunkenness was seen as an important factor in seduction since it weakened judgement and will on the part of both men and women. For much the same reason alcohol was seen as a cause of prostitution. Drinking places were 'masculine preserves' denied to respectable women and often the haunt of prostitutes. It was natural therefore for women to see them as hostile to the family and home, especially when drunkenness could bring a family into poverty or lead to actual physical abuse. The helplessness of women under these circumstances was accentuated by their legal position, which left them almost completely in their husbands' power. In the world of the female novelist, alcoholism and gambling are portrayed as examples of masculine villainy and betrayal and female suffering and superiority (Berg, 1978, p. 137; Papashvily, 1956).

Feminists, therefore, were almost always in sympathy with the ideals of temperance, although temperance workers themselves were not necessarily feminist. What is perhaps more worthy of note is the extent to which feminist leaders began as active temperance workers and sometimes moved to feminism at a later stage in their lives. The best example is probably that of Susan Anthony, born in 1820 and one of the most important of the leaders of the early suffrage campaign. Her father, a Quaker, organized a temperance society for his workers in the cotton mill he owned, and refused to sell liquor in the store he opened. As a young woman she became closely involved with the temperance cause, joining the Daughers of Temperance for which she made her first speech, and for a time was a paid agent of the temperance movement. It was not until the early 1850s that she became interested in feminism, largely through her growing friendship with the prominent feminist leader Elizabeth Cady Stanton. At this time Susan Anthony was becoming deeply involved in the issue of women's right to speak at temperance conventions. Told that women were invited to listen but not to take part in the proceedings, a group of women formed their own association, the Women's State Temperance Society, with Susan Anthony as secretary. For a time, indeed, she was the recognized leader of the women's group. Her campaign to bring feminist issues into the temperance movement, in which she was assisted by Elizabeth Cady Stanton, soon aroused the hostility of other temperance workers. There was, for example, opposition to the bloomer costume that Susan Anthony had adopted at this time, as well as to the claim by Elizabeth Cady Stanton that no woman should remain in the relationship of a wife with a confirmed drunkard (Lutz, 1959; Oakley, 1972). An attempt by Susan Anthony to bar men from their meetings, although briefly successful, ultimately failed, and Elizabeth Cady Stanton was defeated for the presidency. When an attempt was made to rule out all discussions of women's rights both Susan Anthony and Elizabeth Cady Stanton resigned.

Clearly Susan Anthony did not succeed in drawing women temperance workers into feminism. This had to wait another twenty years when Frances Willard united women's suffrage and temperance in the aims of the Women's Christian Temperance Union. For Susan Anthony herself, however, the rebuff she suffered in the temperance organization confirmed her in her feminism. So did her campaign for a prohibition bill for New York, which convinced her that women needed the vote if their influence was to be effectively harnessed to reform. For her, and others like her, the temperance campaign was an important step on the way to feminism, just as moral reform had earlier led some women in the same direction. Other early feminist leaders who were also active in the temperance movement at some time in their careers include Lucretia Mott, Lucy Stone, Elizabeth Blackwell and the Grimké sisters.

In Britain, too, there was an association between the temperance movement and feminism, but on the whole, although women were involved in ladies' temperance committees, along with their involvement in missionary societies, they seem to have played a less dominant role than in the United States. The profession of full-time temperance agent was, for example, exclusively male (Harrison, 1971, p. 153). Nevertheless, from the 1850s women increasingly began to play a more important part. Mrs Wightman, a clergyman's wife, became the leader of the gospel temperance movement when she wrote a bestseller *Haste to the Rescue* in 1859 (Heasman, 1962, p. 132). Women also played a useful part in fund-raising and were valued for their organizing skills (Harrison, 1971, pp. 225–6; Hollis, 1979, p. 290). There is no evidence, however, that feminism became an issue inside the temperance movement as it did in the United States. Even after 1870, as we shall see in chapter 5, the British Women's Temperance Association, founded in 1876, was in sharp contrast to its American counterpart, the Women's Christian Temperance Union, in its relationship to feminism, as indeed in much else. So far as Britain is concerned therefore, we are left with the general impression that, although feminism tended to be sympathetic to temperance, the temperance movement as such played a much less significant part in the development of feminism than seems to have been the case in the United States.

It is in the anti-slavery campaign that we find the most important links between the evangelical movement and feminism. Like temperance, the anti-slavery movement was fundamentally a religious and moral issue, which was given fresh impetus by the religious revivals of the early nineteenth century (Carwardine, 1978, pp. 42–3). It was primarily motivated by disgust at the moral evils of slavery, a disgust that at least in the United States included a strong sexual basis. There was a fear that illicit sexual intercourse was embedded in the very conditions of life in the South where the presence of female slaves enabled white men to indulge their sexual needs without disgrace, so widespread was the sexual exploitation of black women. Indeed, vice could even be made profitable, since it produced fresh slaves for the market (Walters, 1973).

There is some evidence that this aspect of slavery aroused the opposition even of Southern women. Anne Firor Scott (1970) has suggested in her study *The Southern Lady* that expressions of anti-slavery feelings run through many personal documents, which also reveal a bitterness on the subject of sexual alliances with slaves and an undercurrent of concern about venereal disease. This aspect of the hostility to slavery is clear in the writings of the Grimké sisters, Southern women who migrated to the North and became leading members of the anti-slavery campaign (Lerner, 1967). We have in consequence a natural affinity between the anti-slavery movement, moral reform and temperance, all of which show an evangelical concern with the virtues of self-control. This may well have been why the anti-slavery movement in both the United States and Britain seemed to have a special appeal for women. From quite an early stage women began forming auxiliary societies while playing an important part both in fund-raising and in collecting signatures. In Britain, too, women's branches were important and their number grew rapidly after 1826. In 1833 for example, Garrison, the American leader, wrote in praise of the British women's achievement, including anti-slavery petitions signed by 80,000 women (Melder, 1977, p. 57). Even in the 1850s the women remained the backbone of the fund-raising effort, largely through their work with bazaars and sewing circles. Women were also important at this time in attempting to persuade the public to abstain from slave-grown products (Billington, 1966, Appendix pp. ii—ix). It seems, however, that women in the United States were pressing for a more important role in the affairs of the movement from quite an early stage. The original impetus to allow women into the men's organization seems to have come in large part from Lucretia Mott, a Quaker minister who had been influenced by Mary Wollstonecraft's *Vindication of the Rights of Women* and may indeed be described as the pioneer of American feminism. By the late 1830s, women were beginning to be accepted into some of the state societies, but there was considerable opposition and the years between 1837 and 1840 were years of controversy over the issue (Melder, 1977, pp. 95—112).

It was at this time, too, that the unconventional behaviour of the

Grimké sisters directed public attention to the role of women in the anti-slavery movement and probably increased the anxieties of those who were opposed to their wider participation. The two sisters were daughters of a wealthy slave-owning family whose hatred of slavery arose as a result of their personal observations. Although their specifically feminist writings came after their involvement in the anti-slavery campaign, the elder sister Sarah had a longing for education, the desire for independence and feelings of uselessness that undoubtedly provided a fruitful background for the development of a more specifically feminist consciousness. In their search for a more sympathetic environment, the two sisters moved to the North, became Quakers and, in the 1830s, became deeply involved in the increasingly active anti-slavery movement, at first in Philadelphia, later in New York. The fact that they had had personal experience of slavery and also their own undoubted abilities made their contribution particularly valuable and they were drawn into an ever more active participation both as writers and lecturers. The very fact that women were involving themselves so openly in political debate aroused considerable opposition, especially from the Churches, but the greatest hostility was aroused by their lectures to mixed audiences. This seems to have happened almost by accident at first, when men arrived at what were intended to be lectures for women, but later on it became deliberate policy. It may well have been the effect of this opposition, particularly from those who were working within the anti-slavery movement, that led the sisters into an increasingly outspoken feminism. In 1837 Sarah's letters on the equality of the sexes started appearing in newspapers and helped to widen the split in the anti-slavery movement, since even men who believed that women might be allowed a greater degree of participation in the movement did not necessarily want to see the anti-slavery issue linked too openly with the arguments for the rights of women, even when they personally believed these arguments to be correct. Indeed Sarah Grimké's feminism was very radical for its time. In a quite remarkable passage she claims that 'whatsoever it is morally right for a man to do, it is morally right for a woman to do' (Lerner, 1967, p. 193).

In 1840 the controversies within the movement reached a head and there was a split into two groups, one that was prepared to support women's wider involvement, the other that wished to confine women to auxiliary societies, represented at delegate conferences by men. It was not, however, only the women's issue that divided the movement. The pro-woman group, under the leadership of Garrison, was altogether more radical. For Garrison, abolition was essentially a moral crusade that must at all costs keep its purity and purpose. His opponents, essentially more political, were trying to extend support for the movement. They were interested in securing votes and making coalitions and did not want to alienate powerful groups like the clergy who were opposed to the women's claims. There were also specifically religious differences underlying the division. Garrison himself had religious views that were distinctly radical for his time. He believed that perfectability was in practice attainable by man (and denied the doctrine of innate depravity) bringing down upon himself the charge of heresy (Kraditor, 1967).

The anti-slavery movement as a whole certainly welcomed women as allies, and the leaders were more than willing to make use of their services so long as they remained subordinate and did not stray from what was then regarded as their proper sphere. Only if they stepped out of line did their support begin to be perceived as dangerous. The Grimké sisters had to suffer not only the attacks of their opponents but the criticism of their friends who urged them to curb their feminist arguments for the sake of the abolitionist cause. On the whole, however, the consequences of women's participation in the anti-slavery movement, as indeed in the movement for temperance and moral reform, were favourable to the development of feminism. At the very least their involvement in these campaigns, often at the invitation of male relatives and friends, gave them valuable experience in such fundamental if routine political activities as fund-raising and collecting signatures for petitions. At the same time, their enthusiasm for what they saw as a supremely moral cause gave some women at least the courage to break out of what they had been taught to regard as their proper sphere, and to brave the hostility that such behaviour aroused. Indeed this very hostility played its part, since by forcing the Grimké sisters to defend their behaviour it led them into a much more self-conscious articulation of women's rights, which became in time a specific demand for equality between the sexes.

Even more important in the history of the feminist movement is the now well-known exclusion of women delegates from the World Anti-Slavery Convention held in London in 1840. The acceptance of women delegates by the Garrisonian wing of the American movement had as one consequence the inclusion of four women in the American delegation to the London convention, one of whom was the influential Quaker Lucretia Mott. As we have seen, American abolitionists themselves were by no means united on the issue of women delegates, and it was probably no great surprise when after a lengthy debate the decision was taken not to admit women to the convention. Opposition to the entry of women into public debate undoubtedly lay behind this decision although it has been suggested that Quaker delegates might have been hostile to Lucretia Mott because she was a member of the Hicksite or radical wing of the Quaker movement (Cromwell, 1958, pp. 85—7). The most significant consequence of the exclusion of women, however, was the friendship that developed between Lucretia Mott and Elizabeth Cady Stanton, then the young wife of an abolitionist leader, which was to result eventually in the Seneca Falls Convention of 1848 and the beginning of American feminism as an organized social movement. The humiliation of the exclusion from the convention seems to have deepened the feminist consciousness already developing in both women.

The London Anti-Slavery Convention also makes clear the difference between the American and British movements. In spite of the presence of women in the British movement there is no evidence that these activities extended much beyond the fund-raising that was their main function, and there is no sign of any demand for a greater degree of participation in the general movement. At no time does there seem to have been a British equivalent of the Grimké sisters, and even as late as 1853 the Bristol and Clifton Ladies' Anti-Slavery Society appealed for a gentleman to organize public meetings, since this was still believed to be outside the scope of a ladies' society (Billington, 1966, p. 274). Nevertheless, in Britain as in the United States, the anti-slavery movement accustomed women to participate, even if in a subordinate role, in a political campaign, and gave them lessons in tactics that some of them were to turn to good account later on in pursuit of specifically feminist goals. Moreover, the exclusion of the American delegates does not seem to have gone unnoticed by British women. Indeed in the case of Anne Knight, a Quaker abolitionist, it led her in a few years to produce the first British leaflet on women's suffrage (Melder, 1977, pp. 116—17).

It would be wrong to leave this account of the evangelical movement as a source of feminism without drawing particular attention to the part played by the Quakers. Strictly speaking, Quakers were not part of the evangelical movement in that they were relatively untouched by the revivalism that was perhaps its most outstanding characteristic (Gilbert, 1976, pp. 40—1; Strout, 1974, p. 30). Nevertheless, the Quakers certainly shared the moral earnestness of the Evangelicals, and the Quaker faith like the ·evangelical enthusiasm provided a religious motivation for humanitarian reform. Nowhere is this more clearly expressed than in the abolition movement, which derived its earliest impetus, both in the United States and in Britain, from Quaker repugnance at the idea of slavery, even if, at a later stage, the leadership in Britain passed to Evangelicals like Wilberforce and in the United States to men like Theodore Weld and William Lloyd Garrison (Annan, 1955; Strout, 1974, pp. 142—9). Certainly Quakers and Evangelicals were happy to work together, even in Britain, where the Evangelicals, much less broadly based than in the United States, disapproved of Dissenters but were prepared to join with them whenever their interests coincided (Jones, 1952, p. 95).

Even more important for our purposes, however, is the significance of the Quaker movement as a source of feminism, providing as it did some of its earliest and most important leaders. This was particularly so in the United States, perhaps because of the greater significance of the anti-slavery campaign in contributing to feminist consciousness in that country, but perhaps also because of the different part played by religious motivation in the origins of the feminist movement in Britain and the United States.

The reason most usually given for the prominence of Quaker women amongst the early feminists in both countries is the special place afforded to women in their organization. Although there had been women preachers in many of the early sects, the Quakers were alone amongst the larger religious groups in allowing women not only to speak at meetings but to become ministers. This unusual religious freedom would have been most important in the early years of the movement when the prejudice against women speaking in public was very strong, and this probably helps to explain the pioneering work of Lucretia Mott in the United States and Elizabeth Fry in Britain, both of whom began their careers as Quaker ministers. Lucretia Mott was active in founding women's anti-slavery groups in the early 1830s and was already a significant figure in the movement when she was chosen as a delegate to the World Anti-Slavery Convention in 1840. Later she was, with Mrs Stanton, the moving spirit behind the Seneca Falls Convention in 1848 and remained an active and outspoken feminist until her death. Elizabeth Fry was never a feminist as such, but in her work for prison reform she was forced into public life and in 1818 became the first woman to be called to give evidence before a committee of the House of Commons. Criticized for neglecting her home and family, she defended herself in a short book written in 1827 aimed at ladies who wished to organize committees for prison reform. Denying any desire to 'persuade women to forsake their right province', she nevertheless went on to urge on women the claims of the 'helpless, the ignorant, the afflicted and the depraved of their own sex' (Whitney, 1937, pp. 240—1).

The association between Quaker women and feminism was to continue however. In Britain, Anne Knight, a Quaker and an abolitionist, was, as we have seen, responsible for the first leaflet on women's suffrage published in 1847, which led eventually to a petition to the House of Lords in 1851. Later, in the 1860s, Quaker women formed a powerful group in the National Society for Women's Suffrage (Ramelson, 1967, pp. 72, 81). Later still, in the 1870s Quakers were to be an important group in the campaign for the repeal of the Contagious Diseases Acts (Walkowitz and Walkowitz, 1974, pp. 194—6). In the United States, Quaker women were heavily involved in the Seneca Falls Convention. The small group who decided to call the conference were almost all Quakers (Flexner, 1974, p. 74) and among those who signed the Declaration the largest single religious affiliation was the Society of Friends (Paulson, 1973, p. 36).

This should not be taken to imply that the Quakers as a body were feminists either in principle or practice. Nor were their anti-slavery principles always carried forward whole-heartedly, which may explain why leadership in the movement passed into the hands of the Evangelicals. The Grimké sisters joined the Quakers as part of their fight against slavery but found that the views of the Philadelphia Quakers were too restricting to allow them the freedom to pursue their anti-slavery activities as they wished. By the time they were speaking and writing in both the abolitionist and feminist causes they had left the Quakers and were associating with radical, anti-slavery leaders like Lloyd Garrison and Theodore Weld. Nor did the British Quakers appear to have provided much support for the women delegates at the 1840 Anti-Slavery Convention in London when Lucretia Mott and her fellow-delegates were prevented from taking their seats (Stanton and Blatch, 1922, pp. 80—1).

The philanthropic and humanitarian zeal of both the Quakers and the Evangelicals clearly provided a fruitful background from which feminist ideas might emerge, but it is clear that even a deep involvement in such issues did not necessarily lead women to question their traditional role. As we have seen, women were often confined to very routine and limited tasks, carried out under male direction, and these must frequently have meant no more to the women involved than the traditional concern of women for dispensing charity to the poor. Indeed Nancy Cott (1977, pp. 156—7) has argued that a limited involvement in philanthropic activity could divert women from any desire for change by compensating them for their isolation and subordination. It must also be accepted that even those women who were led by their religious involvement to extend their view of women's role and to claim for them a share in the public sphere did not necessarily change their view of the feminine character. When Elizabeth Fry appealed to women to help 'the helpless, the ignorant, the afflicted, and the depraved' she was calling on qualities that were traditional aspects of femininity.

Moreover even when, in time, women preachers became popular within the evangelical movement, their message was unlikely to be a feminist one. Mrs Phoebe Palmer for example, who began her work in the United States in 1835 and who visited England to preach in 1859, expressly disclaimed any intention of urging women's rights or of seeking to revolutionize women's social or domestic relationships, even though she was radical enough in her practice to start speaking to sexually mixed audiences in 1839. She did, however, claim for women the right to play a larger part in the evangelical community (Carwardine, 1978, p. 188).

By the 1860s female preachers were an accepted part of the evangelical movement, associated with a fresh outbreak of revivalist sentiment and the establishment of full-time lay evangelists. Although in practical terms this extended the employment opportunities open to middle-class women, it was not associated with the emerging feminist movement and did not lead to the spread of feminist ideas. Indeed, Olive Anderson has argued that it often involved, for the women concerned, an explicit rejection of feminist theories. Catherine Booth, for example, accepted that a wife's subordination to her husband was part of Eve's punishment for her sin (Anderson, 1969).

To a large extent, therefore, the effect of the evangelical movement on feminism was to be conservative rather than radical, and even when it led women outside the home it was primarily in order to bring the domestic virtues into the public domain. There was little desire, in short, to change either the idea of femininity or the nature of domestic life; in so far as it was radical at all, it was in the attempt to 'feminize' the public sphere by bringing to it the values associated with the home. This tendency is already clearly apparent in the interest of the early feminists in such issues as temperance and the double standard and, as later chapters will show, was to become even more evident in the later years of the nineteenth century.

Nevertheless, women did move from evangelicalism to a feminism of a much more radical kind, and amongst these we must number those unknown women of the New York Female Moral Reform Society, whose interest, springing originally from revivalist fervour, spread from moral reform to such issues as women's low wages and poor employment opportunities and, as early as the 1860s, to the demand for the vote. The Grimké sisters moved from an initial interest in slavery to a far-reaching claim for women's rights, while Susan Anthony, one of America's best-known suffragists of the nineteenth century, was converted to feminism only after an early career in the temperance movement.

Other women, however, entered feminism by a different route. Lucretia Mott, for example, although a tireless worker in the anti-slavery movement, seems to have been influenced less by the evangelical movement than by the arguments of the Enlightenment. Moreover there is evidence, to be explored later, that this tradition was more prominent in the emergence of feminism in Britain, where, as we have seen, evangelicalism did not play so large a part in introducing women to feminism, although it introduced them into some forms of political activity. It is therefore to this second tradition in feminist thought that we must now turn.

3

The Campaign for Equal Rights

The arguments that inspired the French Revolution and justified the rights of man did not necessarily lead to the advocacy of the rights of women, since it was quite possible to define women as having a different nature from that of men. Nevertheless, the French school of rationalism was important in the development of feminist ideas and the question attracted a good deal of attention from French philosophers in the eighteenth century (Bouten, 1975, p. 52). Montesquieu, Diderot and Voltaire, for example, were all sympathetic to women's rights, although Rousseau was strongly anti-feminist and believed that women should be subordinate to men. Later, Concordet gave women's rights his unequivocal support, basing his argument clearly on woman's common humanity with man. Moreover, although the French Revolution did little to further the emancipation of women in France (Tomalin, 1974, ch. 13), the ideas behind the revolution were to be important in the development of feminism in England and in America. The Enlightenment emphasis on reason, natural law and equality of rights can be seen clearly in the writing of Mary Wollstonecraft, whose *A Vindication of the Rights of Women*, published in 1792, was one of the earliest feminist statements in England. A friend of many of the important radical intellectuals of the day, including men like Paine, Priestley and Godwin, Mary Wollstonecraft was well grounded in this tradition and had already written a defence of the rights of man before moving to the rights of women (Walters, 1976). Like William Godwin, later to become her husband, she shared the Enlightenment denial of all innate qualities, and this was extended to women both by Mary Wollstonecraft (Bouten,

1975, p. 7), and by later feminist writers like John Stuart Mill. This belief in the influence of the environment, and particularly education, on forming the differences between men and women is not only crucial to an understanding of all Mary Wollstonecraft's writings; it remained an important ingredient in equal rights feminism throughout the whole of the nineteenth century, and has had a profound influence on feminist thinking down to the present day.

Immediately successful, although later to fall into obscurity (McGuinn, 1978), *A Vindication of the Rights of Women* was to influence feminist thinking in both England and the United States. An early American pamphlet on the rights of women published by Hannah Mather Crocker in 1818 admitted a heavy debt to Mary Wollstonecraft (Flexner, 1974, p. 24). Lucretia Mott, one of the most important of the early feminists, kept a copy of *A Vindication of the Rights of Women* at a centre table in her home for forty years (Cromwell, 1958). Elizabeth Cady Stanton was another enthusiast and she and Lucretia Mott discussed Mary Wollstonecraft and her ideas at the World Anti-Slavery Convention in London in 1840 (McGuinn, 1978, p. 192).

The American Revolution, on the other hand, was able to provide a more direct influence on the American feminist movement (even if the revolution itself helped them no more than did the French Revolution the women of France), since the wording of the Declaration of Independence was the inspiration for the feminist principles that emerged from the Seneca Falls Convention in 1848. This convention, widely regarded as the beginning of organized feminism in the United States, arose out of a renewal of the friendship between Lucretia Mott and Elizabeth Cady Stanton when the Motts visited friends at Seneca Falls, the home of the Stantons. In a sentence-by-sentence paraphrase of the Declaration of Independence the authors claimed that men *and women* are created equal and share in the inalienable rights endowed by their Creator. They therefore specifically applied the language of natural rights to the relationship between men and women and laid claims to the equality of the sexes that is at the centre of the campaign for equal rights feminism.

In England the feminist doctrines of the Enlightenment were kept alive by groups of radical thinkers, of whom the Unitarians were probably the most important. Like the Enlightenment philosophers the Unitarians believed in the power of reason. They shared in the concepts of natural rights, of freedom and of toleration. In theology they rejected the doctrines of original sin, human depravity and absolute predestination (Holt, 1938, pp. 75, 279). They were ardent advocates of parliamentary reform, and were such enthusiastic supporters of the French Revolution that, in the years that followed, they suffered a good deal of persecution. Political reform and religious toleration continued to be important goals in the nineteenth century but Unitarians were very prominent in the anti-slavery campaign and, later, the campaign for the repeal of the Corn Laws.

In addition, the Unitarians, and particularly the more radical of their members, were highly responsive to the doctrine of women's rights. Evidence for this comes from the large number of early feminists who were Unitarians or who came from a Unitarian background (Holt, 1938, p. 19). One reason for this seems to have been the superior education given to girls in Unitarian families, but a contributory factor must also have been the strong tradition of reform characteristic of many of these households. To cite but one example we may take the case of Barbara Leigh Smith, later Barbara Bodichon, one of the first of the active feminist organizers. Her father was both a Unitarian and a radical MP, and her grandfather was William Smith, Wilberforce's lieutenant in the House of Commons during the slave trade campaign. She was given a very liberal upbringing and as a young woman was allowed an unchaperoned Continental tour with her friend and fellow feminist Bessie Parker. When Barbara came of age she was, most unusually, given her own income as if she had been a boy. It is also of interest that Bessie Parker too came from a Unitarian family, and was the great grand-daughter of the Unitarian Joseph Priestley whose sympathy for the French Revolution exposed him to mob violence (Burton, 1949).

The Unitarians as a group seem to have been particularly sensible to the education of girls, and many of those working in the educational wing of the feminist movement were from Unitarian backgrounds. Mary Wollstonecraft was a Unitarian and so was Harriet Martineau for many years of her life. As early as 1823 the *Monthly Repository,* the journal of the Unitarians, published an article by Harriet Martineau 'On Female Education' that denied the inferiority of the female mind and, like Mary Wollstonecraft, argued the necessity for an improvement in the education of girls if they were to fulfil their obligations as wives and mothers (Mineka, 1972, p. 159).

Under the editorship of William Fox the *Monthly Repository* was to become even more feminist in its outlook, and in 1832 it published an outspoken article by Fox himself that included the idea of female suffrage. When, however, Fox went on to argue for the liberalization of the divorce laws, he seems to have gone too far for many of the Unitarians and there were protests in 1833 at the tone and content of articles in the journal on divorce. Matters were further complicated by Fox's own marital difficulties, which became public knowledge at that time and probably contributed to his views on the need for divorce reform. In the ensuing dispute, the majority of Fox's own congregation remained loyal but he was expelled from the Unitarian Church and the *Monthly Repository* ceased to represent the Unitarians (Mineka, 1972, pp. 193—6).

Fox is also important as a friend of John Stuart Mill, and so provides a link between the Unitarians and the philosophic radicals, who were themselves sympathetic to feminism and whose journal *The Westminster Review* also published essays on feminism in the early 1830s. It was Fox who introduced John Stuart Mill to Harriet Taylor, a Unitarian and one of Fox's congregation. Indeed, it is possible that Harriet Taylor's ideas on feminism influenced both Fox and John Stuart Mill (Rossi, 1970, pp. 3—63). Both the philosophic radicals and the Unitarians were, however, very clearly influenced by Enlightenment principles in the development of their feminism. This is abundantly clear, for example, in John Stuart Mill's famous essay on *The Subjection of Women* where we find him placing the rights of women as part of a universal process in which the rule of force is replaced by the rule of reason. Furthermore, he draws a direct analogy between the power of the husband and that of the despotic ruler or slave-owner, and sees the female struggle for independence as a continuation of the struggle of the people to be free of the rule of the tyrant. It is in this context, as we shall see, that the struggle for the suffrage came to seem the culmination of the women's rights movement.

Strangely enough, the Unitarians seem to have played a smaller part in the feminist movement in the United States than they did in Britain. Pioneering feminists, as we have seen, tended to come from Quaker backgrounds, or sometimes, as in the case of the Grimké sisters, came to join the Quakers because of their position on slavery. Susan Anthony is rather exceptional in that, although originally a Quaker, she became a Unitarian when the Society of Friends in Rochester were unfriendly to the anti-slavery movement (Lutz, 1959, p. 24). Elizabeth Cady Stanton also moved towards Unitarianism in the 1840s (Melder, 1977, p. 157).

Originally at least, the American Unitarians certainly seem to have shared many of the radical political characteristics of the British movement. The leaders of the American Revolution were deistical or Unitarian rather than Calvinist in their religious beliefs and both Adams and Jefferson were in fact Unitarians. By the early years of the Nineteenth century, however, the Unitarian movement in America was swamped by the evangelical revivals, and although Jefferson expected Unitarianism to become the majority religion in America, by 1850 more than 90 per cent of the churches were located in New York and New England with especial prominence in Boston. It is possible too that by becoming, as Cushing Strout describes it, 'a badge of the prestigious social and literary establishment of Boston' it changed into a predominantly intellectual movement and lost some of its sympathy for any active involvement in reform (Strout, 1974, p. 126). Daniel Walker Howe (1970, pp. 125—301) has depicted the Boston Unitarians as political conservatives, followers of Burke rather than Paine, who habitually hesitated even on the issue of slavery.

This should not be taken to mean that Unitarians were entirely absent from American reform movements during these years. Unitarians were indeed active in the anti-slavery campaigns, but it was as individuals and in a purely unorganized way (Howe, 1970, p. 277). Nor do we have any reason to suppose that they were unsympathetic to feminism, and certainly their doctrines, which included the perfectability of man and the influence of the environment upon personal character (Howe, 1970, p. 305), were quite compatible with feminist aspirations. Indeed Melder (1977, p. 157) claims that in Massachusetts and New York many feminists were Unitarians, and Cott (1977, pp. 204—5) that in Ithaca, New York, feminists were more likely to come from the Unitarians than from the Evangelicals. On the other hand, Unitarians were not as prominent as they were in Britain in providing either the initial impetus or the leadership of the newly emerging movement, and it is perhaps significant that in her history of feminism Eleanor Flexner (1974) includes nine page references to the Quakers in the index and none at all to the Unitarians.

The evidence on the Unitarians, therefore, tends to support the argument set out in the previous chapter that the Evangelicals were a more important influence on feminism in the United States than in Britain, where the Enlightenment tradition, operating to a large extent through the Unitarians, seems to have been stronger. This is not to suggest that Enlightenment ideas were absent from

American feminism — attention has already been drawn to the use made of the Enlightenment-inspired Declaration of Independence at the Seneca Falls Convention in 1848. Moreover, as we have seen, both the Quaker Lucretia Mott and Elizabeth Cady Stanton were deeply influenced by the Enlightenment doctrines of Mary Wollstonecraft. We are concerned in short with a difference in emphasis only, and there is no doubt, as we shall see, that a concern with natural rights was never entirely absent from the American feminist movement. If, however, the leadership of the British movement was more likely to have come from the more rationalist Unitarians or, in the case of John Stuart Mill, the philosophic radicals, it is necessary to consider the effect of this on the nature of the British movement.

In the first place it must be admitted that, in spite of the early example of Mary Wollstonecraft and her influence on both sides of the Atlantic, feminism as a social movement was slower to start in Britain than in the United States. There seems to have been nothing strictly comparable to the self-conscious feminism of the 1830s, which saw not only the writing and lecturing of the Grimké sisters and of Lucretia Mott, but their very active involvement in the anti-slavery movement. The militant stance of the American Female Moral Reform Society on the double standard was also taking on strongly feminist overtones at this time. Nevertheless the 1830s in Britain were by no means devoid of an interest in feminist ideas. I have already noted the stand taken on women's rights and specifically women's suffrage by the philosophic radicals and some of the more radical Unitarians, which resulted in the publication of several journal articles on this theme. Female suffrage was also discussed, albeit briefly, by the Chartists, and a number of women's political associations were founded specifically to further Chartist aims, thus introducing women to the tactics of political campaigning even if not specifically for themselves (Thompson, 1976). The 1830s and 1840s were also years during which Saint-Simonians and Owenites were active in propagandizing their views on women's rights (Pankhurst, 1957, p. 123). These years also saw the first attempts to improve the education of girls, to find alternative employment for women and to raise the issue of married women's rights to the guardianship of their children. They were years, therefore, that saw much public debate on the position of women in society even if there was as yet nothing that could be called a movement. Even in the United States, however, the feminist movement cannot properly be said to have begun until the

Seneca Falls Convention of 1848 brought together a group of women organized around a specifically feminist platform. The anti-slavery campaign had been of great importance in laying the groundwork for American feminism but the men in the movement were always anxious that feminist claims would harm the cause of the Negro. Consequently, although some of its leaders were sympathetic, at no time was the campaign openly feminist; indeed it was to abandon the women's cause altogether at the end of the Civil War. Similarly, although the American Female Moral Reform Society through its journal attacked low wages and demanded expanded opportunities for women, it does not seem to have become the nucleus of an organized movement. Nor do there seem to have been any links between its membership and the women who came together at Seneca Falls, or those who were drawn into the group subsequently. Further research may throw up such links, but the leading feminists of the 1840s and 1850s seem, from the account we have, to have been drawn into feminism through the anti-slavery and temperance movements rather than moral reform.

In Britain it was 1856 before an organized feminist movement may be said to have come into existence. This was the celebrated circle that gathered around Barbara Leigh Smith and Bessie Rayner Parkes, sometimes known as the 'Ladies of Langham Place', both of whom, as was described earlier, were from radical Unitarian backgrounds. In 1856 Barbara Leigh Smith organized a committee to collect petitions for the Married Women's Property Bill then before Parliament. In 1858 in association with Bessie Rayner Parkes and Mrs Jameson, a noted feminist author, they founded the *Englishwoman's Journal,* which quickly became a major forum for the discussion of women's problems. In 1859 a Society for Promoting the Employment of Women was founded with offices in the same building in Langham Place and from this nucleus sprang a Ladies Institute with a reading room and a small club. The group at Langham Place was not only a centre for feminist activity, it was also, and perhaps even more importantly, a source of recruitment to the movement. Emily Davies, leader of the campaign to open higher education to girls, and Elizabeth Garrett Anderson, the first woman doctor, were both drawn into the circle almost from the first (Burton, 1949). Moreover, it was this same group of women who started the suffrage campaign in the 1860s. To a very large extent, therefore, the activities of this group may be taken as almost synonymous with feminism at this time, just as the little group that clustered around Elizabeth Cady Stanton represent the core of mid-century feminism in the United States. It is to the specific activities of these two groups, therefore, that we must now turn.

The immediate impetus behind the establishment of the Langham Place circle was the reform of the legal position of married women. This had been raised initially by Caroline Norton, not herself a feminist but a woman who had in her own person suffered from the disabilities imposed by the law on married women's property and on the guardianship of children. Her efforts had helped to secure a limited improvement in the law with respect to infant custody in 1839, but it was not until the 1850s that the issue of married women's property became a matter for political debate. In 1854 Barbara Leigh Smith, with the help of a family friend, the Recorder of Birmingham, drew up and published a pamphlet on the legal position of women. The issue was taken up by the Law Amendment Society, which recommended changes in the law, and in 1857 a Married Women's Property Bill passed its second reading in Parliament. In fact, however, much of the support for the bill came from sympathy with the hardships of separated wives, hardships, for example, that Caroline Norton had suffered and that she was now urging on the attention of Parliament. When the Divorce Bill of 1857 offered protection to such women, the strongest case for a more radical bill was removed (Holcombe, 1977). Not until 1882 and after much further campaigning did the Married Women's Property Act give to married women, as of right, their property and earnings (Strachey, 1928, pp. 272—6).

The legal rights of women were also part of the objectives of the early feminist movement in the United States. The Seneca Falls Declaration gave prominence to a number of legal disabilities, and claimed the rights of married women to property and earnings, the guardianship of children and equal rights in divorce. Elizabeth Cady Stanton was deeply involved in these issues ever since, as a young girl, she had seen the effects of the law, as it then stood, in the cases that came to her father's law office (Stanton and Blatch, 1922, p. 33). Indeed post-revolutionary changes in property law had had the effect of worsening the position of American women, as for example in the ending of equity trusts to protect the property of married women from their husbands (Sachs and Wilson, 1978, pp. 75—7). Such trusts, which were in common use in wealthy families in Britain, did not allow a wife the use of her property but protected it from fortune-hunters.

Between 1839 and 1865 many states had passed some kind of legislation recognizing the right of married women to hold property, but these changes not only were limited in their extent, and for example frequently excluded earnings, but were not principally the result of feminist agitation. Indeed the very earliest of the Acts in Mississippi in 1839 was passed without any feminist pressure at all (Riegal, 1970, pp. 96, 216). Similarly the 1848 Married Women's Property Act in New York State was the work of the leaders of the Dutch aristocracy who were concerned to keep their property out of the hands of shiftless sons-in-law (Stanton and Blatch, 1922, p. 149). Andrew Sinclair (1966, p. 87) claims that it was introduced by a conservative judge who wanted to secure his wife's property against his creditors in case of financial disaster.

This is not to suggest that women played no part in the campaigns. In New York State, for example, Mrs Ernestine Rose was collecting signatures for petitions from 1836 to the passing of the Act in 1848 (Flexner, 1974, p. 65). Later on, in 1854, Susan Anthony began a further campaign in the state aimed to secure for women the right to control of their own earnings and to the guardianship of their children in the case of divorce, neither of which was part of the original Act. Elizabeth Cady Stanton was also heavily involved, presenting her case to the New York State legislature in 1854 and again in 1860. A woman was also active in initiating the campaign in Massachusetts that led to the passing of a Married Women's Property Bill in 1854 (Flexner, 1974, pp. 85—93). Moreover, Sachs and Wilson claim that wherever the women's movement was particularly active 'property reforms affecting women, though quite limited, were more comprehensive than where there were no organized female activists' (Sachs and Wilson, 1978, p. 79).

Thus the battle for legal rights was an important aspect of the early feminist movement in both the United States and Britain. In part this was a consequence of the inability of the law to protect the interests of women left defenceless by the doctrine of the unity of married couples. Without a legal identity of her own, a deserted or ill-treated wife was unable to use the law to defend her interests. Moreover, within marriage she had no rights over her own person, her own property (for even if protected by trusts she was denied the use of it), her earnings and even her own children. It was not difficult, either in Britain or the United States, to collect examples of husbands who squandered their wives' property, abused them physically or denied them access to their young children. What is more, there was no protection for the wife in the knowledge of her own innocence since these rights belonged to the husband however badly he infringed the century's own moral code. Indeed, it was perhaps this more than anything else that aroused not only the anger of the feminists, but the sympathy of women uncommitted to the feminist cause and of the men who helped to change the law. Legislators and lawyers also supported the Acts for less altruistic reasons, particularly in the United States where the various Married Women's Property Acts were used as an alternative to the system of trusteeship, which protected what was essentially family property from fortune-hunters and preserved it for heirs. For those who acted from this kind of motive there was no necessary connection between the legal changes they supported and the doctrine of equal rights for women. Those, both men and women, who sympathized with the wife defrauded of her property or deprived of her children often saw little need for any extension of these rights to women living with their husbands.

To those of the feminists and their male supporters who were influenced by more general principles the issue was a wider one, even if they too were moved by cases of individual hardships. This is made very clear in the feminist writings of John Stuart Mill, who perceived the authority of the husband over the wife as one of domestic tyranny comparable with that of the power of an absolute ruler over his subjects or a slave-owner over his slaves. To those who argued that not all husbands were tyrants in practice, he pointed out the folly of judging an institution by its best instances and argued that 'the relation of superiors to dependants is the nursery of those vices of character, which, wherever they exist, are an overflowing from that source' (Rossi, 1970, p. 165). Mill's phrases were echoed by Susan Anthony in 1872 at the time of her trial for exercising what she claimed to be her right to vote. Describing the legal and political position of women, like Mill, as one of servitude, she went on to ask, 'is all this tyranny any less humiliating and degrading to women under our democratic-republican government today than it was to men under their aristocratic, monarchical government one hundred years ago?' (Sachs and Wilson, 1978, p. 89).

By the time Susan Anthony spoke these words, however, the feminist movement in both countries was increasingly occupied in the battle for the vote, and less and less attention was paid to legal reform. In Britain the struggle continued to some extent until the success of the Married Women's Property Bill of 1882 removed the worst of the legal disabilities facing married women, but in the United States by 1870 the suffrage campaign occupied the centre of the stage. During these years there was very little change in the legal position of married women. Moreover, as we shall see later, in spite of some reforms in the years immediately after the granting of suffrage to women, it was left to the new women's movement emerging in the 1960s to take up these legal issues again.

The struggle to change the legal position of married women was, however, only one of the issues that occupied the early years of the feminist movement. An even greater preoccupation was the struggle to enlarge employment opportunities and, as a necessary prerequisite to this, to improve the educational qualifications of those seeking employment. This was particularly true in Britain where a Society for Promoting the Employment of Women was founded by the Langham Place group in 1859. The new society was inspired by an article by Harriet Martineau published in the *Edinburgh Review* in 1859. Although not herself one of the Langham Place circle and indeed unwilling to identify herself too closely with the women's rights movement, she was nevertheless a life-long feminist. Born, like so many other feminists at this time, into a Unitarian family, she overcame many difficulties to establish herself as a highly successful writer. The collapse of her father's business after his death forced her to face the problem of a young middle-class woman who suddenly has to support herself. For a time, indeed, she worked at sewing and basket making, before her literary success made her financially independent. Like Mary Wollstonecraft before her, she believed firmly in the need to educate girls to their fullest capacities and her writings returned again and again to this theme (Walters, 1976).

In her article in the *Edinburgh Review* she drew upon the census of 1851 to illustrate the problem of 'surplus' women who could never marry, simply because there were not enough men to go round. This anxiety about 'surplus' or 'redundant' women was indeed one that was to agitate Victorian society for many years to come, a problem exacerbated by the higher rates of male emigration, by the postponement of marriage by the middle classes and by the unwillingness of men in the upper and middle classes to marry at all (Banks, 1964, pp. 27—30). The remedies for this situation were not necessarily feminist, indeed it is probable that most were not, but there is little doubt that the recognition of this problem, and the anxiety it caused, gave some powerful argument to the feminists and rallied support to their campaign.

The newly formed Society for Promoting the Employment of Women set to work with vigour. Not only did it operate an employment exchange, but, perceiving the extent of the problems, it set in motion a series of experimental ventures to place women in hitherto masculine occupations (Holcombe, 1973, p. 16). These included the Victoria Press, a printing business run by women compositors, and a law stationer's office. From the Langham Place circle, too, came the first impetus to open the professions to women. A series of lectures by the first American woman doctor, Elizabeth Blackwell, were given under their auspices, and it was these lectures that inspired Elizabeth Garrett, later to become the first woman doctor in Britain, to take up the study of medicine herself (Manton, 1965, p. 49). Elizabeth Garrett had been inspired initially by reading articles on eminent women in the *English-woman's Journal* and later was drawn into the Langham Place circle. The journal, indeed, played a very important part in the campaign for the employment of women, not only urging the need for extending employment opportunities but waging a battle with those who tried to maintain a traditional view of women's role (Banks, 1964, pp. 33—4).

It was clearly recognized, however, that the work of opening careers for women was dependent upon the provision of suitable qualifications, and the necessary educational background. Even that traditional standby of impecunious middle-class girls, the profession of governess, needed an education beyond that possessed by most of those trying to enter it, and the Langham Place group found that they needed not only to seek out possible openings but also to provide girls with the necessary training. At the same time they supported, by their writing and by personal encouragement, moves to improve secondary education for girls and, more especially, the attempts to open up higher education for women.

Arguments for an improvement in the education of girls were not of course new, since they dated at least from the eighteenth century. Nor was a critique of the frivolity characteristic of girls' education in the middle and upper classes confined to the feminists. A conservative Evangelical like Hannah More believed as strongly in the necessity to revolutionize the system of female education with its stress on 'accomplishments' as did Mary Wollstonecraft. For Hannah More, girls needed an education that would better enable them to fulfil their customary duties as wives and mothers and as guardians of the traditional religious virtues. The new educational regime she suggested was therefore designed to emphasize women's duties rather than their rights and different from the context of natural rights in which Mary Wollstonecraft framed her plea for a better education for girls (Jones, 1952). Yet, like Hannah More, Mary Wollstonecraft also claimed that education would make women better mothers and, as we shall see, this attempt to argue that education both gave women economic independence and prepared them more effectively for the role as wife and mother was to be typical of nineteenth-century feminist thinking.

The drive for a change in the education of girls came therefore both from an evangelical opposition to frivolity, which was shared by other groups like the Quakers, as well as from an Enlightenment concern with human rights and human rationality. Nor indeed were the first moves in the campaign that eventually changed the situation specifically feminist in intent. In 1841, anxiety at the plight of governesses led to the founding of the Governesses' Benevolent Institution, which was largely a philanthropic organization concerned with the provision of financial aid to governesses in distress. At this stage in fact it was one of the charitable endeavours that I have described as part of the evangelical tradition. The growing belief that these women would best be helped by improving their qualifications led in 1847 to a series of lectures and a year later to the foundation of Queen's College for Women, largely inspired by the Christian socialist Frederick Maurice who, although not unsympathetic, was by no means a feminist. The college itself was governed by men, and Maurice, although he later changed his mind, was opposed to women entering men's professions (Strachey, 1928, p. 168). In 1849 however Bedford College was founded, this time largely under Unitarian auspices with the aim of providing a non-denominational college. Bedford, unlike Queen's included both men and women in its management. However, the colleges did not differ greatly in their courses, which at this stage were nearer to secondary than higher education, and they were both to be important in giving the necessary impetus to a much wider movement for the establishment of an effective secondary education for girls. The two famous headmistresses, Miss Buss and Miss Beale, both of whom began their work in the 1850s, had attended classes at Queen's College and their work furnished the pattern for the schools of the future (Holcombe, 1973, p. 27).

It was in higher education, however, that the main feminist

struggle was to be fought out, and this was largely the work of Emily Davies, herself one of the Langham group. She met Barbara Leigh Smith, by now Barbara Bodichon, in 1857 and thereafter became increasingly involved with the group, particularly after 1864 when she settled in London. She was envious of her brother's career at Cambridge, where he was President of the Union, and devoted her life to opening higher education to women. Although chiefly associated with her work in the establishment of Girton College at Cambridge, which she started to plan with Barbara Bodichon in 1867, she was active on a wide front, campaigning for women to be admitted to matriculation at London University for example, and supporting Elizabeth Garrett in her fight to gain a medical training. It is, however, in her determination to resist special examinations for women that Emily Davies must be seen as specifically feminist in her attitude to the education of girls. She was the acknowledged leader of what Sara Delamont (1978, p. 154) calls the 'uncompromising' campaigners, who feared that special courses would be of little use in demonstrating women's ability to compete with men on equal terms. Nor would such courses be of use in the campaign to open professional occupations to women. She therefore adopted an attitude of unyielding hostility to the other Cambridge college, Newnham, which, under the leadership of Anne Jemima Clough, was prepared to accept different standards for girls (Tullborg, 1975, p. 50). The same struggle also occurred at Oxford, where the uncompromisers founded Somerville in opposition to Lady Margaret Hall.

To some extent the opposition between the two groups was one of tactics. To compromise often seemed the better policy in the beginning, since it took account of the weaknesses in the educational background of women students and the difficulties they faced in following the same courses as the men over the same period of time. Similarly, to compromise meant to avoid some of the hostility that was aroused by direct competition with men, and to avoid the charge that to expose girls and women to the same curriculum as boys and men, and to expect from them the same standards, would be ruinous to their health and happiness (Atkinson, 1978). There were also the arguments of men like Henry Sidgewick who did not want to perpetuate the weaknesses of the existing system and feared, rightly or wrongly, that imitation by the women students would stand in the way of reform (Tullborg, 1975, pp. 39—45). For some, therefore, the acceptance of separate standards was largely a policy of gradualism, and it is certainly true that the separatist colleges soon became identical with those that had from the start operated on principles of strict equality.

On the other hand, there were many, even within the ranks of the educational reformers, who believed that the education of girls should proceed permanently on different lines from that of boys. Even Miss Beale, for example, disagreed with the policy of presenting girls for the same examinations as boys, believing that the spirit of rivalry that it might encourage would endanger 'the true woman's ornaments of a meek and quiet spirit' (Raikes, 1908, pp. 146—7). As we have noticed, moreover, many of those who supported a less frivolous education for girls took a predominantly conservative view of women's role. Even so convinced a feminist as Emily Davies, therefore, had to proceed cautiously, and although she was quite uncompromising on educational standards she was forced to submit to many conventional opinions on ladylike behaviour. Moreover, the educational campaign had to dissociate itself not only from such unsavoury controversies as the campaign for the repeal of the Contagious Diseases Acts but even from the fight for women's suffrage. But to accept separate educational standards for girls and women was to abandon altogether the principles of equality on which feminists like Emily Davies rested their faith. It would have implied, as Sara Delamont (1978, p. 159) has argued, the confinement of women 'in an intellectual and spiritual purdah', which was the very negation of the equality of opportunity that equal rights implied.

In the United States the reform of girls' education came earlier than in Britain partly, it has been suggested, because in America an ornamental education was associated with an outmoded aristocratic vanity and subservience to European mores. It is likely, too, that the seriousness of purpose that accompanied the evangelical revivals and that was probably more widespread in the United States, also played a part. Certainly, articles putting forward a plea for educating women for their maternal and domestic role, rather than in frivolous 'ornaments', were commonplace as early as the 1820s, and when Emma Willard submitted her proposal for a state-sponsored seminary for girls in 1819 it was based on women's duties as wives and mothers (Cott, 1977, pp. 117—21). In 1821 she opened the pioneering Troy Seminary for Girls, which made a serious attempt to raise standards and was to be an important model for later developments. Even in the South the inadequacy of women's education was a favourite topic, and the years 1830 to 1860 saw the foundation of colleges, seminaries and academies for women. As in the North, however, the debate was couched in terms of the better fulfilment of their female responsibilities (Scott, 1970, p. 71).

One of the most important figures in the American movement for the reform of the education of girls was Catherine Beecher (Sklar, 1973), who combined the role of practical reformer with that of philosopher and propagandist. She opened her first school in 1823, soon after Emma Willard opened Troy Seminary, and by 1831, when she left, it was one of the most celebrated academies in New England. Like Emma Willard, she too saw the need to raise the intellectual standard of girls' education in strictly separatist terms. In neither case was any attempt made to copy the content of boys' education, and domestic economy featured as a significant aspect of the curriculum. In no sense, it is true, did Beecher subscribe to the view of women as inferior to men although she recognized that they might need to be subordinate. Indeed, in some respects women were conceived as superior, since they were the moral guardians of the social code and hence the potential saviours of the nation. Nevertheless, their civilizing mission was based squarely on their domestic role. Fully accepting the doctrine of separate spheres, she saw women as exerting their influence chiefly in the better fulfilment of their traditional domestic and maternal tasks within the home. One of her most successful ventures was an influential Treatise on Domestic Economy, which was reprinted nearly every year from 1841 to 1856.

While she recognized that not all women would, or indeed could, marry — since, in the East at least, there was a 'surplus' of women so that they needed to be able to be self-supporting if necessary — she saw their future in an extension of the domestic role in nursing and especially teaching, which she considered as a particularly suitable occupation for women. Indeed, she worked for many years to gain acceptance for the idea of teaching as a female profession as well as campaigning for an improvement in teacher education. In her stress on the difference between male and female roles, and in her emphasis on women's duties, Catherine Beecher was therefore poles apart from those feminists who argued for an extension of women's rights. In 1837 she specifically challenged the Grimké sisters in what was to become a two-year public debate. She strongly disapproved of the attempts of the sisters to enter into public life and argued that women should remain within the domestic and social circle. For this reason she continued to oppose the plea for equal political rights for women.

Moreover, although she recognized the importance of economic independence, she did not at first support equal pay and used women's low cost as an argument for the employment of female teachers. In later life she modified her views a little, and by 1871 was prepared to support equal pay. On the other hand, her concern with the economic independence of the unmarried woman meant that at no time can she be regarded simply as a conservative so far as the position of women is concerned.

Something of the same ambiguity is revealed in the attitude of Elizabeth Blackwell, the first woman doctor. Born in England in 1821 and emigrating to the United States as a girl, she came, like so many others of her generation of feminists, from a strongly anti-slavery background and had serious ideas about reforming society. In the 1830s she read and was influenced by the Grimké sisters (Wilson, 1970). Her decision to become a doctor in 1846 followed an unhappy love affair, and was suggested by a dying friend who stressed the need for women doctors. On the other hand, although two of her brothers married active feminists (Henry married Lucy Stone and later Sam married Antoinette Brown), she was never closely involved in the fight for equal rights. Indeed, when her brother Henry married Lucy Stone in 1855 she disapproved of Lucy's refusal to take his name, as she did of the bloomer costume that Lucy, like other feminists, was wearing at this time. Her attitude to women doctors also shows some similarities with the views of Catherine Beecher on women teachers. In her lectures in London in 1859 she stressed the special contribution that women can make to medicine through women's ability to subordinate the self to the welfare of others, and pointed out that the great essential fact of woman's nature is the spiritual power of maternity.

The main opposition to Catherine Beecher's views on education came from equal rights feminists like Susan Anthony. In early life a school teacher, she won in 1853 the right for women to speak at the state teachers' convention in Rochester where she argued for equal pay, claiming that the low wages of women were the cause of the low status of teaching. Opposed to the idea of educating women for motherhood, she championed coeducation and argued that there was no more need for a special education for mothers than there was a need for a special education for fathers (Lutz, 1959).

By the last quarter of the nineteenth century it was possible to find women's colleges that were insisting on the same curriculum and the same entry standards for girls as in the best of the men's colleges. Bryn Mawr is perhaps the most famous of these, and its founder Martha Carey Thomas was determined to provide women with the knowledge, skills and prestige previously preserved for men (Cross, 1965, p. 31). She was a fierce opponent of all special courses for women and from the age of 14 set out to 'show that women can learn, can reason, can compete with men' (Delamont, 1978, p. 156; Wein, 1974).

On the other hand, many other colleges continued to confine women to a special curriculum and to define women's education in terms of their vocation as wives and mothers. Even Oberlin College, one of the earliest examples of coeducation in higher education, discriminated between its male and female students in many ways. The women students, for example, were expected to cook and clean for themselves and for the male students (Conway, 1974). The home economics movement, too, with its traditional conception of women's role, was to continue to play an important part in the development of women's education during the nineteenth century (Weigley, 1974). Even elite women's colleges did not necessarily follow the line of approach of Bryn Mawr. Wellesley College, for example, tried to combine high intellectual standards with a concern for women's future domestic role, and Bryn Mawr was to remain the exception rather than the rule. Even Bryn Mawr itself was to become more traditional as the influence of Carey Thomas declined and, by 1910, the period that 'had produced Bryn Mawr's sharply characterized independent women had passed' (Wein, 1974, p. 45).

The movement for the better education of girls and women was therefore a highly complex one, involving as it did both an evangelical emphasis on the preparation of women for their moral duties as wives and mothers, and an equal rights claim for equal opportunities for women in terms both of their right to intellectual development and of their need for better employment opportunities. Practical problems, like the needs of the so-called 'surplus women', also played their part, and the attempt to give such girls the education and training needed to support themselves was often received sympathetically, especially when it did not pose any threat to male monopolies in the professions or in skilled employment (Deacon and Hill, 1972). Indeed, in the last quarter of the century there were great improvements in girls' secondary education and a start was made in opening up higher education to women. At the same time, employment opportunities for woman expanded, partly through the growth of semi-professions like nursing and teaching, partly through the enormous expansion of white-collar employment (Holcombe, 1973).

The evangelical tradition therefore continued to play its part within feminism, upholding as it did the domestic ideal of woman as wife and mother in direct opposition to the equal rights feminists who tried to challenge women's narrow confinement to these roles. Indeed, for many of these women the search for economic independence through education meant more than providing for 'surplus women' who could not hope to marry. Even more important, perhaps, was the freedom it bestowed on women not to enter a loveless marriage or, in some cases, not to marry at all. By the end of the nineteenth century, celibacy had become for some women an alternative life style in which useful work and economic independence were seen as equally if not more satisfying than the traditional home and family. Indeed, of the Bryn Mawr women who graduated between 1889 and 1908, only 45 per cent ever married (Wein, 1974). Moreover, by arguing that girls be admitted to the same education as boys, be judged by the same examinations as boys and, ultimately, compete with men for entry into professions that had become accepted as male preserves, the equal rights feminists were forced into defending the Enlightenment position that there were no natural differences between the sexes, either in intellectual ability or in physical fitness (Atkinson, 1978, p. 129).

In contrast, Catherine Beecher stressed the differences between men and women, in terms of both their natural abilities and their social roles. Nevertheless, the importance she gave to the domestic values and women's part in maintaining them, whether inside the home or outside it in such occupations as teacher or nurse, justifies us in placing her, as does her biographer (Sklar, 1973, p. 137), firmly within the feminist camp. The emphasis on women's moral superiority that was part of Beecher's teaching and its significance for the survival of moral values within society itself is an essential ingredient of the doctrine of female superiority that led many later feminists, as we shall see, to believe that it was woman's mission to re-shape the whole of society. Moreover this reforming zeal, which came to characterize a great deal of feminism, especially in the United States, sprang directly from the spirit of the evangelical revival anxious not only to save souls but also, and in a sense perhaps even more importantly, to destroy sin.

The struggle between evangelical and equal rights feminism, with their different and indeed opposed views of female nature, which emerges clearly in the educational debate, was to continue to characterize the feminist movement and will indeed be a major theme of subsequent chapters. First, however, it is necessary to describe the third feminist tradition, that of socialism, and to examine the ways in which it has contributed to feminist thinking. The following chapter therefore will look at the feminism of the early socialists and its relationship with the organized feminist movement.

4

Feminism and the Socialist Tradition

The previous chapter has traced the influence of the French
Enlightenment on feminism through the writings of feminists like
Mary Wollstonecraft and of Unitarians like William Fox, but French
thought was also to be significant for the feminist movement in the
work of the Saint-Simonians through their British and American
disciples. Saint-Simon himself had little to say specifically on
women, but his disciples, and particularly Enfantin, placed great
emphasis not only on sex equality but on the position of women
within their own organization (Pankhurst, 1957). Their ideas were
introduced into Britain by converts like Anna Wheeler, a woman
whose unhappy marriage provided her with practical examples on
which to base her feminist views (Pankhurst, 1954a, b). In 1818,
having left her dipsomaniac husband several years previously, she
became the centre of one of the earliest Saint-Simonite circles in
Caen. After her husband's death in 1820 she became involved in
the various reform movements in London, where she was a close
friend of Jeremy Bentham. She was also the inspiration behind the
feminism of William Thompson, whose book *Appeal of one half
the human race* is the most important feminist treatise to come
after Mary Wollstonecraft's similar appeal thirty years earlier.
Inspired initially by James Mill's opposition to female suffrage, it
argued not only for an end to the legal, political, educational and
economic disabilities of women, but for equal rights in marriage
and an end to the double standard of sexual morality and men's
sexual abuse of women. Although appearing under his name, he
acknowledged her share in its authorship and, indeed, the
passionate language clearly comes from personal experience.

48

Later, Anna Wheeler became a frequent writer and lecturer on feminism. She was an important link between the Saint-Simonians and the English Owenites, and was one of the first to welcome Saint-Simonian missionaries to England, including Flora Tristan who made as many as four visits between 1826 and 1839. Indeed, during the 1830s the Saint-Simonian missionaries were very active in London and attracted a great deal of popular interest, including that of the young Tennyson (Killham, 1958, pp. 50—7).

To a large extent, of course, the views of the Saint-Simonians and of Anna Wheeler and William Thompson have their roots in the Enlightenment philosophers, and in many respects are identical with those of utilitarian feminists like John Stuart Mill and Unitarians like Fox. Indeed, both Mill and Fox were prepared to go a long way with the Saint-Simonians not only in the demand for greater sexual equality but also in their plea for a change in the marriage laws to allow for divorce for incompatibility (Mineka, 1972, p. 295). It was in their economic doctrine that the socialists parted company with the utilitarians, and it was in their belief that the principles of cooperation must replace those of competition, and especially in their advocacy of socialism or cooperative communities, that their feminism took on its most distinctive and indeed its most radical aspect.

The English communitarian movement originated in the ideas and activities of Robert Owen, although, as we have seen, there were close links between the Owenites and the Saint-Simonians from the 1820s. As early as 1812 Owen was 'convinced of the need for communal alternatives to the individual family system' (Harrison, 1969, p. 59). He saw the family as 'the main bastion of private property and the guardian of all those qualities of individualism and self-interest to which he was opposed' (Harrison, 1969, pp. 59—60). In order to reduce the effect of the family he advocated such measures as communal dining rooms and kitchens, and nursery schools. The main aim, it seems, was to strengthen community relationships, but it would also have the effect of emancipating women from household drudgery. Owen, like most of the Saint-Simonians, did not advocate the abolition of marriage and its replacement by completely free sexual relationships. Nevertheless, he did believe that affection, not property considerations, should be the basis of marriage and argued for a system of easy but regulated divorce. Moreover, although Owen himself was not an advocate of birth control, many of the later Owenites, like William Thompson and Owen's son Robert Dale

Owen, were amongst the earliest and most outspoken of the nineteenth-century birth-controllers (McLaren, 1978).

The feminist thinking of the Owenites is most clearly expressed in the life and work of Frances Wright. Born in 1795 in Dundee, the daughter of a radical, she fell under the spell of Byron and rejected religion. Like Thompson she became a friend of Jeremy Bentham but in America in 1824 she became converted to the idea of cooperative communities through a visit to the Owenite colony of New Harmony, and was inspired to found her own colony along even more radical lines (Lane, 1972). In 1828, while still in America, she began, in association with Robert Dale Owen, a campaign of lectures and articles that achieved great notoriety not only from the novelty of a woman lecturer but also because of the radical nature of her arguments, which combined feminism, socialism and the abolition of slavery with arguments against religion and the advocacy of birth control. Later, in 1833, she returned to lecture in England at a time when the Saint-Simonian missionaries were already arousing public interest in matters of this kind.

The communitarian movement was also influenced at this time by the ideas of the Frenchman Charles Fourier. His feminism was even more radical than that of most of the Owenites and the Saint Simonians since he argued that women should be free to form sexual alliances as they pleased. He was indeed remarkably permissive in his attitude to sexuality, especially for his time. In his utopia the sexes would be equal and both would be free to choose any kind of work, since domestic duties and the care of children would be carried out communally (Gray, 1944, pp. 191—2). Although Fourier had disciples in both France and England, and was indeed acquainted with Anna Wheeler, he was particularly influential in the United States where, in the 1840s, Fourierism became the dominant form of communitarianism. A number of short-lived communities were established, although not necessarily based very closely on Fourier's original plans (Muncy, 1973, pp. 67—92).

It was in the Oneida community, however, that the abolition of marriage was to be carried to its most extreme form. Founded in 1841 by John Humphrey Noyes, who was influenced by Fourier, the community was based on a form of group marriage in which every man was in theory the husband of every woman. Indeed, men and women were not simply allowed but expected to extend their sexual relationships widely, since to limit them was to allow personal ties to intrude into the ideal of the community; couples who showed a marked personal preference were separated. Sexual intercourse was deliberately detached from the procreation of children by the insistence on 'male continence' (in actuality a form of coitus reservatus) and the birth of children was decided on eugenic principles. Strong measures were also taken to reduce the ties between parent and child. The community was egalitarian up to a point, although sexual initiative was still a male prerogative in that the man, through an intermediary, sought permission for sexual intercourse, which the woman concerned could reject if she wished. Moreover, although housework and child-rearing were carried out communally, they were still regarded as female tasks. Nevertheless, the women were certainly allowed a greater degree of freedom than in the society around them (Muncy, 1973, pp. 164–92; Gordon, 1972).

Although part of the largely Fourier-influenced communitarianism of the 1840s, the inspiration behind Oneida was mainly religious. Taking its source in the enthusiasm of the earlier revivals, and influenced by the 'perfectionist' heresy and the quest for the regeneration of American society, the millenarianism of the early Evangelicals was now transformed into a belief in a purely earthly utopia (Cross, 1950, pp. 240–8, 324–7). It is not without significance in this connection that a splinter group of the evangelical New York Female Moral Reform Society followed Noyes into Oneida (Pivar, 1973, p. 42). The sexual communism of Oneida was based on a belief in the sacred nature of all love, both earthly and heavenly. Sexual intercourse, provided it was carried out within the rules of the community, was simply another way of binding the members together in the ties of love.

Although Oneida must therefore be placed in a religious rather than specifically socialist tradition, there are close links between it and the anti-religious Owenite communities since, like Oneida, these were inspired by the ideal of the perfect society in which conflict and competition would be replaced by harmony and cooperation. Moreover, like the socialist communities, Oneida sought to achieve feminist goals through changes in the structure of the family and in the cooperative organization of household work and child care.

If, however, feminist goals were an aspect of communitarian socialism, it remains to consider the extent to which they remained an aspect of socialism when the communitarian phase was over. Even in the 1830s during the height of the interest in the ideas of Saint-Simon and the Owenites there were some doubts expressed, in the radical socialist press, as to the wisdom of some of their views on women and marriage. In particular it was feared that such ideas would distract the mind of the public from the more important changes in property that must come first (Pankhurst, 1957, pp. 133—8). The Chartists were also highly ambiguous in their treatment of women. Although strongly influenced by the Owenites, and by William Thompson in particular, they never allowed feminism more than a peripheral place in their aims and objectives. William Lovett, it is true, included women's suffrage in the original draft of the People's Charter, but this was later omitted even if for tactical reasons rather than on grounds of principle. There is evidence, too, that women also played an active part in Chartist campaigns. Often these activities were auxiliary and traditional in that they involved preparing suppers, decorating halls and waggons, making banners and flags, but there is also evidence that they attended meetings and were often active in riots and demonstrations. Once Chartism was under way, however, there is no sign that they took any part in the formal organization of the movement (Thompson, 1976). Nor indeed does their involvement in Chartism seem to have led to any widespread demand by women for feminist goals.

This ambiguous attitude towards women was to continue to characterize socialist thinking throughout the rest of the century. It was also, as we shall see in detail in chapter 7, to characterize the developing trade union movement in both Britain and the United States. Some socialist thinkers were strongly anti-feminist. Babeuf, for example, saw women's nature as posing a threat to communist society, and advocated limiting women's education and maintaining their domestic subordination. Proudhon was also violently opposed to feminism, believing that woman's sensual nature represented a snare from which man must be protected by women's subordination. Similarly, half a century later, Sorel saw women as representative of the destructive power of sexuality, which must be restrained (McLaren, 1976). Although these were all more influential in France than in England, Hyndman and others in the Social Democratic Federation took an uncompromisingly conservative view of women (McLaren, 1978, pp. 159—63).

For Marx and Engels the emancipation of women remained a somewhat marginal question. Indeed Marx seems to have given it little thought. However neither can be described as anti-feminist in his views, and an examination of Engels' writings on the subject reveals a striking similarity with those of the communitarian socialists. For Engels, the key to women's inequality with men lay in their exclusion from socially productive work. Emancipation, then, was to be achieved by a liberation of women from housework and their large-scale participation in production. In the process the private sphere of housework and child care was to become a collective and therefore a public responsibility. This would only be possible however, according to Engels, with the abolition of private property and the coming of socialism. Consequently, the fortunes of women were irretrievably linked to the future of the working classes. Marriage under capitalism was also seen as part of the system of property relationships in which women were bought and sold, either legally within marriage itself or illegally as in prostitution. With the abolition of private property, marriage too would be freed to become a system of voluntary relationships based on love. In fact, Engels believed that working-class women were already less oppressed under capitalism than middle-class women because their marriages were less bound by property considerations. Engels therefore, like most of the communitarian socialists, did not envisage the abolition of either marriage or the family under socialism but rather its transformation. Nor does he seem to have envisaged an end to the traditional division of labour even after many of the woman's previous functions within the family have been socialized (Delmar, 1976).

It remains now to look at the reaction of the feminist movement to the socialist tradition of feminism. Clearly there were many points of contact between the beliefs of the feminists and the feminism of the socialists, grounded as they both were in the Enlightenment doctrine of equality. They could agree on the need to grant women equal rights before the law and the right to economic independence. Both groups also deplored the sexual oppression of women, whether inside or outside marriage, and wanted to put an end to the double standard of sexual morality. It might seem, therefore, that the socialists would have been the natural allies of the newly emerging feminist movement in Britain and the United States. In fact, however, this was very far from being the case, and indeed the organized feminist movement and the socialist movement tended to draw further apart as the nineteenth century progressed.

In the first place, even socialists who were also feminists might be unsympathetic to the organized feminist movement because of the limited nature of its goals. Thus Eleanor Marx, daughter of Karl Marx, argued in 1885 that 'it is with those who would revolutionize society that our work as women lies' (Tsuzuki, 1967, p. 24). In a pamphlet written in association with Edward Aveling (Aveling and Marx, 1886), she expressly repudiated the goals of the feminists, particularly suffrage and higher education, arguing that an improvement in the position of women would come along after the socialist revolution.

The feminists, on the other hand, were alarmed by the radical transformation of society envisaged by the socialists, including their unorthodox views on marriage and the family. By the phrase 'free love', of course, the socialists often meant no more than free choice. They were opposed to marriages arranged by parents with property considerations in mind, and to marriages entered into simply for economic support. The only proper basis for marriage was love. Opposition to the loveless marriage was, however, taken further and in a much more controversial direction by their attitude to divorce. Some of the socialists seem to have envisaged marriage under socialism as a series of free unions made and broken at will, but such views were exceptional and most of those who advocated divorce envisaged that it would be regulated by the community. Many socialists indeed, including Eleanor Marx and Edward Aveling (Aveling and Marx, 1886) believed that only under socialism would true monogamy be able to prevail. The Oneida community was exceptional in taking the belief in community to the extent of holding wives in common and this, as we have seen, had a religious rather than a socialist inspiration.

This attitude to the loveless marriage was shared to a large extent by the feminists. They too believed that marriage should be based on love and not on property, and they deplored the pressures, economic and social, that not only forced women into such marriages but kept them in a husband's power after marriage. As we have seen in the previous chapter, most of the work of the early feminists in Britain centred on such issues, whether in the field of education and employment opportunities or the reform of the laws on married women.

There is evidence also that in the 1830s issues of marriage and divorce were discussed in the radical Unitarian circle in which John Stuart Mill and Harriet Taylor moved (Rossi, 1970, p. 25). In 1833 Fox startled the Unitarian readers of the *Monthly Repository* by articles advocating divorce to free men and women from incompatible marriage (Mineka, 1972, pp. 286—95). John Stuart Mill himself, in an essay written in 1832, had argued that whereas the indissolubility of marriage had worked to the advantage of women in the past, the effect at the present time was to increase their dependency. Clearly, however, he was thinking chiefly of errors in choice that divorce could remedy, and he anticipated that normally the first choice would be adhered to, especially where there were children. Harriet Taylor, always more radical than Mill, went further and argued that there should not be any laws on marriage and that a woman should take responsibility for her own children (Rossi, 1970, pp. 65—88). Neither of these essays was intended for publication however, and indeed they were not published until 1951. Moreover in Mill's *The Subjection of Women*, published in 1869, there is no mention of his views on divorce. This was deliberate, partly because he did not wish to link the issue of divorce with that of equality between the sexes, partly because he felt that its discussion should wait until equality had been achieved (Rossi, 1970, p. 60).

Both Fox and Mill had strong personal reasons for wishing for easier divorce, and this certainly must have influenced their thinking on the matter. On the other hand, there was plenty of evidence that the propagation of such views was dangerous. Fox came under attack for his articles on divorce and even more because of his own irregular relationship with Eliza Flower. The result was a split in his congregation, and eventually in 1835 he was expelled from the Unitarian ministry (Mineka, 1972, pp. 193—6). The reputation of Mary Wollstonecraft also suffered from her liaison with Imlay and contributed to the neglect of her work by later generations (McGuinn, 1978). It is possible, therefore, though we cannot say with certainty, that the avoidance, on the part of the feminists, of socialist theories on marriage and divorce was due to prudence rather than to any essential disagreement of principle. There is also ample evidence, as we shall see later, that the women working for suffrage, and those in the campaign for higher education, held themselves aloof from Josephine Butler's campaign for the repeal of the Contagious Diseases Acts for reasons of expediency, although many were in full agreement with her views.

Some further light is thrown on these issues, however, if we look at the situation in the United States, where the question of divorce actually became a matter of controversy amongst the feminists, since Elizabeth Cady Stanton, for many years one of the principal leaders of the movement, was herself an ardent advocate of the liberalizing of the divorce laws. According to her own account, her feelings were stirred by the sufferings of a close friend, and, indeed, as early as 1852, she argued at a temperance convention that no woman should remain in the relationship of a wife with a confirmed drunkard (Oakley, 1972, p. 56). Letters written by her between 1853 and 1857 show that she was taking an interest in the divorce laws, and in 1860, at the time of an unsuccessful bill before the New York legislature, she introduced the topic at the Women's Rights Convention, speaking for over an hour (Stanton and Blatch, 1922, pp. 185—9). Her speech, however, merely revealed the strength of the opposition within the women's movement itself. Horace Greeley, whose editorial support meant a great deal, was violently opposed to divorce and antagonized by its inclusion. Others, like Lucy Stone, believed that a loveless marriage was immoral, but thought it a dangerous topic to introduce into a women's rights discussion. Other male supporters, like Wendell Phillips and Garvison believed the issue of divorce was not relevant to women's rights (Hays, 1961, pp. 169—70). Although Elizabeth Cady Stanton had the support of her loyal friend Susan Anthony, she was not to carry the movement with her on this issue.

Later, Elizabeth Cady Stanton's views on marriage and divorce came to be one of the reasons for the split in the American woman's movement in 1869, which divided it into two separate groups, the National Woman Suffrage Association and the American Woman Suffrage Association (Riegal, 1962). The immediate reason for the split was the opposition of Elizabeth Cady Stanton and Susan Anthony to the decision by the male abolitionist leaders to sacrifice woman's suffrage to the Negro cause (Dubois, 1978). Their association, the 'National', was deliberately for women only. There may also have been personal rivalry, especially between Susan Anthony and Lucy Stone, who, with her husband Henry Blackwell, was the main impetus behind the 'American'. Behind these immediate reasons, however, were more fundamental differences in the attitude to feminism. The American believed that suffrage was the important goal and that it could only be won by refusing to alienate influential and even conservative members of the community. The National took a much broader view of feminism and tried to combine the suffrage campaign with a discussion of social issues that included marriage and divorce (Riegal, 1962).

Already in 1867 there had been trouble when Elizabeth Cady Stanton and Susan Anthony accepted the support of a rather questionable financier, George Francis Train. He accompanied them on the Kansas suffrage campaign and later provided the money for a feminist journal, *The Revolution,* although later he withdrew his support and the journal had to be abandoned. Train's own views combined anti-Negro sentiments with support for labour as well as feminism, a combination unlikely to appeal to the anti-labour, pro-Negro views of Lucy Stone and Henry Blackwell. Lucy Stone, indeed, thought that no decent woman should be in his society (Riegal, 1962, pp. 490—1).

There were further problems when *The Revolution* championed the cause of Mrs McFarlane whose divorced husband was not only acquitted of the murder of her lover on the grounds of insanity but was given custody of her 12-year old daughter (Lutz, 1959, p. 174). *The Revolution* not only spoke out in her defence but came out in open support of easier divorce. It was, however, in the Victoria Woodhull scandals that the issue of 'free love' was to pose its greatest threat to the feminists. Victoria Woodhull was a woman of great beauty, intelligence and charm who, from very unpromising beginnings, rose to a position of wealth and status (Meade, 1976). In 1870 she and her sister started publication of the *Woodhull and Chaflin Weekly,* which was not only pro-feminist but remarkably outspoken on such issues as birth control, abortion, venereal disease and female sexuality. Her campaign against the double standard of morality included a refusal to accept advertising from abortionists and brothels. She also became well known as a lecturer for her advocacy of 'free love', which appears to have meant rather more than a liberalizing of the divorce laws. In a speech in 1873, for example, she claimed that 'I will love whom I may, that I will love as long or as short a period as I can: that I will change this love when the conditions to which I have referred indicate that it ought to be changed' (Schneir, 1972, p. 154).

Helped by Congressman Butler she addressed Congress in 1871 on women's suffrage in an able speech that won over Elizabeth Cady Stanton and Susan Anthony in spite of Woodhull's reputation. Not only was she invited to speak at the Women's Rights Convention but the three women became friendly for a time. Later, however, her attempt to form a new political party eventually turned Susan Anthony against her. When, in 1871, Victoria Woodhull printed details of a prolonged love affair between Henry Ward Beecher and Elizabeth Tilton, the ensuing scandal also did little to help the feminist cause, since both Beecher and Tilton were known supporters of woman's suffrage. In the eventual trial in 1875 the jury remained undecided — as, indeed, do historians to this day (Clark, 1978, pp. 223—30) — but the link in the public mind between feminism and free love was undoubtedly strengthened (Lutz, 1959, p. 221).

In the years that followed, only Elizabeth Cady Stanton seems to have retained her radical views and to have continued to express them against increasing opposition from time to time. It is perhaps significant that in reply to criticism of Victoria Woodhull's unconventional sexual behaviour she wrote, 'We have already women enough sacrificed to this sentimental, hypocritical prattling about purity, without going out of our way to increase the number. Women have crucified the Mary Wollstonecrafts, the Frances Wrights and the George Sands of all ages' (Schneir, 1972, p. 144). Moreover, she was one of the few feminists at this time who seem to have had sympathy with the early socialists, not only in their views on marriage and divorce but also in their attitude to communities. While living at Seneca Falls in the year before the Seneca Falls Declaration, she was physically isolated and often lonely because her husband was frequently away. Burdened with the care of a large household and a growing number of young children, she later confessed that Fourier's 'community life and cooperative household had a new significance for me' (Stanton and Blatch, 1922, p. 144). It was to be many years, however, before these ideas were to be revived by feminists at the turn of the century, and in neither Britain nor America did the feminist movement concern itself with changes in marriage and the family.

Of the three intellectual traditions described here, the socialist tradition was the most whole-heartedly feminist, though it had the smallest part to play in nineteenth-century feminism. Evangelical Christianity was not, in most of its manifestations, feminist at all, although, as we have seen, it led some of its women followers into feminist beliefs and feminist action. The doctrine of equal rights had more obvious links with feminism, simply because it was only a short intellectual step from the rights of man to the rights of woman, but it was a step that many in that tradition in fact refused to make. Although the early feminists drew, in some measure, from all these traditions, it was to the doctrine of equal rights that they owed most of their inspiration. Increasingly they defined the emancipation of women in terms of equal rights, and eventually in both Britain and the United States these came to be interpreted almost exclusively in terms of women's suffrage. However, the evangelical tradition became not less but more important as the feminist movement itself grew respectable and as its leaders became convinced that only by accepting the moral standards of the middle classes could they hope to gain sufficient support from both men and women to achieve their aims. There is evidence, too, that the growing conservatism of the feminist leaders in the 1870s and after was not just a response to the need for an outward appearance of respectability but an expression of their own attitudes.

Within socialism, the feminism of the Owenites and Saint-Simonians was short-lived and left no very large impact on the movement. Although Marxism was always feminist in *theory,* the doctrine that socialism must come first has meant that rarely has it been feminist in practice. The growing significance of the trade union movement has also worked against feminism, because it has tended to accept a traditional view of women and the family. The more radical vision of the early socialists has remained the property of small extremist groups and has had little practical effect.

It will be the purpose of Part II to explore in more detail the development of feminism in the years between 1870 and 1920. This was a period during which the movement changed from a minority movement of radical men and women to what can fairly be described as a mass movement. They were years that saw the success of a number of feminist campaigns and, most significant of all, the triumph of the suffrage movement in both Britain and the United States in what was virtually the same year. Indeed, at the time, and even for long afterwards, it seemed to many that the feminists had won and that the emancipation of women had at last been achieved. During this period the movement became more conservative in its attitude to women in society. They were years, especially in the United States, when the evangelical tradition became the dominant influence on feminism. It was during this period, too, that feminism was forced to come to grips with the realities of social class, which came, in time, to divide the movement. Although, in most histories, the suffrage campaign dominates feminism between 1870 and 1920, the struggle for the vote is given only brief treatment here. Instead an attempt will be made to set the campaign against changing ideas not only of women's rights in general, but of femininity and of women's role in the family and in society generally.

PART II

The Golden Years, 1870—1920

5

The Pursuit of Moral Reform

The demand for an end to the double standard of sexual morality was, in one respect, no more than an aspect of the claim for equality of treatment that, as we have seen, was common to all the intellectual traditions on which feminism was based, and indeed it seems to have been a universal target of feminism down to the present day. What is unusual is that, for most of the feminists, an end to the double standard of sexual morality did not mean, as in the case of most feminist claims, the opening up to women of opportunities already available to men. Rather, it demanded from men the sexual repression that nineteenth-century morality required from women. It cannot, therefore, be understood as a simple expression of equal rights, but is rather an aspect of the religious tradition that enjoined chastity as a duty for men and women alike. To some extent this was an expression of ascetic attitudes towards sexuality within Christianity itself, but it also represented an essentially evangelical striving after the millennium. The belief in male chastity was reinforced by an emphasis on the domestic virtues and the importance of family life, particularly within the middle classes, which deplored alike the moral libertinism of the aristocracy and the vices of the lower classes. In the United States in particular this was complicated by the impact of successive waves of immigration upon a largely rural Anglo-Saxon population (Berg, 1978).

It has been claimed that the unmistakable improvement in the manners and morals of early nineteenth-century England was due to the Evangelicals, whose concern with a religious revival took the form, in large part, of an attack on sexual immorality, as well as on the neglect of religious observances (Brown, 1961, p. 4). The

63

Society for the Suppression of Vice, founded in 1802 by the Evangelical, Wilberforce, attempted to suppress sabbath breaking, blasphemous and licentious books, theatres, dancing, fairs, brothels and gaming houses. Of these goals, however, it was Sunday observance that was pursued most energetically and most successfully (Brown, 1961, pp. 429—30). Although a belief in male chastity is implicit in the work of the society, it mainly took the form of protecting the young of both sexes from a knowledge of evil. It was for this reason that censorship was so important. It was equally important that the senses should not be excited, whether by novels or plays or by the sight of female flesh, which must be covered. There was a need for euphemisms, and a language of propriety developed that included not only parts of the body but also clothing.

Brothels, and prostitutes soliciting on the streets, were seen largely as temptations to young men, and there seems to have been little of the concern for the prostitute herself seen, for example, in the work of the New York Female Moral Reform Society described in chapter 2. Brothels were condemned, it is true, along with gaming houses, but provision for the prostitute herself took the form of refuges that were largely punitive in their nature. Nor, at this time, do women seem to have been much involved in this work. Although the London Society for the Protection of Young Females, founded in 1835, uncovered methods of entrapment similar to those later revealed by Stead, an attempt in 1843 to enlist women in a campaign for legislation for the protection of girls failed to get off the ground (Bristow, 1977, p. 62). During the 1860s, women engaged in rescue work in larger numbers, but it was not until the efforts of Josephine Butler in 1870 that women broke through the taboos surrounding the subject and became actively involved in moral reform.

The campaign for the repeal of the Contagious Diseases Acts has been well documented (McHugh, 1980; Petrie, 1971). Intended for the protection of the armed forces against venereal diseases, these Acts, which were applicable only to certain districts, required women designated as prostitutes to undergo periodic medical examination and, if necessary, to submit to treatment. Feminist opposition originated with Harriet Martineau, who wrote against the idea in the *Daily News* in 1863, but this attracted little attention at the time; it was an attempt to extend the Acts to other parts of the country that eventually sparked off the campaign. A meeting of men, sponsored by prominent Wesleyans and Quakers, held at the 1869 Social Science Congress, led to the formation of a national association for the repeal of the Acts, and it was at their instigation that Josephine Butler took up the work (Walkowitz and Walkowitz, 1974). Already deeply involved in the movement for the extension of higher education to women, she had also campaigned for the provision of better employment opportunities, believing that prostitution was caused primarily by lack of work for girls and their low pay. She did not take up the uncompromising view of Emily Davies, but rather supported the more moderate position of Ann Jemima Clough, who had first interested her in the movement. It was her work with prostitutes, however, that suggested her as the most likely candidate to enlist women in the campaign. She had become convinced that prostitutes were the victims, not only of women's economic position, but also of a double standard of morality that enabled men to sin with impunity. Nevertheless, in spite of her strong feelings on the issue, it was only with deep reluctance that she took up the campaign, fearing the effect on her reputation and that of her husband. Her fears were indeed vindicated, since in the years that followed she was subjected not only to vilification from the press but to actual physical violence (Petrie, 1971). Moreover, her actions wrecked her husband's career in the Church (McHugh, 1980, p. 273).

The religious motivation behind the campaign is very clear from the nature of its support, in which Quakers and Nonconformists were prominent (Walkowitz and Walkowitz, 1974; McHugh, 1980). Josephine Butler herself was a deeply religious woman for whom the whole campaign was not simply a social but also a religious crusade. Her opposition to the Acts was that they provided a 'licence to sin', and she resolutely refused to accept any argument that depended on the necessity of unchastity. To this religious argument, which was undoubtedly widely accepted within the nonconformist religious community, she also added a feminist slant by her sympathy for the prostitutes involved and the humiliation to which they were subjected. As Bristow (1977, p. 82) has pointed out, compulsory examination was defined as physical rape, and was central to the feminist case. Furthermore, Josephine Butler saw prostitutes as victims and, listening to the stories of seduction from the prostitutes she befriended, she too, like the women in the New York Female Moral Reform Society, wished to see seduction punished by prison.

Apart from drawing on religious and feminist sentiments, the campaign was also able to attract the support of the growing trade union movement, which saw the Acts as a threat to all working-class girls whose way of life made them more vulnerable to unjust accusation (Walkowitz and Walkowitz, 1974; McHugh, 1980, pp. 112—19). Josephine Butler too was very much aware that the Acts gave considerable power to the police. This led to abuse, which the campaign was quick to publicise, thus gaining the support of those like John Stuart Mill who saw the Acts as a threat to individual liberty (McHugh, 1980, p. 64).

Within the feminist movement itself there was considerable support for the campaign. *The Women's Protest,* published in 1870, was signed by notable women like Harriet Martineau, Florence Nightingale and Mary Carpenter. Other feminist supporters included Elizabeth Wolstenhome and Lydia Becker, both leading suffragists (Scott, 1968, p. 123). However, there were many, especially in education, who, like Emily Davies, did not feel that they could come out in open support even if they themselves approved of the campaign. Within the suffrage movement, too, there were those, like Millicent Fawcett, who believed that it should not be entangled with so unpopular an issue, and for a time there was a split in the suffrage ranks, so deep were the feelings that were aroused (Strachey, 1928, pp. 266—9). But the most serious opposition from within the feminist movement came from the women doctors, who supported the medical profession's general approval of the Acts. Elizabeth Garrett, for example, alienated her friends at Langham Place by her attitude, which was based on the injustice of leaving innocent wives and children unprotected (Manton, 1965, pp. 178—80).

There was also, interestingly enough, a connection between support for the Acts and anti-feminism. Thus McHugh has pointed out that prominent repealers such as Stansfield and Jacob Bright were enthusiastic suffragists, whereas their leading opponents, Pulston, Osborne Morgan and Cavendish-Bentinck, opposed women's suffrage. Other leading anti-suffragists also supported the Acts and indeed not only did repealers provide a large proportion of the vote for women's suffrage but those in favour of the Acts 'were the mainstay of the anti-suffrage vote' (McHugh, 1980, pp. 244—5).

The campaign against the Contagious Diseases Acts was widened in the 1880s into an organized protest against child prostitution, and particularly the traffic in English girls to state-regulated brothels in Belgium. As the campaign mounted, pressure was brought on the government but nothing was done until in 1885

Stead's disclosures in the *Maiden Tribute of Modern Babylon* roused public opinion on the issue (Terrot, 1959). The debate over the age of consent was central to Stead's campaign. This had been raised from 12 to 13 in 1875, but, as a result of this new agitation, was raised to 16 in 1885. This was a compromise between those who thought 12 or 13 adequate and the social purity campaigners who wanted an age of 21 (Gorham, 1978). The lower age was accepted by those who saw prostitution as necessary and inevitable and who were convinced that girls entered the profession from choice (Stafford, 1964, p. 50).

The publicity given to Stead's articles, like the controversy over the Contagious Diseases Acts, did a great deal to break down the taboo surrounding the subject of prostitution and to draw women into work with prostitutes. It also did much to hasten a change of emphasis from the reform of individual girls to the extension of protection for girls and women, both by changes in legislation and by other means. Ellice Hopkins, for example, founded the Ladies' Association for the Care of Friendless Girls, which attempted to prevent girls falling into prostitution as well as performing rescue work amongst the prostitutes themselves (Bristow, 1977, pp. 97—9). By 1885 there were Ladies' Associations in about 85 towns. In 1873 she founded the White Cross Army as a movement for chastity amongst young men and later on, in 1884, the Gospel Purity Association. This had both men and women members, the men's groups pledging themselves to purity and the girls' promising to offer no enticement to men (Heasman, 1962, pp. 159—63). Amongst her other activities were attempts to remove children from brothels (Walkowitz and Walkowitz, 1974). Another woman active in the social purity campaign was Mrs Ormiston Chant who addressed over 400 meetings in the twelve months from July 1885. Later she became celebrated for her attacks on music halls (Bristow, 1977, p. 111).

It has been pointed out that much of the work of the purity campaigners was repressive in its implications (McHugh, 1980, pp. 263—4). Although designed to protect women and children, its effect was often to give the police power over them (Walkowitz and Walkowitz, 1974, p. 219). The pressure to raise the age of consent to 21 is a good example. The emphasis on social control is also demonstrated by the National Vigilance Association, which was launched as a direct consequence of Stead's campaign. In many ways this was a return to the principles of the earlier Society for the Suppression of Vice, for it was concerned with such issues as the suppression of brothels and the control of immoral literature. Moreover, Deborah Gorham has pointed out that most purity reformers were insensitive to the economic and social reality of working-class girls, and that their activities were as much concerned with controlling these girls as with protecting them. Indeed, she goes as far as to suggest that there is evidence that the girls involved knew that they were being hired as prostitutes, as the opponents of Stead continually claimed (Gorham, 1978). Most important of all perhaps, the reforms increasingly turned away from the social and political questions raised by prostitution, and especially the issue of women's earnings, which had been regarded as central by Josephine Butler, to focus almost exclusively upon the moral implications (Walkowitz and Walkowitz, 1974).

In this process the purity movement became less directly feminist, in spite of its obvious appeal to women. Nevertheless, there is little doubt that many of the feminists were behind the campaign. The events of 1885 converted Millicent Fawcett to active vigilant work (Bristow, 1977, pp. 120—1) in spite of her doubts about Josephine Butler's earlier campaign (Stafford, 1964, p. 234). The meeting to launch the National Vigilance Association was attended by representatives of suffrage societies as well as by working-class contingents from the East End, and speakers included Henry Broadhurst, the trade union leader, and Richard Pankhurst (Gorham, 1978). As in the case of the earlier agitation against the Contagious Diseases Acts, however, Elizabeth Garrett Anderson stands out as a notable exception. She thought Stead's articles disgusting and untrue, and opposed any involvement in this particular crusade (Kamm, 1966, p. 125).

The association between feminism and purity can be seen clearly in the review of Josephine Butler's *Personal Reminiscences of a Great Crusade* that appeared in the feminist journal, *The Englishwoman's Review,* in 1897. Commenting on the Langham Place work in the field of employment and education, they compared it with Josephine Butler's efforts 'to drain a slough — the Slough of Despond of immorality and vice'. The review went on, 'The two lines of effort are distinct, but they are in harmony . . . Both are needed . . .' (quoted in Banks, 1964, p. 96). Moreover the association between the two sides of feminism was to be long-lasting, as can be seen in the 1913 slogan 'votes for women, purity for men' and above all in Christabel Pankhurst's famous pamphlet on venereal disease, *The Great Scourge and how to end it* (Banks, 1964, p. 112).

If we turn now to the situation in America we find that, if there are differences in timing, the pattern of events and the attitudes expressed are strangely similar. Moreover, if anything the association between feminism and purity is even stronger. I have already noted at some length the activities of the New York Female Moral Reform Society in the 1830s and 1840s, inspired directly by an evangelical revival and turning from a concern with the reform of prostitutes to an active feminism that embraced much more than a concern for the double standard of morality. This seems to have gone far beyond anything in Britain at this period. The society's most marked feature, and one that shows a strong affinity with the position taken later by Josephine Butler, was its sympathy for the prostitute and its feminist protest against the unequal apportionment of blame. It therefore made use of threats to publish the names of the clients of brothels, and campaigned to make seduction a crime.

After the Civil War, a small group of abolitionists turned to the idea of moral education as a means to purify society. Moral education societies came into existence, often organized by women themselves (Pivar, 1973). The purity crusade operated on a wide front, which included a successful campaign for women matrons in prisons and the protection of girls away from home. By the end of the century the purity reformers were strongly committed to censorship and opposed to ballet and to nudity in art. In 1891 the inclusion of two nude canvasses in a Pennsylvania Academy for Fine Art occasioned a protest by 500 prominent women that was reported in the press as a war of righteous women. Most important of all, however, was the campaign against legalized prostitution. After the Civil War, purity reformers defeated regulation bills in New York in 1868, 1871 and 1875. But it was the St Louis battle that probably attracted most attention. Although led by men, women rallied strongly to their support. In Washington, too, women club members publicized their objections and shocked Washington newspapers. The fifteen-year battle to raise the age of consent was also amongst their more successful endeavours. During these years, age of consent legislation made substantial gains, especially in the West. As in England, the aim of the reformers was the age of 21, and although they did not achieve this they were more successful than their English counterparts in so far as some states were persuaded to adopt the age of 18. As in England, too, the campaign for a time gained working-class support when the Knights of Labor joined in the organizing of a gigantic petition as part of a national campaign.

The purity campaigners found considerable support amongst

the leaders of the feminist movement. The *Woman's Journal*, the only woman's suffrage paper after the early collapse of Susan Anthony's *Revolution*, was a firm supporter of moral reform. Lucy Stone, the editor and one of the suffrage leaders, wrote in support of expurgated texts of the classics for both male and female students. In line with this approach, the journal supported Comstock, a staunch upholder of the most repressive kind of purity legislation (Haney, 1960). Indeed the Comstock Act of 1873, by imposing a strict censorship on the mails, limited debate on sexual subjects until well into the twentieth century. The journal also launched an attack on Sarah Bernhardt as an unmarried mother (Hays, 1961, p. 261). In the presidential contest of 1854 Lucy Stone campaigned against Cleveland on the grounds that, because of his involvement in a scandal, to place him at the head of the government was an indignity to women. 'The purity and safety of the home', she argued, 'means purity and safety in the State and nation' (Hays, 1961, pp. 280—1).

Although one of the most radical of the feminist leaders, Susan Anthony was also deeply involved in the campaign against legalized prostitution in 1867, 1871 and 1872. She toured widely during these campaigns and addressed capacity crowds (Pivar, 1973, pp. 52—7). She did, however, emphasize the economic rather than the moral causes of prostitution and neither she nor Elizabeth Cady Stanton seems to have been involved in the wider issues of the purity campaign that interested Lucy Stone. Indeed, as we have seen, Elizabeth Cady Stanton deplored some of the more puritanical aspects of American society, and her liberal views on divorce and her championship of Victoria Woodhull place her somewhat apart from the other feminists of her time.

Elizabeth Blackwell, the first woman doctor in the United States, also supported the movement for male chastity. 'Purity in women', she wrote in 1879, '. . . cannot exist without purity in men' (Walton, 1974, p. 156). Like many other feminists she thought the moral element in society especially embodied in women, and her interest in feminism was in fact largely a moral one. She dreamed of a moral reform society that would work mainly through sex education (Wilson, 1970, p. 259). Moreover, like other purity reformers she attacked not only prostitution but also masturbation and obscene literature.

When we turn to a later generation of suffrage leaders we find a continuation and even an intensification of the association between purity and feminism. Frances Willard, for example, although perhaps better known for her work on temperance (which will be described later), was active, during the 1880s in particular, in campaigns for the protection of girls and especially the raising of the age of consent (Earhart, 1944, pp. 185—6). Like Lucy Stone she was prepared to accept censorship in the interests of moral purity (Pivar, 1973, p. 182). She was also closely involved in the work of the White Cross movement in the United States, adding a female equivalent, the White Shield. Under the auspices of the Women's Christian Temperance Union, the White Cross societies became a mass movement, attracting women at a rate unprecedented by any other reform in the history of the Women's Christian Temperance Union (Pivar, 1973, pp. 113—15). Like many other suffrage leaders of the period she also linked the issue of purity with the demand for the vote.

The feminists, therefore, had no wish to challenge the conventional sexual morality as it applied to women. The insistence on female chastity was not seen by them as oppressive but, with very few exceptions, as both natural and necessary. To understand why this should have been so, and indeed continued to be so even after conventional ideas had begun to change, it is necessary to look briefly at their conceptions of both male and female sexuality.

It was widely and indeed generally held during the whole of the nineteenth century that there was a basic division between the male and the female in their sexual nature. There were some who denied the existence of any natural sexual feeling in women at all, but even those who accepted the fact of female sexuality believed that men's needs were much stronger. In particular, whereas men's sexuality was held to be spontaneous, women, if they experienced sexual desire at all, needed first to be aroused (Gordon, 1971, pp. 225—6). It was for this reason more than any other that it was possible to argue that women were more moral than men.

This belief in women's natural moral superiority is in sharp contrast to the earlier view, firmly entrenched in Christian thinking, that women were fundamentally evil, temptresses who would lead men into sin (Hays, 1966). Basic to this attitude, of course, was a conception of sex as itself evil, but it also implied a view of women as actively sexual creatures and not, as in the nineteenth century, passive victims of male lust. Moreover, only the celibate life was strictly moral; marriage was very much a second-best alternative. Protestantism did not greatly change the basic asceticism of Christianity, but its rejection of celibacy paved the way for a change in the status of women by the value that was increasingly placed on marriage and family life. Women moved from 'natural allies of the devil to godly companions of their husbands' (Hamilton, 1978, p. 64). It also permitted the development of an ideal of conjugal love that allowed a woman to be regarded as pure even as a wife and mother.

An important aspect of this doctrine was to make a sharp distinction between love and lust. The difference was not simply between sexual relationships within marriage and outside it, although this was certainly important. Lust could also exist inside marriage, and the Puritan solution was to purge the marriage bed of its erotic components. Thus men and women were urged to avoid 'sensual excesses, wanton speeches, foolish dalliance' (Hamilton, 1978, p. 61). The price, however, seems to have been the denial of any active female sexuality. Although unchaste women could still be seen as temptresses and feared and hated as such, it was the destiny of the pure woman to protect rather than destroy male chastity, and the duty of the wife was to dampen rather than arouse the sexual ardour of her husband. Women were therefore trained to repress their sexual feelings, so that it is not surprising if it came to be believed by some, both men and women, that, unless they had been corrupted, women had little if any sexual desire.

During the nineteenth century, evangelical enthusiasm revived Puritan fears of sexual pleasure. Moreover, these specifically religious anxieties were strongly reinforced by the views of doctors and health reformers on the harmful effects of sexual intercourse on health. Thus Sylvester Graham in his health crusades in the United States led an attack on sexual indulgence not only outside but also within marriage, and, along with his health diet, recommended that sexual intercourse should be limited to no more than twelve times a year (Haller and Haller, 1974, pp. 97—8). Graham was no isolated crank. His gospel spread with startling rapidity and, if women proved his most ardent supporters, his views also became popular amongst physicians (Pivar, 1973, pp. 38—9). Acton, an English doctor whose *Functions and Disorders of the Reproductive Organs* (published in 1857) was influential on both sides of the Atlantic, argued not only that women had little if any sexual passion, but that sexual intercourse was a drain on the nervous system of the male and should be performed not only as infrequently but also as quickly as possible. The belief that the loss of semen was in itself a strain on both physical and nervous energy was also behind the ferocious warnings on masturbation typical of the period. In the United States, where purity authors, often women, began to monopolize marriage manuals in the 1870s, anything that stimulated erotic feelings was proscribed. This included not only romantic novels but stimulants such as tea, coffee, alcohol and even meat (Haller and Haller, 1974, p. 197). For the unmarried man, masturbation was as harmful as unchastity and it was argued that the 'healthy male could live until marriage without the loss of a single drop of seminal fluid' (Haller and Haller, 1974, p. 201). Clearly this attitude to sex pressed just as hard on men as on women!

Such a view was certainly not typical of all nineteenth-century thought and the purity campaigners were a minority in both the United States and Britain, even if at times their views were able to prevail. Nevertheless, the belief that men both should and could control their sexuality was particularly attractive to women and it is this that underlies both their support for the purity campaign and the alliance between the purity campaigners and the feminists. This belief also lay behind all their attacks on the double standard of morality and their horror at any social policy that suggested that prostitution was necessary. There is no doubt too that they believed that sexuality was a male rather than a female characteristic, and there was widespread agreement amongst them that the male was always the sexual aggressor, the female his unwilling victim. Josephine Butler's argument in opposing the Contagious Diseases Acts — that 'it is unjust to punish the sex who are the victims of a vice, and leave unpunished the sex who are the main cause, both of the vice, and its dreaded consequences' (Banks, 1964, p. 111) — expressed a very general feeling amongst feminists in both Britain and in the United States. This is why they repeatedly claimed that seduction should be punished by law, and why more militant feminist groups threatened from time to time to publicize the clients of brothels.

To get more direct evidence on the feminists' attitude to their own sexuality is, however, more difficult, given the taboos that surrounded the subject, especially for women. Only at the end of the nineteenth century was it possible for women to write openly about such issues, and for much of the period our information has to come from diaries and letters. These, in so far as they are available, show that feminists did not necessarily accept Acton's view that women had no sexual feelings. Elizabeth Blackwell, for example, believed that women's lack of sexual response was not natural, but a consequence of fear of childbirth and previous painful sexual relationships (Haller and Haller, 1974, p. 100).

Elizabeth Cady Stanton, the most radical of the organized feminists and, as we have seen, one who quite unusually was prepared to defend those feminists whose lives were unorthodox, not only condemned the dogma that sex is a crime but in 1885, as a woman of 65, wrote, 'a healthy woman has as much passion as a man' (Schneir, 1972, pp. 144—5; Gordon, 1977, p. 99). In this respect she does not seem to have differed very greatly from Victoria Woodhull, the unorthodox advocate of 'free love' who, in 1873, spoke out against sexual intercourse without pleasure and the sexual starvation of the unmarried (Schneir, 1972, p. 153). Whereas, however, Woodhull publicized her views and gained almost universal discredit, Elizabeth Cady Stanton kept her opinion on the subject discreetly hidden. Nevertheless, if not prepared to deny female sexuality, Elizabeth Cady Stanton certainly shared with the rest of the feminists the belief that male sexuality needed to be brought under control. She wrote to Susan Anthony in 1853, 'man in his lust has regulated this whole question of sexual intercourse long enough' (Sinclair, 1966, p. 72).

Lucy Stone, Elizabeth Cady Stanton's rival for leadership of the suffragists, demonstrates the more conservative and more typical view that sexual intercourse should be restricted to procreation. In letters to her brothers in 1837 she advocated that couples should practise sexual intercourse only for the propagation of children and then, in order to avoid the burden on the wife of frequent child-bearing, only at periods three years apart (Lerner, 1967, pp. 308—9). Even Elizabeth Blackwell, in spite of her often-quoted opposition to Acton on the nature of female sexuality, was very far indeed from Victoria Woodhull's demand for sexual pleasure. Instead she believed that the goal was greater chastity for both sexes (McLaren, 1978, p. 128). If she believed that there was little difference, in nature, between male and female sexuality, it was because men were allowed and encouraged a level of sexuality that was actually *unnatural.*

It was in their attitude to birth control that the feminists revealed most clearly their attitude to sex. It is now generally agreed that neither in the United States nor in Britain was the feminist movement prepared to countenance contraception (Gordon, 1977; Banks, 1964; McLaren, 1978). Far from seeing artificial birth control as a step towards their emancipation, they perceived it as yet another instance of their subordination to man's sexual desires. Along with many others at that time, the feminists tended to see the propagation of birth control techniques as leading to an inevitable degradation of morals, since it would encourage extra-marital sexuality. This was indeed precisely the argument used against the Contagious Diseases Acts, which, so it was believed, took away the punishment from sin. Similarly, even within marriage, birth control could easily be seen as immoral, since the whole object was to allow the pleasures of sex without its consequences. For those who defined all sexual pleasure as sinful, this was to allow lust to corrupt the purity of the marriage relationship itself (Haller and Haller, 1974, p. 124). For the feminists, then, birth control allowed men to indulge their sensuality unchecked both inside and outside marriage. Thus, for example, we find Elizabeth Blackwell in the late 1880s opposing contraceptive devices as 'artifices to indulge a husband's sensuality' (Banks, 1964, p. 93). This attitude was to persist even into the early decades of the twentieth century. The militant suffragette, Christabel Pankhurst, claimed in 1912 that sex was to be used only 'reverently and in a union based on love, for the purposes of carrying on the race' (Banks, 1964, p. 113; McLaren, 1978, p. 20).

Annie Besant, one of the leading campaigners for birth control in Britain, was of course feminist in her views, but she was never associated with the organized feminist movement in any of its different aspects. Nor did she receive even the degree of support granted to Victoria Woodhull by at least some of the American feminists. The trial in 1877 of Bradlaugh and Besant for the publication of birth control propaganda was passed over in silence by the feminists, and an appeal for support to the suffragist leader Millicent Fawcett and her husband Henry Fawcett was repulsed with horrified indignation (Banks, 1964, pp. 92—9). Of the feminist leaders, only Elizabeth Cady Stanton seems so far as we know to have been in sympathy with their position. On a visit to England in 1877 she confided to her diary, 'my sense of justice was severely tried by all I heard of the prosecution of Mrs Besant and Mr Bradlaugh for their publication of the right and duty of parents to limit procreation' (Stanton and Blatch, 1922, p. 303).

This is not to imply that the feminists approved of large families. Indeed, it seems very likely that the views of Lucy Stone on the desirability of 'spacing' children were popular with many of them at least from the 1870s onwards when there was much discussion of the issue (Gordon, 1977, p. 109). Elizabeth Blackwell, it is true, cautioned against 'the grave national danger of teaching men to repudiate fatherhood and women to despise motherhood' (Banks, 1964, p. 93), but she does not seem to have been against family limitation altogether in spite of her opposition to artificial methods of birth control. The principle of voluntary motherhood was, however, interpreted by the feminists as the right of the wife to refuse her husband's sexual demands. Thus Paulina Wright Davis at the National Woman Suffrage Association in 1871 attacked the law 'which makes obligatory the rendering of marital rights and compulsory maternity' (Gordon, 1977, p. 104). Moreover this demand for rights over their own bodies was seen not simply as a method of birth control, although this was important, but as freedom from excessive sexual demands made by husbands on their wives. It is for this reason that it is not adequate to explain feminist attitudes to sex as just a reflection of the absence of adequate techniques of birth control. It was precisely because birth control techniques sought to separate sex from procreation that they were disliked and feared by the feminists, who saw clearly enough that the effect would be to increase the sexual demands made upon women both inside and indeed outside marriage. As Linda Gordon has convincingly demonstrated (1977, pp. 95—115), even the small free love groups, successors to the perfectionist reform groups described in chapter 4, were opposed to artificial methods of birth control, on somewhat similar grounds to the feminists and the moral reformers. The Oneida community, in spite of its radical attitude to marriage and its apparent moral laxity, was in reality very much concerned with the control of sexuality. This was evidenced not only by the rigid self-control associated with their method of coitus reservatus, but by the strict manner in which they regulated the choice of sexual partners. After 1870 the free love movement, of which Victoria Woodhull was at one time an active advocate, was more closely associated with free thought than with religion. Their opposition to marriage was that it stifled love, but in no sense were they concerned with freeing sexuality from moral restraints. Indeed, according to one of its most important exponents, Ezra Heywood, free love would mean a reduction in sexual drives and ideally 'the amount of sexual intercourse that men and women desired would be exactly commensurate with the number of children that were wanted' (Gordon, 1977, p. 103). Not until the very end of the nineteenth century did the free love movement turn away from the association between sexuality and self-restraint (Gordon, 1977, p. 177).

To some extent this opposition to sexuality was expressed in the growing support for celibacy as a life style, which was noted in chapter 4. Although partly a desire simply for economic independence, there does seem to have been involved in it a rejection of the idea of women as no more than female animals. Thus it was suggested that 'the modern dislike of the celibate has its root in the natural annoyance of an over-sexed and mentally-lax generation at receiving ocular demonstration of the fact that animal passion can be kept under control' (Banks, 1964, p. 112). Haller and Haller (1974, pp. vii—xiii) interpret this turning away from sex as women's resentment at their role as sex objects, and Linda Gordon (1977, pp. 105—6) sees it as their reaction to sexual intercourse 'dominated by and defined by the male in conformity with his desires and a disregard of what might bring pleasure to a woman'. Moreover sexual intercourse brought not only the fear of conception but also anxiety about the risk of the transmission of venereal disease. The discussions on venereal disease at the time of the contagious diseases campaigns had brought these issues very much to attention in the 1870s and the purity campaigners kept them before the public eye. The hysteria that fears of venereal disease might give rise to is nowhere better expressed than in Christabel Pankhurst's claim in 1913 that 75—80 per cent of men were infected by gonorrhoea and in her warning to women to avoid marriage with men whose moral standards 'continue to be lower than their own' (Banks, 1964, p. 112).

The sacrifice of their own sexual needs — paid for, the Hallers (1974, p. 102) argue, by hysteria and sexual neurasthenia — was made easier by the feminists' attitude to sexuality itself. To some extent this was simply an acceptance of the view, expressed by Acton amongst others, that normally women had little if any sexual passion. Thus women were taught to see not only men's sexual desires as immoral but their own as well. As Trudgill has put it (1976, p. 62), 'although initial pain might give way to pleasure this might only frighten the woman more since she might have learnt that only lascivious women enjoyed sexual pleasure'. Even more important, however, was the view that sexuality itself was a manifestation not so much of a natural human drive but of the 'beast in human nature' (Banks, 1964, p. 111). This attitude to sexual love is indeed well expressed by the American feminist writer Margaret Fuller who, writing of the love of woman for woman and man for man, described it as the 'love we shall feel when we are angels'. It was 'purely intellectual and spiritual, unprofaned by any mixture of lower instincts' (Melder, 1977, p. 30). The fear of woman's sexuality was therefore a fear not only of sexuality itself but of man's animal nature; it was the need to control this 'beast in man' that was fundamental to the evangelical tradition by which feminism had been so deeply influenced (Christ, 1977, p. 160).

However, the urge to reform the morals of society, essentially evangelical in inspiration, went beyond a concern simply with sexual matters, and, as we saw in an earlier chapter, lay behind women's involvement both in the anti-slavery movement and in temperance campaigns. By the 1870s, the links between feminism and the anti-slavery movement had ended but, in the United States at least, temperance and feminism were to become even more closely involved. As we noticed previously, women were attracted to the idea of temperance from the start and were particularly useful for their organizing and fund-raising skills, just as they were in the anti-slavery campaigns. Even more important was the fact that many pioneer feminists were also temperance reformers.

The years after 1870 saw women becoming increasingly important in temperance crusades. In large part this seems to have reflected the entry of women in large numbers into public and indeed political life, since by this time the prejudice against women speaking in public was declining rapidly. I have already noted the extent to which women were drawn into the various aspects of the purity campaign, taking, in the case of Josephine Butler for example, a leading rather than a simply supporting role. Women still, it is true, organized themselves in separate associations but these now become significant and sometimes even powerful groups in their own right. The most outstanding example is undoubtedly the Women's Christian Temperance Union, which under the leadership of Frances Willard, brought large numbers of American women not only into work for temperance but, increasingly, into the suffrage campaign.

Frances Willard (Earhart, 1944) was born in 1839 and from her early years showed that rebellion against the orthodox female role typical of many of the pioneer feminists. She was, for example, jealous when her brother went away to school, and even more so when she found that she was not allowed to vote. Her attempts at getting an education for herself, and later on a job, were successful only by pitting herself against an authoritarian father. Later, she was to break off an engagement, possibly because her fiancé showed the same inclination to domination as her father. Her early career was in teaching, but eventually her interest in women's education led her, reluctantly at first, into the more conservative wing of the suffrage movement. Her interest in temperance was aroused in 1874, with the outbreak in that year of a spontaneous temperance campaign amongst women in Western towns. She was gradually drawn into the newly formed Women's Christian Temperance Union and she was made first corresponding secretary and then, in 1879, the president. A gifted orator, she was to travel ceaselessly in its service during the 1880s, and it was only in the 1890s, when increasing illness and visits abroad weakened her influence, that her power began to wane.

A feminist before she was a temperance worker, Frances Willard worked unceasingly to unite the two causes and finally succeeded in 1883 when the national convention voted to include women's suffrage in their programme. By uniting temperance and suffrage in this way she was able to win conservative women to the suffrage cause and also help to break down the radical image caused by the scandals of the 1870s and the association in the public mind between women's suffrage and free love. Gradually the WCTU became the largest organization of women in the land. It increased its membership from 135 to 1874 to 345,949 in the 1920s (Mezvinsky, 1961, p. 18). As an organization they were exceedingly active. They petitioned Congress and state legislatures, printed and distributed pamphlets, magazines and newsletters, held public meetings and attempted to influence other organizations and institutions. One of their most successful campaigns was that for temperance instruction in schools. Not only did they secure the passage of legislation in states throughout the country, but by putting pressure upon publishers were able to control the writing and use of hygiene and physiology textbooks. Although a women's organization, run by women, it was recognized as a powerful influence winning public opinion over in favour of prohibition (Mezvinsky, 1961, p. 21). Nor did the association between feminism and temperance end with Frances Willard's death. The new generation of feminist social workers like Jane Addams also supported prohibition. Jane Addams herself never outgrew the attitude that drinking, especially for women, was a sin (Davis, 1967, p. 277).

The British counterpart to the WCTU was the British Women's Temperance Association founded in 1876 under the presidency of Lady Henry Somerset and with a membership including many leading women Evangelicals. It had a fairly wide programme, ranging from the provision of homes for women who were drunkards to clubs for single women, but it never indulged in the wide programme of the American association (Heasman, 1962, p. 134). When Frances Willard visited England in 1892 she was amazed to find that the British Women's Temperance Association had remained limited simply to the temperance issue. Moreover her attempts to widen its scope met with disapproval (Earhart, 1944, p. 324). To a large extent, therefore, the temperance movement in Britain remained outside organized feminism and temperance was not linked as in the United States to women's suffrage.

Nevertheless there is no doubt that feminists and women generally in both Britain and the United States were in sympathy with the temperance movement even if the British temperance movement did not become feminist. This was in part at least because of the association between alcohol and violence. Women were more likely to be the victims of drunken violence because of their greater vulnerability to physical abuse, whether outside or inside the home. The dependence of women and children on a man's earnings also made alcohol an economic threat, and the saloon came to be seen by some of them as depriving them of their husband's earnings as well as his company (Kingsdale, 1973). It was for this reason that the women's crusades of 1873—4 consisted of attacks on saloons in an attempt to force them to close. Carrie Nation, who broke up rum-shops in Kansas with a hatchet at the turn of the century, is a later and more violent example (Sinclair, 1962).

There was also, in both countries, an alliance between the temperance movement and the purity campaigners. Such an alliance was a very natural one, since both causes shared a very similar ideology and there was much common ground between them. As we have seen in an earlier chapter, both drunkenness and sexual immorality were interpreted as a failure of self-control, and, because drunkenness weakens judgement and will, it was seen not simply as analogous to sexual immorality but one of its major causes. Thus temperance was a moral virtue not only in and for itself but also because of its significance in leading men and women into sexual temptation.

I have already noted the significant part played by Frances Willard in the purity campaign. Not only did she attack legalized prostitution but she was active in the campaign for raising the age of consent. Moreover, just as she was enthusiastic for temperance education, so she was interested in the preventive side of the purity campaign, which explains both her support of censorship and her activities on behalf of the educationally oriented White Cross movement. At this time, indeed, the feminist movement in the

United States was very largely an alliance between suffrage, temperance and social purity associations (Paulson, 1973, pp. 118—20), an alliance in which Frances Willard and the WCTU played a major role.

In Britain the temperance movement itself was less significant for feminism. Nevertheless there were strong links between temperance and the purity campaign. The British Women's Temperance Association formed an active social purity department and their president, Lady Henry Somerset, was involved in criticisms of stage nudity and *tableaux vivants* in the 1890s (Bristow, 1977, pp. 135, 212). Ellice Hopkins, although mainly a purity campaigner, toured British garrisons lecturing on both temperance and purity (Bristow, 1977, p. 96). None of this was necessarily feminist and indeed in 1897, much to the horror of her friend Frances Willard, Lady Henry Somerset actually came out in support of the contagious diseases legislation (Earhart, 1944, p. 366). On the other hand, the Association for the Repeal of the Contagious Diseases Acts had attracted many who were involved in the temperance as well as the educational and suffrage campaigns, and its journal *The Shield* had a large teetotal membership (Walkowitz and Walkowitz, 1974; McHugh, 1980).

Brian Harrison has drawn attention to the way in which a number of what may be very broadly termed moral reform societies were, in the late nineteenth century, linked together not only with each other but also with feminism. They shared not only common attitudes and techniques but also what can be described as an interlocking membership (Harrison, 1974, p. 319). His investigation into fourteen organizations in 1884 revealed not only linkages between temperance and sabbatarian movements, which might have been predicted, but also a relationship between them and animal welfare societies. Evangelicalism tended to provide the hard core of original leaders, but moral reform later became less overtly religious in character and opened up the possibility of unions between Evangelicals and utilitarians. There remained, however, differences in emphasis. Whereas the Evangelicals were keen sabbatarians and temperance workers, the utilitarians kept out of the sabbatarian movement and avoided some aspects of the temperance movement (Harrison, 1974, pp. 291—4).

The interest of the moral reformers in animal welfare was in part an expression of their concern for the weak and helpless, and this was behind their support for the anti-vivisection movement. Moreover, the anti-vivisection movement appealed particularly to women who were not only heavily represented in the membership but were even prominent in the leadership. Indeed Frances Power Cobbe, one of the most active of the anti-vivisectionists, was also an enthusiastic feminist who believed in women's suffrage as a means of raising the moral level of society. For her, feminism and the anti-vivisection movement were part of the same crusade (French, 1975). It is also interesting to note the prominent part played in the anti-vivisection movement by Cardinal Manning, who was not only a leading temperance worker but an enthusiastic feminist (Dingle and Harrison, 1969). Bearing in mind the association between Unitarianism and feminism, it is also perhaps not surprising to find a connection between Unitarianism and anti-vivisection. Stevenson (1956) has pointed out that, although Evangelicals and their sympathizers occupied most of the leadership positions, some of the early contributions to anti-vivisectionist literature in Britain in the 1830s were from the pens of Unitarians. McHugh (1980, pp. 244—58) has similarly drawn attention to the alliances between the movement for the repeal of the Contagious Diseases Acts and a whole constellation of other reform movements, including feminism and temperance, but also the campaigns against vivisection, compulsory vaccination and the compulsory notification of infectious diseases. He sees the reformers united in a dislike for the military and the aristocracy, and also for what they believed to be the arrogance of medical experts. To some extent also this opposition to medicine was part of the religious objection to science itself (French, 1975).

Although much of moral reform and certainly the temperance movement and the purity campaign have been described as attempts to propagate the middle-class way of life, there is little doubt that these attitudes were also shared by large numbers of the 'respectable' working class. In Harrison's words, it was a repudiation 'of the whole complex of behaviours associated with race-courses, fairs, wakes, brothels, beer-houses and brutal sports', which was the world not only of the 'rough' working class but also of the aristocracy. It was also, of course, an essentially masculine world and contrasted sharply with the family-oriented life style to which the 'respectable' working man aspired, and who 'if he drank at all ... drank soberly, without neglecting his wife and family' (Harrison, 1971, p. 25). This emphasis on the domestic virtues encouraged an alliance between the feminists and the respectable working class, and we have indeed already noticed the success with which Josephine Butler appealed to working men in her campaign against the Contagious Diseases Acts.

In the United States moral reform drew most of its strength from the rural Protestant middle classes, faced with the growth of cities and an increasing tide of immigrants, many of them Catholics (Sinclair, 1962; Gusfield, 1972). There was also however, as in Britain, support for moral reform from the 'aristocracy of labour'. Under the leadership of Terence Powderly, a life-long abstainer, the Knights of Labor supported temperance and so did four big railway brotherhoods (Timberlake, 1963, p. 95). Frances Willard was also able to gain his support for her purity petitions and women from the WCTU frequently appeared on platforms with the Knights at their annual meetings (Earhart, 1944, pp. 247, 250). By the end of the century the American Federation of Labor had triumphed as the leading union and the alliance between labour and prohibition had ended. Divided on the issue, it nevertheless continued to provide strong support for temperance principles (Timberlake, 1963, p. 95; Sinclair, 1962, p. 122).

If, however, moral reform made for alliances between middle and working classes and between moral reformers and feminists, it also produced conflict between those with voluntaristic and individualistic principles and those who were committed to the idea of an extension of state intervention in the interests of social control. To some extent the main thrust of moral reform in the nineteenth century was towards a greater emphasis on constraint. This is clearly seen in the temperance movement, which passed from an emphasis on individual self-control that accepted some moderate drinking, to an argument for total prohibition (Paulson, 1973, pp. 183–4; Gusfield, 1972, pp. 6–7). The same movement of ideas is also true of Britain (Brown, 1961, p. 508), and we have already noticed the growing repressive tendencies of the purity campaign. To some extent, however, the conflict between libertarianism and authoritarianism was present in moral reform from the start. The evangelical movement in Britain was never, in fact, a radical movement, as Ford K. Brown (1961, p. 155) has demonstrated. Moreover, the thrust of their activities was repressive. The Society for the Suppression of Vice was concerned from its earliest years with the use of state power to prohibit and punish sabbath-breaking, brothel-keeping and gambling.

This conflict within the moral reform movement is clearly expressed in its political manifestations. Although the Liberals, rather than the Conservatives, were associated with moral reform, and later with female suffrage, the Liberal Party was in fact divided, and the moral reformers as well as the suffragists remained a ginger group to the left of the party (Harrison, 1974, p. 291) — although the association between Liberalism and moral reform was to grow after Gladstone's return to active politics in 1876 (McHugh, 1980, p. 208). Moral reform, however, always enjoyed something of a following in the Conservative Party, largely through its paternalistic interest in social control. The Liberal reformers found this quite unacceptable, and this coloured their support for moral reform. Thus John Stuart Mill placed sabbatarianism and temperance at the head of his unjust interferences with individual freedom (Harrison, 1974, pp. 296—7). His disapproval of the Contagious Diseases Acts was on exactly the same grounds. Josephine Butler, too, was concerned with individual responsibility in her dislike of the Acts, although she approved of the prosecution of brothel-keepers and the raising of the age of consent.

The tensions in the moral reform movement between authoritarianism and voluntarism, and between conservative and radical, are reflected within feminism itself. During the years between 1870 and 1914 most of the radicalism that the pioneering feminists had inherited from the Enlightenment disappeared. As feminism grew in influence and became, in the great suffrage campaign of the early twentieth century, something of a mass movement, it shed not only its more radical goals but its more radical conception of womanhood. Most significantly of all, it passed from a concern with the social construction of the female based ultimately upon Enlightenment views on the effect of the environment upon human nature, to an acceptance of the essential uniqueness of the female. By the end of the nineteenth century, the feminist movement was based, not so much on the doctrine of male and female equality as on a notion of female superiority that was accepted not only by women but by many of their male supporters.

6

The Ideal of Female Superiority

In the seventeenth century, during which the Protestant view of marriage evolved, the notion of partnership between husband and wife included a substantial economic element. During the eighteenth century however, to use Roberta Hamilton's words, the bourgeois home became 'only a place to live, not a place to work' (1978, p. 44). Moreover, the removal of the economic function from the home, which occurred within the working class as well as the bourgeoisie, was accompanied, in the case of the latter, by the exclusion of both wives and daughters from the world outside the home. Increasingly, therefore, the women of the bourgeoisie were confined to a narrowly domestic role. Moreover, as this class grew in affluence, more and more domestic tasks were taken over by servants, so that daughters in particular performed a largely decorative role (Hamilton, 1978, pp. 23—49; George, 1973).

The Protestant ideal of a marriage partnership did not at any time mean equality within the marriage relationship and wives were expected to be subordinate to their husbands (Hamilton, 1978, pp. 50—75). Nor had this changed very much by the nineteenth century. Not only, as we have seen, were wives subject to their husbands by law, but the spate of books on woman's sphere that characterized the 1830s and 1840s and were to continue to appear right through the century stressed that 'it is a man's place to rule, and a woman's to yield' (Banks, 1964, p. 60).

By this time, however, the Protestant emphasis on the domestic virtues had blossomed into a cult of domesticity that endowed the home with symbolic and indeed transcendental qualities that it was woman's special and indeed sacred mission to preserve. Its central core was an opposition between the home, which was safe, civilized and 'ideal', and the world outside, which was harsh, competitive and 'real' (Davidoff *et al.,* 1976). Home was a sanctuary, an 'inner space' (Wood, 1972), a place of beauty and peace, a refuge from the market-place, even, in Ruskin's words, a 'walled garden', ruled not by the cash nexus but by love (Banks, 1964, p. 59). This was as true of America as of Britain (Cott, 1977, pp. 65—70). The home and the world were therefore two quite separate spheres: the one, woman's special realm; the other, to a large extent, forbidden to her.

Alongside the doctrine of separate spheres was the development of the cult of true womanhood. This was based in part on the notion of man as the stronger and the harder sex. Men were less emotional, more rational, as well as physically better able to stand the stern and ruthless world of the market-place. If, however, women needed the protecting walls of home because they were weak, they also had other qualities, derived in large part from their maternal nature, that made them specially fitted to be both protectors as well as protected. These were the softer virtues of patience, gentleness and loving kindness, which they could use to succour and comfort their husbands as well as their children. Above all, perhaps, their greater moral purity fitted them to be the moral inspiration of their husbands as well as the moral guardians of their children (Welter, 1966; Kuhn, 1947, pp. 43—5).

The doctrine of separate spheres was, as we have seen, challenged by the feminists who claimed for women the right to break out of both their confinement to domesticity and their legal and political subordination to man. I have traced in earlier chapters their campaign for legal rights, for education and for economic independence, and a later chapter will examine their struggle for the vote. In order to do this, however, they had to re-examine for themselves both the cult of domesticity and its corollary, the doctrine of true womanhood, because these were not only the justification for woman's separate sphere but the basis on which the anti-feminists attacked the feminists' cause. In the process, as we shall see, the feminists changed, sometimes in highly significant ways, the view of women's character and destiny without ever totally rejecting the basis of the doctrine, which implied not only a special feminine nature but also a grounding of that nature in women's domestic and, ultimately, her maternal role. It is with this process that this chapter is concerned.

The opposition to the feminist demands was varied in its nature and sometimes rested on no more than a religious prescription that derived ultimately from the Adam and Eve myth. More frequent, however, was the argument that women's emancipation would unfit them for their domestic role, and particularly for their function as mothers. In the eyes of some anti-feminists this argument was based quite simply on the belief that to admit women to exciting and perhaps lucrative employment or to involve women actively in the political process would make them discontented with the obscurity and even the tedium of their home-bound lives (Banks, 1964, pp. 43—4). At a deeper level was the fear that experience of the world was dangerous for women; that their special characteristics of tenderness, affection and moral purity were a consequence not so much of innate differences between men and women as of the protection from the wickedness of the world that allowed the maintenance of that state of innocence on which women's nature depended.

To some extent the corrupting influence of experience of the world, and particularly of evil, was something that applied to both sexes. Frequently, however, the view was expressed that women were weaker than men, not only physically but also mentally and morally, so that their protection from evil was absolutely essential if they were to remain pure and good. Thus their lack of reasoning power, their lack of self-control, their failure to calculate consequences, were all put forward to explain women's special need for dependence (Banks, 1964, p. 47). The claim that women were weaker than men was a powerful argument in opposition to the employment of women, especially, although not necessarily, in areas that were regarded as male preserves. Medicine is a particularly interesting case, and one where the battle was particularly hard fought, since it was argued not only that its study was physically and intellectually too difficult for women, but that its indecency was also a threat to the preservation of female purity. Later on, when it was successfully demonstrated that women could compete with men on their own terms and, as happened spectacularly in higher education, even beat them, the argument was reformulated so that such competition was seen as dangerous in the long term, especially to women's future role as mothers (Duffin, 1978a; Atkinson, 1978).

In examining the feminist defence against these accusations, we have to consider the different traditions within feminism itself, for, although there might be temporary alliances in support of particular goals, there was considerable variation in approach depending on whether the dominant tradition was primarily evangelical or reflected the more radical philosophy of the Enlightenment. Amongst the evangelical feminists no one was more important, at least in the United States, than Catherine Beecher whose influential educational philosophy has already been described in chapter 2. Like the Grimké sisters, she passionately wanted to extend women's influence in society, but unlike them she perceived it as different in kind, and in the method of its application, from the influence of men. To a considerable extent, indeed, she accepted a view of woman as basically different from man in character and temperament, a difference arising essentially from woman's domestic and indeed maternal role. Woman's great mission, she wrote 'is self-denial . . . if not for her own children, then for the neglected children of her father in heaven' (Cross, 1965, p. 83). She is 'necessarily the guardian of the nursery, the companion of childhood' (Cross, 1965, p. 67). Consequently she thought that when they worked women should take up employment as teachers or nurses or similar occupations that were largely natural extensions of their duties as mothers. Nevertheless, she was fully prepared to see women exercising these domestic functions in the world, as well as the home, and argued that teaching should become a predominantly female occupation in spite of the fact that at that time it was dominated by men. Moreover, by suggesting that businessmen should imitate the self-denying ethics of the home, she was claiming that feminine virtues should be accepted and acted upon by men themselves. At the same time she wanted to see a lessening of the isolation of the home from the world. Although certainly no advocate of greater sexual freedom, she believed that it was wrong to keep women in ignorance of the sin in the world, since only knowledge could protect women from sin (Sklar, 1973).

Conservative as she undoubtedly was, therefore, Catherine Beecher was also a significant innovator in breaking down some of the walls that confined and isolated women in their separate sphere (Kuhn, 1947, pp. 56—7 and 180—4). By arguing that women had a special reforming role in society, she provided the rationale for the entry of large numbers of women into moral reform, whether in the cause of purity or temperance, which eventually led feminism into the attempt to use the vote to transform society itself. The cost however, as we shall see, was that feminism was trapped into a view of womanhood that came dangerously close to the traditional view from which the feminists were trying to escape.

We can see many of the ideas of Catherine Beecher repeated in the writings of later American feminists, especially those who were involved in moral reform. Elizabeth Blackwell, for example, based her claim for women doctors on a view of woman that did not differ materially from that of the anti-feminists. 'The great essential fact of woman's nature', she claimed in her important London lectures in 1859, 'is the spiritual power of maternity . . . the subordination of self to the welfare of others' (quoted in Wilson, 1970, pp. 366—7). She believed that the 'moral element is specially embodied by women' (Walton, 1974, p. 156), who thus had a special responsibility for the moral development of society. The Women's Christian Temperance Union also took the view that women not only had a God-given mission to reform the world but were by *nature* better fitted than men to do this. Frances Willard believed that God had chosen women as the 'apostles of reform' and had given them 'a sense of perception, a measure of hope and faith, and a respect for justice and right superior to those possessed by men' (Mezvinsky, 1961, p. 19). Margaret Fuller was another feminist who in 1855 emphasized the special genius of woman and drew attention to the great radical dualism between male and female. She looked forward to a new age when the 'feminine side', the 'side of love, of beauty, of holiness was now to have its full chance' (Alaya, 1977, p. 263).

In Britain, too, some of the views of the anti-feminists were also shared by the feminists. Mary Wollstonecraft had based her plea for a better education for girls on the need to prepare women to become better wives and mothers (McGuinn, 1978, pp. 189—90) and the leading feminists of the 1850s and 1860s continued to urge the importance of the 'paramount duties of a mother and wife' (Banks, 1964, p. 48). As we have seen, many of the British educationists, as in the United States, preferred a different curriculum for girls, and even so unconventional a woman as George Eliot shared to some extent the fear that women would be unsexed. 'We can no more afford', she wrote, 'to part with that exquisite type of gentleness, tenderness, possible maternity suffusing a women's being with affectionateness, which makes what we mean by the feminine character, than we can afford to part with . . . human love' (Banks, 1964, p. 47). Moreover, even if it is no surprise that Josephine Butler believed in the special and redemptive mission of women, it is perhaps more unexpected to find Mrs Jameson, one of the Langham Place circle, writing in 1852 of the 'coming moral regeneration and complete and harmonious development in the whole human race through the feminine element in society' (Trudgill, 1976, p. 262).

This is not to suggest, of course, that the feminists accepted the traditional view of women as they found it. In the hands even of the most conservative of them the cult of domesticity became transformed into the ideal of female superiority, and the doctrine of separate spheres into the attempted invasion of the masculine world not simply by women but, potentially even more revolutionary in its impact, by womanly values. Moreover, the process by which this change occurred was bound up, as we have seen in the previous chapter, with the transformation of woman from Eve the eternal temptress to Eve the innocent victim. According to this new ideology, it was now the male who was naturally evil; the female was essentially good, and through her goodness and purity was able to redeem mankind from sin.

Fiedler (1960) has pointed out that this reversal of attitudes to women was associated with a conversion of Calvinist dogma into sentimental piety or, as he himself calls it, the Sentimental Love Religion. It was, he argues, part of 'a genteel transformation of Christianity from a religion of duty and the conviction of sin to one of benevolence and the conviction of innocence' (Fiedler, 1960, p. 52). This increasing 'feminization' of religion, as it has been called, was associated partly with the increasing importance of women in the congregation, partly with a growing stress on the softer feminine virtues of love and forgiveness (Welter, 1974). As Stevenson (1956, p. 137) puts it, 'the harshness of an earlier era was slowly melting throughout the nineteenth century, like an iceberg in warmer seas'. In the United States this transformation of Calvinism is associated particularly with Henry Ward Beecher, a brother of Catherine Beecher and an active supporter of women's suffrage in the 1860s, although in later years the scandal associated with his alleged adultery with Elizabeth Tilton was actually to harm the suffrage cause. Beecher preached a 'new experiential Christianity that emphasized God's love for man and the availability of salvation for all'. The new religion was a 'religion of the heart, an appeal to the feelings and emotions that replaced the cold, formalistic evangelical theology of the previous generation' (Clark, 1978, p. 4).

It is perhaps not surprising to find Beecher believing that women have been divinely appointed for 'the moral refinement of the race' (Hogeland, 1971, p. 113). In Britain too, Cardinal Manning, a noted social reformer, saw women as a powerful force for good in society, believing, for example, that prohibition would follow naturally if women were given the vote. His views in fact closely resembled those of Frances Willard, since he saw the home that he regarded as the centre of morality threatened by materialist and indeed masculine values (Dingle and Harrison, 1969). Nor were such views necessarily confined to religious leaders. Trudgill cites a poem by the working-class radical Gerald Massey in which he looks forward to a 'new world of moral purity' brought about by women (Trudgill, 1976, p. 262). Even Ruskin, one of the central figures in the cult of domesticity, with his analogy of the walled garden, did not deny the purifying power of women, not only within the walls of home but also in their influence on the world outside. Like the feminists, Ruskin believed that women's mission was to rescue humanity from sin (Sonstroem, 1977).

By the second half of the nineteenth century this ideal of female superiority appears to have gained wide acceptance not only amongst moral reformers, both male and female, but amongst women writers catering for the emotional needs of middle-class women not necessarily either feminists or moral reformers. The novels of the period portrayed women not only as fundamentally different from men, but as basically superior creatures. Less forcefully, but along very similar lines, they present such feminine traits as sensitivity, consideration and the expression of emotions as more desirable than the more aggressive masculine qualities. This is symbolized in the happy endings in which the male figure is himself weakened by suffering and eventually subjugated by the female (S. Mitchell, 1977; Papashvily, 1956).

Perhaps, however, the ideal of woman as moral saviour reached its fullest development at the close of the nineteenth century and in the early years of the twentieth century, which saw, particularly in the United States, the involvement of middle-class women in social reform on an unprecedented scale. Although, as we have seen, such women were active in moral reform throughout the nineteenth century, the 1890s in particular saw them embark, through the women's club movement, on a wide-ranging programme of civic improvement projects that took them considerably beyond the concern with issues like temperance that had tended to dominate earlier organizations like the Women's Christian Temperance Union. Not that this distinction should be applied too literally. Clearly temperance involves social as well as moral issues and much of the work of the women's clubs, on the exploitation of child labour for example, had a moral basis. Nevertheless, in the changing political climate at the turn of the century there was concern with social rather than individual problems and particularly with the problems produced by the growth of great cities. Moreover, the impetus to take part in reform was more secular, and less and less inspired by evangelical fervour. At this time, too, a number of factors were making it easier for middle-class women to be drawn outside the home. These included smaller families, a proliferation of labour-saving devices and more easily maintained homes (Wilson, 1979, p. 86).

The women's club movement was chiefly effective at the local level, since its members were often important and influential members of their communities (O'Neill, 1969a, p. 88). The clubs were involved in a very wide range of issues that included education, pure food, the protection of women and children in industry, and the reform of criminal justice (Wilson, 1979, p. 99). Moreover, although in some respects conservative and holding aloof from the suffragist struggle until its later stages, there is little doubt that the movement, and especially its leaders, subscribed to the view of woman's special reforming mission. Speaking in 1897, the president of the General Federation of Women's Clubs claimed their purpose to be 'to make woman a practical power in the great movements that are directing the world and for giving her the ability to serve the highly developed and complex civilization that is awaiting her influence' (Wilson, 1979, p. 103).

More important even than the women's clubs, however, was the settlement movement. This grew very rapidly from 1891, when there were only six settlement houses, to 1910, when there were 400. Whereas the clubs appealed to married women, settlement workers were mainly single and were deeply committed to the idea of social work in the great cities. Indeed, although some of this work was voluntary, the growth of the settlement movement was closely linked to the development of professional social work and shared very much the same outlook. Although, like the women's clubs, the settlement workers were concerned with the environment of the cities and especially the condition of the slums, they were also deeply involved with the exploitation of women and children by industry. Their work in this field brought them into contact with working-class women and also with the trade union movement in ways that will be discussed in chapter 7. It was primarily the settlement workers who led the fight to abolish child labour and who were responsible for the setting up of a Children's Bureau in 1912. They were also in the forefront of the attempt to improve the wages and conditions of working women. The crusade against prostitution that was part of their campaign for cleaning up the cities was also linked quite explicitly with low wages and poor working conditions for women, which their campaign for protective legislation for women and children in industry was designed to prevent (Davis, 1967).

Amongst the many women in the settlement movement perhaps the names of Florence Kelley, Julia Lathrop and Jane Addams stand out above the rest. All three came from reformist families with fathers who had supported equal rights for women. Indeed Julia Lathrop's father drafted the bill enabling women in Illinois to be admitted to the bar (Addams, 1974, p. 25). Florence Kelley was appointed Chief Inspector for Factories in Illinois in 1893, and in 1899 was invited to set up the Consumer League, an organization that campaigned against child labour, sweatshops, low wages and long working hours (Goldmark, 1953, p. 59). With Julia Lathrop she was deeply involved in the agitation for a Children's Bureau and during and after the first world war she was active in the fight for maternity and infant legislation.

It is, however, Jane Addams who is the most celebrated of the group. Born in 1860, she was one of the first generation of college women and had to reject the demands of her family in order to live an independent life of her own. At one stage medicine attracted her, but eventually she became the virtual founder of the settlement movement in the United States, and this was followed by a life-time of social reform. Although a suffragist, and radical enough to demand independence for the unmarried woman, she did not challenge many of the conventional views on women's place in society. Instead she adapted them to the cause of social reform, stressing above all the relationship between domestic and municipal housekeeping (Davis, 1973, p. 187). Moreover, as the suffrage campaign gained momentum in the early years of the twentieth century, the need to clean up the city became one of the most important reasons for giving women the vote (Kraditor, 1965, pp. 68–70). In the process, Frances Willard's argument that women needed the vote to protect the home was extended to include in its scope not simply the city but eventually, through the link between women and peace, the whole world.

Jane Addams was certainly a feminist, but her feminism did not include any abstract principle of equality. Indeed, she expressly denied that, in asking for the vote, women aspired either to be men or to be like men. In her own words, 'we still retain the old idea of womanhood — the Saxon lady, whose mission it was to give bread unto her household' (Addams, 1960, p. 103). By a neat reversal, therefore, the world of politics, which was once seen as part of the man's realm and so forbidden to women, was now claimed, in many at least of its manifestations, as no more than an extension of woman's domestic role within the household. She had indeed not only a right, but a duty, to bring her womanly qualities to bear both upon the city and ultimately upon the world so that it too, like the nineteenth-century home, would become clean and orderly, and pure.

Perhaps the most interesting of the feminists at this period was Charlotte Perkins Gilman, who has been described by Degler as the 'major intellectual leader of women's rights during the first two decades of the twentieth century' (Degler, 1956, p. 22). Born in 1860, she married in 1884, but was later separated from her husband and supported herself and their child while campaigning for a wide variety of feminist causes. It was women's economic independence from men that was fundamental to her argument for women's eventual emancipation. She was, therefore, much more radical than most other feminists at that time, who saw the vote as the key issue. Feminine qualities of weakness, helplessness and ignorance were not, in her view, essentially female, but were a product of women's constant shelter and protection within the confines of the home. Her remedy was to end women's economic dependence and social isolation by bringing them out of the home into paid employment, which would enable them to take on some of the hitherto masculine qualities and to become less narrow, less emotional and less personal. In order to make this possible, and also to avoid the waste implicit in the isolation of the housewife in individual domestic units, she advocated the adoption of nurseries for babies and young children, central restaurants instead of individual kitchens, and other collective means of carrying on woman's traditional functions in the home. Even more radically, although she saw cleaning, cooking, etc., as women's work, even if collectively organized, she called for a greater involvement of men in the care and education of children (Gilman, 1972).

She did not, it is true, criticize either marriage as such or nineteenth-century feminist views on female sexuality. Indeed, she firmly believed that, because women were forced to rely on their sex appeal for economic support, the consequence was an increase in the sexuality of both male and female, so that she saw the future in terms of a diminution rather than a heightening of sexual expression, and was, as we shall see, deeply disturbed by the sexual freedom of the 1920s and 1930s, as were indeed other feminists of her generation like Jane Addams and Caroline Catt. Moreover, like those other more conservative feminists, and in spite of her views on the artificiality of the female character, she still maintained much of the doctrine of female superiority and saw woman by virtue of her maternal role as having a special part to play in evolution. The twentieth century, she argued, gave the first chance to woman as mother 'to rise to her full place . . . to remake humanity . . . to rebuild the suffering world' (Gilman, 1935, p. 331).

In Britain, the doctrine of female superiority is less in evidence within feminism than it is in the United States, and it is possible that it was less significant, especially in the campaign for the suffrage. This would certainly be in line with the rather weaker links that have already been demonstrated between, for example, temperance and the suffrage movement, as well as the stronger Enlightenment tradition in the early years of British feminism. Nevertheless there is some evidence that the settlement movement in Britain had much in common with the settlement movement in the United States, and that the emerging social work profession had strong ties with the higher education of women and the settlements, which, for women, acted as a training ground for social work (Walton, 1975). It seems likely too that even when on School Boards or as managers of particular schools women 'exercised a strong welfare role' (Walton, 1975, p. 64). This is not to suggest that all social workers were feminist. Indeed Octavia Hill (1838—1912), a pioneer in housing management as a career for women, although approving of the educational movement, thought suffrage a red herring. Mary Carpenter (1807—1877), whose work was mainly with deprived children, also came late to women's suffrage, although she was from the first a strong supporter of the campaign for the repeal of the Contagious Diseases Acts and as a young woman had been intensely interested in the anti-slavery movement. By the end of her life, however, she had gradually come to a belief that women should have the power of voting on the same terms as men (Schupf, 1974). Of a later generation of social workers, Violet Markham also opposed suffrage initially, although she changed her mind and in 1918 was a Liberal candidate for Parliament (Walton, 1975, pp. 72—3, 158).

On the whole though, at least by the time of the main suffrage campaign, social workers in Britain were strong suffragists. Cecile Matheson, warden of Birmingham's Women's Settlement from 1909 to 1915, argued in an article published during the first world war that 'social workers have all the instincts of reformers and to such political helplessness must be galling'. While rejecting the idea that votes for women would mean a 'sudden social regeneration', she hoped it would mean an alteration in the balance of parliamentary programmes. Moreover, in citing the changes she expected, she followed in precisely the footsteps of her American counterparts by mentioning, in particular, 'pure milk, infant care' and 'the terrible social evil' (Walton, 1975, p. 76).

The attempt to base the case for women's suffrage on what O'Neill has called the 'maternal mystique' (O'Neill, 1968, p. 287) was, of course, a very far cry from a feminism that stressed the similarities between men and women. The Grimké sisters, for example, had argued for women's political and legal rights on the grounds that 'God had made no distinction between men and women as moral beings' (Flexner, 1974, p. 47). In Britain, John Stuart Mill, firmly grounded in the Enlightenment tradition, had asserted that 'what is now called the nature of women is an eminently artificial thing' (Rossi, 1970, p. 148). Yet it seems that increasingly during the nineteenth century, and especially perhaps in the United States, the feminists themselves without in any sense abandoning their claims for political and legal equality based it now upon the view not that men and women were essentially similar but that they were essentially different. Moreover, and this is perhaps the most important point, these differences sprang from women's essential femininity rather than from the rational morality that, the Enlightenment thinkers had argued, women shared with men. In effect, while they challenged women's traditional role, they accepted much of the traditional conception of womanhood, which they, like the anti-feminists, saw as rooted in women's domestic situation and above all in her potential if not her actual maternity.

It is true that not all the feminists embraced the 'maternal mystique'. Those women in both Britain and the United States who fought against a separate curriculum in higher education were certainly more concerned with women's economic independence than with their role as moral reformers and were anxious, indeed, to demonstrate in women those qualities of rationality that the anti-feminists deemed appropriate for men. Emily Davies in Britain and Carey Thomas in the United States are both good examples of women who ceaselessly and uncompromisingly pursued the goal of opening to women the knowledge, skills and prestige previously reserved for men.

On the whole, however, even when they argued like Addams for economic independence and political rights, feminists tended to base their arguments on women's moral superiority. Somewhat naturally, this view of women as the redeeming force in society was more common amongst the moral reformers, but, as was suggested in the previous chapter, the cause of moral reform, although an aspect of feminism from the very beginning, became increasingly prominent as the nineteenth century developed. Moreover, significantly, and even ironically, this concept of female superiority was carried over into the cult of celibacy, which, as we have seen, became an important aspect of feminism by the end of the century.

Celibacy was important to the feminists because it attempted to set up an alternative role for women apart from the traditional female sphere of marriage and motherhood, an alternative, indeed, that was followed from choice by many of the pioneers. It enabled them to avoid the sexual and economic subordination of marriage, while at the same time pursuing for themselves an interesting and challenging career. In fact it is surprising to see how many of the feminists chose to turn down offers of marriage in order to remain independent. This was true, for example, of Florence Nightingale, Dorothea Beale and Frances Buss in Britain, and Elizabeth Blackwell and Jane Addams in the United States. Others like Elizabeth Garrett Anderson and Lucy Stone succumbed to their suitors only after a lengthy period of wooing. Those who chose to marry were sometimes criticized for betraying the feminist cause. Susan Anthony's bitter complaints to Lucy Stone when children hindered her work for the movement have been well documented (Lutz, 1959, p. 72; Hays, 1961, pp. 150—1), and Elizabeth Garrett had to face opposition to her marriage from her friends in the Langham Place circle (Manton, 1965, pp. 213—14).

The urge for independence, however, far from arising from a desire to emulate men, may in some women have arisen from an aversion to masculine society. Taylor and Lasch (1963, p. 35), describing female friendships in the nineteenth century, see them as a direct consequence of the emphasis on female superiority that led women, even when they were married, to 'retreat almost exclusively into the society of their own sex'. They dreamed, indeed, of a 'world without men, of the perfect friendship of women unalloyed by baser and coarser natures'. Certainly some of the leading feminists, as for example Susan Anthony and Jane Addams, had close and even passionate relationships with other women, although these relationships were certainly not lesbian in any conscious sense. Clearly the concept of sisterhood implicit in much feminism would be particularly attractive to those whose dislike of men had this element in it, and this is demonstrated clearly enough, as we shall see, in the modern movement. The bonds of sisterhood may, however, have been equally as attractive to those who had simply absorbed the doctrine of female superiority (Melder, 1977, p. 30). Nor was this dislike of men shared by all feminists, even those who never married. Nevertheless, what is also clear is that even the rejection of marriage and maternity implicit in the choice of celibacy did not necessarily mean the rejection of the 'feminine mystique'. Even a woman like Jane Addams, who deliberately rejected the claims of domesticity and chose for herself independence and a career, was also, as we have seen, one of the main contributors to the doctrine that women's political role was essentially a moral one, and that in putting right the affairs of the city she was still the traditional Saxon lady giving bread to the poor.

The social workers and settlement workers in the closing years of the nineteenth century in both Britain and the United States were typical of the first generation of college women, many of whom chose to remain celibate in order to follow a career but who still saw that career in terms of women's traditional role. They formed the basis of the 'social feminists' who O'Neill suggests took over from the radical feminists and gave nineteenth-century feminism in particular its conservative character. Writing in the context of American feminism, O'Neill has criticized social feminism harshly for its failure to perceive 'the danger presented by even partial accommodation to the maternal mystique' (O'Neill, 1968, p. 287). Delamont and Duffin, however, have shown how necessary it was for the feminists if they were to be successful to articulate their ideas 'in a form acceptable to . . . dominant male opinion' (Delamont and Duffin, 1978, p. 16) and, we may add, although they do not, dominant female opinion as well. Even O'Neill himself, although he criticizes the feminists because they did not attack the nuclear family, demonstrates in his account of the Woodhull scandal the dangers to feminist goals in any radical departure from middle-class norms (O'Neill, 1969a).

Nevertheless, even if we conclude, with Delamont and Duffin, that the feminists could not have pursued a more radical strategy, given all the circumstances in which they found themselves, it is still true that their acceptance of the maternal mystique was to prove a dangerous enterprise and one that ultimately led them 'back to the home from which feminism was supposed to liberate them' (O'Neill, 1968, p. 287). The chapters that follow will be concerned to demonstrate this thesis, not only for the 'social feminists' that O'Neill is concerned with but, to some extent, even for the modern movement. For the moment, however, I am concerned with the period at the close of the nineteenth and beginning of the twentieth century, and the trap that the 'maternal mystique' led the feminists into at this time was the eugenics movement.

The appeal that eugenics had for feminism was the very positive role that it offered to motherhood. In the United States in particular Linda Gordon (1977, p. 112) has argued that a 'concern with eugenics was characteristic of nearly all feminists of the late nineteenth century'. Moreover, this concern was shown not only by the more conservative feminists but also, and perhaps therefore more strikingly, by the radical 'free love' feminists like Victoria Woodhull. Eugenics and feminism were combined to produce 'evocative romantic visions of perfect motherhood'. Feminists used eugenic arguments to buttress such feminist issues as better education for girls and voluntary motherhood, as well as many of the arguments of the social purity movement. Even so radical a feminist as Charlotte Perkins Gilman made use of eugenic arguments and claimed that the 'passing of the power to choose a mate from the women to the man was a major cause of the hereditary decline of the human race' (Gordon, 1977, p. 126).

However, as Gordon (1977, p. 130) also points out, 'every eugenic argument was in the long run more effective in the hands of the anti-feminists rather than the feminists'. This was particularly the case once the fall in the birth rate had provoked fears of 'race suicide' and for which the new generation of educated and emancipated women were given much of the blame. Even some of the feminists actually joined with Theodore Roosevelt, himself not always unsympathetic to the feminist cause, in attacking women's selfishness in seeking independence and preferring the smaller family.

In Britain, too, the eugenics movement appeared to be pro-woman in so far as women were given a crucial role in the future of the race. Indeed the eugenicists even went so far as to adopt the term 'eugenic feminism' to describe their programme (Duffin, 1978b, p. 83). At the same time, however, by placing motherhood and emancipation essentially in opposition to each other, they were often anti-feminist by implication even if not always by intention, since the eugenics movement tended to oppose all those feminist reforms that guaranteed women independence. Even work for improved maternal and infant welfare could be motivated by eugenic rather than feminist principles. In the field of education the eugenicists believed that girls should be educated for motherhood, and to educate them like men, as Emily Davies had advocated, was not only, perhaps to harm them physically but ultimately to unsex them (Duffin, 1978b, pp. 85—6). The effect, as it had been in the United States, was to emphasize the place of domestic science in schools for girls.

The 'mystique of motherhood' and even eugenics itself also exerted a fascination on many of those in the socialist movement. To some extent this had its source in utopian socialism, particularly the Saint-Simonians, who, in spite of their Enlightenment heritage and their conscious feminism, held an essentially dualistic view of the male/female differences that resembled in many ways the ideal of female superiority. The Saint-Simonians wished to organize society around cooperation or love, rather than competition or conflict, and in their eyes women had a special talent for loving. Consequently women deserved respect and even reverence (Killham, 1958, pp. 20—1, 186).

The Saint-Simonian doctrine was, therefore, ambiguous. It could be used, as it was by some of the British Owenites and especially Anna Wheeler and William Thompson, to justify a strongly feminist position. At the other extreme, in the hands of Comte, it became essentially anti-feminist: women, however respected and admired, were rigidly confined within the domestic sphere (McLaren, 1976, pp. 483—4). French socialist thought, indeed, as was noted in chapter 3, tended to be anti-feminist throughout the whole of the nineteenth century and into the twentieth century.

If socialist opinion in Britain was more likely to be feminist, this did not prevent many individual socialists holding essentially conservative opinions on women and the family. This was perhaps most clearly represented in the Social Democratic Federation, which, under Hyndman, tended to hold an 'organic view of society in which the sexes had complementary roles' (McLaren, 1978, p. 163). Moreover, by the end of the century prominent Fabians like the Webbs and H. G. Wells were clearly flirting with eugenic principles. Both Sidney Webb and Wells approved the idea of endowed motherhood and Beatrice Webb was critical of women who wanted to ape men and take up men's pursuits (McLaren, 1978, p. 189). In a phrase redolent of the 'maternal mystique', she argued that it was 'needful for women with strong natures to remain celibate, so that the special force of womanhood — motherly feeling — may be forced into public work' (Webb, 1926, p. 222).

Havelock Ellis, too, was strongly attracted by the eugenicists. Like them he believed firmly in the biological differences between male and female, and although he did not by any means deny sexual feelings to women he saw the female as naturally passive and the male as the active partner. Nor did his view of women as more affectionate and sympathetic than men and his stress on their maternal function differentiate him from conventional and even specifically anti-feminist views of the time. Although he recognized that women needed the vote, he thought the feminists wrong to seek the same opportunities as men, and his feminist sympathies were concentrated more and more on glorifying motherhood (Rowbotham and Weeks, 1977, pp. 168—73). He accepted the feminist principle that women should have control of their own bodies and was radical enough to approve contraception and abortion — but in the interests of eugenics rather than independence and self-expression. Edward Carpenter was another thinker whose sympathy for feminism concealed some conservative features, although he was much more radical than Ellis. He hoped for a freer and more equal relationship between men and women with even some interchange of function with women doing some of men's jobs and, even more unusually, men helping with housework. Nevertheless, he believed in an essential biological femininity even if it had been exaggerated by social factors (Rowbotham and Weeks, 1977, p. 113).

Olive Schreiner, who in the 1880s was friendly with both Ellis and Carpenter, was a much more radical feminist than either of them, but she too combined her feminism with views on women that, if not conservative, were certainly ambiguous. She differed from Ellis in taking a more positive view of women's sexuality and in making their economic independence the only way out of their essential parasitism. At the same time she was ambivalent on sex differences and on the maternal instinct, as well as on marriage itself. An enemy of prudery, she was suspicious of the erotic appetite, which she felt diverted women from their progress towards independence (Berkman, 1979). It was perhaps, however, in the work of the Swedish feminist Ellen Key that the maternal mystique may be seen in its fullest development. For her, feminism had nothing to do with taking over men's tasks, but everything to do with the social recognition of motherhood. Havelock Ellis was deeply influenced by her ideas and so were many American feminists, including the pioneer of birth control, Margaret Sanger, whose work will be discussed in chapter 10.

By the end of the nineteenth century feminism in both the United States and in Britain was, therefore, involved in contradictions between different definitions of feminism and different and indeed opposing concepts of femininity (Alaya, 1977). Thus we have an opposition between women's rights and women's duty, between the similarities between men and women (and the differences), between women's need for independence and their need for protection. These contradictions were not just between feminists and anti-feminists, as of course they were, but within feminism itself, and suggest indeed that there is not one feminism, but two. Moreover, these different aspects of feminism are all too often facing not only in different but actually in opposite directions, so that feminism is in a very real sense facing both ways.

It will be the purpose of Parts III and IV to explore this division within feminism as it manifested itself both in the quiet period between the suffrage campaign and the emergence of the new women's movement and in the new movement as it is taking shape today. Many of the themes of this and the preceding chapter as they relate to female sexuality, the maternal mystique and social feminism will be reintroduced and explored in greater detail, and their significance for the dual character of feminism will be a major concern. For the moment, however, it is necessary to turn to an aspect of feminism that has so far been almost completely ignored, that is, its interrelationship with social stratification. This will form the major element in both the remaining chapters in this Part, first of all in examining the relationship between feminism and the trade union movement and finally in looking at the way in which social stratification as well as party politics became involved in the struggle for the vote. In the process, the contradictions and even at times the conflict between what I have called the two faces of feminism will be further explored.

7

The Protection of the Weak

The separation of home and work that gave increasing leisure to the women of the middle classes, especially those who were unmarried, had quite a different effect on working-class women, who found themselves doing familiar work but in a different location (Scott and Tilly, 1975). In many instances, of course, the location itself did not even change, since many women were employed in domestic service and others continued as before to work within the home (Richards, 1974). For other women the transition to the factory system or the effect of factory legislation meant a change of occupation or, in the case of married women, a retreat from productive labour into domesticity. Nevertheless, the nineteenth century saw the beginning of the gradual transference of women's work from the home to the work-place, which, as we shall see, placed them, potentially at least, in direct competition with men. Increasingly, women workers were seen by men as rivals who, by accepting lower wages, reduced a man's ability to support his family, and this more than anything else underlies the relationship between women and the trade union movement throughout both the nineteenth and twentieth centuries. One consequence was the demand by male trade unionists that women be withdrawn from factory work, the other the gradual acceptance by them of equal pay, not as a principle of equal rights, but as a way to end undercutting by women workers.

On the other hand, the development of a factory system, which drew women out of the home, first in textiles and later in many of the light industries that began to expand towards the end of the nineteenth century, provided at least the potential for some degree of emancipation of women from the control of the family, even if this was only enjoyed by unmarried girls. At the same time, it provided the conditions for the development not only of class consciousness on the part of women, but also a consciousness of their identity as women. The way was at least open, therefore, for the development of feminist activity by working-class women to parallel, if it did not join, the attempts of middle-class women to form feminist organizations to press for equal rights for women. In fact, the development of such a feminist consciousness by working-class women, with certain exceptions, had to wait until the twentieth century, for reasons that will be explored in this and subsequent chapters.

In both Britain and the United States, working-class women were from time to time involved in political and industrial action within the trade union movement, often in a supportive role but sometimes on their own initiative and for their own benefit. Indeed, the role of working-class women in trade unionism resembles even if it does not exactly parallel the part played by middle-class women in social and moral reform campaigns. In neither country was the trade union movement feminist, although its leaders were sometimes sympathetic to some at least of the feminist goals. The alliance between feminism and trade unionism was, like that between feminism and the abolition of slavery movement, a highly complex one in which the position of the feminists, whether male or female, was often ambiguous, and where the pull of different loyalties produced stresses and even antagonisms both within the trade union movement and, on an even wider scale, within feminism itself. A number of studies have recently looked at the history of women's trade union membership both in Britain and the United States and these will provide the main sources for this chapter. Its main purpose, however, is not simply to repeat the outlines of a history already presented in detail elsewhere, but to explore the links between feminism and the trade union movement as they influenced the development of feminism itself.

In the United States, the 1840s were years of considerable initiative amongst women textile operatives in New England. The Lowell Female Labor Reform Association was organized in 1845 by women themselves, who set in train a very widely based programme in support of the Ten Hours Movement (Dublin, 1977, pp. 57—9). In Britain, too, working-class women took an active part in the radical movement that swept the country in the late 1830s. There is ample evidence not only of the part they played in demonstrations and meetings but of the existence of independent organizations of women; there were also female lodges of many male societies (Thompson, 1976, pp. 117—18).

The existence of these early examples does not, however, allow us to ignore the fact that much of the political and industrial activity of working-class women was unorganized and took the form of marches, meetings and similar forms of mass protest, and when organizations were formed they were short-lived, so that working women, unlike working men, remained almost entirely outside the growing trade union movement. This was partly because women were rarely permanent members of the labour force, and partly because they were employed in relatively unskilled work, which was itself largely ignored by the predominantly craft-based unions (Baer, 1978, pp. 17—21). Many trade unions, indeed, refused to accept women members (Soldon, 1978, p. 15), and, in both Britain and the United States, there were efforts to keep women as well as children out of industry altogether, as women's earnings, once a useful adjunct to the family income, now came to be looked upon as a threat to men's livelihood. Women's wages were so low that the danger of undercutting was always present, and their use from time to time as blacklegs in strikes was a further source of anxiety to the trade union movement (Boone, 1942, p. 49). Although it was recognized that for the very poor a wife's earnings were a necessity, increasingly the goal of the movement became the 'family' wage, which would allow a man to support both his wife and family. By the end of the century it had become a source of shame that a man had to send his wife out to work (Lewenhak, 1977, p. 41; Kleinberg, 1977, pp. 22—9).

The first deliberate and consistent attempt to organize women workers in Britain was made by Emma Paterson, who founded the Women's Protective and Provident League in 1874 (later the Women's Trade Union League). A feminist who had worked for a short time as a secretary to a woman's suffrage committee, and had helped Emily Faithful set up her printing society, she became, in 1875, the first woman to attend the TUC. The initiative behind the League came, however, not from the working classes but from middle-class women. Emma Paterson was the daughter of a headmaster, and, although she had to earn her own living, she did so as a white-collar worker (Goldman, 1974). Trade unionism had failed to gain a real foothold amongst women, and even where women had entered mixed unions, as in textiles, they took very little part in the leadership (Neale, 1972, pp. 150—3). It was the hope of the League to provide the encouragement and support that the struggling women's unions needed.

During the years that Emma Paterson was in charge of the League she tried not only to encourage the formation of women's trade unions, but to change the attitude of the TUC to the place of women in industry. At this time the influential trade union leader Henry Broadhurst was strongly opposed to the employment of married women, on the grounds that they should remain 'in their proper sphere at home' and should not compete against 'the great and strong men of the world' (Boone, 1942, p. 25; Goldman, 1974, p. 71). Consequently Broadhurst, along with many others, supported not only the campaign for a family wage that would make the employment of married women with husbands unnecessary, but protective legislation that it was hoped would both improve the working conditions of women workers generally, both single and married, and remove some of the threat of undercutting men's wages that was at the heart of the opposition to women's employment. Such protective legislation involved not only limits on the number of hours worked and the prohibition of night-work for women but also the exclusion of women altogether from certain kinds of work. Such protective legislation must, of course, be differentiated from Acts designed to protect male and female workers equally, whether by restricting the hours of work or by improving working conditions.

The official feminist movement at this time was opposed to protective legislation for women on the grounds that such legislation restricted their opportunities for competition with men, and Henry Fawcett, husband of the suffrage leader Millicent Fawcett and one of the main feminist spokesmen in Parliament, had actually put this case unsuccessfully to the House of Commons in debates throughout the 1870s on the restriction of the hours of employment of women. Later, in the 1880s, Millicent Fawcett and the suffrage societies helped to organize protests against restrictions on pit-brow work by women and on women nail and chain makers (Strachey, 1928, pp. 234—7).

Emma Paterson shared these views, and took them into the trade union movement itself. She saw protective legislation, not without justification, as an attempt to restrict the employment of women. Little attention was paid, for example, to the appalling working conditions of women in occupations where they were not in competition with men. While recognizing both that women workers were exploited and that, because of their willingness to work for low pay, undercutting was a real problem for the unions, she argued that the remedy was not protective legislation but the unionization of women workers. It was for this reason that she worked to encourage women to join trade unions, either alongside men, if men would permit it, or alternatively in unions of their own (Lewenhak, 1977, pp. 64, 72; Soldon, 1978, pp. 17—19; Goldman, 1974, pp. 37—8).

However, the opposition to protective legislation, while perfectly consistent with the equal rights tradition of feminism, did not take account of the difficulties involved in the unionization of the women workers. Moreover, the policy of collective bargaining, which was suiting the skilled workers well enough, did little to protect even the low-paid male worker let alone the army of low-paid and often unskilled women whose employment in any case was often intermittent if not actually casual. Protective legislation therefore was an attractive proposition not only to those male trade unionists who were concerned with the elimination of undercutting, but to many women, including some feminists, whose humanitarian concern for the plight of women, especially those in the sweated trades, was more important than their commitment to the principle of equal rights. Consequently, although feminists like Millicent Fawcett and her husband, whose liberal politics inclined them in any case towards a laissez-faire solution, continued in opposition, the League itself was soon to be committed to protective legislation almost as ardently as it had formerly been against it.

The change was brought about when the leadership passed from Emma Paterson to Lady Dilke in 1886 (Soldon, 1978, p. 29). Although both Lady Dilke and her husband Sir Charles Dilke were feminists, and Sir Charles was active in both the suffrage campaign and the campaign for married women's property rights (Strachey, 1928, pp. 118, 274), she seems to have believed like Henry Broadhurst and Ben Tillett that married women should not work (Lewenhak, 1977, p. 94). Under her guidance, League policy tried to strengthen both trade union organization amongst women and the legal protection of women workers (Boone, 1942, p. 26). At the same time the trade union movement moved away from the attempt to eliminate women from industry and towards the idea of equal pay as a device to end the undercutting by women workers. The first equal pay resolution was passed in 1888 and was actually moved by the Women's Trade Union League (Lewenhak, 1977, pp. 89—91). Increasingly, too, League policy became focused on women's pay. Mary McArthur, who followed Lady Dilke, began life as a shop assistant and was later converted to socialism. She became convinced that only minimum wage legislation could help to raise women's low wages, and it was largely as a result of her efforts that Wages Boards were set up in 1909 (Godwin, 1977, pp. 99—100).

This is not to suggest that all women trade unionists were necessarily converted to all aspects of protective legislation. Efforts to restrict women's hours of work and keep them out of certain trades continued to meet with resistance from some women workers who saw it as a denial of women's right to work. Meacham (1977, pp. 111—12) points out that the issue was a particularly heated one in dressmaking where many workshops depended on seasonal business. In some cases, as in the mineral water bottling trade, men workers replaced women when overtime hours for women were restricted by legislation in 1896. Some women trade unionists also resented the attempt to force married women into the home, and advocated communal facilities for child care as the better solution (Liddington and Norris, 1978, pp. 238—40). On the whole, however, women trade union leaders were increasingly committed to the idea of protective legislation, and this was to be the position after the 1914—1918 war not only of the trade union movement but also of the Labour Party. Moreover, although there were still feminists who took up a position similar to that of the Fawcetts' in the 1870s and 1880s, and the 1920s in particular were years in which the issue was debated within British feminism, trade union women like Marion Phillips and Margaret Bondfield were inclined to dismiss their arguments as 'bourgeois' and due to a lack of underestanding of conditions in industry (Cook, 1978, p. 170). Indeed, women trade unionists in Britain have continued to support protective legislation for women even under its attack by certain sections of the modern feminist movement (Sachs and Wilson, 1978, p. 206).

It will be necessary, in later chapters, to consider in more detail the part that protective legislation played in dividing and indeed weakening feminism in the years after the success of the suffrage campaign. What is perhaps of more significance for the present is the way in which it split the middle-class feminists not only from the male trade union leadership but also from the women leaders, both working-class and middle-class in origin, who were beginning to emerge in the last decades of the nineteenth century. To some extent this was a dispute between Liberal and Conservative feminists who supported laissez-faire in principle, and those, whether socialist or not, who welcomed the use of state control as a means of reform. Thus some of those who opposed protective legislation for women, including many feminists, were equally hostile to its extension to men, and the support for protective legislation for women by many feminists in the Labour party went along with the expectation that such legislation would eventually apply to men and women alike. At the same time, some of the controversy involved differences about the goals of feminism itself.

If we turn now to the United States we find, in certain respects, a situation that closely resembled that in Britain. In particular, the development of trade unionism amongst women faced the same problems of the nature of women's work and the indifference if not hostility of male workers. Nevertheless, some male trade unionists were helpful and the short-lived National Labor Union, a loosely knit federation of national unions, was sympathetic enough in 1868 to allow women to attend its conference as delegates. This gave Susan Anthony and Elizabeth Cady Stanton the opportunity to try to build a bridge between feminism and the labour movement to replace the alliance, then breaking down, between feminism and the anti-slavery movement. Both Susan Anthony and Elizabeth Cady Stanton attended the conference, which gave its support to both equal pay and the organization of women's trade unions although it would not endorse women's suffrage (Dubois, 1978, pp. 110–25). Susan Anthony, in an effort to encourage women's trade unions, formed the Working Women's Association and became closely involved with the efforts of women printers not only to increase their pay but also to break into the men's unions. This alliance with the trade union movement was, however, broken in 1869 when Susan Anthony's credentials were refused on the grounds that she had encouraged women to be strike-breakers. There were also allegations that her paper *The Revolution* paid non-union wages (Kugler, 1961, pp. 99–100; Dubois, 1978, pp. 133–60). The Working Women's Association, open to all working women, began to be dominated by middle-class women, often writers and journalists, and the brief flirtation between feminists and working-class women came to an end. Moreover, the women's unions established at this period, as in earlier periods, proved short-lived. Dependent all too often upon a particular woman's leadership, they also had to face opposition and prejudice from men who not only feared women as strike-breakers and as competitors but believed their place to be in the home (Dubois, 1978, pp. 158—9; Flexner, 1974, pp. 134—41).

The 1880s saw the first successful attempts to build a national trade union movement, and the Knights of Labor, under the leadership of Terence Powderly, proved sympathetic to the place of women in the movement. This may have been due to the influence of Frances Willard, whose friendship with Powderly arose out of their association in the temperance cause and in the purity campaign. The Knights of Labor and the Women's Christian Temperance Union exchanged delegates and if Frances Willard influenced Powderly towards feminism he also influenced her in the cause of trade unionism (Earhart, 1944, p. 247). Women were admitted to membership in the Knights of Labor in 1881 after a long debate in which Powderly's intervention seems to have been the crucial factor, and in 1885 a women's department was organized to look into women's affairs. Nevertheless there was still opposition at the local level where women were rejected as members. Moreover, many men's unions refused to admit women (Kenneally, 1973, p. 43).

The chief rival and eventual successor to the Knights of Labor was the American Federation of Labor, which was to dominate the scene until the 1930s. It too paid lip-service to the rights of women, but in practice its membership, of craft unions, was perhaps even less committed than the Knights of Labor to the idea of women members. Resolutions confining women to the home continued to be debated right up till 1914 and many individual unions still refused to admit women (Flexner, 1974, pp. 195—202; Kenneally, 1973, p. 45; Boone, 1942, pp. 53—5).

The situation by the end of the nineteenth century was therefore little different from that in Britain. The organization of women's work faced similar problems for similar reasons and the trade union establishment gave somewhat grudging support but little actual encouragement. It was against this background that the Women's Trade Union League was founded in 1903. Like its British counterpart, which to some extent had inspired it, the American League began as an organization of mainly middle-class reformers who were concerned at the plight of women workers. Both Leagues were, however, an attempt to combine the contribution of middle-class and working-class women and to encourage working-class women to take an active share in the leadership. Indeed, the participation of working-class women increased over time in both countries although probably rather faster in Britain than in the United States. There were, of course, great differences in the political context in which the two Leagues were founded, and this undoubtedly had its effect after 1920 when the British League was fully absorbed into the main trade union movement. Nevertheless there are striking similarities in the policies of the two organizations, and nowhere more so than in their attitude to protective legislation.

The moving spirits behind the American League were William Walling, a factory inspector and socialist, and Mary Kenny O'Sullivan, a working-class girl by origin who had been involved in settlement work with Jane Addams and who had also been a former organizer for the American Federation of Labor (Davis, 1967, p. 142). An active trade union element was therefore present from the start, but the settlement workers were also very heavily involved in all their activities. Gompers, the influential leader of the American Federation of Labor, gave his support, but was always doubtful about the middle-class element in the League. He tended to distrust the real commitment of the middle-class reformers to the working-class cause, and certainly many of them disliked violence, and advocated conciliation, although there is no doubt of their involvement in a series of strikes toward which they gave favourable publicity and a degree of financial support (Davis, 1967, pp. 104—5; Flexner, 1974, pp. 242—3).

The American League, unlike its British counterpart, was heavily involved right from the start in lobbying for protective legislation. At no time does it seem to have argued against such legislation in the way that Emma Paterson did in the early days of the League in Britain. Certainly, too, the American League was discouraged at the slow progress of trade union organization and the lack of support from men's unions. The settlement workers were in any case heavily committed to the idea of protective legislation, working not only through the Women's Trade Union League but also through the influential Consumer League under the leadership of Florence Kelley (Davis, 1967, pp. 123—35). An important aspect of the work of the Consumer League was its long struggle to prohibit child labour, and what is interesting for our purpose is the way in which protection for women was seen as a natural extension of the needs of helpless children. Indeed, the needs of women and children were frequently bracketed together as if they were the same.

At this time the main thrust of protective legislation for women took the form of setting limits on their hours of work and prohibiting night-work. The progress in such legislation from state to state was, however, threatened by the attitude of the Supreme Court, which had invalidated all protective legislation on the grounds that it violated the liberty of contract. The case for women's protective legislation therefore had to be made on special grounds, and this was achieved in the *Muller v Oregon* case of 1908, which was fought on the famous Brandeis brief (Sachs and Wilson, 1978, pp. 111—16). In effect, Brandeis argued that women needed special protection partly because of their physical structure or 'disposition' and partly because of their maternal function. Taken together these placed limits upon women's personal and contractual rights so that, in the interest of women themselves and the future of the race, women were denied the liberty of contract granted by the Constitution to men. Although recognizing the significance of women's potential maternity, this doctrine reinforced the view of women as naturally unequal in any competition with men, and indeed stressed their dependency, which was seen as natural and inevitable rather than as an aspect of social conditioning or male dominance.

What is surprising about the Brandeis brief is not that it should have been written, since it was, after all, a view common enough at the time, but that it should have been accepted and indeed welcomed by many feminists. Undoubtedly the women who supported this defence of protective legislation did so because they believed that it would improve the actual position of many women who were working excessive hours and that it would pave the way for further legislation to improve the earnings of women. They may also have seen it as a way to open up the possibilities of such legislation for men (Flexner, 1974, p. 214). They seem, however, to have paid little attention to the way in which not only protective legislation itself but the arguments on which it was based could be used to justify differential treatment for women that was not at all in their interest. In particular, it certainly enabled male-dominated unions to keep women out of certain occupations, such as printing and bar-tending, to restrict them to women's jobs in many industries, and to bar them from promotion when this would involve contravening the protective laws (Sachs and Wilson, 1978, p. 115; Baer, 1978, pp. 34—6).

Although the middle-class settlement workers were amongst the strongest supporters of protective legislation, it was by no means a simple issue of class background. One of the founders of the League, Mary Kenny O'Sullivan, who was of working-class origin, was strongly in favour, and so was Rose Schneiderman, also from a working-class background. There were also middle-class supporters of the League, like Helen Maron, who were strongly opposed to protective legislation for women only (Dye, 1977, p. 237). On balance, however, the League, like the Consumer League, was a pressure group for protective legislation throughout its whole existence.

Gompers, and the American Federation of Labor, had been early supporters of protective legislation for both men and women, but by the end of the nineteenth century Gompers had begun to change his mind. Although originally a socialist, he became convinced over time of the need for industrial rather than political solutions (Reed, 1930). He became fearful of the power of the state, and believed that legislation would ultimately be used to the disadvantage of the workers, particularly the workers' right to strike. He was even suspicious of old age pensions. He did, however, accept the need for legislation to prohibit child labour, and also approved of laws on safety at work. His attitude to protective legislation for women was complex but was undoubtedly influenced by his fear that it would be extended to men. He also believed that it could act to retard the unionization of women workers. Indeed, he seems to have been more of a feminist than many of his supporters, since he seems to have carried over a commitment to women's suffrage from his early socialist days. He then, however, recorded with feeling his indignation at Victoria Woodhull's inconoclastic views and it is clear that his socialism was never at any time influenced by radical views of marriage and the family. Moreover, although his general support for the Women's Trade Union League does not seem in doubt, the opposition of individual unions to women members was too strong for him to give them the active encouragement they needed. At the same time, his general suspicion of intellectuals and his growing doubts about protective legislation would also have put him on his guard (Gompers, 1925, pp. 55—6, 400—3).

There were, therefore, divisions within the trade union movement between the Women's Trade Union League and the American Federation of Labor that were to persist after the 1914—18 war. When the British League became absorbed into the general trade union movement at the end of the war, the American League was to continue as an independent body with its own policy, and one that, in many respects, was in opposition to the main thrust of the movement. Moreover, the absence of anything comparable to the Labour Party prevented the alliance between feminism and labour that, as we shall see, was to be an important element in British feminism.

On the other hand, the tendency for protective legislation to split the feminist movement seems to have been even more pronounced in the United States than in Britain. Although there was certainly opposition to the idea of protective legislation for women amongst pre-war feminists, concern for suffrage seems to have kept any such controversy in the background. After the granting of the vote, however, differences of opinion on the issue were brought into the open by the radical Woman's Party's advocacy of the Equal Rights Amendment. Fearful that it would mean an end to protective legislation, women like Florence Kelley opposed it fiercely. The battle that ensued will form the subject matter of Part III, but it occupied the American feminist movement for a decade and led to a decisive victory for Florence Kelley and her supporters.

The conversion of feminism in both Britain and the United States to protective legislation was in part the consequence of bringing the largely middle-class feminist movement face to face with the problems of working-class women in the context of a changing social conscience that had moved from the idea of individual charity to collective remedies for poverty and injustice. In both countries a developing social work profession largely staffed by women provided leadership in the search for reform. The facts of women's employment, brought home to them by the patient collection of statistics as well as by personal contact, cried out for remedy, and it is not surprising that protective legislation should have seemed the answer. The paternalism inherent in the prohibition of night-work and in the exclusion of women from certain occupations would not have perturbed them since they were used to perceiving the working classes as a group in need of care and protection. This paternalism is also very much in line with earlier reform movements that had proved attractive to feminists. Temperance for example, although at one stage seen as a matter for the individual conscience, became associated with social control, in the form of either prohibition or the limitation of licensing hours. It is not very far from laws on alcohol to protect women from drunken assault to laws on working hours to protect women from unscrupulous employers. There is indeed a very direct link between them in that in the United States in particular working in bars was frequently considered unsuitable for women on specifically moral grounds (Baer, 1978, p. 31).

Working-class men were prepared to accept protective legislation for women partly because they too accepted the ideology of women as in need of protection, partly because they feared their competition. Consequently they used protective legislation to safeguard their own jobs, so that frequently what the legislation protected was not the woman worker but the man's wage. Moreover, this may even have been perfectly acceptable to the married woman at home or to the single girl who saw her occupation as temporary. Working women did in fact, as we have seen, protest from time to time at the effect of protective legislation on their jobs, and sometimes, when they had support, with success. If their women trade union leaders sometimes accepted protective legislation, this was often because it seemed to offer the only solution to specific issues of exploitation, which were more important than equal rights. Indeed, to some extent they may have accepted both the notion of the family wage and the idea that certain kinds of work, or hours of work even, if suitable for men were unsuitable for women.

Protective legislation therefore raises all the issues for feminism that have been discussed in previous chapters. In addition it implies, even when it does not explicitly proclaim, not only the fact of male/female difference but also female weakness and dependence and to this extent at least female inferiority. In this sense, perhaps, it departs both from the Enlightenment tradition of equality and the evangelical version of female superiority. Nevertheless, it shares with the Evangelicals a view of women as victims that allows them, as Levine (1971, p. 181) has argued, to become 'like other victimized groups, sources of social redemption in part because of their weakness'. Levine has also suggested that, by presenting working-class women as weak and helpless while demanding autonomy for themselves, Jane Addams and others like her were making an implicit class distinction. There is much truth in this assertion, and the issue of protective legislation in particular raised the whole question of class conflict within feminism in a way that had not faced the largely middle-class feminist movement throughout the greater part of the nineteenth century.

Nevertheless it is not enough simply to dismiss the issue of protective legislation in these terms. In the first place there were, as we have seen, acute controversies about protective legislation both within the middle-class feminist movement and, to a lesser extent, among the growing number of working-class women involved in the trade union movement. The support for protective legislation by women trade unionists was not universal, and some at least shared the anxiety of some of the middle-class feminists that it would work to the detriment of the industrial workers as well as the white-collar and professional woman. Certainly the evangelical tradition within feminism showed more concern for the weak and the oppressed than for women's rights as such, but even feminists as radical as the Grimké sisters wanted social and political rights for women so that they could work more actively for those who needed their help. Moreover, if we look at the first women doctors, they were motivated more by the conviction that women were needed as doctors than by any personal inclination for the study and practice of medicine. On the other hand, the sympathy for the victim that inspired the early feminists was an aspect not of their class but their sex. Even the campaign for the abolition of slavery was influenced by what they saw as the special wrongs of the female slave. Under these circumstances the demand for traditional feminist goals like suffrage and higher education became not an expression of abstract equality but a way in which women could protect not only themselves but also their weaker sisters.

This was precisely why suffrage was so important to the feminists. It represented not only the status of citizenship but the right to have one's voice heard and one's vote counted. In this connection it is important to remember how often the feminists were disappointed during their campaigns and how easy it became to convince themselves that success would be ensured if only they had a vote. This conviction could be applied in the service of any cause that women wanted to make their own, and it was this that gave the suffrage cause its strength and converted it, in the end, from a radical group to a mass movement. It united almost all the feminists into one single campaign, and disguised the differences between them that were to become all too evident in the years after the vote had been achieved. For the time being, controversy was centred not on goals, but on issues of timing and above all on tactics. In the chapter that follows, the suffrage struggle in both Britain and the United States will be reviewed, but the emphasis will not be on details of the campaign itself. Instead the suffrage movement will be presented as an alliance between the different faces of feminism. It will be argued that the three different traditions in feminism — the Enlightenment, the evangelical movement and socialism — came together in a series of alliances in terms of which the temporary set-backs and eventual success of the campaign must be explained.

8

Votes for Women

The claim for the political emancipation of women is part of the equal rights tradition of feminism, and the demand for this enfranchisement on equal terms with men dates from the very beginning of feminism as an ideology. It was, however, only in the 1860s that it began to dominate the organized movement in both Britain and the United States so that eventually it appeared to both contemporaries and historians alike that the suffrage was feminism. This chapter will be concerned, in the main, with the years when the battle for the vote was at its height. Nevertheless it will be necessary to sketch in, briefly, the gradual emergence of the suffrage issue from one of a number of feminist aims to the dominant position it was later to reach. For purposes of convenience Britain and the United States will be taken separately although, as will be seen later, the campaign was to take on remarkably similar features in spite of considerable differences in the political context in which they took place.

Already in Britain a number of articles advocating female suffrage as a general principle had appeared early in the 1830s and the subject was, as we have seen, a topic of discussion in radical as well as Saint-Simonian and Owenite circles. In 1832 a petition was even presented to Parliament asking for the vote for all unmarried females who possessed the necessary qualifications (Fulford, 1956, pp. 33—6). The Chartists, also influenced very probably by the Owenites and particularly by the feminist and socialist William Thompson, had included female suffrage in their original Charter, although this was later dropped for fear that it might endanger the achievement of adult suffrage for men. On the other hand, the

118

women in the Chartist movement, although undoubtedly active, seem only rarely to have made any specific demands for their own rights, and were mostly content to work for the more general aims of the movement (Thompson, 1976, p. 123).

The activities of the 1830s, doubtless spurred by the debates around the extension of the male franchise in the Reform Act of 1832, were not to result in any substantial campaign for women's suffrage. Indeed working-class women were not to involve themselves in political activity until almost the end of the century. Middle-class women, on the other hand, were, as we have seen, increasingly active in the 1840s on a number of fronts, which included the anti-slavery movement and the Anti-Corn Law League as well as a more general involvement in charitable enterprises of all kinds. Very rarely, though, did this include any activity on behalf of women's suffrage, although in 1847 Anne Knight, a Quaker and a feminist, published a leaflet on the issue, and in 1851, under her influence, a Sheffield Association for Female Franchise was not only founded but succeeded in bringing a petition before the House of Lords (Fulford, 1956, pp. 37—9).

It was not until 1865 that the suffrage campaign may properly be said to have begun, encouraged, as in the 1830s, by debate within Parliament and the country on further proposals for electoral reform. Ten years previously the Langham Place circle had set in motion the activities that may properly be described as the beginning of the organized feminist movement, but, as we have seen, they began their work not with the vote but with such issues as education and employment and the extension of legal rights. Barbara Leigh Smith, one of the founders of the Langham Place group and now Barbara Bodichon, took a leading role both in bringing forward the issue of suffrage, in organizing a petition to Parliament that J. S. Mill was persuaded to present, and in founding the London-based Women's Suffrage Committee (Strachey, 1928, pp. 102—11). It was Barbara Bodichon who converted Lydia Becker, a Manchester woman who not only founded an active and important committee in Manchester but was thereafter to devote her life to the suffrage cause (Fulford, 1956, pp. 54—62). In 1867 a loose federation of local groups became the National Society for Women's Suffrage.

Most of the members of this new organization were well known in other branches of the feminist movement, although Lydia Becker was a new recruit to the cause; indeed the original London Committee was centred upon the Langham Place circle. They were, therefore, already familiar with the running of a feminist campaign. Another notable feature that has frequently been remarked upon is the extent to which the suffragists, and this includes Lydia Becker, had been involved in the earlier campaign for the repeal of the Corn Laws. Although in no sense feminist in its specific aim, this particular movement, like the anti-slavery campaign, made considerable use of women in fund-raising activities and in collecting signatures for petitions and memorials (Hollis, 1979, pp. 287—8, 290—1). Moreover, Richard Cobden, one of the leaders of the campaign, was a supporter of female suffrage and his daughters were active feminists (Rosen, 1974, p. 8). The association with the Anti-Corn Law campaign seems to have been of importance not only in introducing women like Lydia Becker to political activity but also in providing them with lessons in tactics. Petitions, and especially lobbying, were to be the methods of the suffragists until the time of the militants at the beginning of the twentieth century.

Amongst the suffragists the Quakers formed a powerful group (Ramelson, 1967, p. 81). The Unitarians also continued to be important (Holt, 1938, p. 153). Indeed the Unitarians were also deeply involved in the Anti-Corn Law League, and this may explain some of the connection between the League and women's suffrage (Holt, 1938, p. 197). The closest political tie at this time was with the Liberals, although later, as we shall see, the socialists were to become more important. Nevertheless, the Liberals were by no means a feminist party and many of their leaders, like Gladstone and later Asquith, were implacably opposed (Rover, 1967, p. 119).

During the 1870s, and subsequently throughout the century, most years saw a Private Member's bill, so that the issue was frequently before Parliament. The extension of the franchise in 1884, like other such reforms, also saw a special, if equally unsuccessful, attempt to change the law with respect to women. Nevertheless, these years were by no means without disagreement amongst the suffragists themselves. One such breach, at the time of the contagious diseases campaign in 1870 and already described, lasted until 1879 before it was healed and illustrates the endeavour to keep the suffragists 'respectable'. There was also some dispute as to whether or not the suffragists should expressly exclude married women (Rosen, 1974, pp. 10—15). Later on, after the founding of the Women's Liberal Federation in 1886, there was a split between those who wished to work within the Liberal Party, through the Women's Liberal Federation, and those who wished to remain independent (Strachey, 1928, pp. 281—2).

By the end of the 1880s, however, it was becoming clear that in spite of over twenty years of campaigning, and in spite of the support and encouragement of a sector of the Liberal Party both within and outside Parliament, the success of the suffragist cause was as far away as ever. Part of the reason for this was the apparent lack of support for female suffrage amongst women themselves, and most damaging perhaps at this time was the protest against women's suffrage that appeared in the *Nineteenth Century* magazine in 1889 signed by a group of prominent women including Mrs Humphrey Ward and Beatrice Webb (Harrison, 1978, p. 116). Even more telling, in the long run, was the lack of any really widespread support in the Liberal Party. Although a few radicals were deeply committed to the idea, many of those who supported it in principle had no intention of voting for it against the wishes of their leader or when it seemed to jeopardize the fortunes of their party (Morgan, 1975, p. 25).

One of the reasons for Liberal opposition — and this was to apply, later on, to the newly formed Labour Party — was the fear that to enfranchise women would be to increase the Conservative vote. Not only were women generally believed to be naturally conservative, and likely to fall under the influence of the Church, but, because the franchise was tied to property, an extension to women would simply increase the representation of the property-owning classes. To some extent, of course, this argument may have attracted the Conservative Party to the suffragist movement, and certainly individual Conservatives did support it and even acted as sponsors for suffrage bills in Parliament. In fact, at the level of party leadership the Conservative Party may have been no more anti-suffrage than the Liberals. In the rank and file, however, there was less support, and indeed a hard core of opposition that lasted until 1928 (Harrison, 1978, pp. 27—30; Rover, 1967, pp. 110—15). This was in part a suspicion of any move towards democracy, in part a Conservative respect for women's traditional role.

If by the end of the 1880s the suffragists had reached something of a stalemate, by the end of the 1890s and early 1900s the movement had entered a completely new phase. This was largely the result of two new factors in the situation: the growth of support for women's suffrage amongst women themselves, and the increasing importance of the labour movement in British politics. If we are to understand the dramatic change in the fortunes of the suffrage issue that was to take place in the twentieth century it is necessary to look at these two new circumstances in turn. It will not be possible to do this in other than broad outline; indeed, so fully have they been documented, it is hardly necessary to do so, and those who wish to know the details are referred elsewhere.

The growing support for women's suffrage within the new profession of charitable work and in the settlement movement has been mentioned briefly in chapter 6. For these women the vote was seen as a powerful tool for the reformation of society and they began not only to accept its necessity but, in many cases, to join actively in the campaign. Eleanor Rathbone, for example, had a life-long involvement with social reform that took her from social work into Parliament. She became an ardent suffrage supporter in the 1890s and continued active in the suffrage campaign although she never supported the militant side of the movement (Stocks, 1949, p. 64). Mary Stocks' account of the Manchester Settlement draws attention to the very close ties between the suffrage movement and the settlement workers, some of whom, like Alice Crompton, left the settlement to work more actively in the suffrage cause (Stocks, 1956, pp. 34—5). A number of the leaders of the militant suffragettes had also been active in social work. Charlotte Despard was one of the earliest poor law guardians and had founded one of the first child welfare centres in the country (Fulford, 1956, p. 145). Emmeline Pethick Lawrence and her husband Frederick Lawrence, both from a prosperous background, were also involved in social welfare. Emmeline had worked in the West London mission from 1890 until 1895 and afterwards continued in various social work enterprises until she met and married Frederick in 1901 (Pethick-Lawrence, 1938). Frederick had lived in a university settlement for some time and was deeply involved in social welfare (Pethick-Lawrence, 1943). Neither of them was involved in the suffrage issue at the time of their marriage, being more deeply concerned with poverty and the 'economic and social deliverance of the toiling masses of the people' (Pethick-Lawrence, 1938, p. 145). Emmeline was eventually converted by Annie Kenney in 1906 and drew her husband in with her.

The years after 1900, and particularly after the first wave of militancy drew public attention to the arguments for women's suffrage, produced new converts even amongst those who had formerly been in active opposition. In 1889 many women novelists supported the appeal against women's suffrage organized by the novelist Mrs Humphrey Ward, but by 1908 there was a Women

Writers' Suffrage League that carried out pro-suffrage propaganda (Showalter, 1977, p. 218). Similarly, Beatrice Webb, perhaps the most important of the signatories of the appeal, changed her mind in 1906 (Hynes, 1968, p. 97). Violet Markham, a prominent member of the Anti-Suffrage League, was converted in 1912 (Markham, 1953, pp. 95—9).

Most important of all, however, was the support given to women's suffrage by women in the growing labour movement. By the 1890s a number of such women, middle-class in origin but socialist in politics, were campaigning for women's suffrage through their involvement with working-class women. Most significant in this respect was the newly formed Independent Labour Party, which was feminist from its inception — unlike many other socialist groups, as for example the Fabians, who did not adopt a suffrage policy until 1906 (Cole, 1961, pp. 127—9), and the anti-feminist Social Democratic Federation (Rowbotham, 1973a, pp. 95—8). This may have had something to do with the links between the ILP and temperance, and the fact that it was led by active nonconformist preachers and temperance advocates like Keir Hardie (Bealey and Pelling, 1958, p. 8). On the other hand, Budd (1977, pp. 249—50) shows that there was also an association between the Unitarians and the ILP. Some Unitarian congregations at this period moved not only into the ethical movement but out again into the ILP. Indeed, politically, most members of the ethical movement, still largely a development out of Unitarianism, were not only left-wing in politics but suffragists as well. They therefore continued the feminist tradition of the radical Unitarians at the beginning of the nineteenth century. The feminism of the ILP may thus have had a Unitarian as well as a temperance and nonconformist source. Certainly many of the leaders were feminist, and Kier Hardie in particular was one of the most constant and devoted supporters even of the militant suffragettes.

During the 1890s middle-class women like Kathleen St John Conway, later Mrs Bruce Glazier, and Enid Stacey became ILP lecturers, and spread not only socialism but also feminism amongst working-class women. Hannah Mitchell, a working-class member of the ILP, was certainly influenced by these lectures in both her socialism and her feminism and later became active in both campaigns (H. Mitchell, 1977, pp. 86—98). At the same time Esther Roper and Eva Gore-Booth, both middle-class socialists, made women's suffrage into a trade union matter by linking it with women's work and women's wages and bringing it directly to the attention of working-class women trade unionists in the cotton mills (Liddington and Norris, 1978, pp. 77—83).

It was the Co-operative Women's Guild, however, that was to be perhaps the most constant supporter of women's suffrage within the labour movement. Founded originally by the wife of an Oxford don in the belief that Co-operation would benefit the working classes, the Guild was initially conservative, insisting that woman's place was in the home and trying to avoid the antagonism aroused by women's rights. However, after 1889 when Margaret Llewelyn Davies, a niece of Emily Davies and a staunch feminist, became General Secretary it was quickly to change its role (Gaffin, 1977, pp. 114—17). A suffrage petition was organized as early as 1893, and the Guild continued an active campaign for the vote, organizing petitions amongst women textile workers and pressing suffrage petitions upon a somewhat reluctant Co-operative Congress (Webb, 1927, pp. 97—9).

The support for women's suffrage within the labour movement was to prove as problematic, in practice, as support within the Liberal Party, and for very similar reasons. Although some labour leaders were firmly and unshakeably feminist, others remained unconvinced. Moreover many who accepted it in principle were, like many Liberals, totally opposed to a bill that would simply extend the suffrage, limited as it was to householders, to include women. Such a proposal, it was claimed, would tip the scales even further against the working-class man without going very far, if at all, to enfranchise working-class women. The labour movement was therefore split between those who saw a limited suffrage bill as the thin end of the wedge and those who refused absolutely to consider anything less than universal suffrage. Moreover, this was an issue that not only divided the men in the movement but the women as well (Rendel, 1977, pp. 59—63). An Adult Suffrage Society was formed, under the leadership of the woman trade union leader Margaret Bondfield, who saw the issue primarily as one of social class. Although a supporter of women's suffrage, she nevertheless consistently opposed any limited extension of the franchise, pointing out that some of the suffragists like Millicent Garrett Fawcett and Frances Balfour in fact had no interest in adult suffrage. She argued that to wait and work for universal suffrage was the quickest way to real sex equality. Bruce Glasier, the chairman of the ILP, was also a strong opponent of a limited franchise. Like Margaret Bondfield he believed that the achievement of socialism was much more important than women's rights, and his views brought him into conflict with both the Pankhursts and Keir Hardie (Thompson, 1971, pp. 148–50).

Support within the labour movement for a limited suffrage came from a group of what Liddington and Norris call 'radical suffragists'. Some were from the ILP, some from the Women's Co-operative Guild and some from the Women's Trade Union League. They argued that even a limited extension represented an advance for women at a time when adult suffrage was not practical politics. Much of their case rested upon their claim that even an extension of the franchise on the same terms as men would give the vote to large numbers of working women, since widows and spinsters in particular were often householders. They therefore queried the view that a limited franchise extension would necessarily increase the vote against Labour, and a debate on this issue raged hotly for a time (Liddington and Norris, 1978, pp. 180–1; Rosen, 1974, pp. 34–5).

Even so, the issue presented the radical suffragists with an agonizing dilemma since they were able, in a way that many of the militant suffragettes did not, to see both sides of the question. The indecision that followed is reflected in the many debates within the labour movement on the issue and the change of policy that occurred even from year to year, as first one side then the other gained the advantage in the argument (Rendel, 1977, pp. 62–75). Even the Women's Co-operative Guild, otherwise unusually consistent in urging the claims of a limited franchise, wavered from time to time. The Women's Trade Union League was divided, but tended, like the TUC, to favour adult suffrage; the same was true of the newly formed Women's Labour League. On the whole, in the labour leadership itself and in the rank and file, opinion hardened against a limited franchise in spite of the continued support of men like Keir Hardie and George Lansbury, and in 1907 the Labour Party conference rejected any extension of the suffrage based on property qualifications. The result was to paralyse the Labour Party equally with the Liberals, so that the initiative in the battle for the vote passed to the militant suffragettes under the leadership of Emmeline Pankhurst.

The association between the Pankhursts and women's suffrage was a long one, since Emmeline's husband Richard Pankhurst had helped found the Manchester Women's Suffrage Society in 1865 and had worked with Lydia Becker for many years. He had been involved in both the inclusion of women householders in the municipal franchise in 1869 and, later, in the Married Women's

Property Bill (Mitchell, 1967, p. 20). In 1889 he and his wife Emmeline helped to form the Women's Franchise League, which emphasized equal voting rights for married women and equal divorce and inheritance rights. In 1894 their increasing radicalism led them into the Independent Labour Party, but after Richard's death in 1898 Emmeline retired from active politics; it was her daughter Christabel's friendship with Eva Gore Booth and Esther Roper that eventually led Emmeline back into the women's suffrage movement. The Women's Social and Political Union (WSPU), founded by Emmeline Pankhurst in 1903, was drawn initially from ILP members and it was aimed at raising support for women's suffrage within the labour movement. Even as late as 1906 it was still a tiny provincial movement dependent for financial support mainly on the ILP (Rosen, 1974, pp. 15—32). By 1907, however, it had broken both with the labour movement and with the traditional suffragist association with the Liberals, and turned to the Conservative Party for support. At the same time it changed its campaign from one for adult suffrage to one for a limited franchise on the same terms as men (Morgan, 1975, pp. 46—7).

The emphasis on a limited extension of the franchise was now shared by both the moderate suffragists, still led by Millicent Garrett Fawcett, and the WSPU. The difference between them was solely one of tactics. Having failed to convince either the Labour Party or the Liberal Party by argument, the WSPU looked to other methods to press their claim. In the early days the WSPU, although militant, was not violent. The aim of heckling was to seek publicity and to force themselves upon the attention of Parliament. By the use of marches as well as petitions they sought to attract recruits to their cause as well as to demonstrate the extent of their support. The increasing violence that crept into this campaign was partly due to the style of leadership of the Pankhursts themselves, partly to the frustrations of the campaign itself.

It seems clear, in retrospect, that the suffragists militant and otherwise, were overoptimistic about the effect of their tactics. Even in their most violent phase they were never sufficiently a threat to exert real pressure on the government and their action alienated some of their supporters and strengthened the hands of the anti-suffrage campaigners (Rosen, 1974, pp. 242—4; Harrison, 1978, pp. 184—94). Nor did they recognize the strength of the forces ranged against them. Neither the Liberals nor the Labour Party, even though in favour of the principle of women's suffrage, were happy about a limited suffrage bill, which seemed to them to bring electoral advantage largely to their political opponents.

The Conservative Party had no prejudice against a limited extension of the franchise as such, though many members were anti-feminist in principle. Nevertheless there was sufficient support within the Conservative Party to make it seem worthwhile to frame a measure for a limited franchise that would, hopefully, get support from within all the parties sufficient to carry it through. In 1910 a Conciliation Committee was set up and a Conciliation Bill framed, but in 1912 it was finally defeated, faced with strong opposition from both the Liberal and the Labour parties to any measure that merely extended the vote to women householders. Lloyd George for example, although a convinced adult suffragist, was nevertheless not prepared to give 'thousands of votes to the Tory Party' (Rosen, 1974, p. 151). There were many others who shared this view and in spite of the support given by a few Labour leaders and by the Co-operative Women's Guild the rank and file of the Labour Party were against it (Rendel, 1977, p. 68). There were many in the Conservative Party of course who were convinced anti-feminists. So was Asquith, who would not at this time have been prepared to support any women's suffrage measure. Churchill, too, believed that women had no great practical grievance (Rosen, 1974, p. 162). He advocated a referendum to women on the issue, followed if necessary by one to men to see if they were prepared to accept it (Morgan, 1975, p. 88).

By 1912, however, now that the Parliament Act of 1911 had curbed the power of the Lords, adult male suffrage no longer seemed outside the realm of practical politics. Moreover the Labour Party had accepted, although not without a struggle, a conference resolution to oppose any government bill for electoral reform unless it included women. This decision was significant in that it gained for Labour the support of Millicent Garrett Fawcett, as the only party prepared to pledge its support for women's suffrage. Even while the Conciliation Bill was still under discussion, steps were taken towards the introduction of a new Franchise Bill that, by ending plural voting and giving votes to lodgers, virtually gave manhood suffrage. Asquith, while not hiding his personal opposition, agreed to accept an amendment to include women, but, in the event, the decision of the Speaker to refuse to accept such an amendment, on the grounds that it would require a new bill, dashed the suffragists' hopes yet again. The failure of the Conciliation Bill and the Speaker's decision, which was interpreted as betrayal, sparked off the final and most destructive phase of militancy before the outbreak of war brought it to an end. The Speaker's decision also precipitated a Cabinet row that resulted in the withdrawal of the Franchise Bill and the effective postponement of electoral reform until the end of the war (Morgan, 1975, pp. 110—18).

Even if the amendment had been allowed, however, there was no guarantee that it would have been successful. The suffragists in the Conservative Party wanted no part in any radical extension of the suffrage for either men or women, a position that was also taken by some of the Liberals. Asquith was deeply opposed and was able to draw on the support of anti-suffrage sentiment within the Liberal Party. The important Irish vote was also expected to be anti-suffrage since they would do nothing to endanger the Home Rule Bill. Lloyd George, who was, according to Morgan, 'the only man with political force enough to secure the inclusion of women's suffrage and prevent the break-up of the government', was silenced at this time by charges of corruption (Morgan, 1975, p. 107). Even within the Labour Party there was no unanimity. At the 1912 conference the voting had been 919,000 in favour, against an opposition of 686,000 votes, which included the important Mineworkers Federation (Morgan, 1975, p. 92). In 1914, at another turbulent debate, a Fabian resolution asking that the government Franchise Bill be rejected unless it included women's suffrage was rejected by the delegates. Ramsey McDonald, pointing out the great value of the bill to Labour, pleaded that the women's suffrage issue must not be allowed to harm the Labour Party. Indeed, as Morgan points out, even without the issue of women, the Franchise Bill was at risk and, given Asquith's own opposition, the dice certainly seem to have been loaded against the women's cause, although if Asquith had supported women's suffrage the situation might well have been different (Morgan, 1975, pp. 128—9, 152—8).

The outbreak of war postponed electoral reform for both men and women and by the time that it was again a serious possibility the situation had changed in various ways. Asquith, although he had probably little more personal enthusiasm for women's suffrage than he had before the war, was prepared to yield on the issue. Lloyd George was now Prime Minister and, as a convinced adult suffragist, was prepared to place his and the government's weight behind the measure. Moreover, the fact that it was now a coalition government meant that it could draw on support in all parties. There had also been some shift of opinion amongst MPs in favour of votes for women, although certainly there is little evidence of the 'swing' that women's work in the war is sometimes believed to have produced (Pugh, 1974).

Even so, the inclusion of women in the 1917 bill was by no means a foregone conclusion, and Pugh's (1974) analysis of the situation indicates that the acceptance of votes for women was certainly not enthusiastic even in 1917. In the event, the Act in 1918 introduced adult suffrage for men only. For women, the suffrage was limited to those over 30 who were local government electors, or the wives of local government electors, or university graduates. By restricting women's suffrage mainly by age the government allayed the fear that many still had that the country would be governed by women, but it also avoided the obvious Conservative bias of a women's franchise limited by property qualifications. The suffragists themselves were not at all happy with this compromise but were prepared to accept the situation and there was in any case no active suffrage movement at this time to take the initiative in the matter. Moreover, there is no doubt that the main principle had been conceded and the battle for women's suffrage had been won. Frederick Pethick-Lawrence for example, writing in 1943, claimed that in 1918 women's societies 'celebrated the victory with enthusiasm. It did not trouble us overmuch that absolute victory had not been attained. We recognized that it was in accordance with British tradition to proceed a step at a time' (Pethick-Lawrence, 1943, p. 104).

It can be seen, therefore, that the political enfranchisement of women in Britain was complicated by the issue of adult suffrage, which confused considerations of sex and class, dividing the loyalties of men and women alike. The committed feminists were prepared to put the issue of women's rights first, but for those in the labour movement in particular this often produced an agonizing dilemma as they weighed their feminism against their socialism. It does not follow, however, that in the absence of this complication victory would have been achieved much earlier. Certainly there is some evidence that if the Liberal and Labour parties had been prepared to accept a limited extension of the suffrage a measure like that of the Conciliation Bill of 1912 that would just have enfranchised women householders might well have been successful, thus giving some women the vote a few years earlier than they actually achieved it. The active support of Asquith rather than his determined opposition might also have made a difference. Even in 1917, however, when Parliament was at last ready to grant adult suffrage to men, it was not prepared to do so for women. We therefore need to look more closely than we have done previously at the source of the anti-suffrage sentiments that delayed adult suffrage to women until they were finally granted equal suffrage with men in 1928.

As we have seen, the issue of votes for women was not simply a party matter. Some Conservative leaders, even if they opposed adult suffrage, were quite prepared to give equal political rights to property owners, whether male or female, whereas some of the leading Liberals, whether or not they supported adult suffrage, were, like Asquith, determinedly anti-feminist. Even as late as 1920 he said of women electors that they were 'hopelessly ignorant of politics, credulous to the last degree and flickering with gusts of sentiment like candles in the wind' (Pugh, 1974, p. 368). The Labour Party, if perhaps the most sympathetic of the three parties to feminist goals, nevertheless had its share of men whose commitment was little more than a token acceptance of democratic principles that rarely produced any positive action. Labour Party members too were troubled by the belief that women were naturally more conservative than men; an opinion that also influenced the Liberal Party. Nevertheless it is probably true to say that the great bulk of the really hard-core opposition came from within the Conservative Party, which unlike the Labour Party and the radicals within the Liberal Party had no adherence to the principle of democracy.

In general, the political enfranchisement of women was seen by its opponents — as indeed it was — as a further and yet more radical intrusion by women into man's traditional sphere, an intrusion on which they had already embarked in their assault upon higher education and the professions, and that they were now about to complete by entering into the realm of government itself. Harrison (1978, pp. 97—9), in his detailed study of the opposition to women's suffrage, has also drawn attention to the association between the leadership of the anti-suffrage organizations and men's clubs, which represented, even into the twentieth century, male exclusiveness in its most extreme form.

Even men and women who had made a contribution to women's education, like Mrs Humphrey Ward and James Bryce, could nevertheless draw the line at the prospect of women as legislators (Harrison, 1978, pp. 55—6), so that not all those who were against women's suffrage were necessarily against women's education or their involvement in social welfare. Attitudes had changed over the years and these activities were now frequently recognized as

[handwritten marginalia: changed view of women etc. But still seen as inferior]

belonging quite properly to women's sphere. Violet Markham, an active anti-suffragist until her change of mind in 1912, was influenced by Mrs Humphrey Ward and admired her work for the settlement movement. Moreover in spite of her opposition to women's suffrage in national government, Violet Markham was a firm supporter of women's work in local government. By 1918, however, she had come to see the denial of full political rights to women as 'the stabilization of a status of permanent inferiority' (Markham, 1953, p. 99). Some women indeed, and this included Beatrice Webb, seem to have believed that women could enjoy a great deal of influence on society without the possession of the vote. It was easy, too, for men and women to believe that married women, at least, could be adequately represented by their husbands, and that votes for married women were simply another form of plural voting. It was also claimed quite frequently that Parliament had always been very responsive to the needs of women and that the vote was not necessary (Harrison, 1978, pp. 73—83).

Most deeply felt of all, perhaps, was the fear of government by women and, as we have seen, the Act of 1918 was careful to limit women's franchise precisely in order to avoid any such possibility. To some extent this seems to have been a fear of the irrationality and emotionality of women and the sheer unpredictability of admitting them into the electorate. For others, however, the woman voter roused more specific fears, most frequently from the alliance between temperance and feminism; Harrison points particularly to the opposition of the brewing interests, but feminism's links with moral reform were also a source of anxiety. Thus as Harrison (1978, p. 138) suggests, 'the easy-going atmosphere of the pub, the race-course, and the music-hall found suffragism uncongenial'. It is perhaps not without significance that Churchill, while a cadet at Sandhurst in the 1890s, had been involved in tearing down screens put up to protect the public from prostitutes in the Empire Theatre, Leicester Square. These screens had been part of a social purity campaign launched by Mrs Chant, a member of the London County Council and an active purity campaigner. The virulent purity campaign launched by the Pankhursts in 1913 with the slogan 'votes for women, purity for men' did nothing to counteract this impression. Moreover, by this time the militant movement, now largely in the hands of Christabel Pankhurst, had become violently anti-male, rejecting even political allies (Mitchell, 1967, pp. 31—7).

The fear of an alliance between women and a minority of male reformers was clearly an element in Dicey's anti-feminism. 'It is not certain', he wrote to a friend in 1909, 'that in such circumstances Englishmen would obey and enforce a law that treated as a crime conduct which they in general held ought to be treated as an offence, not against law, but against morality' (Rover, 1967 p. 45). It is not possible to say how important this kind of anxiety was, but Pethick-Lawrence (1943, p. 68) believed that fear of women's impossibly strict standards of morality was the principal cause of the opposition to women's suffrage.

Ironically, the suffrage cause also suffered from accusations of immorality on the grounds that some of its supporters were advocating motherhood outside marriage (Harrison, 1978, pp. 195—6). In no sense, of course, were these views part of the programme of either the militant or the non-militant suffragist movements, and even Christabel's advice to women not to marry was based upon conventional ideas of morality. Nevertheless, there were advocates of a freer morality amongst the feminists and, between 1911 and 1913, these were propagated by a journal *The Freewoman,* which developed a doctrine of free love and discussed female sexuality in a manner quite opposed to that of the Pankhursts. It was edited by Dora Marsden, a graduate of Manchester and a militant suffragist who had been to prison in 1910 (Rowbotham, 1977, p. 11). Such a view, while it reawakened the free love fears that had haunted the feminist movement since its beginnings, was no nearer to representing the main tradition of feminism than it had ever been. It was instead a reincarnation of the romantic communitarian socialism of the Saint-Simonians and the Owenites, in which the establishment of a socialist society involved a radical reassessment of marriage and the family. This tradition of feminism had never disappeared completely from socialism, although it was at no time to be more than an undercurrent within socialist and especially anarchist thought. Moreover the anarchists, even when they were feminists, were not suffragists, as they tended to maintain the need to overthrow the whole system rather than simply to extend the franchise (Rowbotham, 1973a, pp. 99—101).

Nevertheless, there is no doubt that women's suffrage was feared both because it could impose too great a morality on society *and* because it could herald the break-down of the sanctity of the home. In either case women were seen as stepping out of their proper sphere and threatening to replace their former dependence not simply by independence, as in the case of their claim for employment opportunities, but, because of their numerical preponderance, by actual political domination. This, of course, was to exaggerate the significance of the vote itself, on the part of both the suffragists themselves and their opponents. Nevertheless, because of the importance attached to it, political enfranchisement aroused passions out of all proportion to the subsequent consequences. The achievement of the vote, therefore, did in many respects represent the end of an era in feminism. It will be the purpose of subsequent chapters to demonstrate that this was in fact by no means the end of the story. First, however, it is necessary to look at the suffrage campaign in the very different political context of the USA.

As in Britain, suffrage was not so prominent in the early days of the movement as it was to become later. At the meeting at Seneca Falls the suffrage issue was pressed hard by Elizabeth Cady Stanton, but it aroused more controversy than any other issue, and her chief support came, not from the other women present, but from the ex-slave Frederick Douglas. Eventually her resolution on suffrage was carried, but only by a narrow margin as there were fears that such a revolutionary claim might harm the feminist cause in general (Oakley, 1972, p. 47). Another factor may have been Lucretia Mott's acceptance of the Quaker boycott of the vote in a society not yet based on Quaker principles (Paulson, 1973, pp. 39—41). The first campaigns of the newly organized movement were therefore involved, as in Britain, with issues of women's property and earnings, child custody and the double standard (Sachs and Wilson, 1978, p. 81).

During the 1850s and indeed up until the outbreak of the Civil War, suffrage speedily came to take a more important part in the debate, and both Lucy Stone and Susan Anthony lectured widely on the issue, but with the outbreak of war all specifically feminist propaganda ceased and much of the women's effort went into the war effort or into the anti-slavery cause (Flexner, 1974, pp. 110—11). The victory for the North, by raising the issue of the Negro vote, was to thrust women's suffrage to the fore, where it was to remain until it was finally achieved in 1920. Its immediate effect, however, was disastrous, ending the collaboration between the anti-slavery and feminist forces and splitting the still small feminist movement wide apart.

Unlike Britain, where the suffragists were divided on the issue of property qualifications, the United States by this time already had adult white male suffrage, but race was to play a similar role to property in dividing women and their allies on the same grounds of

loyalty and expediency. The Northern victory had made the Negro
vote possible, if by no means certain, and the abolitionist leaders
were not prepared to jeopardize the Negro in the interests of
women. This was partly principle, in that they did not believe that
the injustice and cruelty that faced women was of the same order
that faced the Negro slave. At the same time it was also a matter of
political expediency. If Negro suffrage was uncertain, women's
suffrage was much more so, and to mix the two issues seemed to
doom Negro suffrage to failure, and of the leading male abolitionists
scarcely any remained loyal to women's rights (Dubois, 1978,
pp. 57—63). Even Frederick Douglas, Elizabeth Cady Stanton's
chief ally in 1848, was unable to sustain his feminist beliefs in what
was then regarded as the 'Negro's hour'.

The feminists reacted to this threat by forming their own
organization, the Equal Rights Association, with the aim of working
for adult suffrage, concentrating their efforts on a campaign at the
state level. Its membership included some anti-slavery males, but
the largest group was composed of women who had worked within
the Anti-Slavery Society for both abolition and women's rights. In
1867 all the efforts of the Equal Rights Association were poured
into a state campaign in Kansas, only to meet with an 'overtly anti-
feminist counter campaign waged by the State Republican Party'
(Dubois, 1978, p. 80). The abolitionist leaders, resting all their
hopes for black suffrage on the Republican Party, remained aloof.
The Equal Rights team found that neither the abolitionist nor the
radical press was prepared either to assist or indeed even to
recognize their efforts.

The hostility of the Kansas State Republican Party to women's
suffrage not only deeply disappointed the women campaigners but
led Elizabeth Cady Stanton and Susan Anthony to look to support
from the Democrats. They also, as we saw earlier, accepted the
help of Train, a Democrat and racist who was prepared to endorse
women's suffrage in order to challenge the Republican Party
(Dubois, 1978, p. 93). The result was a breach in the leadership of
the movement between Susan Anthony and Elizabeth Cady
Stanton on the one hand, and Lucy Stone and Henry Blackwell on
the other, who were not prepared to accept either Train or the
abandonment of the Republican cause. Although disappointed in
the party's refusal to support women's suffrage, they still believed
in its commitment to egalitarian principles.

The final break came over the issue of the Fifteenth Amendment,
which prohibited disenfranchisement on the grounds of race, but

excluded women from consideration. Lucy Stone and Henry Blackwell were prepared to accept the amendment in exchange for a promise, never of course kept, for future Republican support (Dubois, 1978, p. 163). Elizabeth Cady Stanton and Susan Anthony, on the other hand, argued that the passing of the Fifteenth Amendment would actually intensify sexual inequality by making sex the only grounds for disenfranchisement. By abandoning the cause of the Negro man, Elizabeth Cady Stanton and Susan Anthony had to face the charge that they were callously disregarding the suffering of the black people whose interest, it was argued, must come first; it is very clear that this consideration weighed heavily with many abolitionists, both male and female, who were not prepared to jeopardize the Negro vote for what was believed to be a less urgent cause. In addition, however, both Susan Anthony and Elizabeth Cady Stanton were led into both racist and elitist arguments that, as we shall see, were to come increasingly to characterize the women's suffrage movement in the future.

Eventually, in 1869, Susan Anthony and Elizabeth Cady Stanton organized the National Woman Suffrage Association, which admitted only women on the grounds that the earlier Equal Rights Association had been duped by men. This was followed by the founding of the American Woman Suffrage Association, a more conservative group in which Lucy Stone and her husband Henry Blackwell were the most dominant members. Whereas the 'American' concentrated narrowly on the suffrage, the 'National' espoused a variety of causes, including, as we saw in chapter 4, divorce and the organization of working women (Dubois, 1978, p. 197). The American had its own journal in opposition to Susan Anthony's *The Revolution. The Woman's Journal,* as it was called, steered clear of controversial topics and tried to appeal to the conservative woman not yet converted to suffrage (Hays, 1961, pp. 253—4, 311).

From the 1870s onwards, however, American feminism, in both the suffrage associations, concentrated increasingly on the vote. A new Women's Declaration of Rights in 1876 prepared by Susan Anthony and the National gave much more emphasis to political enfranchisement than the Seneca Falls Declaration in 1848 (Sachs and Wilson, 1978, p. 110). This was partly because some of the original demands, like the right to speak in public, had been met, partly because of an increasing disillusion with other attempts at reform. As in Britain, the vote began to be seen as the key to all other changes women wanted to see in society whether these were exclusively feminist or not.

The National Association, under the active leadership of Susan Anthony, concentrated on the passage of a federal amendment along the lines of that enfranchising the Negroes, since such a measure would deny any individual state the right to refuse women the vote. First, however, Susan Anthony and a group of women supporters challenged the legality of the exclusion of women from citizenship by actually going to the polls in the presidential election of 1872. Her ploy failed, and she actually stood trial for her offence and was fined, although the fine was never actually enforced (Sachs and Wilson, 1978). Thereafter the main strategy, as in Britain, was political lobbying with the aim of keeping pressure on Congress. Meanwhile the other society, the American, pursued a policy of campaigning at state level, convinced that this was a more realistic way of attaining their goal. However, this method was no more successful in the long run. Between 1870 and 1910 seventeen state referenda were held, mostly in the West, with only two victories, Colorado and Idaho, although there were some limited gains. By 1890, for example, nineteen states had granted partial suffrage, such as the municipal ballot or elections for the School Board.

But two Western territories, Wyoming in 1869 and Utah in 1870, had already granted women suffrage without any active campaigning by the suffragist societies. A great deal of effort has been expended in trying to explain these two isolated cases, although not with complete success. Certainly the importance of women in the West, arising from their scarcity, may have been one factor, since Western states were more ready to accept women's suffrage than those in either the South or the East, even in the twentieth century. On the other hand, these two territories were exceptional even in the West, and it was to take more than thirty years of hard campaigning before the West as a whole began to follow suit (Larson, 1971, p. 14). The evidence seems to suggest that in both Wyoming and Utah special circumstances gave these early victories to the suffragist cause *in advance* of the general move in that direction in the early years of the twentieth century.

In the first place it should be emphasized that both Wyoming and Utah were territories at this time, and not yet states. Consequently it required only an enactment of the territorial legislature and not, as in the states, a referendum in which men alone of course had the right to vote (Grimes, 1967, p. 26). In

Wyoming too, in spite of the absence of a suffragist campaign, individual feminists played a part in influencing some of the legislators, especially Edward Lee, an ardent suffragist who had been impressed by Anna Dickinson (Larson, 1971, p. 6). What is less clear is the reason why others supported him, since some of them were saloon keepers who might, given the link between feminism and temperance, have been expected to be anti-suffragist. It is possible that some men wanted to increase the number of women settlers and hoped that this would achieve it, or alternatively hoped that it would strengthen the forces of law and order in the territory (Grimes, 1967, p. 58). Also significant, as we shall see later, was the absence of any organized opposition, such as was to feature in later unsuccessful campaigns.

If we turn to Utah, we find an even more unusual situation, for Utah was a Mormon territory, and the Mormon religion was certainly not in any obvious sense feminist. Plural marriage was not allowed to women, its main intention being to provide a suitable role, as wife and mother, for 'surplus' women. Moreover, the Mormons established a rigid hierarchy within the family based upon the Old Testament patriarchs in which women played a subordinate even if essential role. There is, however, also evidence that Mormon women were allowed to vote in church congregations and they were encouraged to form their own organizations for relief work and similar duties (Alexander, 1970). The immediate incentive for their enfranchisement, however, was the attack on polygamy in Congress, which seems to have led the Mormon leaders to believe that to enfranchise Mormon women would demonstrate their wives' support for polygamy. At the same time, perhaps less convincingly, it has been suggested that the Mormons feared an invasion of non-Mormon immigrants and hoped to strengthen the Mormon vote (Grimes, 1967, pp. 28—40).

The confidence of the Mormon leaders does not seem to have been misplaced and there is no evidence of any *organized* opposition to polygamy by Mormon women. Indeed, at a later date, they sent several petitions to Congress demanding that their families should not be destroyed by legislation against polygamy (Arrington and Bitton, 1979, p. 230). This suggests that, under the circumstances of the time, polygamy may have appeared as an advantage to some women, especially perhaps to those who would not otherwise have been married at all. Nor were all wives necessarily anxious to have exclusive possession of their husbands. One of the first Mormon women legislators, herself a plural wife, pointed out that, if a husband has four wives, each wife 'has three weeks of freedom every month' (Arrington and Bitton, 1979, p. 230). It is not clear what it was freedom from, but it is quite possible, given the feminist attitude at the time, that this was an oblique reference to freedom from sexual advances. Moreover, polygamy appears to have personally involved only about 5 per cent of Mormon men and about 12 per cent of Mormon women, a relatively small minority of the population. By the 1880s, however, it had lost whatever popularity it had once had; the numbers entering into plural marriage was declining, and the Mormons themselves voted overwhelmingly to prohibit it (Arrington and Bitton, 1979, p. 203). At this time Mormon women were disenfranchised by Congress, which aroused them to vigorous protest encouraged by Susan Anthony and the National Association (Arrington and Bitton, 1979, p. 229; Grimes, 1967, p. 40). They were finally enfranchised in 1896 as part of a new state constitution.

Colorado was the first state to grant women's suffrage by referendum and this was not in fact achieved until 1893, twenty years after Wyoming and Utah had granted women the vote. Moreover these were years of vigorous campaigning, chiefly in the Western states and quite without success. The victory in Colorado was largely the consequence of a union between the suffragists and the Populist Party, which, as a new party, needed votes and hoped women would supply them. Much the same reason produced a victory for women's suffrage in Idaho in 1896 (Grimes, 1967, pp. 97—9). It is significant, too, that in neither Colorado nor Idaho was there very much organized opposition (Flexner, 1974, p. 222). Once the Populist Party declined, however, women's suffrage lost its appeal also, and it was not until 1910 that the Western states began to accept women's suffrage in any numbers (Grimes, 1967, pp. 97—9).

Of most significance in determining the fate of particular suffrage campaigns during these years of failure was probably the relationship that had developed between suffrage and temperance, largely as a result of the efforts of the temperance reformer Frances Willard. At first, in spite of her feminist leanings, Frances Willard had held herself aloof from the organized suffrage movement. This was during the 1860s, when the scandal of Henry Ward Beecher and Mrs Tilton and the free love reputation of Victoria Woodhull had given an unfortunate notoriety to the two suffrage societies. Shunning the suffrage movement itself, she joined the Association for the Advancement of Women, a conservative group for the exchange of ideas amongst women. Later however, under the influence of Mary Livermore, she joined the American Suffrage Association. Her chief work for suffrage was in swinging her own association, the Women's Christian Temperance Union, to the suffrage cause in 1883. She also played a leading part in bringing together the WCTU and the National Prohibition Party, although, because of opposition to women's suffrage in the South where the Prohibition Party was strong, she was never able to bring it solidly behind women's suffrage (Earhart, 1944, pp. 133—8, 226, 243).

Although Frances Willard must be given credit for her work in mobilizing conservative women to a belief in the vote as the key to temperance legislation, the association in the public's mind between temperance and women's suffrage was not by any means always to the advantage of the suffrage campaign. As in the British context, it served to mobilize the brewers and the liquor interests generally in what amounted to a concentrated campaign financed by the brewers to oppose women's suffrage in state campaigns. The suffrage movement was well aware of the situation and counted the brewers as their chief opponents. Indeed some leaders, including Susan Anthony herself, were a little wary of emphasizing too closely the link between temperance and suffrage for this very reason. Nevertheless, she did recognize the important part played by Frances Willard in breaking down the opposition of the Church to suffrage (Lutz, 1959, p. 245).

The brewing interests certainly took the suffrage threat very seriously indeed, pouring money into the anti-suffrage campaign. They were charged not only with unlawful expenditure on elections, but with bribing the electorate, and it was claimed that in Arizona the saloons checked women's suffrage for eleven years (Catt and Shuler, 1969, p. 129). Surveying the evidence of the suffrage campaign during these years, Paulson has concluded that whenever the opposition 'was chrystallized by the liquor interests' the outcome was bound to be unfavourable (Paulson, 1973, p. 137; Morgan, 1972, pp. 158—63).

At other times the battle for women's suffrage was lost because it seemed to threaten not a particular commercial interest, but the party in power (Paulson, 1973, p. 137). Sometimes even women suffrage leaders put party politics before the suffrage cause, as in the Kansas campaign in 1894. The head of the Kansas State Suffrage Association became president of the Republican Woman's Association in the state and felt it necessary to endorse her party's rejection of women's suffrage (Flexner, 1974, p. 223).

In the meantime, the division between the two suffrage societies began to seem less and less meaningful, and in 1887 the younger women in both the American and National Associations began to press for union. The old rivalries were dying down and the differences in both policies and tactics seemed less important than the need for a wider approach. The new association, founded in 1890, was named the National American Woman Suffrage Association (NAWSA). At first the union failed to make any appreciable difference to the campaign. Indeed, for many years the situation seemed to have worsened, as organizational and personnel problems at the centre hampered the work of the new society, and between 1896 and 1910 the situation, at both the state and the national level, was one of stalemate.

This period of doldrums was discouraging to the suffrage workers but, beneath the surface, support for women's suffrage seems to have been growing steadily, as more and more women came to accept the necessity of political enfranchisement. During these years, not only did feminism become narrowed down to the possession of the vote, but the suffrage cause itself became more respectable and no longer, as it had been in 1848, the dream of a few radical men and women. Elizabeth Cady Stanton, in some respects the most radical of them all, was now an old woman and, although granted the respect of a pioneer, was increasingly out of touch with the mood of the movement. She spent much of her time on her 'Woman's Bible', as she became convinced that established religion was the chief cause of women's position in society. The first volume, published in 1895, caused strong opposition amongst the suffragists and produced what amounted to a rebellion at the 1896 convention. Susan Anthony publicly supported her old friend but privately regarded the enterprise as a futile digression (Lutz, 1959, p. 278). In spite of her support, a resolution was passed disavowing any connection with the Woman's Bible. Carrie Chapman Catt, who played a leading part in carrying the resolution, was later to lead the suffrage campaign to victory. She represented the younger women in the movement who saw the issue of suffrage as paramount and were deeply resentful of any expression of opinion that might alienate its acceptance (Peck, 1944, pp. 87—9; Kraditor, 1965, pp. 77—86).

The growing conservatism of the suffrage movement at this time is reflected in the support for the 'educated vote', which Elizabeth Cady Stanton shared. By 1903 this view was the dominant one at the NAWSA convention (Kraditor, 1965, pp. 133—6). This was a reaction, in part, to the experiences in the state campaigns in which immigrant groups, perhaps because of the suffrage and temperance association, were often strongly anti-suffrage. It also represented the not altogether unnatural resentment of middle-class educated women at the knowledge that newly arrived immigrant men had an automatic right to the suffrage that was denied to them just because they were women. At another level, of course, the alliance between temperance and suffrage was in itself an expression of the concern for social order that characterized the native-born middle-class Protestants, whether male or female, and that the growing tide of immigrants seemed to threaten (Grimes, 1967, pp. 100—4). In the process, however, votes for women, which had once been an expression of equal rights, became an issue of social privilege.

The change in the mood of the suffrage leaders can also be seen in the attitude towards race. The loyalty of the feminists towards the Negro cause had, as we have seen, been threatened by the repudiation of women's suffrage by the abolitionist leaders, and the alliance between the woman's and the Negroes' cause came to an end. By the closing years of the century it was commonplace in the South for racist arguments to be used in support of women's suffrage. The development of a suffrage movement was slow to develop in the South and in the 1860s there were only individual women voicing suffragist opinions. Interest was, however, stimulated by Frances Willard and WCTU, and by the 1890s there was some degree of suffrage organization in every state (Scott, 1970, pp. 150, 177). These leaders now began to play an active part in NAWSA and women's suffrage for white women only was used as an argument for the retention of white supremacy. Moreover, suffragists in the North were quite prepared to accept this strategy if it seemed necessary (Kraditor, 1965, pp. 165—6, 173—83).

By 1910, however, the suffrage movement was picking up new recruits, both from amongst social reformers and settlement workers on the one hand, and from trade unionists and socialists on the other. Besides widening the basis of support for women's suffrage, it now became possible to make advances in the East. Moreover, partly under vigorous new leadership, gains began to be achieved in the West. Thus Washington was won in 1910 and California in 1911. In 1912 no less than three states granted women's suffrage and it began to seem that the tide had at last begun to turn.

The growing support for suffrage is demonstrated by Campbell's

(1979, pp. 134—40) sample study of 879 entrants from the 9,000 prominent women featured in Woman's Who's Who of 1914. She found that 53.5 per cent favoured suffrage, with 23.8 per cent active in support of the movement. Only 9.5 per cent of the sample were actually anti-suffrage. Of the women following professional careers, as many as 38.7 per cent were active suffragists. Women with an interest in social reform were also strong supporters of women's suffrage. Women against suffrage, on the other hand, were more likely to be those with interest in religious and humanitarian rather than social reform, and to be non-career women.

It was at this time, too, that fresh vigour was injected into the campaign for a federal amendment. This had passed through its period of doldrums in which the interest in the topic on the part of Congress had declined rather than increased, but in 1912 the newly formed Progressive Party under Theodore Roosevelt placed women's suffrage as a plank in its presidential election campaign. The conversion of Roosevelt, who had been unsympathetic as late as 1908, must be attributed in large part to Jane Addams, who seconded his nomination and brought with her the support of many social workers. A vice-president of NAWSA in 1911, Jane Addams had worked actively for women's suffrage since 1906, and continued to play a part in the campaign until the outbreak of war. Initially, a group of prominent social reformers had presented a platform of welfare provisions to the Republican Party that included national insurance, better housing, the protection of women and children in industry, and women's suffrage. This was ignored by the Republicans, but when Roosevelt formed his own new party he adopted the platform, including the women's suffrage provision. Although she had little hope of victory for the Progressive Party, Jane Addams saw an alliance with the Progressives as a chance to publicize the cause of both social reform and women's suffrage (Davis, 1973, pp. 184—7, 198). Florence Kelley, another prominent social reformer who worked for protective legislation for women and children, was also an active suffragist and, like Jane Addams, a vice-president of NAWSA (Goldmark, 1953, p. 182).

The association between suffrage and the Progressive platform was, however, like the alliance between suffrage and temperance, only a mixed blessing for the suffrage cause. While it brought social workers and social reformers of the Progressive persuasion, whether male or female, into the suffrage campaign, the opponents of the Progressive platform, and particularly the 'big business' interests, became active workers in the anti-suffrage movement. Flexner (1974, pp. 229—302, 370) has documented some of the ways in which business interests opposed women's suffrage, usually in secret, by means of large donations to anti-suffrage campaigners. Amongst the anxieties aroused by the prospect of a woman's vote was the apparent threat to the supply of cheap labour posed by the concern, expressed in suffrage publications, for the working conditions of women and children. Moreover, the men from Northern states who led the fight against women suffrage in the Senate represented business interests, and this is reflected in the general pattern of their voting. Thus Senator Wadsworth of New York, a determined suffrage opponent, also voted against the income tax, the taxation of war profits and an investigation of Wall Street. Not surprisingly, business interests were often anxious at the links between feminism and socialism.

Although the trade union movement had a long history of support for women's suffrage, there was, as in Britain, little real feeling behind the policy. Terence Powderly, a friend of Frances Willard and both a feminist and temperance advocate, had welcomed suffrage delegates to Knights of Labor conventions and pressed for suffrage resolutions (Kenneally, 1978, p. 16). Gompers, if much less ardently, also supported women's suffrage, and his union, the American Federation of Labor (AFL), approved universal suffrage in 1890 (Kenneally, 1978, p. 129). The Women's Trade Union League (WTUL) had also been committed to women's suffrage from the beginning and they joined the social workers, with whom, as we have seen, they were closely associated, in pressing for a reform platform that contained both protective legislation for women and children and women's suffrage. In so far as there was any contact between the middle-class suffragists in NAWSA and women trade unionists, it came through the WTUL, but in the main there were separate suffrage societies for working-class women, the first being organized in San Francisco in 1908 or 1909 (Jacoby, 1977, pp. 213—15).

Many women in the Socialist Party, although rarely suffragists in the narrow sense of the term, combined work for woman's suffrage with active campaigning for primarily socialist causes (Flynn, 1960). These years also saw a group of young women in Greenwich Village who tried to combine their socialism and their feminism into a new way of life. Largely upper class and college educated, they advocated birth control and communal child care to free women for goals beyond the home. The men involved in this group were feminist too, and Max Eastman, brother of Chrystal Eastman, organized the first men's League for Women's Suffrage in 1909 (Sochen, 1972, p. 73).

- As in Britain however, the attempt to combine socialism and feminism was not altogether easy, and if some of these men and women were active campaigners for suffrage, others were wary of it. Emma Goldman, one of the idols of the Greenwich Village group (Sochen, 1972, p. 63), criticized the whole women's suffrage movement for its stand against labour and its excessive puritanism. An early and forceful supporter of the birth control movement (Drinnon, 1970, p. 169), she condemned the traditional feminists for their attempt to banish men from their emotional lives. While by no means wishing to deny women a political voice, she shared the anarchist suspicion of the vote, and believed the faith in equal suffrage to be mistaken. She saw women's disabilities lying less in external restraints and more in ethical and social conventions (Drinnon, 1970, p. 153). Another woman who thought the emphasis on the vote misguided was the outstanding trade union organizer Mary Harris Jones, known affectionately as Mother Jones. She attacked both suffrage and temperance as directing women's interests away from the real culprit, the organization of industry. It may also be argued, however, that Mother Jones was not really a feminist either, since she believed that women's task was the rearing of children, and, as late as 1930, that the solution to the problem of women in industry was the 'family wage' (Kenneally, 1978, pp. 111—12). On the whole however, as in Britain, socialist women tended to be behind the suffrage campaign, seeing equal suffrage as something that would ultimately be to the benefit of working-class women.

The widening support for women's suffrage at this time also had its effect on the campaign itself. Some of the credit for this must go to Harriet Stanton Blatch, daughter of Mrs Stanton, who had married an Englishman and, now widowed, had returned to New York fresh from the early exploits of the militant suffragists in London. Appalled by the rut in which she found NAWSA, she organized in 1907 her own body, which soon became the Women's Political Union. She recognized the need to bring working-class women into the movement and involved women from the WTUL in her campaigns. New tactics were also employed borrowed from the British militants, which included parades and open air meetings (Flexner, 1974, pp. 251—3).

NAWSA itself still remained in the doldrums faced by weaknesses at the leadership level, but fresh impetus was given to the work for the federal suffrage amendment when Alice Paul and Lucy Burns founded the Congressional Union in 1913. Fresh from working with the Pankhursts, these two lively young women brought not only new tactics but a new philosophy into the American movement. Their main aim was to put pressure on Congress, which they did with such effect that in 1913 the subject was debated for the first time since 1887 (Irwin, 1921, p. 39). Their tactics included the increased canvassing of Congress members and large demonstrations, but their energy and enthusiasm also brought in both money and recruits (Irwin, 1921, p. 21).

It was not long, however, before there was friction between NAWSA and the Congressional Union, which resulted eventually in a complete split and the formation by Paul and Burns of the Woman's Party in 1914 (Flexner, 1974, pp. 265—6). The most important source of disagreement was NAWSA's continuing support for the policy of state campaigns. The Woman's Party argued strongly that only a federal amendment, forcing states to concede the issue, could break the deadlock. It contended that all efforts should be concentrated on Congress, and in particular on the person of the President, Mr Wilson. There was also friction between the two groups when the Woman's Party decided to oppose all Democratic candidates, whatever their view on suffrage, since only by threatening the election chances of the Democratic Party as a whole would it be brought to support votes for women. NAWSA, on the other hand, tried to be non-party and to support all candidates if they were pro-suffrage in their personal views (Irwin, 1921, pp. 74—5). Carrie Chapman Catt believed that the success of women's suffrage depended upon support from both parties, and thought it wrong to campaign against men who were prepared to support the suffrage cause (Peck, 1944, pp. 240—1; Kraditor, 1965, pp. 232—45). Force was given to this policy, in a way that was impossible in the British context, by the existence of states that had granted women's suffrage. Thus the Woman's Party worked to defeat Democratic candidates (including Mr Wilson himself) in the equal suffrage states in 1914 and again in 1916 (Flexner, 1974, pp. 277—8).

The year 1916 turned out to be a critical year, and one in which, as Flexner points out, the tide began to turn. Carrie Chapman Catt, a woman of superb organizing ability, had taken charge of NAWSA in 1915 and the effect of the change in the quality of leadership became apparent straight away. By this time too, with women voters in twelve states, politicians were becoming anxious about the women's vote; also the parties felt the need to make some kind of stand on women's suffrage. It was the year of the presidential election and Wilson had been won over sufficiently to pledge his personal support, although he would not make it a party issue. On the whole, the political parties preferred to leave it as an issue to be decided by the states themselves, as this did not involve them in charges that they were undemocratic (Irwin, 1921, p. 161).

Once Wilson was re-elected the campaign continued. NAWSA, under Carrie Chapman Catt's leadership, continued its endeavour to win over a few more states, while working meanwhile to get the federal amendment submitted to Congress. The Woman's Party, convinced still that pressure on Wilson was the answer, started to picket the White House in 1917. Although never militant, the presence of these pickets, particularly after war was declared, provoked violence and ultimately the arrest of the women themselves (Irwin, 1921, pp. 227—35). Whether or not the picketing helped or hindered the cause of the women's suffrage is a matter of dispute. Certainly NAWSA was afraid that the picketing was harmful, and took pains to dissociate itself from the pickets. Morgan, in the most systematic study of this period to date, sees the Women's Party acting as a catalyst, galvanizing the suffragists to action and presenting to the government the spectre of large-scale disorder (Morgan, 1972, pp. 186—90).

By 1918, however, opinion was moving more decisively in favour of women's suffrage, and this was reflected in victories in several states. During 1917 several states were won, no less than three in one week, and including one Southern state. Most significant perhaps was the success of the New York referendum, with its eleventh hour decision by Tammany Hall to abstain from its traditional opposition. Finally, in 1918 the President agreed to commit the Democratic Party to the measure. This was by no means the end of the struggle since victory still had to be secured in both the House of Representatives and in Senate. Moreover, there was powerful opposition within the party, largely from the Southern states, which were still predominantly anti-suffrage. This was partly because of Southern conservatism with respect to women and the family, partly because of fears of arousing once more the issue of Negro rights. Morgan suggests also that the association between women's suffrage and child labour reform posed a serious threat to the Southern cotton industry, which depended on the cheap labour of women and children (Morgan, 1972, pp. 174—7).

In the final event, the Democrats were split, although the Republicans showed a majority in favour. Apart from the Southern states, there was opposition from industrial states such as Massachusetts, Pennsylvania, New Jersey and Ohio. It was therefore 1919 before the amendment was finally approved by Senate, in spite of special personal appeals by Wilson anxious to secure the women's vote, particularly for his peace plan, which, he felt, would command their support. The Senate victory then had to be followed by the campaign for state ratification by the requisite thirty-six states which was waged for another fourteen months before the issue was finally settled in August 1920.

The description of the campaign (Flexner, 1974, pp. 306—24) reveals that opposition to women's suffrage was still strong, especially, but not entirely, in the Southern states. Indeed, the passage of women's enfranchisement seems to have been much easier, in its final stages at least, in Britain than in the United States. Once the issue of the property qualification had been largely settled, there remained by 1918 no barrier to women's suffrage comparable to the opposition from the American South. There were of course other differences, in the federal nature of American government, in the different relationships between the two Houses in the two countries, in the fact that the Act was passed by a coalition government in Britain, and in the absence in the United States of anything comparable to the British Labour Party. The fact that women's suffrage in Britain was limited to householders, wives of householders and women of 30 and over, thus enfranchising not much more than half the total number of adult women, must also be taken into account. When women's suffrage came to the United States it came to women on exactly the same terms as to men.

In the United States, as in Britain, the struggle for women's suffrage took place against a background in which the simple issue of women's equality and arguments about women's nature were complicated by the political issue of party advantages. Indeed, by the time the struggle was at its fiercest, straightforward anti-feminism, if we can call it such, although by no means absent, was perhaps less important than the calculations of politicians on the possible consequences of women voters on the fortunes of the parties. While on the whole their anxieties on this score made them unwilling to support the suffragists, there came a time when party rivalry could be turned to women's advantage. This was most in evidence, of course, when the balance of opinion began to swing in favour of woman's suffrage, which then seemed to come within the realm of practical politics. At last politicians began to perceive women as potential voters and to see the granting of women's suffrage as a bribe with which to buy the women's vote for their side. Certainly this was very much in Wilson's mind as he wrestled with the Southern senators, because the issue was one to which the Republicans were in fact more sympathetically inclined and he wished to gain the credit for the Democrats.

Party advantage however, although all important in the exact timing of the event, was perhaps less important in itself than the way in which women came to be identified with certain specific values. As we have seen already, the support for women's suffrage was powerfully reinforced by the linkage between votes for women and the issue of both moral and social reform of all kinds. Women as varied as temperance workers in the United States and textile workers in Britain's northern towns turned to the suffrage campaign as the best way, if not the only way, to ensure victory for their cause. It did not matter, at least at the time, that their goals were different, nor even that at times they were contradictory. All that mattered was that they were united behind the demand for women's votes.

It is not surprising, therefore, that certain groups became increasingly anxious as the suffragists became more numerous and more militant. In both countries, if in different degrees, commercial interests were opposed to the suffrage campaign. Liquor interests combined with those who wanted to maintain a supply of cheap labour and feared protective legislation and the demand for a minimum wage. Nor were only commercial interests involved, although these were perhaps the most powerful of the pressure groups involved. Many men clearly came to see the women as at worst narrow-minded and bigoted, and at best hopelessly idealistic. Thus they feared women voters as moralistic busybodies who would attempt to legislate on matters not susceptible to legal control, if not actually harmful to both profit and employment.

In the event, of course, the forces working for women's suffrage, which included not only the suffragists themselves but also those who approved of their reforming tendencies, were finally the more powerful. Women achieved the vote, although not finally in Britain until 1928. Nor can we fail to acknowledge that, however powerful their allies, a decisive element was the demand by women themselves for their political enfranchisement, a demand that was a consequence of women's increasing involvement in public life and in moral and social reform. In this upsurge of women's consciousness at this time we must also take account of the improvement in girls' education and particularly women's opportunities in higher education. College graduates in both Britain and the United States had a very important part to play in providing active support for the suffrage campaign (Campbell, 1979; Delamont, 1978). If, however, educated women were often suffragists, this by itself is not sufficient to explain the growing support for the campaign. The years after 1900 revealed not only dedicated leaders but a mass following amongst all classes of the population. Although originally inspired by middle-class women, the campaign spread to the working classes in such organizations as the Independent Labour Party and the Co-operative Women's Guild in Britain and the Women's Trade Union League and the Socialist Party in the United States. At this period, feminism, in its united stand for suffrage, was for the first time truly representative of both middle-class and working-class women.

Meanwhile, and this was to be vital later, the unity of the suffrage period was to a large extent illusory. True all these very different women wanted the vote, but they wanted it for different reasons. To some extent the alliances that developed between feminism and other reform movements were genuine. Early feminists were often both temperance workers and purity campaigners. By the turn of the century, reformers like Jane Addams combined both of these concerns with a campaign for protective and welfare legislation and saw women's suffrage as the key to them all. Even prostitution, she believed, could not survive the woman's vote (Davis, 1973, p. 179). Yet at the same time new themes were emerging that would divide women once the vote was won. The controversy over protective legislation, already in evidence, was to split the feminist movement deeply in both Britain and the United States. The struggle for welfare legislation and the welfare state to which many feminists were already committed would direct many women away from feminism altogether. The vote itself, which had united women of different social backgrounds in the struggle to achieve it, would soon separate them once it had been achieved, as women began to vote, like men, along party lines. The mass appeal of the suffrage campaign, which had spread the conviction of women's rights and women's wrongs to all sections of society, would not survive the victory and was not destined to reappear until the new movement of the 1960s. Feminism was entering a deeper and more prolonged doldrums than ever before since it had begun, and it would appear that feminism as a social movement had disappeared, never to be reborn.

We now know that this was very far from the truth. Nevertheless, the years from roughly 1920 to 1960 still need to be explained. We must try to understand what happened not only to feminism as an ideology but also to the feminists who anticipated this victory of the suffrage with such high expectations but who seem to vanish from the stage once the vote has been won. The next Part will attempt to follow their fortunes through the inter-war years. It will attempt in addition to explore the different alliances into which they entered and into which, subsequently, feminism as an ideology was swallowed up.

In this way we can perhaps see that feminism did not altogether disappear, only to be reborn anew in the women's liberation movement. Perhaps it is best to describe what happened as a splitting into its constituent parts so that what eventually occurred in the 1960s was a new and distinctive combination of elements that, as I hope to show, had been in feminism from its earliest beginnings. First, however, using such evidence as is available, it is necessary to look at what can perhaps be called the years of intermission when, for the time at least, feminism seemed to have come to an end.

PART III

The Intermission, 1920–1960

9

Women and Welfare

In attempting to relate the history of feminism after the suffrage victory there is immediately a problem of sources. Since feminism, as such, seemed to have reached its main goal, both chroniclers of the movement (Flexner, 1974; Strachey, 1928) and historians generally (Freedman, 1974) felt it unnecessary to explore in detail the subsequent developments in feminist organizations or, except in a few cases, to follow the careers of the feminists themselves. It is noteworthy, for example, that Flexner ends what is in many ways still the standard history of the American movement in 1920, while Strachey, who does the same thing for Britain, devotes only a few pages to the 1920s, and this only because adult suffrage was not achieved by all British women until 1928. It is fortunate, however, that in recent years several American historians, many of them inspired by the resurgence of interest in feminism, have started to explore some of these issues, and we have a number of studies, especially of the inter-war years, with, no doubt, many more still to come. In Britain, in contrast, there is still remarkably little actually published, although the recent interest in feminist studies will certainly produce some of the necessary research before very long. The consequence, for Britain even more than the United States, is that many aspects of this period are still under-explored if not, indeed, unexplored altogether, so that further research may well necessitate a reappraisal on matters both of detail and inter-pretation. On the other hand, it is at last beginning to be possible to trace the major developments in feminism through the 1920s and after and to understand some of the causes of the apparent break in continuity that led to the founding in the 1960s of what seemed to

153

women at the time a totally new movement, without any direct links with a feminist past.

The granting of the suffrage in 1920 left the United States with a powerful suffrage organization that had been mobilized fully for the arduous campaign of state ratification, which was necessary before the federal amendment was finally law. There were two major associations, NAWSA and the Woman's Party, both committed to suffrage if using different tactics and headed by rather different kinds of leaders. These women now had to consider the future of their organizations. If they were to continue at all, it must be around a different set of issues, and this involved decisions about the meaning and purpose of the 'woman's vote', as well as about their attitude to the traditional feminist issues of equality of educational opportunity, equal pay and equality in law.

NAWSA, under the leadership of Carrie Chapman Catt, was the largest and oldest suffrage society. In 1920 it changed its name to the League of Women Voters, and began a mainly educational movement, dedicated to equip women for their new political role. Carrie Chapman Catt, although she never joined a political party herself, was of the decided opinion that women needed to work within the existing parties and 'move right up to the centre' (Peck, 1944, p. 325). The League therefore remained determinedly non-partisan, and, in so far as it was political at all, it acted mainly as a pressure group to further a number of issues about which women might be expected to speak with a common voice. On the other hand, in line with Carrie Chapman Catt's views, and in spite of some opposition from Jane Addams, the League did not try to mobilize the woman's vote for a woman's party. At the same time the League joined with a number of other women's groups to form the Women's Joint Congressional Committee. This was an umbrella organization, established to coordinate all activities involving legislative changes.

The greatest effort of both the Congressional Committee and the League during their early years went into pressure for welfare legislation, and particularly for maternity and infant provision. Still fresh from their suffrage victory, the Women's Joint Congressional Committee lobbied extensively for the Sheppart—Towner Maternity and Infancy Protection Bill, which became law in 1921. In the final week of the debate its subcommittee conducted interviews with congressmen at the rate of fifty a day and forced the bill through a reluctant Congress (Lemon, 1973). An important ingredient in its success was the fear by politicians of a woman's party, a fear that must have been given credence by the remarkable unanimity of women's organizations on the issue. Even the National Federation of Business and Professional Women and the highly conservative Daughters of the American Revolution supported the bill at this time. The only woman then in Congress, the anti-suffragist Alice Robertson, opposed the bill, but her vote carried little weight in the overwhelming support that seemed to come from women generally. The bill was opposed strongly by those who feared it as a form of German paternalism or even as an insidious move towards Bolshevism (Davis, 1973, p. 269). The medical profession saw it as a step towards state medicine and also reacted vigorously against it, although, significantly, the small but radical Medical Women's National Association gave it its approval.

In addition to the pressure for the Sheppart—Towner Act, the Congressional Committee put strenuous efforts into winning extra funding for the Women's Bureau and the Children's Bureau, products of the pre-war progressive movement for social welfare. Other issues taken up by the League included prohibition, electoral and civil service reform, and even public ownership. In the years between 1924 and 1928, for example, it conducted an extensive study of the development and regulation of the power industry that so alarmed the power interests in the United States that they infiltrated the League to spy on its activities (Lemon, 1973).

Another issue that united women's organizations behind the progressive reform movement was the campaign against child labour. In the years after the war the Child Labour Committee, along with the Consumer League, the Women's Trade Union League and the League of Women Voters, worked together, largely unsuccessfully, to prevent the exploitation of children. They were opposed by business and especially agricultural interests who depended on the cheap labour of children, as well as by those who feared the invasion of the rights of individual states. The Roman Catholic hierarchy feared any extension of government as an encroachment upon the Church and there were others who saw the proposals, like those for maternity and child welfare, as a step towards Bolshevism (Chambers, 1963).

In fact, however, this unity amongst women was to be short-lived. Not only did the progressive element in Congress weaken after 1924, indicating a change of mood in the country, but even more significantly many women's organizations seemed to share this mood and to become more and more conservative. Lemon

(1973) has documented this in detail, showing that by the end of the 1920s neither professional women nor women's clubs were any longer interested in issues of social welfare. The Daughters of the American Revolution, who had joined the Women's Joint Congressional Committee in 1920, moved to extreme militarism and isolationism.

Even more serious for any united front of women's organizations was the split within the feminist movement over protective legislation. After suffrage had been achieved, the leaders of the Woman's Party caried out a legal survey that revealed evidence of considerable discrimination against women, particularly over issues of property, the guardianship of children and the laws on divorce. In some states women were not allowed to hold political office and most denied women the right to sit on juries. The Woman's Party, consequently, wanted to work for a federal equal rights amendment that would enforce legal equality throughout the states on the model of the amendment that had guaranteed women the vote. Immediately the supporters of protective legislation were alarmed at the possible consequences of such an amendment on their hard-won protection for women in industry. Florence Kelley, although herself a prominent member of the Woman's Party, had been one of the leaders of the movement for protective legislation, and proved herself to be one of their most determined opponents (Lemon, 1973, pp. 185—8). She argued that an equal rights amendment would make protective legislation that applied only to women illegal, and would also threaten such special measures as widows' pensions and maintenance for deserted wives. Indeed she argued that women in employment needed special treatment, rather than equality, because of their youth, their inexperience and their lack of stability in employment (Goldmark, 1953, pp. 182—6). The members of the Woman's Party were accused of being 'theoretical ultra-feminists' who did not have to work for a living (Chambers, 1963, pp. 77—8).

In the debates that followed there were attempts at compromise, but none were effective and not only the Consumer League but also the Women's Trade Union League and the League of Women Voters took action to oppose all equal rights laws, killing them in five states and preventing their introduction in a number of others. When, in 1923, the Woman's Party submitted an equal rights amendment to Senate the Women's Joint Congressional Committee formed a subcommittee to oppose it (Lemon, 1973, p. 191). The Women's Bureau v as also solidly behind protective legislation and a report in 1928 argued that it did not, in fact, handicap women (Lemon, 1973, p. 196).

The campaign for legal equality was, therefore, maintained by the small Woman's Party; although it continued to work for an equal rights amendment, it was never, in fact, more than a small group of activists that failed to recruit new members and became smaller and more exclusive as time went by (Chafe, 1972, p. 114). Other women's organizations concerned themselves with a variety of general issues, among which their campaigns for the welfare of women and children came closest to feminism.

At the same time a number of women who had been active in the suffrage campaign now began to devote their whole attention to the cause of peace. This had first become apparent in the years before the first world war when an active peace movement joined together women as divergent as the progressives Jane Addams and Lilian Wald and the socialist Chrystal Eastman (Cook, 1978, pp. 11–16). After the war both Jane Addams and Carrie Chapman Catt dedicated themselves to the peace movement. Many other women who had been involved in the suffrage movement followed them, and Chambers has argued that 'almost every woman's group regardless of the specific domestic problems it espoused, was married to the cause of peace' (Chambers, 1963, pp. 232–3). In the 1930s a women's peace lobby in Washington was directly responsible for an investigation into the munitions industry (Chafe, 1972, p. 37). This is not to suggest that the peace movement was, for these women, an abandonment of their feminism. Peace was seen as something of particular importance to women, partly because of their role as mothers, partly because of those female characteristics that gave them their moral superiority. Indeed, for many of them, their work for peace was part of the same impulse for social order that had led them into temperance and moral reform, but whereas in the nineteenth century women's increasing involvement in reform united them behind the suffrage campaign, in the twentieth century the attraction of the peace movement for women, like the split over the equal rights amendment, helped to separate the broad stream of the suffrage movement into distinct and even rival channels.

It was the alliance between women and welfare that was to prove most significant for the way in which feminism was to develop in the years of intermission. To a very considerable extent the demand for welfare legislation and the belief in state intervention as a means of social reform were kept alive during the 1920s by those women's organizations that remained loyal to the progressive platform of the pre-war years. The ideals of the settlement movement lived on in the Consumer League, the Women's Trade Union League, the League of Women Voters and above all perhaps in those creations of the settlement social workers, the Women's Bureau and the Children's Bureau. In these organizations, at least, the goal of welfare legislation survived the fears of Bolshevism that were such a marked feature of the 1920s, and that were used, if not indeed manufactured, by those who were opposed to child labour legislation, maternity and child welfare, and other measures designed largely for the protection of women and children. In fact there were accusations during this period of an interlocking directorate of women's organizations that was part of an international conspiracy to promote Bolshevism, an accusation that was given some credence by the involvement of many of the women's leaders in organizations like the Women's International League for Peace and Freedom (Lemon, 1973).

The continuing support of women for these measures was particularly important in the United States because of the attitude of organized labour. Both Gompers, and his successor William Green, were committed to voluntarism and deeply suspicious of anything that appeared to increase the power of the state. The AFL policy favoured collective bargaining and was opposed even to unemployment insurance as a threat to a free labour market (Chambers, 1963). The Women's Trade Union League, in contrast, had a history of support for welfare measures of all kinds, including minimum wage legislation not only for women but for all workers.

The Depression, of course, brought a change in attitude. The New Deal meant that the tide of opinion that had turned against welfare legislation in the 1920s was now flowing more strongly in its favour. Even within the trade union movement, support for a measure of social security gained ground during the 1930s. Most important of all, however, Roosevelt began to make use of women's services in his administration and to seek their advice (Chambers, 1963). As Graham has argued, 'women progressives almost invariably followed their progressivism straight into the arms of the New Deal' (Graham, 1967, p. 169), largely because the New Deal was in fact implementing the programme they had long supported. The fact that, as Graham shows, these particular women were almost entirely from the field of social work illustrates the link between both social work and welfare, and welfare and feminism. The emerging social work profession had supported the suffrage campaign because it had seemed to open the way, through the woman's vote, to the reformation of the whole society.

There is, of course, nothing anti-feminist about a concern for women and children, and one of the main aims of the suffrage movement had been to give women a voice in decisions about their own needs. As we saw in chapter 7, however, one of the main legacies of the progressive movement was a concern for the protection of the weak, whether they were women and children or more generally simply the poor. In setting their face so determinedly against an equal rights amendment, the women in this tradition were therefore rejecting not simply the amendment itself, but the view of women that it entailed. The equal rights tradition that had informed so much of nineteenth-century feminism was abandoned altogether in favour of a view of women as essentially different. This did not necessarily imply that women were inferior, either physically or mentally, although this was sometimes presumed (as in the famous Brandeis decision), but it almost always assumed that women had different needs arising from their actual or indeed, and this was even more harmful, their *potential* role as mothers, which made the search for equality not only irrelevant but possibly dangerous. In the process attention was turned away from the issues that had concerned earlier generations of feminists. Not only legal equality, but the drive for economic independence and educational opportunity, were either ignored altogether or relegated to secondary concern. If equal pay still remained a live issue, especially amongst trade union women, it was often seen as a less important goal than limiting the hours of work or establishing a minimum wage.

The Depression itself did a great deal to reinforce this tendency to conservatism. Women were seen as in competition with men, as indeed in some cases they were, and the Depression years saw an increase in marriage bars, especially in white collar and semi-professional jobs like teaching and the civil service. Although there was some protest from the Women's Trade Union League against such measures (Boone, 1942, p. 203), many prominent women saw restrictions on married women at work as justified. Frances Perkins, for example, the Secretary of Labour under Roosevelt, and the first woman to be in such a position, denounced women who did not need to work and supported the idea of the family wage (Kenneally, 1978, p. 161). Another influential woman who took a traditional view of woman's place was Mary Dewson; she did an impressive job of organizing the Women's Division of the Democratic Party in 1932. She believed in the distinctive attributes of women and in the sanctity and security of the home (Chafe, 1972, p. 40). The Women's Bureau, always a strong supporter of protective legislation, was also inclined to stress the view that the married woman's place was in the home (Chafe, 1972, p. 64). Organized labour had of course taken this view before the first world war, and the policy of the family wage and the opposition to married women in the work force not only continued afterwards but during the Depression was even intensified. Thus in 1931 the AFL urged that preference should be given in employment to those with dependants (Kenneally, 1978, pp. 137—52).

Given the high rate of unemployment, such a view is at least understandable. More surprising is its persistence after the second world war, when the shortage of labour brought about the subsequent increase in the proportion of married women at work. Nor was it shared only by male trade unionists, since Alice K. Leopold, in charge of the Women's Bureau under Eisenhower, continued to attest that home-making was woman's most important function (Kenneally, 1978, p. 181). Furthermore, support for protective legislation for women continued, even though in 1938 the Fair Labour Standards Act had established the precedent of wage and hour limitation for both men and women. In 1948 for example, at a further hearing to debate an equal rights amendment, opposition was still forthcoming from the same organizations on precisely the same grounds as in the 1920s. Its opponents included the League of Women Voters, the Association of University Women, the National Consumer League, the CIO and its Congress of Women's Auxiliaries, and the AFL and its women's affiliates. Moreover it was still maintained that such an amendment would benefit only women of property and means (Green and Melnick, 1965, pp. 277—301). Not until the 1960s would support for an equal rights amendment spread within women's organizations and eventually reach the trade union movement itself.

If the main pressure from women's organizations came therefore for welfare rather than equality, much the same is also true of the more direct influence of women in politics. The granting of female suffrage not only gave women the vote, it also gave them the right to sit in Congress, and, although slow to start, the number of women politicians, particularly in the House of Representatives, did grow, as did the numbers in state legislatures and in other political appointments. It is necessary, therefore, to look at their record, and to consider to what extent they contributed either separately or together to what may be called a woman's policy. It should first be pointed out, however, that not only has there never been any but a small number of women in Congress, estimated by Chamberlin in 1973 as never more than 3.7 per cent (Chamberlin, 1973, p. 3), but the proportion of those in powerful positions such as committees and chairmanships has been even smaller. Moreover, a sizeable number of women members, particularly in the early years, have been widows of members who were simply keeping the seat warm for a short while without having any active involvement in politics. Even at the local level, where women's participation has been highest, it is still very far from equal (Amundsen, 1971, pp. 76—82), and women are active in politics mainly at the level of the party worker, a role in which they continue to perform similar functions to those carried out by women in the reform organizations of the nineteenth century. Women's political voice, therefore, whatever its direction, has not been a very large or very influential one.

When Carrie Chapman Catt argued against a Woman's Party in favour of women entering party politics it was claimed by her opponents that these women would be lost in the party organization and would cease to speak for women's needs; to a large extent this is exactly what has happened. Women politicians, and indeed women voters, have been loyal to their party rather than to their sex and in neither case has there ever been anything approaching a woman's vote (A. Campbell, 1960, pp. 485—93). Not until the 1960s is there any evidence in Congress of a consciousness of women's interests that was able to unite the women members in either of the two houses. On the other hand, a number of issues appear to attract the woman politician and it is no surprise that a concern with welfare legislation is perhaps the most obvious. Thus Mary Norris, elected to the 1925—1927 Congress and therefore amongst the earliest members, has been described as having an obsession with welfare (Chamberlin, 1973, p. 57). She worked to clean up the slums and to provide old age pensions. As chairman of the Labor Committee she had the task of pushing through Roosevelt's Wage and Hour Bill. Caroline O'Day, elected in 1932, had begun her career in the suffrage movement. She was a social worker and a member of the Consumer League. Not surprisingly, she opposed an equal rights amendment because of its feared effect on protective legislation. These are typical of the more active women elected during the inter-war years. It is not until after the second world war, and particularly in the 1960s, that we find a small group of women politicians actively working on issues of sex discrimination.

An overview of the research on the ninety-five women who have served in Congress shows their interest has been in such issues as hunger, poverty and racial discrimination. Even as late as 1965 women Democrats in California were found to be more public service oriented than men. Moreover, although women voters are often found to be more conservative than men, women members of Congress have been found to be more liberal than their party leaders (Bernard, 1979). In state government, women have been found to pay special attention to health, public welfare, education, consumer protection and delinquent children. The only feminist issue that seems to have concerned them is equal pay (Gruberg, 1968, p. 171).

Our examination of women in politics, therefore, does not really alter the general picture. Women used their new power to seek what we may broadly define as 'welfare' rather than feminist goals. Moreover the 'welfare' that they sought was not, save in the most general sense, for themselves, since the women in politics, like those in social work and most women's organizations, were middle-class white Americans. Women who tried to work for the legal and economic equality that would have benefited middle-class women were, as we have seen, condemned as narrow and selfish. The sexual discrimination in the professions, for example, which a later generation of women was to uncover in the 1960s, was either dismissed as of little consequence or even more likely passed unnoticed altogether. To some extent this was because the women involved in the welfare movement were married and had little interest in the problems of the career woman, but even single women seemed to share the traditional view that woman's role was primarily a domestic one.

Thus, although the Woman's Party kept alive the demand for equal rights throughout this period, supported, as we shall see later, by groups of professional women, the years between 1920 and 1960 were dominated by a tradition of feminism that had little to do with the Enlightenment. Instead its origins lie in the evangelical tradition of moral reform and it depended upon an ideal of female superiority that gave women a special commitment to a new moral order. The enthusiasm for welfare legislation was thus a modern equivalent of the nineteenth-century feminist support for the abolition of slavery and temperance. If women were led to seek changes in their own position this was not for the purpose of personal satisfaction or self-expression but in order to bring about their own particular view of a new society. Consequently, while this might well involve sweeping, and indeed revolutionary, aims like the abolition of war, the imposition of chastity on men and the total rejection of alcohol, it did not necessarily challenge the traditional view of women. Not only were women seen as different and indeed 'better' than men, but their superiority was based on their role as wives and mothers. Thus, however 'radical' in their attitudes to welfare legislation, the women reformers were largely conservative in their view of woman's nature and role.

If we turn now from the United States to Britain we find a marked variation in the political context, which complicates and to some extent obscures a similarity, especially in mood, that was eventually to give feminism in Britain a fate surprisingly similar to that of the United States. At first sight, however, the fortunes of the movement seem very different. The militant campaign had ended at the very start of the war and its leaders, the Pankhursts, became enthusiastic chauvinists leading a national drive to recruit women into munitions (Rosen, 1974, pp. 250—1). Towards the end of the war their organization, the Women's Social and Political Union, was renamed the Woman's Party and Christabel became a candidate, opposing the Labour Party on an anti-Bolshevist platform; but by 1919 it too had ceased to exist. Christabel became a travelling evangelist, and neither Christabel nor Emmeline Pankhurst was again to be active in the British movement (Rosen, 1974, pp. 269—70). Although the Pethick-Lawrences' Women's Freedom League still remained active (Pethick-Lawrence, 1938, pp. 331—2), the most important suffrage society was the long established non-militant National Union of Women's Suffrage Societies. In 1919 this was renamed the National Union of Societies for Equal Citizenship (NUSEC), which acted, along with the Women's Freedom League and several other pressure groups (like the Six Points Group founded by Viscountess Rhondda (1933)) to ensure that women's rights were constantly brought to the attention of Parliament.

Undoubtedly the fact that Britain had not yet achieved complete adult suffrage was an important element in the lively activity shown by the women leading the British movement, many of whom had been militant suffragists in the years before the war. Equal suffrage was in the forefront of their campaign, but their other aims included equal guardianship of children, the opening of the legal profession to women, equal pay, equal standards of morality, and a widow's pension plan (Hopkinson, 1954, p. 95). The 1920s, therefore, if they did not in any sense replicate the fervour of the early 1900s, were by no means years in which feminism was a spent force. Not only were there several groups working together both nationally and internationally with other feminist groups overseas, but their leaders were 'an articulate and socially well-connected group of women' (Lewis, 1973, p. 2) who not only publicized their activities in deputations, meetings and letters to influential newspapers like *The Times,* but promoted Private Member's bills, sometimes through one of the still small number of women MPs, sometimes through a sympathetic man.

Moreover in the main this campaign was successful, at least in so far as it depended on legal changes for its implementation. The 1920s saw an impressive programme of legislation that speedily gave women many of the rights they were demanding, so that by the time full suffrage was gained in 1928 much of this programme had been achieved. This is not the place to go into this legislation in detail but, in brief, the 1919 Sex Disqualification Act gave entry to the learned professions and to learned societies. It also gave British women the right, denied for many years to women in the United States, to sit on juries. These same years also saw women granted equal guardianship of infants and equal rights in divorce. Other successful measures included better maintenance allowances after separations, improvements in the position of unmarried mothers, and, for the first time, widows' pensions for civilians (Hopkinson, 1954, pp. 95—6; Rathbone, 1936). What is perhaps most striking is the ease with which these successes were achieved. The House of Commons was sympathetic and many of the measures were passed with little opposition, so that it is hard not to accept that politicians at this time were still anxious to gain what was still believed to be the woman's vote. When there was opposition it was often from outside Parliament, as in the struggle to achieve entry into the higher ranks of the civil service.

Another reason for the success of so much feminist legislation was the alliance between feminism and the Labour Party. I have already noted that, in spite of the continued support of the Liberal radicals, it was the newly formed Labour Party that was most staunchly behind the suffragist movement in the years immediately before the war. This may have been in part a consequence of the socialist tradition of feminism that characterized both the Owenites and Saint-Simonians and some at least of the Marxists, but the nonconformist roots of the Labour Party also had its links with feminism. Moreover, whether because of its sympathy for feminist ambitions or its democratic basis, there is little doubt that women's groups and auxiliaries had much more influence on the policy of the Labour Party than similar groups within the other two main parties. In addition, some of the leaders of the Labour Party before and after the war were as staunchly feminist as any of the women involved in the movement. We may cite Keir Hardie and George Lansbury in the pre-war period for example, and in the post-war years Frederick Pethick-Lawrence, who had suffered imprisonment and a hunger-strike as well as financial losses during the militant phase of the movement. But even those men who were not themselves feminist were steadily pressured towards feminist policies by the women in the party.

The most strongly feminist of the women's auxiliaries, at least in the early years of the Labour movement, was the Women's Co-operative Guild. Ardent suffragists, they were also active campaigners for a number of other issues concerned specifically with women and children. In the years immediately before the first world war they ran influential campaigns for equal divorce laws for men and women, for better maternity and infant welfare and for maternity benefits to be paid to mothers. Moreover, they were fully prepared to push their views in the face of opposition. Their views on cheaper and easier divorce, for example, not only brought them into conflict with Catholics within the co-operative movement but meant the withdrawal of their grant for several years while they demanded the right to full control over their own policy. Their campaign to give maternity benefits to mothers rather than fathers also aroused some hostility within the Labour Party (Webb, 1927, pp. 125—31, 152—8; Gaffin, 1977, pp. 128—37). The Women's Labour League, founded in 1906 with the object of persuading women to take an active interest in political affairs, also concerned itself with issues affecting women and children. There were lengthy campaigns on school meals, medical inspections in schools, the provision of nursery schools, and pit-head baths. The League also played a major role in the passing of the Maternity and Child Welfare Act of 1918. If these issues had more to do with 'welfare' than with feminism, the League also took part in the years after the war in demands for equal pay in both the civil service and the teaching profession (Middleton, 1977, pp. 26—55).

The consequence of this pressure from within their own ranks was to make the Labour Party receptive to many policies that were also of importance to the feminists. Maternity and infant welfare, for example, which in the United States was almost entirely a feminist issue, was a significant aspect of Labour Party policy, as were numbers of other measures to safeguard the health and well-being of women and children, such as school meals, medical inspection in schools and pensions for civilian widows (Davies, 1918, pp. 31—8). This alliance between feminism and the Labour Party was not paralleled in the United States until Roosevelt's New Deal, which ended the isolation of feminist reformers and social workers.

Not all feminists in Britain were Labour Party supporters, and Lady Rhondda, one of the most influential figures of the 1920s, had no socialist tendencies of any kind (Cook, 1978, p. 103). Nevertheless a number of the leading feminists at this time were prominent in the Labour Party, like the militant Pethick-Lawrences, who were in fact socialists before they became feminists (Pethick-Lawrence, 1938, pp. 145—336). Frederick Pethick-Lawrence became a Labour MP after the war, and although his major interests were in the economy and in foreign affairs his maiden speech was on pensions for widowed mothers (Pethick-Lawrence, 1943, p. 107). He was also involved in the final achievement of adult suffrage in 1928. For such men and women, equal rights for women and welfare legislation were not, as they appeared in the United States, contradictions, but part of one single crusade.

For the most part, therefore, feminists of different political persuasions worked harmoniously together during the 1920s, and until almost the end of the decade there was nothing approaching the split that had divided the American movement into two hostile camps. Nevertheless, beneath the surface, tensions were developing between those whose main emphasis was on equality and those whose objective was social reform. Initially, as we have seen, the feminist programme was mainly devoted to extending the suffrage and securing an end to the legal disabilities that feminism had been attacking for nearly 100 years, but there were those within the movement who, without rejecting the goal of equality between men and women, gave as much, if not more, attention to the need to protect the rights of women and children, and particularly those most in need of such protection, namely, widows, unmarried mothers, women working in sweated industry and the wives and children of the poor. Consequently, the efforts of the movement were expended as much on these welfare goals as on equal rights, which in retrospect were counted equally as feminist goals. Thus, writing in 1938, Emmeline Pethick-Lawrence (pp. 331—2) cited a new attitude to public health as the most significant effect of women's suffrage. In 1943, her husband, Frederick, also emphasized the benefits to women and children, and cited in particular widows' pensions and maternity and child welfare (1943, pp. 105—7).

If, however, the 1920s saw feminist organizations like the National Union of Societies for Equal Citizenship pursuing both equal rights and welfare goals, the middle of the decade brought into the open a debate between those who, like Lady Rhondda, simply wanted the movement to end the existing disabilities that affected women, and others who were concerned to develop what they called a 'new feminism', which would take account of women's special needs and aspirations. Based essentially on the differences between men and women, and accepting above all the centrality of women's maternal role, it sought to recognize and enhance women's function as wives and mothers. Such a conception was not of course new; as we have seen in previous chapters, much feminist theory, especially in the United States, was based upon doctrines of moral superiority that emphasized woman's actual and potential maternity rather than on the Enlightenment tradition of equal rights. What is significant for the present chapter is the form in which the argument now appeared.

Already in 1917 the publication of the *Oxford Essays on Feminism* (edited by Gollancz) had accepted the need to think beyond equal rights if feminist goals were to become a reality, but it was Eleanor Rathbone who brought the debate fully into the open in her presidential address to the NUSEC in 1925. She claimed that the way ahead was to change the structure of society to reflect women's experience rather than simply to open up opportunities previously claimed by men. In practical terms this meant a new recognition of the rights of motherhood by means of a policy of family endowment that would deliberately reallocate society's resources to mothers. This would not only eliminate the economic subjection of the wife, but open the way to equal pay, since it would remove the argument that a man had to support his family (Stocks, 1949, pp. 62—3; Rathbone, 1936, pp. 57—61).

In its emphasis on economic independence there was a great deal in this policy that was in accord with traditional feminist arguments, although the nineteenth-century feminists had been more concerned with giving women economic independence outside marriage than within it. Indeed most of the earlier feminists, including many of the socialists, had conceived of economic autonomy for married women as well as single as arising from their equal entry into the labour market. Eleanor· Rathbone's scheme was therefore by implication at least, a radical one. These implications were never realized in practice, however, and Eleanor Rathbone herself saw family endowment primarily as a means to strengthen both the family and women's traditional part in it rather than to explore possibilities for change. Moreover she was always chiefly concerned with the economic plight of mothers and especially children (Stocks, 1949, pp. 117—18).

By no means all the feminists were prepared to go along with Eleanor Rathbone in her views on the 'new feminism', and Millicent Garrett Fawcett was strongly opposed to family endowment as weakening family responsibilities. The tendency of the 'new feminists' to stress the differences between men and women was a source of anxiety (Lewis, 1973, p. 7). Liddington and Norris also claim that working women in the cotton industry were unfriendly to the idea (Liddington and Norris, 1978, pp. 259—60). Nevertheless, there was strong support from amongst the feminist ranks, and a number of leading women in the post-war movement like Eva Hubback and Mary Stocks were prominent in the family endowment campaign. Feminist approval was, in the long run however, less important than that of socialists who saw family allowances as a way of redistributing the resources of society to the benefit of the poor. The Labour Party and the trade union movement feared for a long time that such a scheme might hinder the family wage, but the women's organizations were early converts (Webb, 1927, p. 100). Like Eleanor Rathbone, these Labour women saw family endowments as enhancing the status of working-class women and I have already noted their campaign, before the first world war, to pay maternity benefits to mothers rather than fathers. Family endowments were a further, and more far-reaching, way of putting money into the hands of mothers, but it would also, it was believed, give working-class women a better chance of escape, by separation or divorce, from an unhappy marriage. On the other hand, it was seen as a way of removing most married women from the labour market altogether since the main economic reason for their labour would be ended. In this sense, therefore, the family endowment scheme was seen as strengthening the traditional family (Davies, 1918, pp. 31—8).

It was as children's allowances that the family endowment scheme eventually gained acceptance in 1945, but by this time they

were seen as additions to the family income to encourage couples
to have larger families and were not even paid for the first child. It
is also a significant illustration of the change of emphasis that in the
original formulation of the bill they were to be paid to fathers,
although Eleanor Rathbone and an organized campaign of women's
societies were successful in forcing an amendment for payment
direct to mothers (Stocks, 1949, p. 310).

If, however, Eleanor Rathbone's 'new feminism' and advocacy
of family endowment introduced controversy into feminism in the
1920s, it was the issue of protective legislation that was finally to
split the movement. As we saw in chapter 7, there were differences
of opinion on this issue from the beginning. Although initially the
women's trade union movement was opposed to such legislation, it
speedily changed its mind and, by the first world war, most of the
women trade union leaders were firmly behind it. The middle-class
suffrage societies, on the other hand, had tended to oppose it on
the grounds that it hampered women's right to work.

By the 1920s this situation had changed very little. The feminist
groups like the National Union of Societies for Equal Citizenship
and the Women's Freedom League, both largely middle-class in
membership, still opposed it (Cook, 1978, pp. 160—4), while the
trade union movement and the Labour Party were united in its
support (Macarthur, 1918, pp. 20—5). Within the trade union
movement, it is true, there were sometimes differences of opinion.
Liddington and Norris (1978, pp. 239—40), for example, have
drawn attention to the opposition, immediately before the first
world war, on the part of women textile workers to attempts to
restrict women's hours of work and to exclude them from certain
trades. After the war this opposition continued to surface from
time to time. In 1925, Crystal Eastman recorded a conversation
with Mary Bell-Richards, the head of the Women's Section of the
National Union of Boot and Shoe Operatives, in which she argued
that you could not protect women without handicapping them in
competition with men (Cook, 1978, pp. 170—1). Women in printing
unions have also been strong supporters of shift- and night-work
for women. On the whole, however, the labour and trade union
movement and its leaders have been behind protective legislation
and have attempted, indeed, to extend and strengthen it. Thus the
Labour government of 1929—31 tried to abolish an Act of 1920
that permitted shift-work in certain trades. An attempt in 1933 by
the ILO to argue for the exemption of women managers from
restrictions on night-work was opposed by the woman representing

the TUC on the grounds that it might open the door to night-work for all women (Lewenhak, 1977, p. 212).

Controversy within the feminist movement itself emerged in 1927 at a time when a new Factories Bill was before the House of Commons that raised anew the whole issue of protection for women workers. A year previously, a new society, the Open Door Council, had been founded, made up of representatives of the four main British societies and including both Lady Rhondda and the socialist Emmeline Pethick-Lawrence. Its declared aim was to oppose protective legislation based solely on sex and to secure for women, irrespective of marriage or childbirth, the right to paid work. In 1927 the NUSEC called a conference that confirmed its opposition to protective legislation for women chiefly on the grounds that it limited their earning capacity. It was argued that limitations on night-work and on overtime effectively excluded them from many trades and that, in fact, such legislation could be used to eliminate their competition. The main opposition at this conference seems to have come from delegates from women's trade unions, although it is perhaps significant that the Secretary of the Association of Women Clerks and Secretaries was more sympathetic than other trade unionists to the feminist point of view (Cook, 1978, pp. 215—19). The Women's Trade Union Conference of that year reaffirmed its support for protective legislation and attacked the policy of the Open Door Council (Soldon, 1978, p. 126).

In that same year, however, the apparent unanimity of the feminist organizations was shattered by the resignation of the equal rights members of the council of the NUSEC. The protest occurred at the annual conference and was apparently brought to a head by a successful attempt on the part of Eleanor Rathbone to modify the opposition to protective legislation by bringing it more into line with the view of women trade unionists. Her amendment was eventually carried after hours of heated discussion by a vote of 81 to 80. A further amendment that tried to relegate such issues as family endowment and birth control to a secondary place while giving priority to equal rights in the franchise, equal moral standards and equal pay and opportunities at work was also lost. Defeated on both counts, the equal rights group on the council resigned altogether, leaving the society in the hands of what Chrystal Eastman, herself an equal rights supporter, called the 'humanitarians' (Cook, 1978, pp. 229—31).

Ultimately, therefore, the British movement, exactly like the

American movement, was weakened by internal divisions centring upon protective legislation but representing, as Chrystal Eastman observed at the time, the distinction within feminism between the equal rights tradition and the movement for social reform. To some extent this was a division along social class lines, with the representatives of working-class opinion in favour of protective legislation and the professional and propertied woman in opposition. On the other hand, as we have seen, middle-class social workers and social reformers could be as solidly behind protective legislation as any trade union leaders, especially in the United States where middle-class social reformers and settlement workers were in the forefront of the campaign. At the same time, some working-class women were against many aspects of such legislation, including for example the prohibition of night-work, since they saw it as limiting their own earnings and opportunities. Middle-class socialists, like Chrystal Eastman, could also be doubtful about some of its effects, perceiving clearly the ways in which it could be used to harm women in industry as well as to help them (Cook, 1978, pp. 222—3).

Behind the dispute over protective legislation was another even more fundamental argument. The feminists like Eleanor Rathbone who wanted a 'new feminism' based not upon equality but on women's special needs were still working within a traditional framework of women's roles. According to this view, even if single women needed employment, married women were expected to remain at home, their lives centred upon and even bounded by maternity. Women in the labour movement, too, tended to see women's issues as revolving around the needs of children, and for many of them women were on the whole regarded as temporary members of the labour force. The trade union movement supported the idea of the family wage and continued to view women, much as they had done in the nineteenth century, as competitors who, by their acceptance of lower pay, threatened the standard of living of the family. During this period it was trade union policy to try to reduce the number of women seeking work, and they held to the general rule that one income going into the household had to suffice (Lewenhak, 1977, p. 185). For this reason the trade union movement often approved of marriage bars (Lewenhak, 1977, p. 226).

If, by the end of the 1920s, the equal rights feminists were no longer dominant within the women's movement, the 1930s accentuated their decline still further so that, as in the United

States, feminism became almost synonymous with welfare. Moreover, this was brought about, to a considerable extent, by the abdication of the equal rights group, who not only resigned from the NUSEC but from the equal rights battle itself. Lady Rhondda, perhaps the most important figure during the 1920s, has recorded how, after equal suffrage was finally achieved in 1928, the 'only big purely legal inequality' was ended, and she now felt free to 'drop the business' (Rhondda, 1933, p. 299). Emmeline Pethick-Lawrence, equally, found her interest moving away from feminism and, in her case, back to the socialism that was her first love before the Pankhursts converted her to militancy (Pethick-Lawrence, 1938, p. 336). Eva Hubback, who had been parliamentary secretary to the NUSEC and had helped to edit its weekly paper the *Woman's Leader,* had been closely involved in lobbying for the equal rights legislation of the 1920s. From 1924, however, she had also been involved in the family endowment campaign with Eleanor Rathbone, and during the 1930s most of her energies went into the issue of healthier families. She became president of the Children's Minimum Council to stimulate an improvement in social services concerning children, and for several years she was a member of the council of the Eugenics Society (Hopkinson, 1954). Mary Stocks, although regarded as one of the 'equalitarians' (Stott, 1978, p. 18), was mainly occupied, during both the 1920s and the 1930s, with the family endowment campaign and with family planning.

Within the NUSEC the final achievement of adult suffrage in 1928 brought changes that turned it even further away from an active involvement in equal rights issues. At this time there were 300 local suffrage societies whose work was now completed, and the question of what should be done with them had to be decided. Eventually, largely on the initiative of Eva Hubback, the NUSEC split into two organizations, the National Council for Equal Citizenship, which had the task of pressing for further equal rights legislation, and a union of Townswomen's Guilds, modelled on the Women's Institutes, whose function would be primarily educational. While this plan, as initially conceived, allowed for the possibility of political campaigning on such issues as equal pay, the abolition of the marriage bar and barriers to promotion in the civil service, in practice, while the educationally oriented guilds grew in numbers, the political societies declined. Already by 1932 there were 51 delegates from the 'political' societies and 183 from the newly organized guilds, and in future the number of guilds was to grow rapidly, and the political societies shrink still further (Stott, 1978, p. 16).

Furthermore, even as educational groups, the Townswomen's Guilds were scarcely feminist in their orientation. Home-making and craft skills were their most popular activities, and there was little interest in political issues, and especially in any active involvement in politics. Indeed from the start the aim seems to have been to avoid controversy and to be strictly non-partisan. The chief political function of the guilds in so far as they have had one, has been indirect, since they have trained women in the practical activities of running an organization and speaking in public, so preparing them as individuals for a more direct involvement in politics. In this way a number of women have been drawn into local politics. Even when the guilds have become more directly involved in a political issue, this has rarely been specifically feminist, and on the whole they have acted as a representative of housewives. Issues such as litter, shopping facilities and consumer protection, which have all interested the guildswomen from time to time, arise directly from their housekeeping function. Other topics, like the care of the mentally defective and the ill, were a part of the general concern of many women's groups at this time for an increase in welfare provision. The concern for moral standards in films and on television, which has been a continuous interest over the years, also reflects the alliance between women and moral reform, which, as we have seen, was characteristic of women's groups in the nineteenth century. Occasionally however, in common with other women's organizations, the guilds have pressed for changes that still reflect their feminist origins. The campaign during the 1930s for women police is a good example, and in 1937 they were part of a more general pressure from women to improve the pensions scheme for dependent wives. Later on, in the 1950s, they joined with other organizations in a campaign, ultimately successful, against turnstiles in public lavatories. In this respect, although never pioneers, they represented a source of organized pressure that could from time to time be captured for more specifically feminist goals when these were able to command, as did the issue of public lavatories, considerable general support from women. They were therefore similar to the women's club movement in the United States, which in the early twentieth century, in spite of its general conservative orientation, acted as a pressure group for both consumer and welfare legislation and, later on, for suffrage itself.

If, however, the very success of the suffrage movement turned women's attention away from equal rights, during the 1930s there were other reasons why welfare seemed to many a more important goal than equality. The Depression and its consequences had focused attention on poverty, and a number of studies published at that time illustrated starkly the hardships endured by working-class wives and mothers in particular. Such studies paved the way both for the comprehensive health service and for the social insurance and social security schemes that, after the war, became the foundation of the new welfare state.

The international situation also occupied the attention of many in the feminist movement. As in the United States, although possibly not to the same degree, some of the feminist leaders, Eleanor Rathbone amongst them, devoted much of their time to the peace movement and to international affairs (Stocks, 1949, pp. 199—209), and many former suffrage workers became active in the branches of the League of Nations Union (Bussey and Tims, 1965). Indeed, now that the temperance campaign no longer exerted the moral appeal that it had once had for the women of the middle classes, peace and international understanding seem, to some extent at least, to have taken its place. Nor was this confined to middle-class women, and after the first world war the Women's Co-operative Guild also placed a growing emphasis on peace and international affairs (Gaffin, 1977, p. 137).

After the second world war, the provisions of the welfare state incorporated many of the policies that had first been advocated by women's organizations and that were designed to improve the health and well-being of women and children. The most striking example is family allowances, which, as we have seen, originated as a specifically feminist programme during the first world war and which were only accepted as Labour Party policy much later on. Many other aspects of the new welfare legislation had been put forward by women's organizations, much of it even earlier than the first world war, and only much later adopted as Labour Party policy. Nevertheless, to a large extent we may see the welfare state in Britain as a product of an alliance between welfare feminism and the Labour Party.

This is not to say, however, that this alliance, significant as it was, always worked smoothly. The assumption behind much of the legislation, and firmly endorsed by Beveridge himself, that married women were economically dependent on their husbands, was challenged by those feminists who wished women to have a greater degree of independence, although protests from women's organizations in 1946 met with little sympathy (Wilson, 1977, p. 154). More successfully, we have already noticed the way in which Eleanor

Rathbone and an organized campaign of women's societies forced the government to pay family allowances to mothers rather than fathers (Stocks, 1949, p. 310). These years also saw attempts within Parliament to raise the economic status of dependent housewives by giving them a share in the matrimonial income. Thus in 1943 Edith Summerskill (1967, p. 144) unsuccessfully took up the case of a housewife whose husband claimed her savings from her Co-operative dividend.

However, in spite of the feminism of individual women MPs like Lady Astor and Eleanor Rathbone and, later, Edith Summerskill, it is only very rarely that women MPs in Britain as in the United States have united to form a common front. In 1932 a group headed by Lady Astor campaigned, with the support of the labour movement, against the exclusion of married women from the working of the National Health Insurance and Contributory Pensions Act (Wilson, 1977, p. 120). In 1940, also led by Lady Astor, there was a campaign to get better use made of professional women as part of the war effort (Stocks, 1949, p. 290). Indeed, to some extent, women MPs have tried to avoid being typecast as women and relegated to women's issues (Vallance, 1979, p. 72). Nevertheless Vallance (p. 107) has calculated that of twenty-five private bills introduced by women, three have related to drunkenness, three to the protection of animals, nine to women and children, and four to consumer interests. This suggests that, in spite of their efforts, the association both between women and welfare and between women and moral reform has by no means come to an end.

To conclude then, we can see that, in Britain as in the United States, the alliance between feminism and welfare dominated the feminist movement in the years after women's suffrage had at last been granted. This alliance, moreover, had its origins in the earlier association between feminism and moral reform, an association that itself sprang from the evangelical tradition in feminism with its notions of individual perfectability and, later on, social utopias. The effect was to turn feminism increasingly away from its roots in the Enlightenment doctrine of equal rights and to give support to the ideal of male and female differentiation.

The form that their differences took during the 'welfare' phase of feminism, as it had done earlier, was based essentially upon woman's actual or potential maternity, which was seen as influencing her nature to a degree utterly different from man's role as a father. In so far as this was considered at all, it was always in terms of his role as breadwinner or family 'provider'. In keeping with the tendency within the evangelical tradition to idealize women, the wider significance of the maternal role was constantly stressed, so that through their role as mothers women, as in the nineteenth century, were seen potentially at least as saviours of the race. Moreover, because welfare feminism was concerned with social as much as, if not more than, with moral issues, it constantly stressed the contribution of the mother to the physical well-being of the child. It is no accident, therefore, that feminism at this time had a close association with the eugenics movement, an association that will be more fully explored in the following chapter in connection with feminism and birth control.

Welfare feminism thus accepted the traditional male and female roles in the family to almost the same extent as the nineteenth- and early twentieth-century anti-feminists who had feared the effect of women's emancipation on women and the family. It would be quite mistaken, however, to argue that welfare feminism was not feminism at all. If its adherents accepted that women were, first and foremost, mothers, and that their interests as women were primarily in the needs of mothers and children, they were both active and indeed radical in their proposals for meeting these needs. The family endowment scheme is a good example of a proposal that, if it had been implemented as it was originally conceived, would have reduced the economic dependence of wives on their husbands. Other measures, if less radical in their implications, certainly did much to improve the actual situation of women, especially those living in poverty, since they needed the financial benefits, like maternity grants, just as they needed the maternity and child welfare services, medical and dental care, and school meals. There is plenty of evidence, too, that both in the United States and in Britain women's organizations were the spearhead of the pressure for welfare legislation of this kind.

Undoubtedly, therefore, welfare feminism has helped to bring the needs of women and children into the forefront of practical politics although it is highly doubtful if it would have succeeded without the help of other forces working towards the introduction of some form of welfare state. In this context the similarities between the two countries are more important than the differences. Certainly in Britain the alliance between feminism and the labour movement made a difference, both in the timing and in the nature of the welfare legislation when it came. The absence of a labour party did not, however, alter the allegiance of American feminism to welfare, although it perhaps made their contribution to it, especially in the early years, even more significant than in Britain. It also appears, from the evidence that we have, that the dramatic and even violent split that occurred in the ranks of American feminism in the 1920s had no real parallel in Britain. There were differences of opinion, some of them leading to open conflict, but for most of the time the issues that divided the American movement so dramatically were contained within the British movement. In both countries, however, welfare feminism had virtually triumphed by the 1930s.

This is not to suggest, on the other hand, that equal rights feminism was dead. In Britain, as we have seen, some women MPs and some women's organizations continued to raise specific feminist issues, even if somewhat haphazardly and often unsuccessfully. Within the women's trade union movement, as we shall see in chapter 11, the fight for equal pay was never really abandoned and neither was opposition to the marriage bar. In the United States, too, the small Woman's Party still campaigned annually for an equal rights amendment with, as the years went by, an increasing number of allies. However, it was only with the awakening of equal rights feminism in the 1960s that these small and largely unsuccessful endeavours could be seen in their true perspective. For most of the welfare feminists, the equal rights tradition, as we have seen in the case of Eleanor Rathbone, seemed not only dead but actually outmoded.

Welfare, then, gave its imprint to the feminism of both the inter-war period and the years after the second world war. Its chief character, as we have seen, was its concern for the welfare of mothers and children, and its influence has been felt largely in legislation designed to that end. It is for this reason that I have argued that, in spite of its traditional attitudes to the family, it is still feminist in intent. It must be accepted, however, that its adherents all too easily came to place their entire emphasis on welfare, ignoring or forgetting the feminist purpose behind the welfare goals. To some extent this arose from their sympathy for the poor. Such sympathy not only deflected some former suffragists like the Pethick-Lawrences away from feminism and into socialism, but drew some of the younger women MPs like Ellen Wilkinson towards socialism rather than feminism. Even those who still remained feminist were often forced to compromise in search of allies. The Labour Party was, as we have seen, sympathetic to many feminist ideas, but was never whole-heartedly committed to feminist doctrines, and the same was true of parties to the left of the Labour Party. The trade union movement continued to remain very traditional in its attitude to marriage and the family. There was therefore conflict as well as cooperation between the feminists and the labour movement as a whole, of which perhaps the most deeply felt and sustained was the conflict over birth control to be described in the next chapter. Most significant of all was the assumption, made very explicit by Beveridge, that the basis of the welfare state was the traditional family with its concept of the family wage and the dependent wife. Feminists, as we have seen, were not always happy at some of the implications of this doctrine, particularly for insurance benefits and contributions, but it was not until the new feminist movement that its fundamental anti-feminism was fully exposed.

At the same time, the issues that had been at the heart of equal rights feminism remained largely unexplored. Equal pay, it is true, continued to be a feminist goal, although some welfare feminists were in doubt about its practicability, but equal opportunities in employment and in education were almost totally ignored. So were many of the legal disabilities that were later on to be raised by the new feminist movement. Indeed, the welfare feminists in the United States, even after the war, were still opposing an equal rights amendment as a threat to protective legislation.

This is not the place to discuss the challenge offered by the new feminist movement to welfare feminism, since this will be the subject matter of Part IV. It is sufficient at this stage to point out that, in some respects at least, the resurgence of equal rights feminism that occurred during the 1960s was not only a return to an earlier tradition but also a reaction against some of the central concepts upon which welfare feminism was based. More particularly, it was a critique of women's traditional role that welfare feminism was not prepared to make, so that welfare feminism itself trapped women in the cult of domesticity from which earlier generations of feminists had tried to free themselves.

Before taking these arguments further, however, it is necessary to examine another aspect of these years of intermission. Dating from even before the end of the nineteenth century, new ideas on sexual morality were to transform the lives of women, especially those of the middle classes. Feminism as such was not in fact very important in producing these changes, but it clearly had to come to terms with them. Consequently the twentieth century saw feminists exploring new attitudes on love and morality, marriage and divorce, contraception and abortion, and, perhaps most important of all, the nature and extent of female sexuality. Nineteenth-century feminism, it is true, had opinions on all these issues, even if they could not always be expressed very openly, and earlier chapters have described them in so far as the evidence allows. For the new feminist movement, as we shall see, attitudes to these issues have become of overriding importance in maintaining its character. Moreover, the ideas that are expressed on most of them are often diametrically opposed to those of their nineteenth-century predecessors. The following chapters will examine the changes in feminist ideology on these issues that occurred during the first half of the twentieth century and that paved the way for the women's liberation movement and the new feminism of today.

10

The New Woman

Although during the early years of the twentieth century the attention of the feminists was upon the campaign for women's suffrage and its consequences, a much greater impact was being made upon women's lives by changes that had little directly to do with the feminist movement and that involved, in both Britain and the United States, a loosening of manners and morals and an emancipation, for the young middle-class girl in particular, from those suffocating conventions that had restricted her within the narrow world of Victorian morality. These changes did not, of course, occur suddenly. Some had been set in train during the last years of the nineteenth century, which in Britain saw both a greater mixing of the sexes in leisure activities and more opportunities to escape from the confines of the home. The popularity of cycling in the 1890s was an important factor in giving young middle-class women greater mobility, although it met with a great deal of hostility at first, both from the notorious anti-feminist Mrs Ellis and other conventional people and from the working classes (Rubinstein, 1977).

Changes in the education of girls and the growth in higher education also had a part to play, although, as we have seen, both schools and colleges had to bow to convention in their early years, even when they were inspired by the most feminist of principles. By the turn of the century, however, the most rigid of the restrictions had gone, even if many irksome restraints still remained. The generation of students who entered college in the years just before the first world war were no longer so hedged around with rules, and had considerable social and intellectual freedom at least by earlier standards.

Another important source of freedom for young women of the middle classes was the growing custom of working before marriage, either in the greatly expanding field of white-collar employment or, for the more fortunate few, in professional or semi-professional work. Although it was to become more general later, the breakthrough of young women into this kind of occupation occurred before the first world war, and not after (Wilson, 1979; Holcombe, 1973). Moreover, although it had been one of the aims of the early feminists, the actual expansion of employment opportunities for these young women was more a consequence of changes in the demand for labour than of the feminist campaign, which had little success in opening the more lucrative male occupations to women. It was in the growing job market in offices and shops and in the semi-professions like nursing and teaching that the young women of the middle classes found a degree of economic independence and, perhaps even more significantly, an escape from the constant adult surveillance of the parental home. These years also, as we have seen, drew many young women of the upper middle classes into social work, whether voluntarily or, as time went on, as a professional career (Pethick-Lawrence, 1938).

Along with this growing freedom from many conventional restraints went a reform of women's dress. Rational dress reform had indeed been a project very dear to the heart of the American feminists in the 1850s and 1860s, and they had experimented with the bloomer costume for a number of years, enjoying its freedom but hurt by the ridicule and even hostility it aroused. Eventually they abandoned it as something of a lost cause (Riegal, 1963). In Britain, the early feminists seem to have set more store by appearing 'lady-like', but a Rational Dress League was founded in 1898, inspired to some extent by the cycling craze. Lady Harberton, a leading figure in the League, was later to become a prominent suffrage worker (Rubinstein, 1977). When it came, however, the sudden change to shorter skirts and shorter hair and the virtual death of the corset owed little to any particular campaign but were expressed through the normal working of fashion.

At one time it was customary to date the final arrival of the 'new woman' in the early 1920s or, at the very earliest, during the first world war. More recently, however, American historians have suggested that this is an error. Amongst the middle and upper classes, at least, changes in hair styles, cosmetics and fashions, in smoking and drinking habits, and in a more permissive sexual morality, occurred before the war; the effect of war-time was to quicken and deepen the revolution but not to cause it. McGovern suggests that the real change occurred after about 1910 when already there was a new and more boyish ideal in figure and dress that anticipated the flappers of the post-war period. By this time, too, smoking and drinking in public were becoming fashionable (McGovern, 1968). In Britain, Cominos (1963) has dated the emergence of the 'new woman' in the mid-1890s along with modern psychology, liberal socialism and the historical method of thought.

The change in outward behaviour was also accompanied by quite significant movements of opinion, particularly with respect to sexuality. The deep suspicion of sexual pleasure characteristic of much of the nineteenth century and brought to its fullest expression in the writings of the purity campaigners was by the 1890s already beginning to decline. This is not to suggest that no vestige of Victorian morality remained. Indeed, the very loosening of restraints on public discussion produced something of a backlash so that these are years that also witnessed the effects of revived purity campaigns in both Britain (Hynes, 1968, pp. 162, 279—80, 287) and in the United States (Gordon, 1977, pp. 177—8). Nor of course was all nineteenth-century opinion in accord with the purity campaigners' view of sexual restraint. Early birth-controllers like Drysdale, for example, considered that enforced celibacy, whether before marriage or in the form of moral restraint during marriage, was physically harmful to both men and women (McLaren, 1978). It was only towards the end of the nineteenth century, however, that such ideas began to become acceptable to a wider circle.

The survey carried out by Mosher in the United States in the 1890s on a small group of highly educated women of the middle and upper classes sheds light on this transitional period in which ideas amongst the educated middle classes appeared to be changing. Few women in this survey gave procreation as the only justification for sexual intercourse, although it is noteworthy that it was the most *frequent* reason given, with pleasure rating only second place. The actual figures of frequency for intercourse show a rate about half that given by the Kinsey survey, and there is evidence that couples were using self-control as one of the means of birth control, which was by that date widely practised by the middle and upper classes. Other methods used included the safe period and coitus interruptus; mechanical techniques clearly had not yet been widely accepted. Most of these women saw sexual pleasure as important but still, in the main, as more significant for the man than for the woman (Campbell, 1979). Degler (1974) has used this survey to argue that sexual pleasure was experienced widely throughout the nineteenth century by women as well as by men, but it is doubtful, as Campbell argues, if it is legitimate to interpret it in this way. It seems more reasonable to regard it as Campbell does, as representing a transitional period in attitudes towards sexuality.

A study of the treatment of sex in marital education literature in the United States shows that during the twentieth century the idea that sex was acceptable only for procreation steadily declined and there was a growing emphasis on the need for mutual sexual satisfaction. After the first world war there was a growing emphasis on sexual techniques as a guide to what was now seen as essential to marital happiness. There was also a growing appreciation of the sexual needs of women, but female sexuality was still represented as more general, less diffuse and, perhaps most significantly, less urgent than that of the male (Gordon, 1971).

From the 1920s, too, in so far as evidence from the United States indicates, there was a reassessment of pre-marital sexual relationships. This involved a convergence between male and female rates of pre-marital sexual intercourse so that, although the rates were increasing for men, the increase was proportionately greater for women. This suggests that the change in behaviour affected women rather than men and allowed unmarried girls, especially of the middle classes, a degree of freedom that had not normally been possible in the days of greater parental control (Gordon, 1977, pp. 192—3).

There is no really comparable material from Britain, but what evidence we have suggests that the pattern was very much the same. Certainly, even if the actual timing was different, there is every reason to suppose that the direction was identical. If we look, for example, at the change in attitude towards birth control on the part of the Church of England, we see even there a gradual, if slow, movement away from nineteenth-century attitudes. As late as 1913 the Church was still maintaining unequivocally that sexual relationships even within marriage were sinful if indulged in for their own sake. Birth control was sternly condemned, continence and self-control commended, and large families approved. Christian men and women, it was argued, 'must bear the cross and keep themselves in purity and temperance' (F. Campbell, 1960, p. 135). By the 1930s, however, the Church was prepared to admit that sexual desire within marriage had its value and importance, and by 1958 family planning had the full support of the Lambeth conference of bishops. The Roman Catholic Church, it is true, still retained the tie between sex and procreation, but for the Protestant churches it had ended (Leathard, 1980). Finally, the decision in 1964 by the London County Council to give family planning advice to unmarried people provided official endorsement of a changed attitude even to pre-marital sexual relationships (Fryer, 1965, p. 269).

The older generation of feminists, however, did not look approvingly at the growing sexual permissiveness. In the United States, Charlotte Perkins Gilman, looking back in the years after the first world war, recalled regretfully the time when 'there was a fine earnest movement toward an equal standard of chastity for men and women, an equalizing upward to the level of what women were then' (Gilman, 1935, p. 323). Like many feminists of today, she saw female sexuality as a trap to keep women pregnant and domesticated (Gilman, 1972, p. xvii), but, instead of anticipating a time when women would be free to enjoy their sexuality, she looked forward to a society where there would be much less emphasis on sex (Gordon, 1977, p. 184). Carrie Chapman Catt also carried into the twentieth century a nineteenth-century admiration for continence. Thinking along similar lines to Gilman, she argued that men's control over women had turned them into sex slaves with the result that not only men but women too had become oversexualized (Gordon, 1977, p. 238). Finally, Jane Addams, writing in the 1920s, could not understand or sympathize with 'the outstanding emphasis upon sex' (Davis, 1973, p. 277).

In Britain, before the first world war, Beatrice Webb protested against the tendency in modern literature to harp on the theme of sexual attraction and condemned the idea of 'sexual emotion for its own sake and not for the sake of bearing children' (Hynes, 1968, pp. 113—14). Moreover, even if it is argued that Beatrice Webb was no feminist, we find her attitude paralleled by Christabel Pankhurst who expressly limited sex to procreation in her notorious pamphlet on venereal disease in 1913 (Banks, 1964, p. 113). Even Maude Royden, in 1917, who was prepared to criticize the idea that women disliked sex and to argue that this was only because they had been taught to do so, clearly believed in the nineteenth-century feminist ideal that both men and women should come chaste to marriage and condemned the abandonment of self-control as the pathological side of sex (Royden, 1917, pp. 41—7).

In the years after the first world war, however, the views of feminists gradually changed. We can document this change most fully if we examine the feminist reaction to those specific controversies that involved most closely a re-examination of nineteenth-century ideas of sexuality. Of these, perhaps the most important for our purposes are birth control and abortion, although this chapter will also include a discussion of the more complex issue of divorce. As we have seen, none of the three was a feminist goal in the nineteenth century. The great majority of the feminists at this time condemned both birth control and abortion, while divorce law reform remained an area of great controversy that many feminists, whatever their private views, preferred to ignore. In the twentieth century this was to change, and the growing centrality of abortion in particular for the new feminism is one of the most significant aspects of the modern movement.

Even in the nineteenth century many feminists were prepared to welcome family limitation and to advocate smaller families, but the use of mechanical or artificial methods of contraception was repugnant to them precisely *because* it threatened to separate sexual intercourse and procreation not only within marriage but also outside it. Consequently it could all too easily seem to imply an increase in the sexual abuse of women and even a flight on the part of men from marriage itself. By the early years of the twentieth century, however, this picture was already changing. In both the United States and Britain the idea of contraception as a method of family limitation was beginning to appeal to a growing number of feminists, particularly those linked to the political left, and some of these began to adopt birth control as part of their political and feminist platform, culminating eventually in a birth control movement that aimed not simply at argument but at practical advice and help.

In Britain both Edward Carpenter and Havelock Ellis were influential in changing attitudes towards sexuality. If many of the older feminist leaders were hostile to this new current of thought, Carpenter in particular was popular in the socialist movement and his book *Love's Coming of Age* was widely read. There is evidence that in small discussion groups up and down the country the work of both Carpenter and Ellis formed an important topic for those involved in both socialism and feminism (Rowbotham and Weeks, 1977, pp. 16—17).

In 1911 a new feminist journal *The Freewoman* was founded that was committed to the new morality and opposed the puritanism of suffragists like Christabel Pankhurst. Amongst those who wrote for it was Rose Witcop, a revolutionary socialist who later became a passionate advocate of birth control (Rowbotham, 1977, pp. 16—17). Another contributor was Stella Browne, who in 1912 used the ideas of Havelock Ellis to protest against the denial of female sexuality. Later Stella Browne, too, was to become significant in the birth control campaign. In 1914, she was active in a campaign organized by the Malthusian League to spread contraceptive knowledge amongst the working classes. Eden and Cedar Paul were two other socialists who became involved in the birth control movement. In 1917 they edited a symposium *Population and Birth Control* that included contributions from German socialists (Rowbotham, 1977, pp. 11—19). Marie Stopes, who was one of the best known and most important of the birth control campaigners, was also influenced by both Carpenter and Ellis, especially in her views on female sexuality. Her book *Married Love,* published in 1918, was a significant milestone, not only in the frank discussion of female sexuality but also in the part it played in breaking down the belief that sexual pleasure was a sin (Hall, 1977).

In the 1920s, the birth control movement was to enter a new phase, which involved not only a greater openness in the discussion of such issues but, even more significantly, steady and widespread pressure to bring information on birth control, already available to and used by the middle classes, within the reach of the working classes. Most important of all for our purposes was the virtual abandonment by organized feminism of its opposition to the birth control movement.

The year 1921 saw the opening of the first British birth control clinic by Marie Stopes, and this was followed very soon afterwards by a number of others, mainly under the auspices of the newly formed Society for the Provision of Birth Control Clinics. Such clinics, in spite of their success, could however meet only a fraction of the need and were always short of funds. Consequently, it was not long before a campaign was under way to provide birth control advice at the maternity clinics under the control of the Ministry of Health, sparked off by the dismissal in 1922 of a health visitor in Edmonton because she had given information on birth control. Edmonton's action was subsequently supported by Dr Janet Campbell, from the Ministry of Health, who ruled that such advice was outside the scope of maternity centres. The issue was taken up by the Women's Co-operative Guild at their 1923 conference and by 1924 a vigorous protest was under way in which Dora Russell was to take a prominent part. There was a debate at the Labour Women's conference that year and also a deputation to the Minister of Health, who, as a Catholic, proved unsympathetic. The result was the launching of the Workers' Birth Control Group to bring the issue to the attention of the labour movement (Russell, 1975; Rowbotham, 1977; Leathard, 1980).

There is little doubt that at this time the Birth Control Group had wide support within the women's sections of the labour movement. Indeed there is evidence that Co-operative women, in particular, had a long history of interest in contraceptive information (Fryer, 1965, pp. 257—8). The problem at this stage was largely to convert the men, and this was not an easy task. Much of the opposition came from the Catholics within the movement, who waged a very fierce and largely successful battle within the Labour Party against it (Leathard, 1980). Indeed, even in 1935, Edith Summerskill, as a candidate in Bury with a large Catholic population, had to face hostility from the Roman Catholic Church because of her support for birth control (Summerskill, 1967, pp. 53—4). Not all of the opposition was of this kind, however. There was a long tradition of anti-Malthusianism within the whole of the socialist movement based upon the anti-socialism of many in the Malthusian League. The Malthusian argument that large families were the cause of poverty, and the opposition of the League to trades unionism and to strikes, came into direct conflict with the socialist doctrine that the system, not the individual, was to blame. Family limitation therefore was seen as a matter for individual families to decide for themselves, or even as an attack on the poor man's right to have children (McLaren, 1978, pp. 158—60; Ledbetter, 1976, pp. 87—116). Within the Communist Party, Stella Browne's fight for birth control to become party policy came into conflict with anti-Malthusian views and she eventually resigned from the party in 1923 because of her differences with them on the issue of birth control and abortion (Rowbotham, 1977, pp. 23—9).

Nor were all the opponents men. Dora Russell relates how Marion Phillips, Woman Organizer of the Labour Party, told her that sex should not be dragged into politics and that she would 'split the Party from top to bottom' (Russell, 1975, p. 172). Later, she was to be converted through the pressure of women within the party (Rowbotham, 1977, p. 55). Women doctors, too, appear to have been as likely to oppose birth control as were their male colleagues (Fryer, 1965, pp. 247—8). One of its most vigorous opponents was Dr Anne Louise McIllroy, Professor of Obstetrics and Gynaecology at the Royal Free Hospital. She spoke out against it in 1921 at the Medico Legal Society and was later involved in a court case in opposition to Marie Stopes. Unmarried herself, she recommended moral restraint as the proper method of family limitation. Later, however, she was converted and was to provide birth control advice. Other medical opponents included Dr Josephine Fairfield, Assistant Medical Officer to the LCC, and Dr Mary Sharlieb, consulting gynaecologist at the Royal Free Hospital. These women were part of the first generation of women doctors and clearly reflected the older feminist attitude to sex. Indeed, in 1918 Dr Sharlieb had advocated drill halls and tea gardens to take men's minds off women and drink.

Within organized feminism however, opinions were changing, and in 1925 the National Union of Societies for Equal Citizenship passed a resolution approving of birth control and calling on the Ministry of Health to give birth control advice at the maternity clinics. A pamphlet written in that year by Mary Stocks, setting out the reasoning behind the resolution, claimed birth control as an explicitly feminist reform. While recognizing that amongst NUSEC's members there were some, albeit a minority, who would only accept family limitation through moral restraint, the pamphlet explicitly rejected the view that linked sex exclusively with procreation. Pointing out that information was already available for the well-to-do, it made a plea for the rights of the poor and uninformed (Stocks, 1925).

Mary Stocks was deeply committed to the campaign for birth control and opened one of the first of the provincial clinics in Manchester, where she was living. She was also active in the attempt to persuade the Ministry of Health to give birth control advice in its own clinics. Eleanor Rathbone also spoke and voted with those who succeeded in committing NUSEC to birth control, although she did not personally play a very active part in the campaign. Eva Hubback, another prominent NUSEC member in the 1920s, was also an active worker in the birth control movement, especially in the 1930s (Hopkinson, 1954, p. 160).

If the feminists became converted to the birth control movement, the movement itself gradually became less radical. The very success of the campaign meant that it was no longer the focus of such controversy, especially after the Ministry of Health in 1930 allowed local authorities some limited power to give birth control advice. Increasingly, a new generation of doctors no longer regarded the practice as harmful and even the Church (the Roman Catholics excepted) began, as we have seen, to accept the view that sex and procreation, at least within marriage, could be separated without harm and indeed with benefit to married life (Leathard, 1980).

During these years, too, the practice of birth control had become so widely accepted that by the late thirties and early forties there were fears of a fall in population and this deeply influenced some of those in the forefront of the campaign. Eva Hubback, for example, was by 1948 stressing the need for larger rather than smaller families (Hubback, 1947). The National Birth Control Council, formed in 1930 to coordinate the five existing birth control societies, began to emphasize clinic advice for sterility and the positive side of planned parenthood. To further this broadening of aims the Council changed its name to the Family Planning Association (Leathard, 1980, pp. 67—8). Moreover, now that large families were concentrated mainly amongst the poor, there was a concern for the quality of the population, and birth control became more closely associated with eugenics than with feminism. Indeed, Eva Hubback was for some years a member of the council of the Eugenics Society. Neo-Malthusianism and eugenics had always been linked (Ledbetter, 1976, pp. 204—5, 218) and, as we have seen, some socialists had been attracted by it in the early years of the twentieth century. Havelock Ellis, too, held that eugenics was central to social reform, and these views of his hardened with age (Rowbotham and Weeks, 1977, pp. 174—80).

Most important of all perhaps was the way in which the campaign for birth control information became part of the growing demand for better welfare facilities for women and children. It was argued that it was needed above all for the improvement of the maternal health of working-class mothers and to reduce the volume of working-class abortions. Since there was considerable public concern at the rise in maternal death rates, as well as the high level of abortions, this made it possible, as Leathard (1980, p. 55) points out, to turn the argument for birth control into a 'safe public health topic'. While aiding the birth control campaign, however, it also helped to turn the birth control movement away from feminism.

In the years after the war, birth control was seen increasingly as bringing the benefits of smaller families to the poor either for eugenic reasons or simply as an extension of welfare. Later still, when population growth again became an anxiety, birth control became a matter of international rather than simply national concern, but once again eugenic considerations, this time about the white race, or alternatively about the future world food supply, were in the forefront of political concern. It was in this context, therefore, that the search for alternative and more efficient methods of contraception was made. The link between birth control and feminism, always a tenuous one, was not to be revived until the new feminist movement once again claimed it as a feminist goal.

The argument for birth control — like that for family allowances, with which it was, indeed, frequently linked — could also be used to sustain rather than challenge woman's traditional role, by emphasizing and even idealizing her maternal nature. Marie Stopes, for example, in spite of her radical views on female sexuality, was ambiguous in her attitude toward women. She believed they had a right to their own intellectual development, and during the 1920s organized an unsuccessful campaign against the decision by the Rhondda Valley education authority to sack all their women teachers. At the same time she believed that marriage and maternity were a woman's chief goal in life. Moreover, while she believed, like modern feminists, that a woman's body was essentially her own, she disapproved of pre-marital sex, abortion, masturbation and lesbianism (Hall, 1977).

Havelock Ellis, too, in spite of his views on the pleasures of sex for male and female alike, remained wedded to a belief in the natural differences between men and women, rooted biologically in women's maternal functions. He did not, in any sense, wish to change the role of women, only to make it more satisfying and more effective. In this, he was influenced in particular by the Swedish feminist Ellen Key, who saw feminism largely in terms of the social recognition and elevation of motherhood. Ellis's later views had much in common with welfare feminism as it developed in the 1920s and 1930s, and as it later became enshrined in the welfare state. After the war, it was to underpin the 'baby boom' and feminine ideology that characterized the 1950s and provided the background against which the new feminism rose in revolt.

The changing attitude of the feminists towards birth control is, therefore, less revolutionary than it sounds. Their conversion parallels and reflects conventional behaviour and conventional attitudes, when birth control ceased to be radical in itself, and when it was beginning to be linked to population policies and welfare reform rather than feminism as such. Only for a brief period in 1920, when, under the leadership of radical feminists like Stella Browne and Dora Russell, women in the movement tried to change the policies of the Labour and Communist parties, do we meet with a specifically feminist approach. Not only was birth control linked more clearly and obviously with the control of women over their own bodies, but there was a serious, if largely unsuccessful, attempt to challenge the overwhelming male leadership in the socialist movement. Both these issues, as we shall see, became significant in the new feminism of the 1960s and 1970s, but they were to disappear almost completely in the 1930s.

The relationship between feminism and the birth control movement is paralleled by the links between the feminist movement and abortion law reform. There was, in fact, no organized movement either to change the law itself or to spread knowledge of abortion during the nineteenth century or, indeed, until the twentieth century was well under way. The leaders of the birth control movement not only made no attempt to argue for easier abortion but were deeply anxious to avoid any charge that they had this in mind. From the beginning, birth control techniques were advocated as the most effective means of reducing artificial abortions and infanticide. The Malthusian League, the main vehicle of birth control propaganda, far from supporting abortion, condemned it as a crime, the murder of the child in the womb (Ledbetter, 1976, p. 132).

The open advocacy of abortion was pioneered, therefore, not by the birth control movement as such, but by a few of the sexual radicals. Havelock Ellis was one of its earliest advocates (Rowbotham and Weeks, 1977, p. 178), and it was probably his views that influenced Stella Browne, who called publicly for the legalization of abortion as early as 1915. Unlike the Malthusian League, Ellis and Browne saw both abortion and birth control as necessary for an effective policy of family limitation that would give women control over their own bodies. Indeed, given the nature of the available forms of contraception, Stella Browne saw early abortion as erotically preferable for some women (Rowbotham, 1977, pp. 113—21). Her views are astonishingly modern and anticipate the modern feminist movement to an extraordinary degree. She opposed, for example, the limitation of abortion to women in certain kinds of need and proclaimed for all women their absolute right to an abortion if they wished.

After the first world war Stella Browne and a number of other feminists, including Alice Jenkins and Janet Chance, tried to bring the abortion issue into the birth control debate, but there were others in the group, like Dora Russell, who, while sharing many of

Stella Browne's ideas, feared that to raise abortion law reform would harm their main aim, the spread of birth control information to the working classes. Certainly this must have seemed sensible tactics at the time since they already had wide support for their stand on birth control. As we have seen, even the National Union of Societies for Equal Citizenship endorsed birth control in 1925. They would still have nothing to do with abortion however, and Mary Stocks, in her pamphlet on family limitation, specifically mentioned her detestation of 'abortifacient practices' (Stocks, 1925, p. 3). Indeed a clause in the 1924 Children and Young Persons Bill that provided even harsher penalties for abortion was supported by the feminist Six Point Group (Rowbotham, 1977).

During the 1930s, however, attitudes on abortion began to change. In 1934 the Women's Co-operative Guild overwhelmingly passed a resolution to legalize abortion. They were moved in particular by the persistently high maternal death rate and the evils of the 'back-street' abortionist. They also wanted an amnesty for women in prison for procuring an abortion. Perhaps encouraged by this resolution, in 1936 a tiny Abortion Law Reform Association was founded, including Janet Chance, Alice Jenkins, Freda Larkin, Dora Russell and Stella Browne among the executive (Rowbotham, 1977, p. 35). Janet Chance, Stella Browne and Alice Jenkins had met originally in the Workers' Birth Control Group. Indeed the founders as a whole were radical in politics, free-thinking in religion and active feminists (Hindell and Simms, 1971, pp. 58—62). The National Birth Control Council, however, considered the abortion issue too hot to handle (Leathard, 1980, p. 63).

Meanwhile, within the British Medical Association itself there was fresh thinking about the case for abortion. In 1935 a committee on abortion was set up that recommended legalizing abortion in cases of rape or of danger to the physical and mental health of the mother, and when there was reasonable certainty that serious disease would be transmitted to the child. This was followed by the Birkett Committee, a government interdepartmental committee, which also gave cautious approval to cases involving danger to life or health although it had doubts about rape victims on the grounds that an assault could be feigned. This report also expressed anxiety about the falling birth rate and falling standards of sexual morality (Hindell and Simms, 1971).

Opinion was therefore moving slowly in the direction of a limited change in the law, although it was to be a long time before any such change was to be achieved in practice. During these years, the

ALRA was too small to be an effective pressure group, and, as the years went by and its original leaders grew older, it became less and less effective. At its instigation, an unsuccessful Private Member's bill was introduced in 1951, but by the 1960s, when opinion was turning decisively in favour of abortion, the ARLA had less than 200 members. Its failure to attract new members reflected the state of feminism itself, and it is not surprising that in 1963 the old organization was virtually taken over by a younger generation of women with different ideas and different methods — women who were forerunners of the new feminism, which was to find abortion of crucial significance in the fight for woman's right to her own body.

It is noteworthy, too, that apart from the small group of radical feminists the argument for abortion that developed during the 1930s and was continued after the war was primarily a medical one. It was based almost entirely on the health of either the mother or the child; even the victim of rape was, as we have seen, offered scant consideration by the Birkett Committee in 1939. Dorothy Thurtle, wife of the vice president of the ALRA and a member of the Birkett Committee, had submitted her own minority report, but even this, although including victims of rape and incest, added only 'eugenic' grounds and women who had already had four pregnancies to the recommendations of the Birkett Committee (Hindell and Simms, 1971, p. 74). Moreover, in their evidence to the Birkett Committee in 1937 the ALRA had defended abortion mainly on the grounds of reducing maternal deaths, presumably because it believed this to be the best and safest argument. Undoubtedly, it was reasons such as this that swayed members of the medical profession in its favour, as well as the desire to bring all abortions under medical control. The knowledge that the well-to-do could already buy illegal abortions so that existing law pressed chiefly on the poor was another factor in changing opinion in favour of law reform. Moreover, while some were certainly motivated by sympathy for the weak and oppressed, others were moved by the eugenic issues involved and were concerned to make abortion, as they had done birth control, an aspect of eugenic policy.

As with birth control, therefore, much of the case for the legalizing of abortion had little to do with feminism as such. This is not to suggest that access to both contraception techniques and safe abortion is irrelevant to women's needs. As we have seen however, a concern to protect women does not in itself necessarily have much to do with feminism and may indeed, as in the nineteenth-century concept of the walled garden, bind women even more securely in their traditional role. To a large extent this had happened, even to the feminist movement, by the 1950s, and issues like birth control and abortion had to be re-examined by the new feminist movement in the 1960s so that they could be placed in a context that was wider than a simple concern for women's welfare. In the process, abortion, as we shall see in chapter 12, takes on a significance that is entirely absent from any previous stage of the feminist movement.

For the moment, however, it is necessary to leave the campaign for abortion law reform and to look briefly at changes in the feminist attitude to marriage and divorce. In the nineteenth century the British feminist movement had avoided the issue of divorce even though early feminist men, like John Stuart Mill and Fox, had certainly favoured some relaxation of the law, partly because of their own personal situation. As the organized movement developed, however, it concentrated its efforts on securing education and employment for girls and protecting the property and earnings of married women. In so far as it was involved in the debates on divorce that took place in the 1850s, it was largely to safeguard the financial interests of divorced and separated wives. Opposition to the double standard, however, made the movement critical of the provision in the 1857 Act that made the adultery of a wife grounds for divorce but not the adultery of a husband.

An important part of the feminist case was the need to free girls from a forced marriage. Economic independence, through educational and employment opportunities and changes in the law of property, was, in effect, the passport that enabled a woman not only to choose not to marry at all but even, under certain circumstances, to leave her husband. The feminists were therefore by no means traditional in their attitude to marriage and divorce. They denied the doctrine that women could only find happiness through marriage and maternity, even if they expected most women to marry (Banks, 1964, pp. 48—9). Nor did they expect women to submit docilely to the view of marriage that denied them rights to a legal identity and placed them in perpetual subordination to their husbands.

On the other hand, the nineteenth-century feminist movement was, as we have seen, anxious to dissociate itself from any charge of advocating 'free love' or any other kind of loosening of sexual morality. Indeed, in its association with the purity campaign it wanted to raise moral standards by ending the acquiescence in an attitude to sexual morality that allowed men to indulge their sexual desires freely at the expense of women. Right into the twentieth century, the organized feminists were respectable, even puritan, in their attitude to marriage. In so far as they wished to equalize the legal position of women and men in divorce, it was simply to free wives from dissolute husbands and not in any sense to win more sexual freedom for themselves.

At the same time, as we have seen, during the 1880s and especially in the 1890s, there was a revival of some of the earlier utopian views of the communitarians that sought to link socialism and feminism around new and indeed alternative ways of living, which included a new view of human sexuality and a resurrection of the old socialist idea of 'free love'. By free love, as we saw in chapter 4, the socialists did not necessarily mean promiscuity, since free unions, as they came to be called, could, in theory at least, involve life-long monogamy. They did, however, recognize no constraints but love itself, so that in practice they could involve many changes of partners, depending on the strength and persistence of the mutual affection. In the anarchist movement in particular, 'free unions' were seen as part of the attempt to work out a new philosophy of life, and a number of women, attracted by both anarchism and feminism, entered into such unions in the years immediately before the first world war (Rowbotham, 1973a, pp. 98—104). Dora Russell accepted these views as a young woman growing up during these years, and has described vividly her 'feeling of disgrace' when she at last agreed to marry Bertrand Russell in order to legitimize their coming child (Russell, 1975, pp. 68—9, 148). The opposition to marriage was specifically feminist, in that what Dora Russell and others in her circle objected to was the view of marriage enshrined in the marriage laws and rights of possession of persons. Like the desire to maintain their own name and to have their own career, it was an aspect of the desire for independence as a person that is one of the roots of feminism. It was also an opposition to the divorce laws as they were then, with their refusal of divorce by mutual consent and their insistence upon blame. The rejection of marriage as possession might also involve, as it did for Dora and Bertrand Russell, the rejection of the concept of sexual exclusiveness (Russell, 1975, pp. 73, 80, 155—6).

The concept of 'free love' was therefore used by these feminists as a personal and individual response to the social and legal constraints that a conventional marriage laid upon them. By remaining free, they hoped to retain not only their independence but those rights that, in spite of some change in the law, they still lost on marriage, including rights over the custody of their children (Russell, 1975, p. 68). For most, however, even amongst the radical feminists, the social disapproval of such a union proved too great, and, like Dora Russell, they eventually married. Undoubtedly, though, it reflected an important mood within radical feminism in the period just before and just after the first world war, which was to be lost in the more conventional mood of the 1930s.

An alternative approach to the rejection of marriage is reform of the laws relating to marriage and divorce, and it was this path that organized feminism had taken right from the start. It was concerned, as we have seen, at the financial consequences of divorce for wives, and at the way the double standard of morality was enshrined in nineteenth-century divorce law. There was also concern during the 1870s that the provisions of the 1857 Act, unsatisfactory as these were, were not available to the poor because of the cost of divorce. The feminist Frances Power Cobbe, in a pamphlet *Wife Torture* published in 1878, proposed that wife assault be made grounds for a legal separation. Her campaign influenced the Matrimonial Causes Act of 1878, which gave a wife the right to a legal separation, with maintenance and with custody of any children under 10 years of age, for aggravated assault (McGregor, 1957, pp. 22—4). A series of Acts that followed gave magistrates further powers to enforce maintenance orders, although it has been suggested that it was mainly poor law administrators who provided the impetus for these reforms, since otherwise the women would have been a burden on the rates (Minor, 1979).

By the beginning of the twentieth century, dissatisfaction with the 1857 Act was beginning to mount and pressure to reform the law gained strength, especially with the foundation of the Divorce Reform Union. Eventually, in 1909, a Royal Commission was appointed to examine divorce law reform. Neither socialists nor feminists were active in the agitation that led up to the Commission (Minor, 1979); indeed the feminists were fully occupied at that time with the fight for the vote. Millicent Fawcett, however, gave evidence and made a plea for an end to the situation in which men were placed on 'a lower plane than women as regards marital fidelity'. She argued that equal divorce laws would in fact make for a levelling up of moral standards since men would have to obey the rules formerly imposed only on women (McGregor, 1957, p. 21).

For feminists like Millicent Fawcett, therefore, the aim was still to equalize moral standards by using criteria that had formerly only applied to women, rather than to extend to women the liberty that had previously been enjoyed by men.

The Women's Co-operative Guild provided the only evidence from a working-class women's organization. Basing themselves on a circular sent out to branches, they demonstrated the hardships caused by the expense of divorce and by the unequal treatment of women. When the Royal Commission Majority Report recommended cheaper divorce, an end to the double standard for men and women and extension of the grounds of divorce, it welcomed these recommendations, as did both the Labour Party and the Women's Labour League. The Women's Co-operative Guild however went further, and urged divorce by mutual consent after two years' separation, a view that was startlingly advanced for its time. Indeed, the views of the Guild on divorce aroused the determined opposition of the Co-operative movement's Catholics and led to a withdrawal of their grant for several years before the split was finally healed (Gaffin, 1977, p. 137). Minor (1979) has criticized the Guild for its stand, arguing that easier divorce did not solve the economic barriers to divorce and ignored the prevalence of common law marriage.

Of the recommendations of the Royal Commission, only the one dealing with the double standard was implemented, and that only in 1923 when it was passed in response to feminist pressure from NUSEC in the years when it was still an active feminist lobby. Nor, in spite of the stand taken by the Women's Co-operative Guild in the years before the first world war, is there any evidence after the war of a campaign within the women's sections of the labour movement for divorce reform. Certainly there is no sign of anything comparable to the campaign for birth control information during the 1920s and 1930s. The radical feminists' desire for the independence of a 'free union' did not therefore represent feminism in the twentieth century any more than the free love movement represented feminism in the nineteenth century. Although they resented the double standard and wanted women to have the right to divorce an adulterous husband, once this was gained, divorce reform no longer seems to have been of interest to the feminists, or to women's organizations generally.

Indeed, once easier and cheaper divorce became a reality in the years after the second world war, it was seen by some feminists as against the interests of women. This was largely due to the belief that easier divorce would allow men, in particular, to treat marriage more lightly. When, in 1963, Leo Abse sought to introduce a bill to liberalize the divorce laws, the Married Woman's Association opposed it in the interests of the first wife. Edith Summerskill also spoke against it, on the grounds that it did not recognize the different meaning that marriage had for women. In her autobiography she expresses perfectly the views of an earlier generation of feminists on female sexuality by arguing that 'the married woman only wants a second man in her life if the first has failed her in some way' (Summerskill, 1967, pp. 240—2). In addition were the greater financial problems that divorce presented to women, especially as the law then stood with respect to matrimonial property (McGregor, 1972, p. 53; Rover, 1970, pp. 158—9). The issue of divorce has always reflected some of the ambiguities that the feminists have felt about marriage, seeing it sometimes as haven, sometimes as trap. Moreover, feminism embraces both the socialist communitarian tradition of free love and the evangelical belief in Christian marriage. Consequently, liberal divorce laws may represent either the path to freedom or, in Edith Summerskill's own words, a 'Casanova's Charter' (Adam, 1975, p. 196). It is not surprising, therefore, if divorce has been seen by the feminists as largely an issue of equal rights, whether in the custody of children or the transfer of property. It is only with the modern movement that some of the deeper questions raised not only by divorce but by marriage itself have become central issues for feminism as a whole.

For the moment, however, it is necessary to look briefly at the response of American feminists to birth control and abortion, and, also briefly, to the issue of divorce law reform. I can be brief because the pattern of response in the two countries shows so many similarities that most of the significant arguments have already been made. In both countries, for example, feminist support for birth control came from radical feminists, not from the organized feminist movement. Moreover, radical feminism in the United States, as in Britain, had its source partly in socialism in one of its several forms and partly in the writings of the radical sex reformers of whom, in the United States as in Britain, Edward Carpenter and Havelock Ellis were the most important.

Consequently, we find a group of feminists, often known to one another, who not only combined their feminism with socialism but advocated, for women as well as for men, freedom to indulge in sexual pleasure as well as the economic independence sought by the more orthodox feminists. June Sochen has described just such a group of women living in Greenwich Village in the years between 1910 and 1920, of whom Chrystal Eastman, Henrietta Radman and Ida Rauh are typical examples. Often involved, for a time at least, in 'free unions', they also advocated crèches and other types of communal facilities for working women as well as a motherhood endowment fund. Most supported birth control, and Max Eastman, the brother of Chrystal Eastman, argued in his radical paper *The Masses* that it was as essential to women's emancipation as the vote (Sochen, 1972).

One of the idols of *The Masses* was the feminist anarchist Emma Goldman. An ardent free love advocate, she was a fierce critic of the institution of marriage, which she believed turned women into sex objects (Drinnon, 1970). Like other anarchists on both sides of the Atlantic, she thought the struggle for the vote an illusion, and condemned both the anti-socialist and puritan stands that had always been present in the American feminist movement. She took issue with feminists like Charlotte Perkins Gilman in their response to sex and believed that ethical and social conventions were as much the enemy as external tyrannies. She became an advocate of birth control in 1900 when she attended a neo-Malthusian conference in Paris and was an active campaigner in the movement until 1917 when she turned to other issues.

The most influential of the American birth-controllers was, however, not Emma Goldman but Margaret Sanger. In her early life she, too, was attracted by anarchism, but even more influential in the long run were the British sex radicals Havelock Ellis and Edward Carpenter. On a visit to Britain she met Havelock Ellis and they became lovers. He influenced her away from anarchism and persuaded her to devote herself to the birth control campaign (Rowbotham, 1977, pp. 15—17). At first, however, and certainly until the end of 1915, she worked within the socialist movement and had a great deal of support from socialist groups. They sent her letters of advice and support, distributed her pamphlet *Family Limitation,* and invited her on speaking tours (Gordon, 1977, pp. 266—9).

In 1916 she organized her first clinic and although this led to trouble with the police, it also gave publicity to her cause, which was beginning to gain support outside the socialist movement (Kennedy, 1970). From 1920 onwards, her association with the radicals declined as the birth control campaign became increasingly respectable. Although, as in Britain, the Catholic Church continued its opposition, and there was still a good deal of anxiety that birth control knowledge might get into the hands of the unmarried, it became more and more obvious that birth control was here to stay. It was this realization more than any other that, as in Britain, brought together the birth control movement and eugenics. Now that the middle classes were limiting their families, it became more and more important to enable the poor to do so as well. Birth control came to be seen as an alternative to sterilization in limiting the numbers of 'unfit'. Sanger herself became involved in eugenic arguments and during the 1920s and 1930s the alliance between birth control and eugenics replaced that between birth control and socialism (Gordon, 1977, pp. 281—90, 330—1).

If part of the reason for this move to the right on the part of the birth control movement was a search for respectability, it was also in part a response to a lack of enthusiasm within the parties of the left for the birth control cause. As in Britain, although individual socialists were enthusiasts for birth control, the movement as a whole was decidedly ambiguous towards it (Gordon, 1977, p. 240). There were many reasons for this, including suspicion of neo-Malthusian arguments, a fear that it would divert attention away from the class war, a fear of the association between birth control and free love, a fear of sexuality, and a traditional stance towards the family, all attitudes that were common within the American socialist and trade union movement just as they were common within the British labour movement. Consequently, the socialist movement never accepted birth control as part of its official programme. In any event, the socialist movement in the United States was itself on the defensive in the years after the first world war. Preoccupied with other issues, it simply did not see birth control as relevant or important to its political future.

Feminism, too, turned its back on the birth control movement. As we saw in chapter 5, nineteenth-century feminism had never accepted artificial contraception, preferring moral restraint as a method that protected women from excessive sexual demands. In the twentieth century, the organized movement continued to hold the birth control movement at arm's length. As late as 1927 the Woman's Party avoided birth control as an issue for fear of splitting their organization. Even in 1930, the more conservative League of Women Voters declined to consider a resolution that merely called for the study of birth control. Nor, throughout the 1930s, would the Children's Bureau acknowledge the importance of contraception until persuaded to do so by Eleanor Roosevelt in 1942 (Kennedy, 1970, pp. 137, 261—2).

Many individual feminist leaders continued to fear contraception for the same reasons they had feared it in the nineteenth century. They saw it simply as allowing more sexual exploitation of women both before and after marriage. As we have seen, feminists like Carrie Chapman Catt and Charlotte Perkins Gilman looked to a future in which sexuality played less part in the lives of both men and women; they had little sympathy with the ideas of the sex reformers for maximizing sexual pleasure. They both therefore had reservations about Margaret Sanger's campaign, even if they admitted it might also do good, although Gilman later on came out in support of legalizing birth control in 1932 (Gordon, 1977, pp. 236—8).

The Greenwich Village feminists who had been prominent birth control advocates tended to move out of political action after 1920. Some of those who had been prominent before the first world war died; others moved out of politics altogether. The new generation of young women in Greenwich Village accepted the new teaching on sexuality but did not carry it through into political action (Sochen, 1972, p. 126). Feminists in the Woman's Party concentrated on a narrow interpretation of equal rights that excluded any wider conceptions of feminism, while other women's organizations either turned away from feminism altogether or limited it to considerations of welfare.

Margaret Sanger herself, it is true, never completely lost her feminism (Gordon, 1977, p. 358). She continued to emphasize that birth control was a necessary condition for the enjoyment by women of their sexual nature. Nevertheless, her style of feminism was derived from Havelock Ellis and Ellen Key. Like Marie Stopes she retained an ideal of feminism that stressed women's differences from men; differences moreover that had their source in the maternal impulse. She argued that women should develop their powers in their own sphere and not try to compete with men (Kennedy, 1970, pp. 133—4). She thus paved the way for the idealization of femininity that was to characterize the 1950s.

By the 1930s birth control in the United States, as it had in Britain, was beginning to become admissible not simply as a resource for individuals but as an aspect of public policy. Largely because of the Depression and its consequences, some states began to offer birth control services as part of their public health programme (Gordon, 1977, pp. 330—5). As in Britain, it began to be perceived as one of the services of the developing welfare state, and as such could be introduced for primarily eugenic reasons or to benefit the health and welfare of mothers of large families. By the 1940s it was accepted as one aspect of what became known as planned parenthood, and by the 1960s it was incorporated into population policy in both the United States and the Third World (Gordon, 1977, p. 346).

The fortunes of the birth control movement in the twentieth century were, therefore, remarkably similar in Britain and the United States. In neither country was it for very long primarily a feminist cause, although the feminist movement played a larger role in Britain than in the United States, largely because of feminist activity in Britain during the 1920s. Its subsequent history, during the post second world war years in particular, shows quite remarkable similarities as in both countries it becomes absorbed into population policy, its connection with feminism almost forgotten.

Abortion law reform in the United States also follows the same pattern. The birth-controllers, as in Britain, presented contraception as an alternative to abortion, although in 1913 Margaret Sanger, perhaps influenced by Havelock Ellis, defended a woman's right to an abortion, something she was never to do at any later time (Gordon, 1977, p. 223). In contrast to Britain, however, where the ALRA was founded by feminists in 1936, there was no feminist call for a change in the abortion laws until the new feminist movement in the 1960s (Mohr, 1978, p. 263). Indeed, it was not until 1959 that the first steps to abortion law reform were taken in the United States when the American Law Institute recommended abortion be allowed for such reasons as the health of the mother, grave physical or mental defect in the child, or rape and incest (Hole and Levine, 1971, p. 283).

Similarly, divorce law reform has been no more central to American feminists than it has to the British movement. Certainly Elizabeth Cady Stanton tried to make divorce a feminist issue but, as we saw in chapter 5, her efforts met with very little success, and in neither the nineteenth nor twentieth century did the organized movement press for more liberalized divorce laws. As we have seen, it was preoccupied with suffrage until the vote was won, and afterwards a commitment to welfare feminism dominated the leaders of the movement and turned them away from such traditional feminist issues as legal rights and economic independence. Only the small Woman's Party, with its largely unheeded call for an equal rights amendment, persisted in drawing attention to legal discrimination against women. Even those individual feminists like Charlotte Perkins Gilman who defended divorce did so because they believed it freed women from sexual dependence on men (O'Neill, 1965).

Within American feminism, as in Britain, only the feminists in the socialist tradition accepted divorce as a way of freeing both men and women for a fuller and more satisfactory sex life. Indeed, some of the men and women in this group not only criticized the divorce laws but were opposed to marriage itself, preferring free unions (Sochen, 1972, pp. 76—82). As we have seen, however, this alliance between socialism and feminism did not outlast the first world war. From 1920 onwards feminism in the United States was represented either by welfare feminism or by the elitist feminism of the Woman's Party, which concerned itself largely with the interests of propertied and professional women and had no enthusiasm either for socialism or for sexual freedom. In this respect the United States was more conservative than Britain, where the link between socialism and feminism was vigorous throughout the 1920s and into the 1930s, and where intellectuals like Dora Russell could and did join forces with working-class women in both the labour movement and the Co-operative movement to press 'for issues like birth control and abortion law reform.

In neither country, however, did feminism survive the combined assault of both the Depression and the second world war. The mood of the United States in the 1950s was dominated by the feminine mystique (Friedan, 1963) that celebrated women's domestic role. Debates in the late 1940s and 1950s on women's role showed a strong anti-feminist swing in which Freudian psychology played an important part (Chafe, 1972, pp. 204—9). In Britain, too, the theories of John Bowlby were used to glorify motherhood (Adam, 1975, p. 165; Wilson, 1977, pp. 972, 1567). Moreover, in both countries these were years of the so-called 'baby-boom' in which a high birth rate and early marriages combined to reinforce the dominant ideology of women's essentially domestic destiny, and in which it did not seem unreasonable to believe that feminism as a movement was dead. Nevertheless, it is against this unpromising background that the first signs of the new feminism were already beginning to appear. The sources of this new mood amongst the post-war generation of young women, many of them products of the 'baby-boom' that had trapped their mothers, and the new directions into which it led feminism, will be the subject of the next Part.

PART IV

The Modern Movement

11

The Re-Birth of the
Equal Rights Tradition

In neither the United States nor Britain did the pressure for equal rights die out completely. Individual women, many of them veterans of the suffrage struggle, as well as groups of one kind or another continued to maintain a steady, if almost completely unsuccessful, pressure for legislation that would end the discrimination against women that continued even after the vote had been achieved. When the new equal rights feminism emerged in the 1960s, therefore, it was not entirely a re-birth, since nineteenth-century feminism had not completely disappeared. It is necessary therefore to look briefly at those who carried the standard of equal rights feminism during those discouraging years when the tide of events seemed to have turned altogether against them — years of the Depression, of a world war, and of a feminine mystique that trapped twentieth-century woman, like her nineteenth-century counterpart, in a largely traditional role.

In the United States it was the small Woman's Party that carried the struggle for equal rights forward throughout the whole of this period. Every year from 1923 onwards their pressure resulted in an equal rights amendment being brought before Congress that sought to end discrimination in such areas as marriage, divorce, work, property and jury service (Sachs and Wilson, 1978, p. 118). As we have seen, however, their stand brought them into collision with the welfare feminists who feared the effect of the amendment on protective legislation and who believed that the Woman's Party represented a small number of career women and women of property who were motivated only by their own interests. Genuinely believing that such legislation would be against the interests of most women, the welfare feminists combined with the anti-feminists to fight against the equal rights amendment, and most women's organizations remained adamantly opposed to it until well into the 1960s.

The Woman's Party, however, did not stand entirely alone. The National Federation of Business and Professional Women's Clubs, although never an overtly feminist organization, was aware from its members' own experience that protective legislation was a double-edged tool that frustrated some women while it protected others. It was never, therefore, as whole-hearted a supporter of such legislation as most of the women's groups and, after a period of doubt and controversy within its ranks, finally endorsed the equal rights amendment proposal in 1937. Within particular states the Business and Professional Women's Clubs fought against protective legislation that attacked the interests of white-collar women. In California in 1927, for example, they successfully opposed an attempt to impose an eight-hour day on all women other than nurses, housemaids and cannery workers, and similar battles were fought in Indiana and New York (Lemon, 1973, pp. 46, 202—3).

Other professional women's groups were also active in an attempt both to illustrate the discrimination against them and to try to bring it to an end. The American Medical Woman's Association, for example, exposed such issues as the lack of training facilities for women in hospitals and their lack of promotion. However, since women doctors, after 1915, could also join the AMA, by no means all joined the AMWA, which remained too small to be effective. Its radical stance on such issues as birth control and socialized medicine also meant that some women doctors opposed it (Hummer, 1978, pp. 90—2, 116—20). The National Association of Women Lawyers was also a small organization that did not succeed in attracting all the women lawyers, many of whom did not want to work specifically for women, since, after 1918, they could join the American Bar Association. Like the Business and Professional Women's Clubs it too fought against protective legislation when it tried to include professional women, and in the 1930s moved into strong support for the idea of an equal rights amendment (Hummer, 1978, pp. 124—5). Even in the 1930s, therefore, opinion amongst professional and white-collar women was moving against protective legislation. But such women's organizations could make little headway against the continuing support for protective legislation of those groups representing married women at home, the determined weight of the whole trade union movement, and those organizations, including the Women's Bureau, concerned with women employees in low-paid, unskilled work, for whom protective legislation still seemed the only hope for better wages and working conditions.

If the trade union movement and the welfare feminists remained determinedly opposed to the idea of an equal rights amendment as such, this was not so for equal pay. This had been accepted by a predominantly male trade union leadership as the best protection for male earnings and was officially endorsed by both the American Federation of Labor and the CIO in the 1930s (Kenneally, 1978, pp. 161, 164). Nevertheless, at the local level in particular there was little interest in equal pay as an issue and little support for women trade unionists, who remained under-represented at both local and national levels of the leadership. Feminists, however, remained faithful to the idea of equal pay, and when, in 1945, equal pay legislation was introduced into Congress, it gained the active support of many women's organizations, as well as women trade unionists who continued to work actively for it (Kenneally, 1978, pp. 181—2). The Women's Bureau too, in spite of its attitude to the equal rights amendment, was a consistent supporter of the rate for the job. Moreover, in 1936 Mary Anderson, then head of the Bureau, drew up a charter containing demands for equal rights in politics, education, law, and employment that, although it received little support at the time from women's organizations, demonstrated that the equal rights tradition was not dead (Lee, 1977, p. 15).

During the 1940s the struggle to promote the equal rights amendment entered a new phase when, for the first time, it was endorsed by the Republican Party in 1940 and by the Democratic Party in 1944. In 1943 it was also approved for the first time by the General Federation of Women's Clubs, although the trade union movement, the League of Women Voters and the Women's Bureau remained implacably in opposition. In 1945 it was passed by the House of Representatives, although not by Senate, again for the first time. Support for the amendment was clearly growing, although its opponents were still much the stronger group and managed to block its progress throughout the 1940s and the 1950s. Clauses were added that, by allowing exceptions on the basis of biological and social functions, retained protective legislation and so destroyed some of its effectiveness. It also had to face the determined hostility of Emmanuel Celler, chairman of the House Judiciary Committee, who persistently refused to allow it out of the committee stage (Greenberg, 1976, pp. xiv—xv).

With the amendment blocked, several women members of Congress worked actively on the equal pay issue; they were eventually rewarded by the Equal Pay Act of 1963, the first piece of equal rights legislation and one that anticipated the spate of lobbying that heralded the new equal rights movement of the 1960s. Prominent in the fight in Congress for equal pay was Edna Kelly, who had worked for the Act for twelve years before the success of the campaign, as well as Edith Green and Martha Griffiths, one of the most outspoken feminists in Congress (Chamberlin, 1973). Interestingly, however, administrative, executive and professional women were not included until 1972.

It is clear, therefore, that by the end of the 1950s pressure was building up both within Congress and outside it for legislation to end discrimination against women, particularly in the area of employment. Undoubtedly, a major factor here was the dramatic change in the pattern of the female labour force brought about partly by changes in demand and partly by demographic factors, such as the low birth rate of the 1930s and the early marriages of the 1950s, which had reduced the supply of women (Oppenheimer, 1967). The resulting increased demand for women's labour brought large numbers of married women into the labour market, not only into manual work but, more significantly for our present purpose, into clerical and service occupations. This influx of married women into non-manual work was not, however, accompanied by any real increase in the proportion of women in professional and higher administrative employment. Indeed, although the *number* of women in professional employment had increased, the *proportion* shows an actual, if small, decline between 1940 and 1964 (Knudsen, 1969). Moreover, this decline was in spite of a dramatic increase in women's participation in higher education during the same period. It is not altogether surprising therefore if women, and especially middle-class women in professional and semi-professional careers, were becoming dissatisfied with their conditions of employment and ready to look sympathetically at the idea of legislation against discrimination in pay and employment opportunities.

There were other changes in the 1960s that were likely to predispose women towards an equal rights version of feminism and away from the emphasis on the maternal function that feminists and anti-feminists had come, in their different ways, to share. The decline in the American birth rate, after the years of the 'baby boom', had started in 1957 and was to continue throughout the

1960s. Women were not only having fewer children, but they were also marrying later, and, in the middle classes, more of them were going on to graduate- as distinct from undergraduate study. Moreover, as Jessie Bernard has pointed out, all these changes had started some years *before* Betty Friedan wrote her celebrated attack on the feminine mystique in 1963 (Bernard, 1971, p. 17). This suggests that her critique, and especially its astonishing reception, was a consequence rather than a cause of a new mood amongst middle-class women. Jo Freeman has also pointed out that the decline in the numbers of books on women that started in the mid-1920s had already begun to be reversed as early as 1959 (Freeman, 1973, p. 1).

The 1960s were also years of acute manpower shortage, and womanpower, as in war-time, began to be seen as a valuable asset, in sharp contradiction to the mood of the Depression when women, and especially married women, were feared as competitors to men. In the years immediately after the war, as had been the case after the first world war, the chief concern had been to give men back their jobs, and women were expected to retreat from industry back to the home. Soon, however, expanding employment opportunities were to draw them back again in greatly increased numbers. By the mid-1960s politicians as well as employers began to welcome women's increased role in the economy, and in 1966 President Johnson himself asked employers to explore the possibility of using women for jobs normally filled by men (Bird, 1970, pp. 158—9). Both employers and politicians therefore were concerned with ways in which they could make employment more attractive to women.

It was against this background, so different from the 1930s, that in 1961 President Kennedy set up his Commission on the Status of Women. The motives of Kennedy himself are not altogether clear, although we know that the idea originated with Esther Peterson, who had been on Kennedy's campaign staff and had then been appointed to take charge of the Women's Bureau (Hole and Levine, 1971, p. 19). Initiative also came from the Business and Professional Women's Clubs, whose leaders were active on the Commission and the several State Commissions that followed (Gruberg, 1968, p. 107). Hole and Levine (1971, p. 19) have also suggested that Kennedy might have seen it as a way to reward women who had helped in his campaign. Nevertheless, it seems reasonably certain that for many of its chief supporters the main aim was to block the equal rights amendment by making concessions to sex equality.

The 'awful equal rights amendment', as she called it, was certainly in Esther Peterson's mind, and the hope of finally killing the amendment seems to have been behind Emmanuel Celler's long-term support for a Commission of this kind.

The Report, when it appeared, was relatively modest in its proposals, although it documented many areas of discrimination, thus playing a significant role in reinforcing the consciousness of inequality in the minds of individual women, especially those already active in politics, a role also played with considerable effect by the State Commissions that followed (Freeman, 1973, p. 37). However, the Equal Rights Amendment itself was opposed, the Commission proposing instead that an end to discrimination in employment should be achieved by voluntary effort. Equal pay nevertheless was approved, and legislation to this effect, as we have seen, followed shortly after. The Report also came out in favour of an end to certain forms of legal discrimination, particularly in the area of marriage and property (Hole and Levine, 1971, pp. 20—2).

By 1964, however, the Civil Rights Act had already made the Commission's preference for voluntary effort out of date. Intended originally to deal with racial discrimination, the word sex was added by a Southern congressman in what appeared to be a last-minute attempt to kill the bill. In fact the amendment was accepted and the amended bill was passed, so that women were now included, almost by accident, in the brief of the Equal Employment Opportunities Commission set up to administer the Act. Even the Commissioners themselves were unenthusiastic about the inclusion of sexual discrimination in their brief, and the first Director sought to ignore the issue of sex, arguing that its inclusion was a fluke (Hole and Levine, 1971).

Perhaps the most immediate effect of the refusal of the Equal Employment Opportunities Commission to enforce the sexual provisions of the Act was the impetus it gave to the foundation of the National Organization of Women, or NOW as it is more usually called. The President's Commission, and later the State Commissions, had brought together a number of politically active women (Freeman, 1975, p. 53) who became increasingly aware of the need for a new feminist pressure group. Eventually, action was taken at a National Conference of State Commissions in 1966 and the new organization began its work by trying to place pressure on the Equal Employment Opportunities Commission to implement the Civil Rights Act as it applied to women (Hole and Levine, 1971, pp. 82—4). Although there have been and indeed continue to be serious problems of implementation, the effect of NOW has been to increase the attention paid by the Commission to sexual discrimination, largely by the political pressure it has applied to state legislatures, Congress and enforcement agencies, as well as by support for individual female defendants (Freeman, 1975, pp. 188—96; Sachs and Wilson, 1978, pp. 210—18). Indeed, without pressure from NOW it seems likely that the sex discrimination aspect of the Act would have remained virtually a dead letter.

The establishment of NOW was followed by a number of other equal rights groups, often with more specialist interests, some of which split off from NOW as its programme widened and became more radical. The Women's Equity Action League, for example, founded in 1968, was a group of largely professional women who focused their action chiefly upon discrimination in education and employment, although they also campaigned against tax inequalities. The National Women's Political Caucus, founded in 1971, was formed to support the entry of more women in political office. In 1969, academic women began to organize themselves into professional associations, and by the end of 1971 there were women's groups in no less than thirty-three professional associations. On the whole, however, the academic women's movement, although highly active and even successful, was concerned almost exclusively with improving women's status in their own profession (Klotzburger, 1973).

In the meantime, attitudes towards the Equal Rights Amendment continued to change. The Women's Bureau, one of its most consistent and determined enemies since the 1920s, changed significantly in 1969 with the appointment of Elizabeth B. Koontz as its head. Under her guidance the Bureau was drawn into the women's rights movement and reversed its attitude completely (Hole and Levine, 1971, p. 53). Changing attitudes were also reflected in President Nixon's Task Force on the Status of Women, which, in direct contradiction to President Kennedy's earlier Commission, came out in support of the Equal Rights Amendment in 1969.

At first the trade union leadership refused to follow the Women's Bureau in its change of mind and, indeed, chided it for abandoning its traditional attitude to protection. Some women trade unionists, however, took a different view, and as early as 1947 there was dissent in the Women's Trade Union League over the prohibition of night-work, when it was argued that such legislation could affect women adversely. By the 1960s some women's unions were beginning to challenge the accepted trade union line and to argue that protective legislation had in fact been used selectively to benefit men rather than women. The Equal Rights Act of 1964, by making protective legislation illegal, was also a significant factor in changing attitudes, especially when it began to be demonstrated that it was in fact working-class women who were involved in bringing cases to the attention of the EEOC ·(Kenneally, 1978, pp. 184, 197—9). Eventually the AFL/CIO was forced to reassess its position under pressure from women trade unionists and abandoned its opposition in 1973 (Freeman, 1975, pp. 164—6).

NOW, after a brief internal struggle, was in support of the amendment from the start, and it was pressure from NOW, as well as from women within Congress like Martha Griffiths, that brought it before the Senate Judiciary Committee in 1970 and then on to the full House. Eventually, after a series of defeats, it was approved by Senate in 1972 and started on the long process of ratification before it could finally become law. Its successful passage through Congress was a consequence of a period of intense political lobbying at both the national and grass-roots level (Hole and Levine, 1971, pp. 55—7) in which even not overtly feminist organizations took part. This large measure of public support helped women in Congress to prove that there was a real demand for the amendment (Freeman, 1975, pp. 220, 234).

Of particular significance in demonstrating the grass-roots nature of support for equal rights was the strike organized in 1970, which perhaps for the first time made the potential power of the movement apparent. It also produced a massive increase in the membership of NOW, particularly from amongst the white-collar labour force, so that its membership jumped from 1,000 to 40,000 between 1967 and 1974. Housewives also began to join, and this led NOW away from a preoccupation with employment into a much wider range of issues, in ways that will be discussed in more detail in the next chapter (Freeman, 1975, pp. 84—5).

The period 1970—1972, in fact, was a time when the unity of the women's movement was at its height and opposition even came to seem politically dangerous (Greenberg, 1976, pp. xv—xvi). In 1970 the number of women in Congress rose to fifteen (Chamberlin, 1973, p. 332) and more of them than ever were committed to feminist issues. The 1972—74 Congress, in particular, passed a large batch of women's rights legislation at the instigation of individual women members (Freeman, 1975, p. 204). At this stage, too, opposition to the amendment was still largely unorganized. The feminist movement was now united in its support, and even the traditional trade union hostility was in the process of change. It was easy, therefore, for both friends and enemies to exaggerate the degree of consensus in its favour.

It can be argued, however, that all the equal rights legislation of this decade was, in a real sense, in advance of public opinion, as witnessed by the difficulties in its implementation. Neither the equal pay legislation nor the legislation on equal employment opportunities was able to do very much to break down the widespread and deeply rooted discrimination against women in employment (Sachs and Wilson, 1978, pp. 210—24). Moreover, if the tide seemed to be in favour of equal rights legislation for both Negroes and women during the 1960s, the 1970s were years of a growing conservatism in politics. Consequently, if at first the ratification of the Equal Rights Amendment appeared to go smoothly (with twenty-eight states ratifying in the first year), an organized opposition developed quickly and progress has in fact been slow, with some states actually attempting to rescind their original ratification (Sachs and Wilson, 1978, pp. 219—20). By 1979 the deadline had still not been met and Congress agreed to an extension until 1982, so that the final outcome of the amendment is currently in the balance.

The opposition to the amendment is largely conservative rather than from the left (although some left-wing groups remain opposed), and is frequently from ultra-conservative groups like John Birch, the Ku Klux Klan and the American Nazi Party. Conservative women's groups, too, are prominent, including the Daughters of the American Revolution, and there has been a determined effort to rouse women in particular against the amendment on the grounds that it will lose them a number of privileges including a husband's obligation to support his family and exemption from the draft. To a large extent, the STOP-ERA campaign has concentrated its efforts on the South and on rural areas, and has tried to appeal to those women who take a traditional view of their place in society. The stand taken by feminists on abortion and homosexuality has also brought into active opposition the National Council of Catholic Women and a number of anti-abortion groups like the National Right to Life campaign as well as those opposed to homosexual rights (Sachs and Wilson, 1978, p. 220).

The feminists, meanwhile, have been unable to sustain either the intensive lobbying or the grass-roots support that characterized the campaign at the national level. This is partly because of the tendency, already indicated, to splinter into separate groups following specific and often narrow goals, and partly, even within NOW itself, as we shall see, a move away from equal rights and towards the more radical implications in the concept of women's liberation. For these radical feminists the search for alternative life styles becomes more important than legislative reform.

Finally, the achievement of some measure of equal rights through legislation has coincided with a change in the economy from boom to recession. If the equal rights movement started in a manpower crisis in which womanpower was an asset to be placated, its implementation has had to take place in an atmosphere of falling opportunities, which like the Depression of the 1930s turns women into rivals. It is not surprising, therefore, if recent years have seen such set-backs in the implementation of equal rights as the complaint of 'reverse discrimination' on the part of white males (Sachs and Wilson, 1978, p. 216).

In Britain, too, the 1960s saw a revival of the equal rights tradition of feminism, although, as we saw, the prolongation of the suffrage fight until 1928 kept that tradition alive longer than in the United States. So did the women's groups in the labour movement who represented a radical tradition in feminism almost entirely absent from the American scene. Women politicians, like those in the United States, were few in number, but some of them were influential, and a few active feminists continued to keep the feminist point of view before Parliament. Within the trade union movement, the opposition to the marriage bar and the campaign for equal pay was pressed consistently, especially by the white-collar unions. It is necessary, therefore, to look briefly at the fortunes of equal rights feminism in the years between the final granting of suffrage in 1928 and the new feminist movement that emerged, as it did in the United States, during the 1960s.

Feminist groups in the 1920s and on into the 1930s had campaigned for equal pay, for the right of married women to work and for the redress of inequalities in unemployment and health insurance (Soldon, 1978, p. 127), but there is little doubt that the bulk of the struggle was caried out by women in the trade union movement. Within the civil service unions in particular there was a strong tradition of support for equal pay, and as early as 1911 the Civil Service Typists Association, which fought against higher rates for male typists, claimed 90 per cent membership

(Humphreys, 1958). After the first world war the strongly feminist Federation of Women Civil Servants fought bitterly against separate treatment and unequal pay for women. However, it later lost members to the Clerical Officers Association, which recruited both men and women, so that by the 1930s the Federation acted mainly as a pressure group for equal pay. At a higher level, the Council of Women Civil Servants had as its main objective the battle for equal opportunities for women. On the whole, the men in the civil service unions were not opposed to the principle of the rate for the job in spite of certain doubts, because lower pay for women resulted in the downgrading of men's jobs. Consequently, when equal pay in the public service became a political possibility in 1952 there was strong pressure in its support from the civil service unions as a whole.

Within the trade union movement in general, however, the situation was less clear cut. Although equal pay in principle had been accepted as early as 1885, this was mainly, on the men's side, seen as a way of reducing their fear of women undercutting men's earnings. Moreover, there were problems at the rank and file level where there was opposition from both men and women. Women manual workers, less confident than women white-collar workers, feared that it might lead employers to favour men. On the men's side there was resentment when women's earnings rose, largely because of the belief that women did not have families to support (Soldon, 1978, p. 116).

After the first world war the Women's Trade Union League merged with the TUC and there was no separate voice for women trade unionists. Instead, a TUC General Council Women's Group represented the interests of women. By 1923, however, the need for a special 'ginger group' for women led to a special annual Women's Conference. Later, in 1931, a National Women's Advisory Committee was formed, to try and raise the level of support for trade unionism amongst women workers. Within these bodies women were able to debate issues of special concern to them, although their failure to gain union office meant that they had only a small voice in the trade union movement as a whole (Lewenhak, 1977).

After the second world war, militant women trade unionists became increasingly active and increasingly important both within the Women's Advisory Committee and in the wider movement. From 1945 to 1960 the militants battled insistently with the trade union leadership on a variety of issues of which equal pay was perhaps the most important (McCarthy, 1977, p. 170). Active women trade unionists were indeed the most consistent supporters of equal pay and, at this time, its most persistent advocates. Moreover, although individual unions like the National Union of General and Municipal Workers (Soldon, 1978, p. 142) and the Union of Shop, Distributive and Allied Workers (Lewenhak, 1977, p. 237) came out in opposition at different times, by the end of the second world war increasing fear of being replaced by women had actually strengthened male trade union support for equal pay (Lewenhak, 1977, p. 249).

In the 1960s the campaign for equal pay gained ground under increasing pressure from women trade union militants and encouraged in particular by the eventual achievement of equal pay in the public service in 1961. There was also a revival of male demands for equal pay, and the return of a Labour-government in 1964, committed, in principle at least, to equal pay, also served to encourage the hopes of the campaigners. The imposition of a wage freeze, however, meant a refusal by the government to implement their policy, in spite of support from within Parliament by such women as Edith Summerskill, Joyce Butler and Irene Worth, as well as strong pressure from the Women's Advisory Committee (Lewenhak, 1977, pp. 278–83).

In the next few years the fight for equal pay by women trade unionists was to combine with the re-awakening of the women's movement in Britain and it will be examined later in this context. What is clear from this account, however, is the extent to which equal pay as a feminist issue was kept alive by women activists within the trade union movement. During the 1920s and 1930s women trade unionists joined with feminist groups to protest at the imposition of marriage bars in the civil service and local authorities (Soldon, 1978, p. 127). At this time such a bar was often official trade union policy as a way to reduce the competition from married women, and the opposition was largely confined to women's groups and organizations, who saw such a bar as an infringement of women's rights to work. Women workers may also have differed from their male colleagues. When, for example, the London County Council Staff Association voted on its own marriage bar, the majority of men voting wanted it retained, but over half the women wanted it lifted (Lewenhak, 1977, p. 226).

The Women's Advisory Committee also frequently took up a feminist stance, sometimes in opposition to the movement as a whole. There were unsuccessful requests for a women's industrial charter in the 1930s, and in 1944 the Conference had criticized the lack of science teaching for girls. The pressure for an industrial charter was renewed after the war and in 1963 such a charter was approved by the TUC. Anticipating many of the demands of the new movement, it asked not only for equal pay, but also for better employment opportunities, better apprenticeships and training facilities, retraining for older women, and health and welfare facilities for women at work (Lewenhak, 1977, pp. 234–5, 276).

Within the Labour Party, itself, women's groups also supported the issue of equal pay, although with less insistence than the women trade unionists. During the 1960s the issue was revived and there were repeated resolutions at National Labour Women's Conferences (McDonald, 1977, p. 149). By the end of the 1960s Labour Party women were actively involved in the general issue of discrimination against women, which was part of the new women's movement and will be described in more detail later. Without their pressure, indeed, it is likely that the Labour Party as a whole would have been far less responsive to women's rights. As we have seen, however, women in the labour movement have had a long history of campaigning on behalf of women and, although they were particularly active during the suffrage struggle, they did not lose this interest even in the 1920s and 1930s when feminist organizations as such began to lose their influence. In 1935, for example, they campaigned against the denial of unemployment benefit to married women in industrial work. Again, in 1941 they argued for proper compensation for housewives injured in the war. They also campaigned, along with many other groups, to allow British women to retain their British nationality on marriage (McDonald, 1977, p. 148).

Clearly, therefore, the active feminism that existed as early as the end of the nineteenth century in the Independent Labour Party, in the Co-operative Women's Guild and in the women's trade union movement did not die out altogether with the coming of women's suffrage. It remained as a small but growing pressure within a labour movement that was largely indifferent to, if not at times even hostile to, feminist demands. Moreover, there are clear signs that this pressure from women activists was growing in intensity and significance even before the new women's movement reached Britain from the United States. The British equal rights legislation of the early 1970s, therefore, which will be discussed in detail shortly, like the earlier American legislation, does not owe its origin to the new feminism, even if a new feminist awareness helped to create the mood in which such legislation could be better achieved.

It is necessary at this stage to look briefly at the part played by women in Parliament in maintaining a tradition of equal rights feminism on which the new movement could be based. On the whole, it is true, women MPs, whatever their party, have not formed themselves into a caucus or group to pursue women's interests. Vallance, in a recent study, concludes that they have tended to accept 'men's views of what was important' (Vallance, 1979, p. 86). Nevertheless they have, from time to time, taken concerted action to advance the position of women. During the war, for example, they acted as a group to claim a more responsible role for women in the war effort. This led to a committee of women MPs that campaigned for greater equality of opportunity for women.

Nor have women MPs always been feminists, and even if they were they have not necessarily seen their role in Parliament in these terms. For some, indeed, their feminism has taken the form of direct competition with men, and they have sought to avoid women's issues and to achieve success in what are seen as the masculine province of foreign policy or economic affairs (Vallance, 1979). For many women in the Labour Party, too, socialism has taken precedence over feminism and they have worked for what seemed to them a greater goal.

Nevertheless there have been a few women MPs who have seen themselves perhaps first and foremost as feminists. The first woman MP, Nancy Astor, must certainly be regarded as one of these. She cooperated closely with feminist groups during the 1920s and much of her work in Parliament was on strongly feminist lines. Even her interest in temperance, which led to the first successful private bill to be introduced by a woman, the Intoxicating Liquors (Sales to Persons under 18) Act of 1923, is firmly in the feminist, if not the equal rights, tradition. Moreover, in 1925 she introduced an unsuccessful bill on prostitution that would have ended the special restrictions on women and replaced them by legislation on 'annoyance', which would have been equally applicable to both men and women. The result of pressure by the Association for Moral and Social Hygiene, the bill was part of the long-standing feminist attack on the double standard of sexual morality (Cook, 1978, pp. 130—1).

By the end of the 1920s, however, although the number of

women MPs grew, if very slowly and with constant set-backs, their feminist consciousness seems to have declined with its decline in the world outside. Eleanor Rathbone, perhaps the most important feminist in Parliament at that time, became absorbed in the family allowances campaign and in foreign affairs, and this illustrates, perhaps as well as anything, the prevailing mood of the time.

In 1938, Edith Summerskill entered Parliament, and she was to prove to be the most active and forceful of the feminist politicians of the next two decades. An early advocate of birth control, she also campaigned on such issues as clean food and the power of the drug industry, but it is as an advocate of the rights of the housewife that her feminism is most clearly expressed. For some years she was president of the Married Women's Association, founded in 1938 to improve the economic position of the wife in the home. As early as 1943 she took up, unsuccessfully, the case of a housewife whose husband claimed her savings from her Co-op dividends — a case that demonstrated that legally the housekeeping money was the sole property of the husband. In 1952 she was equally unsuccessful when she introduced a bill to protect women whose husbands had defaulted on the payment of maintenance orders. In 1963, however, she successfully introduced a Married Woman's Savings Bill, which eventually became law and entitled a woman to half her savings. This meant that a married woman who had no earnings of her own could nevertheless claim to have contributed, by her work for the family, to the family income, a principle that was later to become an important plank in the new feminist programme.

There were therefore, even during the unpromising 1950s, signs that equal rights feminism was not only alive but struggling to make itself heard. So far, it is true, it had achieved little success and even in the early 1960s there were few indications of the enormous change of mood that was to come. Edith Summerskill's bill, it was true, had been successful, and equal pay in the public service had finally been achieved, but equal pay in general had been blocked by the wage freeze and there seemed little real prospect of any immediate solution.

In 1968 it was both Human Rights Year and the fiftieth anniversary of the suffrage campaign, and these focused attention on equal rights as a political issue. The equal rights legislation in the United States provided a useful model, and so did race relations legislation in Britain. Rumours of an upsurge of feminism in the United States may also have added to the new mood (Rowbotham,

1972). Most significant of all, however, was a quite new and apparently spontaneous outbreak of militancy on the part of women workers against discrimination. In June, for example, there was a strike of women at Ford's for equal pay that was given a lot of publicity and aroused considerable public sympathy. Also in that year there was a small but very militant revolt of bus conductresses against the trade union policy of not allowing them to be bus drivers (Lewenhak, 1977, pp. 286—91). Rowbotham (1972) draws attention, too, to the rather different campaign by fishermen's wives to improve conditions on trawlers.

Trade union women activists were already disturbed by the failure of the Labour government to implement its election policy on equal pay, and organized a National Joint Action Committee for Women's Equal Rights that pressed hard for action on equal pay (Lewenhak, 1977, pp. 286—7). Barbara Castle was eventually persuaded to lend her support and an Equal Pay Bill was introduced by her, and passed, with the united support of almost all the women MPs, by a Labour government in 1970 (Vallance, 1979, pp. 45—6).

It was at this time that the issue of discrimination against women became a major political issue. In 1967 Betty Lockwood had become the chief woman officer and Assistant National Agent of the Labour Party, and from this time the party began to take an increasing interest in sex equality. In 1968 the National Council of Labour Women considered a report, *Discrimination Against Women,* which led to a Green Paper published in 1972 when the Labour Party was in opposition (McDonald, 1977, p. 149). In the meantime the Labour MP Joyce Butler had introduced a Sex Discrimination Bill that was supported by women's organizations, like the Townswomen's Guilds, that were by no means overtly feminist (Stott, 1978, p. 173). Pressure continued from the National Labour Women's Advisory Committee, and there was a period of intense discussion within the Labour Party. In 1974 a Labour government White Paper, *Equality for Women,* superseded the earlier Green Paper and was followed in 1975 by the Sex Discrimination Act, which made such discrimination unlawful in education, advertising and the provision of public facilities. An Equal Opportunities Commission was also set up with wide powers of investigation and publicity to implement the Act (Sachs and Wilson, 1978, p. 203).

As in the United States, however, the passage of equal rights legislation did not in itself guarantee that discrimination would cease. Indeed in both countries, in the short term at least, the effect has been very small. I have already noted the virtual failure of the Equal Pay Act in the United States to change the pattern of women's earnings, and this seems also to have been true in Britain. Not only does the Act not apply to those jobs that are clearly stratified by sex, but employers have been reluctant to implement the Act, and tribunals have tended to apply the law conservatively (Sachs and Wilson, 1978, p. 204). The issue of protective legislation also creates problems, since equal pay is dependent on the elimination of different conditions of work as between men and women. Yet both the TUC and most women trade unionists are still basically in favour of the retention of protective laws for women, and efforts of employers to use equal pay to end restrictions on night-work, for example, have sometimes met with opposition from the women themselves (Rowbotham, 1973b, pp. 92–3).

The Equal Opportunities Commission, like its American counterpart, has been criticized for its unwillingness to take the vigorous action necessary as well as for limitations on its powers. This is not to suggest that the legislation itself has been valueless since it can be effective in individual cases, as indeed can the Equal Pay Act; it may also, as Sachs and Wilson point out, have a part to play in educating public consciousness as well as the consciousness of women themselves. The results, however, have underlined the limitations of legislation as the main weapon in the battle for equal rights and, as in the United States, have emphasized the necessity for the equal rights movement to look elsewhere for an answer to the problem of discrimination.

The drive for the traditional equal rights claimed by feminists since the early days of the movement is, however, only one aspect of the new feminism and in many ways perhaps the least distinctive part. The movement known as Women's Liberation in fact had its own beginning in the United States independently of the equal rights movement and independently too of the whole tradition of feminism as it had developed in the past. Later, it is true, it was to search for, and discover, its founders, but initially at least it was a spontaneous response of a group of young women to their own experience of discrimination. Later, the liberation movement and the equal rights movement were to lose their distinctive identities, and in Britain at least they were never so far apart as they were in the United States. Nevertheless, if the division is at times an arbitrary one, it is useful as well as convenient. The following chapter, therefore, will be concerned with those aspects of the new feminism that take us beyond equal rights, and, making use of a

12

Radical Feminism

The origins of radical feminism — or, in the more popular terminology, the women's liberation movement — have often been described and there is no need here to do more than summarize the main events from which the movement sprang (Hole and Levine, 1971; Freeman, 1975; Carden, 1974; Bouchier, 1978). Like the equal rights campaign it began early in the 1960s, when small groups of women activists in the civil rights movement, and later in the New Left, began to be conscious of the limited role assigned to women in the movement, and in particular their exclusion from decision-making and their relegation to domestic and other auxiliary chores. Such a role was of course typical of women's political involvement, but the women making the protest were not only themselves highly educated but part of a movement that stressed an equal rights ideology. It is no coincidence, therefore, that radical feminism in the 1960s and the first wave of nineteenth-century feminism in the 1830s arose within the context of natural rights and moved from a consideration of justice for the Negro to justice for women.

However, the attempt by these women to raise the issue of women's rights met not only with a refusal to listen to their arguments, but with a level of contempt and ridicule that did a great deal to stimulate the incipient feminism of the women involved. Hostility to their male colleagues led eventually to open revolt, and in 1967 women's groups were founded in New York and Chicago respectively and women's liberation as a movement was born. The next few years were filled with intense activity. Groups sprang up more or less spontaneously, some of them the result of a

225

split within existing groups as a feminist ideology gradually developed. Journals and articles added to the intellectual excitement and to controversies between different sections of the new movement. Demonstrations of one kind and another gave publicity that, if not always favourable, spread knowledge of the new feminism and its ideas to women who had previously had little political involvement of any kind. Fundamental to these groups, however, was that they were not simply feminist, but female. The principle of male exclusion, which is still a characteristic of radical feminism, seems to have been initially at least a direct consequence of male rejection. The women had attempted, at first, to develop their feminism within the civil rights, New Left and other radical movements. It was only later that they moved out of these male-dominated organizations to form their own groups in which women, as women, could discuss their problems together. Later, male exclusion as a principle was to become a significant aspect of the developing ideology.

It is not altogether clear why the men should have responded with such extreme hostility to the women's demands. There has always been an element of feminism in left-wing thinking, which might have led to a certain sympathy with the women even if it had fallen short of actual support. The argument that issues of class or race must take precedence, which was certainly used by the men to oppose the inclusion of feminist aims, does not explain the tone of the opposition and the contempt with which the women were treated. In particular it can hardly excuse the sexist and indeed sexual language that was used against the women (Carden, 1974, p. 62). It has been suggested that the New Left during these years adopted an increasingly male imagery, with heroes drawn from rock music, black power and the Cuban revolution (Young, 1977, pp. 367—9). The result was an emphasis on masculinity as hardness and toughness, which went along with a contempt for women that reduced them to servants and campfollowers (Roszak, 1969, pp. 92—3). Whatever the truth of this, it seems certain that some of the more violent anti-male attitudes taken up by some of the radical feminists at this time, as for example the manifesto of the Society for Cutting-Up Men or SCUM (Morgan, 1970), were a result of the humiliation some of them had experienced personally at the hands of men they had sought as allies. In fact the split was never healed, and the attempts later on of male-dominated groups to take over made male sympathizers seem even more dangerous than opponents (Bouchier, 1978, pp. 133—4).

In the next few years radical feminism continued as a very loose federation of independent groups. It did, however, develop certain characteristics that served to define it as a movement, if not as an organization. During these years, the radical feminists had to work out their relationship with the New Left and particularly that between feminism and socialism (Hole and Levine, 1971, pp. 129—31; Bouchier, 1978, pp. 105—8). The result was a feminism that differed considerably both in ideology and tactics from the equal rights feminism that was developing at the same time. Moreover, these differences sprang directly from the origins of the women's liberation movement in radical politics. Thus, whereas NOW began as a political pressure group with little grass-roots involvement, radical feminism was deliberately anti-elitist. There were attempts within it, not always successful, to break down traditional leadership roles and to create new kinds of structure with the emphasis on participation (Hole and Levine, 1971, pp. 145, 161). There was a preference for direct action, as for example the demonstration in 1968 against the Miss America pageant, rather than the political lobbying that certainly characterized equal rights feminism at this time. A particular invention of the radical feminists was the consciousness-raising group, which spread rapidly as it seemed to meet the needs of many women to talk over their problems with other women and to discover shared experiences (Carden, 1974, pp. 34—7).

Ideologically, radical feminism has no single doctrine and no simple set of goals or aims. Indeed its opposition to organization, and its respect for spontaneity and self-expression, meant not only that each group developed its own programme, but that there were constant splits as groups divided on issue of both ideology and strategy (Hole and Levine, 1971, pp. 129—61). On the whole, however, the movement is united in its opposition to what it sees as patriarchy or women's oppression by man — a concept that, in its implications, is far wider and more radical than the equal rights concept of feminism. Much of the energy of the feminists, and especially of the feminist intellectuals, has therefore gone not simply into action, or even propaganda, but into a search for the *source* of man's power over women; one of the main lines of division is to be found in the alternative answers that individuals and groups have provided to this crucial question.

The Marxist feminists, who represent one kind of answer, try to retain their loyalty to both socialism and feminism. Consequently they continue to give priority to issues of class, although they no longer see feminism, as do many orthodox socialists both male and female, as a necessary consequence of a socialist victory. They are agreed, however, that feminism without socialism is impossible (Mitchell, 1971, p. 95) and for this reason, if for no other, the struggle for socialism is given pride of place. At the same time, those women who wish to maintain the link between feminism and socialism find that they can only do so by what amounts to a very radical critique of orthodox Marxist views on the position of women (Mitchell, 1971, pp. 82—88; Kuhn and Wolpe, 1978, p. 8).

Radical feminists, on the other hand, see sex as a form of oppression independent of social class. Indeed patriarchy, the oppression of women by men, is seen as not only pre-dating capitalism but continuing after capitalism itself has been superseded. Consequently man himself becomes the exploiter and women the major oppressed class. For some radical feminists, indeed, socialism becomes quite irrelevant, since it will merely succeed in replacing one group of men by another. Nevertheless it is important to realize that even those radical feminists who seem to depart most widely from orthodox Marxism betray in countless ways their origin in the New Left (Bouchier, 1978, pp. 111—12). This is revealed most clearly not in the actual content of their ideology, which is often very unMarxist, but in the kind of concepts they employ and the manner in which they employ them. It will be argued later that it is the particular style this gives to the movement that provides women's liberation with its special characteristics and serves to differentiate it quite sharply from other kinds of feminism. It is this, certainly, that marks it, potentially at least, as revolutionary rather than reformist in its orientation, and that indeed, because of the basic and also far-reaching implications of sex-role divisions in society, makes it even more radical than Marxism in the extent of the changes it proposes. At the same time, by emphasizing sexual rather than economic exploitation, radical feminist writers often treat men as an exploiting class as if they were completely analogous to the ruling class in Marxist orthodoxy, except that the class war becomes a war between the sexes. Indeed, Kate Millett (1971) simply replaces class by sex. This gives great force to the ideology but raises problems for the movement that we must return to later. Concepts like consciousness raising, sisterhood and many more were also derived fairly directly from Marxist ideology. Moreover, not only do many radical feminists still see themselves in some respects at least as Marxists but many Marxist feminists are attempting to redefine Marxism by taking account in a much more sympathetic way than before of the radical feminist critique of sexism in society. Consequently the division between radical feminists and Marxist feminists should not be taken too literally. They are ideal-types rather than clear-cut divisions within feminism.

One of the most original of the radical feminists to arise in the early days of the American movement was Shulamith Firestone. She based women's oppression in the very fact of reproduction itself, and saw no answer to the problem until artificial child-bearing was technologically a possibility. This would enable the family as we know it to disappear, although Firestone, unlike some later feminists, did not propose that men and women should no longer live together. Only by thus breaking the tie between women and reproduction, Firestone (1971) argued, can women achieve both economic independence and sexual freedom. Moreover, because the cultural division between male and female is also based on biological reproduction, artificial reproduction would allow such distinctions to be broken down and men and women to share in characteristics hitherto sharply sex linked.

It is interesting to notice that, although her theory is not at all Marxist in its essentials, she is still trying to maintain a general Marxist framework and terminology, and describes herself as a socialist. In the process, however, she falls into a rigidly conceived technological determinism and her critics have pointed out that artificial reproduction could still be used to continue and even enhance male domination unless women were able to control the manner of its introduction (Rose and Hanmer, 1976). Nevertheless, Firestone's analysis is important because it stresses precisely those aspects of women's position that are crucial in the ideology of radical feminism. The emphasis she lays on women's reproductive functions, and the part played by marriage and the family in the oppression of women, have been and to a large extent remain central to the women's liberation movement both in the United States and elsewhere. Radical feminists therefore, quite unlike the equal rights feminists, have tended, as Jo Freeman (1975, pp. 50—1) has pointed out, to concentrate on the 'traditional female concerns of love, sex and children', even if they have been concerned about them in a very untraditional way.

To criticize marriage is not of course necessarily *new,* since nineteenth-century socialists, and indeed many feminists at that time and later, were opposed to marriage laws that denied women legal rights, just as they were opposed to an economic system that

forced women into loveless marriages and kept them tied to cruel
and perhaps dissolute men. The radical feminists go further
however, alleging that marriage is at the very root of woman's
subjection to the man because through it man controls both her
reproduction and her person. Few aspects of marriage and the
family remain unscathed in this attack, although perhaps it is the
position of the wife as 'unpaid domestic labourer' and the traditional
sex roles within marriage and the family that come under the
heaviest and most frequent fire. Romantic love is another favourite
target since it is seen as a way of trapping women into accepting
their own oppression.

The alternatives to marriage and the family put forward by the
radical feminists are not necessarily new either, with the exception
of Firestone and her advocacy of artificial reproduction. The free
love union that is sometimes advocated was, for example, a
favourite remedy with some groups in the nineteenth century.
Even the attack on individual love as possessive and the advocacy of
group marriage have their counterpart in the nineteenth-century
Oneida community and indeed elsewhere. There is also a renewal
of the ideal of celibacy that attracted some of the most conservative
of the early feminists, although the open advocacy of lesbianism,
the final symbol of sisterhood, could not have occurred at any
earlier time. What is new, however, is the way in which these ideas,
attractive to isolated individuals or small groups, have now become
the very core of radical feminism.

New, too, is the strong emphasis on alternatives to traditional
patterns of child-rearing, whether through state-supported services
or the self-help of some kind of commune. This was certainly a
preoccupation of some nineteenth-century communitarian socialists, and later of a few feminists, of whom Charlotte Gilman is
perhaps the most notable example, but most feminists paid little
attention to such ideas. Welfare feminism, it is true, was very
concerned to ease the burden of the mother, especially if she was
living in poverty, but it rarely used this concern to challenge
traditional views on the role of the woman in child-rearing. Both
state-supported services and family allowances were seen as aids to
the traditional family and not as alternatives.

Radical feminism has also shown a deep concern with the issue
of female sexuality. To some extent, as we have seen, this concern
has never been absent from the feminist movement; from its
earliest days it has criticized the way in which women have been
made the victims of male lust, both within and outside marriage.

The form this took was, as we have seen in some detail in earlier chapters, a retreat from sexuality altogether. The radical feminists too are deeply concerned with male violence towards women, expressed in such issues as rape, and see sexual violence in particular as a significant consequence of male domination and female oppression. What is new, however, is the serious exploration by the radical feminists of the nature of female sexuality and the conditions under which it can flourish. The argument that the sex act itself is defined in male terms, for male pleasure, and that female satisfaction requires different techniques and a different approach (Gordon, 1977, pp. 381—3) is a good example of the attempt of the radical feminists to come to terms with women's needs without either denying them altogether or subordinating them to male demands.

This attempt to redefine female sexuality is combined with a new look at the effect of sexual permissiveness on women. Increasingly, greater sexual freedom has come to be seen as a doubtful benefit, operating as it does in the interests of men rather than women. By being 'persuaded to shed their armor' Shulamith Firestone (1971, pp. 160—1) has argued, 'a new reservoir of available females was created'. Consequently, sexual permissiveness, *in itself,* is no longer seen as necessarily liberating but, like romantic love, part of the sexist trap into which women are led by men. Much feminist thinking has therefore gone into the problem of how to allow women sexual freedom without at the same time contributing to their domination, and it is in this context that we must understand the preoccupation with such issues as abortion law reform and, on a wider front, the attack on male-dominated medicine and the demand, central not only to radical feminism but, as we shall see later, to feminists of almost every kind, that in political decisions and in personal relationships women are allowed to control their own bodies. The radical feminist attack on beauty contests and their dislike, in advertising and elsewhere, of the presentation of women as 'sex objects' is another aspect of this campaign.

The separatism of the radical feminists, to which attention has already been drawn, and the emergence, after 1970 in particular, of radical lesbianism as an important force in the movement have exaggerated the tendency in some sections of the movement to advocate the replacement of heterosexual love either by celibacy or by lesbianism, an advocacy made more plausible by the acceptance of a view of female sexuality that not only sees it as different from that of men but argues that its satisfaction does not necessarily involve a heterosexual relationship (Koedt, 1973a). Undoubtedly the influence of the feminist lesbians has been important here, but it is likely that some of those who advocated and practised lesbianism were drawn to it by their ideological commitment to feminism and particularly to sisterhood. Lesbianism in such circumstances (Hole and Levine, 1971, p. 241) was much more than a sexual preference and could become an important part of the sex war. Thus Dana Densmore (1973, pp. 117–18) argues, 'if it were true that we needed sex from men it would be a great misfortune, one that might almost doom our fight'.

While it is easy to exaggerate the importance of lesbianism as an aspect of radical feminism, the association of the two was sufficiently close to make Koedt herself (1973b, p. 254) feel the need to repudiate the claim that a radical feminist need necessarily be a lesbian. Moreover, the definition of man, and by implication all men, as the enemy — the repudiation of men as friends and allies and the exclusion of men not only from consciousness-raising sessions but from other activities — had given powerful 'pro-woman' emphasis to some sections of the movement. Women are seen not only as innocent victims but also as 'good', whereas men are not only oppressors but also 'bad', a view that vividly recalls the ideal of female superiority that characterized much earlier feminist thinking. For some radical feminists the elimination of male domination, if not of men altogether, would free the world not only of the oppression of the female by the male but of oppression itself. Moreover, in their forms of organization, radical feminists often try to eradicate characteristics that they classify as male, which include hierarchy, competition and aggression. Consequently, the qualities that they perceive as female and wish to encourage and perpetuate include just those 'soft' qualities (Roszak, 1969, p. 103) of affection, cooperation and even tenderness that were part of the ideology of femininity in both the nineteenth and the early twentieth centuries. There is little discussion, however, of the source of what are perceived as these more desirable feminine qualities and the extent to which they are the result of societal processes rather than 'nature' (of which perhaps the most important is the very oppression from which all the feminists want to free women).

In addition, for some although by no means all parts of the movement, the rejection of both maleness and the male have accompanied an intensification if not idolization of the maternal role, which is not only centred explicitly on biology but makes the mother—child relationship central (Glennon, 1979, p. 123). This takes many forms in practice. It may involve no more than the demand that mothers should always have the ultimate responsibility for their children, but at the other extreme are the communities that deliberately exclude men and in which groups of women care communally for the children. The effect is to weaken if not altogether to destroy not only the traditional male/female relationship but also the tie between father and child, whereas the maternal role is strengthened, even though child care may be collectively rather than individually organized. On the other hand, the tendency for men to become simply temporary sexual partners and to lose their paternal role seems to be a tendency even in mixed sex communes (Abrams and McCulloch, 1976, pp. 143—5, 215—16; Berger, 1973, pp. 362—3).

The pro-woman version of feminism accepts that sexism involves sex-role stereotyping but argues that procreation and children have been made to be oppressive by men. The removal of male domination would allow women not only to be free but also to be female; this view thus depends on a notion of the essential difference between men and women. While some radical feminists like Firestone want to free women from biological maternity there is another version of feminism that seeks only to free maternity from male domination. This involves on the one hand the return of childbirth to the care of women themselves, on the other the progressive removal of the rights *and* duties of fatherhood. The goal of such a version of feminism is neither equal rights nor androgyny, but matriarchy (Glennon, 1979, p. 138).

The presentation of what may be described as the ideology of radical feminism in this way makes it appear more systematic and certainly more unified than it really is, and it is necessary to stress once again that radical feminism is not a 'movement' in any concrete sense of the term and that it in fact represents a wide variety of positions. Even the difference often drawn between Marxist feminism and radical feminism is, as we have seen, by no means as clear-cut as it seems. Consequently, within radical feminism there are a variety of positions, not only existing side by side but competing with one another vigorously, and sometimes even violently, for acceptance. Even the issue of male exclusion, which has been a very dominant aspect of the ideology, can mean very different things to different people, and the argument that men should be excluded from the movement does not necessarily imply for all women that they must also be excluded from their lives.

Problems also arise from the very weakness of the theory on which radical feminism is based. As David Bouchier (1979, p. 390) has rightly pointed out, it amounts 'to little more than the bald statement that men were and always had been the oppressors of women, that women could discover this oppression through their own experience, and that that discovery was a revolutionary act'. From this sprang the emphasis on consciousness raising and the definition of man as the oppressor, but there was little in such a theory to guide the feminists on how power was to be taken from men, or the place of men in the new society. If men in themselves were the enemy, as many radical feminists believed, then the solution could well come to seem the abolition not simply of marriage, or even the family but of men, whether by their exclusion from women's society or, more radically, their abolition. It is not likely that many women in the movement actually envisaged the physical destruction of men, and certainly it is difficult to see this as a practical possibility, but there is no doubt that the dream of a world without men, which, as we have seen, haunted some nineteenth-century women, was a powerful attraction to many of the radical feminists who saw no other end to their oppression. Shulasmith Firestone, it is true, hoped to free women from child-bearing and so provide a new basis for the relationships between men and women, but other feminists, while rejecting men, have by no means rejected maternity, and Firestone's ideas have not been taken up by the movement generally (Bouchier, 1979). It could be argued that, by defining men as the source of women's oppression, women's fate appeared not only as universal and unchanging but even as biologically determined. If, however, women are indeed oppressed by biology itself, only the most radical solutions appear to offer an answer, whether in the form of Firestone's hope of an end to biological motherhood or in the proposals for a life apart from men.

Most of those who have attempted to examine the development of radical feminism are agreed that it was seriously weakened by internal disputes, by its lack of formal structure and by the theoretical weaknesses that continued to plague it. The years just before 1970 were its heyday, and through the 1970s it has fallen into a decline, its most committed followers retreating into feminist communes where they could practise only a kind of personal redemption. Others have moved into political action at the level of feminist issues like rape and abortion, the significance of which is reformist rather than revolutionary in its implications (Bouchier, 1979, p. 395).

If the 1970s saw the decline of radical feminism, they were also years in which equal rights feminism was increasingly radicalized as NOW moved into many of the positions originally occupied by the radical feminists. This had in fact started before 1970 with the adoption by NOW of abortion as a feminist issue. Introduced for the first time in 1967, it aroused considerable controversy and caused the more conservative elements in NOW to form the Women's Equity Action League, which concentrated on issues of employment, education and tax inequalities (Hole and Levine, 1971, pp. 95—8, 279). By 1970, the strike organized by NOW centred upon three issues — abortion on demand, 24-hour child care centres, and equal opportunity in employment and education — that took the organization firmly beyond a narrow equal rights policy (Freeman, 1973, p. 13). Lesbianism was another highly controversial issue within NOW when lesbians tried to claim it as a feminist issue, but after 1970 lesbianism was acknowledged by NOW as a legitimate concern of feminism (Deckard, 1979, pp. 374—8) even if some leading feminists continued to be anxious about the effect of a lesbian image on the movement (Friedan, 1977, p. 129).

Thus, over time, NOW broadened its activities and began to explore issues of female sexuality and alternative life styles borrowed from the radical feminists. To some extent this arose from changes in the membership of NOW itself, as the publicity attracted initially by radical feminists drew much larger numbers of women into the organization. There was also within NOW a growing awareness of the inadequacy of a narrow equal rights feminism. Nevertheless, the net effect has been what Bouchier has described as the de-radicalization of radical feminism. If the goals of NOW have extended beyond the concept of equal rights, the solutions they propose are often vastly different from those of the radical feminists, and the end result has been a 'moderate' feminism with policies that, like those of equal rights, are essentially reformist in character. Bouchier (1979) has argued that this was brought about partly by a surrender from within radical feminism itself, weakened as it was by internal disputes and a lack of structure, partly by the media, which distorted and ridiculed the message of the radicals, and partly by what amounted to a takeover by the better-organized NOW, which enabled it to capture the new recruits who were being attracted into feminism at this time.

The practical effect of this de-radicalization has been an increasing limitation of feminism to specific feminist issues and a move away from a radical critique of society. These issues include attempts to change the laws on abortion, birth control, divorce and property, to improve child care facilities, to change the image of women in the media, and to end discrimination against women in education and employment, some of which do not go very far beyond the equal rights tradition. More radical perhaps are the attempts to provide help and support by women for women in such areas as abortion and rape (Deckard, 1979, pp. 429—38), but even these are essentially reformist rather than revolutionary in aim, whatever their ultimate implications.

One of the most significant of the issues that has joined radical feminists and NOW has been the abortion campaign (Hole and Levine, 1971, pp. 279—302). As we saw in chapter 10, historically the movement for change in the abortion laws has been based on the health of the mother and the child. Public discussion during the 1960s was stimulated by both the thalidomide scare and the German measles epidemic; pressure for some degree of reform built up and some states made minor revisions in their abortion laws. It was left to the feminists to demand the right to abortion as a matter of justice, an aspect of a woman's right to control her own reproduction, and this became a part of NOW's campaign as well as of the radical feminists. There were, however, divisions on tactics, with NOW preferring the more traditional method of lobbying and the radical feminists more direct action, such as picketing, demonstrations and civil disobedience. There was also some disagreement on whether to work only for total repeal or whether to work within the abortion law reform movement for a limited measure of reform (Cisler, 1973). Finally in 1973 a Supreme Court decision came near to allowing abortion on demand, although there were still restrictions on the timing of the abortion and it was still largely in the control of the medical profession, restrictions that feminists continue to oppose. There has also been the need to combat the attempts, since 1973, to overturn the Supreme Court decision, and anti-abortion groups, as we have seen, are important opponents of the feminist movement and the Equal Rights Amendment (Deckard, 1979, pp. 426—7). As part of the right to abortion campaign, feminist groups have also set up abortion referral services to help women get around the inadequacies of the system.

Another consequence of the de-radicalization of feminism has been a move away from the sex war and the politics of confrontation between men and women to the position that the existing relationship between the sexes, and in particular the present sex-role stereotyping, oppresses both men and women. According to this version of feminism, the institutions of marriage and the family need to be changed, but by reform rather than abolition. The solution lies in what is frequently termed androgyny, or role-sharing, in which both personality and role behaviour will cease to be sex-typed. Moreover, since it is the system, rather than men, that is seen as oppressive, change depends not upon a revolutionary struggle but upon the conversion of both men and women to a new system from which both will gain (Yates, 1975, pp. 126—32). This will require a change both in the system of child care and in life styles, so that the burden of child care does not fall solely on women, and in sex stereotyping, through changes in the educational system.

Such a position departs from the equal rights tradition by demanding radical change in the position of men and women in society, but it is very far indeed from the radical feminists who view man as the oppressor. It is also largely outside a Marxist perspective, although conceivably some version of androgyny could be combined with Marxism. Its appeal perhaps is particularly to those who, like Betty Friedan, dislike the sex-war analogy, which, she claims, 'makes a woman apologize for loving her husband or children' (Friedan, 1977, p. 121). She asks for a 'two sex movement for human liberation' and an end to the 'obsolete sex roles, the feminine and masculine mystiques, which torment us mutually' (Friedan, 1977, p. 125).

The androgynous approach is by no means without serious weaknesses at the theoretical level and may represent no more than an attempt to avoid the revolutionary confrontation inevitable in both Marxist and radical feminism. At the same time, by accepting the need for quite large changes in male/female roles, it avoids some of the difficulties that have increasingly become apparent in equal rights feminism. For this reason it is likely to continue to be an important element in feminism, particularly in the United States where Marxist feminism has remained un-developed. Indeed it is possible, and this possibility will be examined again in the Conclusion, that social and economic changes, irrespective of feminist pressures, are already pointing towards a more androgynous society. Before passing on to these more general issues, however, it is necessary to move on to a survey of radical feminism as it has developed in Britain and in particular to examine the ways in which it has differed from the movement in the United States.

As in the United States, radical feminism arose from within the revolutionary left, although it was, from the first, strongly influenced by the American movement, news of which came from American women in London and from the network of radical journals (Rowbotham, 1972, p. 93; Bouchier, 1978, p. 109). Groups began to be formed in 1969, some associated with existing male revolutionary groups, others independent. An important landmark was the Oxford conference in 1970, which attracted some 600 participants; its success may be said to have started the movement in Britain. The policy that emerged from the conference centred upon equal pay, improved education, 24-hour nurseries, free contraception and abortion on demand (Rowbotham, 1972, p. 97), policies that indeed reflect the practical orientation of the British movement.

Perhaps the main difference between the United States and Britain, however, is the closer link in Britain between socialism or Marxism and feminism. Although by no means sympathetic to women's claims, there was never the deep rift between radical men and women that occurred, and indeed persisted, in the United States and kept the two groups not only apart but hostile to each other. Consequently Marxist feminism has continued to be much stronger in Britain than in the United States, and many of the most influential British feminists have tried to reconcile Marxism and feminism rather than to develop an independent feminist theory (Bouchier, 1978, p. 133; Mitchell, 1971; Kuhn and Wolpe, 1978). The concern with Marxism at the theoretical level is, however, only one aspect of the relationship. There is more concern in Britain with the economic exploitation of women and closer ties between feminism and women in the trade union movement, so that issues like equal pay and child care provision have a more immediate and practical significance.

This is not to suggest that radical British feminists do not share, to some extent at least, the anti-male perspectives of their American counterparts. Within the British movement the practice of excluding men has been followed just as strongly in meetings, conferences and seminars, extending, at times, to a retreat from heterosexuality itself (Whiting, 1972, p. 211). Moreover, all the themes of radical feminism in the United States can be found within the writings of the British movement. It does seem, nevertheless, that the extreme version of the anti-male ideology has not taken root to such an extent in Britain as in the United States (Bouchier, 1978, p. 113). Furthermore, radical feminists in Britain have been active in a large number of political campaigns that have tended to bring them into an alliance with both equal rights feminists and women in the labour and trade union movements. These issues, of which there are many, include the campaign against anti-abortion laws, better provision for battered wives, changes in the law on rape, better social security provision and improved child care facilities (Bouchier, 1978, p. 129). Such work, because it involves political tactics of one kind or another, may well involve working with or through men. Women in the trade union movement, for example, forced their unions to back demands for day nurseries (Lewenhak, 1977, p. 290).

The campaign against the abortion laws is perhaps the most successful and the most impressive of the radical feminists' excursions into politics and is worth examining in a little more detail. As we have seen in chapter 10, the campaign initially had as its chief concern the health and well-being of the mother and child. As in the United States, it was the thalidomide scare that was perhaps the most powerful influence in turning public opinion towards the idea of reform, and this occurred before the emergence of the new feminism in the late 1960s (Hindell and Simms, 1971, p. 108). Even when, in 1963, a younger generation took over leadership of the Abortion Law Reform Association and there was a dramatic increase in its level of activity and in the size of its membership, this was not linked to any specifically feminist argument. Indeed at this time the argument that it was a woman's right to choose was rejected by the ALRA (Potts *et al.*, 1977, p. 296).

There was considerable support for some measure of reform from women's organizations (Hindell and Simms, 1971, p. 127), many of which were by no means specifically feminist in their orientation, although it may well have been considered by them as an issue of special relevance to women. On the other hand, support for a change in the law did not come only from women, and during the 1960s the campaign seems to have been part of a general movement to liberalize the legal system in the direction of more individual freedom especially, although not exclusively, with respect to sexual morality. During the early 1960s, for example, such issues as homosexuality, divorce and euthanasia, as well as abortion and contraception, became of increasing concern to groups that had previously ignored them. The British Humanist Association took a great interest in these issues at this time, whereas in the past it had tried to dissociate itself from the free love tradition in progressive thought. It is significant, therefore, that when Baroness Wootton opposed a clause of the Abortion Bill in 1968 she was not re-elected to the vice-presidency of the Association (Budd, 1977, p. 260). It must also be noted that the older generation of feminists did not see abortion on demand as part of the feminist case either. Edith Summerskill, for example, feared that if abortion was too easy it might be used as an alternative to birth control (Summerskill, 1967, p. 229).

The Act, which came into operation in 1968, went a considerable way to liberalize the abortion law, although the restrictions that it imposed, and the difficulties of implementing the Act, meant that, in the final event, it was a long way from free abortion on request. Moreover, in the years since its passage, the energies of the reformers, as in the United States, have perforce been concentrated on maintaining the Act rather than on pressing for further reforms. What is interesting for our purpose, however, is that the case for abortion has come to be seen increasingly in feminist terms. Already by the early 1970s, as we have seen, abortion was a key issue in the women's liberation groups, and in 1971 a national woman's demonstration made free contraception and abortion on demand one of its main aims (Leathard, 1980, p. 175).

The feminist involvement in the abortion issue can be seen very clearly in the first serious threat to the 1967 Abortion Act in 1975. A Woman's Right to Choose campaign was organized that brought feminist arguments and feminists themselves into the very centre of the battle. Even the Abortion Law Reform Association was won over; it not only adopted the feminist slogan 'a woman's right to choose' but argued the feminist case for the right to abortion on request (Leathard, 1980, p. 205). By 1979 the labour and trade union movement was deeply involved in the controversy and in that year the TUC and the women's movement organized a joint protest march that brought the two groups together for the first time. In the case of abortion law reform, therefore, the radical feminists in Britain have played an important part in radicalizing not only feminism itself but also reform movements concerned with feminist issues. The same case could be made with respect to rape and to violence against wives, since it is largely the radical feminists who have raised these as significant legal and political issues rather than as personal and psychological problems.

As in the United States, however, the feminist movement in the late 1970s has had to meet both an ideological backlash, partly produced by its own earlier successes, and the challenge of an economic recession, which threatens the gains that women have actually won. The heady optimism of the early 1970s has indeed gone, and it is possible that we may be entering another period of decline such as that which characterized the Depression of the 1930s and, in that instance, lasted for a whole generation. Whether this will occur again is a matter, perhaps, for speculation rather than prediction, although an attempt will be made to suggest some answers. Before looking to the future, however, it is time to return to the past and, in a final chapter, to turn from description to analysis and, by examining the results of this exercise in historical comparison, to seek to learn something more of the nature of feminism, and its strengths and weaknesses as a social movement.

13

Conclusion

In looking at feminist ideology the point has been made many times that we are dealing with not one but three traditions, which, if they have some things in common, are also to a large extent not only different but even contradictory. In consequence, feminism has displayed contradictions both in its philosophy and in its programme that have opened it to attack both from its enemies and indeed from within its own ranks. Thus it has seemed to stand for both sexual repression *and* free love, for independence *and* protection for women, as identical with *and* essentially different from men. Indeed, if all feminists are agreed that women's position needs to be changed, they sometimes seem to be united about little else. Opposition to feminist goals can come not only from what are usually described as anti-feminists but, sometimes just as bitterly, from those who are themselves part of the feminist movement. The split in the American movement in 1869 is one such example, but the division in the 1920s was probably even more deeply felt. In Britain there were also periods of antagonism, most notably the struggle within both the Liberal and Labour parties over adult suffrage. Sometimes these controversies have been simply over questions of tactics, but often, as in the case of the issue of protective legislation, different ideologies have divided the movement.

Apart from contradictions between different traditions, there are also problems that arise from within the traditions themselves. Thus, as we have seen, evangelical feminism, in spite of the moral fervour that it brought to the movement and that has been such an important source of inspiration, is essentially conservative in its

242

attitude to women. Its most powerful influence has been in motivating women to move out of the home into the public sphere, but if women's realm is thereby widened it is not in its essential nature changed. Even radical feminism still bears traces of this evangelical feminism, glorifying woman in her maternal role and looking to her in her specifically feminine attributes to reform the world. It is no accident that feminists of this persuasion tend to look *backwards* in time to a golden age of mother rule.

The equal rights tradition has been concerned largely with formal equality and this has been both its strength and its weakness. It has brought about legal changes in property rights; it has won the vote for women and the possibility, if not always the actuality, of political power; it has broken down legal and institutional barriers that kept women out of certain roles and organizations; it has made discrimination illegal; and it has legislated for equal pay. It is not surprising, therefore, if equal rights has sometimes been equated with feminism itself, and if the struggle for such rights has absorbed all the energies of feminist organizations. Nor should the victories this kind of feminism has won be dismissed as of no importance; each has had some part to play in breaking down male privilege and opening the way to greater equality for women, even if it has more to offer to those, mainly propertied and educated, women who are better able to take advantage of the opportunities it provides.

Nevertheless, the emphasis on formal equality that characterizes this tradition is based on an overoptimistic assumption of the power of legislation to effect changes in society. It overlooks the limitations of legal reform and the inability of legislation to change attitudes and behaviour rooted in the division of labour and in the work place. The failure of women to take an equal place in the professions or in politics, and the difficulties of implementing the legislation on equal pay, are but a few examples that have led to a disenchantment within feminism with purely legislative solutions. Thus the equal rights tradition, in spite of its Enlightenment emphasis on the fundamental similarities of men and women, has tended, like the evangelical tradition, to leave unchanged, and indeed at times even unchallenged, the traditional division of labour and the traditional role of women.

At first sight, therefore, the communitarian socialist tradition of feminism seems the most promising. It offers a much more radical vision of feminist goals, including formal equality but going beyond it to advocate changes in marriage and the family, in child-rearing, and, in its most radical formulation, in sexuality itself. However, communitarian experiments were usually much less radical in practice than in ideology; the Oneida community stands out as one that went further than most in its rejection not only of private property but also of marriage and the family. However, communities of this kind were short-lived, some lasting only a few years, others, like Oneida, not surviving the loss of their original leader.

Moreover, communitarian socialism was not destined to be long-lived even as an ideology, and the versions of socialism that replaced it gave much less attention to new patterns of living. Feminism itself, however, remained part of the official ideology and there was a sympathy for feminist goals that was sometimes given active expression, as in the support for suffrage campaigns, particularly by individuals like Keir Hardie and George Lansbury in Britain. On the other hand, expressions of official support, as in the case of equal pay for example, could often go hand in hand with an unwillingness to take any positive action, and even at times with outright opposition to the implementation of what was agreed in principle. Socialism and the labour and trade union movements, in spite of their feminist traditions, have thus been uncertain and sometimes unwilling allies of the feminist movement. Moreover, as we have seen in earlier chapters, positive support for feminist goals has frequently been brought about only as a result of pressure from women's groups within the socialist and labour movements.

Modern feminism, and especially radical feminism, to a much greater extent than nineteenth-century feminism, has recognized that feminist goals cannot be achieved without changes in the relationship between men and women that entail the transformation of traditional sex roles and the traditional family. To this extent it is perhaps closer to communitarian socialism than to either the equal rights tradition or evangelical Christianity, and it is no accident that radical feminists have a predilection towards communitarian solutions. Nevertheless, radical feminism contains many contradictory and indeed conflicting elements, some inclining towards androgyny, others towards a kind of matriarchy that bears a distinct resemblance to the evangelical tradition of female superiority.

Perhaps the most interesting tendency of modern feminism is the attempt to re-think Marxist theory on the position of women and to forge an alliance between Marxism and feminism that goes beyond the lip-service paid by earlier generations of Marxist and indeed other kinds of socialists to feminist goals and aspirations. This has involved a serious attempt, too complex to be described here, to amend traditional Marxist theory on the position of women so that it includes an analysis of women's domestic labour, an abandonment of the idea that socialism will *necessarily* emancipate women and an attempt to explore the concept of patriarchy as it operates *both* with *and* outside capitalism (Kuhn and Wolpe, 1978). However, socialist or Marxist feminists still claim that feminism cannot succeed without socialism, so that for many of them socialism still retains its essential priority. Moreover, this pull of loyalties is likely to continue until there is a solution to the problems of the relationship between feminism and socialism that can satisfy the goals of socialists on the one hand and feminists on the other.

Ideology, however, is only one aspect of feminism. A social movement must also have an organization of some kind, however loosely structured; it must have leaders with strategies; and above all it must have supporters, and in some circumstances allies, if it is to fight and win campaigns. This issue of support, to which we must now turn, is by no means independent of ideology. Supporters are attracted to a movement by its ideology, but may also be repelled by it, so that the ideology to a large extent determines the membership, just as, in the opposite direction, the membership determines the ideology. This can be seen very clearly in the American suffrage movement in the late nineteenth century. Frances Willard persuaded large numbers of religious and conservative women that the vote would promote temperance and safeguard the home, thus attracting large numbers of new supporters to the suffrage movement. In the process, however, the ideology of the suffrage movement became more conservative.

It is for this reason that O'Neill (1968) is wrong in his argument that nineteenth-century feminism failed because it was not radical enough. True, it might be argued, as he does, that without changes in monogamy and the conjugal family many feminist issues cannot be resolved, but it was not the absence of an ideology that prevented nineteenth-century feminism from realizing these goals. As we have seen, a radical reassessment of marriage and the family was central to the ideology of communitarian socialism in both Britain and in the United States, which indeed saw most of the practical experiments in putting such an ideology into practice. Moreover, there were always adherents of this ideology, and by the turn of the century there were socialist feminists in both countries prepared to follow these ideals in their own lives. Yet the way of life they adopted would not have appealed to the much greater number of women who were working for suffrage, embracing as it did not only a new attitude to sexuality, but the equally radical doctrines of socialism or anarchism. To assume otherwise is to ignore the very real differences between what I have called the three traditions of feminism. Those whose chief inspiration was evangelical Christianity were removed from the socialist feminists by an intellectual gulf that a common belief in feminism could not bridge. Indeed, if my previous arguments are correct, they held little in common, even in their idea of feminism.

It is necessary, therefore, to examine in some detail what we have learned about the nature of support for feminism, how it has changed over time, and how both the source of the support and its extent relate to ideology, on the one hand, and success and failure on the other. To do this it will be necessary to make a distinction between a mass movement, a pressure group and a radical sect, because feminism, throughout its history, has been all of these. In its origin, as we have seen, feminism was a radical ideology presenting a role for women so different from what was customary that public opinion was outraged. It is difficult at the present time to realize to the full what it cost these early feminists to break away from convention even when we read their own accounts, so commonplace today are the acts they performed or the changes they advocated. The earliest feminists were exceptional women, with great courage and unconventional minds. Even the men who supported them had to display unusual capacities and it is no surprise that the women's first male allies in the United States had already suffered hatred and violence in their advocacy of the abolition of slavery.

If, however, feminism was to achieve its aim, it had to win support for its arguments, and this involved it, from the start, in a search for allies as well as in an educational programme to convert women to the cause and turn feminism into a mass movement. A problem in the search for support was the necessity to appeal to men as well as to women. This was not simply to give a broad base to the movement, but because women were excluded not simply from the vote but from most, if indeed not all, significant areas of decision-making. In the early years of the movement, therefore, there was a constant search to secure men as allies, whether, at one extreme, to act as chairmen in mixed meetings or, at the other, to instigate and carry through new legislation on such issues as property rights, or ultimately, the vote. Later, especially once the vote was won, women were no longer so dependent on men. Furthermore, experience had taught them that the majority at least would always put their own interests first. In the twentieth century, therefore, women themselves became a political force, occasionally in the role of a politician, but more usually organized as a group, whether this was a women's club, a professional association or, particularly in Britain, women in the trade union movement, the Labour Party or the Co-operative Women's Guild. Finally, in parts of the modern movement, men are rejected altogether. They are sought neither as allies nor as converts.

It has been one of the weaknesses of feminism that women as a whole have not been enthusiastic feminists. There have always been prominent women to argue an anti-feminist cause, and this is as true today as it was in the nineteenth century. Women, too, are always prominent in anti-feminist organizations. For much of its history feminism has appealed to a small minority of women and it is only occasionally, as for example during the suffrage campaign or, more recently, at the start of the new feminism, that it begins to approach a mass movement. Studies in the United States show that, when men and women are polled on issues of women's rights, women are not very different from men in their answers. Moreover, there is evidence to support the view that the greatest change over time since 1945 has been in the opinions of men, who are now much more likely to support equal rights for women. Education and age are related to attitudes however, and education in particular seems to make a great deal of difference, particularly to women (Bozeman *et al.*, 1977). However, even on such a feminist issue as abortion, women as a whole are *less* likely to support it than are men (Francome, 1979). It is not, therefore, a case of simple confrontation between men and women.

Women's organizations, on the other hand, while not necessarily feminist, have at times rallied to support feminist goals, and one important aspect of most successful feminist campaigns has been the way in which the support of women's groups that are not normally overtly feminist provides not merely numbers but the appearance, and indeed the reality, of respectability for the cause in question. What has significantly failed to happen is the organization of women's votes into anything even approaching a woman's party. In the United States, it is true, such a party was formed, but it remained a very small elite group and was never a party in any real sense of the term. Women have increasingly made use of their vote, but they have not used it in the interests of women. Nor have women politicians, as we have seen, organized themselves other than sporadically in this way, and many, in fact, have avoided what they regard as 'women's questions'.

It is for this reason that the vote has been dismissed as unimportant for women. Such a view has its attractions and there is no doubt at all that women's suffrage has failed to achieve the hopes of those who campaigned for it. Nevertheless, it overlooks the fact that women are no longer altogether without political power and that, potentially at least, this must be taken into account, and indeed has sometimes been taken into account by politicians anxious not to lose what they at least conceive of as the 'woman's vote'. Moreover, even if that power has not been used in the past, either by voters or indeed by women in politics, there are at least some indications especially on issues like abortion law reform, that it might be used more effectively in the future.

The failure, for most of its history, to secure mass support for its policies has meant that the feminist movement has relied to a large extent on pressure group policies. While never ignoring either petitions or processions, feminist leaders in both countries have relied mainly on lobbying and other tactics to exert direct pressure on legislators. Almost all the early feminist victories, while the movement as a movement was almost non-existent, were achieved in this way, and it remained a favoured tactic even after the vote was won. In the 1920s, for example, both the Women's Party in the United States and the various feminist organizations in Britain made use of this method, and it was also the chief tactic of the modern equal rights movement in both Britain and the United States. While sometimes successful in securing legislation reforms, it is however unsuitable for securing the larger changes that the more radical feminsits require. Nor is it likely to be successful unless the legislators themselves can be convinced either that the change is in itself desirable or that a large body of opinion is in its favour. For this reason feminism has always needed the support of a mass movement, and when there is general apathy about feminist goals the movement languishes.

The alliances into which feminism has been drawn in its need for support have also had an important influence upon the movement. To some extent the choice of allies has been determined by ideological considerations and in some cases, as we have seen, individual women were drawn into feminism after they had already become committed to another cause. The main nineteenth-century alliances — with the anti-slavery movement, with temperance and with moral reform — were all of this kind. On the other hand, by the end of the century there were many feminists whose attachment to feminist principles was secondary to their concern for welfare or for socialism. For such women, feminism was one of a cluster of causes inspired by moral or social principles that derived in large part from an evangelical tradition of utopianism and moral perfectability. Even the commitment of twentieth-century feminists to welfare has much the same origin, deriving as it does essentially from nineteenth-century evangelical philanthropy. If such a version of feminism had in common with evangelical Christianity its moral fervour and its commitment to reform, it also shared its attitude to sexuality, which, while condemning the double standard of sexual morality, also denied many of the pleasures of sex to both men and women.

The strength of the evangelical tradition in feminism has also resulted in opposition on the part of many feminists to alliances with causes deriving from different traditions. Perhaps the most obvious, and indeed the most important, of these was the resistance of nineteenth-century feminists to the birth control movement. Fundamentally secularist, even hedonist, it came into inevitable conflict with the evangelical background to feminism. Not surprisingly, the socialist feminists in the late nineteenth century embraced the birth control movement with whole-hearted enthusiasm, and these women in both Britain and the United States looked for their allies to the new writers on female sexuality, like Havelock Ellis, and to socialist or anarchist movements of the extreme left. In their alliances therefore, as in their ideologies, the socialist and evangelical traditions are in conflict. Occasionally, feminists from different traditions come together to work towards a common goal. The campaign for the vote is the most obvious example of a union between feminists of different traditions, particularly in the United States where there was no division between adult suffrage and a property vote. Such periods of unity are, however, usually short-lived, since the contradictions between the traditions cannot be obscured for very long.

Nothing that has been said so far in this chapter allows us to place the feminists in their social context. We need to know in more detail not only the appeal of feminism, but the appeal of different kinds of feminism to different groups of women. This is not a question that can be answered with a great deal of precision, partly because we do not have the necessary information, partly because the issue is more complex than it at first appears. Nevertheless the preceding chapters can provide us with at least some tentative answers.

Perhaps the most frequent way to classify feminists is in terms of their social class background, and on such a system of classification most of them emerge as overwhelmingly middle class. This is as true of the modern movement as of the nineteenth century; the only exceptions are women in the trade union movement and women in working-class organizations like the Labour Party and the Women's Co-operative Guild. Even in these organizations, middle-class women often took the lead, as we can see for example in the part played by Dora Russell and other middle-class women in the Labour Party campaign for providing birth control information to working-class women in the 1920s. It would be a mistake, however, to assume from this that feminism was simply a reflection of middle-class discontent. Certainly much feminism, including the modern movement, represents middle-class attitudes and aspirations, but this is not by any means a simple expression of self-interest. In order to understand it we must take account of the powerful impetus within feminism towards philanthropy, which finds strong expression in both evangelical and socialist feminism.

It is equal rights feminism, of course, that reflects in its clearest and most obvious form the middle-class nature of the feminist protest. Much of it was concerned with opening the professions to middle-class girls, improving their education and securing their property after marriage. Not all of the women who worked for these aims were personally involved in the outcome, but all were restricted in their outlook to women of their own class. Even the campaign for the vote was, as we have seen, often conducted in elitist and, in the United States, racist terms. Similarly, some of the fight for equal rights in education and employment in the modern movement has been represented as in the interest of educated women only. This is not to suggest that all of the benefits won for women were available only to the middle clases. Rather the argument is that middle-class women, and sometimes only middle-class women, were in a position to take advantage of these provisions.

It is when we turn to the other traditions that the situation becomes more complex, since in neither evangelical nor socialist feminism were the middle-class women working for themselves. In the evangelical tradition the motives were clearly philanthropic.

Women worked for temperance, for moral reform, for protective legislation and minimum wages, for increased welfare for mothers and children, and eventually even for birth control and abortion, for what they perceived as the needs of the poor. To reinterpret their motives as self-interest it is necessary to argue that they were concerned to protect middle-class values and the middle-class ways of life, that in doing so they sometimes, perhaps even always, misinterpreted the needs of the poor, or that, in relation to the true needs of the poor, their efforts were only ameliorative and indeed were intended to preserve the status quo and prevent the possibility of any real change. There is some truth in all of these assertions, although in some of their forms they falsify the motives of some of the individuals involved, and they certainly overlook the real benefits that some of the reforms conferred. At the very least, however, we must concede that there were aspects to all of these campaigns that were not in the interests of those they were intending to help, and I need perhaps only give the example of protective legislation to make the point. Moreover, there was a tendency for each one of these causes to pass over from simple philanthropy to social control. Temperance and moral reform are perhaps easy examples, but I have already noted the tendency of the birth control movement to merge with eugenics. Finally, in the alliance between feminism and each of these issues, there was a strong tendency for the feminist arguments to be weakened and even to be lost altogether so that in some instances, as in some aspects of the welfare state, the result was anti-feminist in its implications.

Socialist feminists, to a considerable extent, have also been middle-class in origin, and to some extent too have been motivated by similar philanthropic principles as the evangelical feminists. The difference perhaps lies in the greater tendency to work with and through working-class groups themselves. It is in this context certainly that one hears the authentic voice of organized working-class women. This is also, of course, one of the most important features distinguishing British feminism from feminism in the United States, and it is a difference, interestingly, that characterizes modern feminism just as much as feminism in the past. Working-class feminism, when it emerges, appears to be determinedly practical and to make demands for birth control and abortion, day nurseries and other measures designed to make the lives of working-class wives and mothers easier, and there is no evidence that it supports the more radical critique of marriage and the family that is often argued by both socialist and radical feminists in the modern movement.

Social class background is, however, only one way of dividing women. An alternative classification, and one that appears to have special relevance for feminism, is marriage. The particular significance for single women of nineteenth-century equal rights feminism has often been pointed out. Indeed the problem of unmarried women, especially of the middle classes, was often used by feminists and others as a justification for the provision of better educational facilities for girls and of employment opportunities for women. Moreover, the feminists were concerned with the provision of alternatives to marriage not only for those women who could not marry but for those who actually preferred a life of celibacy. Indeed, as we have seen, in both Britain and the United States the first generation of college girls did in fact marry less frequently, although this tendency was not maintained after the first world war. This is not to suggest that marriage and a career were never combined in practice. In general, however, throughout the inter-war years and into the 1950s a career and marriage tended for most girls to appear as alternatives (Roland and Harris, 1979). Moreover, by this time the surplus of women had disappeared and marriage rates reached an unprecedented level.

It was not until the late 1950s that middle-class women began in any numbers to continue with their work after marriage. In consequence, in the years between 1920 and the 1950s many of the issues that had been of central concern to nineteenth-century feminists almost disappeared from view. In part this was because the success of many equal rights campaigns led a lot of feminists to believe that the battle was over. By the 1920s not only was the vote won, or virtually won, but women had succeeded in opening most of the doors not only to higher education but to professional associations. Some institutions, like Cambridge for example, remained obstinately closed, but Oxford had yielded; and if the Church was barred to women this was no longer true of medicine and law. What was not realized to the full until much later was the limited extent to which women took advantage of these opportunities, and the disadvantages experienced by those who did. Women in the professions were often well aware of the particular problems they faced with respect to both earnings and promotion (Hummer, 1978), but these issues did not become of general concern until the resurgence of equal rights feminism in the 1960s.

Undoubtedly the Depression was a factor here, since it not only increased discrimination against women but led to the imposition of marriage bars in, for example, the civil service and teaching that made it impossible for women in these occupations to combine marriage and a career even if they had wished. Moreover, after the war early marriage and the baby boom turned even educated girls away from the idea of a career. The consequence was to equate issues of equal rights in education and employment, even in the minds of feminists, with the needs of a limited number of *single* professional women.

This is not to suggest that nineteenth-century feminism was exclusively concerned with the problems of single women. In both Britain and the United States organized feminism was involved in legal struggles over such issues as women's rights to their property and earnings and to the custody of children. However, whatever the abstract justice of these claims, and whatever the hardships of individual women involved, there is little doubt that most married women in the middle classes were not personally involved in disputes about property and earnings or the custody of children. Only when divorce became widespread after the second world war were issues of this kind of very general concern to married women in both the middle and the working classes.

Evangelical feminism shared with equal rights feminism both a concern with the double standard of sexual morality and, by claiming that low wages were a cause of prostitution, an interest, shown very clearly by Josephine Butler, in the education of girls and job opportunities for both middle-class and working-class women. Nevertheless, the main thrust of evangelical feminism was philanthropic, and this is apparent both in its links with temperance and the purity campaigners and, later, in its involvement in the development of welfare legislation. Moreover, as we have seen, much of the emphasis of evangelical feminism was on a traditional view of marriage and the family. Indeed it has been argued that welfare feminism, in its support of the welfare state, did a great deal to buttress ideas of the family wage, with the husband as the breadwinner and the wife as a dependant. Family allowances, which might have been developed in the direction of economic independence for housewives, were allowed to become part of a welfare policy for the relief of poverty. Protective legislation, especially in the United States, was also developed along lines that emphasized the differences between men and women. Although welfare feminism paid a great deal of attention to the needs of women and children, almost all of its effort went into the attempt to protect the traditional family.

Very much the same arguments can be applied to the feminism of the labour movement. The trade unions, as we have seen, were committed to the 'family wage' throughout virtually the whole period of this study and this was, and to a large extent still is, generally advocated by the labour movement in its conception of the welfare state. Even the organized women in the movement have tended to accept the arguments of the welfare feminists and to have placed their claims in the context of better welfare provision for women and children. On the whole, therefore, when feminism has turned to a consideration of the special needs of married women, there has been a preoccupation with the health and welfare of working-class women and especially with the relief of poverty, rather than with pressing for changes in the role of women in the family.

It may be argued, of course, that married women themselves have no fault to find with the traditional family and their traditional roles. It is significant that the welfare feminists, some of whom were married, turned their attention almost exclusively to the problems of poverty and ill-health of working-class mothers and did not, until the rise of the modern movement, seriously question the role of women as wives and mothers in either middle- or working-class families, nor indeed did they issue any real challenge to the authority vested by either custom or law in the husband and father. Yet such a critique is absolutely central to modern feminism. Undoubtedly, whatever discontent was felt by individual women it did not during these years find expression in any organized movement or organized protest. Women who were dissatisfied may have blamed themselves, or even their husbands, but they did not, at this time, blame the institution of marriage itself.

The acceptance by women of their role in the traditional family is also important in understanding both the lack of widespread support for those feminists who do criticize women's role in the family as well as the tendency of women to embrace anti-feminist beliefs and organizations. The current anti-ERA campaign in the United States, organized by a woman and campaigning to women, is only one example of the opposition by women to feminist aims. Similarly we may note the active presence of women in anti-abortion campaigns.

One of the most important ways in which women may come to challenge their traditional role is through involvement in the labour market. Indeed it is precisely by this means, according to orthodox Marxist theory, that the emancipation of women will eventually be brought about. It is frequently argued, too, that the move by married women, and particularly middle-class women, into jobs in the 1950s and 1960s has had an important part to play in the rise of the new feminist movement. Faced by discrimination in employment, by lack of promotion possibilities, by the failure to achieve equal pay, married women in employment began to support the campaigns of NOW and similar organizations, turning what had been essentially a lobbying campaign into a mass movement. At the same time, it is assumed that the growing number of married women in industry is likely to increase the numbers of women trade unionists, so making it possible for women to have a greater voice in trade union affairs and trade union policies.

It is clear that the simple involvement of married women in either manual or white-collar employment will not in itself provide the conditions for emancipation. Women in such employment suffer from the division of labour in the family and the work-place both in societies like Britain and the United States and in communist countries like the USSR and Czechoslovakia (Heitlinger, 1979; Garnsey, 1978). The personal frustrations that this gives rise to may easily remain at the personal level, and the opportunities for the politicization of discontent provided for example by the trade union movement, or by political parties or by feminist groups themselves, may not be taken by women already overburdened by their dual role. Nor, for most women, does employment provide the economic independence that would enable them to break their traditional dependence on marriage for their economic as well as their emotional needs. It is not likely therefore, in itself, to lead to any change either in women's objective position or, even, in their attitude to marriage and the family unless it is accompanied by a specifically feminist consciousness. Possibly, however, and some aspects of the modern women's movement give grounds to believe that this has been so, it provides the conditions for a feminist critique that not only examines discrimination in the work-place but explores the consequences of the present allocation of roles in the home.

Finally, we may examine the part played in the modern movement by the increase in single-parent families, which has mainly been the consequence of the rapid rise in divorce in recent years (Friedan, 1977, p. 175). Such families challenge both the notion of the traditional conjugal family and the traditional conception of male and female roles. Moreover, they do this both at the personal level, where men and women are forced to take on unaccustomed tasks, and at the political level, where the basic assumptions of the welfare state on family roles completely break down. It is not possible to assess, at this stage, the contribution that this kind of rethinking has made to the resurgence of feminism. Certainly, as we have seen, a section of the radical feminists see the family of the future as some combination of women and children with the state providing either financial assistance or child care, or a combination of both, but in either case independent, or more or less independent, of male support. Whether these alternatives to traditional marriage will ever become commonplace is a matter for conjecture, but what is interesting for our purpose is that this particular ideological challenge to the dominance of the conjugal family comes at a time when the institution itself is in the process of change. It is possible, therefore, that those women who have themselves passed through the experience of marital breakdown are more willing to accept the radical feminists' critique for the conjugal family.

With these divisions in mind, it becomes very clear that women can only be described as a class in a very limited sense. Although all women share some experiences in common, there is also a great deal that divides them, and the needs of working-class women differ from those of middle-class women just as those of single women are not the same as those of married women, or those of women at work the same as those of housewives at home. We can see these conflicting interests at work, for example, in issues like equal pay and the marriage bar. Women supporting themselves, and perhaps supporting dependants as well, often argue that married women should not work, especially at times when unemployment is high. Consequently, support for the marriage bar and the 'family wage' is not confined to men. Similarly, equal pay may appear as a threat to women who fear that it is only their low wages that make them attractive to employers. Protective legislation, too, may appear in quite a different guise to women seeking promotion or the entry to skilled trades. Moreover, women who have spent their lives in a successful adaptation to their traditional role and whose whole identity is absorbed in that of the wife and mother have a personal investment in marriage and the family that the radical feminists are not likely to share. Such women may well be not simply indifferent but violently anti-feminist.

It is also important to recognize that the relationship of men and women is not that of other opposing groups in society since both marriage and motherhood involve a level of emotional inter-dependence that is not found in any other relationship. This is fully recognized by the radical feminists and this is why they attack at both the political and the personal level in their slogan 'the personal is political'. Moreover, they condemn not only male aggression in the form of rape or other violence against women, but tenderness and affection, seeing both equally as aspects of the domination of the male. It is for this reason that the more extreme of them advocate the rejection of heterosexual relationships so that women can be emotionally free. This position is a perfectly logical one and may well appeal to those who have no desire for such relationships or who have been hurt by them, but for other women, and especially those already involved in such relationships, it is more likely to turn them against feminism than to convert them.

The relationship between ideology and support is therefore a very complex one. A particular ideological position both attracts recruits to a social movement and reflects the needs and aspirations of those who are already members. To look at a social movement over time is to see a process of change in ideology and in membership in which both interact with each other but also reflect the changing social context in which the movement is set. To understand the rise of modern feminism we need to take into account a whole complexity of interrelationships, in which the political mood of the 1960s and the changing position of women, and especially middle-class women, in the work force as a result of an economic boom and a shortage of labour were perhaps the most important although certainly not the only ingredients. The radical direction taken by feminist ideology reflects both the left-wing context in which the movement has developed and the nature of the membership, which is predominantly both highly educated and middle class. Such an ideology, however, also repels those who find its radicalism uncongenial and it is not surprising to find studies indicating that housewives in particular find it inimical (Welch, 1975; Stott, 1978, p. 214). On the other hand, the very success of a social movement can change its ideology, making it more conservative. This happened, as we have seen, to the American suffrage movement, but it has also happened to radical feminism, which, Bouchier has argued, has become more reformist as it has attracted a wider range of supporters. Indeed he suggests that, for a movement like radical feminism, 'in order to gain a hearing as a legitimate group, major concessions may have to be made in the direction of reformism' (1978, p. 164).

What then can be said about the future of feminism? Clearly it would be foolish to assume that the present level of feminist activity will continue, and there are in fact already signs that perhaps it has passed its peak. Nevertheless, without venturing into prediction, it is possible to estimate chances for the future, and at the very least to indicate some of the conditions that are favourable for the success of a feminist movement and those that are not. From this point of view it is obvious that feminists can hardly be optimistic. The very conditions that gave rise to the modern movement have already gone: the radical political mood is over and the economic boom that gave women most of their opportunities in the work force has been replaced by recession and unemployment. To the extent that modern feminism owed not only its existence but its success to these two factors, the future must be in doubt. Nor is it safe to assume that the set-back to women's aspirations in the field of employment will lead to a heightening of feminist consciousness. The unemployment of the 1930s, which certainly harmed women's opportunities, especially of married women in professional and white-collar employment, had the effect of depressing feminist aspirations, and these were years in which feminism as both an ideology and a movement began seriously to decline. Whether this will happen again depends, to some extent, on the ability of women's groups to retain both members and commitment, but if there is a large-scale return of women to domesticity, especially in the middle classes, then there is little reason to expect such commitment to survive.

At the same time it also has to be recognized that the current depression finds a feminist movement more aggressive and more unified than feminism in the early 1930s. Attempts to impose marriage bars, for example, may meet with much more organized opposition than in the 1930s. Consequently, even if feminist advances are unlikely, the movement may be more successful in blocking measures that are actually retrogressive. So far, for example, British feminists, if they have made no progress in the 1970s towards their goal of abortion on demand, have at least prevented any change in the law that would make abortion more difficult.

In general, too, the mood of modern feminism is less complacent than in the early 1930s. In the 1920s and 1930s feminism in Britain and the United States was still largely under the influence of the evangelical tradition with its conservative assessment of women's role. Moreover, many feminists at that time believed that, with the success of the suffrage campaign, the battle was virtually won and that all that remained was the task of educating women for their political responsibilities. Today the dominant tradition, particularly in Britain, is socialist feminism, and this provides it not only with a radical, not to say revolutionary, ideology but with organizational ties with the socialist and labour movements. In the United States, where such a tie is absent, the future is more precarious. Much of the impetus in the 1960s came from equal rights feminism and this may not survive the change in political mood and economic climate. Radical feminism, in spite of its origins within the American left, has developed isolationist and exclusionist tendencies that may have left it vulnerable. Perhaps its greatest significance for the future, and this may also be true of Britain, is in its grass-roots organization, which, if it can be maintained, is a powerful source of mass support when it can be mobilized for particular issues.

It may also be argued, although this is highly speculative, that a number of changes are occurring in Britain and the United States that may be conducive to the development of feminist consciousness. The rise of the one-parent family has already been mentioned, since it provides both men and women with experiences that take them outside the traditional division of labour within the family. There is also some evidence that fathers spend more time with their children, even if only in the more 'attractive' aspects of child care. Given that this trend continues, it may go some way to break down the rigid sex-role stereotyping that, by seeing women as 'natural' mothers, denies fathers both the physical care of young children and the qualities of caring and tenderness that are associated with this role. Moreover, recent moves, often feminist inspired, to reduce sex-typing in schools and to break down the stereotyping of men's and women's occupations will, if they succeed, challenge the traditional division of labour in the workplace. Such developments suggest that notions of femininity and masculinity *may* be less rigid in the future as women are allowed to develop more of their 'male' and men more of their 'female' nature. On the other hand, it is all too easy to be overoptimistic, and the attempts of the feminists to change the schools may be as unsuccessful as their attempts to legislate for equal pay.

Role sharing within marriage *is* possible, but it cuts across the demands of the work situation, threatening a highly competitive career and, even when that is not an issue, depriving the husband of much of his leisure time. It would seem that only those men deeply committed to the principle of equality are prepared for the sacrifices that it entails. For a few families, paid domestic help is at least a partial solution, for others the decision not to have children, but for most couples the answer lies in structural changes that allow a greater community involvement in child care or, alternatively, in a change in the nature of work that enables it to combine with domestic responsibilities rather than, as at present, to conflict with them. This would allow both husbands and wives to participate on equal terms in the world of work and in the care of children within the family. The goal of androgyny, therefore, does not depend simply on changing attitudes, although this is necessarily a part of it. Even if it does not, as radical feminism does, demand the abolition of either marriage or the family, it cannot be achieved without quite drastic changes in the structure of both the family and the work-place.

All of this, however, implies some level of agreement about the nature of feminism, and one of the arguments of this book has been that such agreement is limited and that the different faces of feminism actually point in different directions. For this reason feminists themselves differ in their assessment both of what is wrong with the position of women in society and of what is needed to put it right. While part of this disagreement stems from a different analysis of the causes of women's disabilities, part stems also from a different perception of the nature of woman herself. An emphasis on the essential similarity of men and women is difficult to reconcile with the idealization of women that lies behind some versions of modern feminism, just as it has characterized evangelical feminism in the past. Firestone's essentially androgynous solution conflicts therefore with those other radical feminists who celebrate women's maternal function. Indeed the androgynous solution, in contrast to the exclusionist tendencies in much radical feminism, would seem, in its implications at least, to be trying to draw men and women closer together.

A further and deeply significant controversy within modern feminism is concerned, fundamentally, with what one may call the limits of reform. Socialist feminists, in particular, see the present division of labour in the family and the work-place as so *necessary* to capitalism that only the transition to socialism can break it down. Consequently they believe that both equal rights feminism and the development of a more androgynous society can have only the most limited effects on the essentially patriarchal nature of capitalist society. However, while it can be demonstrated that patriarchy serves the needs of capitalism, it is also perfectly clear that it can serve the needs of socialism equally well. This is now widely recognized, and socialist feminists are currently trying to work out the links between both feminism and capitalism and feminism and socialism at a more satisfactory theoretical level. In the meantime, however, the problem of the limits of feminist reform within both capitalism and socialism still remains unresolved.

It is the limitations of socialist feminism as a theory that lie behind the radical feminists' attempt to define the problem as one of patriarchy and to see this as a universal, even indeed a historically constant, source of oppression. As we have seen, however, this often is no more than the descriptive statement that men have power over women, and the solution offered is sometimes no more than the decision to exclude men from women's lives. Equal rights feminists, of course, have always argued that men occupy positions of power in society, but their solution, in which the fight for suffrage was the most important, was to win for women the right to share power with men. The androgynous position within feminism takes this further by trying to make it easier for women to do this by greater role sharing within the family and by minimizing sex-role socialization within the family and the school. The radical feminists, on the other hand, do not trust men to share power, and reject this solution as unworkable. Certainly the record of men as allies is not a very inspiring one, and the attitude of the radical feminists is at least understandable. Nevertheless, if it is perhaps too distrustful of men, it is certainly too trustful in its attitude to women. The concept of sisterhood, if politically valuable in the development of a feminist consciousness, is unreliable in practice if it leads to a romanticized view of woman that sees her as the repository of all the virtues. Yet this is the natural consequence of an ideology that sees men as the enemy. The androgynous solution, which sees both masculinity and femininity as artificial constructs and seeks to preserve the best of each, if perhaps also decidedly on the romantic side, seems to be closer to reality and to offer more possibilities for feminism as a practical ideology in the future. Like equal rights feminism, however, it may prove to offer only limited opportunities for change.

This comparison of feminism in Britain and the United States, if it has emerged with any conclusions at all, has tended to do so for both Britain and the United States. What was most striking in actually making the comparison were not the differences but the similarities between the two countries. Time and time again developments occurred at the same time in the two countries, in spite of very large differences in the social and political context as well as in the style of leadership. This is not to suggest that the two movements were identical, for there were clearly divergences, but these were few and relatively unimportant compared with those aspects that were shared in common. In the case of suffrage, for example, the differences appear as variations on a theme, when we consider the almost identical timing of the two campaigns. Another fascinating parallel is the relationship between the birth control movement and feminism, which again was almost identical in the two countries, even to the striking similarities in the personalities of both Marie Stopes and Margaret Sanger.

Moreover, the main source of such differences as were found was not the nature of the leadership but the different social and political context in which developments took place. Of these, the study has singled out the greater strength of evangelical feminism as perhaps the most important way in which feminism in the United States differed from feminism in Britain and this is quite clearly a reflection of the much greater impact of the evangelical movement on American society. The other major difference is the much greater significance of the labour movement in Britain, and this is just as clearly linked to the weakness, if not indeed virtual absence, of such a movement in America. However it might be argued that these are still differences in emphasis and do not destroy the picture of two movements sharing a very similar if not identical chronology, a similar if again not identical set of ideologies, and similar if not identical goals and strategies.

In so far as one of the aims of the study was to use the differences between the two countries to explore the nature of feminism as a general phenomenon, the extent of the similarity is somewhat disappointing. Nevertheless, from another point of view the very similarities suggest that the conclusions that have been drawn, albeit tentatively, may have wider implications. No attempt has been made to use the framework of analysis developed here to examine, even cursorily, the development of feminism elsewhere, although clearly such a further comparison would be eminently desirable. In particular it would be useful to examine countries like France, which are characterized by the absence of a feminist movement. Indeed, France is particularly interesting because it is the home not only of the Enlightenment tradition but also of communitarian socialism. Yet neither led to an organized feminist movement of the kind that developed not only in Britain and the United States but also in Germany (Evans, 1976). If feminism, where it has occurred, shows the similarity suggested by the present study, cases of its absence would seem to have a particularly valuable part to play. Moreover it would seem that attention might need to be paid not only to Protestantism but also to evangelical Christianity, as well as to the economic changes that resulted in the rise of the bourgeoisie, the separation of home and work and the cult of domesticity. Only in this way will some of the seeming paradoxes that still obscure many aspects of feminism be resolved.

Bibliography

Abrams, Phillip and McCulloch, Andrew (1976) *Communes, Sociology and Society* Cambridge, Cambridge University Press.

Adam, Ruth (1975) *A Woman's Place 1910—1975* London, Chatto and Windus.

Addams, Jane (1960) *A Centennial Reader* (edited by Emily Cooper Johnson) New York, Macmillan.

Addams, Jane (1974) *My Friend, Julia Lathrop* New York, Arno Press. Originally published New York, Macmillan, 1935.

Alaya, Flavia (1977) 'Victorian science and the "genius" of woman' *Journal of the History of Ideas* 38, pp. 261—80.

Alexander, Thomas G. (1970) 'An experiment in progressive legislation: the granting of woman suffrage in Utah in 1870' *Utah Historical Quarterly* 38, pp. 20—30.

Amundsen, Kirsten (1971) *The Silenced Majority. Women in American Democracy* Englewood Cliffs, NJ, Prentice Hall.

Anderson, Olive (1969) 'Women preachers in mid-Victorian Britain: some reflections on feminism, popular religion and social change' *Historical Journal* 12, pp. 467—84.

Annan, N. G. (1955) 'The intellectual aristocracy' in J. H. Plumb (ed.) *Studies in Social History* London, Longman, pp. 241—87.

Arrington, L. J. and Bitton, D. (1979) *The Mormon Experience* London, Allen and Unwin.

Atkinson, Paul (1978) 'Fitness, feminism and schooling' in Delamont and Duffin, pp. 92—133.

Aveling, Edward and Marx, Eleanor (1886) *The Woman Question* London, S. Sonnenschein.

Baer, Judith A. (1978) *The Chains of Protection. The Judicial Response to Women's Labor Legislation* London and Westport, Greenwood Press.

264

Banks, J. A. and Olive (1964) *Feminism and Family Planning in Victorian England* Liverpool, Liverpool University Press.

Bealey, Frank and Pelling, Henry (1958) *Labour and Politics 1900—1906* London, Macmillan.

Berg, Barbara (1978) *The Remembered Gate: Origins of American Feminism. The Woman and the City 1800—1860* New York, Oxford University Press.

Berger, Bennet M. (1973) 'Child-raising practices of the communal family' in Rosabeth Moss Kanter *Communes, Creating and Managing the Collective Life* New York, Harper and Row.

Berkman, Joyce Avrech (1979) *Olive Schreiner. Feminism on the Frontier* London, Edens Press.

Bernard, Jessie (1971) 'The status of women in modern patterns of culture' in Cynthia Fuchs Epstein and William J. Goode (eds) *The Other Half. Roads to Women's Equality* Englewood Cliffs, NJ, Prentice Hall.

Bernard, Jessie (1979) 'Women as voters. From redemptive to futurist role' in Jean Lipman Blumen and Jessie Bernard (eds) *Sage Studies in International Sociology* London, Sage Publications.

Billington, Louis (1966) 'Some connections between British and American reform movements 1830—1860 with special reference to the anti-slavery movement' MA thesis, University of Bristol.

Bird, Caroline (1970) *Born Female. The High Cost of Keeping Women Down* New York, David McKay.

Boone, Gladys (1942) *The Women's Trade Union League in Great Britain and the U.S.A.* New York, AMS Press.

Bouchier, David (1978) *Idealism and Revolution. New Ideologies of Liberation in Britain and the United States* London, Edward Arnold.

Bouchier, David (1979) 'The deradicalisation of feminism' *Sociology* 13, pp. 387—402.

Bouten, Jacob (1975) *Mary Wollstonecraft and the Beginnings of Female Emancipation in France and England* Philadelphia, Porcupine Press.

Bozeman, B. *et al.* (1977) 'Continuity and change in opinions about sex roles' in Marianne Githens and Jewel L. Prestage *A Portrait of Marginality. The Political Behavior of American Women* New York, David McKay.

Bristow, Edward J. (1977) *Vice and Vigilance. Purity Movements in Britain since 1700* Dublin, Gill and McMillan.

Brown, Ford K. (1961) *Fathers of the Victorians: The Age of Wilberforce* Cambridge University Press.

Budd, Susan (1977) *Varieties of Unbelief. Atheists and Agnostics in English Society 1850—1960* London, Heinemann.

Burton, Hester (1949) *Barbara Bodichon 1827—1891* London, John Murray.

Bussey, Gertrude and Tims, Margaret (1965) *Women's International League for Peace and Freedom 1915—1965* London, Allen and Unwin.

Campbell, Angus (1960) *The American Voter* New York, John Wiley.

Campbell, Barbara Kuhn (1979) *The 'Liberated' Women of 1914. Prominent women in the progressive era* London, UMI Research Press.

Campbell, Flann (1960) 'Birth control and the Christian churches' *Population Studies* 14, pp. 131—47.

Carden, Maren Lockwood (1974) *The New Feminist Movement* New York, Russell Sage.

Carwardine, Richard (1978) *Transatlantic Revivalism. Popular Evangelism in Britain and America 1790—1865* London, Greenwood Press.

Catt, Carrie Chapman and Shuler, Nettie Rogers (1969) *Woman Suffrage and Politics. The Inner History of the Suffrage Movement* London, University of Washington Press. Originally published in 1923.

Chafe, W. H. (1972) *The American Woman. Her Changing Social, Economic and Political Roles 1920—1970* New York, Oxford University Press.

Chamberlin, Hope (1973) *A Minority of Members. Women in the United States Congress* New York, Praeger.

Chambers, Clarke A. (1963) *Seed-time of Reform. American Social Service and Social Action 1918—1933* Minneapolis, University of Minnesota.

Christ, Carol (1977) 'Victorian masculinity and the Angel in the House' in Martha Vicinus (ed.) *A Widening Sphere. Changing Roles of Victorian Women* Bloomington and London, Indiana University Press.

Cisler, Lucinda (1973) 'Abortion law repeal (sort of) A warning to women' in Anne Koedt *et al.* (eds) *Radical Feminism* New York, Quadrangle.

Clark, Clifford E. Jnr (1978) *Henry Ward Beecher. Spokesman for a Middle Class America* Urbana, Chicago, London, University of Illinois Press.

Cole, Margaret (1961) *The Story of Fabian Socialism* London, Heinemann.

Cominos, Peter T. (1963) 'Late Victorian sexual responsibility and the social system' *International Review of Social History* 8, pp. 216—50.

Conway, Jill K. (1974) 'Perspectives on the history of women's education in the United States' *History of Education Quarterly* 14, pp. 1—12.

Cook, Blanche Wiesen (ed.) (1978) *Chrystal Eastman. On Woman and Revolution* London, Oxford University Press.

Cott, Nancy F. (1977) *The Bonds of Womanhood. 'Woman's Sphere' in New England 1780—1835* New Haven and London, Yale University Press.

Cromwell, Otelia (1958) *Lucretia Mott* Cambridge, Mass., Harvard University Press.

Cross, Barbara M. (1965) *The Educated Woman in America* New York, Teachers College Press.

Cross, Whitney R. (1950) *The Burned over District. The Social and Intellectual History of Enthusiastic Religion in Western New York 1800–1850* New York, Cornell University Press.

Davidoff, Leonore *et al.* (1976) 'Landscape with figures: home and community in English society' in Juliet Mitchell and Ann Oakley (eds) *The Rights and Wrongs of Women* Harmondsworth, Penguin.

Davies, Margaret Llewelyn (1918) 'The claims of mothers and children' in Marion Phillips (ed.) *Women and the Labour Party* London, Headly Bros.

Davis, Allen F. (1967) *Spearheads for Reform. The Social Settlements and the Progressive Movement 1890–1914* New York, Oxford University Press.

Davis, Allen F. (1973) *American Heroine. The Life and Legend of Jane Addams* New York, Oxford University Press.

Deacon, Allan and Hill, Michael (1972) 'The problem of "surplus women" in the nineteenth century. Secular and religious alternatives' in *A Sociological Yearbook of Religion* London, SCM Press.

Deckard, Barbara Sinclair (1979) *The Women's Movement* (2nd edition) New York, Harper and Row.

Degler, Carl N. (1956) 'Charlotte Perkins Gilman on the theory and practice of feminism' *American Quarterly* 8, pp.21–39.

Degler, Carl N. (1974) 'What ought to be and what was: Women's sexuality in the nineteenth century' *The American Historical Review* 79, pp. 1467–90.

Delamont, Sara (1978) 'The contradictions in ladies' education' in Delamont and Duffin (eds).

Delamont, Sara and Duffin, Lorna (eds) (1978) *The Nineteenth Century Woman. Her Cultural and Physical World* London, Croom Helm.

Delmar, Rosalind (1976) 'Looking again at Engels' "Origins of the Family, Private Property and the State" ' in Juliet Mitchell and Ann Oakley *The Rights and Wrongs of Women* Harmondsworth, Penguin.

Densmore, Dana (1973) 'Independence from the sexual revolution' in Anne Koedt *et al.* (eds) *Radical Feminism* New York, Quadrangle.

Dingle, A. E. and Harrison, B. H. (1969) 'Cardinal Manning as temperance reformer' *The Historical Journal* 12, pp. 485–510.

Donnison, Jean (1977) *Midwives and Medical Men. A History of Interprofessional Rivalries and Women's Rights* London, Heinemann.

Drinnon, Richard (1970) *Rebel in Paradise. A Biography of Emma Goldman* Boston, Beacon Press.

Dublin, Thomas (1977) 'Women's work and protest in the early Lowell mills' in Milton Cantor and Bruce Laurie (eds) *Class, Sex and the Woman Worker* London, Greenwood Press.

Dubois, Ellen Carol (1978) *Feminism and Suffrage. The Emergence of an Independent Women's Movement in America 1848—1869* Ithaca, London, Cornell University Press.

Duffin, Lorna (1978a) 'The conspicuous consumptive: woman as invalid' in Delamont and Duffin (eds).

Duffin, Lorna (1978b) 'Prisoners of progress: women and evolution' in Delamont and Duffin (eds).

Dye, Nancy Schrom (1977) 'Creating a feminist alliance: sisterhood and class conflict in the New York Women's Trade Union League 1903—1914' in Milton Cantor and Bruce Laurie (eds) *Class, Sex and the Woman Worker* London, Greenwood Press.

Earhart, Mary (1944) *Frances Willard. From Prayer to Politics* Chicago, University of Chicago Press.

Evans, Richard J. (1976) *The Feminist Movement in Germany 1894—1933* London, Sage Publications.

Evans, Richard J. (1977) *The Feminists. Women's Emancipation Movements in Europe, America and Australasia 1840—1920* London, Croom Helm.

Fiedler, Leslie A. (1960) *Love and Death in the American Novel* New York, Criterion Books.

Firestone, Shulasmith (1971) *The Dialectic of Sex. The Case for a Feminist Revolution* London, Jonathan Cape.

Flexner, Eleanor (1974) *Century of Struggle. The Woman's Rights Movement in the United States* New York, Atheneum.

Flynn, Elizabeth Gurley (1960) 'Women in American socialist struggles' *Political Affairs,* April, pp. 33—9.

Francome, Colin (1979) *Breaking Chains* London, the Abortion Law Reform Association, December/January 1979/80.

Freedman, Estelle B. (1974) 'The new woman. Changing views of women in the 1920's' *Journal of American History* 61, pp. 372—93.

Freeman, Jo (1973) 'Women on the move: roots of revolt' in A. Rossi and A. Calderwood (eds) *Academic Women on the Move* New York, Russell Sage.

Freeman, Jo (1975) *The Politics of Women's Liberation* New York, David McKay.

French, Richard D. (1975) *Anti vivisection and Medical Science in Victorian Society* Princeton, Princeton University Press.

Friedan, Betty (1963) *The Feminine Mystique* New York, Norton.

Friedan, Betty (1977) *It Changed My Life. Writings on the Women's Movement* London, Gollancz.

Fryer, Peter (1965) *The Birth Controllers* London, Martin Secker and Warburg.

Fulford, Roger (1956) *Votes for Women. The Story of a Struggle* London, Faber and Faber.

Gaffin, Jean (1977) 'Women and co-operation' in Lucy Middleton (ed.) *Women in the Labour Movement. The British Experience* London, Croom Helm.
Garnsey, Elizabeth (1978) 'Women's work and theories of class stratification' *Sociology* 12, pp. 223—43.
George, Margaret (1973) 'From goodwife to mistress: the transformation of the female in bourgeois culture' *Science and Society* 37, pp. 152—77.
Gilbert, A. D. (1976) *Religion and Society in Industrial England. Church and Chapel in Social Change 1740—1914* London and New York, Longman.
Gilman, Charlotte Perkins (1935) *The Living of Charlotte Perkins Gilman: An Autobiography* New York and London, Appleton-Century.
Gilman, Charlotte Perkins (1972) *The Home, its Work and Influence* Urbana, Chicago, London, University of Illinois Press. Originally published in 1903.
Glennon, Lynda M. (1979) *Women and Dualism. A Sociology of Knowledge Analysis* New York and London, Longman.
Godwin, Anne (1977) 'Early years in the trade union movement' in Lucy Middleton (ed.) *Women in the Labour Movement: The British Experience* London, Croom Helm.
Goldman, Harold (1974) *Emma Paterson. She Led Woman into a Man's World* London, Lawrence and Wishart.
Goldmark, Josephine (1953) *Impatient Crusader. Florence Kelley's Life Story* Urbana, University of Illinois Press.
Gollancz, Victor (ed.) (1917) *The Making of Women. Oxford Essays in Feminism* London, Allen and Unwin.
Gompers, Samuel (1925) *Seventy Years of Life and Labour* London, Hurst and Blackett.
Gordon, Linda (1977) *Woman's Body, Woman's Right. A social history of birth control in America* Harmondsworth, Penguin.
Gordon, Michael (1971) 'From an unfortunate necessity to a cult of mutual orgasm. Sex in American marital education literature 1830—1940' in James M. Henslin *Studies in the Sociology of Sex* New York, Appleton Century Croft.
Gordon, Michael (ed.) (1972) *The Nuclear Family in Crisis. The Search for an Alternative* London, Harper and Row.
Gorham, Deborah (1978) 'The "Maiden Tribute of Modern Babylon" Re-examined: child prostitution and the idea of childhood in late Victorian England' *Victorian Studies* 21, pp. 353—79.
Graham, Otis L. Jnr (1967) *An Encore for Reform. The Old Progressives and the New Deal* New York, Oxford University Press.

Gray, Alexander (1944) *The Socialist Tradition. Moses to Lenin* London, Longman.

Green, Arnold W. and Melnick, Eleanor (1965) 'What has happened to the feminist movement?' in A. V. Gouldner (ed.) *Studies in Leadership* New York, Russell and Russell.

Greenberg, Hazel (1976) *The Equal Rights Amendment. A Bibliographical Study* London, Greenwood Press.

Grimes, Alan P. (1967) *The Puritan Ethic and Woman Suffrage* New York, Oxford University Press.

Gruberg, Martin (1968) *Women in American Politics* Wisconsin, Academic Press.

Gusfield, Joseph R. (1972) *Symbolic Crusade. Status Politics and the American Temperance Movement* (3rd edition) Urbana, Chicago, London, University of Illinois Press.

Hall, Ruth (1977) *Marie Stopes* London, Deutch.

Haller, John S. and Haller, Robin M. (1974) *The Physician and Sexuality in Victorian America* Urbana, Chicago, London, University of Illinois Press.

Hamilton, Roberta (1978) *The Liberation of Women. A Study of Patriarchy and Capitalism* London, Allen and Unwin.

Haney, Robert W. (1960) *Comstockery in America* Boston, Beacon Press.

Harrison, Brian (1971) *Drink and the Victorians. The Temperance Question in England 1815—1872* London, Faber and Faber.

Harrison, Brian (1974) 'State intervention and moral reform in nineteenth century England' in P. Hollis *Pressure from Without in Early Victorian England* London, Edward Arnold.

Harrison, Brian (1978) *Separate Spheres. The Opposition to Women's Suffrage in Britain* London, Croom Helm.

Harrison, J. F. C. (1969) *Robert Owen and the Owenites in Britain and America* London, Routledge and Kegan Paul.

Hays, Elinor Rice (1961) *Morning Star. A Biography of Lucy Stone 1818—1893* New York, Harcourt Brace and World.

Hays, H. R. (1966) *The Dangerous Sex. The Myth of Feminine Evil* New York, Pocket Books.

Heasman, Kathleen (1962) *Evangelicals in Action. An Appraisal of their Social Work in the Victorian Era* London, Bles.

Heitlinger, Alena (1979) *Sex Inequality in the Soviet Union and Czechoslovakia* London, Macmillan.

Hindell, Keith and Simms, Madaleine (1971) *Abortion Law Reformed* London, Peter Owen.

Hogeland, Ronald W. (1971) ' "The female appendage" feminine lifestyles in America 1820—1860' *Civil War History* 17, pp. 101—14.

Holcombe, Lee (1973) *Victorian Ladies at Work. Middle-class working women in England and Wales 1850—1914* Newton Abbott, David and Charles.

Holcombe, Lee (1977) 'Victorian wives and property. Report on the married women's property law 1857—1882' in Martha Vicinus (ed.) *A Widening Sphere. Changing Roles of Victorian Women* Bloomington and London, Indiana University Press.

Hole, Judith and Levine, Ellen (1971) *The Rebirth of Feminism* New York, Quadrangle.

Hollis, Patricia (1979) *Women in Public 1850—1900* London, Allen and Unwin.

Holt, Raymond V. (1938) *The Unitarian Contribution to Social Progress in England* London, The Lindsay Press.

Hopkinson, Diana (1954) *Family Inheritance. A Life of Eva Hubback* London, Staples Press.

Howe, Daniel Walker (1970) *The Unitarian Conscience. Harvard Moral Philosophy 1805—1861* Cambridge, Mass., Harvard University Press.

Hubback, Eva (1947) *The Population of Britain* Harmondsworth, Penguin.

Hummer, Patricia M. (1978) *The Decade of Elusive Promise. Professional Women in the United States 1920—1930* London, UMI Research Press.

Humphreys, B. V. (1958) *Clerical Unions in the Civil Service* London, Blackwell and Mott.

Hynes, Samuel (1968) *The Edwardian Turn of Mind* London, Oxford University Press.

Irwin, Inez Haynes (1921) *The Story of the Woman's Party* New York, Harcourt Brace and Co.

Jacoby, Robin Miller (1977) 'The Women's Trade Union League and American feminism' in Milton Cantor and Bruce Laurie (eds) *Class, Sex and the Woman Worker* London, Greenwood Press.

Jones, M. G. (1952) *Hannah More* Cambridge University Press.

Kamm, Josephine (1966) *Rapiers and Battle-axes. The Women's Movement and its Aftermath* London, Allen and Unwin.

Kenneally, James J. (1973) 'Women and trade unions 1870—1920. The quandary of the reformer' *Labour History* 14, pp. 42—55.

Kenneally, James J. (1978) *Women and American Trade Unions* St Albans, Vermont, Eden Press.

Kennedy, David M. (1970) *Birth Control in America. The Career of Margaret Sanger* London, Yale University Press.

Killham, John (1958) *Tennyson and the Princess. Reflections of an Age* London, University of London Press.

Kingsdale, Jon M. (1973) 'The "poor man's club". Social functions of the urban working-class saloon' *American Quarterly* 25, pp. 473—89.

Kleinberg, Susan J. (1977) 'The systematic study of urban women' in Milton Cantor and Bruce Laurie (eds) *Class, Sex and the Woman Worker* London, Greenwood Press.

Klotzburger, Kay (1973) 'Political action by academic women' in A. Rossi and A. Calderwood (eds) *Academic Women on the Move* New York, Russell Sage.

Knudsen, Dean (1969) 'The declining status of women. Popular myths and the failure of functionalist thought' *Social Forces* 48, pp. 183—93.

Koedt, Anne (1973a) 'The myth of the vaginal orgasm' in Anne Koedt *et al.* (eds) *Radical Feminism* New York, Quadrangle.

Koedt, Anne (1973b) 'Lesbianism and feminism' in Anne Koedt *et al.* (eds) *Radical Feminism* New York, Quadrangle.

Kraditor, Aileen S. (1965) *The Ideas of the Woman Suffrage Movement 1890—1920* New York and London, Columbia University Press.

Kraditor, Aileen S. (1967) *Means and Ends in American Abolitionism: Garrison and his critics on strategy and tactics 1834—1850* New York, Pantheon.

Kugler, Israel (1961) 'The trade union career of Susan Anthony' *Labour History* 2, pp. 90—100.

Kuhn, Anne L. (1947) *The Mother's Role in Childhood Education. New England Concepts 1830—1860* London, Yale University Press.

Kuhn, Annette and Wolpe, Ann Marie (eds) (1978) *Feminism and Materialism: women and modes of production* London, Routledge and Kegan Paul.

Lane, Margaret (1972) *Frances Wright and the Great Experiment* Manchester, Manchester University Press.

Larson, T. A. (1971) 'Emancipating the West's dolls, vassals and hopeless drudges. The origins of woman suffrage in the West' in R. Daniels (ed.) *Essays in Western History in Honor of Professor T. A. Larson* Laramie, University of Wyoming Publications.

Leathard, Audrey (1980) *The Fight for Family Planning* London, Macmillan.

Ledbetter, Rosanna (1976) *A History of the Malthusian League, 1877—1927* Columbus, Ohio State University Press.

Lee, Marcia M. (1977) 'The Equal Rights Amendment: public policy making by means of a constitutional amendment' in David A. Caputo *The Politics of Policy Making in America. 5 Case Studies* San Francisco, W. H. Freeman.

Lemon, J. Stanley (1973) *The Woman Citizen. Social Feminism in the 1920's* Urbana, University of Illinois Press.

Lerner, Gerda (1967) *The Grimké Sisters from South Carolina: Rebels against Slavery* Boston, Houghton Mifflin.

Levine, Daniel (1971) *Jane Addams and the Liberal Tradition* Madison, State Historical Society of Wisconsin.

Lewenhak, Sheila (1977) *Women and Trade Unions* London and Tonbridge, Ernest Benn.

Lewis, Jane (1973) 'Beyond suffrage: English feminism in the 1920s' *The Maryland Historian* 6, pp. 1—17.

Liddington, Jill and Norris, Jill (1978) *One hand tied behind us. The Rise of the Women's Suffrage Movement* London, Virago.

Lutz, Alma (1959) *Susan B. Anthony. Rebel, Crusader, Humanitarian* Boston, Beacon Press.

Macarthur, Mary (1918) 'Women trade unionists' point of view' in Marion Phillips (ed.) *Women and the Labour Party* London, Headley Bros.

McCarthy, Margaret (1977) 'Women in trade unions today' in Lucy Middleton (ed.) *Women in the Labour Movement. The British Experience* London, Croom Helm.

McDonald, Oonagh (1977) 'Women in the Labour Party today' in Lucy Middleton (ed.) *Women in the Labour Movement. The British Experience* London, Croom Helm.

McGovern, James R. (1968) 'The American woman's pre-World War I freedom in manners and morals' *Journal of American History* 55, pp. 315—33.

McGregor, O. R. (1957) *Divorce in England* London, Heinemann.

McGregor, O. R. (1972) 'Equality, sexual values and permissive legislation. The English experience' *Journal of Social Policy* 28, pp. 44—59.

McGuinn, Nicholas (1978) 'George Eliot and Mary Wollstonecraft' in Delamont and Duffin (eds).

McHugh, Paul (1980) *Prostitution and Victorian Social Reform* New York, St Martin's Press.

McLaren, Angus (1976) 'Sex and socialism: the opposition of the French left to birth control in the nineteenth century' *Journal of the History of Ideas* 37, pp. 475—92.

McLaren, Angus (1978) *Birth Control in Nineteenth Century England* London, Croom Helm.

Manton, Jo (1965) *Elizabeth Garrett Anderson* London, Methuen.

Markham, Violet (1953) *Return Passage* London, Oxford University Press.

Meacham, Standish (1977) *A Life Apart. The English Working Class 1890—1914* London, Thames and Hudson.

Meade, Marion (1976) *Free Woman. The Life and Times of Victoria Woodhull* New York, Knopf.

Melder, Keith E. (1977) *Beginnings of Sisterhood. The American Woman's Rights Movement 1800—1850* New York, Schocken Books.

Mezvinsky, Norton (1961) 'An idea of female superiority' *Midcontinent American Studies Journal* 2, pp. 17—26.

Middleton, Lucy (1977) 'Women in labour politics' in Lucy Middleton (ed.) *Women in the Labour Movement. The British Experience* London, Croom Helm.

Millett, Kate (1971) *Sexual Politics* London, Rupert Hart Davis.

Mineka, Francis E. (1972) *The Dissidence of Dissent. The Monthly Repository 1806–1838* New York, Octagon Books.

Minor, Iris (1979) 'Working class women and matrimonial law reform 1890–1914' in David E. Martin and David Rubinstein (eds) *Ideology and the Labour Movement* London, Croom Helm.

Mitchell, David (1967) *The Fighting Pankhursts. A Study in Tenacity* London, Jonathan Cape.

Mitchell, Hannah (1977) *The Hard Way Up* London, Virago.

Mitchell, Juliet (1971) *Woman's Estate* Harmondsworth, Penguin.

Mitchell, Sally (1977) 'Sentiment and suffering: women's recreational reading in the 1860s' *Victorian Studies* 21, pp. 29–45.

Mohr, James C. (1978) *Abortion in America. The Origins and Evolution of National Policy 1800–1900* New York, Oxford University Press.

Morgan, David (1972) *Suffragists and Democrats. The Politics of Woman Suffrage in America* East Lancing, Michigan State University Press.

Morgan, David (1975) *Suffragists and Liberals. The Politics of Woman Suffrage in England* Oxford, Blackwell.

Morgan, Robin (ed.) (1970) *Sisterhood is Powerful, An Anthology of Writings from the Women's Liberation Movement* New York, Random House.

Muncy, Raymond Lee (1973) *Sex and Marriage in Utopian Communities* Bloomington and London, Indiana University Press.

Neale, R. S. (1972) *Class and Ideology in the Nineteenth Century* London, Routledge and Kegan Paul.

Oakley, Mary Ann B. (1972) *Elizabeth Cady Stanton* New York, The Feminist Press.

O'Neill, William L. (1965) 'Divorce in the progressive era' *American Quarterly* 17, pp. 203–17.

O'Neill, William (1968) 'Feminism as a radical ideology' in A. F. Young (ed.) *Dissent. History of American Radicalism* Illinois de Kalb, Northern Illinois University Press.

O'Neill, William (1969a) *Everyone was Brave: the rise and fall of feminism in America* New York, Quadrangle.

O'Neill, William (1969b) *The Woman Movement: Feminism in the United States and England* London, Allen and Unwin.

Oppenheimer, Valerie K. (1967) 'The interaction of demand and supply and its effect on the female labour force in the United States' *Population Studies* 21, pp. 239–59.

Pankhurst, Richard (1954a) 'Anna Wheeler — a pioneer socialist' *Political Quarterly* 25, pp. 132—43.
Pankhurst, Richard (1954b) *William Thompson 1775—1833. Britain's Pioneer Socialist, Feminist, and Co-operator* London, Watts and Co.
Pankhurst, Richard (1957) *The Saint Simonians* London, Sidgwick and Jackson.
Papashvily, Helen Waite (1956) *All the Happy Endings* New York, Harper and Brothers.
Paulson, Ross Evans (1973) *Women's Suffrage and Prohibition: A Comparative Study of Equality and Social Control* Glenview, Ill., Scott Foresman and Co.
Peck, Mary Gray (1944) *Carrie Chapman Catt. A Biography* New York, H. W. Wilson and Co.
Pethick-Lawrence, Emmeline (1938) *My Part in a Changing World* London, Gollancz.
Pethick-Lawrence, F. W. (1943) *Fate has been Kind* London, Hutchinson.
Petrie, Glen (1971) *A Singular Iniquity. The Campaigns of Josephine Butler* London, Macmillan.
Pivar, David J. (1973) *Purity Crusade: sexual morality and social control 1868—1900* Westport, Conn., London, Greenwood Press.
Potts, Malcolm *et al.* (1977) *Abortion* Cambridge, Cambridge University Press.
Prochaska, F. K. (1974) 'Women in English philanthropy 1790—1830' *International Journal of Social History* 19, pp. 426—45.
Pugh, Martin D. (1974) 'Politicians and the woman's vote 1914—1918' *History* 59, pp. 358—74.

Raikes, Elizabeth (1908) *Dorothea Beale of Cheltenham* London, Constable.
Ramelson, Marian (1967) *The Petticoat Rebellion* London, Lawrence and Wishart.
Rathbone, Eleanor (1936) 'Changes in public life' in Ray Strachey (ed.) *Our Freedom and Its Results* London, Hogarth Press.
Reed, Louis S. (1930) *The Labor Philosophy of Samuel Gompers* Port Washington, New York, Kennikat Press.
Rendel, M. (1977) 'The contribution of the Women's Labour League to the winning of the franchise' in Lucy Middleton (ed.) *Women in the Labour Movement. The British Experience* London, Croom Helm.
Rhondda, Viscountess (1933) *This was my world* London, Macmillan.
Richards, Eric (1974) 'Women in the British economy since about 1700: an interpretation' *History* 59, pp. 337—57.
Riegal, Robert E. (1962) 'The split in the feminist movement in 1869' *Mississippi Valley Historical Review* 49, pp. 485—96.
Riegal, Robert E. (1963) 'Women's clothes and women's rights' *American Quarterly* 15, pp. 390—401.

Riegal, Robert E. (1970) *American Women. A Study of Social Change* Rutherford, Fairleigh Dickinson University Press.

Roland, Alan and Harris, Barbara (1979) *Career and Motherhood* New York, Human Sciences Press.

Rose, Hilary and Hanmer, Jalna (1976) 'Women's liberation, reproduction and the technological fix' in Diana Leonard Barker and Sheila Allen (eds) *Sexual Divisions and Society: Process and Change* London, Tavistock.

Rosen, Andrew (1974) *Rise up Women! The Militant Campaign of the Women's Social and Political Union 1903—1914* London, Routledge and Kegan Paul.

Rosenberg, Carroll Smith (1971) *Religion and the Rise of the American City. The New York City Mission Movement 1812—1870* Ithaca and London, Cornell University Press.

Rossi, Alice S. (ed.) (1970) *Essays on Sex Equality. John Stuart Mill and Harriet Taylor Mill* Chicago and London, University of Chicago Press.

Roszak, Theodore (1969) 'The hard and the soft: the force of feminism in modern times' in Betty and Theodore Roszak (eds) *Masculine/ Feminine: Readings in Sexual Mythology and the Liberation of Women* New York and London, Harper and Row.

Rover, Constance (1967) *Women's Suffrage and Party Politics in Britain 1866—1914* London, Routledge and Kegan Paul.

Rover, Constance (1970) *Love, Morals and the Feminists* London, Routledge and Kegan Paul.

Rowbotham, Sheila (1972) 'The beginnings of women's liberation in Britain' in Micheline Wandor *The Body Politic. Writings from the Women's Liberation Movement in Britain 1969—1972* London, Stage I.

Rowbotham, Sheila (1973a) *Hidden from History* London, Pluto Press.

Rowbotham, Sheila (1973b) *Woman's Consciousness, Man's World* Harmondsworth, Penguin.

Rowbotham, Sheila (1977) *A New World for Women* London, Pluto Press.

Rowbotham, Sheila and Weeks, Jeffrey (1977) *Socialism and the New Life: The Personal and Sexual Politics of Edward Carpenter and Havelock Ellis* London, Pluto Press.

Royden, A. Maude (1917) 'Modern love' in Victor Gollancz (ed.) *The Making of Women. Oxford Essays in Feminism* London, Allen and Unwin.

Rubinstein, David (1977) 'Cycling in the 1890s' *Victorian Studies* 21, pp. 47—71.

Russell, Dora (1975) *The Tamarisk Tree* London, Virago.

Sachs, Albie and Wilson, Joan Hoff (1978) *Sexism and the Law. A study of male beliefs and judicial bias* Oxford, Martin Robertson.

Schneir, Miriam (ed.) (1972) *The Essential Historical Writings* New York, Random House.

Schupf, Harriet Warm (1974) 'Mary Carpenter' *Victorian Studies* 17, pp. 301—17.

Scott, Anne Firor (1970) *The Southern Lady. From Pedestal to Politics 1830—1930* Chicago, University of Chicago Press.

Scott, Benjamin (1968) *A State Iniquity. Its Rise, Extension and Overthrow* New York, Kelley, 1968.

Scott, Joan W. and Tilly, Louise A. (1975) 'Women's work and the family in nineteenth century Europe' *Comparative Studies in Society and History* 17, pp. 36—64.

Showalter, Elaine (1977) *A Literature of their Own. British Women Novelists from Bronte to Lessing* Princeton, Princeton University Press.

Sinclair, Andrew (1962) *Prohibition. The Era of Excess* London, Faber and Faber.

Sinclair, Andrew (1966) *The Emancipation of the American Woman* New York, Harper and Row.

Sklar, Kathryn Kish (1973) *Catherine Beecher. A Study in American Domesticity* New Haven and London, Yale University Press.

Sochen, June (1972) *The New Woman. Feminism in Greenwich Village 1910—1920* New York, Quadrangle.

Soldon, Norbert C. (1978) *Women in British Trade Unions 1874—1976* Gill and Macmillan.

Sonstroem, David (1977) 'Millett versus Ruskin: a defence of Ruskin's "Of Queen's Garden" ' *Victorian Studies* 20, pp. 283—97.

Stafford, A. (1964) *The Age of Consent* London, Hodder and Stoughton.

Stanton, Theodore and Blatch, Harriet Stanton (eds) (1922) *Elizabeth Cady Stanton as Revealed in her Letters, Diaries and Reminiscences* New York and London, Harper and Brothers.

Stevenson, Lloyd (1956) 'Religious elements in the background of the British anti-vivisection movement' *Yale Journal of Biology and Medicine* 29, pp. 125—57.

Stocks, Mary D. (1925) *Family Limitation and Women's Organization* London, National Union of Societies for Equal Citizenship.

Stocks, Mary D. (1949) *Eleanor Rathbone. A Biography* London, Victor Gollancz.

Stocks, Mary D. (1956) *Fifty Years in Every Street* (2nd edition) Manchester, Manchester University Press.

Stott, Mary (1978) *Organization Woman. The Story of the National Union of Townswomen's Guilds* London, Heinemann.

Strachey, Ray (1928) *The Cause. A Short History of the Women's Movement in Great Britain* London, Bell and Sons.

Strout, Cushing (1974) *The New Heaven and the New Earth. Political Religion in America* London, Harper and Row.

Summerskill, Edith (1967) *A Woman's World* London, Heinemann.

Taylor, William R. and Lasch, Christopher (1963) 'Two "kindred spirits". Sorority and family in New England, 1839—1846' *The New England Quarterly* 36, pp. 23—41.

Terrot, C. (1959) *The Maiden Tribute* London, Muller.

Thompson, Dorothy (1976) 'Women and nineteenth century radical politics. A lost dimension' in Juliet Mitchell and Ann Oakley (eds) *The Rights and Wrongs of Women* Harmondsworth, Penguin.

Thompson, Lawrence (1971) *The Enthusiasts. A Biography of John and Katherine Bruce Glasier* London, Gollancz.

Timberlake, James H. (1963) *Prohibition and the Progressive Movement 1900—1920* Harvard University Press.

Tomalin, Claire (1974) *The Life and Death of Mary Wollstonecraft* London, Weidenfeld and Nicolson.

Trudgill, Eric (1976) *Madonnas and Magdalens. The Origin and Development of Victorian Sexual Attitudes* London, Heinemann.

Tsuzuki, Chushichi (1967) *The Life of Eleanor Marx 1855—1898. A Socialist Tragedy* Oxford, Clarendon Press.

Tullborg, Rita McWilliams (1975) *Women at Cambridge. A Men's University — though of a Mixed Type* London, Gollancz.

Vallance, Elizabeth (1979) *Women in the House. A Study of Women Members of Parliament* London, Athlone Press.

Walkowitz, Judith R. and Walkowitz, Daniel J. (1974) 'We are not beasts of the field. Prostitution and the poor in Plymouth and Southampton under the Contagious Diseases Acts' in Mary Hartman and Lois Banner *Clio's Consciousness Raised. New Perspectives on the History of Women* London, Harper and Row, pp. 192—225.

Walters, Margaret (1976) 'Mary Wollstonecraft, Harriet Martineau and Simone de Beavoir' in Juliet Mitchell and Ann Oakley (eds) *The Rights and Wrongs of Women* Harmondsworth, Penguin.

Walters, Ronald W. (1973) 'The erotic South. Civilization and sexuality in American abolitionism' *American Quarterly* 25, pp. 177—201.

Walton, R. G. (ed.) (1974) *Primers for Prudery* Englewood Cliffs, NJ, Prentice Hall.

Walton, S. G. (1975) *Women in Social Work* London, Routledge and Kegan Paul.

Webb, Beatrice (1926) *My Apprenticeship* London, Longmans Green.

Webb, Catherine (1927) *The Woman with the Basket: the Story of the Women's Co-operative Guild* Manchester, CWS.

Weigley, Emma Seifrit (1974) 'It might have been euthenics. The Lake Placid conferences and the home economics movement' *American Quarterly* 26, pp. 79—96.

Wein, Roberta (1974) 'Women's colleges and domesticity, 1875—1918' *History of Education Quarterly* 14, pp. 31—47.

Welch, Susan (1975) 'Support among women for the issues of the women's movement' *Sociological Quarterly* 16, pp. 216—27.

Welter, Barbara (1966) 'The cult of true womanhood 1820—1860' *American Quarterly* 18, pp. 151—74.

Welter, Barbara (1974) 'The feminization of American religion 1800—1860' in Mary S. Hartman and Lois Banner *Clio's Consciousness Raised. New Perspectives on the History of Women* London, Harper and Row.

Whiting, Pat (1972) 'Female sexuality. Its political implications' in Micheline Wandor *The Body Politic. Women's Liberation in Britain 1969—1972* London, Stage I.

Whitney, Janet (1937) *Elizabeth Fry* London, Harrap.

Wilson, Dorothy Clark (1970) *Lone Woman. The Story of Elizabeth Blackwell the first woman doctor* London, Hodder and Stoughton.

Wilson, Elizabeth (1977) *Women and the Welfare State* London, Tavistock.

Wilson, Margaret Gibbons (1979) *The American Woman in Transition: The Urban Influence 1870—1920* London, Greenwood Press.

Wood, Ann Douglas (1972) Mrs Sigourney and the sensibility of the inner space' *New England Quarterly* 45, pp. 163—81.

Yates, Gayle Graham (1975) *What Women Want. The Ideas of the Movement* Cambridge, Mass., Harvard University Press.

Young, Nigel (1977) *An Infantile Disorder? The Crisis and Decline of the New Left* London, Routledge and Kegan Paul.

Index of Names

280

Subject Index

284